CECELIA AHERN

A Place Called Here

Thanks for the Memories

HARPER

Harper
An imprint of HarperCollins*Publishers*
77–85 Fulham Palace Road,
Hammersmith, London W6 8JB

www.harpercollins.co.uk

This omnibus edition 2009
1

A catalogue record for this book is
available from the British Library

ISBN 978-0-00-785089-1

Set in Sabon by Palimpsest Book Production Limited,
Grangemouth, Stirlingshire

Printed and bound in Great Britain by
Clays Ltd, St Ives plc

Before embarking on her writing career, Cecelia Ahern completed a degree in Journalism and Media Communications. At twenty-one years old, she wrote her first novel *PS, I Love You*, which instantly became an international bestseller and was adapted into a major motion picture starring Hilary Swank. Her successive novels *Where Rainbows End, If You Could See Me Now, A Place Called Here, Thanks for the Memories* and *The Gift* are also number one bestsellers. Her books are published in forty-six countries and have collectively sold over nine million copies. Cecelia has also co-created the hit ABC Network comedy series *Samantha Who?* which stars Christina Applegate.

To sign up for the exclusive Cecelia Ahern HarperCollins newsletter and discover all about Cecelia's books, as well as interviews, photographs and much more, log onto www.cecelia-ahern.com

Praise for Cecelia Ahern:

'Enchanting and unexpected.' *You*

'Captivating.' *Irish Independent*

'There's more than a touch of fairytale about Cecelia Ahern's novel . . . thanks to a liberal sprinkling of magic.' *Glamour*

'A beautifully written love story.' *Closer*

'A contemporary fairytale.' *Irish Times*

'An enchanting blend of magic and whimsy.' *Daily Mail*

Also by Cecelia Ahern

PS, I Love You
Where Rainbows End
If You Could See Me Now
The Gift

A Place Called Here

For you, Dad –
with all my love.

Per ardua surgo

*A missing person is anyone whose
whereabouts are unknown whatever the
circumstances of disappearance.
The person will be considered 'missing'
until located and his/her wellbeing,
or otherwise, established.*

An Garda Síochána

1

Jenny-May Butler, the little girl who lived across the road from me, went missing when I was a child.

The Gardaí launched an investigation, which led to their lengthy public search for her. For months every night the story was on the news, every day it was on the front pages of the papers, everywhere it was discussed in every conversation. The entire country pitched in to help; it was the biggest search for a missing person I, at ten years of age, had ever seen, and it seemed to affect everyone.

Jenny-May Butler was a blonde-haired, blue-eyed beauty, who smiled and beamed from the TV screen into the living room of every home around the country, causing eyes to fill with tears and parents to hug their children that extra bit tighter before they sent them off to bed. She was in everyone's dreams and everyone's prayers.

She too was ten years old, and in my class at school. I used to stare at the pretty photograph of her on the news every day and listen to the reporters speak about her as though she was an angel. From the way they described her, you never would have known that she threw stones at Fiona Brady during yard time when the teacher wasn't looking, or that she called me a 'frizzy-haired cow' in front of Stephen Spencer just so he would fancy her instead of me. No, for those few months she had become the perfect being and I didn't think it fair to ruin that. After a while even I forgot about all the

1

bad things she'd done because she wasn't just Jenny-May any more: she was Jenny-May Butler, the sweet missing girl from the nice family who cried on the nine o'clock news every night.

She was never found – not her body, not a trace of her; it was as though she had disappeared into thin air. No suspicious characters had been seen lurking around, no CCTV was available to show her last movements. There were no witnesses, no suspects; the Gardaí had questioned everyone possible. The street became suspicious, its inhabitants calling friendly hellos to one another on the way to their cars in the early morning but all the time wondering, second-guessing, and visualising surprisingly distorted thoughts they couldn't help about their neighbours. Washing cars, painting picket fences, weeding the flowerbeds, and mowing lawns on Saturday mornings while surreptitiously looking around the neighbourhood brought shameful thoughts. People were shocked at themselves, angry that this incident had perverted their minds.

Pointed fingers behind closed doors couldn't give the Gardaí any leads; they had absolutely nothing to go on but a pretty picture.

I always wondered where Jenny-May went, where she had disappeared to, how on earth anyone could just vanish into thin air without a trace without *someone* knowing *something*.

At night I would look out my bedroom window and stare at her house. The porch light was always on, acting as a beacon to guide Jenny-May home. Mrs Butler couldn't sleep any more, and I could see her perpetually perched on the edge of her couch, as though she was on her marks waiting for the pistol to be fired. She would sit in her living room, looking out the window, waiting for someone to call by with news. Sometimes I would wave at her and she'd wave back sadly. Most of the time she couldn't see past her tears.

Like Mrs Butler, I wasn't happy with not having any answers. I liked Jenny-May Butler a lot more when she was gone than when she was here and that also interested me. I missed her, the *idea* of her, and wondered if she was somewhere nearby, throwing stones at someone else and laughing loudly, but that we just couldn't find her or hear her. I took to searching thoroughly for everything I mislaid after that. When my favourite pair of socks went missing I turned the house upside down while my worried parents looked on, not knowing what to do but eventually settling on helping me.

It disturbed me that frequently my missing possessions were nowhere to be found and on the odd time that I did find them, it disturbed me that, in the case of the socks, I could only ever find one. Then I'd picture Jenny-May Butler somewhere, throwing stones, laughing and wearing my favourite socks.

I never wanted anything new; from the age of ten, I was convinced that you couldn't replace what was lost. I insisted on things having to be found.

I think I wondered about all those odd pairs of socks as much as Mrs Butler worried about her daughter. I too stayed awake at night, running through all the unanswerable questions. Each time my lids grew heavy and neared closing, another question would be flung from the depths of my mind, forcing my lids to open again. Much-needed sleep was kept at bay and each morning I was more tired yet none the wiser.

Perhaps this is why it happened to me. Perhaps because I had spent so many years turning my own life upside down and looking for everything, I had forgotten to look for myself. Somewhere along the line I had forgotten to figure out who and where I was.

Twenty-four years after Jenny-May Butler disappeared, I went missing too.

This is my story.

2

My life has been made up of a great many ironies. My going missing only added to an already very long list.

First, I'm six foot one. Ever since I was a child I've been towering over just about everyone. I could never get lost in a shopping centre like other kids; I could never hide properly when playing games; I was never asked to dance at discos; I was the only teenager that wasn't aching to buy her first pair of high heels. Jenny-May Butler's favourite name for me – well, certainly one of her top ten – was 'daddy-longlegs' which she liked to call me in front of large crowds of her friends and admirers. Believe me, I've heard them all. I was the kind of person you could see coming from a mile away: I was the awkward dancer on the dance floor, the girl at the cinema that nobody wanted to sit behind, the one in the shop that rooted for the extra-long-legged trousers, the girl in the back line of every photograph. You see, I stick out like a sore thumb. Everyone who passes me, registers me and remembers me. But despite all that, I went missing. Never mind the odd socks, never mind Jenny-May Butler; how a throbbing sore thumb on a hand so bland couldn't be seen was the ultimate icing on the cake. The mystery that beat all mysteries was my own.

The second irony is that my job was to search for missing persons. For years I worked as a garda. With a desire to work solely on missing persons cases, but without working in an actual division assigned to these,

I had to rest solely upon the 'luck' of coming across these cases. You see, the Jenny-May Butler situation really sparked off something inside me. I wanted answers, I wanted solutions and I wanted to find them all myself. I suppose my searching became an obsession. I looked around the outside world for so many clues I don't think that I once thought about what was going on inside my own head.

In the Guards sometimes we found missing people in a state I won't ever forget for the rest of this life and far into the next, and then there were the people who just didn't want to be found. Often we uncovered only a trace, too often not even that. Those were the moments that drove me to keep looking far beyond my call of duty. I would investigate cases long after they were closed, stay in touch with families long after I should. I realised I couldn't go on to the next case without solving the previous, with the result that there was too much paperwork and too little action. And so knowing that my heart lay only in finding the missing, I left the Gardaí and I searched in my own time.

You wouldn't believe how many people out there wanted to search as much as I did. The families always wondered what my reason was. They had a reason, a link, a love for the missing, whereas my fees were barely enough for me to get by on, so if it wasn't monetary, what was my motivation? Peace of mind, I suppose. A way to help me close my eyes and sleep at night.

How can someone like me, with my physical attributes and my mental attitude, go missing?

I've just realised that I haven't even told you my name. It's Sandy Shortt. It's OK, you can laugh. I know you want to. I would too if it wasn't so bloody heartbreaking. My parents called me Sandy because I was born with a head of sandy-coloured hair. Pity they didn't foresee that my hair would turn as black as coal. They didn't know either that those cute podgy little legs would soon stop kicking and start growing at such a fast rate, for so long. So Sandy Shortt is my name. That is who

I am supposed to be, how I am identified and recorded for all time, but I am neither of those things. The contradiction often makes people laugh during introductions. Pardon me if I fail to crack a smile. You see, there's nothing funny about being missing and I realised there's nothing very different about being missing: every day I do the same as I did when I was working. I search. Only this time I search for a way back to be found.

I have learned one thing worth mentioning. There is one huge difference in my life from before, one vital piece of evidence. For once in my life I want to go home.

What bad timing to realise such a thing. The biggest irony of all.

3

I was born and reared in County Leitrim in Ireland, the smallest county in the country with a population of about 25,000. Once the county town, Leitrim has the remains of a castle and some other ancient buildings, but it has lost its former importance and dwindled to a village. The landscape ranges from bushy brown hills to majestic mountains with yawning valleys and countless picturesque lakes. But for a two mile coastal outlet on Donegal Bay, Leitrim is all but landlocked, bounded to the west by Sligo and Roscommon, to the south by Roscommon and Longford, to the east by Cavan and Fermanagh, and to the north by Donegal. When there, I feel it brings on a sudden feeling of claustrophobia and an overwhelming desire for solid ground.

There's a saying about Leitrim and that is that the best thing to come out of Leitrim is the road to Dublin. I finished school when I was seventeen, applied for the Guards and I eventually got myself on that road to Dublin. Since then I have rarely travelled back. Once every two months I used to visit my parents in the three-bedroom terraced house in a small cul-de-sac of twelve houses where I grew up. The usual intention was to stay for the weekend but most of the time I only lasted a day, using an emergency at work as the excuse to grab my unpacked bag by the door and drive, drive, drive very fast on the best thing to come out of Leitrim.

I didn't have a bad relationship with my parents. They were always so supportive, even ready to dive in front of bullets, into fires and off mountains if it meant my happiness. The truth is they made me uneasy. In their eyes I could see who they saw and I didn't like it. I saw my reflection in their expressions more than in any mirror. Some people have the power to do that, to look at you and their faces let you know exactly how you're behaving. I suppose it was because they loved me, but I couldn't spend too much time with people who loved me because of those eyes, because of that reflection.

Ever since I was ten they had tiptoed around me, watched me warily. They had pretend conversations and false laughs that echoed around the house. They would try to distract me, create an ease and normality in the atmosphere, but I knew that they were doing it and why, and it only made me aware that something was wrong.

They were so supportive, they loved me so much and each time the house was about to be turned upside down for yet another gruelling search they never gave in without a pleasant fight. Milk and cookies at the kitchen table, the radio on in the background and the washing machine going, all to break the uncomfortable silence that would inevitably ensue.

Mum would give me that smile, that smile that didn't reach her eyes, the smile that made her back teeth clench and grind when she thought I wasn't looking. With forced easiness in her voice and that forced face of happiness, she would cock her head to one side, try not to let me know she was studying me intently and say, 'Why do you want to search the house again, honey?' She always called me 'honey', like she knew as much as I did that I was no more Sandy Shortt than Jenny-May Butler an angel.

No matter how much action and noise had been created in the kitchen to avoid the uncomfortable silence, it didn't seem to work. The silence drowned it all out.

My answer: 'Because I can't find it, Mum.'

'What pair are they?' – the easy smile, the pretence

that this was a casual conversation and not a desperate attempt at interrogation to find out how my mind worked.

'My blue ones with the white stripes,' I answered on one typical occasion. I insisted on bright coloured socks, bright and identifiable so that they could be easily found.

'Well, maybe you didn't put both of them in the linen basket, honey. Maybe the one you're looking for is somewhere in your room.' A smile, trying not to fidget, swallow hard.

I shook my head. 'I put them both in the basket, I saw you put them both in the machine and only one came back out. It's not in the machine and it's not in the basket.'

The plan to have the washing machine switched on as a distraction backfired and was then the focus of attention. My mum tried not to struggle with losing that placid smile as she glanced at the overturned basket on the kitchen floor, all her folded clothes scattered and rolled in messy piles. For one second she let the façade drop. I could have missed it with a blink but I didn't. I saw the look on her face when she glanced down. It was fear. Not for the missing sock, but for me. She quickly plastered the smile on again, shrugging like it was all no big deal.

'Perhaps it blew away in the wind. I had the patio door open.'

I shook my head.

'Or it could have fallen out of the basket when I carried it over from there to there.'

I shook my head again.

She swallowed and her smile tightened. 'Maybe it's caught up in the sheets. Those sheets are so big; you'd never see a little sock hidden in there.'

'I already checked.'

She took a cookie from the centre of the table and bit down hard, anything to take the smile off her aching face. She chewed for a while, pretending not to be thinking, pretending to listen to the radio and humming the tune of a song she didn't even know. All to fool me into thinking there was nothing to be worried about.

'Honey,' she smiled, 'sometimes things just get lost.'

'Where do they go when they're lost?'

'They don't *go* anywhere,' she smiled. 'They are always in the place we dropped them or left them behind. We're just not looking in the right area when we can't find them.'

'But I've looked in *all* the places, Mum. I *always* do.'

I had, I always did. I turned everything upside down; there was no place in the small house that ever went untouched.

'A sock can't just get up and walk away without a foot in it,' Mum false-laughed.

You see, just like how Mum gave up right there, that's the point when most people stop wondering, when most people stop caring. You can't find something, you know it's somewhere and even though you've looked *everywhere* there's still no sign. So you put it down to your own madness, blame yourself for losing it and eventually forget about it. I couldn't do that.

I remember my dad returning from work that evening to a house that had been literally turned upside down.

'Lose something, honey?'

'My blue sock with the white stripes,' came my muffled reply from under the couch.

'Just the one again?'

I nodded.

'Left foot or right foot?'

'Left.'

'OK, I'll look upstairs.' He hung his coat on the rack by the door, placed his umbrella in the stand, gave his flustered wife a tender kiss on the cheek and an encouraging rub on the back and then made his way upstairs. For two hours he stayed in my parents' room, looking, but I couldn't hear him moving around. One peep through the keyhole revealed a man lying on his back on the bed with a face cloth over his eyes.

On my visits in later years they would ask the same easy-going questions that were never intended to be intrusive, but to someone who was already armoured up to her eyeballs they felt as such.

'Any interesting cases at work?'

'What's going on in Dublin?'

'How's the apartment?'

'Any boyfriends?'

There were never any boyfriends; I didn't want another pair of eyes as telling as my parents' haunting me day in and day out. I'd had lovers and fighters, boyfriends, men-friends and one-night-only friends. I'd tried enough to know that anything long term wasn't going to work. I couldn't be intimate; I couldn't care enough, give enough or want enough. I had no desire for what these men offered, they had no understanding of what I wanted, so tight smiles all round while I told my parents that work was fine, Dublin was busy, the apartment was great and no, no boyfriends.

Every single time I left the house, even the times when I cut my visits short, Dad would announce proudly that I was the best thing to come out of Leitrim.

The fault never lay with Leitrim, nor did it with my parents. They were so supportive, and I only realise it now. I'm finding that with every passing day, that realisation is so much more frustrating than never finding anything.

4

When Jenny-May Butler went missing, her final insult was to take a part of me with her. I think we've established that after her disappearance there was a part of me that was missing. The older I got, the taller I got, the more that hole within me stretched until it was gaping throughout my adult life, like a wide-eyed jaw-dropping fish on ice. But how did I physically go missing? How did I get to where I am now? First question and most importantly, *where* am I now?

I'm here and that's all I know.

I look around and search for familiarity. I wander constantly and search for the road that leads out of here but there isn't one. Where is *here*? I wish I knew. It's cluttered with personal possessions: car keys, house keys, mobile phones, handbags, coats, suitcases adorned with airport baggage tickets, odd shoes, business files, photographs, tin openers, scissors, earrings scattered among the piles of missing items that glisten occasionally in the light. And there are socks, lots of odd socks. Everywhere I walk, I trip over the things that people are probably still tearing their hair out to find.

There are animals too. Lots of cats and dogs with bewildered little faces and withering whiskers, no longer identical to their photos on small-town telephone poles. No offers of rewards can bring them back.

How can I describe this place? It's an in-between place. It's like a grand hallway that leads you nowhere, it's like a banquet dinner of leftovers, a sports team

15

made up of the people never picked, a mother without her child, it's a body without its heart. It's almost there but not quite. It's filled to the brim with personal items yet it's empty because the people who own them aren't here to love them.

How did I get here? I was one of those disappearing joggers. How pathetic. I used to watch all those B-movie thrillers and groan every time the credits opened at the early morning crime scene of a murdered jogger. I thought it foolish that women went running down quiet alleyways during the dark hours of the night, or during the quiet hours of the early morning, *especially* when a known serial killer was on the prowl. But that's what happened to me. I was a predictable, pathetic, tragically naïve early morning jogger, in a grey sweat suit and blaring headphones, running alongside a canal in the very early hours of the morning. I wasn't abducted, though; I just wandered onto the wrong path.

I was running along an estuary, my feet pounding angrily against the ground as they always did, causing vibrations to jolt through my body. I remember feeling beads of sweat trickling down my forehead, the centre of my chest and down my back. The cool breeze combined to cause a light shiver to embrace my body. Every single time I remember that morning I have to fight the urge to call out to myself and warn me not to make the same mistake. Sometimes in that memory, on more blissful days, I stay on the same path, but hindsight is a wonderful thing. How often we wish we'd stayed on the same path.

It was five forty-five on a bright summer's morning; silent apart from the theme tune to *Rocky* spurring me on. Although I couldn't hear myself I knew my breathing was heavy. I always pushed myself. Whenever I felt I needed to stop I made myself run faster. I don't know if it was a daily punishment or the part of me that was keen to investigate, to go new places, to force my body to achieve things it had never achieved before.

Through the darkness of the green and black ditch

beside me, I spotted a water-violet up ahead, submerged. I remember my dad telling me as a little girl, lanky, with black hair, and embarrassed by my contradictory name, that the water-violet was misnamed too because it wasn't violet at all. It was lilac-pink with a yellow throat but even still, wasn't it beautiful and did that make me want to laugh? Of course not, I'd shaken my head. I watched it from far away as it got closer and closer, telling it in my mind, *I know how you feel.* As I ran I felt my watch slide off my wrist and fall against the trees on the left. I'd broken the clasp of the watch the very first moment I'd wrapped it around my wrist and since then it occasionally unlatched itself and fell to the floor. I stopped running and turned back, spotting it lying on the damp estuary bank. I leaned my back against the rugged dark brown bark of an alder and, while taking a breather, noticed a small track veering off to the left. It wasn't welcoming, it wasn't developed as a rambler's path but my investigative side took over; my enquiring mind told me to see where it led.

It led me here.

I ran so far and so fast that by the time the play-list had ended on my iPod I looked around and didn't recognise the landscape. I was surrounded by a thick mist and was high up in what seemed like a pine-tree-covered mountain. The trees stood erect, needles to attention, immediately on the defensive like a hedgehog under threat. I slowly lifted the earphones from my ears, my panting echoing around the majestic mountains, and I knew immediately that I was no longer in the small town of Glin. I wasn't even in Ireland.

I was just here. That was a day ago and I'm still here.

I'm in the business of searching and I know how it works. I'm a woman who packs her own bags and doesn't tell anyone where I'm going for a straight week in my life. I disappear regularly, I lose contact regularly, no one checks up on me and I like it that way. I like to come and go as I please. I travel a lot to the destinations of where the missing were last seen, I check out the area, ask around. The only problem was, I had just arrived in this town that morning, driven straight to the Shannon Estuary and gone for a jog. I'd spoken to no one, hadn't yet checked into a B & B, nor walked down a busy street. I know what they'll be saying, I know I won't even be a case – I'll just be another person that's walked away from my life without wanting to be found; it happens all the time – and this time last week they probably would have been right.

I'll eventually belong to the category of disappearance where there is no apparent danger to either the missing person or the public: for example, persons aged eighteen and over who have decided to start a new life. I'm thirty-four, and in the eyes of others have wanted out for a long, long time now.

This all means one thing: that right now nobody out there is even looking for me.

How long will that last? What happens when they find the battered, red 1991 Ford Fiesta along the estuary with a packed bag in the boot, a missing persons file on the dashboard, a cup of, by then, cold not yet sipped coffee and a mobile phone, probably with missed calls, on the car seat?

What then?

5

Wait a minute.

The coffee. I've just remembered the coffee.

On my journey from Dublin, I stopped at a closed garage to get a coffee from the outside dispenser and he saw me; the man filling his tyres with air saw me.

It was out in the middle of nowhere, in the midst of the countryside at five fifteen in the morning when the birds were singing and the cows mooing so loudly I could barely hear myself think. The smell of manure was thick but sweetened with the scent of honeysuckle waving in the light morning breeze.

This stranger and I were both so far from everything but yet right in the middle of something. The mere fact that we were both so completely disconnected from life was enough for our eyes to meet and feel connected.

He was tall but not as tall as I; they never are. Five eleven, with a round face, red cheeks, strawberry-blond hair, and bright blue eyes I felt I'd seen before, which looked tired at the early hour. He was dressed in a pair of worn-looking blue denims, his blue and white check cotton shirt crumpled from his drive, his hair dishevelled, his jaw unshaven, his gut expanding as his years moved on. I guessed he was in his mid-to-late thirties, although he looked older, with stress lines along his brow and laughter lines . . . no, I could tell from the sadness emanating from him that they weren't from laughter. A few grey hairs had crept into the side of his temples, fresh on his young head, every strand the result of a harsh lesson learned. Despite the extra weight he looked strong, muscular. He was someone who did a lot of physical work, my assumption backed up by the heavy work boots he wore. His hands were large, weather-beaten but strong. I could see the veins on his forearms protruding as he moved, his sleeves rolled up messily to below his elbows as he lifted the air pump from its stand. But he wasn't going to work, not dressed like that, not in that shirt. For him this was his good wear.

I studied him as I made my way back to my car.

'Excuse me, you dropped something,' he called out.

I stopped in my tracks and looked behind me. There on the tarmac sat my watch, the silver glistening under the sun. Bloody watch, I mumbled, checking to see that it wasn't damaged.

'Thank you,' I smiled, sliding it back onto my wrist.

'No problem. Lovely day, isn't it?'

A familiar voice to match the familiar eyes. I studied him for a while before answering. Some guy I'd met in a bar previously, a drunken fling, an old lover, a past colleague, client, neighbour or school friend? I went through the regular checklist in my mind. There was no further recognition on either side. If he wasn't a previous fling, I was thinking I'd like to make him one.

'Gorgeous.' I returned the smile.

His eyebrows rose in surprise first and then fell again, his face settling in obvious pleasure as he understood the compliment. But as much as I would have loved to stay and perhaps arrange a date for sometime in the future, I had a meeting with Jack Ruttle, the nice man I had promised to help, the man I was driving from Dublin to Limerick to see.

Oh, please, handsome man from the garage that day,

please remember me, wonder about me, look for me, find me.

Yes, I know; another irony. Me, wanting a man to call? My parents would be so proud.

6

Jack Ruttle trailed slowly behind an HGV along the N69, the coast road, which led from North Kerry to where he lived in Foynes, a small town in County Limerick, a half-hour's drive from Limerick city. It was five a.m. as he travelled the only route to Shannon Foynes Port, Limerick's only seaport. Staring at the speedometer, he telepathically urged the truck to go faster while he gripped the steering wheel so tightly his knuckles turned white. Ignoring the advice of the dentist he had seen just the previous day in Tralee, he began to grind his back teeth. The constant grinding was wearing down his teeth and weakening his gums, causing his mouth to throb and ache. His cheeks were red and swollen, and matched his tired eyes. He'd left the friend's couch he was sleeping on in Tralee to drive home through the night. Sleep wasn't coming easily to him these days.

'Are you under any stress?' the dentist had asked him while studying the inside of Jack's mouth.

An open-mouthed Jack had swallowed a curse and fought the urge to clamp his teeth down on the white surgical finger in his mouth. *Stressed* wasn't even the word.

His brother Donal had disappeared on his twenty-fourth birthday after a night out with friends in Limerick city. After a late-night snack of burger and chips in a fast-food café he had separated himself from his friends and staggered off alone. The chipper was too packed for any particular person to be noticed; his four friends were too drunk and too distracted by their attempts to bring a female home for the night to care.

CCTV showed him taking €30 out of an ATM on O'Connell Street at 3.08 a.m. on a Friday night, and later he was caught on camera stumbling in the direction of Arthur's Quay. After that, his trail was lost. It was almost like his feet had left the earth and he'd floated up towards the sky. Jack prepared himself for the fact that in a way, maybe he had. His death was a concept he knew he could eventually accept if only there was a shred of evidence to support it.

It was the not-knowing that tortured him; the worry and fear that kept him awake every night and the inconclusive search of the Gardaí that fuelled his continuous quest. He had combined his trip to the dentist in Tralee with a visit to one of Donal's friends who had been with him the night he went missing. Like the rest of the crowd that were there that night, he was a person Jack felt like punching and hugging all at the same time. He wanted to shout at him, yet console him for his loss of a friend. He never wanted to see him again, yet he didn't want to leave his side in case he remembered something – something he'd previously forgotten that would suddenly be the clue they were all looking for.

He stayed awake at nights looking through maps, rereading reports, double-checking times and statements while, beside him, Gloria's chest rose and fell with her silent breathing, her sweet breath sometimes blowing the corners of his papers as her sleeping world crept in on his.

Gloria, his girlfriend of eight years, always slept. She had slept soundly through the entire year of Jack's horrid nightmare, and still she dreamed. Still she had hopes for tomorrow.

She had fallen into a deep sleep after hours spent at the garda station, the first day they worried about not hearing from Donal after four days of silence. She slept after the Gardaí had spent the day searching the river for his body. She slept after the day they'd spent hours attaching photos of Donal to shop windows, supermarket notice boards and lampposts. She slept the night they thought they had found his body down an alley in the town and slept the next night when they discovered it wasn't him. She slept the night the Gardaí said there was nothing more they could do after months of searching. She slept the night of his mother's funeral, after seeing the coffin of a grief-stricken mother being lowered into the dirt, to join her husband at long last after twenty years in this life without him.

It frustrated Jack, but he knew it wasn't a lack of caring that caused Gloria's lids to close. He knew this because she held his hand when they sat through the questions at the garda station that first time. She stood beside him as the wind and rain lashed at their faces, by the river, watching the divers appear on the surface of the grey murky water with faces more gloomy than when they had disappeared to the world below. She had helped him stick posters of Donal to windows and poles. She had held him tightly when he cried the day the Gardaí stopped looking and she stood in the front row of the church and waited for him while he helped carry his mother's coffin to the altar.

She cared all right, but one year on, she still slept at night during the longest hours of his life. The hours when Jack cared most about everything but the hours when, deep in her sleep, Gloria didn't and couldn't care at all. Every night he felt the distance grow between her world and his.

He didn't tell her about coming across the woman, Sandy Shortt, from the missing persons agency in the Golden Pages. He didn't tell her he had called her. He didn't tell her about the late-night phone calls all last week and the new sense of hope this woman's determination and belief had filled his head and heart with.

And he didn't tell her that they had arranged to meet on this very day in the next town because . . . well, because she was sleeping.

*   *   *

Jack finally managed to overtake the long vehicles, and as he neared home he found himself alone on the now quiet country road in his twelve-year-old rusting Nissan. The interior of his car was silent. Over the past year he found he was intolerant of unwanted noise; the sound of a TV or a radio in the background was merely a distraction to his pursuit of answers. Inside his mind was manic: shouting, screaming, replays of previous conversations, imaginings of future ones all leaped around his head like a bluebottle trapped in a jam jar.

Outside the car the engine roared, the metal rattled, the wheels bounced and fell over every pothole and bump in the surface. His mind was noisy in the silent car, his car clattered in the quiet countryside. It was five fifteen on a sunny Sunday morning in July and he needed to stop for air, for his lungs and for the front deflated wheel.

He pulled over at the deserted petrol station, which would be closed until later in the morning, and parked beside the air pump. He allowed the birdsong to fill his head temporarily and push out his thoughts while he rolled up his sleeves and stretched his limbs from the long journey. The bluebottle momentarily settled.

Beside him a car pulled up and parked. The population of the area was so small he could spot an alien car a mile away . . . and the Dublin licence plate gave it away too. Out of the tiny battered car, two long legs dressed in grey sweatpants appeared, followed by a long body. Jack stopped himself from gawking but from the corner of his eye he watched the curly-black-haired woman taking long strides to the coffee dispenser by the door of the shuttered garage. He was surprised that someone of her height could even fit into the small car. He noticed something fall from her hand and heard the sound of metal against the ground.

'Excuse me, you dropped something,' he called out.

She looked behind her in confusion and walked back to where the metal was glistening on the ground.

'Thank you,' she smiled, sliding what looked like a bracelet or a watch onto her wrist.

'No problem. Lovely day, isn't it?' Jack felt the pain in his swollen cheeks worsen as they lifted in a smile.

Her green eyes sparkled like emeralds against her snow-white skin and glinted as they caught the sunlight streaming through the tall trees. Her jet-black curls twirled around her face playfully, revealing parts of her features, hiding others. She looked him up and down, taking him in as though analysing every inch of him. Finally she raised an eyebrow. 'Gorgeous,' she replied, and returned the smile. She, her jet-black curly hair, the Styrofoam cup of coffee, legs and all, disappeared into the tiny car like a butterfly into a Venus flytrap.

Jack watched the Ford Fiesta drive into the distance, wanting her to have stayed, and once again he noted how things between him and Gloria, or perhaps just his feelings for her, were changing. But he hadn't time to think about that now. Instead he returned to his car and leafed through his files in preparation for his meeting later that morning with Sandy Shortt.

Jack wasn't religious; he hadn't been to church for over twenty years. In the last twelve months he had prayed three times. Once for Donal not to be found when they were searching the river for his body, the second time for the body in the alley not to be him, and the third time for his mother to survive her second stroke in six years. Two out of three prayers had been answered.

He prayed again today for the fourth time. He prayed for Sandy Shortt to take him from the place he was in and to be the one to bring him the answers he needed.

7

The porch light was still on when Jack arrived home. He insisted on it being left on all night for Donal's sake, as a beacon to guide his brother home. He turned it off now that it was bright outside and tiptoed around the cottage quietly, careful not to wake Gloria, who was enjoying her Sunday lie-in. Scouring through the linen basket of dirty clothes, he grabbed the least crumpled garment he could find and quickly changed out of one check shirt and into another. He hadn't washed as he didn't want the electric shower and ceiling fan in the bathroom to wake her. He'd even held back from flushing the toilet. He knew it wasn't his overflowing generosity that was causing him to behave that way and yet he couldn't quite summon the shame in knowing that it was exactly the opposite. He was deliberately keeping his meeting with Sandy Shortt a secret from Gloria and the rest of his family.

It was as much to help them as it was to help him. In their hearts, they were beginning to move on. They were trying their utmost to settle back into their lives after the major upheaval and upset of suffering the loss of not one but two family members in one year. Jack understood their positions, they had all reached a point where no more days off work could be taken, sympathetic smiles were being replaced by everyday greetings, and conversations with neighbours were returning to normal. Imagine, people were actually talking about other things and not asking questions or offering advice.

29

Cards filled with comforting words had stopped landing on his doormat. People had gone back about their own lives, employers had moved around shifts as much as possible and now it was back to business for all concerned. But to Jack it felt wrong and awkward for life to resume without Donal.

Truthfully it wasn't Donal's absence that held Jack back from joining his family in bravely carrying on with the rest of his life. Of course he missed him but, as with the death of his mother, he could and would eventually get through the grief. Instead it was the mystery that surrounded his disappearance; all the unanswered questions left question marks dotting his vision like the aftermath of flash photography.

He closed the door behind him to the cluttered one-bedroom bungalow where he and Gloria had lived for five years. Just like his father, Jack had worked as a cargo handler at Shannon Foynes Port his entire working life.

He had chosen Glin village, thirteen kilometres west of Foynes, for the meeting with Sandy Shortt as it was a place none of his family inhabited. He sat in a small café at nine a.m., a half-hour before they were due to meet. Sandy had said on the phone that she was always early and he was eager, fidgety and more than willing to give this fresh idea a go. The more time they had together, the better. He ordered a coffee and stared at the most recent photograph of Donal on the table before him. It had been printed in almost every newspaper in Ireland and seen on notice boards and shop windows for the past year. In the background of the photo was the fake white Christmas tree his mother had set up in the living room every year. The baubles caught the flash of the camera and the tinsel twinkled. Donal's mischievous smile grinned up at Jack as though he was taunting him, daring him to find him. Donal had always loved playing hide-and-seek as a child. He would stay hidden for hours if it meant winning. Everyone would become impatient and declare loudly that Donal was the winner just so that he could leave his place with a proud beaming smile. This was the longest search Jack had ever endured and he wished his brother would come out of his hiding place now, show himself with that proud smile and end the game.

Donal's blue eyes, the only similar feature between the two brothers, sparkled up at Jack and he almost expected him to wink. No matter how long and hard he had stared at the photograph, he couldn't inject any life into it. He couldn't reach into the print and pull his brother out; he couldn't smell the aftershave he used to engulf himself in, he couldn't ruffle his brown hair and ruin his hairstyle as he annoyingly had, and he couldn't hear his voice as he helped their mother around the house. One year on he could still remember the touch and smell of him, though unlike the rest of his family, to him the memory alone wasn't enough.

The photo had been taken the Christmas before last, just six months before he went missing. Jack used to call round to his mother's house once a week, where Donal was the only one of six siblings who remained living there. Apart from the habitual short casual conversations between Jack and Donal that lasted for no more than two minutes at a time, that Christmas was the last occasion Jack had spoken to Donal properly. Donal had given him the usual present of socks and Jack had given him the box of handkerchiefs his oldest sister had given him the year before. They'd both laughed at the thoughtlessness of their gifts.

That day, Donal had been animated, happy with his new job as a computer technician. He'd begun it in September after graduating from Limerick University; a ceremony at which their mother had almost toppled off her chair such was the weight of her pride for her baby. Donal had spoken confidently about how he enjoyed the work and Jack could see how much he had matured and become more comfortable after leaving student life behind.

They had never been particularly close. In the family

of six children, Donal was the surprise baby, nobody more surprised than their mother, Frances, who was forty-seven at the time she learned of the pregnancy. Being twelve years older than Donal meant that Jack had moved out of home by the time Donal was six. He lost out in knowing the secret sides to his brother that only living with someone brought, and so for eighteen years they had been brothers, but not friends.

Jack wondered, not for the first time, if he had known Donal better, whether he could have solved part of the mystery. Maybe if he'd worked harder at getting to know his little brother or had had more conversations about something rather than nothing, then perhaps he could have been out with him on the night of his birthday. Maybe he could have prevented him from leaving that fast-food restaurant or maybe he could have left with him and shared a taxi.

Or maybe Jack would have found himself in the same place as Donal was right now. Wherever that place was.

8

Jack slugged back his third cup of coffee and looked at his watch.

Ten fifteen.

Sandy Shortt was late. His legs bounced up and down nervously beneath the table, his left hand drummed on the wood and his right hand signalled for another coffee. His mind stayed positive. She was coming. He knew she would come.

Eleven a.m., he tried calling her mobile number for the fifth time. It rang and rang and finally, 'Hello, this is Sandy Shortt. Sorry I'm not available at the moment. Leave a message and I'll call you back as soon as I can.' Beep.

Jack hung up.

Eleven thirty, she was two hours late, and once again Jack listened to the voice message Sandy had left the previous night.

'Hi, Jack, Sandy Shortt here. I'm ringing to confirm our meeting tomorrow at nine thirty a.m. in Kitty's Café in Glin. I'm driving down tonight.' Her tone softened. 'As you know, I don't sleep,' she laughed lightly, 'so I'll be there early tomorrow. After all our conversations I look forward to finally speaking to you in person. And, Jack,' she paused, 'I promise you I'll do my best to help you. We won't give up on Donal.'

*   *   *

Twelve o'clock, Jack played it again.

At one o'clock, after countless cups of coffee, Jack's fingers stopped drumming and instead made a fist for his chin to rest on. He had felt the café owner's gaze on his back as he sat for hours waiting nervously, watching the clock and not giving up his table to a group willing to spend more money than he. Tables filled and emptied around him, his head snapped up every time the bell over the door rang. He didn't know what Sandy Shortt looked like; all she had said was that he couldn't miss her. He didn't know what to expect but each time the bell tinkled, his head and his heart both lifted with hope and then fell as the newcomer's gaze flitted past him and settled on another.

At two thirty, the bell rang once more.

After five and a half hours waiting, it was the sound of the door opening and closing behind Jack.

9

For almost two days I'd stayed in the same wooded area, jogging back and forth, trying to recreate my movements and somehow reverse my arrival here. I ran up and down the mountainside, testing different speeds as I struggled to remember how fast I'd been running, what song I'd been listening to, what I'd been thinking of and what area I was in when I first noticed the change in my location. As though any of those things had any part in what happened. I walked up and down, down and up, searching for the point of entry and, more importantly, the point of exit. I wanted to keep busy. I didn't want to settle like the personal possessions scattered around; I didn't want to end up like the backless earrings that glinted from the long grass.

Thinking you're missing is a bizarre conclusion to arrive at – I'm well aware of that – but it wasn't a sudden conclusion, believe me. I was hugely confused and frustrated for those first few hours but I knew that something more extraordinary than taking a wrong turn had occurred because, geographically, a mountain couldn't just rise from the ground in a matter of seconds, trees that had never grown before in Ireland couldn't all of a sudden sprout from the ground, and the Shannon Estuary couldn't dry up and disappear. I knew I was somewhere else.

I did of course contemplate the fact that I was dreaming, that I had fallen and hit my head and was currently in a coma, or that I'd died. I did wonder whether the anomalous nature of the countryside was pointing towards the end of the world and I questioned my knowledge of the geography of West Limerick. I did indeed consider very strongly the fact that I'd lost my mind. This was number one on the list of possibilities.

But when I sat alone for those days and thought rationally, surrounded by the most beautiful scenery I'd ever seen, I realised that I was most certainly alive, the world had not ended, mass panic hadn't taken over and I was not just another occupant of a dump yard. I realised that my searching for a way out was clouding my view of where exactly I was. I wasn't going to hide behind the lie that I could find a way out by running up and down a hill. No deliberate distractions to block out the voice of reason for me. I am a logical person and the most logical explanation out of all of the incredible possibilities was that I was alive and well but missing. Things are as they are, no matter how bizarre.

Just as it was beginning to get dark on my second day I decided to explore this curious new place by walking deeper through the pine trees. Sticks cracked beneath my trainers, the ground was soft and bouncy, covered with layers of fallen, now decayed leaves, bark, pine cones and velvet-like moss. Mist hovered like wispy cotton wool above my head and stretched to the tips of the trees. The lofty thin trunks extended up like towering wooden pencils that coloured the sky. During the day they tinted the ceiling a clear blue, shading wispy clouds and orange pigment, and now by night the charcoaled tips, burned from the hot sun, darkened the heavens. The sky twinkled with a million stars, all winking at me, sharing between them a secret of the world I could never know.

I should have been afraid, walking through a mountainside in the dark by myself. Instead I felt safe, surrounded by the songs of birds, engulfed by the scents of sweet moss and pine, and cocooned in a mist that contained a little bit of magic. I had been in many unusual situations before: the dangerous and the plain bizarre. In my line of work I followed all leads, wandered down all paths and never allowed fear to cause me to turn away from a direction that could lead me to finding someone. I wasn't afraid to upturn every stone that lay in my path or hurl them and my questions around atmospheres with the fragility of glasshouses. When people go missing it's usually under dark circumstances most people don't want to know about. Compared to the previous experiences of delving into the underworld, this new project was literally a walk in the park. Yes, my finding my way back into my life had become a project.

The sound of murmuring voices up ahead stopped me in my tracks. I hadn't had human contact for days and wasn't at all sure if these people would be friendly. The flickering light of a campfire cast shadows around the woods, and as I quietly neared, I could see a clearing. The trees fell away to a large circle where five people sat laughing, joking and singing to music. I stood hidden in the shadows of the giant conifers, but like a hesitant moth being drawn to a flame. Irish accents were audible and I questioned my ludicrous assessment of being outside the country and of being outside my life. In those few seconds I questioned everything.

A branch snapped loudly beneath my foot and it echoed around the forest. The music immediately stopped and the voices quietened.

'Someone's there,' a woman whispered loudly.

All heads turned towards me.

'Hello, there!' a jovial man called excitedly. 'Come! Join us! We're just about to sing "This Little Light of Mine".' There was a groan from the group.

The man jumped up from his seat on a fallen tree trunk and came closer to me with his arms held open in welcome. His head was bald apart from four strands of hair, which hung spaghetti-like in a comb-over style. He had a friendly moon-shaped face and so I stepped into the light and instantly felt the warmth of the fire against my skin.

'It's a woman,' the woman's voice whispered loudly again.

I wasn't sure what to say and the man who had approached me looked back to his group now uncertainly.

'Maybe she doesn't speak English,' the woman hissed loudly.

'Ah.' The man turned back to me. 'Doooo yooooou speeeeeaaaaak Eng-a-lish?'

There was a grumble from the group, '*The Oxford English Dictionary* wouldn't understand that, Bernard.'

I smiled and nodded. The group had quietened and were studying me and I knew what they were all thinking. She's tall.

'Ah, great.' His hands clapped together and remained clasped close to his chest. His face broke into an even more welcoming smile. 'Where are you from?'

I didn't know whether to say Earth, Ireland or Leitrim. I went with my gut instincts and, 'Ireland,' was all that came out of my mouth, which hadn't spoken for days.

'Splendid!' The cheery fellow's smile was so bright that I couldn't help but return it. 'What a coincidence! Please come and join us.' He excitedly led me towards the group with a hop, skip and a jump.

'My name is Bernard,' he beamed like the Cheshire cat, 'and heartiest welcome to the Irish contingency. We're frightfully outnumbered here,' he frowned, 'although it seems that the numbers are rising. Excuse me, where are my manners?' His cheeks flushed.

'Underneath that sock over there.'

I turned to look at the source of the smart comment to see an attractive woman in her fifties, tight silver hair, with a lilac pashmina draped around her shoulders. She was staring distantly into the centre of the fire, the dancing flames reflecting in her dark eyes, her comments flowing out of her mouth as though she were on autopilot.

'Who have I the pleasure of being acquainted with?'

Bernard beamed with excitement, his neck craned up to look at me.

'My name is Sandy,' I replied, 'Sandy Shortt.'

'Splendid.' His cheeks flushed again and he shook my outstretched hand. 'It's a pleasure to meet you. Allow me to introduce you to the rest of the gang, as they say.'

'As who say?' the woman grumbled irately.

'That's Helena. She loves the chat. Always has something to say, don't you, Helena?' Bernard looked at her for an answer.

The wrinkles around her mouth deepened as she pursed her lips.

'Ah.' He wiped his brow and turned to introduce me to a woman named Joan; Derek, the long-haired hippy playing the guitar; and Marcus, who was sitting quietly on the far side. I took them in quickly: they were all of a similar age and seemed very comfortable with one another. Not even Helena's sarcastic comments were causing any friction.

'Why don't you take a seat and I'll get you a drink of some sort—'

'Where are we?' I cut in, unable to take his bumbling pleasantries any longer.

All other conversation around the fire stopped suddenly and even Helena raised her head to stare at me. She took me in, a quick glance up and down, and I felt like my soul had been absorbed. Derek stopped strumming his guitar, Marcus smiled lightly and looked away, Joan and Bernard stared at me with wide frightened Bambi eyes. All that could be heard was the sound of the campfire crackling and popping as sparks sprang out and spiralled their way up to the sky. Owls hooted and there was the distant snap of branches being stepped on by wanderers beyond.

There was a deathly silence around the campfire.

'Is anyone going to answer the girl?' Helena looked around with an amused expression. Nobody spoke.

'Well, if nobody speaks up,' she wrapped her shawl

tighter around her shoulders and grasped it at her chest, 'I'm going to give my opinion.'

Voices of objection rose from the circle and I immediately wanted to hear Helena's opinion all the more. Her eyes danced, enjoying the choir of disapproval.

'Tell me, Helena,' I interrupted.

'Oh, you don't want that, trust me,' Bernard fluffed, his double chin wobbling as he spoke.

Helena lifted her silver-haired head in defiance and her dark eyes glistened as she looked at me directly. Her mouth twitched at the side. 'We're dead.'

Two words said coolly, calmly, crisply.

'Now, now, don't you mind her,' Bernard said in what I imagined was his best angry voice.

'Helena,' Joan admonished, 'we've been through this before. You shouldn't scare Sandy like that.'

'She doesn't look scared to me,' Helena said, still with that amused expression, her eyes unmoving.

'Well,' Marcus finally spoke after his long silence since I'd joined the group, 'she may have a point. We may very well be dead.'

Bernard and Joan groaned, and Derek began strumming lightly on his guitar and singing softly, 'We're dead, we may very well be dead.'

Bernard tutted, then poured tea from a china pot into a cup and handed it to me on a saucer. In the middle of the woods, I couldn't help but smile.

'If we're dead, then where are my parents, Helena?' Joan scolded, emptying a packet of biscuits onto a china plate and placing them before me. 'Where are all the other dead people?'

'In hell,' Helena said in a singsong voice.

Marcus smiled and looked away so that Joan wouldn't see his face.

'And what makes you think we're in heaven? What makes you think *you'd* get into heaven?' Joan huffed, dunking her biscuit into her tea and pulling it up before the soggy end fell in.

Derek strummed and sang gruffly, 'Is this heaven or is this hell? I look around and I can't tell.'

'Didn't anybody else notice the golden gates and the choir of angels as they entered or was it just me?' Helena smirked.

'You didn't enter through golden gates.' Bernard shook his head wildly, his neck wobbling from side to side. He looked at me and his neck continued to shake. 'She didn't enter through golden gates.'

Derek strummed, 'I didn't pass the golden gate nor felt the burning flames of hate.'

'Oh, stop it,' Joan huffed.

'Stop it,' he sang.

'I can't bear any more.'

'I can't bear any more, someone please show me the door . . .'

'I'll show you the door,' Helena warned, but with less conviction.

He continued strumming and they all fell silent, contemplating his last few lyrics.

'Little June, Pauline O'Connor's daughter, was only ten when she died, Helena,' Bernard continued. 'Surely a little angel like her would be in heaven and she's not here, so there goes your theory.' He held his head high and Joan nodded in agreement. 'We're not dead.'

'Sorry, it's over-eighteens only,' Helena said in a bored tone. 'St Peter's down at the gate with his arms folded and an earpiece in his ear, taking instructions from God.'

'You can't say that, Helena,' Joan snapped.

'I can't get in, I can't get out, St Peter, what's it all about?' Derek sang in a gravelled voice. Suddenly he stopped strumming and finally spoke. 'It's definitely not heaven. Elvis isn't here.'

'Oh, *well then*.' Helena rolled her eyes.

'We've got our own Elvis here, haven't we?' Bernard chuckled, changing the subject. 'Sandy, did you know that Derek used to be in a band?'

'How would she know that, Bernard?' Helena said,

exasperated. Bernard ignored her again. 'Derek Cummings,' he announced, 'the hottest property in St Kevin's back in the sixties.'

They all laughed.

My body turned cold.

'What was it you were called, Derek? I've forgotten now,' Joan laughed.

'The Wonder Boys, Joan, the Wonder Boys,' Derek said fondly, reminiscing.

'Remember the dances on a Friday night?' Bernard asked excitedly. 'Derek would be up there on the stage, playing the rock and roll, and Father Martin would be almost having a heart attack at him shaking his pelvis.' They all laughed again.

'Now, what was the name of the dance hall?' Joan thought aloud.

'Oh, gosh . . .' Bernard closed his eyes and tried to remember.

Derek stopped strumming and thought hard.

Helena kept staring at me, watching my reactions. 'Are you cold, Sandy?' Her voice sounded far away.

Finbar's Hall – the name jumped into my head. They had all loved going to Finbar's Hall every Friday night.

'Finbar's Hall,' Marcus finally remembered.

'Ah, that was it.' They all looked relieved and Derek's strumming continued.

Goose pimples formed on my skin. I shivered.

I looked around at the faces of the group, studied their eyes, their familiar features and I allowed all I had learned as a little girl to come flooding back to me. I could see it now as clearly as I had then, when I came across the story in the computer archives while researching a project for school. I had immediately taken interest, had followed up on the story and was more than familiar with it. I saw the young teenage faces smiling up from the newspaper's front page and I saw those same faces around me now.

Derek Cummings, Joan Hatchard, Bernard Lynch, Marcus Flynn and Helena Dickens. Five students from

St Kevin's Boarding School. They disappeared during a school camping trip in the sixties and were never found. But here they were now, older, wiser and their innocence lost.

I had found them.

10

When I was fourteen, my parents talked me into seeing a counsellor after school on Mondays. They didn't have to do much convincing. As soon as they told me I'd be able to ask all the questions I wanted and that this person was qualified enough to answer, I practically drove myself to school.

I knew they felt that they had failed me. I could tell that by their expressions when they sat me down at the kitchen table, with the milk and cookies in the centre and the washing machine going in the background as the usual distraction. Mum held a rolled tissue tightly in her hands as though she had used it earlier to dab away tears. That was the thing with my parents: they would never let me see their weaknesses but yet they would forget to get rid of the proof of them. I didn't see Mum's tears but I saw the tissue. I didn't hear Dad's anger at having failed to help me but I saw it in his eyes.

'Is everything OK?' I looked from one strong face to the other. The only time people can look so confident and as though they can face anything is when something bad happens. 'Did something happen?'

Dad smiled. 'No, honey, don't worry, nothing bad happened.'

Mum's eyebrow lifted when he said that and I knew she didn't agree. I knew Dad didn't agree with his words either but he was saying them none the less. There was nothing wrong with sending me to a counsellor, nothing wrong at all, but I knew that they had wanted to help me themselves. They had wanted their answers to my questions to be enough. I overheard their endless discussions about the correct method of dealing with my behaviour. They had helped me in every way they could and now I could feel their disappointment in themselves and I hated myself for making them feel that way.

'You know the way you have so many questions, honey?' Dad explained.

I nodded.

'Well, your mum and I –' he looked to her for support and her eyes softened immediately as she glanced at him – 'well, your mum and I have found someone that you'll be able to talk to about all of those questions.'

'This person will be able to answer my questions?' I felt my eyes widen and my heart quicken as though all of life's mysteries were about to be answered.

'I hope so, honey,' Mum answered. 'I hope that by talking to him, you won't have any more questions that will bother you. He'll know far more about all the things you worry about than we do.'

Then it was time for my quick-fire round. Fingers on the buzzers.

'Who is he?'

'Mr Burton.' Dad.

'What's his first name?'

'Gregory.' Mum.

'Where does he work?'

'At the school.' Mum.

'When will I see him?'

'Mondays after school. For an hour.' Mum. She was better at this than Dad. She was used to these discussions while Dad was out working.

'He's a psychiatrist, isn't he?' They never lied to me.

'Yes, honey.' Dad.

I think that's the moment I began to hate seeing myself in their eyes, and unfortunately it was the beginning of my dislike of being in their company.

*　　*　　*

Mr Burton's office was in a room the size of a closet, just about big enough for two armchairs. I chose to sit in the dirty olive-green velvet-covered chair with dark wooden handles, as opposed to the stained brown velvet-covered chair. They both looked like they dated from the forties and hadn't been washed or removed from the small room since. There was a little window so high up on the back wall that all I could see was the sky. The first day I met Mr Burton it was a clear blue. Every now and then a cloud passed, filling the entire window with white before moving on.

On the walls were posters of school kids, looking happy and declaring to the empty room how they had said no to drugs, spoken out against bullying, coped with exam stress, had beaten eating disorders, dealt with grief, were clever enough to not have to face teenage pregnancy because they didn't have sex, but on the off chance that they did, there was another poster of the same girl and boy saying how they used condoms. Saints, the lot of them. The room was so positive I thought I was going to be ejected from my chair like a rocket. Mr Burton the magnificent had helped them all.

I expected Mr Burton to be a wise old man with a head of wild grey hair, a monocle in one eye, a waist-coat with a pocket watch attached by a chain, a brain exploding with knowledge after years of extensive research into the human mind. I expected Yoda of the Western world, cloaked in wisdom, who spoke in riddles and tried to convince me that the force in me was strong.

When the real Mr Burton entered the room I had mixed feelings. The inquisitive side of me was disappointed, the fourteen-year-old in me positively delighted. He was more of a Gregory than a Mr Burton. He was young and handsome, sexy and gorgeous. He looked like he had just walked out of college that very day, in his jeans and T-shirt and fashionable haircut. I did my usual calculations: twice my age could work. In a few years it would be legal and I would be out of school. My whole life was mapped out before he had even closed the door behind him.

'Hello, Sandy.' His voice was bright and cheery. He shook my hand and I vowed to lick it when I got home and never wash it again. He sat on the brown velvet armchair across from me. I bet all those girls in the posters invented all those problems just to come into this office.

'I hope you're comfortable in our designer top-of-the-range furniture?' He wrinkled his nose in disgust as he settled into the chair, which had burst at the side and had foam spilling out.

I laughed. Oh, he was so cool. 'Yes, thanks. I was wondering what you would think my choice of chair says about me.'

'Well,' he smiled, 'it says one of two things.'

I listened intently.

'Firstly, that you don't like brown, or secondly that you like green.'

'Neither,' I smiled. 'I just wanted to face the window.'

'Ah-ha,' he grinned. 'You are what we call at the lab a "window facer".'

'Ah, I'm one of *those*.'

He looked at me with amusement for a second, then placed a pen and pad on his lap and a tape recorder on the arm of the chair. 'Do you mind if I record this?'

'Why?'

'So I can remember everything that you say. Sometimes I don't pick up on things until I listen back over the conversation.'

'OK, what's the pen and pad for then?'

'Doodling. In case I get bored listening to you.' He pressed record and said that day's date and time.

'I feel like I'm at a police station, about to be interrogated.'

'Has that ever happened before?'

I nodded. 'When Jenny-May Butler went missing, we were asked to give any information we had at the school.' How quickly talk had come round to her. She would have been delighted at the attention.

'Ah,' he nodded. 'Jenny-May was your friend, wasn't she?'

I thought about that. I looked at the antibullying posters on the wall and wondered how to answer. I didn't want to seem insensitive to this gorgeous man by saying no, but she wasn't my friend. Jenny-May hated me. But she was missing and I probably shouldn't speak badly of her because after all, everyone thought she was an angel. Mr Burton mistook my silence for being upset, which was embarrassing, and the next question he asked his voice was so gentle I almost burst out laughing.

'Do you miss her?'

I thought about that one too. Would you miss a slap across the face every day? I felt like asking him. Once again I didn't want him to think I was insensitive by saying no. He'd never fall in love with me and take me away from Leitrim then.

He leaned forward in his chair. Oh, his eyes were so blue.

'Your mum and dad told me you want to find Jenny-May – is this true?'

Wow. Talk about getting the wrong end of the stick. I rolled my eyes, OK enough of this crap. 'Mr Burton, I don't want to seem rude or insensitive here because I know Jenny-May is missing and everyone is sad but . . .' I trailed off.

'Go on,' he encouraged me, and I wanted to jump on him and kiss him.

'Well, me and Jenny-May were never friends. She hated me. I miss her in a way that I notice she's gone but not in a way that I want her back. And I don't want her back or to find her. Just knowing where she is would be enough.'

He raised his eyebrows.

'Now, I know you probably thought that because Jenny-May was my friend and she went missing, that every time I lose something, like a sock, and try to find it, it's like my way of finding Jenny-May and bringing her back.'

His mouth dropped open a little.

'Well, it's a reasonable assumption, I suppose, Mr Burton, but it's just not me. I'm really not that complicated. It's just annoying that when things go missing, I don't know where they go. Take, for instance, the Sellotape. Last night Mum was trying to wrap a present for Aunt Deirdre's birthday but she couldn't find the Sellotape. Now, we always leave it in the second drawer under the cutlery drawer. It's always there, we never put it anywhere else and my mum and dad know how I am about things like that and so they really do put everything in their places. Our house is really tidy, honestly, so it's not like things just get lost all the time in a mess. Anyway, I used the Sellotape on Saturday when I was doing my art homework – for which I got a crappy C today, by the way, even though Tracey Tinsleton got an A for drawing what looks like a squashed fly on a windscreen and that's considered "real art" – but I promise I put it back in the drawer. Dad didn't use it, Mum didn't use it and I'm almost certain no one broke into the house just to steal some Sellotape. So I searched all evening for it but I couldn't find it. Where is it?'

Mr Burton was silent and slowly moved back and settled into his chair.

'So let me get this straight,' he said slowly. 'You don't miss Jenny-May Butler.'

We both started laughing and for the first time ever, I didn't feel bad about it.

'Why do you think you're here?' Mr Burton got serious again after our bout of laughing.

'Because I need answers.'

'Answers like . . . ?'

I thought about it. 'Where is the Sellotape that we couldn't find last night? Where is Jenny-May Butler? Why does one of my socks always go missing in the washing machine?'

'You think I can tell you where all these things are?'

'Not specifics, Mr Burton, but a general indication would be fine.'

He smiled at me. 'Why don't you let me ask you the questions for a moment and maybe through your answers, we'll find the answers you want.'

'OK, if you think that'll work.' Weirdo.

'Why do you feel the need to know where things are?'

'I have to know.'

'Why do you feel you have to know?'

'Why do you feel you have to ask me questions?'

Mr Burton blinked and was silent for a second longer than he wanted, I could tell. 'It's my job and I get paid to do it.'

'Paid to do it.' I rolled my eyes. 'Mr Burton, you could have my Saturday job stacking toilet rolls and get paid but you chose to study for what – ten million years? – to get all of those scrolls you've hung on the walls.' I looked around at his framed qualifications. 'I'd say you went through all of that studying, all of those exams and ask all these questions for more reasons than just getting paid.'

He smiled lightly and watched me. I don't think he knew what else to say. And so there was a two-minute silence while he thought. Finally he put down his pen and paper and leaned towards me, resting his elbows on his knees.

'I like to have conversations with people, I always have. I find that through talking about themselves people learn things that they didn't know before. It's a kind of self-healing. I ask questions because I like to help people.'

'And so do I.'

'You feel by asking questions about Jenny-May, you're helping her or maybe her parents?' He tried to hide the confusion from his eyes.

'No, I'm helping myself.'

'How does it help you? Isn't *not* getting the answers frustrating you even more?'

'Sometimes I find things, Mr Burton. I find the things that have just been misplaced.'

'Isn't everything that's lost misplaced?'

'To misplace something is to lose it temporarily by forgetting where you put it. I always remember where I put things. It's the things that I *don't* misplace that I try to find; the things that grow legs and walk away all by themselves that annoy me.'

'Do you think it's possible that somebody else, other than you, moves all these things?'

'Like who?'

'I'm asking you.'

'Well, in the case of the Sellotape the answer is clearly no. In the case of the socks, unless somebody reaches into the washing machine and takes out my socks then the answer is no. Mr Burton, my parents want to help me. I don't think that they would move things and then forget about it every single time. If anything, they are more aware of exactly where they put things.'

'So what is your assumption? Where do you think these things are?'

'Mr Burton, if I had an assumption, then I wouldn't be here.'

'You have no idea then? Even in your wildest dreams, during your most frustrating times when you're vigorously searching into the early hours of the morning and you still can't find it, have you any opinion *at all* as to where you think the missing things are?'

Well, he'd clearly learned more about me from my parents than I thought, but having to answer this question truthfully I feared would mean he'd never fall in love with me. But I took a deep breath and told the truth anyway. 'At times like that I'm convinced they are in a place where missing things go.'

He didn't miss a beat. 'Do you think Jenny-May is there? Does it make you feel better to think that she's there?'

'Oh God.' I rolled my eyes. 'If someone killed her, Mr Burton, they killed her. I'm not trying to create imaginary worlds to make myself feel better.'

He tried very hard not to move a muscle in his face.

'But whether she's alive now or not, why haven't the Gardaí been able to find her?'

'Would it make you feel better to just accept that sometimes there are mysteries?'

'You don't accept that, why should I?'

'What makes you think I don't?'

'You're a counsellor. You believe that every action has a reaction and all that kind of stuff. I read up on it before I came here. Everything that I do now is because of something that happened, something somebody said or did. You believe there are answers to everything and ways of solving everything.'

'That's not necessarily true. I can't fix everything, Sandy.'

'Can you fix me?'

'You're not broken.'

'Is that your medical opinion?'

'I'm not a doctor.'

'Aren't you a "doctor of the mind"?' I held up my fingers in inverted commas and rolled my eyes.

Silence.

'How do you feel when you are searching and searching but you still can't find whatever it is that you're looking for?'

I could tell this was the weirdest conversation he had ever had.

'Have you a girlfriend, Mr Burton?'

His forehead creased. 'Sandy, I'm not sure that this is relevant.' When I didn't answer, he sighed. 'No, I don't.'

'Do you want one?'

He was contemplative. 'Are you saying that the feeling of searching for a missing sock is like searching for love?' He tried to ask the question without making me sound stupid but he failed miserably.

I rolled my eyes again. He was making me do that a lot. 'No, it's a feeling of knowing something is missing in your life but not being able to find it no matter how hard you look.'

He cleared his throat awkwardly, picked up his pen and paper and pretended to write something.

Doodle time. 'Boring you, am I?'

He laughed and it broke the tension.

I tried to explain again. 'Perhaps it would have been easier if I said that not being able to find something is like suddenly not remembering the words to your favourite song that you knew off by heart. It's like suddenly forgetting the name of someone you know really well and see every day, or the name of a group who sang a famous song. It's something so frustrating that it plays on your mind over and over again because you know there's an answer but no one can tell you it. It niggles and niggles at me and I can't rest until I know the answers.'

'I understand,' he said softly.

'Well, then, multiply that feeling by one hundred.'

He was contemplative. 'You're mature for your age, Sandy.'

'Funny, because I was hoping you'd know an awful lot more for yours.'

He laughed until our time was up.

That night at dinner Dad asked me how it went.

'He couldn't answer my questions,' I replied, slurping on my soup.

Dad looked like his heart was going to break. 'So I suppose you don't want to go back.'

'No!' I said quickly and my mum tried to hide her smile by taking a sip of water.

Dad looked back and forth from her face to mine questioningly.

'He has nice eyes,' I offered by way of explanation, slurping again.

His eyebrows rose and he looked to my mum, who had a grin from ear to ear and flushed cheeks. 'That's true, Harold. He has very nice eyes.'

'Ah, *well then*!' He threw his arms up. 'If the man has nice eyes for Christsake, who am I to argue?'

Later that night I lay on my bed and thought about

my conversation with Mr Burton. He may not have had answers for me but he sure cured me of searching for one thing.

11

I went to see Mr Burton every week while I was at St Mary's Secondary School. We even met up during the summer months when the school remained open to the rest of the town for summer activities. The last time I went to see him there was when I had just turned eighteen. I'd finished my leaving certificate the previous year and I'd found out that morning I'd been accepted into the Gardaí Síochána. I was due to move to Cork to train at Templemore in a few months.

'Hello, Mr Burton,' I said as he entered the small office that hadn't changed one bit since the first day we met. He was still young and handsome and I loved every inch of him.

'Sandy, for the hundredth time, stop calling me Mr Burton. You make me sound like an old man.'

'You are an old man,' I teased.

'Which makes you an old woman,' he said lightly, and a silence fell between us. 'So,' he became business-like, 'what's on your mind this week?'

'I got accepted into the Gardaí today.'

His eyes widened. Happiness? Sadness? 'Wow, Sandy, congratulations. You did it!' He came over and gave me a hug. We held on a second longer than we should have.

'How do your mum and dad feel?'

'They don't know yet.'

'They'll be sad to see you go.'

'It's for the best.' I looked away.

'You won't leave all your problems behind in Leitrim, you know,' he said gently.

'No, but I'll leave behind the people who know about them.'

'Do you plan on coming back to visit?'

I stared him directly in the eyes. Were we still talking about my parents? 'As much as I can.'

'How much will that be?'

I shrugged.

'They have always supported you, Sandy.'

'I can't be who they want me to be, Mr Burton. I make them uncomfortable.'

He rolled his eyes at me calling him that, at my deliberate attempts to build a wall between us. 'They just want you to be you, you know that. Don't be ashamed of how you are. They love you for who you are.'

The way he looked at me made me wonder again if we were talking about my parents at all. I looked around the room. He knew everything about me, absolutely everything, and I sensed everything about him. He was still single and living alone, despite every girl in Leitrim town chasing him. He tried to tell me week after week to accept things as they were and move on with life, but if there was one man who had put his life on hold to wait for something, or someone, it was him.

He cleared his throat. 'I heard you went out with Andy McCarthy at the weekend.'

'And?'

He rubbed his face wearily and allowed a silence to fall between us. We were both good at that. Four years of therapy, of me baring my soul, yet every new word was a word further from discussing the very thing that consumed my thoughts most moments of most days.

'So come on, talk to me,' he said softly.

Our last session and I couldn't think of anything. He still had no answers for me.

'Are you going to the fancy-dress party on Friday?' He picked up the mood of the atmosphere.

'Yes,' I smiled. 'I can't think of a better way to say

goodbye to this place than to walk out being dressed as something else.'

'What are you dressing up as?'

'A sock.'

He laughed so hard. 'Andy isn't going with you?'

'Do my socks ever come as a pair?'

He raised his eyebrows, indicating he wanted more.

'He didn't get why I turned his flat upside down when I couldn't find the invite.'

'Where do you think it is?'

'With everything else. With my mind.' I rubbed my eyes wearily.

'You haven't lost your mind, Sandy. So you're going to be a garda.' His smile was shaky.

'Worried about the future of our country?'

'No,' he smiled. 'At least I know we'll be in safe hands. You'll be questioning criminals to death.'

'I learned from the best.' I forced myself to smile.

Mr Burton turned up at the fancy-dress party that Friday night. He was dressed as a sock and I laughed so hard. He drove me home that night and we sat in silence. After so many years of talking neither of us knew what to say. Outside my house he leaned over and kissed my lips hungrily; long and hard. It was like our hello to one another and a goodbye all at once.

'Pity we're not the same pattern, Gregory. We would have made a good pair,' I said sadly.

I wanted him to tell me that we'd make the most perfect odd pair around but I think he agreed because I watched him drive away.

The more partners I had, the more I realised Gregory and I were the best pair I'd ever come across. But in my pursuit of answers to all the difficult questions in my life, I missed out on the obvious ones right in front of my very eyes.

12

Helena was watching me curiously through the amber blaze of the campfire, the shadow of the flames dancing upwards to lick her face. The other members of the group had continued with their reminiscing of Derek's rock-and-roll days, happy to move the subject away from my question about where we were. Excited chatter had resumed but I remained on the outside, though I was not alone. Finally, I lifted my eyes from the ash floor and allowed them to meet Helena's.

She waited for a silence to fall between the group before asking, 'What do you do for a living, Sandy?'

'Oooh, yes,' Joan said excitedly, warming her hands around her tea cup. 'Do tell us.'

I had everyone's attention and so I considered my options. Why lie?

'I run an agency,' I began and then stopped.

'What kind of an agency?' Bernard asked.

'A modelling agency, is it?' Joan asked in hushed tones. 'With long legs like yours I'll bet it is.' Her tea cup rested in her hands not far below her lips, her baby finger was erect and standing tall like a dog on the hunt.

'Joan, she said she *runs* the agency, not is a *member* of one.' Bernard shook his head and his chin wobbled.

'Actually, it's a missing persons agency.'

There was a silence as they searched my face and when they all looked at each other, they erupted in laughter. All except Helena.

'Oh, Sandy, that was a good one.' Bernard wiped the corners of his eyes with his handkerchief. 'What kind of agency is it really?'

'Acting.' Helena jumped in before I had a chance to answer.

'How do you know?' Bernard asked her, rather in a huff that she knew something before him. 'You're the one who asked the question in the first place.'

'She told me while you were all laughing.' She waved her hand dismissively.

'An acting agency.' Joan looked at me with wide eyes. 'How wonderful. We put on some excellent plays in Finbar's Hall,' Joan explained. 'Do you remember that?' She looked around at her friends. '*Julius Caesar*, *Romeo and Juliet* to name but two of Shakespeare's finest works. Bernard was—'

Bernard coughed loudly.

'Oh, I'm sorry.' Joan blushed. 'Bernard *is* a fantastic actor. He played quite a convincing Bottom in *A Midsummer Night's Dream*. No doubt you would love him to be in your agency.'

And they fell into their usual chatter of swapping old stories. Helena made her way round the fire and sat next to me.

'I must say, you excel in your occupation,' Helena chuckled.

'Why did you do that?' I referred to her interjection.

'Oh, you don't want to tell them that, especially Joan with her voice so hushed she feels the need to tell everybody everything just to make sure she's heard,' she teased, but watched her friend fondly. 'If anyone finds out you run a missing persons agency you'll be swamped with questions. Everyone will think you'll have come to bring us all home.' I wasn't sure whether she was joking or asking me a question. Either way, she didn't laugh and I didn't answer.

'Who else is there to tell around here?' I stared into the silent black woods. I hadn't come across any others for two days.

Helena looked at me curiously again. 'Sandy, there *are* others, you know.'

Apart from Ewoks, I found it hard to believe anybody else inhabited the dark and silent surroundings.

'You know our story, don't you?' Helena kept her voice low so that the others couldn't hear.

I nodded, took a deep breath and recited, '"Five students are missing after disappearing during a school camping trip in Roundwood, County Wicklow. Sixteen-year-olds Derek Cummings, Helena Dickens, Marcus Flynn, Joan Hatchard and Bernard Lynch from St Kevin's Boarding School for Girls and Boys in Blackrock were due to visit Glendalough but were missing from their tents that morning."'

Helena was gazing at me with such childlike intent and tear-filled eyes I felt a duty to recite the newspaper article word-perfect, tone-perfect. I wanted to express the feeling in the country during that initial week, on behalf of the country; I wanted to convey accurately the outpour of love and support complete strangers had displayed towards the missing five students. I felt I owed it to all those people who prayed for their return. I felt Helena deserved to hear it.

'"The Gardaí today said that they were following leads although they couldn't confirm ruling out foul play. They ask for anyone with any information to contact the Roundwood or Blackrock Gardaí. The students of St Kevin's have all gathered to pray for their fellow students and locals have been placing flowers near the scene."'

I was silent.

'What's wrong with your eyes, Helena?' Bernard asked worriedly.

'Oh,' Helena sniffed, 'it's nothing. Just a spark from the fire jumped into my eye, that's all.' She dabbed her eyes with the corner of her pashmina.

'Oh dear,' Joan said, moving over and peering in her eye. 'No, it looks fine to me, just red and watery. It probably just stings a bit.'

'I'm fine, thanks,' Helena dismissed them all, embarrassed by their care, and the others continued chatting amongst themselves.

'With acting like that you could join my agency,' I smiled.

Helena laughed and fell silent again. I felt I should say something.

'They never gave up looking for you, you know.'

Her mouth let out a tiny sound. A sound that was beyond her control to stop, a sound that had worked its way up straight from her heart.

'Your father championed every new Garda Commissioner and Minister for Justice that took office. He knocked on every door and searched between every blade of grass to find you. He made sure they searched the entire area with a fine-tooth comb. As for your mother, your amazing mother . . .'

Helena smiled at the mention of her mother.

'She set up an organisation to help counsel families suffering the effects of missing loved ones, named Porch Light, as many families of the missing leave their front lights on as a beacon, hoping that someday their loved ones will return. She was tireless in her charity work, setting up bases all around the country. Your parents never, ever gave up. Your mother still hasn't.'

'She's alive?' Her eyes widened and filled once again.

'Your father – I'm sorry – passed away some years ago.' I allowed her to process the information before moving on. 'Your mother is still actively involved with Porch Light. I attended their annual lunch last year and had the pleasure of meeting her and telling her how wonderful I thought she was.' I looked down at my hands and cleared my throat, the role of messenger not always proving easy. 'She told me to continue with my efforts as she wished I could find her beloved daughter for her.'

Helena's voice was barely a whisper. 'Tell me about her.'

And so I forgot about my own worries and settled down by the warmth of the campfire to do just that.

'I never wanted to go on the camping trip.' Helena was exhilarated and full of emotion after I had filled her with knowledge of her mother. 'I pleaded with them not to make me go.'

I knew all this but I listened intently, fascinated to hear the story I knew so well from one of its main characters. It was like seeing my favourite book come alive on stage.

'I'd wanted to go home that weekend. There was a boy . . .' She laughed and looked at me. 'Isn't it always about a boy?'

I couldn't relate but smiled all the same.

'A new boy had moved into the house next door to us. Samuel James was his name, the most beautiful creature alive.' Her eyes were bright, as though the fire's sparks had leaped in and set her pupils alight. 'I met him that summer and fell in love, and we had the most wonderful time together. *Sinful*.' She raised her eyebrows and I smiled. 'I'd been back at school for two months and I missed him dreadfully. I begged and pleaded with my parents to let me go home but to no avail. They were punishing me,' she said with a sad smile. 'I'd been caught cheating in my history exam in the same week I'd been caught smoking behind the gymnasium. Unacceptable, even by my standards.' She looked around the group. 'And so I was stuck going away with this lot as though separating me from my best friends would suddenly make me an angel. All the same, it turned out to be a punishment I don't think I entirely deserved.'

'Of course not,' I empathised. 'How did you get here?'

Helena sighed. 'Marcus and I made arrangements early in the evening to meet up when everyone had gone to sleep. He was the only one who had a packet of cigarettes so the other two boys went with him and, well, Joan,' Helena looked at her friend on the other side of the campfire with fondness, 'she was afraid to stay in the tent by herself so she came too. We moved away from the camp so our teachers wouldn't see the cigarettes alight or smell the smoke. We didn't walk that far at all, just a few minutes or so, but we found ourselves here,' she shrugged. 'I can't really explain it any other way.'

'That must have been terrifying for you all.'

'No more than it was for you.' She looked at me. 'And at least we had each other. I couldn't imagine going through it all alone.'

She wanted me to talk but I wouldn't. It wasn't in my nature to open up. Not unless it was with Gregory.

'You can't even have been born when we went missing. How do you know so much?'

'Let's just say I was an inquisitive child.'

'Inquisitive indeed.' She studied me again and I looked away, finding her glare intrusive. 'Do you know what has happened to everybody's family here?' She nodded at the rest of the group.

'Yes.' I looked around them all, seeing their parents' faces in each of them. 'I made it my life's work to know. I followed up on all of you every year, wanting to see if anyone came home.'

'Well, thank you for helping me feel one step closer to it now.'

A silence fell between us, Helena no doubt lost in her memories of home.

Eventually, she spoke again. 'My grandmother was a proud woman, Sandy. She married my grandfather when she was eighteen years old and they had six children. Her younger sister, who they could never seem to marry off, embarked on a mysterious affair with a man she would never name and to everybody's shock, gave birth to a baby boy,' she chuckled. 'That my grandfather's face was written all over that child was not lost on my grandmother, nor were the shillings that disappeared from their savings just as the new clothes appeared on the child. Of course, those things are entirely coincidental,' she said in a singsong voice, stretching her legs out in front of her. 'There are a great many brown-haired, blue-eyed men in the country and the fact my grandfather had a fondness for drinking would explain the dents in their savings.' Her eyes twinkled at me.

I looked at Helena in confusion. 'I'm sorry, Helena, I'm not sure why you're telling me this.'

She laughed. 'That you have ended up here with us could be one of life's great coincidences.'

I nodded.

'But my grandmother didn't believe in coincidences. And neither do I. You're here for a reason, Sandy.'

13

Helena added another log to the dying fire and its weight sent a pile of adolescent ashes racing one another down the side of the burning tower. The flames were awakened from the embers and sleepily began to climb up the log, casting out heat to Helena and me.

I had been talking to her for hours, filling her in on all the details of her family life that I knew of. An unusual feeling had stirred within me as soon as I'd realised whose company I was keeping. It washed over me in waves, each wave relaxing me, making my eyes that little bit heavier, causing my mind to tick that little bit slower, and for the tension in my muscles to relax just a little bit more. It was just a little bit, mind you, but it was something.

All of my life people had told me that my questions were irrelevant, that my over-interest in cases of missing persons unnecessary, but right there in the woods every stupid, embarrassing, irrelevant and unnecessary question I had ever asked about Helena Dickens meant the world to her. I knew there had been a reason for my endless searches, my infinite interrogations of myself and of others. And the greatest thing of all was that there wasn't just one reason for it all; sitting next to me by the campfire there were four others.

Oh, the relief. That's what the feeling was. The first sense of relief my mind had felt since I was ten years old.

The sky was growing brighter; the tips of the trees

that had been burned by the sun by day had been cooled by the night and now shaded the sky a cool blue. The birds that had been silent during the dark hours were now warming their vocal cords, like the idiosyncratic rendition of an orchestra tuning, pre-performance. Bernard, Derek, Marcus and Joan lay asleep in their sleeping bags, covered by blankets and looking how they should have the night of their school camping trip. I wondered, had they slept soundly through that night instead of venturing into the woods, would they have been back in their families' arms all those years ago, or would the secret door to this world have welcomed them in regardless?

Was it an accident that we were all here? Did we stumble upon a blip in the earth's creation, a black hole on the surface, or was this just a part of life that was unspoken throughout the centuries? Were we lost and unaccounted for, or was this where we truly belonged and our 'normal' lives the original error? Was this a place for those who felt like outsiders in life to belong, to finally feel relief? Despite my own relief, my questions kept flowing. The world around me had changed but some things remained constant.

'Were you happy?' I looked around at the others sleeping. 'Was everybody happy?'

Helena smiled softly. 'We've all asked the question of why, and there is no answer that we know of. Yes, we were happy. We were all very, very happy in our lives.' She paused. 'Sandy,' she broke the silence again, watching me with that amused expression as if enjoying a private joke, 'believe it or not we're very happy here too. We've spent more years living here than anywhere else. The past is a distant but pleasurable memory for us.'

I looked around the campfire. They had nothing. Nothing but small overnight bags packed with tea bags, unnecessary chinaware and biscuits, blankets and sleeping bags, wraps and jumpers to keep warm, all of which they undoubtedly retrieved from the piles of belongings scattered around us. These five people had slept under the stars, swathed in blankets with a fire and the sun as their only source of light and heat. For forty years. How could they be truly happy? How could they not be clawing their way back to existence, back to material belongings and craving the companionship of others?

I shook my head as I looked around.

Helena laughed at me. 'Why are you shaking your head?'

'I'm sorry.' I was embarrassed at being caught pitying a life they seemed content with. 'It's just that forty years is such a long time to settle,' I looked around at the clearing, 'well . . . here.'

Helena's face opened in surprise.

'Oh, I'm so sorry,' I backtracked. 'I didn't mean to offend you—'

'Sandy, Sandy,' she interrupted, '*this* is not our whole world.'

'I know, I know,' I backed off. 'You have each other and—'

'No.' Helena started laughing and her forehead crumpled in confusion. 'I'm sorry, I thought you knew this wasn't a permanent thing. We go camping together once a year on the anniversary of our disappearance. I thought you would recognise the date. This clearing is the first place we arrived at forty years ago – well, the first area where we *realised* we weren't at home any more. We all stay in touch during the year but we live more or less separate lives.'

'What?' I was confused.

'People go missing all the time, you know that. Wherever people gather, life begins, civilisation exists. Sandy, fifteen minutes' walk from here, the woods end and a whole new life begins.'

I was stunned. My mouth opened and closed but no words would come out.

'Interesting you should arrive here today of all days,' Helena said, deep in thought.

I scrambled to my feet. 'Come on, let's go now. Show me this place you're talking about. We won't disturb the others.'

'No.' Helena's voice was hard and her smile quickly faded. Her hand sprang up to grab my arm. I flinched and tried to pull away, not liking the contact, but this did not rattle her. I couldn't move; the force of her hold was so strong. Her face was stony. 'We do not just leave each other like that, we do not disappear from one another. We will sit here until they wake.'

She loosened her grip on my arm and wrapped her pashmina tighter around her body; retreating to the guarded woman she had been earlier in the evening. She watched her friends intently as though on duty and I realised it wasn't just me that had been keeping her awake all night. It was just her turn.

'We stay until they wake,' she repeated firmly.

Jack sat on the corner of the bed and watched Gloria sleeping with a small smile on her face. It was the early hours of Monday morning and he had just returned home. After Sandy Shortt's no-show he had spent the entire day checking B & Bs and hotels in all the nearby towns to see if she had checked in anywhere. There were so many things that could have prevented her from arriving at the café; he convinced himself her no-show that morning didn't mean it was the end of their search. She could have just overslept and missed their meeting, or got caught up in Dublin and couldn't leave for Limerick that night. There could have been a death in the family or a sudden lead in another case that took her away from Limerick. She could be heading towards him now, driving through the night to get to Glin. He had thought of the endless possibilities but not one of those theories was the idea that she could have deliberately let him down.

A mistake had been made, that was all. He would return to Glin later today in his lunch break to see if she had arrived. He had lived all week for that meeting and he wasn't going to give up now. Sandy had given him more hope in one week during a few phone conversations than anyone else had succeeded in doing over the entire year. He knew from their talks that she wouldn't let him down.

He was going to tell Gloria, he really was. He reached out to touch her shoulder and shake her gently but his hand stopped mid-air. Maybe he should hold off telling her until he made contact with Sandy again. Gloria sighed sleepily, stretched her body and turned over.

She eventually settled on her side, her back towards Jack and his outstretched hand.

14

Only a week before the no-show from Sandy, Jack had quietly closed the bedroom door adjoining the living room so as not to disturb a sleeping Gloria. The Golden Pages lying open on the couch stared back at him as he paced the far side of the room, one eye on the phone book, the other eye on the bedroom door. He stopped and traced his finger down the page until he came across the advert for Porch Light, the organisation that helped counsel friends and relatives of the missing. Jack and his sister Judith had tried to convince their mother to talk to Porch Light after Donal's disappearance, but her old Irish ways of refusing to speak her private thoughts to a stranger held her back. Below the advert was the number for Sandy Shortt's missing persons agency. He picked up his mobile and switched on the television so as to cover the sound of his voice in case Gloria awoke. He dialled the number he had memorised when he first came across the advertisement. It rang twice before a female answered.

'Hello?'

Jack suddenly couldn't remember what to say.

'Hello?' The voice was softer this time. 'Gregory, is that you?'

'No.' Jack finally found his voice. 'My name is Jack, Jack Ruttle. I got your number from the Golden Pages.'

'Oh, I'm sorry,' the woman apologised and returned to her original businesslike tone. 'I was expecting someone else. I'm Sandy Shortt,' she said.

'Hello, Sandy.' Jack paced the small cluttered living room, tripping over the unevenly rolled, mismatching rugs that adorned the old wooden floors. 'I'm sorry to call so late.' Get to the point he hurried himself, pacing faster while he watched the bedroom door.

'Don't worry. A call at this hour of the night is an insomniac's dream, pardon the pun. How can I help you?'

He stopped pacing and held his head in his hand. What was he doing?

Sandy's voice was gentle again. 'Is somebody you know missing?'

'Yes,' was all Jack could reply.

'How long ago?' He could hear her rooting for paper.

'A year.' He settled on the arm of the couch.

'What is this person's name?'

'Donal Ruttle.' He swallowed the lump in his throat.

She paused, then: 'Yes, Donal,' a tone of recognition in her voice. 'You're a relative?'

'Brother . . .' Jack's voice cracked and he knew he couldn't go on. He needed to stop now; he needed to move on like the rest of his family. He was stupid to think that an insomniac from the phone book with too much time on her hands could succeed where an entire garda search hadn't. 'I'm sorry, I'm very, very sorry. This phone call was a mistake,' he forced out. 'I'm sorry for wasting your time.' He quickly hung up the phone and fell back into the couch, embarrassed and exhausted, knocking against his files and sending pictures of a smiling Donal floating to the ground.

Moments later his mobile rang. He dived for it, not wanting the ring tone to waken Gloria.

'Donal?' he breathed, jumping to his feet.

'Jack, it's Sandy Shortt.'

Silence.

'Is that how you usually answer the phone?' she asked gently.

He was lost for words.

'Because if it is and you're still expecting your brother

76

to call, I don't think your phone call to me was a mistake, do you?'

His heart was hammering in his chest. 'How did you get my number?'

'Caller ID.'

'My number is blocked.'

'I find people, Jack. That's what I do. And there's a chance that I can find Donal for you.'

He glanced at all the photographs scattered around him, the cheeky smile of his younger brother staring up at him, silently daring him to seek him out as he had when he was a child.

'Are you back in?' she asked.

'I'm in,' he replied, and he headed to the kitchen for a cup of coffee in preparation for the long night ahead.

The following night at two a.m., as Gloria lay asleep in bed, Jack lay on the couch, on the phone to Sandy, his hundreds of pages of garda reports scattered around him.

'You've spoken to Donal's friends, I see,' Sandy said, and he could hear her leafing through the pages he'd faxed to her earlier in the day.

'Over and over again,' he said wearily. 'In fact, I'm going to call in to one of his friends again on Saturday while I'm in Tralee. I've got a dental appointment,' he added casually and then wondered why.

'The dentist, yuck, I'd rather have my eyes gouged out,' she murmured.

Jack laughed.

'Don't they have dentists in Foynes?'

'I've to see a specialist.'

He could hear the smile in her voice. 'Don't they have specialists in Limerick?'

'OK, OK,' he laughed. 'So I wanted to ask Donal's friend a few more questions.'

'Tralee, Tralee,' she repeated, rustling through paper. 'A-ha,' the paper rustling stopped. 'Andrew in Tralee, friend from college, works as a web designer.'

'That's him.'

'I don't think Andrew knows anything more, Jack.'

'How do you know?'

'Judging by his answers during questioning.'

'I didn't give you that file.' Jack sat upright.

'I used to be a garda. Conveniently for me, it's about the only place I managed to make friends.'

'I need to see those files.' Jack's heart raced. There was something new, something more for him to stay awake at night analysing.

'We can meet up soon,' she dismissed him politely. 'I suppose talking to Andrew again wouldn't hurt.' There was the sound of her leafing through more pages and she was silent for a long time.

'What are you looking at?'

'Donal's photograph.'

Jack picked it up from his pile and stared at it too. It was becoming too familiar to him; it was looking more like just a photograph and less like his brother every day.

'Good-looking guy,' Sandy complimented. 'Nice eyes. Do you two look alike?'

Jack laughed. 'I feel inclined to say yes after that.'

They continued studying the pages.

'You don't sleep?' Sandy asked.

'No, not since Donal went missing. What about you?'

'I've just never been a great sleeper.'

He laughed.

'What?' she asked defensively.

'Nothing. You being a light sleeper is a great answer,' he said playfully, dropping the pages onto his lap. In the deathly silence of the cottage he listened to the sound of Sandy's breathing and her voice, and tried to imagine what she looked like, where she was and what she was thinking.

After a long silence her voice was gentler. 'I've a lot of missing people on my mind. There's too much to think about, too many places to look to allow sleep to come. You can't find anyone or anything in dreams.'

Jack looked towards the closed bedroom door and agreed.

'But why I told you that, I have no idea,' she grumbled to the sound of more paper being shifted.

'Tell me honestly, Sandy, what's your success rate?'

Paper rustling stopped. 'It depends on the level of the missing case. I'll be honest with you, cases like Donal's are difficult. There has already been a large-scale search and it's rare that I have found someone under these circumstances. But with general missing cases I find people around forty per cent of the time. You should know that not all the people I find return to their families. You have to be prepared for that.'

'I am prepared. If Donal's lying in a ditch somewhere I want him back here so we can bury him and give him a proper funeral.'

'That's not what I mean. Sometimes people go missing deliberately.'

'Donal wouldn't do that,' Jack said dismissively.

'Perhaps not. But there have been situations just like this where I've learned that people just like Donal, from families just like yours, voluntarily move on from their lives without a word to anyone close to them.'

Jack digested this. It hadn't occurred to him that Donal would take off of his own free will and he found this scenario hugely improbable. 'Would you tell me where he was if you found him?'

'If he didn't want to be found? No, I couldn't tell you that.'

'Would you tell me *if* you found him?'

'It depends on how prepared you are to accept being unable to know where he is.'

'All I would want to know is that wherever he is, he's safe and happy.'

'Well, then I would tell you.'

After a long silence, Jack asked, 'Is there much work for you? On the rare occasions that people go missing, don't their families turn to the Gardaí to deal with it?'

'That's true. There aren't many severe cases for me like Donal's, but there's always something or someone to find. There are categories of missing people that the Gardaí can't and won't investigate.'

'Like what?'

'You really want to know this?'

'I want to know everything about it.' Jack looked at the clock: two thirty a.m. 'And besides, I've nothing better to do at this time of night.'

'Well, sometimes I find people that others have merely lost contact with – long-lost relatives, old school friends or adopted children trying to find their biological parents, that kind of thing. I work quite a lot alongside the Salvation Army, trying to trace people. Then there are the more serious cases such as people who have disappeared, many of them of their own volition, and families just want to know where they are.'

'But how would the Gardaí know it was their choice?'

'Some people leave messages behind saying they don't want to return.' He could hear her unwrapping something in the background. 'Sometimes they take their personal effects with them or sometimes people have previously expressed dissatisfaction with their situation.'

'What are you eating?'

'A chocolate muffin,' she replied with her mouth full. She swallowed. 'Sorry, did you hear me properly?'

'Yeah, you're eating a chocolate muffin.'

'No, not that,' she laughed.

Jack smiled. 'So the families come to you for cases the Gardaí can't deal with.'

'Exactly. A lot of my work, using the help of other missing persons agencies in Ireland, is in specifically tracking cases that aren't classed as high risk. If a person has left home of their own accord they won't be accepted as missing but it doesn't ease the worries of their families and friends.'

'So they're just forgotten about?'

'No, a record will be made at the station but the

extent of the enquiries is left to the discretion of the garda in charge of the station.'

'What if somebody who was incredibly unhappy with his life packed his bags to be alone for a while, but then went missing? Nobody would look for him because he previously expressed a dislike of his life. And haven't we all done that at some point?'

Sandy was silent.

'Am I wrong in thinking that? Wouldn't you want to be found?'

'Jack, I can only assume that there's only one thing *more* frustrating than not being able to find someone, and that's not being found. I would want someone to find me, more than anything,' she said firmly.

They both thought it over.

'I'd better go now.' Jack yawned. 'I've to be up for work in a few hours. Will you sleep now?'

'After I go through all these files again.'

He shook his head in wonder. 'Just so you know, if you'd told me you'd never found anyone, I'd still be on this phone.'

She was quiet for a moment. 'And if I'd never found anyone, I would be too.'

15

Jack woke up earlier than Gloria, as usual. Her head rested on his chest, her long brown hair spread across his skin, tickling where it fell down alongside his ribs. He silently and very slowly moved his body from under hers and slipped out of bed. Gloria moaned sleepily and settled back down with a peaceful look on her face. He showered and dressed and left the bungalow before she had even stirred.

Every morning he left their home before she did to be at work at eight a.m. Gloria didn't start work as a guide in Foynes Flying Boat Museum until ten o'clock. The museum was Foynes' number-one tourist attraction, celebrating the era between 1939 and 1945 when Foynes was the centre of the aviation world, with air traffic between the US and Europe. Gloria, always more than willing to talk and help people, worked as a multilingual guide in the museum from March until October.

Apart from the museum, Foynes was famous for one other thing: the invention of Irish coffee. During cold and rainy weather, people waiting at the air terminal needed something stronger than coffee to keep them warm. Thus Irish coffee was born.

In a matter of days from now, Foynes would be overrun by bands playing music on the festival stage, the farmers' market in museum square, the regatta, and the children's street art would decorate the town for the Irish Coffee Summer Festival. As usual, the celebratory fireworks would be sponsored by the

Shannon Foynes Port Company, which was exactly where Jack was headed that morning.

After greeting and consulting his colleagues, Jack took his place in the gigantic metal crane and got to work loading cargo. He enjoyed his job and felt a sense of satisfaction, knowing that someone just like him, somewhere on foreign soil, would unload the gift he had helped wrap. He enjoyed placing things where they belonged. He knew everything and everyone had a place in life: every piece of cargo that lay stocked up on the docks and every man and woman who worked alongside him had a space to slot into and a part to play. Every day he had the same goal: moving things and putting them where they belonged.

He could hear Sandy's voice in his head, repeating the same sentence over and over again. *I can only assume that there's only one thing more frustrating than not being able to find someone, and that's not being found. I would want someone to find me, more than anything.*

He carefully placed the cargo onto the ship, lowered himself to the ground, to the surprise of his watching colleagues, took off his helmet, threw it to the ground and ran. Some watched in confusion, some in anger, but those closest to him viewed his exit with sympathy, for they guessed that even a year on, Jack could no longer sit in his perch high above the ground, so high he felt he could see the entire county and all that was in it, except his brother.

For Jack, running down to his car, all he could think about was finding Sandy, so she could bring Donal back to where he belonged.

Jack's continuous questions about Sandy Shortt to the hotels, inns and bed-and-breakfasts in Glin were beginning to raise eyebrows. Impatience was entering the voices of the once-friendly members of staff, and diversions of his phone calls to duty managers were becoming more frequent. Now, with still no clues as to where Sandy was, Jack found himself taking deep breaths of fresh air down by the Shannon Estuary. The River Shannon had been a prominent feature in Jack's life. Ever since he was a child he had wanted to work in Shannon Foynes Port. He had loved the excitement of the bustling docks that housed the monstrous machines that roamed the river's edge like metal herons with long steely legs and beaks.

He had always felt a connection with the river and wanted to be a part of helping all it carried. His mother and father had brought the family to Leitrim on a summer holiday one year, the holiday that remained more vivid in Jack's mind than any other. Donal wasn't born and Jack hadn't yet reached ten years old. It was on that holiday he learned where and how the great river began, slowly and quietly at first in County Cavan before it picked up speed, gathering the secrets and spirit of each county with each part of soil it eroded. Each tributary was like an artery being pumped from the heart of the country, whispering its secrets in hushed and excited babbles until it eventually carried them to the Atlantic where they were lost with the rest of the world's whispered hopes and regrets. It was like Chinese whispers, starting out small but eventually growing and becoming exaggerated, from the freshly painted wooden boats that bobbed on the surface in Carrick-on-Shannon, to finally carrying steel and metal ships alongside cranes and warehouses that was the grand excitement of Shannon Foynes Port.

Jack rambled aimlessly down a quiet road along the Shannon Estuary, grateful for the peace and quiet. Glin Castle disappeared behind the trees as he walked further down the track. A splash of bright red glowed from behind the greenery in an area that had long ago been used as a car park but was now overgrown and merely used as a walk for ramblers and birdwatchers. The gravel was uneven, the white lines had faded and weeds grew from between every crack. There sat an old red Fiesta, battered and dented, its gleam long ago rubbed away. Jack stopped in his tracks, immediately recognising the car as the Venus flytrap that had captured the long-legged beauty from the garage the previous morning.

His heart quickened as he looked around to find her but there was no sight or sound of any other presence. A coffee-filled Styrofoam cup sat on the dashboard, newspapers piled up on the passenger seat alongside a towel, which led Jack's overactive imagination to believe she was jogging nearby. He moved away from the car in fear she would return to find him peering through the windows. The coincidence of them meeting once again in another deserted area filled him with far too much curiosity for him to walk away. And saying hello to her again would be a welcome joy to a day lacking in results.

After forty-five minutes of waiting around, Jack began to feel bored and foolish. The car looked like it had been abandoned years ago in the forgotten area, yet he knew for sure that he had seen it being driven yesterday morning. He moved closer and pressed his face against the glass.

His heart almost stopped. Goose bumps rose on his skin as a shiver ran through his body.

There on the dashboard, beside the cup of coffee and a mobile phone with missed calls, was a thick brown file with 'Donal Ruttle' written in neat handwriting across the front.

16

I tapped my shoe against the plate that once held the chocolate digestives, causing a loud tinkling sound to echo through the clearing. Around me the four sleeping bodies were lazily stretched out on the forest floor, and Bernard's snores seemed to get louder with every minute that passed. I sighed loudly, feeling like a pesky hormonal teenager who couldn't get her way. Helena, whom I hadn't spoken to for an hour, raised her eyebrows at me, trying to show her lack of amusement although I knew well that she was enjoying every second of my torture. Over the past hour I had 'accidentally' knocked over the china, dropped a packet of biscuits on Joan and had a rather loud bout of coughing. Still they slept and Helena refused to lead or even direct me out of the woods to the other life she had spoken of.

Hearing laughter, I had attempted to make my own way out but, finding my way blocked by thousands of identical leering pines, I decided that getting lost once was enough, to get lost a second time in already unusual circumstances would be just plain stupid.

'How long do they usually sleep for?' I asked loudly in a bored tone, hoping my voice would disturb them.

'They like to get a good eight hours.'

'Do they eat?'

'Three times a day; usually solids. I walk them twice a day. Bernard in particular loves the leash.' She smiled into the distance as though remembering. 'And then they partake in the occasional personal grooming,' she finished.

'I meant do they eat here?' I looked around the clearing in disgust, no longer caring if I insulted their annual camping resort. I couldn't help my agitation but I hated to be pinned down. Usually I came and went in my life as I pleased, in and out of others'. I never even succeeded in staying in my own parents' house for very long, usually grabbing my bag by the door and running. But here, I had no place to go.

Laughter echoed in the distance once again.

'What is that noise?'

'People call it laughter, I think.' Helena settled down in her sleeping bag, looking snug and smug at the same time.

'Have you always had an attitude problem?' I asked.

'Have you?'

'Yes,' I said firmly, and she laughed. I let go of my frown and smiled. 'It's just that I've been sitting in these woods for two entire days now.'

'Is that an apology?'

'I don't apologise. Not unless I really need to.'

'You remind me of me when I was young. Young*er*. I'm still young. What has you so irritable at such a young age?'

'I'm not a people person.' I looked around as I heard another bout of laughing.

Helena continued talking as though she hadn't even heard it. 'Of course you're not. You've just spent the guts of your life working to find them.'

I registered her statement but decided not to respond to it. 'Do you not hear these sounds?'

'I grew up beside a train station. When friends stayed over they'd be kept awake all night by the noise and the vibrations. I was so used to it I couldn't hear a thing, yet the creaking on the stairs when my parents went to bed woke me every time. Are you married?'

I rolled my eyes.

'I'll take that as a no. Do you have a boyfriend?'
'Sometimes.'
'Have you got children?'
'I'm not interested in children.' I sniffed the air. 'What is that smell? And who is laughing? Is there somebody nearby?'

My head whizzed round like a dog trying to snap at a fly. I couldn't discern where the sounds were coming from. They had seemed to be coming from behind me but when I'd turned round the noise appeared to be louder in the other direction.

'It's everywhere,' Helena explained lazily. 'What the new people here compare to a surround-sound system. You probably understand that more than I.'

'Who's making that noise and is someone smoking a cigar?' I sniffed the air.

'You ask a lot of questions.'

'And you didn't when you first arrived here? Helena, I don't know where I am and what's going on, and you're not being much help.'

Helena at least had the decency to look embarrassed. 'I'm sorry. I'd forgotten what it's like.' She stopped and listened to the sounds. 'The laughter and these smells are just entering our atmosphere now. So far, what do you know about people who come here?'

'That they're missing.'

'Exactly. So the laughter, cries and scents that arrive are missing too.'

'How can that be?' I asked, utterly confused.

'Sometimes people lose more than just socks, Sandy. You can forget where you put them first of all. Forgetting things is just parts of your memory missing, that's all.'

'You can remember again, though.'

'Yes, but you don't remember *all* things and you don't find *all* things. Those things end up here, like the touch and smell of someone, the memory of their exact face and the sound of their voice.'

'That's bizarre.' I shook my head, unable to take it all in.

'It's really very simple if you remember it like this. Everything in life has a place and when one thing moves, it must go somewhere else. Here is the place that all those things move to.' She held her hands up to display our surroundings.

A thought suddenly occurred to me. 'Have you ever heard your own laughter or cries?'

Helena nodded sadly. 'Many times.'

'*Many* times?' I asked in surprise.

She smiled. 'Well, I had the great privilege of being loved by many people. The more people who love you, the more people you have out there to lose memories. Don't make that face, Sandy. It's not as desperate as it sounds. People don't intend to lose memories. Although there are always some things that we would rather forget.' She winked. 'It could be that the real sound of my laughter has been replaced by a new memory, or that, when a few months after I went missing my scent left my bedroom and my clothes, the scent they tried so hard to remember was altered. I'm sure the image I have of my own mother's face is very different from how she actually looked but, forty years on and no reminder, how is my mind to know, exactly? You can't hold on to all things for ever, no matter how hard you grip them.'

I thought of the day I'd hear the sound of my own laughter drifting overhead, and I knew it would only happen once because there was only one person who knew the true sound of my laughter and cries.

'All the same,' Helena looked up to the now bright sky with tears in her eyes, 'you do sometimes feel like catching them and throwing them back to where they came from. Our memories are the only contact we have. We can hug, kiss, laugh and cry with them over and over again in our minds. They're very precious things to have.'

Chuckles, hisses, snorts and giggles filtered through the air, floating by our ears on the wind, the light breeze carrying the faint scents like the forgotten smell of a childhood home; a kitchen after a day's baking. There's a mother's forgotten smell of her baby, now grown up: baby powder, Sudocrem, candy-smelling skin. There are older, musty smells of favourite grandparents: lavender for Grandma, cigar, cigarette and pipe smoke for Granddad. There are the smells of lost lovers: sweet perfumes and aftershaves, the scent of sleepy morning lie-ins or simply the unexplainable individual scent left behind in a room. Personal smells as precious as the people themselves. All the aromas that had gone missing in people's lives had ended up here. I couldn't help but close my eyes and breathe in those scents and laugh along with the sounds.

Joan stirred in her sleeping bag and I snapped out of my trance. My heart began to race in anticipation of finally seeing beyond the woods.

'Good morning, Joan,' Helena sang so loudly she succeeded in waking Bernard too. He awoke with a start, raising his head and revealing his spaghetti strips hanging to the wrong side. He looked around sleepily, his hand feeling for his glasses.

'Good morning, Bernard,' Helena said so loudly she succeeded in waking both Marcus and Derek.

I stifled a laugh.

'Here you go, a nice hot drop of coffee to wake you up.' She thrust steaming mugs in their faces.

They looked at her sleepily in confusion. As soon as they'd taken their first sip of coffee Helena threw off her blanket and rose to her feet.

'Well, that's enough hanging around now. Let's go, everybody.' She started folding her blanket neatly and packing away the utensils.

'Why are you talking so loudly and what's the rush?' Joan held her messy bed head and whispered as though she was suffering a hangover.

'It's a brand-new day so let's drink up and we'll head back as soon as you're all done.'

'Why?' Joan asked, sipping quickly.

'What about breakfast?' Bernard moaned like a child.

'We'll have that when we get back.' Helena grabbed his mug from him, threw the remainder of the coffee over her shoulder and packed the mug in a bag. I had to look away out of fear of laughing.

'What's the rush?' Marcus asked. 'Is everything OK?' He watched her intensely, still unsure of my presence.

'Everything's fine, Marcus.' She placed a hand on his shoulder caringly. 'Sandy just has some work to do.' She smiled at me.

I did?

'Oh, how lovely. Are you staging a play? It's been such a long time since we've done a play,' Joan said excitedly.

'I do hope you give us notice of the auditions well in advance because we'll need time to prepare. It's been a while,' Bernard said worriedly.

'Don't worry,' Helena jumped in, 'she will.'

My mouth dropped open but Helena held a hand up to stop me from protesting.

'Have you ever thought of doing a musical?' Derek asked, packing away his guitar. 'There would be huge interest in taking part in a musical.'

'That's a very strong possibility.' Helena spoke as though dismissing a child.

'Will they be group auditions?' Bernard asked, a little panicked.

'No, no,' Helena smiled, and I finally knew what she was up to. 'I think Sandy will want to spend a little time with everyone alone. Well,' she lifted Bernard's blanket from off his shoulders and began folding it while he watched open-mouthed, 'let's get ourselves ready so we can show Sandy around. She'll need to find a good venue for the show.'

How quickly Bernard and Joan got ready.

'By the way, I meant to ask you,' Helena whispered, 'were you working when you arrived here?'

'What do you mean exactly?'

'Were you on a job or following the trail of somebody

at the time you arrived here? It's such an important question but I forgot to ask it.'

'Yes and no,' I replied. 'I was jogging by the Shannon Estuary when I found myself here but my reason for being in Limerick was work-related. I had just taken on a new case five days beforehand.' I thought back to the phone call that I'd received from Jack Ruttle late one night.

'The reason I ask is because I wonder what it was about *that* person out of all the missing people you've searched for, that brought you here. Had you a strong link to him?'

I shook my head but knew I wasn't quite telling the truth. The late-night phone calls with Jack Ruttle had been very different from all my other cases. They were phone calls I enjoyed receiving, he was someone I could talk with about other things besides business. The more I spoke to the likeable Jack, the harder I worked trying to find his brother. There was only one other person in my life who could allow me to feel similarly.

'What was the missing person's name?'

'Donal Ruttle,' I said, remembering the playful blue eyes from the photograph.

Helena thought about it. 'Well, we might as well start now. Anyone here know a Donal Ruttle?' She looked around.

<h1 style="text-align:center">17</h1>

Jack paced alongside the red Ford Fiesta, feeling a mixture of impatience, frustration and anxiety. Occasionally he would stop, stare in the passenger window and will the door to open so he could grab the file and hungrily scoff the information on the pages. Then he'd calm down and pace again. He looked around, not wanting to venture far from the car in case Sandy Shortt returned and drove off without him.

He couldn't believe Sandy Shortt was the woman from the petrol station. They had passed by each other as though they were strangers but just as when he'd been speaking over the phone, he had felt something when he saw her, a bond that linked them. At the time he had thought it was because they were the only two in the place so early in the morning, but now he knew that connection was more. And now, here again, he had come across her in a hidden place. Something was drawing him to her. What he'd give to go back to that moment so he could talk to her about Donal. So she had come to Glin after all. He knew she wouldn't have let him down, and she had driven through the night just as she'd promised. Finding her car in this desolate spot only raised more questions than he already had. If she was in Glin, where had she been on Sunday when they were due to meet?

He looked at his watch. Three hours had passed since he'd come across the car and there was still no sign of her. A more important question reared its ugly head: where was she now?

He sat down on the dilapidated kerb by the car and did what he had become accustomed to doing over the past year. He waited. And he wasn't going to budge an inch until Sandy Shortt came back to her car.

I followed the group through the trees, my heart beating so loudly I could barely hear Bernard, who was chatting to me constantly about his previous years' acting experience. I nodded now and then when I felt his eyes on me. Disappointingly, there had been no reaction to Donal's name when asked; just shrugged shoulders and mumbles of 'I don't know'. But a reaction had stirred within me as soon as Helena mentioned his name to the others because hearing it made it all become real to me. I would be seeing people I had been searching for, for years.

I felt as though all my life's work led up to this moment. Nights of no sleep, distancing myself from possible friends and caring parents had left me living a solitary life I had been content with, but it was a life haunted by friendships and relationships with people I'd never met. I knew everything about them: their favourite colours, their best friends' names, their favourite bands, and I felt that with every step I took I was closer to meeting my long-lost friends, my missing parents, uncles, aunts and family. Recognising these emotions alerted me to the island I had become. None of those missing people I thought of so fondly would even know me. When their eyes fell upon me they would see a stranger, yet my eyes would see anything but. Though we had never met, family photos of past Christmases, birthdays and weddings, first days of school, debutante balls were firmly imprinted in my memory. I had sat with crying parents and been shown photo album after photo album, yet I couldn't remember a day when I had shared a couch with my own family and done the same. The people I lived for didn't even know of my existence and I hadn't acknowledged that of the people who lived for me.

I could see up ahead where the trees ended. The stillness of the woods was dissipating and instead there was lots of movement, noise and colour. So many people. I stopped walking with the group and shakily held out my hand to hold on to the trunk of a pine.

'Sandy, are you OK?' Bernard asked, stopping beside me.

The group stopped walking and turned to look at me. I couldn't even smile. I couldn't pretend everything was OK. The master of lying was caught in a web of lies I'd weaved myself. Helena pushed her way from the front of the group and rushed over to me.

'Go ahead, all of you. We'll meet you later on,' she dismissed them, and when they didn't move: 'Go on!' Slowly they turned round and reluctantly left the shade for the light.

'Sandy.' Helena softly placed her hand on my shoulder. 'You're trembling.' She put her arm round my shoulders and held me to her. 'It's OK, you've nothing to fear here. It's perfectly safe.'

It wasn't the safety of the place my body shook for. It was the fact that I had never felt as if I belonged anywhere. I had spent my life detaching myself from anyone who wanted to be close, dissociating myself from friends and lovers because they never answered my questions or tolerated or understood my searches. They made me feel like I was wrong and, without them knowing it, maybe even a little crazy, but I had a passion to just *find*. Finding this place was just one big answer to a life-long question that had caused me to sacrifice everything. I'd hurt so many people that loved me in order to help those that I couldn't see and now as I was just about to see them I was afraid to let them in too. I used to think that I was a saint, just like Jenny-May Butler on the nine o'clock news; I thought I was Mother Teresa with a missing persons file, making sacrifices to help others. In reality I'd sacrificed nothing. My behaviour suited me and only me.

The people in this place were the people I had clung to. When I grabbed my bag by the door of my family home in Leitrim it was for these people. When I ended relationships and turned down invitations to nights out it was for these people.

But now that I'd found them, I had no idea what to do.

18

Helena and I stepped out of the darkness of the shaded woods and entered a world of colour. I held my breath at the sight before me. It was as though grand red curtains had parted to welcome a production on such a grand scale I could barely focus on one thing for long enough. What welcomed my eyes was an entire bustling village of nations gathering. Some people were walking alone, others gathering in twos, threes, groups and in crowds. Sights of traditional costumes, sounds of combined languages, scents of cuisine from all over the world. It was rich and alive, bursting at the seams with colour and sound as though we'd followed the path of a pulse to reach the heart of the woods. And there it pumped, people flowing here, there and everywhere.

Sophisticated wooden buildings lined the street, with doors and windows decorated with ornate carvings. Each building was constructed from a different timber, the varying shades and grains camouflaging the village so that it and the woods were combined and almost one. Solar panels lined the roofs – hundreds of roofs into the distance. All around were wind turbines, up to one hundred feet tall, with blades going round and round in the blue skies, their dark shadows circling on rooftops and roadways. The village was nestled among the trees, among mountains, among wind machines. Before me, hundreds of people, dressed in traditional costumes from all eras, *lived* in a lost place that looked real and smelled real, and when I held out my hand

and felt the fabric of someone rush by, it felt real. I fought with myself to believe it.

It was a scene I was familiar yet unfamiliar with all at the same time because everything I could see was composed of recognisable elements from home, but used in such very different ways. We hadn't stepped back or forward, we had entered a whole new time. A great big melting pot of nations, cultures, design and sound mixed to create a new world. Children played, market stalls decorated the road and customers swarmed around them. So much colour, so many new sounds, unlike any country I'd been in. A sign beside us said 'Here'.

Helena linked my arm, a gesture I would have shrugged off had I not physically needed her to prop me up. I was stunned. I was Ali Baba who'd stumbled across the cave of treasures, Galileo after his discoveries through the telescope. More importantly, I was a girl of ten years old who had found all her socks.

'Every day is market day,' Helena explained softly. 'Some people like to trade whatever bits they've found for other things of value. Sometimes they're of no value at all but it's become a bit of a sport now. Money has no value – all we need is found readily on the streets – so there is no need to work for pay to provide for ourselves. There is, however, a requirement to work to help the village, age, health and other personal reasons permitting. Our occupations are more of a community service rather than for self-gain.'

I looked around in awe. Helena continued talking softly in my ear, holding my arm as my body shook.

'The turbines are something you will see throughout the land. We have many wind plants, most of them among the mountain gaps that produce wind funnelling. One wind machine can produce enough electricity for up to four hundred homes a year, and the solar panels on the buildings also help generate energy.'

I listened to her but barely heard a word. My ears were tuned into the conversations around me, to the sounds of the monstrous wind turbine blades breaking through the air. My nose was adjusting to the crisp freshness that seemed to fill my lungs with cool air in one small breath. My attention turned to the market stall closest to us.

'It's a mobile phone,' a British gentleman explained to an elderly stall owner.

'What use have I for a mobile phone?' the Caribbean stall owner dismissed him, laughing. 'I've heard those things don't even work here.'

'They don't, but—'

'But nothing. I have been here forty-five years, three months and ten days.' He held his head high. 'And I don't see how this music box is a fair trade for a phone that doesn't work.'

The customer stopped fuming and appeared to view him with more respect. 'Well, I've been here only four years,' he explained politely, 'so let me show you what phones can do now.' He held the phone up in the air, pointed it at the stall owner and it made a clicking sound. He showed the screen to the salesman.

'Ah!' He started laughing. 'It's a camera! Why didn't you say?'

'Well, it's a camera *phone* but, even better, look at this. The person who owned it took a whole pile of photos of themselves and whatever country they live in.' He scrolled down the phone.

The stall owner handled it gently.

'Somebody here might know these people,' the customer said softly.

'Ah, yes, mon,' the salesman replied gently, nodding. 'This is very precious indeed.'

'Come on, let's go,' Helena whispered, leading me by the arm.

I began to move as though on autopilot, looking around open-mouthed at all the people. We passed the customer and stall owner; they both nodded and smiled. 'Welcome.'

I just stared back.

Two children playing hopscotch stopped their game

on hearing the men's salutation. 'Welcome.' They both gave me toothless grins.

Helena led me through the crowd, through the choruses of welcomes, the nods and smiles of well-wishers. Helena acknowledged them all politely for me. We walked across the street towards the large wooden two-storey building with a decked porch across the front. An intricate carving of a scroll and theatrical feathered pen decorated the door. Helena pushed the door open and the scroll and feather halved as though bowing and holding out their arms to make way for us.

'This is the registry. Everyone comes here when they first arrive,' Helena explained patiently. 'Everybody's name and details are logged in these books so that we can keep track of who is who and how many people are here.'

'In case anybody goes missing,' I said smartly.

'I think you'll find that nothing goes missing here, Sandy.' Helena was serious. 'Things have no place else to go and so they stay here.'

I ignored the chill of her implication and instead tried unsuccessfully to inject humour into the situation. 'What will I do with myself if I've nothing to look for?'

'You'll do what you've always wanted; you'll seek out those you searched for. Finish the job you started.'

'Then what?'

She was silent.

'Then you'll help me get home, right?' I asked rather forcefully.

She didn't respond.

'Helena,' a cheery fellow called out from where he was sitting behind a desk. On the desk a series of numbers was displayed. Beside the main door there was a board with all the countries of the world, their associated languages, some I'd never even heard of, and their corresponding numbers. I matched one of the numbers on his desk to a familiar one on the board. 'Country: Ireland. Languages: Gaelic, English.'

'Hello, Terence.' Helena seemed glad of the interruption to our conversation.

It was then I looked around the room for the first time. There were dozens of desks in the large room. Each desk had a series of numbers and behind each desk sat a person of a different nationality. Queues had formed before the tables. The room was quiet and filled with the tension of hundreds of people who had just arrived, who couldn't yet comprehend their situation. They each looked around the room nervously with wide terrified eyes as they hugged their own bodies for comfort.

I noticed Helena had joined Terence at his desk.

He looked up as I approached them. 'Welcome,' he smiled softly. I sensed sympathy in his voice and his accent revealed his Irish roots.

'Sandy, this is Terence O'Malley. Terence, this is Sandy. Terence has been here for . . . oh gosh, how many years has it been now, Terence?' Helena asked him.

Eleven years, I thought.

'Almost eleven years now,' he replied with a smile.

'Terence worked as a—'

'Librarian in Ballina,' I cut in before even thinking about it. Ten years on, he was still recognisable as the single, fifty-five-year-old librarian who had disappeared on his way home from work eleven years ago.

Helena froze and Terence looked confused.

'Oh, yes, I told you that before we came in,' Helena jumped in. 'Silly me. I must be getting old, repeating myself like that,' she laughed.

'I know the feeling,' Terence laughed, pushing his sliding spectacles back up his nose.

I'd always thought his nose was exactly like his sister's. I studied it some more.

'Well,' Terence began to fidget under my glare and he turned to Helena for backup, 'let's get down to business now, shall we? If you wouldn't mind taking a seat, Sandy, I'll help you go through this form. It's very simple really.'

As I took a seat before the desk I looked at the queues around me. To my right a woman was helping a young boy onto the chair before her desk.

'*Permettimi di aiutarti a sederti e mi puoi raccontare tutto su come sei arrivato fin qui. Avresti voglia di un po' di latte con biscotti?*'

He looked at her with big brown eyes, as lost as a puppy, and nodded. She nodded to someone behind her, who disappeared through a door behind the desk and returned moments later with a glass of milk and a plate of cookies.

To my right, a bewildered-looking gentleman stepped up to the top of the queue. The man at the desk, name tag revealing 'Martin', smiled at him encouragingly. '*Nehmen Sie doch Platz, bitte, dann helfe ich Ihnen mit den Formularen.*'

'Sandy.' Terence and Helena were calling me, trying to get my attention.

'Yes, what, sorry,' I snapped out of my trance.

'Terence was asking you where you are from.'

'Leitrim.'

'Is that where you lived?'

'No. Dublin.' I looked around as more people were led into the room, looking dazed.

'And you went missing in Dublin,' Terence confirmed.

'No. Limerick.' My voice was quiet as all the thoughts in my head got louder and louder.

'You know Jim Gannon . . . Leitrim town . . . ?'

'Yes,' I replied, watching a young African woman draping her ochre-coloured blanket tighter around her body as she looked about her strange surroundings in fear. Armbands of copper, weaved grasses and beads decorated her skin. We locked eyes for a moment before she quickly looked away and I continued speaking to Terence as though I wasn't really there. 'Jim owns the hardware store. His son taught me geography.'

Terence laughed happily about it being a small world.

'A lot bigger than I thought,' I replied, my voice sounding like it was coming from somewhere else.

Terence's voice came and went in my head as I looked around at all the faces, all the people who had one moment ago been on their way to work, or walking to the shop and who had suddenly found themselves here.

'. . . for a living?'

'She's involved in theatre, Terence. She runs an acting agency.'

Some more mumbling as I tuned out.

'. . . is that right, Sandy? You run an agency of your own?'

'Yes,' I said absentmindedly, watching as the little boy beside me was led by the hand through a door behind the Italian registry desk.

He watched me with big worried eyes all the way. I smiled at him and his frown softened. The door was closed behind him.

'Where does that door lead?' I asked suddenly in the middle of one of Terence's questions.

He stopped. 'Which door?'

I looked around the room and noticed for the first time there was a door behind each desk.

'All of them. Where do they all lead to?' I asked faintly.

'That's where people are briefed on what we know, where we are and what happens here. There's counselling services and employment opportunities, and we arrange for somebody from here to come to greet them so that they can guide them around for however long they're needed.'

I looked at the large solid oak doors and didn't say anything.

'As you have already met Helena, she will be your guide,' Terence said gently. 'Now we'll just get through the last of these questions and then you can get out of here, which I'm sure you're looking forward to do.'

The main door opened and sunlight filled the room again. Everyone looked up to see a young girl, no older than ten years old, with soft bouncing blonde curls and big blue eyes, walk into the room. She sniffled and wiped her eyes, following the guide who led her into the room.

'Jenny-May,' I whispered, my head becoming dizzy again.

'And your brother's name?' Terence asked, working his way down the form.

'No, hold on a minute. She doesn't have a sister,' Helena interrupted. 'She told me earlier she was an only child.'

'No, no,' Terence sounded slightly agitated, 'I asked her if she had any sisters and she said Jenny-May.'

'She mustn't have heard you correctly, Terence,' Helena said calmly, and the rest of their sentences turned to murmuring in my ears.

My eyes continued to follow the little girl as she was led through the room; my heart beat faster just as it always had when Jenny-May Butler was within a few feet of me.

'Maybe you could clear this up.' Terence looked at me. His face appeared and faded from my vision.

'Maybe she's not well, Terence. In fact, she looks very pale.' Helena's voice was close to my ear now. 'Sandy, would you like to—'

That's when I passed out.

19

'Sandy . . .'

I could hear my name being called and felt a warm breath on my face. The smell was familiar: sweet coffee, which sent my heart into its usual flutter, fanning my body and causing excited chills to chase one another just below the surface of my skin.

Gregory's hand softly brushed back strands of hair from my face as though gently brushing away sand on an excavation site to reveal something far more precious than me. But that's what he was, my excavator, the one who unearthed all that was buried beneath to discover my hidden thoughts. One hand was placed at the back of my neck as though I was the most fragile thing he'd ever held; the other softly traced the line of my jaw, occasionally running up my cheeks and through my hair.

'Sandy honey, open your eyes,' the voice whispered close to my ear.

'Move back, everybody!' a louder and more aggressive voice shouted nearby. 'Is she OK?' His voice got louder, closer.

The comforting hand moved from my hair to my hand and grasped it tightly, his thumb soothingly stroking my skin as he spoke quietly. 'She's not responding. Call an ambulance.' His voice was distorted and it echoed in my head. My head hurt.

'Oh, Mother of Jesus,' the voice muttered.

'Sean, get the kids back into the school. Don't let them watch this,' my saviour said calmly.

Sean, Sean, Sean. I knew that name. Knew that voice.

'Where's that blood coming from?' he panicked.

'Her head. Get the kids away.' My hand was held tighter.

'He hit her hard, the bastard.'

'I know, I saw. I was watching her from the window. Call the ambulance.'

Sean's shouts to the kids to go inside moved further away and I was left in the echoing silence with the angel. I felt soft lips on my hand.

'Open your eyes, Sandy,' he whispered. 'Please.'

I tried to but they felt like they were glued together, like a lotus nestled in the mud, forced to open its petals ahead of time. My head was heavy, my thoughts clumsy and slow as it throbbed and pulsated repeatedly with abnormally strong force in the protective hand that cradled it. The ground felt cold and rough beneath me. Concrete. Why was I on the ground? I struggled to get up but my body resisted the action, and still my eyes wouldn't open.

I heard the ambulance in the distance and I fought to open my eyes. They opened just a slit. Ah. Mr Burton. My saviour. He held me in his arms, looking down at me as though he'd just discovered gold in the Leitrim tarmacadam. He had blood on his shirt – was he hurt? His eyes looked hurt as they searched my face. I suddenly remembered the great big spot on my chin that I wished all day I'd popped that morning. I tried to move my hand to cover it but it felt like my hand had been dipped in concrete and left to dry.

'Oh, thank God,' he whispered, his hand holding mine tighter. 'Don't move yet. The ambulance is almost here.'

I had to cover my spot. I was finally this close to Mr Burton after four years and I looked a mess. My seventeen-year-old's hormones were ruining the moment I'd been dreaming of. Hold on, he'd said, ambulance. What had happened? I tried to speak and a croak passed my lips.

'It's going to be OK,' he hushed, his face close to mine.

I believed him and forgot my pain for a moment while I once again self-consciously felt for my spot.

'I know what you're trying to do, Sandy, so stop it.' Gregory attempted to laugh lightly while carefully removing my arm from my face.

I groaned, words still not coming to me.

'He's not so awful, you know. His name is Henry, he's been keeping me company while you've been so rudely passed out. Henry, meet Sandy; Sandy, meet Henry, although I don't think you're a very welcome guest here.' He ran his finger across my chin, lightly brushing the spot as though it were the most beautiful thing about me.

So there I was with blood running from my head, a spot named Henry on my chin and a face so aflame it could have powered the entire town. I began to close my eyes again. The sky seemed so bright it pierced my pupils and sent spears of pain through my sockets and into my already throbbing head.

'Don't close your eyes, Sandy,' Gregory said more loudly.

I opened them and caught the worry in his face before he had a chance to hide it.

'I'm tired,' I finally whispered.

'I know you are.' He held me tighter. 'But stay awake with me for a while. Keep me company until the ambulance gets here,' he pleaded. 'Promise me.'

'Promise,' I whispered, before shutting them again.

A second siren arrived on the scene. A car pulled up nearby. I could feel the vibrations on the concrete near my head and I feared the tyres would run over me. Doors opened and slammed.

'He's over there, Garda.' Sean was back, shouting. 'He drove straight into her, wasn't even looking,' he panicked. 'This man here saw it.'

Sean was quietened down, I heard a man crying. Heard garda voices trying to comfort, radios crackling and beeping, Sean being led away. Footsteps came closer to me, there was a mumbling above my head of concerned voices. All the time Gregory whispered in my ear words that sounded pretty, the vowels easy in my ringing ears. The sounds shut out the sirens, the cries of fear, the shouts of panic and anger, the feel of the cold concrete and the sticky wet trickling down my ear.

As the ambulance sirens got louder, Gregory's tones became more urgent as I began to drift away in his arms.

'Welcome back.'

I awoke to see a worried Helena wafting a fan in my face.

I groaned and my hand flew to my head.

'You've got a nasty bump so I'd advise you not to touch it,' she said gently.

My arm kept moving.

'I said don—'

'Ouch.'

'Serves you right,' she said haughtily, and walked away.

I squinted around the unfamiliar room, feeling the egg-sized bump that had formed above my temple. I was on a couch; Helena was at a sink facing a window. The light was bright and illuminated her, blurring her around the edges as though she were a holy vision.

'Where are we?'

'My home.' She didn't turn around, continued rinsing a cloth.

I looked around. 'Why do you have a couch in the kitchen?'

Helena laughed lightly. 'Of all the questions you could have asked, that is the first one you chose.'

I was silent.

'It's not a kitchen, it's a family room,' was her reply. 'I don't cook here.'

'I don't suppose you have electricity.'

She grunted. 'Once you get a chance to look around outside you'll see we have a system of what we call *solar panels*.' She dragged out the words as though I was slow. 'They're similar to the ones found on pocket calculators and they generate electricity from the sun. Each house has its own power voltage system,' she said excitedly.

I lay back on the couch, feeling dizzy, and closed my eyes. 'I'm aware of how solar panels work.'

'They exist there too?' She was surprised.

I ignored her question. 'How did I get here?'

'My husband carried you.'

My eyes flew open and I winced with the pain. Helena still didn't turn around and the water still flowed.

'Your husband? You can get married here?'

'You can get married anywhere.'

'Not technically true,' I protested meekly. 'My God, electricity *and* marriage? This is too much for me,' I mumbled, the ceiling beginning to swirl above me.

Helena sat beside me on the couch and held a cold face cloth over my forehead and eyes. It was soothing on my throbbing, burning head.

'I had the most awful dream that I was in a bizarre place where all the missing things and people in the world go,' I grumbled. 'Please tell me that was a dream or at least a nervous breakdown. I can handle a nervous breakdown.'

'Well, if you can handle *that* then you can handle the truth.'

'What is the truth?' I opened my eyes.

She was silent as she stared at me, then sighed. 'You know the truth.'

I closed my eyes and fought the urge to cry.

Helena grabbed my arm, squeezed it and leaned in with urgency in her voice. 'Hang in there, Sandy. It will make sense to you after a while.'

I didn't think that possible.

'If it makes you feel better, I haven't told anybody else what you've told me. *No one*.'

It did make me feel better. I could figure out whatever it was I had to do in my own time.

'Who is Jenny-May?' Helena asked curiously.

I closed my eyes and groaned, remembering the scene at the registry. 'Nobody. Well, not nobody, she's somebody. I thought I saw her in the registry, that's all.'

'It wasn't her?'

'Not unless she stopped ageing the day she arrived here. I don't know what I was thinking.' Frowning, I reached to my pounding head again.

There was a light tap on the door and it was gently opened by a man so tall and broad he filled the doorframe. White light impatiently squeezed itself through the small spaces he didn't fill, shooting into my eyes like spears of fire direct from the sun. He was of similar age to Helena, with shining ebony skin and intense black eyes. He stood well over my own six foot one height and for that reason alone I immediately liked him. His figure dominated the room yet brought with it a feeling of safety. A small smile revealed snow-white teeth, while eyeballs like purified sugar melted around pupils of black coffee. He was hard, but softened around the edges. His cheekbones sat high and proud on his face, his jaw square yet, above it, cushioned lips for his words to bounce from and launch themselves into the world.

'How is our kipepeo girl doing?' The rhythmic sound of his words revealed his African roots.

In confusion I looked to Helena, who was looking at the man in surprise, the surprise I could tell, not for his sudden presence but for the words he had spoken. She knew this man and I assumed knew his words. I didn't know what the words meant but I guessed the speaker of them to be her husband. We locked eyes and I felt drawn to his gaze, trapped in his and he trapped in mine as though a magnet drew us together. He held a plank of wood in his large hands; sawdust covered his white linen clothes.

'What does "kipepeo" mean?' I asked the room. The room didn't answer, but knew.

'Sandy, this is my husband, Joseph,' Helena introduced us. 'He's a carpenter,' she added, referring to the plank of wood in his hand.

My unusual introduction to Joseph the carpenter was interrupted by a little girl who entered the kitchen through Joseph's legs, giggling while her curly black hair bounced with each childish skip. She ran to Helena and grabbed her leg.

'And who's this, the immaculate conception?' I asked, the little girl's shrieks sounding like wails in my pounding head.

'Almost,' Helena smiled. 'She's our daughter's immaculate conception. Say hello, Wanda.' She ran her hand through the little girl's hair.

A toothless smile greeted me before she shyly ran out of the room under her grandfather's legs. I looked up from where she had disappeared to Joseph's eyes again. He was still watching me. Helena looked from him and back to me, not with suspicion but with . . . I couldn't quite figure it out.

'You must sleep.' He gave a single nod.

Under the gaze of Helena and Joseph, I placed the face cloth over my eyes and allowed myself to drift. For once I was too tired to ask questions.

'Ah, there she is now.' My father's voice greeted me as though I was suddenly pulled up out of the water. Muffled sounds gradually became audible, faces eventually recognisable. It was as though I was reborn into the world, facing my loved ones from a hospital bed once again.

'Hello, honey.' My mother rushed to my side and took my hand. Her face appeared close to mine, too close for me to focus and so she remained a lavender-scented blur with four eyes. 'How do you feel?'

I hadn't yet had time to feel before I was asked and so concentrated on it before answering. I didn't feel very good.

'OK,' I responded.

'Oh, my poor baby.' Her cleavage dominated my view as she leaned over to kiss my forehead, glossy lips leaving my skin sticky and ticklish. I looked around the room after she'd moved and saw my father, scrunched cap in hand and looking older than I remembered. Perhaps I had been underwater longer than I'd thought. I winked, he smiled, relief written all over his face. Funny how it was the job of the patient to make the visitors feel better. It was as though I was on stage and it was my turn to entertain. The walls of the hospital had rendered everyone speechless and awkward as though we had met that day for the very first time.

'What happened?' I asked after sipping water through a straw from a cup that had been thrust at me by a nurse.

They looked nervously at one another. Mum decided to do the honours.

'A car hit you, honey, just as you were walking across the road from the school. He came around the corner . . . he was just a young lad, only on his provisional licence. His mother didn't know he'd taken the car, bless her heart. Luckily Mr Burton saw it all happen and could give the Gardaí a full witness report. He's a good man, is Mr Burton,' she smiled. 'Gregory,' she added to me a bit more quietly.

I smiled too.

'He stayed with you all the way into the hospital.'

'My head,' I whispered, the pain suddenly entering my body as though hearing the story had reminded it it needed to do its job.

'Your left arm is broken.' Mum's glossy lips glistened in the light as they opened and closed. 'And your left leg,' her voice shook lightly, 'but apart from that you're very lucky.'

It was only then I noticed my arm in a sling and my left leg in a cast, and found it amusing that they thought I was lucky even after being hit by a car. I started to laugh but the pain stopped me.

'Oh, yes, and you've a cracked rib,' my father added quickly, looking apologetic for the lack of warning.

When they had left, Gregory rapped lightly on the door. He looked more gorgeous than ever with his tired concerned eyes and messy hair that I could imagine he ruffled as he paced with worry. He always did that.

'Hi,' he smiled, walking in, and kissed me on the forehead.

'Hi,' I whispered back.

'How are you feeling?'

'Like I've been hit by a bus.'

'Nah, it was only a Mini. Stop looking for attention.' A smile tickled the sides of his lips. 'You've heard the bad news, I assume?'

'That I have to do my Leaving Cert exams orally?' I lifted up the cast covering my left arm. 'I think the Guards will still accept me,' I smiled.

'No,' he said seriously, and took a seat on the bed. 'We lost Henry in the ambulance. I think it's the oxygen mask that took him out.'

I started laughing but had to stop.

'Oh shit, sorry.' He immediately stopped joking around at seeing me in pain.

'Thanks for staying with me.'

'Thanks for staying with me,' he replied.

'Well, I did promise,' I smiled, 'and I'm not planning on disappearing anywhere anytime soon.'

20

Jack sat on the gravel surface beside what he assumed to be the now abandoned car. His overactive mind contemplated every possible scenario as to where Sandy Shortt was, why her car was in the middle of the trees in an old car park, why she hadn't turned up to their meeting the previous day and why she hadn't returned to her car for the entire day. Nothing made sense to him any more. He hadn't moved from the car's vicinity all day. A quick search of the surroundings showed no sign of her – or of any other life, for that matter. It was late now. The forest area was black, the only lights being those from distant ships out at sea and Glin Castle in the distance behind the tall pines. Jack could barely see past the end of his nose. The blackness of the night was thick and engulfing, yet he was afraid to leave in case he missed her, in case somebody towed the car away, which in turn would take away Donal and all possible traces of him.

The file sat on the dashboard. The mobile phone beside it was the only immediate source of light, flashing every few seconds to signal a dying battery. If Sandy wasn't going to arrive at her car anytime soon, Jack needed to get his hands on that phone to see her recent call list and, with luck, trace somebody from her phone book who would help find her. If her battery went dead it was possible he wouldn't be able to switch it back on without a pin code.

His own mobile phone rang again: Gloria looking

for him, no doubt. It was eleven o'clock and he couldn't bring himself to answer; he didn't know what he could possibly say to her. He didn't want to lie, so lately he had avoided conversation with her altogether, leaving the house before she woke, arriving home after she had fallen asleep. He knew his behaviour would most definitely be upsetting her – sweet, patient Gloria, who never nagged as friends of his claimed their partners did. She always gave him the space he needed and felt secure enough in herself to know that he wouldn't betray her. But he was – he was betraying her patience now and perhaps even driving her away. Maybe that's what he wanted. Maybe it wasn't. All he knew was that Donal's disappearance had brought an end to talks of family and marriage that had previously seemed so important to him, to them both. Right now he was putting their relationship aside and focusing on finding his missing brother. Somehow he felt that by finding Sandy, he would be one step closer to finding Donal, or perhaps that was just another excuse, another obsession to delay moving on with life, to delay confronting Gloria over a relationship he no longer knew how he felt about.

He did the only thing he could think of. He picked up his phone and rang Graham Turner, the guard Jack and his family had been dealing with during the search for Donal.

'Hello?' Graham answered. The background was noisy with shouts, chatter and laughter. Pub noises.

'Graham, it's Jack,' Jack shouted in the silent wooded area.

'Hello?' Graham shouted again.

'It's Jack,' he raised his voice even higher, startling whatever animals had taken refuge in the nearby trees.

'Hold on, I'm going outside,' Graham shouted. The voices and noise grew louder as the phone was carried through the pub. Finally there was silence. 'Hello?' Graham said more quietly.

'Graham, it's Jack.' He kept his voice down now. 'Sorry to call you so late.'

'No problem. Is everything OK?' Graham asked with concern, used to Jack's late-night calls over the past year.

'Yeah, things are OK,' Jack lied.

'Any news on Donal?'

'No, no news. Actually I was calling you about something else.'

'Sure, what's up?'

How on earth was he going to explain this? 'I'm just a bit worried about someone. I was due to meet them yesterday morning in Glin but they didn't show up.'

Silence.

'I see.'

'A message on my answer phone was left before leaving Dublin to let me know they were on their way down but they never showed and the car is parked down by the estuary.'

Silence.

'Yeah.'

'I'm just starting to get worried, you know?'

'Yeah, yeah, I know. You're bound to under the circumstances.'

That one statement suddenly made Jack feel like a raving paranoid lunatic. Maybe he was.

'I know it sounds like nothing but I think it's something, you know?'

'Yeah, yeah, of course,' Graham said hurriedly. 'Sorry, hold on one minute.' The phone was covered as voices became muffled. 'Yeah, another pint. Cheers, Damian. I'll be in as soon as I finish my smoke,' he said, and then came back on the line. 'Sorry about that.'

'No problem. Look, I know it's late and you're out. I apologise for calling.' Jack held his head in his hands, feeling like a fool. His story had sounded stupid and his concern for Sandy unnecessary as soon as he had vocalised them, but he knew deep down that things weren't right.

'Don't worry about it. What do you want me to do? What's the guy's name and I'll ask around?'

'Sandy Shortt.'

'*Sandy* Shortt.' Yep, the guy was a woman.

'Yeah.'

'Right.'

'And you were to meet her . . . ?'

'In Glin yesterday. We passed one another at Lloyds station, you know the one on—'

'Yeah, I know it.'

'Yeah, well, we met there at about five thirty a.m. but she didn't show up later that morning.'

'She didn't say where she was going when you met her?'

'No, we hardly spoke.'

'What does she look like?'

'Very tall, curly black hair . . .' He trailed off, realising he had no idea what Sandy Shortt looked like, he had no reason to believe that the woman he had passed at the petrol station was even Sandy Shortt. The only proof he had was a file on the dashboard with Donal's name on it. The driver could have been anyone. He had allowed all the pieces to fit together nicely without even questioning its sense, which right now seemed like none at all.

'Jack?' Graham was calling him.

'Yeah.'

'She's tall with curly black hair. Know anything else? Her age or where she's from or anything?'

'No. I don't know, Graham. I'm not even sure what she looks like. We only ever spoke over the phone. I don't even know if that was her at the station.' He suddenly had a thought. 'She used to be a garda. In Dublin. She quit four years ago. That's all I know.' He gave up.

'OK, right, well, I'll make a few phone calls and get back to you.'

'Thanks.' Jack felt humiliated; his story was full of holes. 'You'll keep this between us, won't you?' he asked quietly.

'Will do. All well with Gloria?' The tone was accusing. Or maybe it wasn't – it was possible Jack was misjudging everything these days.

'Great, yeah.'

'Good. Send her my regards. You've got a saint there, Jack.'

'Yeah, I know,' he replied defensively.

Silence. Then pub atmosphere.

'I'll get back to you, Jack,' Graham shouted. The line went dead.

Jack thumped his head, feeling like an idiot.

At midnight, as he ran a finger up and down the side of the cold metal car as he paced, his phone rang. He had already texted Gloria to let her know he would be home late, and so he knew it wasn't her when he answered.

'Jack, it's Graham here.' His tone was gentler than before. 'Listen, I made a few calls, asked around the lads to see if any of them knew a Sandy Shortt.'

'Go on.' His heart thumped.

'You should have told me, Jack,' Graham said softly.

Jack nodded in the darkness, though Graham couldn't see him.

Graham continued, 'Seems you shouldn't worry about her. A good few of the lads knew her,' he laughed, and stopped himself. 'They said she disappears all the time without letting anyone know. She's a hermit, keeps to herself and comes and goes as she pleases but always comes back within a week or so. I wouldn't worry about her, Jack. This seems to be in keeping with her usual behaviour.'

'But what about her car?'

'A 1991 red Ford Fiesta?'

'Yeah.'

'That's hers all right. Don't worry about it; she's probably around the area checking out the place. The lads say she's a keen jogger, so she probably parked there and went for a run earlier or maybe the car wouldn't start or something simple as that. Anyway it's been a little over twenty-four hours since you were supposed to meet. There's no need to panic.'

'I thought the first twenty-four hours were supposed

to be the most important,' Jack said through gritted teeth.

'In missing cases they are, Jack, but this Sandy Shortt isn't missing. She likes to disappear all the time. The way it sounds, from speaking to her ex-colleagues, is that she'll contact you within a few days. Apparently that's the way she works. I was told that even her own family never know where she is. They called the guards on three occasions years ago but they don't bother any more. She comes back.'

Jack was silent.

'There's not much I can do. There's nothing to go on, nothing to suggest she's in any danger.'

'I know, I know.' Jack rubbed his eyes wearily.

'As a word of advice, be careful of those kinds of people. Agencies like Sandy Shortt's are just out to make money, you know? I wouldn't be surprised if she's done a runner. There's nothing that they can do that we haven't already done. There aren't any more places to search that we haven't already searched.'

Sandy hadn't asked for a cent, knowing that Jack hadn't got a cent to give.

'I had to do something,' was all he replied. He didn't like how Graham was referring to Sandy. He didn't believe she was crooked, he didn't believe she had gone wandering on an investigation without her phone, her file, her diary and her car, or was still jogging at midnight. Nothing Graham said made sense, yet nothing Jack said aloud seemed to make sense either. He was going entirely by instinct alone, instinct that had been affected by Donal's disappearance and a week of nightly phone calls to a woman he had never met.

'I understand,' Graham responded. 'I'd probably do the same myself if I was in your shoes.'

'What about my stuff that's locked in her car?' Jack bluffed.

'What stuff?'

'I sent her Donal's file and a few other things. I can see them sitting in the car. If she's going to take my money and run, I'd at least like my things back.'

'I can't help you out in that area, Jack, but I wouldn't be asking any questions if by morning your belongings are back in your possession.'

'Thanks, Graham.'

'Anything at all to help.'

A few hours later, as the sun was rising over the estuary, casting orange hues on black ripples, Jack found himself sitting in Sandy's car, leafing through Donal's file and through all the pages of garda reports that only Sandy had been able to retrieve through her contacts. Her diary revealed a plan to go to Limerick city that day to visit one of Donal's friends, Alan O'Connor, who had been out with Donal the night of his disappearance. Hope returned at the possibility of meeting her there. The cramped car smelled sickeningly sweet of the vanilla air freshener that hung from the dashboard mirror, mixed with the tinge of stale coffee from the Styrofoam cup balanced below it. There was nothing about the car that gave him any more clues as to the type of person Sandy was. There were no wrappers left behind, no CDs or cassettes revealing her taste in music. Just an old, cold car with work and cold coffee left behind.

It had no heart; she had taken that part with her.

21

I awoke I wasn't sure how many hours later, to a little girl with wild black frizzy hair perched next to me on the arm of the couch, watching me with the same intense black eyes as her grandfather.

I jumped.

She smiled. Dimples dented her yellow skin and her eyes softened to a dark brown.

'Hi,' she chirped.

I looked around the room that was now almost pitch-black save for the orange light creeping under the kitchen door, lighting the floor just enough for me to be able to make out my surroundings and the little girl half-lit before me. The sky outside the window over the sink was black. Stars, the same stars I never paid the slightest bit of notice to at home, hung above like Christmas lights decorating a toy village.

'Well, aren't you going to say hi?' the little voice chirped happily.

I sighed; I had never had time for children and had even despised being one myself.

'Hi,' I said with disinterest.

'See? That wasn't so hard, was it?'

'Excruciating.' I yawned and stretched.

She hopped off the arm of the sofa and bounced onto the end, joining me but crushing my feet in the process.

'Ouch,' I moaned, tucking my legs closer to my body.

'That can't have hurt.' She lowered her head and viewed me doubtingly.

'How old are you, one hundred and ninety?' I asked, pulling my blanket around me tighter as though it would protect me from her.

'If I was a hundred and ninety, I'd be dead.' She rolled her eyes.

'And what a shame that would be.'

'You don't like me, do you?'

I thought about that. 'Not really.'

'Why not?'

'Because you sat on my feet.'

'You didn't like me before I sat on your feet.'

'True.'

'Most people think I'm cute,' she sighed.

'Really?' I asked in mock surprise. 'I don't get that impression.'

'Why not?' She didn't seem to be insulted, just more interested.

'Because you're three feet tall and you have no front teeth.' I closed my eyes, wishing she'd go away, and rested my head against the back of the couch. The throbbing in my head had dissipated but the chirping at the end of the couch would no doubt bring it back in full force.

'I won't be like this for ever, you know,' she said, trying to please me.

'I hope so, for your sake.'

'Me too,' she sighed, and rested her head on the back of the couch, imitating me.

I stared at her in silence, hoping she'd take the hint and go away. She smiled at me.

'Most people's impression of me is that I don't want to talk to them,' I hinted.

'Really? I don't get that impression,' she imitated me, saying the words with difficulty in her toothless mouth.

I laughed. 'What age are you?'

She held up her hand, displaying four fingers and a thumb.

'Four fingers and a thumb?' I asked.

She frowned and looked at her hand again, her lips moving as she counted.

'Is there a special school kids go to, to learn to do that?' I asked. 'Can't you just say "five"?'

'I can say "five".'

'So what, you think holding up a hand is cuter?'

She shrugged.

'Where is everyone?'

'Asleep. Did you used to have a television? We have televisions here but they don't work.'

'Bummer for you.'

'Yeah, bummer,' she sighed dramatically, but I don't think she cared. 'My grandma says I ask a lot of questions but I think you ask more.'

'You like to ask questions?' I was suddenly interested. 'What kind of questions?'

She shrugged. 'Normal questions.'

'About what?'

'Everything.'

'You keep on asking them, Wanda, maybe you'll get out of here.'

'OK.'

Silence.

'Why would I want to get out of here?'

Not such normal questions after all, it appeared. 'Do you like it here?'

She looked around the room. 'I prefer my own room.'

'No, this *village* place,' I pointed out the window, 'where you live.'

She nodded.

'What do you do all day?'

'Play.'

'How tiring for you.'

She nodded. 'Sometimes it is. I start school soon, though.'

'There's a school here?'

'Not in here.'

She still couldn't get past this room. 'What do your parents do all day?'

'Mama works with Granddad.'

'She's a carpenter too?'

She shook her head. 'We don't have a car.'

'What does your dad do?'

She shrugged again. 'Mama and Daddy stopped liking each other. Have you got a boyfriend?'

'No.'

'Ever had one?'

'I've had more than one.'

'At the same time?'

I didn't answer.

'Why aren't you with any of them now?'

'Because I stopped liking them.'

'*All* of them?'

'Almost all of them.'

'Oh, that's not very nice.'

'No . . .' My mind wandered. 'I suppose it's not.'

'Does it make you sad? It makes Mama sad.'

'No, it doesn't make me sad.' I laughed awkwardly, not feeling comfortable with her gaze or loose tongue.

'You look sad.'

'How can I look sad when I'm laughing?'

She shrugged again. That's why I hated children; there were so many empty spaces in their minds and not enough answers, the exact reason why I'd hated being one myself. There was always a lack of knowledge about what was going on and seldom did I come across an adult who could enlighten me.

'Wanda, for someone who asks a lot of questions you don't know a lot of answers.'

'I ask different questions than you do,' she frowned. 'I know lots of answers.'

'Like what?'

'Like . . .' she thought hard, 'the reason Mr Ngambao from next door doesn't work in the fields is because he has a sore back.'

'Where are the fields?'

She pointed out the window. 'That way. That's where

our food grows and then everyone goes to the eatery three times every day to eat it.'

'The entire village eats together?'

She nodded. 'Petra's mama works there but I don't want to work there when I'm older, or in the fields. I want to work with Bobby,' she said dreamily. 'My friend Lacey's dad works in the library.'

I searched for the importance of her sentence and found none. 'Does anybody ever think of spending their time more wisely, like trying to get the hell out of here?' I asked smartly, more to myself.

'People try to leave,' she said, 'but they can't. There's no way out, but I like it here so I don't mind.' She yawned. 'I'm tired. I'm going to bed. Night.' She climbed down off the couch and made her way to the door, dragging a torn blanket behind her. 'Is this yours?' She stopped, bending over to pick up something from the floor. She held it up and I saw it shine as the light seeping in from under the door hit it.

'Yes,' I sighed, taking my watch from her hands.

The door opened, orange light filled the room, forcing me to close my eyes, and then I heard it shut again and I was alone in the darkness with the words of a five-year-old ringing in my ears.

People try to leave but they can't. There's no way out . . .

That was the other thing I hated about kids: they always said the exact things that deep down you already knew, would never admit, and most certainly never wanted to hear.

22

'So Joseph is a carpenter. What is it that you do, Mary?'
I asked Helena as we strolled along the dusty path of
the village.

Helena smiled.

We had walked through the village and now
wandered beyond, passing fields of glorious golds and
greens, dotted with people of all nationalities, who
stooped and rose as they worked the farm, growing
anything and everything I had ever and never heard of.
Dozens of greenhouses speckled the landscape, the
villagers taking every opportunity to grow what they
could. Like the diverse people, the weather had arrived
in this place in all its fiery yet vital forms. Already in
just a few days I'd experienced the sweltering heat, a
thunderstorm, a spring breeze and a winter chill, incon-
sistent weather I presumed to be the explanation for
the unusual array of plants, trees, flowers and crops
that all managed to successfully live together in the same
environment. The explanation for the humans, I hadn't
yet learned. But it seemed there were no rules regarding
nature in this place. Four seasons in one day was
accepted, welcomed and adapted to. It was warm again
now as we strolled side by side, me feeling revitalised
after sleeping more hours in one night than I had since
I was a child. Since Jenny-May.

'Since Jenny-May *what*?' Gregory would always ask
me. 'Since she went missing?'

'No, just *since Jenny-May* full stop,' I would reply.

That morning I encountered someone I had been searching for for twelve years. Helena had urged me onwards, snapping shut my gaping gob and clicking fingers before my goggling eyes. I was overwhelmed by her presence and I was never overwhelmed. I was dumbfounded, and I was never dumbfounded. I suddenly felt lonely, and I was never lonely. But lately I was a lot of things I never was. After so many years of looking, it was near impossible to remain as serene as Helena when the faces I saw in my dreams passed me in waking hours.

'Stay calm,' Helena had murmured more than once into my ear.

Robin Geraghty was the first of my ghosts to float by. We had been seated at the 'eatery', a stunning timber build on two levels, with a balcony around four sides from which the views of forestry, mountains and fields were displayed to perfection. It wasn't a crammed work canteen, as I had imagined, it was a beautiful building that housed the local villagers for breakfast, lunch and dinner; a scheme created to help ration the food they collected and grew. Money, I learned, had no value here, not even when wallets filled with it arrived on their doorsteps. 'Why spend money on something that arrives in abundance daily?' Helena had asked by way of explanation.

On the front of the building, ornate hand-crafted timber decorated the entrance as it did the registry. Owing to the many languages of the village, Helena explained, these carvings were the most productive and attractive methods of exhibiting the use of the building. Oversized vine of grapes, wine and bread decorated the front, looking so delectable even in its lumber form that I had to run my hand along the smooth curve of the berry.

I was returning from my trip to the buffet-style counter when I saw Robin, causing me almost to drop my tray of doughnuts and frappacino. (It appeared that a box of food had gone missing from a Krispy Kreme delivery van and had arrived on the outskirts of the village that morning, much to my delight. I had visions of a delivery man, clipboard in hand, ignoring the insults of a stressed-out store manager, as he scratched his head in wonder and recounted the contents of his van, parked up on a busy loading bay outside a down-town New York store while I, and a line of hungry people behind me, dived into the basket in a long-lost place.) The appearance of Robin almost caused me to scald myself, it was as though my frappacino got a fright too, wavering slightly in its stance.

Robin Geraghty had disappeared at the age of six. She had gone out to play in her front garden in the suburbs of North Dublin at eleven a.m. but was gone when her mother checked on her at 11.05. Everyone – and I mean *everyone* – the family, the country, the Gardaí, which at that time included me, all thought she had been abducted by the next-door neighbour. Fifty-five-year-old Dennis Fairman, an odd man, a loner, spoke to nobody but Robin each time he passed her, much to her parents' concern.

He said he didn't do it. He swore to me he didn't do it; he kept on repeating that she was his friend and that he couldn't and wouldn't hurt her. Nobody believed him – *I* didn't believe him – yet we didn't have the proof of his guilt. We didn't even have a body. The man became so tormented by his neighbours, by the media, by the constant garda questioning that he ended his own life, a sure sign to the parents and everybody else of his guilt. But as a nineteen-year-old Robin walked by me and made her way to the counter, I felt ill.

Although Robin had disappeared at the age of six, I knew it was her the moment I lifted my ogling eyes from the Krispy Kreme to see the young woman walk by. A computer-generated image of her had been made public and updated every few years. I had memorised it, had used it every day as part of my mind checks when I came across familiar faces. And that face was all of a sudden coming towards me. The computer image hadn't been far off, though her face was fuller, her hair was darker, there was a swing in her hips and a knowledge in her eyes as all she had seen and done had altered all but their colour. All the things a picture couldn't convey. But it was her.

I'd been unable to eat my breakfast; instead I sat at the table with Helena's family in a daze, while Wanda studied me and impersonated my every move. I ignored her and her constant babbling about somebody called Bobby, unable to stop myself from watching Robin while trying to figure out how I felt about seeing this young woman living life as she had done for the past twelve years. My feelings were mixed, my happiness bittersweet, because although all the people I yearned to find surrounded me, it was also the moment I realised that I had spent a colossal portion of my life looking in all the wrong places. It's that moment when you meet your idol, when all your wishes come true; there's a feeling of secret disappointment.

Helena and I stopped walking at an uncultivated multicoloured field filled with bright yellow Bermuda buttercups, blue and mauve milkwort, daisies, dandelions and long grasses; the sweet smell reminding me of the last few breaths I had taken in Glin.

'What's up ahead?' I spotted more buildings peeking out behind a gathering of silver birch, the oak visible against the peeling, papery black and white bark of the trunk.

'That's another village,' Helena explained. 'There are so many new arrivals every day, we couldn't possibly fit into this tiny town. Also, there are so many cultures that wouldn't and couldn't settle for living in environments like this. Their homes are out there.' She nodded towards the faraway trees and mountains.

I hadn't even contemplated that. 'So there are more people I've searched for, over there?'

'Possibly,' she agreed. 'They would have registry offices just as we have here so all the names will be logged, although I'm not sure they'll release the information as it's usually deemed private except in the case of emergencies. Hopefully we won't have to go looking for them. They'll find you.'

I smiled at the irony. 'What exactly is this plan you're hatching?'

'Well,' she smiled and her eyes sparkled mischievously, 'thanks to the list you provided me with, Joan is now taking bookings for private auditions for a new Irish play in about,' she lifted my hand and looked at my watch, 'two hours' time.'

I felt anxious about meeting people like Robin but Helena's plan made me laugh. 'Surely there could have been an easier way to do this.'

'Of course.' Helena threw her lemon pashmina over her right shoulder. 'But this is so much more fun.'

'What makes you think that any of the people on my list will come to these auditions?'

'Are you joking?' She looked surprised. 'Didn't you see Bernard and Joan? Most people here really love to get involved in activities, especially ones held by people from home.'

'Won't the non-Irish communities be jealous?' I half-joked. 'I wouldn't want them to think I'm omitting them from my grand production.'

'No,' Helena laughed, 'everyone will have a laugh at our expense come show time.'

'Show time? You mean we're actually staging a play?' My eyes widened.

'Of course!' Helena laughed. 'We're not dragging twenty people to the auditions just to tell them there's no play, but what exactly that play will be we've yet to decide.'

My headache returned. 'As soon as I start talking to them today they're going to realise the likelihood of my running an acting agency is no more than Bernard's chances of landing a lead role.'

Helena laughed again. 'Don't worry, they won't suspect a thing, and even if they do they won't mind. People tend to reinvent themselves here; they use this

experience as a second chance in life. If what you were
at home was not an acting agent, it doesn't mean that
you're not one here. The longer you're here the more
you'll notice that there really is a good atmosphere
among everyone.'

I had noticed. The atmosphere was relaxed; people
were peaceful and went about their daily duties effi-
ciently yet without rushing or panic. There was room
to breathe, space to think, time to spend wisely and
lessons to be learned. People who were once lost took
time to reflect, to love, to miss and to remember.
Belonging was important, even if it meant joining a
hopeless play.

'Won't Joseph mind that he can't take part?'

'Oh, I don't think that will worry him in the slightest,'
Helena said.

'Joseph is from Kenya?'

'Yes.' We began walking back towards the village.
'Along the coast of Watamu.'

'What was it he called me yesterday?'

Helena's expression changed and I knew she was
feigning ignorance. 'What do you mean?'

'Come on, Helena, I saw your face when he called
me it. You were surprised. I can't remember the word,
Kalla . . . Kappa something, what does it mean?'

Her forehead wrinkled in pretend confusion, 'Sorry,
Sandy, I've no idea. I honestly can't remember.'

I didn't believe her. 'Did you tell him what I do for
a living?'

Her face changed to that same intrigued look from
yesterday. 'He knows now, of course, but he didn't then.'

'He didn't *when*?'

'When he met you.'

'Of course he didn't. I don't expect him to be psychic,
I just want to know what he said.' I stopped walking
out of frustration. 'Helena, please be straight with me.
I can't take riddles.'

Her face pinked. 'You'll have to ask him, Sandy,
because I don't know. Whatever it was, it must have

been in his local Kiswahili language and I'm far from being an expert.'

I was convinced she was lying and so we walked in silence. I looked at my watch again, anxious that I would soon be sharing messages from family members at home. Messages they sent off in their prayers every night to land here and be told. I questioned my ability to transmit their sentiments accurately. What I had said to Helena the previous day was true: I *wasn't* a people person, finding them didn't mean wanting to spend time with them. Wondering where Jenny-May went didn't mean I wanted to go there or wished she'd return.

Helena, as usual, in her own instinctive way picked up on my feelings. 'It was nice being able to tell Joseph about my family at long last,' she said gently. 'We spoke about them until my lids closed and I dreamed about them until the sun came up. I dreamed about my mother and her organisation, about my father and his searching for me.' She closed her eyes. 'I woke up in this place this morning hardly knowing where I was after spending hours in my dreams where I grew up.'

'I'm sorry if I upset you,' I apologised. 'I'm not quite sure how to tell people what it is their families would want me to say.' I played with the watch around my wrist as we walked, wanting to turn back the time that kept ticking on.

Helena's eyes opened and I could see a layer of tears settling on her lower lashes, building up in an invisible reservoir. 'Don't think that about yourself, Sandy. I felt soothed by your words – how could I not be?' Her face brightened. 'I woke up *knowing* I had a mother out there still minding me. Today I feel protected, like I'm swaddled in an invisible blanket. You know, you're not the only one whose life-long questions have been answered. I now have photographs in my mind that I never had before. An entire catalogue has been filed and stored, all in one night.'

I just nodded. There was nothing to say.

'You will be fine with these people; I know you will

be *more* than fine. The people on the list you have given will be arriving in how long?'

I looked at my watch. 'An hour and a half.'

'Right, in ninety minutes, they'll all be there with the full intention of spending a short while of their lives calling Romeo from a balcony or re-enacting the great escape through the art of mime.'

I laughed.

'Anything more you tell them will be a bonus, no matter how you phrase it.'

'Thank you, Helena.'

'No problem.' She gave my arm a comforting pat and I tried to stop myself from stiffening.

I looked down at my clothes. 'There's just one more problem. I've been wearing this tracksuit for days and I would really love a change of clothes. Is there anything you have that I could borrow?'

'Oh, don't worry about that,' Helena said, walking off in the direction of the trees. 'You wait here; I'll be back in a minute.'

'Where are you going?'

'Just a minute . . .' Her voice disappeared, along with her short salt-and-pepper hair and billowing lemon pashmina, into the darkness.

I tapped my foot impatiently, wondering and worrying about where she'd gone. I couldn't lose Helena now. Up ahead I spotted the towering figure of Joseph leaving the woods, carrying logs in one hand, an axe in the other.

'Joseph!' I called.

He looked up and waved with the axe, a motion that wasn't particularly heart-warming, and he made his way towards me. His bald head shone like polished marble, his flawless skin making him appear younger than his years.

'Everything OK?' he asked with concern.

'Yes, I think so. Well, I don't know,' I added with confusion. 'Helena just disappeared into the woods and—'

'What?' His eyes darkened.

'I don't mean *disappeared*.' I realised my error. 'She walked, *walked* into the woods a few minutes ago.' Disappearing from here was impossible, so no wonder Joseph was alarmed. 'She told me to wait here for her.'

He set the axe down and watched the woods. 'She will return, kipepeo girl.' His voice was gentle.

'What does that mean?'

'It means she will come back,' he smiled.

'Not *that* – what does the Kenyan word mean?'

'It is what you are,' he said lazily, his eyes not moving from the trees.

'Which is?'

Before he had a chance to answer the question, Helena reappeared, tugging what appeared to be luggage behind her. 'Found this for you. Oh, hi, sweetheart. I thought I heard you tapping away at the trees. Name on the bag says Barbara Langley from Ohio. Hope, for your sake, Barbara from Ohio has long legs.' She dropped the bag by my feet and dusted off her hands.

'What is this?' I asked open-mouthed, studying the baggage ticket on the handle. 'This was bound for New York over twenty years ago.'

'Great, you'll have a nice retro look,' Helena joked.

'I can't wear someone else's clothes,' I protested.

'Why not? You were going to wear mine,' Helena laughed.

'But I know you!'

'Yes, but you wouldn't have known the person who wore them before me,' she teased, heading off before me. 'Come now, how much time have we left? We're going to the auditions now,' she explained to Joseph, who nodded solemnly and picked up his axe again.

I looked at my wrist. My watch was gone.

'Oh damnit,' I grumbled, dropping the bag back down on the ground and searching around my legs.

'What's wrong?' Helena and Joseph stopped walking and turned round.

'My watch fell off my wrist again,' I grumbled, standing back and scouring the ground.

'Again?'

'The fastener on it is broken. Sometimes it just opens and falls onto the ground.' My voice was muffled as I went down on my knees and searched closer to the ground.

'Well, you were wearing it just a minute ago so it can't have gone far. Just lift the bag,' Helena said calmly.

I looked under the bag.

'That's funny.' Helena came over to where I stood and leaned in to get a closer look at the ground. 'Did you go anywhere when I went into the trees?'

'No, nowhere. I was waiting *right* here with Joseph.' I climbed down onto my knees and began crawling around the dusty floor.

'It can't have gone missing,' Helena said, not at all worried about the situation. 'We'll find it, we always do, here.'

We all stood still as we looked around the small area I hadn't moved from for over five minutes. There was nowhere else it could have fallen. I shook out my sleeves, emptied my pockets, and checked the bag to see if the watch had got caught up. Nothing, no sign, nowhere.

'Where on earth did it roll to?' Helena muttered, examining the ground.

Joseph, who had barely said a word since he'd joined us, stood still in the same place he had been standing all along. His eyes, as black as coal, appeared to have absorbed all light from around him. They were on me the whole time.

Just watching.

23

I spent the next half-hour searching the road for my watch, retracing my steps over and over again in my usual obsessive way. I combed the long grass by the sides of the uncultivated fields and dug my hands deep into the soil lining the forest. The watch was nowhere to be seen, but this brought a strange kind of comfort to me. My mind instantly erased where I was and all that had happened, and for those few moments I was me again with one goal. Finding. As a ten-year-old I would hunt for a single sock as though it had the value of the rarest diamond in the world but this time it was different; the watch was worth far more.

Joseph and Helena watched over me worriedly as I uprooted grass, followed by sods, in order to find the precious jewel that had clung to my wrist for thirteen years. Its inability to remain where it should have been for too much of that time pretty much tallied with the inconsistency of the relationship with the person who had given it to me. But even those times when it released itself from my clutches and flew off, drawn in the opposite direction to the one I was heading, I always looked out for it and wanted to be near it. That way too, exactly like the relationship.

Helena and Joseph didn't pretend, as my parents used to when I had a hunting episode. They looked worried and they were right to, because for people who said nothing could or ever had gone missing in this place, they were finding it difficult having to munch on and digest their own words. At least that's what the obsessive side of me thought. The rational side of me reckoned the more obvious cause for their concern may have just been me, on my hands and knees, covered in dust, dirt, grass stains and muck.

'I think you should stop looking now,' Helena said with a hint of amusement on her face. 'You have lots of people to meet at the Community Hall, not to mention now needing a shower and change of clothes.'

'They can wait,' I said, clawing my way through the grass, feeling soil gathering beneath my fingernails.

'They've waited long enough,' Helena said forcefully, 'and frankly so have you. Stop trying to avoid the inevitable and come with me now.'

I stopped clawing. There was the word I was so used to hearing from Gregory's mouth. 'Avoid'. *Stop avoiding things, Sandy* . . . Was that what I was doing? How I could be avoiding things by concentrating fully on one thing and refusing to leave it, had always been beyond me. Surely avoidance meant walking in the other direction. It was people like Gregory, my parents and now Helena and Joseph who were avoiding dealing with the fact that something had gone missing and couldn't be found. I looked up at Helena, who looked doll-like beside Joseph's huge frame. 'I really need to find that watch.'

'And you will,' she said so easily that I believed her. 'Things *always* show up here. Joseph said he would keep an eye out for you, and maybe Bobby will know something.'

'Who's this Bobby that I keep hearing about?' I asked getting to my feet.

'He works in Lost and Found,' Helena explained handing me the luggage I had abandoned in the middle of the road.

'Lost and Found,' I laughed, shaking my head.

'I'm surprised you didn't end up in the front window,' Helena said gently.

'That's Amsterdam you're thinking of,' I smiled.

Her forehead wrinkled. '*Amsterdam?* What are you talking about?'

Dusting myself off, I left the search scene behind me. 'Helena, you have so much to learn.'

'A wonderful piece of advice, coming from someone who spent the last thirty minutes on her hands and knees trawling through muck.'

We left Joseph standing in the middle of the road, hands on his hips, logs and axe by his feet, surveying the dusty path.

I arrived at the Community Hall dressed as Barbara Langley from Ohio. Her legs, it seemed, were far from long, and she had a penchant for mini skirts and leggings I didn't even dare try on. The other items she unfortunately missed out on wearing on her New York trip were stripy sweaters with shoulder pads that brushed my earlobes and jackets covered with badges of peace signs, Yin and Yang emblems, yellow smiley faces and American flags. I had hated the eighties the first time round; I had no intention of reliving it.

Helena had laughed when she saw me in skin-tight stone-washed jeans that stopped above my ankles, white socks, my own trainers, and a black T-shirt with a yellow smiley face.

'Do you think Barbara Langley was in *The Breakfast Club*?' I asked, trudging out of the bathroom like a child who had been forced to replace her play clothes with a dress and tights for Sunday dinner of green vegetables aplenty.

Helena looked confused. 'I have no idea what clubs she was a member of although I do see others wearing those kinds of clothes here.'

I ended up doing what I had been convinced I would never resort to: grabbing marginally more decent items of clothing lying alongside the roads as we made our way to the village.

'We can go to Bobby's afterwards,' Helena had tried to cheer me up. 'He has a huge collection of clothes to choose from or else there are a few clothes makers around.'

'I'll just get some second-hand clothes,' I preferred. 'I won't be here by the time they finish making me a wardrobe.'

She snorted at that, much to my annoyance.

The Community Hall was a magnificent oak building with a large double-door entrance similar to the others. On it were larger-than-life carvings of people gathered together, arms and shoulders touching and hands holding, while their hair and clothes flapped in a breeze trapped in the walls of wood. Helena pushed open the twelve-foot-tall doors and the crowd parted for us.

A stage stood at the top of the forty-foot-long hall. Around it on three sides were rows of solid oak chairs, and the same above on a second gallery level. A red velvet curtain parted and was held back on both sides by a thick golden rope. On the entire length of the back wall on the stage was a canvas covered in black paint handprints. They were all of different sizes, representing ages from babies to the elderly as they lined up in a row of at least one hundred across and one hundred down. Above it were words written in many languages but reading the English I saw they were 'Strength and Hope'. It was so familiar to me.

'They are the handprints of each person that lives and has lived here over the past three years. Each village has the same in its community hall. I suppose it's our emblem now for here.'

'I recognise it,' I said, thinking aloud.

'Oh, no, you couldn't.' Helena shook her head. 'The Community Hall is the only place you'll see this in the village.'

'No, I recognise it from home. There is a national monument just like it in the grounds of Kilkenny Castle. Each hand was cast from the actual hand of a relative of a missing person. Beside it is a stone with an inscription of the words –' I closed my eyes and recited the inscription I had run my finger over so many times –

'"This sculpture and area of reflection is dedicated to all missing persons. May all relatives and friends who visit find continuing strength and hope." The cast of your mother's hand is there.'

Helena looked as though she was holding her breath as she searched my face, waiting for me to somehow announce that I was joking. I didn't and she exhaled slowly.

'Well, I don't know what to say.' Her voice shook and she turned to look at the mural. 'Joseph thought it would be a nice idea for everyone to do that.' She shook her head in disbelief. 'Wait until he hears what you've told me.'

'Wow,' I said, looking around the rest of the building. It was more like a theatre than a community hall.

'This seats twenty-five hundred people,' Helena explained, moving on from what I had told her, though understandably seeming somewhat distracted. 'The chairs are taken out if we need to hold more but it's very rare that the entire community will attend anything. It's used for lots of different things such as a ballot hall, a discussion forum between the elected council and the community, art galleries, debates, even a theatre for the rare occasions that plays are staged. The list goes on.'

'Who is on the elected council?'

'A representative from each nation in the village. We have over one hundred nations in this village alone and every village has its own council. There are dozens of villages.'

'So what happens at these council meetings?' I asked with amusement.

'The same as everywhere else in the world; everything that needs discussion and decision is discussed and decided.'

'What are the crime levels here?'

'Minimal.'

'How is it kept that way? I don't recall seeing the long hand of the law patrolling the streets on our way here. How is everyone kept on the straight and narrow?'

'There has been a judicial system in place for hundreds of years. We have a courthouse, a rehabilitation institute and a security council, but getting every nation to abide by the same rules isn't always easy. The council at least encourages talk and debate.'

'So this is the sounding house? Do they actually have any power?'

'The power that we have vested in them. Everybody gets one of these in their information pack when they arrive.' Helena took a pamphlet from a display on the wall. 'You should have one too if you bothered to look through your folder. There are voting guidelines.'

I flicked through the pamphlet, reading aloud: '"Vote for those with the ability to listen and to make decisions on behalf of the people in a manner reflecting consensus and serving the wellbeing of all,"' I laughed. 'What else is preached – two legs good, four legs bad?'

'They are the basics of good leadership.'

'Well, does this pamphlet for how to elect a leader work?' I smirked.

'I should think so.' She made her way over to Joan, who was on the far side of the room. 'Seeing as Joseph is on the council.'

My mouth dropped as I watched her cross the room. *'Joseph?'*

'You seem surprised.'

'Yes, well, I am surprised. He seems so . . .' I searched for the correct way to explain without offending her. 'He's a carpenter,' I eventually settled on.

'Those on the council are ordinary people with their own day jobs. He's merely called on to voice decisions when decisions need voicing.'

I couldn't stop smiling. 'I just get the feeling that everybody here is playing "house", you know? It's hard to take seriously,' I laughed. 'Come on. I mean, we're in the middle of *nowhere* and you have councils and courthouses and who knows what else.'

'You think it's funny?'

'Yes! Everywhere I look everyone's playing dress-up

in other people's clothes. How can this place, wherever this place is,' I stressed, 'have any kind of order or rules at all? It exists completely without *logic*. It lacks all sense of *practicality*.'

Helena seemed offended at first but then became sympathetic, which I hated. 'This is *life*, Sandy, *real life*. Sooner or later you'll discover that nobody's playing any games here. We're all just getting on with life and doing what we can to make it as normal as possible, just like everybody else, in every other country, in every other world.' She approached Joan. 'How did you get on with Sandy's list?' she asked, ending our conversation.

Joan looked up in surprise. 'Oh, hello. I didn't hear you both coming. You look,' she gave my eighties outfit the once-over, 'different.'

'Did you get in touch with everyone on the list?' I asked, ignoring her disapproving gaze.

'No, not all of them,' she said, glancing down at her page.

'Let me see.' I grabbed her notepad, my body surged with a sudden rush of adrenalin. My eyes scanned through the list of thirty names I had provided her with: fewer than half of them had ticks beside them. Joan continued talking as I read through the names so quickly I was barely able to take them in. My heart beat wildly, and skipped a beat each time my eyes registered a name and I realised that person was alive and well, and that soon we would be meeting.

'As I was saying,' Joan spoke, angry I had jumped ahead of her story, 'Terence at the registry was no help because he couldn't give out any information unless someone from the council requested it for official reasons.' She eyed Helena warily. 'So I had to just ask around the village. But you'll be pleased to know, Sandy, the Irish community here is so small that everyone knows everyone anyway.'

'Go on,' Helena urged.

'Well, I got in contact with quite a lot of people, twelve in total,' she continued. 'Eight are interested in auditioning, the other four said they'd take part in the production in some way but definitely not on stage. But I didn't get the likes of, let me see . . .' She put her glasses on and lifted the page.

'Jenny-May Butler,' I finished the sentence for her, my heart plunging into the depths of my stomach.

Helena looked at me, obviously recognising the name from the time of my collapse.

'Bobby Stanley,' I read another name, my hopes dashed. I continued, 'James Moore, Clare Steenson . . .' The list of untraceable people went on.

'Well, just because they're not here doesn't mean they're not in the next village,' Joan tried reassuring me.

'What are the chances of that?' I asked, feeling hopeful again.

'I won't lie to you, Sandy. The majority of the Irish community are in this village,' Helena explained. 'Five to fifteen people, at most, arrive each year, and because there are so few of us we tend to stick together.'

'So Jenny-May Butler must be here,' I said forcefully. 'She has to be here.'

'What about the others on the list?' Joan said in a quiet voice.

I scanned it quickly, Clare and Peter, Stephanie and Simon . . . I had sat with their relatives long into the night, thumbed through photo albums and wiped tears through promises of finding their children, brothers, sisters and friends. If they weren't here then it meant I could only suspect the worst.

'But Jenny-May . . .' I started digging into the facts of the case I'd stored in my brain. 'There was no one else. Nobody saw anything or anybody.'

Joan looked confused; Helena sad.

'She has to be here. Unless she's hiding, or else she's in another country; I didn't look into other countries,' I rambled on to myself.

'OK, Sandy, why don't you just take a seat now? I think you're burning up,' Helena interrupted.

'I'm not burning up.' I swatted her hand away. 'No,

she's not hiding and she can't be in another country. She's my age now.' I looked to Joan and everything was clear. 'You have to find Jenny-May Butler, tell everyone that she's my age. She's thirty-four years old. She's been here since she was ten, I know it.'

Joan nodded her head quickly, almost afraid to say no. Helena held out her hands towards me, afraid to touch me yet afraid to move away. I noticed the faces of the two women as they watched me. Worried. I quickly sat down and drank from a glass of water Helena had thrust into my hands.

'Is she OK?' I heard Joan ask Helena as they moved away.

'She's fine,' Helena said calmly. 'She just really wanted Jenny-May for the play. Let's do our best to find her, shall we?'

'I don't think she's here,' Joan whispered.

'Let's look anyway.'

'Can I ask why I was given a list of thirty to find? How does Sandy know they can act? When I contacted them all, they were very surprised. Most of them have never been involved in amateur dramatics. What about all the others who are interested in taking part? They're still allowed to audition, aren't they?'

'Of course everyone's allowed,' Helena fobbed her off. 'The people on the list were just special, that's all.'

Of the two thousand people reported missing in Ireland every year, between five and fifteen will never be found. The thirty people I had chosen were the ones I had spent my entire working life obsessed with finding. Others I had found, others I could give up looking for, knowing something sinister was involved, that harm had sadly come to them or that they'd merely walked away of their own accord. But these thirty on the list – they were the ones that had disappeared without a trace and without reason. These were the thirty that haunted me, the thirty without a crime scene to examine or witnesses to question.

I thought of all their relatives and of how I'd promised I'd find their loved ones. I thought of Jack Ruttle, of how only last week I had made that promise. I thought of how I had failed to show up at our meeting in Glin and how now I had once again failed.

Because according to the list, Donal Ruttle wasn't here.

24

On Tuesday morning, exactly two days since Sandy's no-show, Jack, who had not long returned home with Sandy's file on Donal, stepped out into the fresh July morning air and closed the door to the cottage quietly behind him. Around the town, preparations were being made for the pending Irish Coffee Festival. Banners were rolled up beside telegraph poles, ready to be hung, and the back of a lorry had been opened up as a makeshift stage for the outdoor trad-band performances. The town was quiet now, though, everybody still in the comfort of their beds, dreaming of other worlds. Jack started his engine, the noise of it loud enough in the quiet square to wake the entire town, and he made his way into Limerick city where he would hopefully meet Sandy at Donal's friend Alan's home. He also wanted to pay a visit to his sister Judith.

Judith was the closest of his siblings. Married with five kids, she was a mother from the moment she arrived kicking and screaming into this world. Eight years older than Jack, she had practised her skills of obedience training and nurturing on every doll and every child that lived nearby. The common joke on the street was that there wasn't a doll in the city that didn't sit up straight and shut up when Judith was around. As soon as Jack was born, she turned her attention to him, a real baby whom she could mother and often smother from that day until now. She was the one he ran to for advice and she always found time between school runs, nappy changing and breast-feeding to lend an ear.

As he pulled up outside her terraced house, the front door opened and the wail of a thousand banshees flew past his ears, almost blowing his hair.

'Daaa-deee,' a banshee yelled.

The banshee's father appeared at the door in an off-white creased shirt with an open top button and a loosened tie in an uneven knot. He held in one hand a mug that he clung to for dear life and gulped on with bulging eyes. His other hand gripped a tattered briefcase while the banshee with white-blonde hair, Power Rangers pyjamas and Kermit the Frog slippers clung to his leg.

'Dooon't gooooo,' she yelled, wrapping her limbs around one of his legs as though her life depended on his staying.

'I have to go, sweetie. Daddy has to work.'

'Nooooooo.'

An arm appeared from inside the door, thrusting a slice of toast in Willie's direction. 'Eat,' said Judith's voice over more wails from a second source.

Willie took a bite, slugged down some more coffee and shook Katie from his leg gently. His head disappeared from the doorway, kissed the owner of the arm, shouted, 'Bye, kids!' and the door was slammed. The screams were still audible yet Willie kept a smile on his face. It was eight a.m. and he'd already been through an hour or two of what Jack would consider pure torture. Yet he smiled.

'Hiya, Jack.' His moon-shaped face beamed.

'Good morning, Willie,' Jack said, noticing how his shirt buttons strained at his gut, a coffee stain decorated his shirt pocket and there was toothpaste on his paisley tie.

'Sorry. Can't talk. Escaping,' he chuckled, patting Jack on the back and squeezing into his car. The exhaust let out a bang and off he sped.

Jack looked around the housing estate of tightly

packed grey houses and noticed a similar scene occurring on each doorstep.

He opened the door tentatively, hoping the madhouse wouldn't swallow him whole. He stepped inside and saw fifteen-month-old Nathan running off down the hall, with a bottle hanging from his lips and naked but for a bulging nappy. Jack followed him. Four-year-old Katie, who had only seconds ago clung to her father as though her world was going to end, was sitting a foot away from the television, cross-legged on the floor, a bowl of cereal spilling onto the already stained carpet, completely captivated by dancing bugs singing about the rainforest.

'Nathan!' Judith called pleasantly from the kitchen. 'I have to change your nappy. Come back in here, please!'

She had the patience of a saint, while around her chaos ensued. Toys cluttered every surface, scribbles and drawings were either pinned to the walls or drawn directly *on* the walls. There were baskets of dirty clothes, baskets of clean clothes, clothes horses with drying clothes lining the walls. The television was blaring, a baby was wailing, pots and pans were being banged. It was a human zoo: three girls and two boys, a ten-year-old, an eight-year-old, a four-year-old, a fifteen-month-old and a three-month-old, all running riot and demanding attention, while Judith sat at the kitchen table, dressed in her stained robe, hair wild and unwashed, *things* just everywhere, cluttering every surface and her face a picture of serenity.

'Hi, Jack.' She looked up in surprise. 'How did you get in here?'

'The door was open, and I followed your doorman in.' He nodded at Nathan, who had taken his position on the floor, stinky nappy and all, and had resumed banging pots with a wooden spoon. Three-month-old Rachel was shocked into silence, her eyes widened and her lips parted ready to release bubbles. 'Don't get up.' Jack leaned over Rachel in her cot to kiss Judith.

'Nathan honey, I told you not to unlock the door without Mammy saying so,' Judith explained calmly. 'He keeps turning the lock,' Judith explained to Jack.

Nathan stopped banging and looked up at her with big blue eyes, a double chin with drool dripping from it. 'Dada,' he gurgled in response.

'Yes, you do look like your daddy,' Judith replied, getting to her feet. 'Can I get you anything, Jack? A cup of tea, coffee, toast, earplugs?'

'Tea and toast, please. I've had enough coffee,' Jack replied, rubbing his face wearily as the saucepan banging became almost unbearable.

'Nathan, stop,' Judith said firmly, flicking the switch on the kettle. 'Come on, let's change your nappy.'

She lifted him onto a nappy-changing facility in the kitchen and got to work, giving Nathan her house keys to amuse himself with.

Jack looked away, no longer feeling hungry.

'So why aren't you at work?' Judith asked, holding two podgy legs together at the ankles as though she was about to stuff a turkey.

'I took the day off.'

'Again?'

He didn't answer.

'I spoke to Gloria yesterday. She said you'd taken the day off,' Judith explained.

'How did she know?'

Judith pulled a baby wipe from a container. 'Now is not the time to start thinking your intelligent partner of eight years is stupid. Oh, what's that I hear?' She held her hand to her ear and looked off into the distance. Nathan stopped jangling the keys and watched her. 'Oh, no, I don't hear it any more but I used to hear the sound of wedding bells and the pitter-patter of tiny feet.'

Nathan laughed and continued jangling his keys. Judith popped Nathan back on the floor again, the sound of his feet on the tiles like a duck stepping in puddles.

'Gee, Jack, you've gone awful quiet,' she said sarcastically, washing her hands in the kitchen sink, he noted, over a pile of dirty dishes and cups.

'It's not the right time,' Jack said tiredly, taking the wooden spoon from Nathan, who in turn started screaming, which woke Rachel, who started screaming, which caused Katie to turn up the volume of the television instantly in the living room. 'Besides, this place alone is enough of a contraceptive for me.'

'Yes, well, when you marry a man with the name Willie you pretty much know what you're getting.' In less than one minute Judith had calm again, a cup of tea and a slice of toast on the table before Jack. She finally sat down, removed Rachel from her cot, moved her dressing gown to one side and began breastfeeding while Rachel's tiny fingers opened and closed in mid-air, playing an invisible harp with her eyes closed.

'I've taken the week off work,' Jack explained. 'Arranged it on the way here this morning.'

'You've what?' Judith took a sip of tea. 'They let you have more time off?'

'With a bit of persuasion.'

'That's good. You and Gloria need to spend more time together.' But she could tell by his face that that wasn't the intention. 'What's going on, Jack?'

He sighed, wanting so much to tell her the story but afraid to do so.

'Tell me,' she said gently.

'I came across someone,' he began. 'An agency.'

'Yes?' Her voice was low and questioning like it used to be when he came home from school after being in trouble and was forced to explain such things as why they'd stripped Tommy McGovern naked and tied him to the goal posts in the yard.

'It's a missing persons agency.'

'Oh, Jack,' she whispered, hand flying to her mouth.

'Well, what harm could it do, Jude? What's the damage in one more person having a look?'

'*This* is the damage, Jack. *You*, taking one more week off from work, *Gloria* ringing me, looking for you.'

'She rang?'

'Ten o'clock last night.'

'Oh.'

'So go on, tell me about the agency.'

'No.' He leaned back in his chair, frustrated. 'No, I couldn't be bothered now.'

'Jack, don't be such a child and tell me.'

He waited to cool down before speaking again. 'I came across the ad in the Golden Pages and I gave her a call.'

'Who?'

'Sandy Shortt. I explained the case to her and she told me she'd solved cases like this before. We spoke on the phone until late every night last week. She used to be a garda and she got her hands on a few reports we'd never seen.'

Judith raised her eyebrows.

'She wasn't asking for a penny, Judith, and I believed her. I believed she wanted to help and I believed she could find Donal. She was legit, there's no doubt about it.'

'Why are you speaking about her like she's dead?' she smiled, and then stopped, looking alarmed. 'She's not dead, is she?'

'No,' Jack shook his head, 'but I don't know where she is. We arranged to meet on Sunday morning in Glin. We passed one another at a petrol station but I didn't know it was her until after.'

Judith's forehead wrinkled.

'We'd only ever spoken on the phone, you see.'

'So how do you know it was her?'

'I found her car down by the estuary.'

Judith looked even more flummoxed.

'Look, we were supposed to meet and she left a voice message the night before saying she was on her way over from Dublin but she didn't show up. So I looked around the town, asked for her in all the B & Bs, and when I couldn't find her, I went for a walk by the estuary. That's when I found the car.'

'How can you be sure it was her car?'

Jack opened the bag beside him. 'Because this was on the dashboard.' He placed the file on the kitchen table. 'So was this,' he placed her diary down, 'and this,' her charged mobile phone. 'She labels *everything*, absolutely everything. I went through her bag – all her clothes, her socks, *all* labelled. It's like she's afraid of losing things.'

Judith was quiet. 'You went through her bag?' She shook her head, confused. 'But how did you get these from the car? Maybe she was just taking a walk, Jack. What if she returns to her car and all her stuff is missing? Are you crazy, taking all this?'

'Then I'll have some apologising to do but it's been *two* whole days. That's a long walk.'

Silence while they both remembered how their mother had been desperately worried after two days of Donal's silence.

'I rang Graham Turner.'

'What did he say?' Hands buried her face. The same scenario all over again.

'He said that as it had only been over twenty-four hours and because it was in keeping with her usual behaviour that he didn't think there was any cause to worry.'

'Why, what's her usual behaviour?'

'That she comes and goes as she pleases, keeps to herself and doesn't tell anyone where she's going,' Jack rattled off tiredly.

'Oh.' Judith looked relieved.

'But that doesn't mean you park your car in the middle of trees by the estuary and desert it for two days. That's slightly different from coming and going as she pleases.'

'So let me get this straight,' Judith said slowly. 'The missing persons person is missing?'

Silence.

Judith allowed that thought to roll around in her head, shifting it until it found a place it was comfortable to settle in. She looked contemplative as she moved her jaw from side to side.

Then she snorted and burst out laughing.

Jack sat back in his chair and folded his arms, feeling offended as Judith shook uncontrollably before him. Rachel stopped suckling and watched her bouncing mother, who was now wiping tears from her eyes. Nathan stopped playing with his blocks, stood to his feet to watch his mother. His face broke into a gummy smile and he began laughing, clapping his podgy hands and bouncing his body with delight from the knees up. Eventually Jack felt the corners of his lips tickle and he joined in, laughing deliriously at the ridiculousness of the situation and feeling such relief to let go after so long, even if only momentarily. Once they'd settled down Judith began rubbing Rachel gently on her back, so soothingly it made Jack's eyes feel heavy.

'Look, Judith, maybe Graham is right. Maybe she did just walk away. Maybe she just thought, to hell with all this, and left her car, left her phone, her diary, her life, and gave up. Maybe she's this mad, loony woman who does it all the time with the intention of coming back after a while. Maybe she walked away completely, but *I'm* going to find her, *she's* going to find Donal and *then* she can quit. *Then* I'll let her walk away.'

'You really think this woman could find Donal?' Judith was contemplative.

'She believed she could.'

'What do you think?'

He nodded.

'So if you find her, you'll be helping to find Donal.' She was deep in thought. 'You know, Willie and I were going through the photo album last night with the kids and Katie pointed to Donal and asked who he was.' Her eyes filled. 'Neither Katie or Nathan remember him – they'll *never* have a memory of him – and Rachel,' she looked down at her baby in her arms, 'she doesn't even know he existed. Life is going on without him and he's missing all this.' She shook her head.

Jack couldn't think of anything to say, didn't think there was anything *to* say. The same thoughts ran through his head every second of every day.

'What makes you so sure that a woman you've never even met, a woman you don't know anything about, has the ability to find Donal?'

'Blind faith,' he smiled.

'Since when did you ever have that?'

'Since I spoke to Sandy on the phone,' he replied earnestly.

'There was nothing . . .' she paused and decided to ask anyway, 'there was nothing between you two was there?'

'There was something, but it was nothing.'

'When is something ever nothing?'

He sighed and decided to avoid the question. 'Gloria doesn't know about Sandy – not that there's anything to know – but I don't want her or the rest of the family knowing about the agency.'

Judith didn't look happy.

'Please, Jude.' He grabbed her hand. 'I don't want to bring everyone through all this again. I just want to try by myself. I need to.'

'OK OK.' She let go, holding it up in defence. 'So what are you going to do now?'

'Simple.' He put the file, diary and phone back into his bag. 'I'm going to start looking for her.'

25

I was sixteen years old, in Mr Burton's office. I was sitting on one of the burst velvet chairs, the same since the day I'd arrived over two years ago, but for the extra foam on display. I was staring at the same posters on the walls of the cramped room. The bricked walls had been clumsily painted white, some holes still black and naked of paint, others holding clumps of white. It was all or nothing in this room, never even. Blu-Tack clung to parts of the walls, corners of old posters still hung on to the Blu-Tack. Somewhere in the school I imagined a room fully stocked with corner-less posters.

'What are you thinking about?' Mr Burton finally spoke.

'Corner-less posters,' I replied.

'Ah, that old chestnut.' He nodded. 'How was your week?'

'Crap.'

'Why crap?'

'Nothing very exciting happened.'

'What did you do?'

'School, ate, slept, school, ate, slept, multiplied by five more times and to be multiplied by a million more weeks in my life. My future looks bleak.'

'Did you go out at the weekend? You were saying last week that you'd been asked out by a group of people.'

He always wanted me to make friends. 'Yeah, I went out.'

'And?'

'And it was OK. There was a house party. Johnny Nugent's parents were away, so we all went there.'

'Johnny Nugent?' He raised his eyebrows.

I didn't answer but my cheeks pinked.

'Were you able to forget about Mr Pobbs and enjoy yourself?'

He asked it so seriously, I studied the Blu-Tack again, feeling slightly embarrassed. I'd had Mr Pobbs since I was a baby – a grey, fluffy, one-eyed teddy in blue striped pyjamas, who slept in my bed, and any other bed I stayed in, every night. My parents and I had been away for the week a short time before and as soon as we'd returned I had repacked to go stay with my grandparents for the weekend. Somewhere in changing over my clothes I'd misplaced Mr Pobbs. It had upset me deeply all the time I was at my grandparents', and I'd taken to a two-week-long search of the house on my return, much to my parents' dismay. Last week we had discussed my not wanting to go out with Johnny Nugent at the weekend because I'd have preferred to find Mr Pobbs, my trusted friend, no matter how ridiculous it sounded. It had been difficult leaving the house to go out for the night, knowing that somewhere in there, Mr Pobbs lay hidden.

'So you went out with Johnny Nugent?' Mr Burton went back to the question.

'Yes, I did.'

He smiled awkwardly. He'd obviously heard the rumours too. 'Is everything . . . are you . . . ?' He stopped talking and instead made trumpeting noises with his lips while he thought how to rephrase his question. It was rare to see him awkward as he always seemed to be in control. He was in this room, anyway; other than the small hints of personal information he revealed unwittingly during our, at times, candid talks, I knew nothing of his life outside of these four walls. I also knew not to ask any questions, because he wouldn't answer and because I didn't want to know.

Not knowing, asking and him not answering reminded me that we were strangers in a way. Only inside this room were we familiar. We had created our own world, had rules to follow and had a line between us that, although couldn't be passed, could be danced upon on playful days.

I jumped in and stopped his trumpeting lips from launching into an orchestra of brass instruments. 'Mr Burton, if you're wondering if I'm OK then, please, don't worry. For once in my life I've lost something and I've no intention of searching for it or expect it to come back. I think I'm cured.'

We laughed. And laughed. And when there was an uncomfortable silence while I fantasised about him curing me too, we laughed again.

'Will you see him again? And by that I mean, did you enjoy the company of others? Did you enjoy going out, did you relax, could you forget about all the things that are missing?' He started laughing again. 'Did they manage to reach Scathach's island?'

While my head was banging against the headboard in Johnny Nugent's parents' bed, I'd had an epiphany. I'd remembered where I thought I'd put Mr Pobbs aside before packing my clothes. I had called my gran the next day and expected Mr Pobbs to be found, lying under the bed staring with his one eye at the broken springs beneath. But he wasn't and we had arranged for my search of my grandparents' house the following weekend. Even though Johnny Nugent had asked me out. I was going to explain all this when I was pulled up short. 'Wait a minute, what's Scathach's island?'

Mr Burton laughed. 'Sorry, that just slipped out. It's a bad analogy.'

'Explain!' I smiled, watching his face redden.

'I didn't mean to say it. It just popped out. Never mind, let's move on.'

'Hold on a minute, you don't let me get away with that! I have to repeat *everything* I mumble,' I laughed, watching him squirm for the first time in my life.

He composed himself. 'It's an old Celtic story, and it was a stupid comparison.'

I motioned for more.

He rubbed his face. 'Oh, I can't believe I'm telling you this. Scathach was a great warrior woman who trained many heroes of the time. Legend tells us that it was almost impossible to reach her island, so that anyone who did was considered worthy to be trained in martial arts.'

My mouth dropped. 'You're comparing me to a warrior woman who trains men in martial arts?'

He laughed again. 'The point is that she was a woman that was hard to reach.' He stopped laughing when he saw my face. He leaned forward and grabbed my hand. 'I think you've taken that the wrong way.'

'I hope so,' I said, slowly shaking my head.

He groaned and thought fast. 'It's just that only the strongest, bravest and most worthy people could reach her.'

I relaxed a little, liking the sound of this. 'How would they reach her?'

He relaxed a little too. 'First they would have to cross the Plain of Ill Luck where they would be pierced by razor-sharp grass blades.' He paused while he studied my face to see whether he should go on or not. Happy that I wasn't about to punch him, he continued, 'Then they would face the Perilous Glens with devouring beasts. Their final task was the Bridge of the Cliff, which was a bridge that tilted upwards whenever anyone tried to cross.'

I pictured the people in my life that tried to approach me, that tried to befriend me, that tried to connect with me. I pictured me knocking them back.

'Only real heroes would get across,' he finished.

Goose bumps formed on my skin. My hairs stood up and I hoped he didn't notice.

He ran his hands through his hair and shook his head. 'That wasn't part of the . . .' *job*, he almost said. 'I shouldn't have said that. Sorry, Sandy.'

'It's OK,' I decided, and he looked relieved. 'Just tell me one thing, where are you on this journey?'

Those gorgeous blue eyes bored into mine. He didn't even need to think about it, didn't even look away. 'I'd say I've just passed over the Plain of Ill Luck right this minute.'

I pondered that. 'I'll go easy with my devouring beasts if you promise to just let me know when you've passed the Bridge.'

'You'll know,' he smiled, reaching for my hand and squeezing it. 'You'll know.'

Jack pulled up beside Alan's flat and flicked through Sandy's diary. She had also made an appointment for yesterday for one o'clock at a place with a Dublin number, and he needed to know if she had kept it. He was hoping whoever she was to meet would be able to help him. Though Sandy had made this appointment for yesterday in Dublin, yet she had planned to visit Alan in Limerick today. It must have been an important appointment in Dublin in order for her to make the journey over and back.

With shaking hands he dialled the Dublin number Sandy had written. A woman answered quickly, sounding distracted as other phones rang in the background.

'Hello, Scathach House.'

'Hi, I am wondering if you can help me,' Jack said politely. 'I have your phone number written down in my diary and I can't remember why I've made a note to call you.'

'Of course,' she said politely. 'Scathach House is the office of Dr Gregory Burton. Maybe you wanted to make an appointment?'

I woke up in my Dublin bedsit to the shrill sound of a telephone ringing in my ear. I put the pillow over my head and prayed for the noise to stop. I had a terrible hangover. I peeked over the side of my bed and caught a glimpse of my crumpled garda uniform lying in a ball on the ground. I'd worked a late shift and then gone for a few drinks. A few had clearly turned into a few too many and I had absolutely no memory of coming home. The ringing finally stopped and I breathed a sigh of relief, although it echoed in my head for a few seconds longer. And then it started again. I grabbed the phone from the side of the bed and brought it back under the pillow to my ear.

'Hello,' I croaked.

'Happy birthday to yoooou, happy birthday to yoooou, happy birthday, dear Sandeeeee, happy birthday to yoooou.' It was my mother singing so sweetly as though she was in a church choir.

'Hip, hip . . .'

'Hooray!' That was Dad.

'Hip, hip . . .'

'Hooray!' He blew a party blower down the receiver, which I instantly held far away from my ear, allowing my arm to hang off the bed. I could still hear them celebrating from under the pillow as I drifted off again.

'Happy twenty-first, honey,' Mum said proudly. 'Honey? Are you there?'

I put the phone back to my ear. 'Thanks, Mum,' I mumbled.

'I wish you'd have let us throw you a party,' she said wistfully. 'It's not every day my baby girl is twenty-one.'

'It is actually,' I said tiredly. 'I have three hundred and sixty-four more days of being twenty-one, so we've lots of time to celebrate.'

'Oh, you know it's not the same.'

'You know what I'm like at those things,' I said, referring to the party idea.

'I know, I know. Well, I want you to enjoy your day. Would you think about coming home for dinner at all? At the weekend, maybe? We could just do a small thing, just me, you and your dad. We won't even mention the birthday word,' she tried.

I paused. 'No, I can't this weekend, sorry. Things are really busy at work,' I lied.

'Oh, OK, well, what about if I come to Dublin for a few hours? I won't even stay over; we can have a coffee or something. A quick chat and I'll be gone, I promise.' She gave a nervous laugh. 'I just want to mark the day with you in some way. I'd love to see you.'

'I can't, Mum, sorry.'

There was a silence. For far too long.

Dad came on the phone cheerily. 'Happy birthday, love. We understand you're busy so we'll let you get back to doing what you were doing.'

'Where's Mum?'

'Oh, she, eh, had to answer the door.' He was as bad at lying as I was.

She was crying, I knew it.

'OK, well, have a great day, honey. Try to enjoy yourself, OK?' he added softly.

'OK,' I said quietly, and the phone clicked and went dead.

I groaned, hung the phone back up on my bedside locker and threw the pillow off my head. I allowed my eyes to adjust to the bright light my cheap curtains were incapable of keeping out. It was ten a.m. on a Monday morning and I finally had a day off. What I was going to do with it, I had no idea. I would have preferred to work on my birthday, although I would busy myself with working on a missing case that had recently run into a dead end. A little girl named Robin Geraghty had disappeared while playing in her front garden. All the signs were implicating her middle-aged neighbour next door in Robin's vanishing. However, no matter how hard we'd dug into this case we weren't hitting the treasure chest at the bottom. Recently I had started following up on such cases by myself, unable to switch off when the file was locked away in a cabinet.

I turned to lie on my back and noticed from the corner of my eye a lump beside me in the bed. The lump was on its side, a tousle of dark brown hair lying on the pillow. I jumped, gathering my bedclothes and wrapped them around me tighter. The lump began to move to face me, his eyes opened. Bloodshot tired eyes.

'I thought you were never going to answer that phone,' he said croakily.

'Who are you?' I asked in disgust, clambering out of bed and taking the covers with me, leaving him lying on the bed spread-eagled and naked. He smiled, rested his hands behind his head sleepily, and winked.

I groaned. It was meant to be a silent, inward groan but it forced its way out of my mouth. 'I'm going to the bathroom and when I get back you will be gone.' I picked up what I assumed were his clothes and threw them onto the bed. I picked up my own stray clothes that were resting on a chair, hugged them close to me and banged the door shut. Almost immediately I returned and grabbed my wallet, much to his disgust. I wasn't about to leave that there.

Not after the last time.

I stayed in the bathroom for as long as I could until Mr Rankin from next door began pounding on the door and telling me and everyone else in the building how he was going to burst an area of his body that I didn't care to think much about. I opened the door immediately and went back to my bedsit, hoping the hairy stranger had vanished. No such luck. He was closing the door behind him.

I walked towards him slowly, not knowing what to say. He didn't seem to know either, but nor did he care, his smirk still on his face.

'Did we . . . ?' I asked.

'Twice.' He winked and my insides churned. 'By the way, before you throw me out of your building, some guy called by when you were in the bathroom. I told him he could wait if he wanted, but you probably wouldn't recognise him when you saw him.' He grinned again.

'What guy?' I racked my brain.

'See, I told him you wouldn't remember him.'

'Is he in there?' I looked to the closed door.

'No, I guess he didn't feel like hanging around a bedsit with a naked hairy man.'

'You answered the door naked?' I asked angrily.

'I thought it was you,' he shrugged. 'Anyway, he left this card for you.' He handed me the business card. 'I don't suppose there's any point in me giving you my number?'

I shook my head, took the card from his hand. 'Thanks, eh . . .' I began weakly.

'Steve.' He held out his hand.

'Nice to meet you,' I smiled, and he laughed. He was kind of cute but still I watched him walk down the stairs.

'We met before, by the way,' he called up, not turning around as he made his way down the steps.

I was silent while I tried to remember.

'At Louise Drummond's Christmas party last year?' He stopped and looked up hopefully.

I frowned.

'Ah, it doesn't matter.' He waved his hand dismissively. 'You didn't remember the next morning then, either.' He smiled and was gone.

There was a moment of guilt until I remembered the business card in my hand and the bad feelings vanished. My knees went weak when I saw the name.

It seemed Mr Burton had set up a clinic in Dublin – Scathach House on Leeson Street. Wait a minute – *Dr* Burton; he'd passed his exams at last.

I danced around excitedly on the spot. I heard the toilet flush and Mr Rankin left the toilet with a paper in his hand and caught me dancing.

'You need to go again? I wouldn't go back in there for a while.' He wafted the newspaper.

I ignored him and went back into my bedsit. Mr Burton was here now. He'd found me three years after I'd moved away and that's all that mattered. At last one odd sock had showed up.

26

'Oh, Dr Burton.' Jack sat up in the car seat and pressed the phone closer to his ear. 'I remember why I'd made a note of it now. Actually, it's not me that I'm enquiring about. It's about a friend of mine who had an appointment yesterday with Dr . . .' He stopped, already forgetting the surname.

'Burton,' the secretary finished for him and he could hear another phone ringing in the background. 'I'm sorry, could you just hold for a moment, please, sir?'

'Yes.' Jack waited and listened to Duran Duran playing over the phone while he tried to formulate some sort of a plan. He scribbled Dr Gregory Burton's name and address into his notebook. Later he would go through Sandy's missed calls, received calls and dialled numbers that her phone had recorded over the last few days and he would try to piece together where she had gone, even if it meant ringing everyone in her phonebook.

The secretary returned on the line. 'I'm sorry, it's very busy here today. How can I help you?'

'I was wondering if you could tell me whether my friend Sandy Shortt showed up for her appointment yesterday?'

'I'm sorry, Mr . . . ?'

Jack thought fast. 'Le Bon.' Not fast enough. *Le Bon?*

'I'm sorry, Mr Le Bon, but we can't give out information about our clients.'

'Oh, of course you can't, I understand that, but I'm not looking for any personal information. My friend has been terribly sick lately but she has been afraid to do anything about it in case it's more serious than she anticipates. It's her stomach; it's been giving her trouble for months. I made an appointment for her and she says she went to Dr Burton yesterday but I'm afraid she's lying to us all. The family are all so worried. Could you at least just let us know if she arrived for the appointment? I'm not asking for any personal details.'

'You're enquiring about Sandy Shortt?'

He sat back relieved. 'Yes, Sandy,' he replied happily. 'Her appointment was for one o'clock.'

'I see, well, I'm afraid I can't help you as this is not a medical clinic, Mr Le Bon. It's a counselling centre, so you can't have made the appointment for her regarding stomach problems. Is there anything else I can help you with?' Her voice was firm, angry even.

'Em,' Jack's face was red with embarrassment, 'no.'

'Thank you for calling.' She hung up.

He stared in embarrassment at the appointment made for one o'clock in Sandy's diary. Suddenly Sandy's mobile phone began ringing and the name 'Gregory B' flashed up on the screen. Jack's heart thumped like a drum. He ignored the ring tone, relieved when it finally stopped and beeped to signal a message. He picked up the phone and dialled into her messaging service.

'Hi, Sandy. Gregory here. I've tried calling you a few times but there's no answer. I presume you've gone wandering the deep abyss again. I was just calling to let you know that a man named . . .' he moved his mouth away from the phone, 'Carol, what was his name?'

Jack heard the secretary's voice saying, 'Mr Le Bon.'

'Right, yeah.' Gregory came back on the phone. 'A Mr Le Bon – I assume that's not his real name –' he laughed, 'rang our offices looking for you. He was wondering if you'd made your appointment yesterday for your *stomach* problem?' His voice got quieter. 'Just be careful, OK? I don't suppose there's any chance you've considered getting a real job yet, waitressing or something. There's little chance nuts would be chasing you then. You could go door-to-door, selling bibles; in fact a nice woman dressed head to toe in tweed called to my door last night, which quite obviously made me immediately think of you, so I took her card. Think about calling her. It's a fine uplifting card with Our Lord looking miserable on the Cross. And it's recycled paper, so she really must care,' he laughed again. 'Anyway, if you don't think you could endure the tweed, get a nine-to-five. I don't know if you've heard of it, it's this thing that people do. It allows them to have a life outside of work hours. That's "life", L-I-F-E; you can look it up in your dictionary when you get the chance. Anyway . . .' he sighed and was quiet for a while as if deciding what to say, or more likely he knew exactly what to say and was deciding whether to say it or not. Jack knew that silence well. 'Right,' his voice suddenly got louder and more businesslike. 'Talk to you soon.'

Knuckles rapping loudly on the glass of the passenger side of the car caused Jack to jump and drop the phone. He looked up to see Alan's mother, a round-faced frump of a woman, glaring in the window. He leaned over and rolled down the window.

'Hello, Mrs O'Connor.'

'Who's that?' She scrunched up her face and stuck her head in the window. Wiry hairs escaped from her jawline. Her false teeth unclamped themselves from her gums and moved around in her mouth as she spoke. 'Do I know you?' she shouted, spit landing on Jack's lip.

'Yes, Mrs O'Connor.' He wiped his lip and raised his voice, knowing she had bad hearing. 'I'm Jack Ruttle, Donal's brother.'

'Merciful hour, baby Donal's brother. What are you doing sitting out here? Get out and let me have a look at you.'

She shuffled away in maroon-coloured velvet slippers,

her jaw moving as she looked him up and down, teeth sloshing around in her mouth. She was dressed in the same outfit she appeared to have been wearing since the forties. 'Make Do and Mend' had always been a part of the O'Connors' way of life, recycling textiles around the house to clothe the twelve children she had reared without their father, who came for one thing and left when he got it. Jack remembered Alan coming on a day out with Donal when they were kids, wearing white shorts made from pillowcases. Donal never seemed to care, refusing to mock his friend as the other kids did. Not that Alan endured the taunts, instead choosing to knock the bejaysus out of anyone who even looked at him the wrong way. But he protected Donal from everyone, and his friend's disappearance had hit him particularly hard.

'Com'ere to me, aren't ya all grown up?' She rubbed Jack's hands and tousled his hair as though he had just reached adolescence that very day. 'You're the image of your father, God rest his soul,' she blessed herself.

'Thank you, Mrs O'Connor. You look great too,' he lied.

'Ah, I don't,' she waved her hand dismissively and began to shuffle back towards her ground-floor flat in the high-rise building. Two bedrooms and twelve kids – he wondered how she had managed it. No wonder Alan had spent so much time in the Ruttles' house, being satiated with food by Jack's mother.

'Is Alan here? I came to talk to him.'

'No he's not. He finally moved in with that young wan. In a house now, wouldn't you know. He's only with her because of the house but she only gets it because of her kid, mind you. Fancy houses they get nowadays, the single mothers. I had nothin' like it in my day – not that I was single but I was as good as and all the better for it,' she continued, shuffling to her door.

Jack laughed. Alan was always involved in something, landing on his feet no matter what the circumstances. Donal had named him 'The Cat'.

'I won't disturb you, Mrs O'Connor. I'll go over to Alan at the house, if that's OK.'

'You think he done something wrong?' She looked worried.

'Not to me, anyway,' Jack smiled, and she nodded, relief written all over her hard face.

Alan must have received a phone call from his mother as he was outside in the driveway waiting. He looked thin – thinner than usual – and his face was pale and drawn, paler and more drawn than usual. But didn't they all; hadn't everyone and everything been affected by Donal's disappearance? It was as if, when he left the chipper that night, bumping against the doorframes in his drunken state, he had managed to bump the earth off its axis, causing it to swirl at top speed in the wrong direction on the wrong path. Everything felt out of place.

They greeted one another with a hug. Alan immediately began to cry and Jack fought the urge to join him. Instead he stiffened, allowing the younger man to weep on his shoulder, swallowing back the swelling in his throat, blinking back the tears and trying to focus on everything around him that was real and that he could touch, everything except Donal.

They sat in the living room. Alan's hands shook as he tapped ash from his cigarette into one of the empty beer cans piled alongside the couch. The room was deathly silent; Jack wished they could put on the television as a background distraction.

'I came here to see if a woman had called by today. She's helping me out with looking for Donal.'

Alan's face brightened. 'Yeah?'

'She just wanted to ask you questions about the night – you know, go back over everything again.'

'I've been through that a million times with the guards, and a million times every day with myself.' Alan inhaled deeply on his cigarette and his nicotine-stained fingers rubbed his eyes wearily.

'I know, but it's good to have a fresh eye and ear go

over everything again. Maybe there's something they missed.'

'Maybe,' he said in a small voice, but Jack doubted he believed that. He doubted there was any moment of that night that Alan hadn't analysed, over-analysed and then dissected all over again. To tell him there might be something he was forgetting must surely be an insult.

'She didn't call by?'

Alan shook his head. 'I've been here all day, was here all day yesterday and I'll be here all day tomorrow too,' he said angrily.

'What happened to that last job of yours?'

He made a face and Jack knew not to ask any more questions.

'Do me a favour will you?' Jack handed Alan his phone. 'Ring this number and make an appointment for me with Dr Burton. I don't want them to recognise my voice.'

Alan being Alan didn't ask any questions. 'Hi, I want to make an appointment with Dr Burton,' he said, opening another beer can.

He raised his eyebrows and looked at Jack. 'Yeah, for a counselling session.'

Jack nodded.

'When do I want the appointment?' he repeated the secretary's question, looking at Jack.

'As soon as they can,' Jack whispered.

'As soon as you can,' Alan repeated. He listened and looked at Jack. 'Next month?'

Jack shook his head wildly.

'No, I need it sooner than that. My head is really messed up, you never know what I might do.'

Jack rolled his eyes.

Seconds later he hung up. 'You got a cancellation for noon on Thursday.'

'Thursday?' Jack asked, jumping up from his chair as though moving now would get him there on time.

'Well, you said as soon as possible,' Alan said, handing him back the phone. 'Has that got anything to do with finding Donal, by any chance?'

Jack thought about it. 'In a way, yeah.'

'I hope you find him, Jack.' His eyes filled up again. 'I keep going back over that night again and again, wishing I'd left with him. I really thought he'd be OK getting a taxi down that way, you know?' His eyes looked tortured and his hand shook. Around his feet on the floor lay sprinkles of ash he constantly flicked off with his nicotine-stained thumb.

'You weren't to know,' Jack comforted him. 'It's not your fault.'

'I hope you find him,' Alan repeated, opening another can of beer and slugging it down.

Jack left him sitting there in the silence of the empty house, staring into space, knowing he was rethinking and reliving that night all over again, looking for the vital piece of evidence they had all missed. It was all they could do.

Missing person number one, Orla Keane, entered the great Community Hall, the light shining in from the open door spotlighting her presence. She stopped at the entrance, trying to get her bearings, looking like Alice in Wonderland who had just swallowed an 'Eat Me' beside the monstrous oak door. I cleared my throat nervously and its amplified sound bounced off the walls, raced to the ceilings and back down again like a ping-pong ball let loose. She turned to where I had made the noise and began to make her way towards me, high heels on the wooden floor echoing loudly.

Joan and Helena had set up a table for me to sit behind on the far side of the room and, much to Joan's disappointment, they stepped outside to give me privacy. As Orla walked towards me, I felt star struck. I couldn't believe that this person had stepped out of my 'Missing' photographs and was now a living, breathing person walking directly towards me.

'Hello,' she smiled, her Cork accent still strong, despite her time here.

'Hello.' My voice came out as a whisper. I cleared my throat and tried again. I looked down at the list of names on the table before me. I would have to do this twelve times today, and then again with Joan and Bernard. The thought of seeing all these people thrilled me but the idea of having to discuss such delicate topics so subtly, was draining me already. I had asked Helena earlier once again why on earth it was that I couldn't just let everybody know without having to carry out this charade.

'Sandy,' she had said so firmly that I needn't have even heard a reason. 'When people want to get home they get desperate. For them to learn that you found your way here while looking for them would cause them to believe that they can leave with you. Life wouldn't be worth living here with a few hundred people trailing your every move.'

She had a point. So here I was, playing the role of casting agent and owner of an acting agency, about to wind a conversation about every member of their family and friends into a Hamlet soliloquy.

I had had one more question for Helena. 'Do you think that I *can* lead the people out of here and bring them home?' I had been wondering if that was my purpose for being here, because I was convinced I wasn't staying. The typical victim belief: this can't happen to me, not me of all people.

She smiled sadly and once again I needn't have heard her response because her face said it all. 'Sorry, Moses, I don't think so.' But before I dissolved completely she quickly added, 'But I think you are here for a reason and that reason is, right now, to share your stories with everyone, to tell them about their families and how much they're missed. That's your way of bringing them home.'

I looked up at Orla, who was sitting before me, anxiously awaiting my next move. It was time to bring her home.

She was twenty-six years old now and she looked like she'd hardly changed at all. Nearly six years had passed since she had gone missing. Six years I'd spent looking for her. I knew her parents' names were Clara and Jim and they had divorced two years ago. I knew she had two sisters, Ruth and Lorna, and a brother, James. Her best friends were Laura, and Rebecca, who was also known as 'Fly' due to her regular forgetfulness to zip up her fly. Orla was studying art history at Cork University when she went missing. Her debs dress was purple, and the scar across her left eyebrow was from when she'd fallen off her bike on holiday in Bantry when she was eight. She lost her virginity when she was fifteen at a house party, to Niall Kennedy, the guy who worked at the local video store, and she secretly crashed her parents' car when they were away for a week in Spain but had it repaired on time and they still don't know it to this day. Her favourite colour is lilac, she loves pop music, played the piano until she was fourteen, had secretly dreamed of becoming a ballet dancer since the age of six yet never once took a class, and she had been here for five and three-quarter years.

I looked at her and didn't know where to start. 'So, Orla, tell me a bit about yourself.'

I watched her as though in a trance, watched as the lips I'd seen only in photographs opened and closed, her face animated, *alive*, and I listened to her words. The singsong tone of her Cork accent, the way her long blonde hair moved as she spoke. I was enthralled.

When she got to the part about studying in college I saw my chance to jump in. 'Art history in Cork University?' I repeated. 'I know someone who studied the same year as you.'

'Who?' She almost jumped off her seat.

'Rebecca Grey.'

Her mouth dropped open. 'No way! Rebecca Grey is one of my best friends!'

'Really?' I noticed everything was still in the present. Rebecca was still her best friend.

'Yeah! That's so weird, how do you know her?'

'Oh, I met her brother Enda a few times. He's friends with friends of mine – you know how it is.'

'What's he doing now?'

'Actually, last time I saw him was at his wedding a few months ago. I think I may have met your mum and dad there too.'

She was silent for a moment and when she spoke again her voice was hushed and shaking. 'How are they?'

'Oh, they were in great form, I was talking to one of your sisters – Lorna, I think.'

'Yes, Lorna!'

'She was telling me that she got engaged.'

'To Steven?' She bounced up and down on her seat, clapping her hands excitedly.

'Yes,' I smiled, 'to Steven.'

'Oh, I knew she'd take him back,' she laughed with tears in her eyes.

'Your older sister was there with her husband. She was heavily pregnant, I noticed.'

'Oh.' A tear fell from her eye and she quickly wiped it away. 'What else? Who else did you see? Did my mum and dad say anything? What did they look like?'

And so I brought her home.

A half-hour had passed and Joan coughed rather loudly to let me know another audition applicant had arrived. We hadn't even noticed Joan enter the hall and I looked at my wrist to check the time, forgetting that my watch was still lying somewhere on the road leading out of the village. The familiar feeling of irritation scratched at my body as I thought of it being somewhere yet not being able to find it. I looked up to see the next person I was due to meet – Carol Dempsey, nervously wringing her hands as she stood by Joan – and my irritation disappeared. I became scared all over again.

'I'm sorry, our time is up,' I said to Orla.

Her face fell and I knew she had all of a sudden been whisked away from home and transported and plonked back to the reality of where she was.

'But I haven't even auditioned,' she panicked.

'It's OK, you've got the part,' I whispered, and winked.

Her face lit up as she stood, leaned over and grasped

my hand in both of hers. 'Thank you, thank you so much.'

I watched her leave with Helena, Orla's head awash with a million new thoughts of stories from home. So much to think about now: new thoughts and new memories all raising new questions and a new longing for home.

Carol sat before me. A mother of three, housewife, from Donegal, forty-two years old and a member of the local choir, who went missing while on her way back from choir practice four years ago. She had passed her driving test a week before her disappearance, her husband had celebrated his forty-fifth birthday with the family the night before and her youngest daughter's school play was opening the following week. I looked at her mouse-like face, timid and shy, her brown limp hair tucked behind pink ears, a purse clasped in her hands on her lap, and I instantly wanted to take her home.

'So, Carol,' I said gently, 'why don't we start off by you just telling me a bit about yourself?'

Later in the day we all sat around in a circle in the grand Community Hall. I faced the stage and the thousands of handprints decorating the backdrop. 'Strength and Hope', I repeated to myself. Strength and hope had got me through today; I was still on a high from meeting my idols but knew I would quickly become drained. As usual, as soon as everybody had taken their places, I had chosen to stand back and observe, outside of the circle. Old habits die hard. Helena had called out to me and the chorus of fifteen other voices joined in, coercing me to sit down. I took a seat, aware that I was joining a group, something I had run from doing all of my life. I slowly sat down, all the time battling with my legs, which wanted to run out of the door, and my mouth, which wanted to make an excuse to leave.

After I had spoken to everybody individually, Helena

had come up with the idea of everybody getting to know one another better by sharing the experiences of where and when they had gone missing. She was calling it a team-building workshop all to help the production but I knew she was really doing it for me, to help me with my continuous search for understanding where we all are and how we got here.

One by one the people explained how they had arrived here. It was an emotional experience. Some had been here only a few years, others over a decade, yet the realisation of never returning home was still raw. There were tears from many, as usual, but none from me. It was as though by the time my tears worked their way from my heart to my eyes, they had evaporated and drifted into the air as sad vapours instead. I was fascinated to hear what had happened after they left the scenes that I had examined so many times and arrived here. It was all so simple. I had followed unnecessary routes, suspected all the wrong people, scrutinised every single inch of the road they were last seen on. It was pointless because all they did was wander off here.

While it was painful for the missing, knowing that they wouldn't be returning home, it was a lot better than the alternative. I wished Jenny-May Butler was here, I wished Donal Ruttle was here, I wished the others on my list and the thousands of others that go missing every year were here. I prayed that harm hadn't come to Jenny-May. I prayed that, if it had, it had been quick and painless. But mostly I prayed that she was here.

I was captivated as I watched all of these people. I was a stranger to them but they were best friends to me. I had so many stories of theirs I wanted to tell them, that I knew and understood and had laughed at and could identify with. There were so many people they knew that I wanted to tell them I'd met and laughed with. There were situations that I knew they'd been in that I wanted to tell them I shared. The complete opposite to how I was in life. I wanted to join in, swap stories and belong.

There was a silence and I realised all eyes were on me.

'Well?' Helena asked, adjusting her lemon pashmina around her shoulders.

'Well, what?' I asked, looking around in confusion.

'Aren't you going to tell us your story of arriving here?'

I felt like telling them I'd been here long before them all. But I didn't. Instead I politely excused myself from the hall.

Later that night I sat in the eatery at a quiet table with Helena and Joseph. Candles flickered on every table, bird-of-paradise flowers sat in small tin buckets in the centre. We had just finished a starter of wild mushroom soup and piping hot brown bread, and I sat back in my chair, already full, and awaited my main course. The eatery was quiet on this Wednesday night, people choosing to go to bed before their early starts at work the next day. Each of the people taking part in the production had been granted time off from their work, their involvement in the arts seen by the council to be enough. We were to spend all day every day rehearsing in order to meet the deadline of next Sunday, when Helena had already assured the cast and community the dress rehearsal would be. This was a task that seemed highly ambitious and entirely unrealistic in my eyes, yet Helena assured me that people here threw themselves into their work and were highly productive. But what did I know?

I looked at my wrist for the millionth time since I'd lost my watch and sighed with frustration.

'I have to find my watch.'

'Don't worry,' Helena smiled. 'It's not like being at home, Sandy; things don't just go missing.'

'I know, I know, you keep telling me that, but if that's so, well then, where is it?'

'Wherever you dropped it,' she laughed, and shook her head at me like I was a child.

Joseph, I noticed, didn't smile but changed the subject altogether. 'What kind of play will you do?' he asked in his deep soothing tones.

I laughed, 'We have no idea. Helena managed to steer the conversation away from talk of what the actual play would be every time someone asked. I don't mean to rain on your parade but I think a week is an entirely implausible amount of time to rehearse and perfect a play.'

'It will be a short one,' Helena said defensively.

'What about scripts and costumes and whatever else is needed?' I asked, suddenly realising the extent of what we would have to do.

'Don't worry about all of that, Sandy.' She turned to Joseph. 'There's the belief at home that old theatres are haunted because costumes and make-up are always reported or rumoured to go missing. Well, it's true, they do go missing but it's not due to ghosts, not of the pilfering kind, anyway, because the finest costumes show up here daily. Bobby will have everything we need,' she said calmly.

'She has thought this all through.' Joseph smiled affectionately at his wife.

'Oh, the thinking is all finished, dear. It has already been decided. We are going to stage *The Wizard of Oz*,' Helena said grandly and proudly, swirling her red wine and taking a sip.

I started laughing.

'Why is it funny?' Joseph asked, amused.

'It's *The Wizard of Oz*,' I stressed. 'It's not a play, it's a musical! It's what children do in school shows. I thought you'd come up with something a bit more cultured, like a Beckett play or O'Casey,' I argued. 'But *The Wizard of Oz* . . . ?' I wrinkled my nose.

'My, my, I think we have a snob on our hands.' Helena tried not to smile.

'I'm not aware of this *Wizard of Oz*.' Joseph looked confused.

I gasped. 'Neglected child.'

'It's not something that was shown all the time in Watamu,' Helena reminded me. 'And if you hadn't left rehearsals so early today, Sandy, you would have learned that we are not doing a musical version. It is an adaptation written many years ago by Dennis O'Shea, a fine Irish playwright who has been here for two years. He heard about what we were doing and brought it to me this morning. I thought it was perfect and so it has already been cast and the first few scenes blocked. Mind you, I had to tell them that it was you that had made the decision.'

'You cast them in *The Wizard of Oz*?' I said, totally unimpressed.

'What is it about?' Joseph asked, intrigued.

'Sandy, you do the honours,' Helena said.

'OK, well, it's a *children*'s movie,' I stressed to Helena, 'made in the thirties about a little girl called Dorothy Gale who is swept away in a tornado to a magical land. Once there she embarks on a quest to see the wizard, who can help her return home. It's ridiculous to ask a group of adults to do it,' I laughed, but realised no one was laughing with me.

'And this wizard, does he help her?'

'Yes,' I said slowly, feeling it odd the story was being taken so seriously. 'The wizard helps her and she learns that she could have returned home all the time, all she had to do was tap her ruby heels together and say, "There's no place like home, there's no place like home."'

He still didn't laugh. 'So she returns home in the end?'

There was a silence and I finally understood why. I nodded slowly.

'And what does she do while she's in this magical land?'

'She helps her friends,' I said quietly.

'It doesn't seem such a silly story to me,' Joseph said seriously. 'One the people here will very much like to see.'

I thought about that. In fact, I thought about it all night, until I was dreaming of ruby slippers and tornadoes and of talking lions and houses that fell on witches, until the phrase 'There's no place like home' was echoing so loudly and continuously in my head that I woke up saying it aloud and I was afraid to go back to sleep.

28

I stared up at the ceiling, at the point right above my head where the white paint had bubbled and cracked over the wood. The moon was sitting perfectly framed in the window of the family room I was sleeping in. Blue light cast through the glass, causing an exact reflection of its window squares to appear on the chunky wooden table. There was no moon in the window on the table, I noticed, just a ghostly reflection of pale blue.

I was wide awake now. I felt for my wrist to check the time and remembered again my watch was gone. My heart started to pound as it always did when something of mine was missing; I would immediately become restless and ache to start looking. My hunts were like an addiction, the feeling pre-search like a craving. A part of me was possessed and became obsessed with not resting until my belongings were found. There was very little anybody could do when I was in that mode, there was very little that could be said or done to cause me to screech in my tracks. The people with me always used to tell me it was lonely for them when I left them like that all of a sudden. Everybody I was with was always the victim; didn't they know that it was lonely for me too?

'But the *pen* is not your missing object,' Gregory would always say to me.

'Yes it is,' I would grumble, while rooting in my bag, nose practically touching the bottom.

'No it's not. When you search you are trying to fulfil

a *feeling*. Whether you have the pen or not is completely irrelevant, Sandy.'

'It is not irrelevant,' I would shout back. 'If I have no pen, well then, how can I write down what you are about to tell me?'

He reached into the inside pocket of his jacket and handed me a pen. 'Here.'

'But that isn't *my* pen.'

He would sigh and smile as he always did. 'This idea of searching for lost things is a *distraction*—'

'Distraction, distraction, distraction, distraction. Never mind me; *you* are obsessed with saying that word. You saying the word "distraction" is *your* distraction from saying anything else,' I spluttered angrily.

'Let me finish,' he said sternly.

I stopped rooting immediately and listened to him, feigning interest.

'This idea of searching for lost things is a distract—' he stopped himself, 'is a way of avoiding dealing with something else that's lost in your life *within you*. Now shall we start searching for what that is?'

'A-ha!' I smiled, happily extracting my pen from the bottom of my bag. 'Found it!'

Unfortunately for Gregory, the craving never reared its ugly head anytime we would try to search within me.

If there had been a ten-foot wall surrounding the house I would have scaled it. There was no barrier to my search scenes; all they did was become invisible hurdles. Gregory did have one good thing to say about my searching and that was that he had never seen stamina and determination quite like it. And then he ruined the compliment by saying what a pity it was that I didn't pump that energy into other areas of my life. Still, somewhere in his comment I sensed praise.

The clock on the family-room wall read 03.45. I threw back the covers in the deathly silent house and began rummaging through Barbara Langley's suitcase of eighties nightmare clothes. I settled on a black and white sailor-style top, black drainpipe jeans and flat black pumps. All I needed was an armful of bracelets, hoop earrings and backcombed hair and I'd be dancing to 'The Time Warp'. But then, I already was.

Joseph and Helena seemed so sure that my watch wasn't lost, they seemed so confident that nothing could leave this place. I had to find out. I slipped out of the house silently so as not to wake the family. Outside, the weather was mild. I felt as if I was walking around a toy village in the snowy mountains of Switzerland: little wooden chalets with window boxes, and candles in the windows to help light the way and welcome new wanderers. All was quiet outside. The crackling and the snapping of branches could be heard from the forest as people made their way to the village for the first time. People who'd probably found themselves there during an innocent walk to the shop or a stroll home from the pub. I felt safe in the village, protected by people intent on picking up from where they left off and moving on.

I walked out of the village, following the dusty road that led alongside the fields. The sun was rising over the trees in the distance, casting orange hues over the blue light, like a giant orange squeezing its colourful juice over the villages, the trees, the mountains and fields, and allowing the liquid light to flow like a stream down the pathways.

In the distance I saw a figure rising and stooping in the centre of the road. He stood up and his height and physique revealed him to be Joseph. His figure was jet-black against the rising sun, which was the giant orange sitting at the top of the road, looking like it was about to roll down to us, squashing all in its path. I was just about to approach him when he got down on his hands and knees and began brushing the dusty floor. I jumped into the woods and hid behind a tree, watching him. He'd beaten me to it; I realised he was searching for my watch.

Torchlight flashed through the trees and made its way towards me. I quickly ducked, wondering where on earth it was coming from. Joseph stopped what he was doing to look up at the light. It disappeared, he continued searching and I continued to watch him, wanting to see what he would do when he came upon the watch. But he didn't find it. After an hour of very determined searching, I think Gregory would agree, Joseph finally rose to his feet, placed his hands on his hips, shook his head and sighed.

A chill ran through me. It wasn't there, I *knew* it.

Before Jack went home on Wednesday night he returned to the estuary to see if Sandy's car had upped and gone over the past twenty-four hours.

Gloria had been delighted to learn that he was planning on seeing a psychiatrist, although she was a little confused to say the least as to why he had to travel to Dublin for a session. Still, he hadn't seen her so happy in a long time and it showed him how bad he must have been lately. He could almost hear her thinking and planning wedding, babies, christenings and who knows what else, as he told her. However, she was misguided in thinking the counselling was directly for him. He had no intention of wanting to be cured of wanting to find his brother. To him it was no sickness.

It was dark outside, pitch-black among the trees down by the Shannon Estuary, where owls hooted and creatures moved around in the undergrowth. He took his emergency flashlight out of his car and, as he switched it on, he saw various startled glowing eyes freeze and then dash back into the bushes. Sandy's Ford Fiesta was in its place, untouched since he'd last been there. He shone the light around the trees, at the laneway that led further along the estuary. A pleasant walk for bird-watchers and nature lovers or a jogging path for Sandy? He walked towards it, deeper into the forest where he had looked so many times over the last few days. His inexperience had previously led him to look out for footprints, as if they would be any help to him. He walked further, enjoying seeing creatures leap out of the line of the light into the distance, and he shone the light up into the trees and watched as it found its way up to the sky.

A trail appeared on his left. He stopped walking and immediately stopped trying to work out what was niggling at him. He'd never noticed that trail before. He shone the light up the trail: more trees and blackness were at the end. He shuddered and moved the light away again with the intention of returning in the light of day to wander up the track. As he shone the torch in another direction, shining metal caught his eye and disappeared again. He quickly searched around with the light, afraid whatever it was would vanish. His eye fell upon a silver watch, lying among the long grass beside the trail to his left. He bent to pick it up with his heart thumping in his chest, an image suddenly appearing in his mind.

It was the memory of Sandy bending to pick up her watch in the garage a few mornings ago.

29

'Hello. I hope I've called the correct number for Mary Stanley.' Jack spoke to the answer-phone service. 'My name is Jack Ruttle. You don't know me but I've been trying to get in touch with Sandy Shortt, whom I know you were recently in contact with. I know this seems like a strange phone call but if you hear from her or have any idea where she has gone, could you please contact me on the following number . . .'

Jack sighed and tried another number. All around him on this sunny day in Dublin, people were lying out on the grass of St Stephen's Green. Ducks were waddling around his bench, searching for bits of bread people had dropped while feeding them. They quacked, pecked and hopped back into the glistening water, distracting him momentarily. After spending over an hour trying to find his way around Dublin city's one-way system, and then being stuck in traffic jams, he'd finally managed to find a parking space around St Stephen's Green. He had an hour to spare before his session with Dr Burton, something he was growing increasingly nervous about. Jack wasn't good at discussing his feelings with anyone at the best of times, never mind an entire hour of searching his brain for pretend worries with a psychiatrist, all just to find information about Sandy Shortt. Columbo he was not, and he was growing tired of trying to find backward ways of getting answers.

He had been ringing through the list on Sandy's phonebook all morning, leaving messages with all those who had contacted her over the past few days and those she had made appointments with in previous weeks. He wasn't getting anywhere. So far he'd left six voice messages, he'd spoken to two people who were extremely guarded about giving any information out, and he'd listened for far too long to her fuming landlord, who seemed more upset about not being paid yet that month than where Sandy was.

'Let me warn you now, sonny, before she breaks your heart,' he'd growled, 'unless you want to be hanging around for days on end, waiting for her, then I suggest you cut your ties with her now. You're not the only one, I can tell you that.' He'd laughed heartily. 'Don't be fooled by her. She brings them back all the time, thinking none of us hear her. I'm right above; I hear her comings and goings, if you'll pardon the pun. You mark my words; she'll turn up here in a few days wondering what all the fuss was about, probably thinking she was gone for two hours instead of two weeks. She does it all the time. But if you do see her before then, tell her to get that money to me a.s.a.p. or she'll be turfed out on her arse.'

Jack sighed. If he was going to give up, now was the time to do it. But he couldn't. Here he was in Dublin, a few minutes away from meeting someone he imagined knew more about what went on in Sandy's head than anybody else. He didn't want to pack it all in and head home to . . . nothing. His idea of Sandy was changing. Through their conversations on the phone he had painted a picture of her in his mind: organised, businesslike, in love with her job, chatty, personable. The more he dug around into her life the more that image of her altered. She was still all of those things, but more. She was becoming more real to him. This wasn't a phantom he was chasing; she was a real, complex, layered person, no longer just the helpful stranger he'd spoken to on the phone. Maybe Garda Turner was right, maybe she'd just had enough and was hiding from the world for a while, but that was something her counsellor would surely know.

Just as he was about to dial another number, his phone rang.

'Is that Jack?' a woman asked quietly.

'Yes,' he replied. 'Who is this?'

'This is Mary Stanley. You left a message on my phone about Sandy Shortt.'

'Oh, yes, Mary, hello. Thank you so much for returning my call. It was a peculiar message, I know.'

'Yes . . .' She was guarded, just as the others had been; unsure of this strange man who was looking for their friend without any viable reason whatsoever.

'You can trust me, Mary. I mean no harm to Sandy. I don't know how well you know her, if you're a relative or friend, but let me explain myself first.' He told the story of how he contacted Sandy, arranged to meet her, passed her at the petrol station, and since had lost contact with her. He left out the reason for his meeting her, feeling that wasn't relevant. 'I don't want to raise any alarm bells,' he continued, 'but I've been ringing around people she seems to have maintained close contact with, just to see if they've seen or heard from her lately.'

'I received a phone call from a Garda Graham Turner this morning,' Mary said, and Jack wasn't sure if it was a question or a statement. It was probably both.

'Yes, I contacted him. I'm concerned for Sandy.' Jack had called Garda Turner that morning and told him about discovering Sandy's watch, hoping that would make him sit up and take notice. It obviously had.

'I'm worried too,' Mary said, and Jack's ears pricked to attention.

'How did he know to call you?' Jack asked, meaning, who are you? How do you know Sandy?

'Who else was on your call list?' she asked, ignoring his question, sounding lost in thought.

He flicked open his notepad. 'Peter Dempsey, Clara Keane, Ailish O'Brien, Tony Watts – do you want me to keep going?'

'No, that's enough. You got your hands on a list of Sandy's?'

'She left her phone and diary behind. They were the only ways I could look for her.' Jack tried not to sound guilty.

'Did somebody you know go missing?' Her tone wasn't soft but it wasn't harsh either. He was taken aback by the question, asked so directly, as though missing people happened all the time.

'Yes, my brother Donal.' A lump swelled in Jack's throat every time he mentioned his brother.

'Donal Ruttle – yes, that's right. I remember reading that in the paper,' she said, and was quiet again in thought. 'All those you've mentioned are people whose family members have gone missing,' Mary explained, 'including me. My son, Bobby, has been gone for three years.'

'I'm very sorry,' Jack said softly. It would make sense that all of Sandy's recent contacts were work-related; he had yet to come across any friends of hers.

'Oh, don't be sorry. It's not your fault. So let me get this straight: we all enlisted Sandy to help us find our loved ones and now you're enlisting us to help you find Sandy?'

Even though Jack was on the phone, his face pinked. 'Yes, I guess so.'

'Well, whether the others have replied to you yet or not, I don't care. I'll speak for them. You can count us all in. Sandy's very special to us all; we'll do everything we can to help find her. The quicker we find her, the quicker she can find my Bobby.'

They were Jack's thoughts exactly.

Unable to sleep for the remainder of the night, I lay awake pondering the whereabouts of my watch. My head was dizzy with possibilities, for after finding myself here, there were now a plethora of places I could imagine it inhabiting. Just as I was picturing a world where watches ate, slept and married one another, with grandfather clocks as heads of state, pocket watches as the intellects, waterproof watches that inhabited the waters, diamond watches the aristocracy, and digital watches the mere workers, Joseph's creeping into the house stopped me. I had observed him for what I guessed was a further hour walking up and down the road, looking wide-eyed and fierce in his attempts to find my watch. I now knew what I looked like during my searches, focused and in the zone, completely unaware of all life around, particularly oblivious to a person hiding behind a tree not far away.

A half-hour after I'd returned to my bed, Joseph made his way quietly, but not quietly enough, into the house. I pressed my ear to the wall as I tried to hear the mumblings between him and Helena in the room next to me. The timber was warm against my cheek and I closed my eyes momentarily, hit by a pang of homesickness and a longing for the warm heaving chest I used to rest my head upon in bed. Then there was silence and, feeling like a caged lion, I decided to slip out of the house before anybody stirred again.

Outside, the market stalls were being set up for another busy day of trading. There was the colourful sound of banter mixed with birdsong, laughter, shouting as crates and boxes were being unpacked and stacked. I closed my eyes, hit by my second longing for home that day, and imagined myself as a child walking hand in hand with my mother through the organic farmers' markets in the Market Yard in Carrick-on-Shannon, the scintillating smell of the fruit and vegetables, so ripe and colourful, enticing everybody to touch, smell and taste. I opened my eyes again and was back here.

I arrived outside the Lost and Found building and noticed how the carvings on this building were more colourful and playful: two odd socks, one yellow and pink polka dot and the other purple and orange stripes. I stood thinking of Gregory and me at my final goodbye dance at school, and I laughed. A face appeared in the window, a very familiar face, and I immediately stopped laughing, feeling as though I'd seen a ghost. He was young – nineteen by now, if I calculated correctly. He gave me a cheeky grin, waved and disappeared from the window, and appeared at the now open door like the Cheshire cat. So this was the Bobby from Lost and Found that Helena and Wanda had mentioned.

'Hello.' He leaned against the doorframe with his shoulder, crossed one leg over the other and held out his two hands. 'Welcome to Lost and Found.'

I laughed. 'Hello, Mr Stanley.'

His eyes narrowed at my knowing his name, but his smile widened. 'And you are?'

'Sandy.' I'd heard he was a character, always acting the joker. I had watched countless home videos of him performing for the camera from age six all the way up to sixteen just before his disappearance. 'You were on my list,' I explained, 'for auditions yesterday, and you didn't show up.'

'Ah!' Realisation dawned on him yet he still continued to study me curiously. 'I've heard about you.' He stopped leaning against the doorframe and coolly made his way down the steps with his hands in his pockets. He stopped directly in front of me, folded his arms, then placed one hand to his chin and began to circle me slowly.

I laughed. 'What have you heard about me?'

He paused behind me and I twisted my upper body around to him. 'They say you know things.'

'They do?'

'They do,' he repeated, and continued strolling around me. When he had come full circle he stopped and folded his arms again, twinkles dancing in his blue eyes. He was everything his mother had boasted. 'They say you're the soothsayer of Here.'

'Who are *they*?' I asked.

'The . . .' he looked around to make sure nobody was listening; he lowered his voice to a whisper, '*auditionees*.'

'Ah.' I nodded, smiling. 'Them.'

'Yes, *them*. We have a lot in common,' he said mysteriously.

'We do?'

'We do,' he repeated. 'They say – *they* being,' he looked left and right again before whispering, 'the *auditionees* – say you're the person to go to if you want to know things.'

I shrugged. 'Maybe I know some things.'

'Well, I'm the person to go to if you want to *get* things.'

'Well, that's why I'm here,' I smiled.

He became serious. I think. 'Which one? You're here to get something or to let me know something?'

I thought about that but didn't answer aloud. 'Aren't you going to let me inside?'

'Of course,' he smiled and dropped the act. 'I'm Bobby,' he held out his hand, 'but you already know that.'

'I do,' I smiled. 'I'm Sandy Shortt.' I took his hand and shook it. It felt limp and I looked up to see that his face had paled.

'Sandy *Shortt*?' he asked again.

'Yes.' My heart beat nervously. 'Why, what's wrong with that?'

'Sandy Shortt from Leitrim, Ireland?'

I let go of his limp hand and swallowed. I didn't answer. It seemed that I didn't need to. Bobby took me by the arm and led me to the shop. 'I've been expecting you.' He looked over his shoulder to see that no one was watching one last time before dragging me inside and closing the door.

Then he closed the shop.

30

Leading away from St Stephen's Green, Leeson Street was a fine Georgian street largely intact. The buildings, once grand homes housing the aristocracy, now mainly housed businesses: hotels, offices, and the basements were home to Dublin's 'Strip', a chain of thriving night-clubs and strip clubs.

A brass plate beside the grand black Georgian door announced the building to be Scathach House. Jack took the seven concrete steps up to the door and came face to face with a brass lion's head with a ring clasped between his teeth. He was just about to grasp it and rap it against the door when he noticed a collection of buzzers to the right of the door: modern day's ugly invention mingled with the old. He looked up Dr Burton's clinic; it was on the second floor, a PR agency at the bottom, a solicitor's office at the top. He was buzzed upstairs where he waited in an empty reception area. The receptionist smiled at him and he felt like shouting, 'I'm not here for *me*, there's nothing wrong with *me*, I'm *investigating*!'

But he smiled back instead.

Magazines adorned the table, some a few months old, others a year old. He picked up one and self-consciously flicked through the pages, reading about a member of the royal family of an obscure country who lay across beds, couches, kitchen tables and pianos in the favourite rooms of her house.

The door to Dr Burton's office opened and Jack quickly disposed of the magazine.

Dr Burton was younger than Jack had imagined, mid-to-late forties. He had a tight beard, light brown, speckled with silver in places. He had piercing blue eyes, was five eleven, Jack guessed, and was dressed in jeans and a tan corduroy jacket.

'Jack Ruttle?' he asked, looking at him.

'Yes.' Jack stood up and they greeted one another with a handshake.

The office was busy, the style of furniture and design eclectic with a packed bookshelf, a full desk, a line of filing cabinets, a wall of academic achievements, non-matching rugs, a chair and a couch. The place had character. It suited the man that sat before him in the chair taking his personal details.

'So, Jack.' Dr Burton finished filling out the form and crossed his legs, focusing all his attention on Jack. Jack fought the urge to run out of the building. 'Why is it that you have come here today?'

To find Sandy Shortt, he wanted to say, but instead shrugged and shifted uncomfortably in his seat. He wanted to just get this all over and done with right now. How on earth was he going to find out about Sandy through making up lies about himself? He hadn't fully thought this through, assuming that everything would fall into place as soon as he'd walked into Dr Burton's office. What was it they said in the movies when the shrinks asked them questions? *Think Jack, think.* 'I'm under a lot of pressure,' he said a bit too confidently, pleased with himself for answering a question.

'What kind of pressure?'

What *kind*? Was there more than one kind? 'Just normal kind of pressure.' He shrugged again.

Dr Burton frowned and Jack feared he'd got the question wrong. 'Is it due to work or—'

'Yeah,' he jumped in, 'it's work. It's really . . .' he searched his brain, 'pressurising.'

'OK.' Dr Burton nodded. 'What is it that you do?'

'I'm a stevedore in Shannon Foynes Port Company.'

'And what brings you to Dublin?'

'You.'

'You came all the way to see me?'

'I had to visit a friend too,' he said quickly.

'Oh, OK.' Dr Burton smiled. 'So what is it about work that you find so pressurising? Talk to me about it.'

'Uh, the hours.' Jack made an under-pressure face that he thought was convincing. 'The hours are so long.' He was silent then and he clasped his hands together on his lap and nodded and looked around the room.

'How many hours do you work a week?'

'Forty.' He spoke before thinking.

'Forty hours aren't more than average, Jack. Why is it you feel that you can't cope with these?'

Jack's face pinked.

'It's OK to feel that way, Jack. Perhaps we can get to the root of why work is bothering you, if it is indeed work that is bothering you . . .'

Dr Burton continued talking while Jack tuned out and looked around the room for signs of Sandy, as if she would have scribbled her name across the wall before she left. Jack realised Dr Burton was staring at him in silence.

'Yes, I think that's it,' Jack said, nodding, and looked at his hands, hoping he had said something suitable.

'And what's her name?'

'Whose name?'

'Your partner, the person at home you're having difficulties with?'

'Oh, Gloria,' he said, thoughts switching to her at home and how delighted she was that he was here today, spilling his heart out, when in reality he wasn't even listening. The more he thought about it, the angrier he began to feel inside.

'Do you talk to her about your feelings of stress and pressure?'

'Oh, no,' Jack laughed. 'I don't talk to Gloria about that kind of thing.'

'Why not?'

'Because she always has an answer, she always has a way to fix me.'

'You don't want that?'

'No,' he shook his head. '*I* don't need to be fixed.'

'What needs to be fixed?'

He shrugged, not wanting to be dragged into this discussion.

Dr Burton left a long silence and Jack felt the pressure to fill it. 'It's what's going on around us that needs to be fixed,' he finally answered.

Dr Burton waited for more.

'And . . .' he stalled, 'so that's what I'm trying to do.'

'You're trying to fix what's going on around you,' he repeated.

'That's what I just said.'

'And Gloria's not happy with this.'

Dr Burton was being paid an extortionate amount of money for this, Jack thought incredulously. 'No,' he shook his head, 'she thinks I should move on and forget about everything.' He hadn't actually meant to say any of that, but it hadn't hurt and he still hadn't given anything away.

'What does she want you to forget about?'

'Donal,' Jack said slowly, not sure whether to continue or not. Maybe if he explained, Dr Burton would agree with him and he would finally have someone on his side. 'The rest of the family are the same. They want to forget him, let him go, leave him behind. Well I don't think like that, you know? He's my brother. Gloria looks at me like I'm crazy when I try to explain.'

'Did your brother Donal pass away?'

'No, he didn't,' Jack said as though that was ludicrous, 'but you would think he had. He's only missing. *Only*,' he laughed angrily, rubbing his face tiredly. 'I sometimes think it would be easier if I knew he was dead.'

There was a silence and Jack felt the need to fill it again. He thumped his fist against his hand with every point he delivered. 'He went missing last year on the night of his twenty-fourth birthday.' *Thump.* 'He took cash out of the ATM on O'Connell Street at 3.08 a.m. on Friday night.' *Thump.* 'He was seen on Arthur's Quay at 3.30 a.m.' *Thump.* 'And after that no one saw him again. How can you let that go?' he asked. 'How can you decide to keep on living life when your brother is somewhere out there and you don't know where he is or if he's hurt and needs you? How the hell is everything supposed to become normal?' He became angry now. 'How does anybody expect you to be bothered to do forty hours of pointless work a week, putting cargo on a ship? Boxes I don't even know what's in them, and send them to places I've never been and never will be in. Why is that more important than finding my brother? How can you *not* look around you in all directions, trying to find him every time you're outside? Why is it everywhere I go and everyone I ask I'm met with the same answers?'

His voice raised even louder now. 'Nobody *saw* anything, nobody *heard* anything, nobody *knows* anything. There are *five million* people in this country, there are 175,000 of them living in Limerick, 55,000 of whom are living in Limerick city. How the hell didn't *somebody*, even *one* person, see my brother, *somewhere*?' He stopped shouting now, out of breath, his throat sore and his eyes full of tears he was adamant he wouldn't let fall.

Dr Burton allowed the silence to lengthen. He allowed Jack to gather himself and his thoughts and ponder all that he had blurted out. He went to the water cooler and returned with a plastic cup for Jack.

Jack sipped the water and thought aloud. 'She sleeps a lot, you see. The times when I need her, she's asleep.'

'Gloria?'

Jack nodded.

'Do you have difficulty sleeping?'

'I've so much going on in my head, I've so many

papers to look through and reports to go over. Things people said go through my head over and over again, and I just can't switch off. I have to find him. It's like an addiction. It eats away at me.'

Dr Burton nodded understandingly – not in the patronising way that Jack had thought would be the case, but as if he had a *real* understanding. It was as though Jack's problem was now *their* problem, and it was time for them to figure it out together.

'You're not the only person that feels like this and lives like this, you know, Jack. This is exactly the kind of behaviour expected after a trauma such as yours. Were you advised to speak to a counsellor after your brother's disappearance?'

Jack crossed his arms. 'Yeah, the guards mentioned something, and every day leaflets and fliers landed on my hall floor about joining groups of other "sufferers", they called them.' He waved his hand dismissively. 'Not interested.'

'It's not just a waste of time, you know. You would realise that there are many people in your position suffering from the same effects of losing someone,' and he added, more to himself, 'or even suffer from losing *things*.'

Jack looked at Dr Burton with confusion. 'No, no, you've got me wrong. I can deal with losing *things*, absolutely fine, it's missing family members that I've the problem with. My siblings have lost a brother too and not one of them feels the way I do. I can't imagine anything worse than sitting in a group and having the same conversations as I do at home.'

'Gloria seems supportive of you – you should appreciate that. I'm sure it's been difficult for her to lose Donal, but remember not only has she lost him, she's lost you too. Show that you appreciate her. I'm sure that would mean a lot to her.' Real emotion slipped into Dr Burton's voice and he stood up and walked over to the other side of the room to get himself a cup of water. When he came back, he was back to his cool self.

'Do you love her?'

Jack was silent, then shrugged. He didn't know any more.

'My mother used to say listen to what your heart tells you,' Dr Burton laughed, lightening the mood.

'Was she a psychiatrist too?' Jack smiled.

'As good as,' he laughed. 'You know, you remind me of someone, Jack, someone I know very well.' He smiled lightly, sadly, and then returned to his former self. 'So what are you going to do?' He checked his watch. 'Bearing in mind we only have a few minutes left to tell me.'

'I've already started to do something about it.' Jack suddenly remembered why he was here and saw a way in.

'Talk to me.' Dr Burton leaned forward, resting his elbows on his thighs.

'I found someone in the Golden Pages, an agency, a *missing persons* agency,' he stressed.

Dr Burton didn't flinch. 'Yes?'

'I got in touch with this woman and we spoke at length about her helping me to find Donal. We arranged to meet last Sunday in Limerick.'

'Yes?' He leaned back in his chair, slowly, poker-faced.

'Funny thing is, we passed one another at a petrol station on the way and then she never turned up at the meeting point.' He shook his head. 'I really believed and still believe this person has the ability to find him.'

'Really?' Dr Burton's tone was dry.

'Yes, really. So I started looking for her.'

'The missing persons person?' he stated, deadpan.

'Yes.'

'And did you find her?'

'No, but I found her car and I found my brother's files in her car, and her phone, her diary, her wallet and a bag full of labelled clothes all with her name on them. She labels everything.'

Dr Burton began to fidget in his chair.

'I was so worried about her – I am *still* worried about her – because I believe this woman has the ability to find my brother.'

'So you're fixing your obsession onto this other woman,' Dr Burton said a bit too coldly.

Jack shook his head. 'She said to me on the phone once that the one thing that would be more frustrating than not being able to find someone would be not being found. It's her wish to be found.'

'Perhaps she just wandered off for a few days.'

'The garda I contacted said the very same thing.' Dr Burton's eyebrows rose at the mention of involving the police. 'I contacted a lot of people who know her and they also said the same thing,' Jack shrugged.

'Well, then, you should listen to those people. Leave it alone, Jack. Try to concentrate on dealing with your brother's disappearance before you start worrying about another one. If she's been gone a few days and hasn't been in touch, maybe it's for a reason.'

'I wasn't bothering her, Doctor, if that's what you're implying. There are a few of us that are worried so we've arranged to meet up and do something about it.'

'Maybe she does this a lot,' Dr Burton said. 'Maybe there's nothing at all wrong with her and she's gone off on her own for a few days.'

'Yeah, maybe. But it's been four days since I've seen her and more days since anybody else has, unless I find somebody that tells me differently. If that's the case, then I'll back off and get on with my own life, but I don't think she's *wandering*, as so many people have said,' he said gently. 'I just would really love to find her, to thank her for the encouragement she's given me, for the hope of finding Donal that she has helped me to feel. That hope she's given me has allowed me to realise that I could find her too.'

'What makes you think that she's missing?'

'I'm listening to my heart on this one.'

Dr Burton smiled grimly at having his words thrown back in his face.

'And in case my heart isn't proof enough for you, there's also this.' Jack reached into his pocket and gently placed Sandy's silver watch on the table.

31

It had been three years since I'd seen Mr Burton. From a distance I could tell that time had aged him well. From a distance it appeared that time hadn't aged either of us. From a distance everything was perfect and nothing was altered.

I had changed my clothes six times before leaving the bedsit. Feeling mildly pleased with my appearance, I had made my way to Leeson Street for the fourth time that month. I had danced in the halls when I had received his business card. I had skipped down the stairs like the fourteen-year-old on a Monday morning, knowing what and who lay ahead of me that day. I had run from Harold's Cross to Leeson Street, I had taken the steps up to the grand Georgian door in twos, and I had then frozen as my finger hovered above the intercom button and had quickly retreated to the other side of the road. Close up, it was a completely different picture.

I was no longer the schoolgirl coming to him for help. Now I didn't know who I was, running *from* help. I sat across the road on two more occasions, unable to cross over, instead watching as he arrived in the mornings, left in the evenings and everything else in between.

I sat on the concrete steps on the fourth visit, elbows on my knees, fists under my chin, staring at all the feet and legs rushing by on the sidewalk. A pair of tan shoes beneath a pair of blue jeans crossed the road. They walked towards me. I expected them to pass me by and enter through the door behind me but they didn't. One step, two step, three steps up they stopped and sat down beside me.

'Hi,' the voice said softly.

I was afraid to look up but I did. I came face to face with him, blue eyes as bright as the day I first laid mine on him.

'Mr Burton,' I smiled.

He shook his head. 'How many times do I have to tell you not to call me that?'

I was about to call him Gregory when he said, 'It's *Doctor* Burton now.'

'Congratulations, *Doctor* Burton,' I smiled. I examined his face, taking all of him in.

'Do you think this week you could move away from these steps and make it inside the building? I was getting tired of watching you from a distance.'

'Funny, I was just thinking that sometimes it's easier to see things from a distance.'

'Yes, but it's impossible to hear.'

I laughed.

'I like the name of the building.' I looked over at the brass plate with the 'Scathach House' engraving.

'I came across it advertised for rental in the paper. I thought it was perfect. A good luck sign, perhaps.'

'Perhaps. I don't suppose you're any closer to that Bridge we discussed.'

He smiled and searched my face, took all of me in, and shivers ran through me.

'If you let me take you out for lunch, we could see where we are. That's if your boyfriend doesn't mind.'

'Boyfriend?' I asked, confused.

'The follicley unchallenged young male who answered the door to your place a few weeks back.'

'Oh, him.' I shook my head. 'That was just . . .' I paused, unable to remember his name, 'Thomas,' I lied. 'We're not together.'

Mr Burton laughed, stood up and held out his hand to help me up. 'My dear Sandy, I think you'll find his name was Steve, but not to worry. The more men's names you forget, the better it is for me.' He placed his hand lightly on the small of my back and I felt a jolt of electricity race through my body. He guided me across the road. 'Can we go into my office for just a moment? There's something I want to give you first.'

He introduced me proudly to his receptionist, Carol, and brought me into his office. It smelled of him, it looked like him, everything about it was Mr Burton, Mr Burton, oh, Mr Burton. I felt like I was wrapped in a gigantic hug, embraced in his arms as soon as I stepped in and sat on his couch.

'It's a bit better than the one we used to have, isn't it?' he smiled, retrieving something from a desk drawer and bringing it over.

'It's beautiful.' I looked around and breathed in his scent.

Suddenly he was nervous. He sat opposite me. 'I was supposed to give this to you last month when I called round, for your birthday. I hope you like it.' He slid the box across the veneer cherry table. The box was long, red and velvet. I took it in my hands as though it were the most fragile thing I'd ever held, and I rubbed my fingers along the soft furry velvet. I looked at him; he was nervously eyeing the box. I opened it slowly and held my breath. A silver watch glistened inside.

'Oh, Mr Bur—' I started and he grabbed my hand, stopping me.

'*Please*, Sandy. It's Gregory now, OK?'

It's Gregory now. It's *Gregory* now. It's Gregory *now*. A choir of cherubs sang in my ear.

I nodded, smiling. I took the watch from the box and wrapped it around my left wrist, fiddling with the clasp, still stunned by the unexpected gift.

'If you look at the back, you'll see your name is engraved.' With shaking hands he helped me turn it over. There it was, 'Sandy Shortt'. 'May it never go missing.'

We smiled.

'Don't force it,' he warned, watching me trying to

close it. 'Here, let me help you,' he said just as the clasp made a snapping sound between my fingers.

I froze. 'Did I break it?'

He moved to the couch beside me, all fingers and thumbs as he tried to fix it, his skin brushing against mine and everything, *everything*, melting inside of me.

'It's not broken but the clasp is loosened. I'll have to take it back and get it fixed.' He tried to keep the disappointment from his voice but failed miserably.

'No!' I stopped him from taking it off me. 'I love it, I want to keep it on.'

'It's too loose, Sandy. It may open and fall off.'

'No, I'll keep my eye on it. I won't lose it.'

He looked unsure.

'Just for today at least, let me wear it.'

'OK.' He stopped fiddling with it and we both finally stayed still and looked at one another.

'I'm really giving you this to help you with your time-keeping. Three years without contact are not allowed to pass again.'

I looked down and twisted the watch around my wrist, admiring the links of the wristband, the mother-of-pearl face. 'Thank you, Gregory,' I smiled, loving how the word felt in my mouth, on my tongue as I said it. 'Gregory, Gregory,' I repeated a few more times as he laughed, loving every moment of it.

I let him take me out for lunch and we saw where we were.

Lunch was as close to a disaster as it could possibly have been. We consumed enough Food for Thought to last us our lifetimes. If either of us had any ridiculous notions that this could be the beginning of something special – and we most certainly did – we were brought to earth by the realisation that we were right back where we finished off. Or very possibly right back to Gregory having to walk over razor-sharp grass blades. I was Scathach and my heart was on Scathach's island in all her and its fierce extremities. I had worsened by the years.

Yet I didn't ever, not for one day, take my watch off.

There were times when it fell, but we all do that. It was put back where it belonged, where I felt and knew it to belong. That watch symbolised an awful lot. The positive side to our learning lunch was that it confirmed that we felt inextricably linked to one another, as if there was an invisible umbilical cord joining us both, allowing us to feed off one another, helping us to grow and give one another life.

Inevitably, there was the flip side: that we could tug on the cord whenever we liked, twisting it and knotting it, not caring enough that our twisting and knotting had the ability to choke and suffocate one another slowly.

From a distance everything was great, close up things were completely different. We couldn't fight the effects of time; how it alters us, how with each year an extra layer is glazed upon us, how every day we are something more than we were. Unfortunately for me and for Gregory, it was glaringly obvious that I was something and somebody far less than who I once was.

32

Bobby closed the door of Lost and Found quietly behind us, as though the sound would bring the stall owners outside to a stunned silence. I wasn't sure if this carry-on was just another of his dramatics but I sensed with a mild panic that it wasn't. Bobby let go of my clammy hand and scuttled off into an adjoining room without a word, closing the door over behind him. Through the slit I could see his shadow flickering as he darted by the light, furiously rooting around; moving boxes, scraping furniture across the floor, clinking glasses, making every possible sound, each introducing a new conspiracy theory in my suspicious mind. Finally I averted my eyes from the doorway and looked around the room.

I was faced with walnut shelves floor-to-ceiling high, like in the old grocery stores of decades ago. Baskets were filled to the brim with knick-knacks: Sellotape, gloves, pens, markers and lighters. Others were filled with socks with a handwritten sign excitedly announcing the sale of actual *pairs*. There were dozens of clothes rails lining the centre of the shop, the men's and women's sections separated, everything colour-co-ordinated, styles, eras labelled with dates from the fifties, sixties, seventies and up. There were costumes, traditional clothing and wedding dresses (who loses a wedding dress?). On the opposite wall there was a selection of books, and before that there was a counter displaying jewellery: backs of earrings, single earrings, some pairs

Bobby had matched up despite the difference in their appearances.

There was a musty smell in the shop, everything was second-hand; used, had a history. Thin T-shirts had depth, had layers glazed upon them. There wasn't the same atmosphere as in a shop of shiny new things. Nothing was squeaky clean and young and innocently ready to learn. There were no books unread, no hats not yet worn, no pens not yet held. The gloves had held the hand of an owner's loved one, the shoes had walked distances, scarves had wrapped, umbrellas had protected. These objects knew things, knew what they were supposed to do. They had experience of life and lay in baskets, folded on shelves and hung on rails ready to teach those who wore them. Like most of the people here, these objects had tasted life and then seen it slip away. And like most people here, they waited until they could taste it again.

I couldn't help but wonder about who was looking for them now, who was tearing their hair out to find their favourite earrings. Who was grumbling and searching in the bottom of their bag for another lost pen? Who was on their cigarette break only to find their lighter was missing? Who was already late for work and couldn't find their car keys that morning? Who was trying to hide from their spouse the fact their wedding ring had disappeared? They could look and look till their eyes were sore but they would never find. What a time for me to have such an epiphany. Here in Aladdin's cave of lost possessions far away from home. *There's no place like home . . .* the phrase taunted me again.

'Bobby,' I called, inching closer to the doorway, and shutting out the voice in my head.

'Just a minute,' came his muffled reply, followed by a bang, followed by a profanity.

Despite my nerves I smiled. I ran my finger along a walnut display cabinet, the kind you'd expect to contain good silverware and crockery. Here it contained hundreds of photographs of smiling faces from all over the world, over the decades. I picked up one of a couple standing in front of Niagara Falls and studied it. It looked like it was taken in the seventies; it had the yellowy tint that could only be obtained by being dipped in time. Two forty-something-year-olds in wide flares and raincoats, one second caught and contained among a lifetime of seconds. If they were alive now, they too would be in their seventies with grandchildren looking on and waiting patiently as they leafed through their photo albums, looking for the picture to recall their trip to Niagara. Secretly wondering if they had imagined it all, whether that second among a lifetime of seconds had been true at all, while grumbling to themselves, 'I know I have it here somewhere . . .'

'Nice idea, isn't it?'

I looked up to see Bobby watching me from the doorway. After all his rummaging in the next room, he had nothing in his hands.

'Last week, Mrs Harper found a wedding photo of her cousin Nadine, whom she hadn't seen for five years. You wouldn't believe her reaction when she came across the photo. She sat there all day just staring at it. It was a group photo of all at the wedding, you see. Her entire family were there. Imagine not seeing your family for five years and then suddenly coming across a recent photo of them. She only came in looking for socks.' He shrugged. 'It's times like that when I feel useful around here.'

I put the frame of the couple down. 'You said you were expecting me.' I said it more harshly than I meant to, but I was scared.

He unfolded his arms and placed his hands in his pockets. I thought he was finally going to take something out of them and give it to me but instead he left them there. 'I've been here for three years now.' He had the same haunted face as everyone else had when they recalled the memory of arriving here. 'I was sixteen years old. Two years to go till I finished school, ten years to go till I planned on growing up. I had no idea what I wanted to do with my life. I figured I'd still be at home annoying Mum until she forced me out and made me get a proper job. In the meantime I was happy being the joker at school and having my boxers washed and ironed. I didn't take many things seriously,' he shrugged. 'I was only sixteen,' he repeated.

I nodded, not knowing where this was going. Wondering why on earth he said he'd been expecting me.

'I didn't know what to do when I first arrived here. I spent most of the time on the other side of the woods, trying to find a way out. But there's none.' He took his hands out of his pockets and made a clear signal. 'I'll tell you that now, Sandy, there's *no* way out of here and I've seen people drive themselves demented trying to find a way.' He shook his head. 'I soon realised I had to start life here. I had to, for once in my life, take something seriously.' He shifted uncomfortably in his stance. 'It happened when I was looking for some clothes to wear. I was rummaging through all the gear outside, feeling like a homeless man at a junk site. I came across a sock that was bright orange, glowing from under a business file I imagine someone was fired that morning for losing. It was so bright I couldn't help but wonder how on earth someone had managed to lose something so luminous, something that so clearly stood out from the crowd. But the more I looked at it, the better it made me feel about myself turning up here, because before, I thought it was my fault. I thought it was my complacency that led me to wind up here. I thought that if I'd paid more attention in school and had stopped messing around so much, that I could have prevented myself from coming here.'

I nodded. I knew that very same feeling.

'The sock made me feel better because it was the brightest thing I'd ever seen,' he laughed. 'It was even *labelled*, for Christsake, and I just knew that it was bad luck and *only* bad luck on both our parts for ending up here! There was nothing I could have done to avoid ending up here, no more than the sock could have done.

I felt sorry for the person who'd labelled it, put their address on it, who'd basically done everything to avoid it going missing. So I kept it to remind myself of that feeling, of that day I stopped blaming myself and everybody else. A *sock* made me feel better.' He smiled. 'Follow me.' He went back into the adjoining room.

The next room was much the same as the shop, with walls lined with shelving units, though it was much smaller and was piled high with cardboard boxes, by the looks of it, used for storage.

'Here's the sock.' He gave it to me and I held it in my hands. It was small, that of a child, and was of towelling material. If Bobby thought the sock was going to have the same effect on me as it did on him, he was wrong. I still wanted out of here and blamed myself and everybody else for putting me here.

'After a few weeks of being here, I found myself helping newcomers to find clothes and anything else they needed when they arrived. So I eventually opened this place up. Mine is the only store in this village where you can get everything all under one roof,' he said proudly. My lack of enthusiasm caused his smile to disappear and to continue his story. 'Anyway, as part of owning and running this place, I have to go out every day and collect as many useful things as possible. I pride myself on being the only place that sells actual pairs of shoes, socks, matching outfits and such like. Other people just gather what they find and display them. I search for the other half, kind of like a matchmaker,' he grinned.

'Go on,' I urged, sitting on an old torn chair that reminded me of my first sessions with Mr Burton.

'Anyway, the orange sock wasn't much of a big deal at all until I found this.' He leaned over and took a T-shirt from a box beside him. Again, it appeared to be that of a child. 'And *that* wasn't even a big deal until I found this.' He placed another odd sock on the floor before me and studied my face.

'I don't get it,' I shrugged, throwing the orange sock down to the floor.

He continued to take out the contents of the cardboard box in silence and laid them out on the floor before me while my mind worked overtime trying to decipher the code.

'I thought there was more in this one, but anyway, that's the lot,' Bobby said finally.

The floor was almost covered in items of clothing and accessories and I was about to stand up and demand he start talking sense when I finally recognised a T-shirt. And then I recognised a sock, a pencil case . . . and then handwriting on a piece of paper.

Bobby stood by the empty box, excitement flashing in his eyes. 'You get it now?'

I couldn't speak.

'They're all labelled. The name "Sandy Shortt" is written on every single thing you see before you.'

I held my breath, looking furiously from one item to another.

'That's just *one* box. They're all yours too,' he said excitedly, pointing to the corner of the room where five more boxes were stacked up. 'Every time I saw your name I collected the item and stored it. The more things of yours I found, the more I became convinced that it was only a matter of time before you would come to collect them yourself. And here you are.'

'Here I am,' I repeated, looking at everything on the floor. I got down on my knees and ran my hand across the orange sock. Although I couldn't remember it, I could imagine my frantic searches that night while my poor parents watched. That was the beginning of it all. I took my T-shirt in my hands and saw my name written on the label in my mother's handwriting. I felt the ink with my fingertips, hoping that in some way I was connecting with her. I moved on to the piece of paper with my messy teenage handwriting. Answers to questions on *Romeo and Juliet* from school. I remember doing that homework and being unable to find it in class the next day. The teacher hadn't believed me when I couldn't find it in my school bag. He'd stood over me in a silent class and watched me root in my school bag, my frustration clearly growing, yet his failure to recognise that genuine frustration had meant punishment homework. I felt like grabbing the page and running back to Leitrim, bursting in on that teacher's class and saying, 'Here, look, I told you I had done it!'

I touched every item on the floor, the memory of wearing them, losing them and searching for them coming to mind. After I'd seen every item from the first box, I raced over to the next on the top of the stacked pile in the corner. With shaking hands I opened the box. Staring up at me with his one eye was my dear friend Mr Pobbs.

I took him out of the box and held him close to me, inhaling him, trying to get the familiar scent of home. He had long lost that and was musty, like the rest of the belongings here, but I clung to him and squeezed him to my chest. My name and phone number were still visible on his tag, the blue felt pen of my mother's writing blurred now.

'I told you I'd find you, Mr Pobbs,' I whispered, and I heard the door behind me gently close as Bobby stepped out of the room, leaving me alone with a head and a room full of memories.

33

I don't know how long I'd been in the storeroom – I had lost track of all time. I looked out the window for the first time in hours, feeling cross-eyed and tired from concentrating on my possessions for so long. My *possessions*. I actually had belongings in this place. They brought me that bit closer to home, momentarily linking the two worlds and blurring the boundaries so that I didn't feel so lost as I touched and held things I had once held in my place near the people I loved. Especially Mr Pobbs. So much had happened since I'd seen him. Johnny Nugent and a thousand other Johnny Nugents had happened. It seemed the night Mr Pobbs disappeared from my bed, an entire team of Mr Wrongs had taken his place.

Joseph walked by the window and I sat back and watched as he strode confidently in his white linen shirt with sleeves rolled to just below his elbows and trousers rolled above the ankles of his sandalled feet. He always stood out from the crowd to me. He looked like somebody important, who oozed dominance and power. He spoke little, yet when he did he chose his words carefully. When he spoke, people listened. His words moved from whispers to songs, never anything in between. Despite the strength of his physical demeanour, he spoke softly, which made him all the more superior.

The bell on the shop's front door rang again. The door squeaked and closed.

'Hello, Joseph,' Bobby said cheerfully. 'Did my Wanda not want to see me today?'

Joseph laughed lightly and I *knew* Bobby was funny to have made him laugh, 'Oh, that girl is so in love with you. Do you think she wouldn't be here if she knew I was here?'

Bobby laughed. 'How can I help you?'

Joseph's voice lowered as though he knew I was here and I immediately pressed my ear against the door.

'A watch?' I heard Bobby repeat loudly. 'I have lots of watches here.'

Joseph's voice was lowered to inaudible again and I *knew* it was terribly important for his voice to be so hushed. He was talking about *my* watch.

'A silver watch with a mother-of-pearl face,' I heard Bobby say, and I was thankful for his habit of repeating people. Their footsteps on the walnut floor got louder and I prepared to move away from the door in case it was opened.

'What about this one?' Bobby asked.

'No, it would have been one you had found yesterday or this morning,' Joseph said.

'How do you know?'

'Because it went missing yesterday.'

'Well, I don't know how you could know that,' Bobby laughed awkwardly. 'Unless you've been talking to someone from the other world, which I'm highly doubtful of.'

There was silence.

'Joseph, this watch is exactly what you've described.' I could hear the confusion in Bobby's voice.

'It's not the one I want,' Joseph said.

'Did you see it somewhere? On somebody? Perhaps you could tell them to visit me so I get an idea of what you're looking for. If I come across it, I'll save it for you.'

'It is the very watch I saw somebody wearing that I'm looking for.'

'Someone from Kenya? Years ago?'

'No, from Here.'

'Here?' Bobby repeated.

'Yes, Here.'

'Did somebody from Here give it to me?'

'No, it went missing.'

Silence.

'It can't have. They must have misplaced it.'

'I know but I saw it with my own eyes.'

'You saw it *disappear*?'

'I saw it on her wrist and she didn't move an inch from her place, and then I saw that it was gone from her wrist.'

'It must have fallen off her.'

'Yes, it did do that.'

'So it's on the ground.'

'That's the funny thing,' Joseph said drily, and I *knew* it wasn't funny at all.

'But it can't ha—'

'It did.'

'And you thought it would show up here?'

'I thought you may have found it.'

'I didn't.'

'I can see that. Thank you, Bobby. Speak of this to no one,' he warned, giving me a chill. Footsteps began to move away.

'Hold on, hold on, Joseph. Don't go yet! Tell me, who lost it?'

'You don't know her.'

'Where did she lose it?'

'Halfway between here and the next village.'

'No,' Bobby whispered.

'Yes.'

'I'll find it,' Bobby said determinedly. 'It has to be there.'

'It's not.' Joseph raised his voice to a normal tone but for him it was loud. From the way that he said it I *knew* that it was not.

'OK, OK.' Bobby backed down, still not sounding like he believed it. 'Does the person who lost it know that it's gone? Maybe she knows where it is.'

'She's new here.' That said it all. That meant *she doesn't understand a thing*, and he was right, I didn't, but I was learning fast.

'She's new?' The tone in Bobby's voice had changed. I recognised that and was sure Joseph would too. 'Maybe I can talk to her and get the exact description.'

'I have given you the exact description.' Yes, he noticed it. Footsteps moved towards the door again, the door squeaked and the bell rang.

'Was there a name on the watch?' Bobby called out at the last minute, and the squeak of the front door stopped, it closed again, and footsteps got louder as they neared me again.

'Why do you ask?' Joseph's voice was firm.

'Because sometimes people engrave names, dates or messages on the backs of watches.' Bobby sounded nervous.

'You asked me if there was a name – why did you specifically ask about a name?'

'Some watches have names engraved on them.' His voice went up an octave in defence. 'I should know.' He tapped on glass and I guessed it was the jewellery cabinet.

There was an odd atmosphere outside. I didn't like it.

'Let me know if you find the watch. Be quiet about it, you know how people would react if they found out that things from Here were going missing.'

'Of course, I understand it might give them hope.'

'Bobby . . .' Joseph warned, and a chill ran through me.

'Yes, sir,' Bobby said smartly.

The door squeaked, the bell rang and it was closed again. I waited a while to make sure Joseph didn't come back in. Bobby was silent outside. I was about to stand up when Joseph walked by the window again, closer this time, staring at the building suspiciously. I quickly ducked and lay flat on the floor, wondering why on earth I was suddenly hiding from Joseph.

Bobby opened the door and looked down at me. 'What on earth are you doing?'

'Bobby Stanley,' I sat up brushing the dust off me, 'you have a *lot* of explaining to do.'

He took me by surprise and folded his arms across his chest. 'And so have you,' he said coolly. 'Want to know why I wasn't at your auditions? Because nobody told me about them. Want to know why? Because around here everybody knows me as Bobby *Duke*. Ever since the day I arrived here, I haven't told *anybody* that my name is Bobby Stanley. So how did you know?'

34

'Mr Le Bon, I assume,' Dr Burton addressed Jack, leaning back in his chair and folding his arms.

Jack reddened but he was determined not to back down or be dismissed from Dr Burton's company as a raving lunatic. He leaned forward. 'Dr Burton, there are *many* of us who are trying to find Sandy—'

'I don't need to hear any more.' He pushed his chair back, grabbed Jack's file from the coffee table and got to his feet. 'Our time is up, Mr Ruttle. You can settle the fee outside with Carol.' He spoke with his back turned as he made his way to his desk.

'Dr—'

'Goodbye, Mr Ruttle.' His voice rose.

Jack took the silver watch in his hands and stood. He spoke quietly but quickly while he had the chance. 'Can I just say that a garda by the name of Graham Turner may contact—'

'Enough!' Dr Burton shouted, slamming the file down on the desk. His face reddened and his nostrils flared. Jack froze and was immediately silenced.

'You obviously haven't known Sandy very long *or* intimately. Taking that into consideration, it's glaringly obvious that it's absolutely no business of yours to go snooping around in her life.'

Jack opened his mouth to protest but he was beaten to it again.

'But,' Dr Burton continued, 'I believe that you and your group are genuine and so I will tell you this before you take things any further with the police.' He battled visibly with his anger. 'I'll tell you what the Gardaí will tell you if they start ringing around. I'll tell you what Sandy's own family will tell you,' his anger rose again and he ground his back teeth. 'And what every single person who knows her will tell you and that is this: that *this*,' he threw his arms up helplessly in the air, 'is what Sandy does.'

Jack tried to speak again.

'*All* of the time,' he shouted. 'She floats in and floats out, leaves things behind, sometimes she collects them, sometimes she doesn't.' He placed his hands on his hips, his chest heaving with anger. 'But the point is, she'll come back again. She always comes back.'

Jack nodded and looked down at the ground. He started to cross the room to leave.

'You can leave her things here,' Dr Burton added. 'I'll make sure she gets them and thanks you on her return.'

Jack slowly lowered the rucksack of her belongings to the ground by the door and quietly stepped out, feeling like a scolded schoolboy, but at the same time feeling sympathy for the schoolmaster who had chastised him. It wasn't Jack he was angry at. It was the breeze that came and went, blowing sporadic gusts of hot and cold air from puckered lips, kisses that tickled and air that smelled sweet, but who at the snap of her fingers inhaled it all back in an instant. It was Sandy he was mad at. And himself, for his eternal wait.

Jack left Dr Burton, hands on hips, staring out the Georgian window, grinding his jaw. Jack closed the door softly behind him, locking the atmosphere inside. It was far too precious to allow to creep into the reception for the awaiting people to sense. It would remain locked in the office, hovering around Dr Burton while he took the time to process it, deal with it, allow it to cool, and then eventually dissipate.

The receptionist, Carol, looked at Jack with worry, not sure whether to be frightened of him or sorry for him at the screaming she had heard inside. Jack placed his credit card on the counter and reached down to her desk to pass her a piece of paper.

'Could you please tell Dr Burton that if he changes his mind, here's my phone number and the address of the meeting point later today?'

She read the note quickly and nodded, still defensive of her boss.

He entered his pin code into the machine and retrieved his credit card. 'Oh, and please give him this too.' He placed the silver watch on the counter. Her eyes narrowed as he walked away.

'Mr Le Bon?' he heard her say as he reached the door. A man reading a car magazine looked up at the mention of the peculiar name.

Jack froze and turned to her slowly. 'Yes?'

'I'm sure Dr Burton will be in contact soon.'

Jack laughed lightly. 'Oh, I'm not too sure about that.' He moved to leave again and she cleared her throat, trying to get his attention. He walked back to her desk.

She leaned forward and lowered her voice. The man took the hint and went back to reading his magazine.

'It's usually just a few days each time. The longest was almost two weeks but that was at the beginning. This is by far the longest in a while,' she whispered. 'When you find her, tell her to come back to . . .' she looked sadly at the door to Dr Burton's office, 'well, just tell her to come back.'

As quickly as she'd spoken, she stopped, took the watch from the counter, placed it in a drawer and carried on typing. 'Kenneth,' she called, ignoring Jack now. 'Dr Burton will see you now. Go right in.'

It's difficult beginning a relationship with someone you were never allowed to know anything about.

Our relationship to date had been based on me and I was finding it hard to make the transition to it suddenly being about the both of us. Every week our meetings were centred on how *I* was feeling, what *I* had done that week, what *I* thought and what *I'd* learned. He was allowed to access my mind whenever he wanted. That was the reason alone for our relationship; for him to delve into my mind and try to figure me out. And to try to stop me from trying to figure him out.

A more serious relationship, a more *intimate* relationship was proving to be the opposite. I had to remember to ask him about him and to remember that he couldn't now know everything that was inside my head. Some things had to be held back, for safe-keeping, for self-preservation, and in a way I lost my confidant. The closer we got, the less he knew about me, the more I learned about him.

An hour a week had been intensified and roles had been reversed. Who'd have thought Mr Burton had a life beyond the four walls of the old school? He knew people and did things that I never knew about. Things that I was suddenly allowed to know about but wasn't sure of whether I wanted to. How could a person historically incapable of sharing a bed *and* a head not need to run from all of that? Sure I went missing for days at a time.

No, the age gap didn't matter, it had never mattered. The years weren't the problem; it was the time that was the fault. This new relationship existed without a ticking clock. There was no long hand to dictate the end of a conversation; I could not be saved by the proverbial bell. He could access me at all times. Of course I ran.

There's a fine line between love and hate. Love frees a soul and in the same breath can sometimes suffocate it. I walked that tightrope with all the gracefulness of an elephant, my head weighing me to the side of hate, my heart hoisting me to the side of love. It was a wobbly journey and sometimes I fell. Sometimes I fell for long periods of time but never for too long.

Never for as long as this.

I'm not asking to be liked. I've never yearned to be liked, nor am I asking to be understood; I've never been that either. When I behaved that way, when I left his bed, let go of his hand, hung up the phone and closed his door behind me, even *I* had difficulty liking me, understanding me. But it's just how I was.

How I *was*.

35

Bobby stood at the door of the stockroom, arms folded across his chest, a scowl on his face.

'What?' I scrambled to my feet and towered over him. He didn't seem so confident now that I'd risen to my full six foot one. He dropped his hands by his sides and looked up at me. 'Your name *isn't* Bobby Stanley?'

'No, according to everybody else here, my name is Bobby Duke,' he said defensively, accusingly, childishly.

'Bobby *Duke*?' I rubbed my face in frustration. 'What?' I repeated. 'The guy from the cowboy movies? Why?'

'Never mind the *why*.' His face reddened. 'I think the issue here is that you are the only one who knows my real name. How?'

'I know your mother, Bobby,' I said softly. 'There's no great mystery. It's as simple as that.' The past few days had consisted of secrets, mysteries and little white lies. It was time to stop all that, for now anyway. All I wanted to do was meet the people I had been searching for, tell them all that I knew and then bring them home. That is what I would do. While contemplating all this I suddenly noticed that Bobby had gone completely silent and had whitened ever so slightly.

'Bobby?' I said.

He didn't speak, just backed away a little from the doorway.

'Bobby, are you OK?' I asked a little more gently.

'Yeah,' he said, not looking at all OK.

'You're sure?'

'I kind of knew that,' he said quietly.

'What?'

'I kind of knew that you knew my mum. Not just when I first opened the shop door this morning and you called me Mr Stanley, and not just when everybody from the auditions told me that you knew so much, but I kind of knew when I kept finding all of your things.' He looked beyond me to my lost life scattered on the floor. 'When you're on your own, you look for signs. Sometimes you make them up, sometimes they're actually there, but most of the time you can't tell the difference between the two. I believed in this one the most.'

I smiled. 'You're exactly as she said you'd be.'

His lower lip trembled and he tried to stop it. 'Is she OK?'

'Apart from missing you like crazy, she's OK.'

'Ever since Dad left it was always just her and me. She's on her own now. I hate that she's on her own.' His voice went up and down as he tried to control it.

'She's never alone, Bobby; she has your uncles, aunts and grandparents. Besides, she brings anyone and everyone who'll listen into her home and goes through photo albums and home videos of you. I don't think there's one person in Baldoyle who hasn't seen you score against St Kevin's in the finals.'

He smiled. 'We could have won that match had it not been . . .' he trailed off.

I continued for him, 'Had it not been for Gerald Fitzwilliam getting injured in the second half.'

He raised his head and looked at me, light in his eyes. 'It was Adam McCabe's fault,' he tutted, and shook his head.

'He should never have been put in midfield,' I said, and he laughed. He laughed that loud, cartoon laugh that I'd heard so many times in the home videos, the laugh that his family spoke about so much. The high-pitched, addictively funny sound that instantly made me giggle.

'Wow,' he breathed, 'you know her *well*.'

'Bobby, believe me, you don't need to know your mother well to know that.'

Jack sat in Mary Stanley's home, drinking coffee and watching home videos of her son, Bobby.

'See this bit here.' Mary inched forward suddenly in her chair, coffee spilling over the side of her mug and falling onto her blue jeans. 'Ah,' she jumped back, making a face, and Jack leaped forward, thinking she'd burned herself. 'That's where it all went wrong,' she said angrily.

Jack realised she was still referring to the television and he sat back on the couch.

'See him?' She pointed at the TV, spilling coffee again.

'Watch yourself,' Jack warned her.

'I'm fine.' She rubbed her leg without looking. 'This is where it all went wrong. We could have won that match had it not been for him,' she pointed again, 'Gerald Fitzwilliam, getting injured right there in the second half.'

'Mmm,' Jack replied, sipping his coffee and watching the amateur footage of the match jumping up and down on the screen. Most of the time all he could see was a blur of green followed by close-ups of Bobby's head.

'It was Adam McCabe's fault,' she tutted and shook her head. 'He should never have been put in midfield.'

Bobby brought me up a small winding staircase, which led to his residence above the shop. I sat waiting for him in his living room on an impressive leather couch I imagined somebody had impatiently waited for, for longer than the average four-to-six-week period. He brought me in a glass of orange juice and a croissant and my ravenous stomach gurgled in thanks.

'I thought everybody was supposed to eat in the eatery,' I said, attacking the fresh croissant, which flaked in my hands.

'Let's just say the chef has a soft spot for me. She has a son my age back home in Tokyo. She slips me food every once in a while and I occasionally tease her, disgust her and do other son-like things.'

'Charming,' I murmured, face covered in pastry.

Bobby was staring at me, his food untouched on his plate.

'Whapft?' I said with a mouthful of food. He continued staring and I quickly swallowed. 'Is there something on my face?' I felt around.

'I want to hear more,' he said sombrely.

I looked sadly to the remainder of food on my plate, wanting so much to finish it but knowing by the look on Bobby's face that I owed it to his mother to start talking fast.

'You want to know about your mum?' I washed down the crumbs with orange juice.

'No, I want to know about you.' He got comfortable on the couch while I watched him, suddenly uncomfortable, with my mouth agape.

'I was told you ran an acting agency – was it through the agency that you became friends with my mum?'

'No, not really.'

'I didn't think so.'

'What do you mean by that?'

'You don't run an acting agency, do you? You don't seem like the type.'

My mouth dropped open and I felt oddly insulted. 'Why, what *type* of person usually runs an acting agency?'

'People that aren't like you,' he smiled. 'What do you really do?'

'I search,' I smiled. 'I hunt.'

'For talent?'

'For people.'

'For talented people?'

'I suppose everybody I look for has a talent of some sort, although I'm not too sure about you.' Bobby looked confused and I decided to drop the awkward humour and place my trust in him. 'I run a missing persons agency, Bobby.'

At first he looked shocked. Then, as the realisation hit him, he began to smile, the smile grew into a grin, the grin worked its way into laughter, laughter became the addictively funny sound I knew so well, and then I was laughing too.

Suddenly he stopped. 'Are you here to bring us all home or are you just visiting?'

I looked at his hopeful face and immediately felt sad. 'Neither. I'm stuck here too, unfortunately.'

At moments when life is at its worst there are two things that you can do: 1) break down, lose hope and refuse to go on while lying face down on the ground banging your fists and kicking your legs, or 2) laugh. Bobby and I did the latter.

'OK, here's what you have to do. *Do not* tell anybody else this news,' Bobby said.

'I haven't. Apart from Helena and Joseph, nobody else knows.'

'Good. We can trust them. The idea for the play was Helena's?'

I nodded.

'Clever move.' His eyes glistened mischievously. 'Sandy, you really need to be careful. People were talking this morning at the eatery.'

'People don't usually talk at the eatery?' I joked, tucking into the remainder of my croissant.

'Come on, this is serious. They were talking about you. The group of auditionees must have told their friends and their families here about what you'd told them, who in turn told a few other people, and now *everybody's* talking.'

'Is it really that bad that they know? I mean, what harm will it do if they all know I used to look for missing people?'

Bobby's eyes widened. 'Are you crazy? The vast majority of people here are settled and wouldn't go back to their old ways if you paid them, and not just because money has absolutely no use for them here. But there are a number of people – the kind of people that are how I was when I arrived. These people haven't found their feet yet because they are still trying to find their way out. Those people will latch on to you like you don't know what, and you'll be wishing you'd never opened your mouth.'

'Helena said the very same thing to me. Did that happen before?'

'*My God*, did it happen before! Well, not *exactly* the same circumstances.' He waved his hand dismissively and dropped the dramatics. 'Years ago before I even arrived here, some old guy claimed that some of his things kept going missing. If you ask me it was his mind more than anything. Well, as soon as people heard, there wasn't a toilet he could go to without company. He was followed absolutely *everywhere*. When he went to the eatery, people flocked to his table; they followed him to the shops and even waited outside his home. It was madness. Eventually he had to give up his job because huge numbers would shadow him.'

'What was his job?'

'He was a postman.'

'A postman? Here?' I screwed up my face.

'What's so odd about that? We need postmen here more than anywhere. People need to get letters, messages and packages to others in surrounding villages, as even though we have telephones, televisions and computers, there's no network or service on any of them, just static and a lot of fuzz. Anyway, he couldn't keep cycling into villages with a trail of people behind him. Villagers were giving out about it but the people who followed him thought he was miraculously going to find his way out of here.'

'And what happened?' I asked, now on the edge of my seat.

'They all drove him crazy, even more crazy than he already was. There was nowhere he could go in privacy.'

'Where is he now?'

'I dunno.' Bobby appeared suddenly bored by the story. 'He disappeared. He's probably a few towns away or something. Joseph would know as they were very close. You should ask him.'

A chill entered my body and I shivered.

'Are you cold in here?' Bobby asked, incredulous. 'It's always so hot upstairs, I find. I'm absolutely sweating.' He picked up our plates and glasses.

He may have acted cool, but I saw him. I saw him from the corner of my eye, giving me a long, long look before he exited the room. He wanted to see if his seed had been planted. He needn't have worried. It had.

36

'Come on, we can walk and talk at the same time,' Bobby said, standing and grabbing my hand to pull me up.

'Where are we going?'

'To rehearsals, of course. Now more than anything, you have to keep up this play lark. People will be keeping their eyes on you whether you notice it or not.'

I got chills again and shuddered. Once downstairs, Bobby started throwing clothes at me.

'What are you doing?'

'People will take you a lot more seriously if you stop dressing like Sinbad the Sailor.' He handed me a pair of grey pinstripe trousers and a blue shirt.

'These are the correct sizes,' I said, looking through the tags, impressed.

'Yes, but I did not take into account the very long legs.' He bit his lip looking down at me.

'The bane of my life.' I rolled my eyes, handing the trousers back.

'No problem, I've got just the thing!' He ran off down the end of the shop. 'This entire rail is for people with very long legs.' He rooted through the hangers, while I looked at the clothes like a kid in a sweetshop. Never, *never* had I come across such a luxury.

'My God, I think I might be happy here after all.' I ran my fingers along all the clothes.

'Here you go.' He handed me what looked like exactly

the same trousers, but longer. 'Put them on quick. We don't want to be late for rehearsals.'

We stepped outside into the bright sunny day, my eyes aching after being hidden away in the darkness of the musty walnut building. It was noisy with the business of trade going on. People were shouting, bargaining, laughing and calling out in all different languages, some I had never heard before. A small group of four women turned to stare at Bobby and me as he locked up the shop. I stood on the porch in my new clothes, feeling on show as they whispered to one another.

'There she is,' I heard one whisper very loudly, so loudly I wonder how on earth she thought I wouldn't hear her. One nudged another and she was pushed forward, stumbling towards us as we made our way down the steps.

'Hi.' She stopped us in our tracks.

Bobby went to move around her but she stepped to the left, blocking us again.

'Hi,' she repeated, looking at me and ignoring Bobby.

'Hi,' I responded, aware that the group she had emerged from were watching.

'My name is Christine Taylor?'

Was that a question?

'Hi, Christine.'

Silence.

'I'm Sandy.'

Her eyes narrowed as she searched my face, hunting for my recognition of her.

'Can I help you?' I asked politely.

'I've been here for two and a half years?' she asked again.

'Oh, I see. That's,' I looked to Bobby, who raised his eyes to heaven in response, 'well, that's quite a while, isn't it?'

She studied me again. 'I used to live in Dublin?'

'Really? Dublin's a very nice city.'

'I have three brothers and one sister?' She tried to refresh my memory. '*Andrew* Taylor?' Eyes searched my face. '*Martin* Taylor?' Silence. '*Gavin* Taylor?' Silence. 'My sister is *Roisín* Taylor?' Searched again. 'She's a nurse in Beaumont Hospital?'

'I see . . .'

'Do you know any of them?' she asked hopefully.

'No, I'm sorry, I don't.' I really didn't. 'It was nice to meet you, though.' We started to move away when she grabbed my arm. 'Hey!' I yelped, trying to shake her off. Her grip tightened.

'Hey, let go of her,' Bobby stepped in.

'You know them, don't you?' she said, moving closer to me.

'No!' I said, stepping back, her grip tightening on my arm.

'My mam and dad are Charles and Sandra Taylor.' She spoke more quickly now. 'You probably know them too. Just tell me ho—'

'Get *off* me!' I pulled my arm violently away from her as the crowd around us quietened and turned to stare.

That stopped her talking and she turned to her friends, who stared back, assessing me.

'I'm sorry, but we're late for the rehearsals. We have to go now.' Bobby took me by the sore arm and pulled me away. In shock I allowed him to pull me along, half running, half walking through the crowd, feeling eyes boring into me as we passed.

We finally reached the Community Hall and there was a small queue forming at the door.

'Sandy!' one person called out. 'There she is! Sandy!' Others began to call out and swarmed around me. I felt Bobby tugging me again, I was pulled backwards and the door to the Community Hall slammed behind me. The cast of the play, who sat in a circle, all turned to stare at me and Bobby, who stood panting, with our backs pressed up against the door.

'Well,' I said, catching my breath, and my voice echoed around the hall, 'is this the bloody twilight zone or what?'

Helena jumped up. 'Said Dorothy as she landed in

Oz. Thank you, Sandy, for sharing her first line with us,' she said quickly as horrified faces transformed to understanding nods. 'It will be a modern twist on an old story,' Helena explained. 'Thank you, Sandy, for sharing that with us *so* dramatically.'

Mary finally pressed Stop as Bobby's first class school play ended and she ejected the videotape Jack had secretly fantasised about burning for the last two hours. He knocked back the remainder of his cold coffee in a bid to stay awake.

'Mary, I really have to get back to Limerick tonight,' he hinted, looking at his watch. In all the time he had spent in her company, there hadn't been one mention of Sandy. He felt he was being broken in first, being inducted into Mary's life before they could move on to other matters. All around him in the living room framed photographs cluttered every surface. Bobby as a new-born baby, Bobby as a toddler, Bobby on his first bike, Bobby on his first day of school, Bobby on the day of his Holy Communion, his Confirmation, decorating a Christmas tree, Bobby freeze-frame, leaping into a swimming pool on a sun holiday. From bald, to bleach blond, to mousy-brown hair. No teeth, to missing teeth, to metal train tracks. There were no clocks in this room, time was imprinted in every picture and suspended as if forbidden to tick on from the last photograph; Bobby and Mary on his sixteenth birthday.

Thirty-eight-year-old Mary lived in an apartment above her charity shop, which consisted of clothes, shoes, books, knick-knacks, home accessories and everything else you could imagine. The shop was musty from the smell of second- or third-hand clothes, dusty books that had been well thumbed and old toys that had been outgrown and outlived. Above was the space that Mary had shared with Bobby all of his sixteen years.

Mary stood up. 'More coffee?'

'Please.' Jack followed her to the kitchen where

he found more photographs dotting the walls, lining the window sill. 'Aren't any of the others I called coming to the meeting?' Jack had been expecting a small gathering.

'They can't make it on such short notice. Peter lives in Donegal with his two young children and Clara and Jim live in Cork although they've recently divorced so the chances of getting them in the same room will be slim. It's sad really. Their daughter, Orla, has been missing for six years. I think it's that that drove them apart.' She poured more coffee. 'Things like this, huge dramatic changes in life have the magnet effect. They either drive people apart or bring them together. Unfortunately the latter happened in their case.'

Jack immediately began thinking of Gloria and how this magnetic event had repelled them apart.

'I've no doubt everybody will pitch in to help, though, once we need them for something specific.'

'Sandy helped all of these people?'

'Sandy *helps*, Jack. She's not gone yet. She's a Trojan worker. I know you didn't get the benefit of quite seeing her in action but she keeps in touch with us every week. Even after all these years, she gives us a weekly call to let us know if there's any news. Most of the time, and particularly more lately, the phone calls have been to see how we are.'

'Did anybody hear from her this week?'

'Nobody.'

'And that's unusual?'

'Not *entirely* unusual.'

'I've been told by a few people that it's not unusual for her to lose contact and just disappear for a while.'

'She disappeared all the time, but she'd still ring us from her hiding places. If there's one thing Sandy is committed to it's her work.'

'It sounds like it's the only thing.'

'Yes, I wouldn't be surprised if that's true,' Mary nodded. 'Sandy gave – *gives* –' she corrected herself, 'very little away. She's a pro at not talking about herself.

She never mentions family or friends. *Not once*, and I've known her for three years.'

'I don't think she has any,' Jack said, sitting at the kitchen table with a fresh mug.

'Well, she has us.' Mary joined him. 'You didn't get anywhere with Garda Turner?'

Jack shook his head. 'I spoke to him today. There's really nothing he can do if relatives and friends are saying that this is normal behaviour. Sandy's not a danger to herself or others, and there's nothing suspicious about her disappearance.'

'There's nothing suspicious about a deserted car with all her belongings left inside?' Mary asked in surprise.

'Not if it's what she does all the time.'

'But what about the watch you found?'

'The link on it was broken. She apparently often drops it.'

Mary tutted and shook her head. 'That poor girl is going to be punished for all her previous odd behaviour.'

'I'd love to talk to her parents, see what they think about the whole thing. I have such a hard time dealing with the fact that five days without hearing from a family member isn't something to be worried about.' Jack knew inside that this was all entirely possible. He wasn't particularly close to Donal, or with the rest of his family, for that matter. Apart from Judith, they would often go for weeks without hearing from one another. It was his mother that raised the alarm bells after three days.

'I have their address, if you want.' Mary left the table to rummage around in a kitchen cabinet. 'Sandy quite surprisingly asked me to send something to her there.' Her voice was muffled from inside the press. 'I think she was stranded with the family for Christmas one year and was desperately looking for some work to save her,' she laughed. 'But isn't that what Christmases are all about? Here it is.' Her head finally emerged.

'I can't just drop in unannounced,' Jack said.

'Why not? The worst they can do is not talk to you, but it's worth a try.' She handed him the Leitrim address. 'You can stay here tonight, if you like. It's far too late for you to be travelling to Leitrim and then on to Limerick.'

'Thanks, I might even stay in Dublin a bit longer tomorrow to see if Sandy shows up to another appointment she made.' Jack smiled, looking at a photo of a young Bobby dressed as a dinosaur for Hallowe'en. 'Does it get any easier?'

Mary sighed. 'Never easier but a little less hard, perhaps. It's always at the forefront of my mind, every single waking and sleeping moment. The hurt begins to . . . not quite disappear, but it's as though it evaporates so that it's always there in the air around me, ready to rain down when I least expect it. Then when the hurt goes, anger takes its place, when the anger runs out of steam, loneliness steps in to take over. It's a neverending circle of emotions; every lost emotion being replaced by another. The same isn't so for sons, unfortunately,' she smiled wryly. 'I used to love the great mysteries of life, the uncertainties, the not knowing. I always thought it was so necessary to our journey,' she smiled sadly. 'I'm not so enthusiastic about that any more.'

Jack nodded and they both got lost in thought for a while.

'Anyway, it's not all doom and gloom,' Mary perked up. 'Hopefully Sandy will do what she always does and return home in the morning.'

'With Bobby and Donal in tow,' Jack added.

'Well, here's hoping.' Mary raised her mug and clinked it with Jack's.

37

Jack slept in Bobby's box bedroom that night, surrounded by posters of sports cars and half-naked blondes. On the ceiling were miniature stars and space-ships that once illuminated brightly in the dark but, like Bobby's presence, now merely emitted a faint glow. Stickers that had been stuck to the door and the discoloured wallpaper had been torn off, leaving He-Man without his sword, Bobby Duke without his cowboy hat and Darth Vader without his helmet. The earth's solar system was displayed on the navy-blue duvet cover, every planet and place to be seen but the one Bobby was in.

A writing desk was piled high with CDs, a CD player, speaker phones and magazines containing yet more cars and women. Few school books were piled up in the corner, their place of importance low on the scale. Above the desk, shelves burst with more CDs, DVDs, maga-zines and football medals and trophies. Jack doubted anything had been altered since the day Bobby had left this room and never come back. Jack placed his hands on as few items as possible and tiptoed on the carpet, not wanting to leave his imprint behind. Everything in this room was precious and existed only as a museum.

Peeking out from between the posters of cars and naked glamour models was *Thomas the Tank Engine* wallpaper. Just beneath the surface lay childhood with only a thin layer to separate it from adolescence. It was the room of someone no longer a boy but not yet a

man; of someone in a place between innocence and realisation, on the path of discovery.

Jack once again felt as he had earlier while in the
house. He felt trapped in a time that wasn't allowed to
move on. The door plate reading '*Bobby's Room: KEEP
OUT!*' had been heeded and the door had been firmly
shut, leaving everything inside, all the treasured items
locked away as though the boxroom were a safe. Jack
wondered whether Bobby was elsewhere now, living his
life, whether he had moved on from the image Mary
was fighting to hold on to or whether his journey had
ended. Was he forever to exist in time as no longer a
boy and not yet a man, in an in-between place as an
in-between person with nothing fully whole, nothing
fully realised?

He thought of his own refusal to let go of Donal and
what Dr Burton had said to him about replacing one
search, which had reached a dead end, with another. He
supposed in theory he was, but he was adamant that it
wasn't due to an unwillingness and inability to move
on. He shook away the thought that he was in any way
similar to Mary, hanging on to memories and being stuck
eternally in a moment that had long since passed. He
pulled the duvet over his head and hid from the stars
on the ceiling and galaxy above him. Realistically, his
search for Sandy wouldn't find Donal, but something in
his heart, in his mind, was driving him forward.

Tomorrow would be Friday, and Sandy, if she didn't
wander back into her life, would have been missing for
six days. He needed to make the decision now whether
it was the moment to pull back, to open the door of
his life and allow the trapped time and memories to
escape, to move on and catch up on all it had missed.
Or he could go full steam ahead with this search, peculiar and out of the ordinary though it might be. He
thought about Gloria at home, at the nothingness he
felt towards her, his life and their future, and he decided
that he, like the Bobby that still inhabited the room he
lay in, was embarking on a journey of discovery. He

heard Mary switching off the television and unplugging appliances in the kitchen. A gap in the curtains welcomed a sudden light through into the bedroom, shining a ruler of yellow light onto a poster of a red Ferrari. Realising it was the porch light, Jack was engulfed by a strange sort of calm and he watched the light on the wall until his eyes became heavy.

He awoke at eight forty-five the following morning to the sound of his phone ringing.

'Hello?' he croaked, eyes looking around and momentarily thinking he'd travelled back in time to his teenage years and was waking up at home in his mother's house. His mother . . . he felt a pang of loneliness for her.

'What the hell are you doing?' his sister Judith asked angrily. In the background he heard babies crying and dogs barking.

He groaned. 'Waking up.'

'Yeah?' she said sarcastically. 'Beside whom?'

Jack turned to his right and looked at the blonde wearing not much more than a cowboy hat and boots. 'Candy from Houston, Texas. She likes horse-riding, homemade lemonade and taking her dog Charlie for walks.'

'What?' she shrieked, and a baby cried louder.

Jack started laughing. 'Relax, Jude. I'm in the box bedroom of a sixteen-year-old boy. There's no need to worry.'

'You're *what*?'

Could he hear gunshots?

'JAMES, TURN THAT TV DOWN!'

'Ouch.' Jack moved his head away from the phone.

'I'm sorry, did that noise from *hundreds of miles away* disturb you?' she huffed.

'Judith, why are you so tetchy today?'

She sighed. 'I thought you were only going to Dublin to meet with the doctor.'

'I was but I thought I'd ask around a bit more before I head home.'

'This is still about the missing persons woman?'

'Sandy Shortt, yes.'

'What are you doing, Jack?' she asked softly.

He rested his head back against Babs from Down Under's nether regions. 'I'm putting my life back together.'

'By tearing it apart first?'

'Remember when we used to do the Humpty Dumpty jigsaw together every Christmas?'

'Oh dear, he's lost his mind,' she sang.

'Humour me. Do you remember?'

'How can I forget? The first year it took us till March to finish it and all because Mum cleared it off the good room's dining table in a panic when Father Keogh paid one of his surprise visits.'

They both laughed.

'After Father Keogh had left, Dad came in to help us start again, remember? He taught us to separate all the pieces, turn them all face up first *and then* get to work putting them together.'

'And they said, "All the king's horses and all the king's men",' she sighed. 'So you're gathering all your pieces.'

'Exactly.'

'My philosophical baby brother. What happened to trips to the pub and fart jokes?'

He laughed. 'They're still inside me somewhere.'

She turned serious. 'I understand what you're going through and I understand what you're doing, but do you have to do it all on your own without telling anybody anything? Can't you at least make it back home for the festival this weekend? I'm going tonight with Willie and the kids. There's an outdoor band playing and some games for the kids with the usual firework display on Sunday night. You've never missed one before.'

'I'll try to get there,' Jack lied.

'I don't know where Gloria gets her patience from. She seemed so cool about you staying on, but you're certainly testing her. Are you deliberately trying to push her away?'

Jack was about to launch into another defence of himself but stopped and thought about it for a change. 'I don't know,' he sighed. 'Maybe. I don't know.'

'Good morning,' Mary sang, knocking on the door.

'Come in,' Jack called out, wrapping the bedclothes around him.

There was a rattle and a few clinks as the handle lowered and Mary pushed open the door with a tray filled with breakfast.

'Wow,' Jack said, eyeing the food hungrily.

Mary laid the tray down on the writing desk. She didn't move any magazines or CDs, preferring to allow the tray to rest dangerously on the edge of the desk. Nothing was to be touched. Jack was surprised she had allowed him to sleep in the bed at all.

'Thanks, Mary, everything looks great.'

'You're very welcome. I used to love treating Bobby occasionally to breakfast in bed.' She looked around the room, wringing her hands together. 'Did you sleep well?'

'Yes, thanks,' he replied politely.

'Liar,' Mary said, moving towards the door. 'I haven't slept through one single night ever since Bobby disappeared. I bet you're the same.'

Jack just smiled, grateful to hear he wasn't the only one.

'I have to open the shop now, but take your time. I've left a towel in the bathroom for you.' She smiled, took one more haunted look around the room and was gone.

Jack was glad he'd made a note of all of Sandy's future appointments before handing her diary over to Dr Burton. For today she had written, 'YMCA Aungier Street. 12 Noon – Room 4.' There was no mention at all of what the occasion was, but he noted that she had attended it, or at least made a note of it, once every month. He decided it was best not to call ahead but to go straight there.

He entered the building ten minutes after twelve, thanks to Dublin's dire traffic he had yet to account for in his travel time. There was no one behind the counter at reception. He leaned over the desk, looking left and right, and called out but to no avail. He was faced with many doors and notice boards advertising fitness classes, childcare, computer classes, counselling services and youth work programmes. What was behind door number four, he wondered. He seriously doubted it was another counselling service, but whatever it was he hoped it wasn't a fitness class. Computers he hoped for; he could do with learning about computers. He rapped lightly on the door, looking for signs of what was inside and hoping, *hoping* it was Sandy.

The door opened and a lady with a kind face answered.

'Hello,' she smiled, her voice almost a whisper.

'Sorry to interrupt,' Jack whispered. Whatever was going on behind the door, it was certainly being done quietly. Yoga – he hoped it wasn't yoga.

'Don't worry, people are welcome regardless of the time. Do you want to join us?'

'Em, yes . . . I was actually looking for Sandy Shortt.'

'Oh, I see. Did she recommend this to you?'

'Yes.' He nodded emphatically.

She opened the door wider and a circle of people turned to stare. No mats, he thought with relief, no yoga. His heart beat wildly as he looked for Sandy, wondering if she could see him before he'd spotted her. And if she was looking at him now, would she recognise him? Would she be angry he had found her, hiding in her burrow, or would she be thankful, relieved someone had noticed her absence?

'Welcome, come and take a seat.' The woman held her arm out towards the circle while somebody unstacked a chair from the side of the small room and brought it to the circle. Jack walked towards them, searching from face to face for a sign of Sandy. The circle grew larger as he neared, the movement like an umbrella being opened slowly. He sat down with trepidation. Sandy wasn't there.

'As you can see, Sandy unfortunately isn't with us today.'

'Yes, I see that.' He ground his back teeth together and the familiar pain began to throb at the back of his mouth.

'I'm Tracey,' the woman smiled.

'Hello.' Jack cleared his throat nervously as heads turned to stare at him, assess him, study him, analyse his every awkward move. 'I'm Jack.'

'Hello, Jack,' they all responded in unison and he paused, his eyes widening in surprise at the hypnotic tone of their voices. There was a long silence as he shifted uncomfortably in his seat, not at all sure what it was he was supposed to be here for.

'Jack, would you prefer it if the others spoke first this week, and maybe next week you can tell us your story?'

His *story*? He looked at everybody else; some had notepads and pens in their laps. To one side of the room was a whiteboard with the words 'Written Assignment' circled at the top of the board. From that circle stemmed the words: 'Feelings', 'Thoughts', 'Concerns', 'Ideas', 'Language', 'Expression', 'Tones' among so many others he couldn't take them all in, and finally came to the conclusion that it was more than likely he was in a creative writing class.

'Sure,' he replied with relief. 'I'd like to listen to everyone else first.'

'OK. Richard, can you start off for us by letting us know how you got on this month.'

'Here, I find that this helps,' a woman beside Jack whispered, and handed him a pamphlet.

'Thank you.' He left it on his lap and decided to wait until Richard had finished his story before reading through it. Richard's story was a rather absurd tale about an instantly dislikeable man and his constant fear of acting on violent impulses. He droned on, painfully and miserably reciting the tale of how an equally painfully miserable man constantly felt overly responsible for the safety of others, to the point he was afraid to drive, out of fear he would run over someone with his car. At times Jack shook his head and laughed out loud, thinking it an obvious, however slightly dark, comedy, but he quickly stopped after receiving numerous odd looks from the group.

Minutes, which felt like hours, later, the room was still echoing to the incessant droning of Richard's story, each word sounding twice in Jack's ears, which were already bored from hearing them the first time. As the story moved towards being just plain depressing, with the main character's behaviour the cause of the loss of his wife and child, Jack finally tuned out and began to read the pamphlet scrunched beneath his clammy hands.

His relaxed body stiffened as he finally concentrated on the cover of the thin glossy booklet. Hot waves of colour spread from his neck all the way to the top of his strawberry-blond head within seconds as he read 'Welcome to Obsessive Compulsive Anonymous'.

Jack sat quietly through the remainder of the meeting, feeling embarrassed to be there and generally ashamed by his earlier behaviour during Richard's story. Keeping his head down when the hour was up, he filed out of the room, hiding amongst the rest of the members.

'Jack!' Tracey called out, and he froze. He stopped walking and allowed everyone to file past him, watching their faces as they prepared to leave their safety net and battle the world and all its demons alone. He also saw Dr Burton, who was waiting outside the room, arms folded and a face like thunder. Jack took a few steps back into the room towards Tracey.

Tracey caught up to him and held out her hand to shake his. 'Thank you for coming today,' she smiled. 'You know you coming here was the first step in helping to heal yourself. It's a rocky journey, it will be difficult, but please know that we are all here to help you through it.' Jack heard Dr Burton laugh mirthlessly. 'The twelve steps that we mentioned earlier, as originated by Alcoholics Anonymous, and adapted for OCA *can* bring relief. I've seen that they can reduce and even eliminate our obsessions and compulsions, so do come again next month.' Tracey patted his arm encouragingly.

'Thanks.' He cleared his throat awkwardly, feeling like an impostor.

'Do you know Sandy well?' she asked.

He winced, disliking being asked the question in Dr Burton's company. 'Kind of,' he said uncomfortably, clearing his voice.

'If you see her, tell her to come back to us. It's unusual for her to miss a meeting.'

Jack nodded again and felt glad now that Dr Burton was within earshot. 'I'll do my best.'

'Hear that?' he said to Dr Burton as soon as Tracey was out of earshot. 'She says it's unusual for Sandy not to be here. I wonder where she is.'

38

I went to the OCA meetings every month. I went because every month that I was there I knew it was another month of deserving to be with Gregory.

'Sandy!' I could hear Gregory calling my name. I was downstairs in his house, half-naked at ten past two in the morning, rooting through my overnight bag that I'd placed, as usual, by the front door when I'd walked in.

'Sandy!' he called again.

There was a thump and the floorboards above me creaked as he climbed out of bed and crossed the bedroom. My heartbeat quickened and my search became more frenzied. Feeling a pressure now that Gregory was making his way towards me, I turned my bag upside down and spilled the contents to the floor. I picked items up, tossed them aside, shook out all my clothes, went through the pockets, laid them flat on the floor and ironed each point firmly with the palm of my hand, trying to feel for the hidden lump.

'What are you doing?' His voice was suddenly behind me and I jumped. My heart thudded and adrenalin raced through me as I felt like I'd been caught in the act, as though I'd been doing something criminal like stealing, or immoral like cheating on him. I hated that he made me feel what I was doing was wrong. It was that same look in his face that I had run from in others, the look that, strangely, hadn't chased me away from him yet. Not completely, anyway, although I had run a few times.

The aftershave I bought for him each of the six Christmases we had been together filled the room. I didn't respond to him. I just laid my navy-blue garda uniform out on the carpet, feeling each point for unusual bumps.

'Hello?' he sang. 'I was calling you.'

'I didn't hear you,' I replied.

'What are you doing?'

'What does it look like?' I replied calmly, running my hand down the length of the navy-blue nylon trouser leg.

'It looks like your clothes are being given a deep massage.' I felt him move further into the room and he sat down before me on the couch, wrapped in the robe I'd bought for him this Christmas, wearing tartan slippers I'd bought for him the previous. 'I'm rather jealous,' he murmured, watching me smoothing down the pockets.

'I'm looking for my toothbrush,' I explained, emptying the contents of my washbag onto the floor.

'I see.' He watched me. He just sat there quietly and watched me, yet this made me feel uncomfortable. His disapproving eyes on me made me feel like I was sitting on the floor doing drugs instead of merely looking for something. A few minutes passed of my searching without results.

'You know that you have a toothbrush upstairs in the bathroom already?'

'I bought a new one today.'

'The old one won't do?'

'The bristles are too soft.'

'I thought you liked soft bristles.' He ran his hand through his tight beard.

I smiled for his sake.

He watched me for a little while longer.

'I'm going to make a cup of tea, do you want one?' He had the same method as my parents; they too used to keep an easy tone in their voices to pretend to me that everything was all right, to stop me from picking up negative vibes and panicking because something was lost. When I was younger that's what I thought. Now that I was older, I had learned from Gregory that it wasn't me he was trying to lighten the atmosphere for, it was himself. I stopped searching and watched him moving around the adjoining kitchen as though he made cups of tea at two o'clock every morning. I watched him playing house and pretending that his on/off girlfriend was perfectly normal and correct to be sitting on the carpet half-naked while emptying her bag for a toothbrush she already had sitting in a cup holder upstairs. I watched him pretending to himself, smiling as I fell in love with another flaw I never knew existed within him.

'Maybe it fell out in the car,' I said, more to myself.

'It's raining, Sandy. You don't want to go out now, do you?'

He needn't have asked, he knew the answer, but he was still playing along with his own game. Pretending now that his full-time, eternally faithful girlfriend was going to risk running out into the wet night to look for something. How unusual, how frightfully odd, how attractively kooky. Such fun.

I looked around the living room for a jacket or blanket to throw on. There was none. In this state, although I appear calm on the outside, inside I'm running around screaming, shouting, looking in all directions, anxious to go, go, go. To run upstairs and throw some clothes on would take too long, would take precious minutes away from finding. I looked at Gregory, who was pouring the boiling water into a witty mug I'd got him for the previous Christmas. He obviously saw the desperate search in my eyes, the silent longing for help. He played it cool as usual.

'OK, OK,' he held his hands up in surrender, 'you can have the robe.'

I actually hadn't thought of his robe.

'Thanks.' I got to my feet and walked to the kitchen. He undid the belt and coolly shrugged it off his shoulders, and handed it to me, standing dressed now in only his tartan slippers and the silver chain I had given him for his fortieth birthday the previous year. I laughed and took it from him, but he held on to it, the robe firmly in his grasp. He turned serious.

'Please don't go outside, Sandy.'

'Gregory, don't,' I mumbled, tugging on the robe, not wanting this discussion again, not wanting to go through the same thing all over again, fighting about it, talking in circles, resolving nothing and apologising for nothing but the insults fired between the main issues.

His face crumpled. 'Please, Sandy, *please* can we just go back to bed? I'm up in four hours.'

I stopped tugging on the robe and looked at him, standing before me naked but revealing more in the look on his face alone. Whatever it was about that face, about the way he looked at me, the way he yearned for me not to leave him, the way it seemed so important that I be with him rather than away, something inside me stopped fighting.

My grip relaxed on the robe. 'OK.' I gave in. *I gave in.* 'OK,' I repeated, more to myself this time, 'I'll go to bed.'

Gregory looked surprised, relieved and confused all in one glance, but he didn't push it, didn't question it. He didn't want to ruin the moment, spoil the dream and chase me away again. Instead he held my hand and we went back upstairs to bed, leaving the clutter of my scattered clothes and washbag on the floor by the door. It was the first time I'd turned my back on the situation and headed in the other direction. It was apt that it was Gregory leading me.

In bed I laid my head on his warm heaving chest, felt his heartbeat beneath my cheek and his breath on the top of my head. I felt loved and secure, and thought everything in my life couldn't possibly be any more perfect and wonderful. Before he fell asleep, he whispered to me to remember that feeling. At the time I thought he was referring to us being together, but as the night slowly moved on for me and the niggling returned, I knew he had meant for me to remember the feeling of walking away and the reason that led to that decision. I needed to hold on to that, store it in my memory and call upon it whenever the moment raised its ugly head.

I was restless that night. I only meant to go back downstairs and tidy my belongings away. And then when I had done that, I only meant to go out into the wet night to search my car. But then when it wasn't there, I forgot the feeling that I'd tried to hold on to while in Gregory's arms and Gregory's bed.

He woke up alone that morning and it pains me to imagine his thoughts when he felt around the bed and his hand rested on the cold sheets. Meanwhile, while he was asleep in his bed, pretending in his dreams that I was alongside him, I had returned to a cold bedsit to find my toothbrush still in its packet, lying on the table. For once I got no solace from finding. I was emptier after finding the toothbrush than I had been before. It seemed the more things I found when I was with Gregory, the more I lost inside. I was alone in bed at five in the morning after leaving the warm bed of a man I loved, and who loved me. Of a man who would, as a result, no longer take my calls. A man who after thirteen years of wanting to learn all there was to learn about me had finally given up and wanted to know me no longer.

For a while, I gave up on him too, until I became too lonely, too tired, and my heart became too sore from pretending I cared more about a whole series of nothings with nobodies rather than a single episode of *something* with somebody. I told myself that morning to hold on to that feeling, to remember the foolishness of leaving warmth to walk alone in the cold, the ridiculous loneliness of leaving something for nothing.

He took me back on one condition. That I recognise my problems and attend a monthly meeting called the OCA. The first thing you learn while in OCA, is

that you can't be in OCA for anybody else but yourself. It was a lie from the very beginning. Every extra
month I attended the meeting was another month spent
with Gregory, a happier Gregory, who was content
knowing I was taking steps, twelve to be precise, to
recover. He pretended to himself again because it was
obvious to everyone that there had been no change in
my behaviour. I knew in my heart that I wasn't the
same as the others in the class. I felt it absurd that he
think I was among the likes of those who scrubbed and
cleaned themselves for hours at night before going to
bed until they almost bled, and hours in the morning
before going to work. Or the woman who made tiny
slits with a blade on her own arms, or the man who
touched, counted, arranged and hoarded every little
thing that came into his path. I wasn't like them. My
dedication was confused with obsession. There was a
difference. *I* was different.

Years and years of going to the meetings and I was
still the same as the twenty-one-year-old who sat on the
concrete steps opposite Dr Burton's office building every
week, with my elbows on my knees, chin rested on my
hands, watching the world pass by as I waited to cross
the road.

Every single time, Gregory crossed over for me and
met me on my side. I realise now, I don't think I ever
met him in the middle. And I don't think I ever once
said thank you for that.

But I'm saying sorry now. I shout it a thousand times
a day from this place that he can't hear me from. I say
thank you and sorry and I scream it through the trees,
over the mountains, pour my love into the lakes and I
blow kisses in the wind, hoping that they will reach
him.

I went to the OCA meetings every month. I went
because every month that I was there I knew it was
another month of deserving to be with Gregory.

I missed it this month.

39

After returning from an afternoon rehearsal at the Community Hall, Helena, Joseph, Bobby and I sat around the pine table in their home. Wanda sat opposite me, her head of messy black curls just about visible over the table, and her arms pulled up in a giant effort to clasp her hands together, imitating how I was seated. Joseph had just announced that the council had called a meeting for tomorrow night, which for reasons known only to the others around the table was a cause to become quiet and allow an atmosphere of impending doom to fall over us.

I don't know why, but I found the day-to-day running of this place comical. I didn't and couldn't take their world and their issues seriously, however important they were. I hid my smile beneath my hand as I watched them worriedly looking at one another. I was completely detached from the problem, thankful that whatever was happening was happening to them and not me. It was as though their problems weren't mine because I was an outsider, of my own choosing, and I would do my utmost to remain in that position. Anything to avoid having to deal with the harsh reality of settling here. There seemed to be very little choice involved in that reality. So my feeling while I sat at the table was that my time here would be too short-lived to have to care about whatever it was that affected their world. *Their* world, not mine. Nobody had spoken for a while so I tried to break the frosty atmosphere.

'So what's such a big issue that would cause a meeting to be called?'

'You,' Wanda said perkily, and I could tell her legs were swinging under the table from the way her shoulders rocked.

A chill went through me. I chose to ignore her, annoyed that a child was allowed to sit in on our conversation without being silenced, annoyed that she had transformed me from black sheep to piggy by snatching me from the outside where I felt comfortable and plonked me right in the middle of the equation. I looked to the faces around the table, still glancing worriedly at one another but still not speaking. The only one willing to look me in the eye was Wanda.

'What makes you say that?' I questioned the five-year-old, taking that nobody had corrected her, either because it was the general consensus or they were ignoring her because she was bonkers. I hoped for the latter.

'From the way that everyone was staring at you when we walked from the Community Hall to here.'

'That's enough now, sweetheart,' Helena said gently.

'Why?' Wanda looked up at her grandmother. 'Didn't you see how they all stopped talking and made way for her? It was like she was a fairy princess.' She revealed her gummy smile. Yep, bonkers.

'OK,' Helena patted her on the arm to signal her to stop. Wanda was quiet and I could tell her legs were still.

'The meeting is being called about me.' I absorbed this. 'Is this true, Joseph?' I very rarely, if at all, got nervous for anything and, at the idea of this, curiosity was the only emotion that stirred within me. And yet it was still mixed with the bizarre feeling of thinking it was all very cute and twee. A funny little happening in a funny little place.

'We don't know that it's about you.' Bobby leaped to my defence. He looked at Joseph. 'Do we?'

'I have been told nothing.'

'Do people regularly call meetings about new arrivals? Is that normal?' I asked. I squeezed the stone that was Joseph, for water.

'Normal,' he threw his hands up in the air. 'What do we know of normal? What does our world and the old world, the world who thinks it knows it all, really know of normal?' He stood up and loomed over us.

'Well, do I need to be worried?' I asked, hoping now that he could at least reassure me.

'Kipepeo, one never *needs* to be worried.' He placed his hand on my head and I felt his warmth soothe my pounding headache. 'We will be at the Community Hall at seven p.m. tomorrow. We shall test our understanding of normality then.' With a small smile he drifted out of the room. Helena followed him.

'What did he just call you?' Bobby asked, confused.

'Kipepeo,' Wanda sang, her legs swinging wildly again.

I leaned into the table and Wanda momentarily looked startled. 'What does that mean?' I asked rather aggressively but I was anxious to know.

'Not telling you,' she pouted and crossed her arms across her chest. 'Because you don't like me.'

'Don't be silly. Of course Sandy likes you,' Bobby said.

'She *told* me she didn't.'

'I'm sure you misheard her.'

'She didn't,' I explained, 'I told her directly.' Bobby looked shocked so I made an attempt to wave the white flag. 'Well, tell me what kipepeo means and I might like you.'

'Sandy!' Bobby exclaimed.

I shushed him. Wanda mulled it over. Slowly but surely her face began to crumple. Bobby kicked me in the leg and I leaned forward. 'Wanda, don't worry about it.' I tried to soften my voice as much as I could. 'It's not your fault that I don't like you.' In the background Bobby tutted and sighed. 'If you were ten years older, it's very possible that I could like you.'

Her eyes lit up. Bobby shook his head at me. 'What age will I be then?' she asked, kneeling excitedly on her chair and leaning forward on her elbows on the table to get closer to me.

'You'll be fifteen.'

'Nearly the same age as Bobby?' She was hopeful.

'Bobby is nineteen.'

'Which is four years older than fifteen,' Bobby explained politely.

Wanda seemed delighted by this and gave him a shy gummy smile.

'But I'll be twenty-nine when you're fifteen,' Bobby explained and I saw her face fall. 'Every time you get older, I get older,' he laughed. He was confusing her fallen face with a lack of understanding, and he continued, 'I'll always be fourteen years older than you, you see.' As I watched her face falling along with the penny in her mind, I signalled for him to stop.

'Oh,' she whispered.

Your heart can break at any age. I think that's when I started liking Wanda.

I hated going to sleep in the place they called Here. I hated the sounds at night that drifted into the atmosphere from home. I hated to hear the laughter, I wanted to block my nose to the smells, close my eyes to the people wandering in from the woods for the first time. I was afraid each noise would be me, I was afraid each sound would be a part of me forgotten. Bobby and I shared that fear. We stayed up late into the night, talking about the world he had left behind: music, sport, politics and everything in between, but mostly we spoke about his mother.

Jack returned to Mary Stanley's house after leaving Dr Burton at the OCD meeting. Once again angry words had been shared between them, with the doctor firing threats of stalking charges and everything he could think of to make Jack back off from his search. After wandering around Dublin city for the afternoon, he had left a voicemail on Gloria's phone, telling her he wouldn't be home for another few days; that it was complicated but that it was important. He knew she would understand. He had postponed his trip to Leitrim to visit Sandy's parents after being warned off by Dr Burton. Instead he hoped to share his thoughts and concerns with Mary before he moved on with his search. He needed to know whether to continue or not. He needed to know if he was chasing his own shadow, whether there was any purpose to him searching for Sandy if those who knew her well weren't concerned.

Mary had welcomed Jack to stay with her for another night and they sat in her living room, once again watching a video of Bobby performing in his sixth class school play of *Oliver*. He noticed Bobby had an unusual laugh, a loud chuckle that came from deep inside him, causing everyone around him, including the audience, to smile. Jack found himself with a grin on his face as Mary turned off the tape.

'He seemed like a happy lad,' Jack commented.

'Oh, yes,' she nodded enthusiastically, sipping on her coffee. 'He was that, indeed. He was always cracking jokes, always acting the class clown and letting his words get him into trouble and his laugh get him out of it. People loved him.' She smiled. 'That laugh of his . . .' She looked at a photograph on the mantelpiece, Bobby's face a picture of delight, his mouth wide open mid-laughter. 'It was infectious, just like his grandfather's.'

Jack smiled and they studied the photo.

Mary's smile faded. 'I have a confession to make, though.'

Jack was silent, not sure he wanted to hear it.

'I don't hear that laugh any more.' Her voice was almost a whisper, as though if she said it any louder it would make it true. 'It used to fill the house, it used to fill my heart, my head, all day, every day. How can I not hear it any more?'

From the faraway look in her eye Jack could tell she wasn't asking him for a reply.

'I remember how it used to make me *feel*. I remember the atmosphere just one simple giggle would evoke in a room. I remember people's reactions. I can see their faces and the impact the sound made on them. I can hear it on the videos when I play it back, I can see it on his face in photographs, I hear versions of it, I suppose, echoes of it in other people's laughter. But without all those things, without the photographs, videos and echoes, when I'm lying in bed at night, I can't remember it. I don't hear it and I try to but my head becomes a jumble of the sounds I've made up and the sounds I've recalled from memory. But as much as I search and search, my memory of it is missing . . .' she trailed off. She looked over at the photo on the mantel again, cocked her ear as though listening for the sound. Then her body seemed to collapse into itself as she gave up.

Bobby and I were both tucked up on the couch in Helena's home. Everybody had gone to bed, apart from Wanda, who had sneaked back in and was hiding behind the couch, overexcited by the fact her dear Bobby was staying the night in her house. We knew she was there but ignored her, hoping she would get bored and go to sleep.

'Are you worried about the meeting tomorrow night?' he asked.

'No, I don't even know what reason I have to be worried. I don't see what I've done wrong.'

'You haven't done anything wrong but you know things – you know too much about people's families for everybody's comfort. They will want to learn how and why.'

'And I'll tell them I'm a hugely sociable person. I move around the Irish social scene talking to friends and family of missing people,' I said drily. 'Come on, what are they going to do to me? Accuse me of being a witch and burn me at the stake?'

Bobby smiled lightly. 'No, but you don't want your life being made difficult.'

'They couldn't possibly make it any more difficult. I'm living in a place where lost things go. How bizarre is that?' I rubbed my face wearily and muttered, 'I'm definitely going to need some serious counselling when I get back.'

Bobby cleared his throat. 'You're not going back. You need to get that out of your head, for a start. If you say that at the meeting you'll definitely be asking for trouble.'

I waved him off, not interested in hearing that again.

'Maybe you could start writing your diaries again. It looked like you enjoyed doing that.'

'How do you know I wrote diaries?'

'Well, because of the diary in one of your boxes back at the shop. I found it down by the river just at the back of the shop. It was dirty and damp but when I saw your name written on it I brought it back to the shop and spent a lot of time restoring it,' he said proudly. On my lack of reaction he quickly lied, 'I promise I didn't read it.'

'You must be thinking of somebody else.' I forced a yawn. 'There wasn't a diary there.'

'There was.' He sat up. 'It was purple and . . .' he trailed off, trying to remember it.

I began to pull on a thread on the hem of my trousers.

He snapped his fingers and I jumped in fright, feeling Wanda behind the couch jumping too. 'That's it! It was purple, kind of a suede material which was ruined because of the damp but I cleaned it up as much as I could. Like I said, I didn't read it but I did open up the first few pages and there were doodles of love hearts all over it.' He thought again. '"Sandy loves . . ."'

I pulled on the thread more.

'Graham,' he continued. 'No, it wasn't Graham.'

I tightly wrapped the fine filament around my baby finger, watching my skin squeezing through, watching the blood being caught.

'Gavin or Gareth . . . Come on, Sandy, you must remember. It was written so many times I don't know how you could forget the guy.' He kept on thinking while I kept on pulling the thread, wrapping it tighter and tighter.

He snapped his fingers again. 'Gregory! That's it! "Sandy loves Gregory." It was written all over the inside of the book. You must remember it now.'

I spoke quietly. 'It wasn't in the boxes, Bobby.'

'It was.'

I shook my head. 'I spent hours going through everything. It's definitely not there. I would have remembered it.'

Bobby looked confused and irritated. 'It was bloody well there.'

With that, Wanda gasped from behind the couch and jumped up.

'What's wrong with you?' I asked, seeing her head popping up between mine and Bobby's.

'You've lost something else?' she whispered.

'No I haven't,' I denied, but felt a chill again.

'I won't tell anyone,' she whispered, her eyes wide. 'I promise.'

There was a silence. I fixed my eyes on the black thread that kept on coming. Suddenly and completely inappropriately, I heard Bobby laugh loudly, one of his finest, loudest laughs I had heard from him yet.

'The situation is hardly very funny, thanks, Bobby.'

Bobby didn't reply.

'Bobby . . .' Wanda's childish whisper ran down my back.

I looked up at Bobby, noticed the deathly pale of his face, his mouth hung open as though the words that had run from his vocal cords had chickened out last minute, refused to jump and instead stood on his lips in fear. Tears formed in his eyes and his bottom lip trembled and I realised the laughter hadn't come from his mouth at all. It had floated from there to Here, carried on the wind, over the tree-tops and into this place, landing somewhere amongst us. While I attempted to process all this, the door to the living room was pushed open and Helena appeared sleepy-eyed in her dressing gown, her hair tousled and her face a picture of worry. She froze at the door while she studied Bobby, making sure she had heard correctly. His look said it all and she charged at him, holding her arms out. Plonking herself on the couch, she held his head to her chest and rocked him as though he were a baby while he cried and mumbled through his tears how he'd been forgotten.

I sat on the other end of the couch and kept on pulling the thread. It kept on coming, unravelling more and more with every minute spent in this place, unable to stop detaching itself from the seams.

I have found that the many imbalances within our individual lives result in an overall more worldly balance. What I mean is that no matter how unfair I think something is, I need only look at the bigger picture to see how, in a way, it fits. My dad was right when he said that there was no such thing as a free meal: *everything* comes at a cost to others, most of the time at a cost to ourselves. Whenever something is gained, it has been taken from another place. When something is lost, it arrives elsewhere. There are the usual philosophical questions: why do bad things happen to good people? Within every bad thing I see good, and likewise, within every good thing I see bad, however impossible it is to understand it or see it at the time. As humans we are the epitome of life, in life there is always balance. Life and death, male and female, good and bad, beautiful and ugly, win and lose, love and hate. Lost and found.

Apart from the Christmas turkey my dad won at the Leitrim Arms pub quiz when I was five years old, my dad had never won anything in his life. The day Jenny-May Butler went missing was the day that my dad won £500 on the lotto scratch cards. Maybe he had a good thing owed to him.

It was a summer day. There was only one week left before we were to go back to school and I was dreading even the thought of it, but apart from the anxiety for the week ahead, without having to get up every morning for school over the past few months, I had lost all sense of time. Weekdays were the same as weekends. For a few months a year, the dreaded Sunday nights were the same as Friday and Saturday nights. This night was a Sunday night but, unusually for this time of year, it was a dreaded one. It was six forty p.m., still bright, the cul-de-sac was busy with kids playing, just like me, forgetting what day it was but knowing that whatever day it was, it sure was a great one because tomorrow would be exactly the same. My mother was in the front garden with my grandma and granddad, getting the last few warm evening sunrays. I was sitting at the kitchen table anxiously waiting for the doorbell to ring. I was drinking a glass of milk and watching the clothes in the washing machine go round and round, trying to identify each garment that flashed by, just to occupy my mind.

My dad had eyed me warily as he came back and forth from the TV room to the kitchen, grabbing food he wasn't supposed to be eating while on his new diet. I didn't know whether he was trying to suss me out or whether he was eyeing me to see if I had noticed him stealing food. Either way, he'd asked me three times already what was wrong, and I'd just shrugged and told him nothing. It was one of those occasions when telling someone wouldn't make it any better. He checked on me from time to time, noticing how I'd jumped when the doorbell rang (only my mum, who had forgotten to put the door on the latch). He made a few faces at me to try to make me laugh, cramming a few biscuits into his mouth all at once to pretend he was entertaining me and not his stomach. I smiled for his sake, he seemed happy enough with that and then moved into the TV room again, this time with a Jaffa cake up his sleeve.

You see, I was waiting for Jenny-May to call around.

She had challenged me to a game of King/Queen. It was a game we used to play on the road with a tennis ball. Each person stood in the boxes that were drawn on the tarmac with chalk and then the idea was to bounce the ball first in your own box before passing it into someone else's. They had to do the same and if they missed it, if it failed to bounce in their own box first or if the ball went outside the lines, they were out. The idea was to try to make it to the box at the top, which was the King's box, which was where Jenny-May was for the duration of the game. Everybody used to always say how wonderful she was at playing the game, how amazing and brilliant and talented and fast and precise and how gag, gag, make me puke, she was. My friend Emer and I used to watch the games from our wall. We were never allowed to play because Jenny-May wouldn't allow us. I merely commented to Emer one day that one of the reasons Jenny-May always won was because she always *started* in the top box. This meant that she didn't have to work her way up like everybody else did.

Well, somebody somewhere overheard and word got back to Jenny-May what I'd said and the next day when Emer and I were sitting on the wall kicking our heels against the bricks and flicking ladybirds from the pillars to see how far they'd go, Jenny-May marched up to us with her hands on her hips, surrounded by her posse, and demanded I explain myself, which I did. Red-faced and flustered at being answered back at, she challenged me to a game of King/Queen. As I said, I'd never played this game before and I knew all too well that Jenny-May was good. All I'd meant was that she wasn't *as* good as people were saying. There was something about Jenny-May that made people see more in her than there actually was. I've come across a few people like that in my life and they always make me think of her.

She was clever, though. She made sure that everyone knew that if I didn't show up then she would automatically become the champion, and I suddenly wished my dreaded visit to Aunty Lila was a day early.

Word spread among everyone in the road that Jenny-May had challenged me to a game. They were all going to turn out and sit on the kerb to watch, including

Colin Fitzpatrick, who was way too cool to hang out on our road. He used to go skateboarding with the people around the corner that no one else had the privilege of hanging out with. Word was that even the skateboard gang were all coming to watch.

I barely slept a wink the night before. I got out of bed, put my runners on with my nightdress and went outside to practise King/Queen up against the garden wall. It wasn't much use because the ball kept hitting against the stippled back wall, which sent it flying in all the wrong directions. Plus it was so dark I could hardly see it. Eventually Mrs Smith from next door opened her bedroom window and stuck her head out, which was covered in hair-curlers, which I thought was odd because the next morning her hair was straight, and she sleepily asked me to stop. I went back to bed but didn't sleep much and when I did, I dreamed of Jenny-May Butler being lifted onto everyone's shoulders wearing a crown, while Stephen Spencer, who was on a skateboard, pointed a nail-varnished finger at me and laughed. Oh, and I was naked.

It was my challenge with Jenny-May that alerted her parents to the fact she was missing. During the summer months we all had complete freedom. We stayed outside together all day playing, rarely going inside and sometimes having lunch in one another's house. So I don't blame her parents for not noticing she hadn't been around all day. Nobody blamed them because I knew they all understood. They all knew deep down that it could have happened to them too, that it could have been their child no one had noticed not being around for a few hours that day.

Jenny-May's house and mine were directly opposite each other. Mum and my grandparents had come back inside now that the sun had finally disappeared behind the Butlers' house. I knew everybody was gathering on the kerb waiting for me and Jenny-May to leave our houses and meet in the middle. I saw my dad look out the front window and then back at me. I think he finally understood what was wrong and gave me a small smile. Then he put biscuits on the table and sat with me, munching away.

Eventually, as it struck seven p.m., everybody outside began chanting. Some voices called for me but they were drowned out by chants for Jenny-May. Maybe it was equal but I seemed to hear only her name. All my life, I've heard her name louder than my own. Suddenly there was a big cheer and I assumed Jenny-May had left her house. Then the cheering stopped, there was chattering, then it got quieter and then it was completely silent. Dad looked at me and shrugged. The doorbell rang. I didn't jump this time because something didn't feel quite right. Dad patted my hand. I heard Mum answer the door, as usual her voice friendly and chirpy. Then I heard Mrs Butler's voice, not so friendly, no singsong tone. Dad recognised it too and left the table to join them in the hall. Voices turned to concerned tones.

I don't know why, but I couldn't leave the table. I just sat there thinking of ways to get out of the challenge, but at the same time having the strange feeling that I wouldn't need an excuse. The atmosphere had changed, for the worse, I sensed, but I had that relieved feeling like arriving at school to find out the teacher's sick and not for one second worrying about the teacher. A few minutes later the kitchen door opened and Dad, Mum and Mrs Butler came in.

'Honey,' Mum said softly, 'do you, by any chance, know where Jenny-May is?'

I frowned, confused by the question even though it was perfectly straightforward. I looked back and forth to all their faces. Dad was looking at me with concern, Mum was nodding at me encouragingly and Mrs Butler looked like she was going to cry. She looked like her entire life depended on my answer. I suppose it did, in a way.

When I didn't answer immediately, Mrs Butler spoke quickly. 'The kids outside haven't seen her all day. I thought maybe she would be with you.'

I knew it was wrong but I felt the sudden urge to laugh at the idea that Jenny-May would have spent the day with me. I just shook my head. Mrs Butler called around to all the neighbours to see if they'd seen her daughter. The more doors she knocked on, the more I could see how her face changed from embarrassment to steely determination and then to fear.

I've seen mothers' faces in shopping centres when they turn round and notice their child isn't with them. I studied their faces so intently, completely fascinated by it, because I don't recall ever seeing that look on my mum's face. Not because she didn't love me, of course, but because I was always so tall and out of place there was no way she could lose me. I used to try to get lost sometimes, just to see her face. I would close my eyes, spin around and choose a direction to head in. Other times I deliberately waited for her to turn the corner into the next aisle in the supermarket. I would shiver by the frozen food and count to twenty until I felt she was far enough away but most of the time I would turn the corner and there she would be, studying the calorie content on the back of food packets, not having even noticed my absence. If she ever did notice the lack of my shuffling, lanky body trailing behind her, no more than five minutes would pass before she found me. She only needed to look up and she'd see my head above the clothes rails, or look down to spy my awkward oversized feet poking out from behind a shelf.

From viewing other mothers, I see how the first casual glance over their shoulder changes to panic, how their movements become quicker, head, eyes, limbs darting around, then their abandoning shopping trolleys in search for the only thing that truly feeds their soul. The fear, the panic, the dread, the drive. They say a mother has the strength to lift a car if it means saving her child. I think that week Mrs Butler could have lifted a bus just to find Jenny-May. As it got into the second month she looked as though she could barely lift her own eyes above ground level. Jenny-May had taken a big chunk of her with her too.

It turned out that I was one of the last to see her. When Grandma and Granddad arrived at noon that day, I opened the door to welcome them in and Jenny-May cycled past. She turned to me and gave me a look. One of her looks that I hated so much. A look that could wither you instantly, a look that said I'm better than you and you are going to lose today at King/Queen and then Stephen Spencer will know what an incompetent lanky idiot you are. I looked over my grandmother's shoulder as I hugged her and watched Jenny-May cycling down the road with her head held high, her chin and nose up in the air and her blonde hair falling to the small of her back. I did what anyone in my situation would have done. I wished she would disappear.

That day my dad won £500 in the lotto scratch cards. He was so delighted, I could tell. He sat down in the kitchen with me and tried not to smile but I could see the corners of his lips curling. We could hear Mrs Butler crying in the next room with my mother. He placed his hand over mine and I knew he was thinking right then that he was so lucky, what a lucky father to win money in the lotto and still have his daughter when people like Mr and Mrs Butler were suffering so much. I, in turn, was glad that I hadn't gone missing, and due to Jenny-May's no-show I was now the undisputed champion of King/Queen. I'd also made some new friends now that Jenny-May wasn't around to tell them not to. Things were going great for my family and life couldn't possibly be any worse for Mr and Mrs Butler. My parents stayed up late those nights, talking and thanking God how they had been blessed.

But something inside me felt different. Jenny-May's last stolen glance had taken a part of me with it. That day, Mr and Mrs Butler weren't the only parents to lose a child.

Like I said, there's always balance.

41

Despite Dr Burton's threats and protestations, Jack had decided to continue with his mission and make the journey to Leitrim after all. Another night spent in young Bobby's room had awoken the drive within him to find Donal – not that it had needed much of an awakening. It was the part of him that was constantly wide-eyed and alert, searching around for answers, clues and meaning with every beat of his heart. He was still clinging to the idea that finding Sandy was his way out. She was the medicine his overworked mind needed in order to rest. Why exactly, he didn't know, but he had rarely felt such instincts for something in his life. It was as though the part of him that had been lost along with Donal had been replaced by a strengthened sense. He was like a blind man being led by his heightened sense of smell, by touch he could orientate himself, by sound he could listen to his heart. When Jack had lost Donal he had lost his vision but he'd gained a new sense of direction in his life.

He didn't know what he was going to say to Sandy's parents when he saw them, if indeed they were home or if they would even give him the time of day. He just kept on following the invisible internal compass that had replaced Donal. At noon he found himself sitting in his car around the corner from the housing estate where they lived, taking deep breaths. It was a Saturday, but the small cul-de-sac was quiet. He got out of the car and strolled down the street, trying to look inconspicuous but feeling and knowing he was completely out of place on the tranquil road, the only moving piece on a chessboard.

He stopped outside number four where there was a small two-door silver car in the drive that glistened to within an inch of its life. The front garden was immaculate and was a hive of activity for bees and birds. All the summer flowers were out in their glory, colours of every shade, sweet honey scents, jasmines and lavenders. The grass was an even inch in height all around, the border where it met the soil a razor-sharp line that looked like it could cut any petal that dared to fall. A hanging basket overflowing with petunias and geraniums hung from outside the porch door. An umbrella stand sat inside, Wellington boots and fishing gear beside that. By the entrance a gnome hid under a willow tree, holding a sign saying 'Welcome'. Jack relaxed slightly. Here were not the boarded-up windows, barking dogs and burned-out car from his worst-case-scenario fears.

He opened the lemon-coloured gate, which matched the front door and windowframes, like a perfectly edible candy house. There was no creak, just as he'd suspected. He walked up the even flagstones, not a weed peeking between them. He cleared his throat and pressed the doorbell, its tinkling sound also non-threatening. He heard footsteps, saw a shadow through the obscured glass. Despite the friendly appearance of the woman he assumed to be Sandy's mother, the arrival of a strange man on her doorstep demanded the porch's sliding door remain closed.

'Mrs Shortt?' Jack smiled, giving her the least threatening face he could.

She seemed to relax a bit and stepped into the porch area, the sliding door still a barrier. 'Yes?'

'My name is Jack Ruttle, I'm very sorry to disturb you at home but I was wondering if Sandy was here?'

Her eyes moved fleetingly over him, quickly surveying the man who looked for her daughter, and then she slid the porch door open. 'You're a friend of Sandy's?'

Saying no would probably result in the closing of the door once again. 'Yes,' he smiled. 'Is she here?'

She smiled back. 'I'm sorry, Mr . . . what did you say your name was?'

'It's Jack Ruttle, but just call me Jack.'

'Jack,' she smiled pleasantly. 'She's not here. Is there anything I can help you with?'

'I don't suppose you could tell me where she is?' He kept smiling, knowing it had the potential to be far more of an awkward moment, a perfect stranger interrogating a mother on the whereabouts of her child.

'Where is she?' she repeated thoughtfully. 'I don't know, Jack. Would she want me to tell you where she is?'

They both laughed and Jack shifted uncomfortably. 'Well, I'm not sure how I could possibly convince you of that.' He held his hands out, admitting defeat. 'Look, I don't know what I was expecting when I got here but I just thought I'd take a chance. I'm very sorry for bothering you. Could I leave a message for her? Could you tell her that I'm looking for her and that,' he paused and tried to think of something that could convince Sandy to crawl out of her hiding place if she was in that house listening to him right now, 'could you tell her that I can't do this without her. She'll know what I'm talking about.'

Sandy's mother nodded, studying him all the while. 'I'll pass the message on.'

'Thank you.' There was a pause and Jack prepared to wrap it up.

'You're not a Leitrim boy, by the sounds of it?'

He smiled. 'Limerick.'

She mulled that over. 'She was going to visit you last week?'

'Yes.'

'The one thing I do know about my daughter, she rang me on her way to Glin, was it?' she smiled and it faded quickly. 'She was looking for someone of yours?'

Jack nodded, feeling like a teenager faced by a night-club bouncer and hoping his silence would allow him in.

Mrs Shortt was quiet while she pondered what to do. She looked up and down the road. A neighbour across the road raised a garden glove to her and she waved back. Perhaps feeling less threatened, she made her decision. 'Come inside,' she motioned to him, and moved away from the door, heading back down the hall.

Jack looked up and down the road. The neighbour watched him reluctantly step into the house. He smiled awkwardly. He could hear Mrs Shortt in the kitchen, clattering cups and plates. He heard the kettle go on. The inside of the house was as immaculate as the outside. The front door led directly into the living room. It smelled of furniture polish and fresh air, as though all the windows had been left open for the scents of the garden to rush inside. There was no clutter. The carpet was vacuumed, silver and brasses gleamed, wood shone.

'I'm in here, Jack,' Mrs Shortt called out as though they were life-long friends.

He went through to the unsurprisingly gleaming kitchen. The washing machine was running, RTE Radio 1 was on in the background and the kettle was building up its crescendo to boiling point. From the kitchen there were French doors that led out to the back garden, and it was as well maintained as the front, with a large bird-house, currently accommodating a greedy-looking robin singing between each peck at the seeds.

'You have a lovely home, Mrs Shortt,' Jack said, taking a seat at the kitchen table. 'Thank you for the kind invitation.'

'You can call me Susan, and you're welcome.' She filled the teapot with boiling water, covered it with a tea-cosy and waited. Jack hadn't had tea like that since his mother used to make it. Despite welcoming him into her home Susan was still on guard and stood by the counter with one hand on the tea-cosy, the other fiddling with a tea bag. 'You're the first friend of Sandy's to call by since she was a teenager.' She looked deep in thought.

Jack didn't know how to respond to that.

'Everybody after that knew better,' she smiled. 'How well do you know Sandy?'

'Not well enough.'

'No,' she said more to herself, 'I didn't think so.'

'Every day that I search for her, I learn something new about her,' he added.

'You're searching for her?' She raised her eyebrows.

'That's why I'm here, Mrs Shortt—'

'Susan, please.' She looked pained. 'I look around for Harold's mother and the scent of cabbage when I hear that name. Everything was cabbage, cabbage, cabbage with that woman,' she laughed at the memory.

'Susan,' he smiled. 'The last thing I came here to do is worry you, but I was due to meet with Sandy last week, as you mentioned. She didn't show up and since then I've done everything to try and contact her.' He deliberately left out the details about finding her car and phone. 'I'm sure she's fine,' he insisted, 'but I really want,' he started again, 'I really *need* to find her.' Sending Sandy's mother into a panic was the very opposite of his intention and he held his breath, awaiting her response. He was relieved if not a little shocked to see a tired smile crawl onto her face but it gave up, collapsing in a sad heap, before reaching her eyes.

'You're right, Jack, you certainly don't know our Sandy well enough.' She turned her back to him to pour the tea. 'Now let me teach you another thing about my daughter. I love her very much but she has the ability to hide as expertly as a sock in a washing machine. No one knows where it goes just as no one knows where she goes, but at least when she decides to come back, we're all here, waiting for her.'

'I've heard that from everyone this week.'

She whisked around. 'Who else did you speak to?'

'Her landlord, her clients, her doctor . . .' he trailed off guiltily. 'I really didn't want to have to call on you about this.'

'Her doctor?' Susan asked, not minding at all that she had been left until last. She was more interested in the mention of her daughter's doctor.

'Yes, Dr Burton,' Jack said slowly, not sure whether to reveal Sandy's private information to her mother.

'Oh!' Susan tried to hide a smile.

'You know him?'

'Do you know by any chance if it's *Gregory* Burton?' She tried to hide her excitement but failed miserably.

'That's him, but he isn't so keen on me, in case you're talking to him.'

'Indeed,' Susan said thoughtfully, not hearing what he'd said. 'Indeed,' she repeated with her eyes alight, answering a question Jack wasn't privy to. She was clearly delighted but, remembering Jack was in the room, she composed herself, intrigue taking the place of a mother's excitement. 'Why is it that you want to find Sandy so much?'

'I was worried about her when she didn't turn up to meet me in Glin, and then I was unable to contact her, which made me even more concerned.' It was partly true but it sounded lame and he knew it.

Susan appeared to know it too. She raised her eyebrows and spoke in a bored tone. 'I've been waiting for three weeks for Barney the plumber to come and fix my sink but I haven't yet planned on visiting his mother.'

Jack looked absentmindedly at her sink. 'Well, Sandy *is* looking for my brother. I even got in touch with a member of the Gardaí in Limerick.' He felt his face flush as Susan let out a sound of surprise. 'Graham Turner is his name, in case he calls.'

Susan smiled. 'We called the police on three occasions at the beginning but we've learned not to now. If

Garda Turner asks around he'll know not to continue with his investigations.'

'He's already done that,' Jack said grimly and then he frowned. 'I don't understand all this, Susan. I can't understand where she's gone. I can't fathom how she can disappear so cleverly without anyone knowing where she is, without anyone *wanting* to know where she is.'

'We each have our hiding places and we each put up with the little quirks of the people we love.' She rested her head on her hand and seemed to study him.

He sighed. 'That's it?'

'What do you mean?'

'That's it? Just let people vanish? No more questions asked? Come and go as you please? Flutter in and out. Disappear, reappear and disappear again? No problem!' he laughed angrily. 'Nobody worry about a thing! Don't bother caring about all the people at home that love you and that are worrying themselves sick about you.'

There was silence.

'You love Sandy?'

'What?' he screwed his face up.

'You said . . .' she trailed off. 'Never mind.' She sipped her tea.

'I've only ever spoken to Sandy on the phone,' Jack said slowly. 'There was no . . . relationship between us.'

'So by finding my daughter, you find your brother?' He didn't have time to answer the question. 'Do you think your brother's hiding place is the same as Sandy's?' she asked boldly.

And there it was. Said by a complete stranger, someone who had met him no more than ten minutes before had summed up the ridiculous notion behind his frantic search in one question. Susan allowed a few moments to pass before offering, 'I don't know the circumstances of your brother's disappearance, Jack, but I know he's not in the same place as Sandy. Here's another lesson,' she said softly, 'a lesson Harold and I have learned over the years. No one ever finds the other sock in the washing machine, not through actively looking, anyway.' She waved her hand dismissively. 'Things just turn up. You can drive yourself crazy trying to find them. It doesn't matter how neat and tidy you keep your life, it doesn't matter how organised things are.' She paused and laughed sadly. 'I'm a hypocrite. I pretend to myself that a tidy house will make Sandy come home more often. I think, if she can just *see* everything, if she can see that everything is in order and has its place then she won't have to worry about things going missing.' She looked around the spotless kitchen. 'Anyway, it doesn't matter how much, how often or how closely you keep an eye on things, you can't control it. Sometimes things and people go,' she waved her hand through the air, 'just like that.' Then she placed a comforting hand over his. 'Don't destroy yourself trying to find out where.'

They said their goodbyes at the door and Susan, trying to hide her embarrassment, said, 'Talking about things turning up, if you do come across Sandy before we do, tell her I found her purple diary with the butterflies. It was in her old bedroom, unusual because I've cleaned out that wardrobe dozens of times but never came across it,' she frowned. 'Anyway, it would be important for her to know.'

She looked up and waved again across the road and Jack turned to see a woman of similar age to Susan. 'That's Mrs Butler,' she said, although it was of no importance to Jack. 'Her daughter, Jenny-May, went missing when she was ten years old, the same age as Sandy. Such a lovely little girl, an angel, everyone said.'

Jack, suddenly interested, studied the woman some more. 'Did they find her?'

'No,' Susan said sadly, 'they never did but she has left that porch light on every single night for twenty-four years hoping she'll come home. She'll barely go away on holiday, she's so afraid she'll miss her.'

Jack slowly walked back to his car, feeling odd, different, as though he had switched bodies with the man who had only an hour ago entered the Shortt household. He stopped walking, looked to the sky and contemplated all that he had learned through meeting Sandy's mother. He smiled. And he cried as relief washed over him like a waterfall raining down. Because for the first time in a year, he felt like he could finally stop.

And start living again.

42

Bobby was in no mood to discuss hearing his laughter enter this atmosphere the previous night but he needn't have spoken a word because it was clear that the air had been let out of his once ballooned spirit and all that was left was its deflated shell. It broke my heart to see him that way, to see a bird that had once soared now lie defeated on the ground, a broken wing stopping his flight. The few times I had attempted to raise the issue the more still he lay. There wasn't a whimper, there wasn't a tear; it was his silence that screamed the words he couldn't or wouldn't voice. It appeared he was going to concentrate on my problems until he felt fit to deal with his own – not an altogether alien method of dealing with life, for me.

'Why do you always leave your bag by the door?' Bobby spoke for the first time as we entered his shop.

I looked to where Bobby was staring to see my bag or, dare I say, Barbara Langley's bag, that had been quite absentmindedly placed beside the door. Like a cowboy in a Western who parked his horse up by the saloon door, it was to enable a swift departure from any situation. To help ease the feelings of claustrophobia I would feel in the rooms and company of those I wasn't altogether comfortable with, my parents included. Gregory included. My own home included. Rarely were there places I would keep my bag on my person. I would look to the door, see my bag, and feel secure knowing there was a way out and there, as proof, were my belongings not far from that exit to freedom.

I shrugged. 'Just habit.' How all of my life's complications and complex idiosyncrasies could be reduced to a shrug and two words. How nothing words could be.

Bobby wasn't in the mood to question me any further and we returned to the storeroom containing my boxes of belongings.

'So,' I broke the silence and looked to Bobby, who was staring as though lost, as though he had never before encountered this room, 'what are we doing back here?' I asked.

'We're going to empty your boxes.'

'Why?'

He didn't respond; not because he was ignoring me but because I think he didn't hear me. There was so much more for him to hear now. He began emptying the top box, placing Mr Pobbs very carefully on the floor. He lined up each item in a row from wall to wall, then moved to the next box and did the same. I helped him, though I didn't understand why. After twenty minutes, my belongings from Here were lined neatly in six rows across the walnut floor. I looked down at each item and couldn't help smiling. Each one, from the impersonal, the stapler, to the personal, Mr Pobbs – all opened the doors to previously locked-away memories.

Bobby was looking at me.

'What?'

'Do you notice anything?'

I looked back to the floor, running my eyes along the rows. Mr Pobbs, stapler, T-shirt, twenty odd socks, engraved pen, work file I got in trouble for losing . . . Was I missing the point? I turned to him questioningly.

'What about the passport?' he stated lifelessly.

I looked back to the floor, smiling already. When I was fifteen years old my parents had arranged for us to go to Austria on a hiking holiday but the night before we were due to travel, my passport was nowhere to be found. I hadn't wanted to go away at all. I had been complaining about the trip for months. A week away had meant missing two sessions with Mr Burton but not only that, any fear, any irrational phobia, tends to affect normal daily life. I stopped enjoying trips away due to my fear of losing things, and if something was lost in a place like Austria, a place I had never been to, a place I would more than likely never return to again, well then, how on earth was I supposed to find anything again? The night I lost my passport I had a quick change of heart. The two sessions with Mr Burton were forgotten – all of a sudden I wanted to find the passport and I wanted to go on the trip. Anything that meant not missing another possession in my life.

The trip was cancelled as it was too late to get a replacement or temporary passport but for once, my parents were genuinely as flummoxed as I was, and had searched as frantically as I had. Finding it here after all those years, tattered and worn and complete with gawky photograph of me aged eleven, had been an incredible moment. But as I looked around the floor my smile faded. It was no longer there.

I stepped over the rows of items, kicking some in my rush to get to the cardboard boxes where I frantically searched. Bobby left the room to give me my space, or so I thought, but he returned with a Polaroid camera. He motioned for me to step aside, which I did without question. He pointed the camera at the ground, took a photograph, extracted the square photo, shook it, examined it and then slid it into a plastic folder.

'I found this camera years ago,' he explained, sadness echoing in his words. 'It's difficult to find the cartridges that go with it. I don't even know if they make them any more, but now and again I come across boxes of the right ones. I have to be careful with the photographs I take; I can't waste them. I don't mind being careful but it's difficult to know which second among a lifetime of seconds is more special. Often when you realise how precious those seconds are, it's too late for them to be captured because the moment has passed. We realise too late.' He was silent for a moment, lost in thought, frozen as though his batteries had run out. I touched his arm and he looked up, surprised to see me in the room. He looked down at the camera in his hands, surprised to see it there too. Then he rebooted, the light returned behind his eyes and he continued, 'This is how you refill it. Take photos of these items on the floor every morning from now on.' He handed it to me and added before walking away, 'And then I suggest you start taking the other photos.'

'What other photos?'

He stopped at the doorway and suddenly looked even younger than his nineteen years, like a little lost boy. 'I don't know much about what goes on around here, Sandy. I don't know why we're all here, how we all got here or even what we're supposed to be doing. I never knew that when I was at home with my mum either,' he smiled. 'But as far as I can see, you followed all your belongings here and now, day by day, items disappear. I don't know where they're going, but wherever that is, I suggest that when you find yourself there, you have proof that you were ever here. Proof of us.' His smile weakened. 'I'm tired now, Sandy. I'm going to go to bed. See you at seven for the council meeting.'

43

Barbara Langley hadn't much in the way of clothes suitable for community meetings, most likely because the doomed New York holiday, which resulted in the loss of her luggage over twenty years ago, didn't call for being put on trial by an entire community. But then again, you never know.

I chose to stay away from rehearsals at the Community Hall, knowing that my presence there later would be enough and that Helena had all under control the play I really wasn't interested being involved in. I passed the day by covering the shop for Bobby, who had quite understandably decided to stay in bed the entire day. I busied myself; I *pleasured* myself rooting around the long-legged people's section, diving into bargain buckets with all the ferocity of a bear that had stumbled upon a picnic park. Excitedly I pulled out outfits I dreamed of having at home. Ecstasy-fuelled purrs escaped my lips as I tried on shirts with sleeves that reached my wrists, T-shirts that covered my belly button and trousers with hems that fell to the floor. A tingle rushed through my body each time the feel of fabric covered an area of skin so used to being bare and exposed. What a difference an inch of fabric made. Particularly on a cold morning standing at the bus stop, stretching the sleeves of a favourite jumper just so it covered a racing angry pulse. That small inch, insignificant to most, everything to me, was the difference between a good day and a bad, between internal peace and outward loathing, denial and the realisation of an overwhelming, albeit temporary, desire to be like everyone else. A few inches shorter, a few inches happier, richer, content, warmer.

Every once in a while the bell over the door sounded and just like the end of my playtime at school, the climax would come to an abrupt end. The majority of shoppers that day had come to the shop with one goal in mind: to have a look at me, the one they had heard about, the one who knew things. People from all nations would lock eyes with me, hoping for recognition, and when there wasn't any, would leave, disappointment weighing heavy on their shoulders. Each time the bell rang and another pair of eyes bored into mine, I became more nervous for the evening ahead, and no matter how hard I wanted to prevent the many clocks on the wall from ticking, the hands raged on and the night was suddenly upon me.

It seemed the entire village had decided to attend the council meeting at the Community Hall. Bobby and I pushed our way through throngs of people slowly filing towards the giant oak door. News of somebody with the capacity to know all about families at home had caused people of all nationalities, races and creeds to flock in their thousands to the building. The hot orange sun was disappearing behind the pines trees, giving the effect of strobe lighting as we walked briskly alongside them. Above us, hawks circled low in the sky, dangerously skimming the tree-tops. Around me, I felt eyes on me, watching, waiting to pounce.

The carvings of people shoulder to shoulder, upon the giant doors, parted and bodies began to file in. The theatre had been transformed from the informal arrangement of rehearsal hours. I felt deceived, realising it was more than it had originally appeared to be, capable of more than it had shown itself to me, and now here it was elegantly dressed, standing upright and proud; royalty when I had thought it a servant. Hundreds of rows of seats led from the stage, the red velvet curtains pulled back by a chunky golden twist with tassels bowing, their overturned heads of hair skimming the ground. On stage rows of representatives sat on tiered seating, some wearing their countries' traditional costumes, others choosing modern dress. There were three-piece suits next to embroidered dishdash, sequined jellabahs, silk kimonos, kippas, turbans and jilbab, bead, bone, gold and silver jewellery, women in elaborately patterned khanga, upon them Swahili proverbs offering pearls of wisdom I could not understand, and men in fine hanbok. There was everything from khussa shoes to Jimmy Choos, Thousand Mile sandals and flip-flops to polished leather lace-ups. I spotted Joseph in the second row wrapped in a purple gown with gold trimming. The vision was stunning, the mixture of fine cultured clothes side by side a treat. Despite my feelings on the evening ahead, I lifted the Polaroid camera and took a photo.

'Hey!' Bobby grabbed the camera from my hands. 'Stop wasting the cartridges!'

'Wasting?' I gasped. 'Look at that!' I pointed to the stage of representatives from all nations, sitting grandly overlooking the sea of villagers, who watched them expectantly, desperately awaiting news of the old world they had left behind. We sat in seats halfway up the auditorium to ensure I wasn't in the first row for the firing line. We spotted Helena towards the front of the room, desperately scouring the crowds with an alarming look of concern or fear – I couldn't tell which. Assuming it was us she was looking for, Bobby waved at her wildly. I couldn't move. My body sat frozen in this new fear I was experiencing, in a theatre that had very quickly become full with the noise of thousands of people becoming louder and louder in my ears. I glanced over my shoulder. Dozens more stood at the back of the hall, blocking the exits, unable to find seats. The banging shut and locking of the gigantic doors reverberated around the room and everybody instantly fell silent. The breathing of the man behind me was loud in my ears, the whispering of the couple in front of me like a loudspeaker. My heart began a drumbeat of its own. I looked at Bobby for reassurance I didn't get. The harsh lights from above didn't allow anybody or their reactions to hide. Everyone and everything was revealed.

Helena had been forced to take her seat when the door had shut and silence had ensued. I tried my best to keep thinking that this was a silly little place, a figment of my imagination. It was all a dream, unimportant, not real life. But no matter how much I pinched myself and tried to zone out, the atmosphere pulled me back in, leaving me with the foreboding sense that this was as real as the beating of my heart.

A woman walked up the outside aisle with a basket of earphones. They were taken by the person at the end seat and passed along the rows like a church collection. I looked to Bobby questioningly and he demonstrated, plugging the headphone set into a socket in the chair in front. He placed them over his ears as a man stood before the microphone on stage. He began speaking Japanese, a word of which I could not understand but was so transfixed by the scene before me I failed to remember to put my earphones on. Bobby elbowed me and I jumped, quickly placing them over my ears. A heavily accented English voice offered the translation. I had missed the beginning of his announcement.

'. . . this Sunday evening. It's rare that so many of us all gather together. Thank you for the wonderful turnout. There are a few reasons why we are here tonight—'

Bobby elbowed me again and my headphones came off. 'That's Ichiro Takase,' he whispered. 'He's the Rep President. It changes person every few months.'

I nodded and the headphones went back on again.

'. . . Hans Liveen wishes to speak to you about the plans for the new mill scheme but before we address that we will deal with the reason why so many of you have attended this meeting. Irish Representative Grace Burns will speak to you about this.'

A woman who appeared to be in her fifties stood from her seat and made her way to the microphone. She had long wavy red hair, her features were pointed as though chiselled from a rock and she was dressed in a sharp black business suit.

I removed my headphones.

'Good evening, everybody.' Her accent placed her from the north of Ireland, Donegal. Many of the non-Irish English speakers put their headphones back on for the translation. 'I'll make this brief,' she said. 'I was approached this week by many people from the Irish community with news that a newcomer from Ireland had information on various villagers' families. Despite the rumours, this of course isn't unusual, given Ireland's size. I was also told that an item belonging to this person – I understand that it's her watch – has gone missing,' she said in her matter-of-fact tones.

People that understood English immediately gasped, although the majority of them were surely aware of this rumour already. A few seconds later, there was a second gasp as the interpreters translated. Murmuring began in the hall and the Irish Representative held her arms up to silence everyone. 'I understand this news has had an effect on the entire village. News like this disrupts our attempts at normal living and we are keen to put the rumours to rest.'

My heart began to beat a little less dramatically.

'We've called the meeting tonight to assure you that the matter is in hand and it will be dealt with. As soon as it is, we will immediately inform the community, as we always do, as to the outcome. I believe this newcomer is among us tonight,' she announced, 'and so I wish to address this person.'

Instantly my heart began to palpitate again. People around me looked about, murmuring, jabbering excitedly in foreign tones and eyeing one another suspiciously, accusingly. I looked to Bobby in shock. He gaped back at me.

'What will I do?' I whispered. 'How do they know about the watch?'

The nineteen-year-old in him shrugged back, eyes wide.

'We all think it's best to deal with this privately and quietly so that the person can remain anonymous—'

There was a heckling of boos from the crowd, some people laughed and my skin crawled.

'I see no need for dramatics,' Grace continued in her official, no-nonsense tone. 'If the newcomer could just present us with the alleged missing item then this will be dropped and forgotten once and for all so that the congregation can get back to spending their valuable time in their usual greatly productive ways.' She smiled cheekily and there were chuckles from around the room. 'If the person in question could familiarise themselves with my office tomorrow morning and bring the watch with them, then this can be dealt with swiftly and privately.'

More boos by members of the audience.

'I'll take a few questions on this and then we will move on with the more important matter of the plans to build further past the wind farm.' I could tell she was being deliberately blasé about the whole thing. An entire village had turned out to hear about me, about how I knew intimate details of people here and their family members. In a few sentences she had brushed it all under the carpet. People looked around at each other unhappily and I sensed a storm brewing.

Many people raised their hands and the representative nodded to one. A man stood. 'Ms Burns, I don't think it's fair that this matter be dealt with privately. I think it's clear from the turnout tonight that this issue is more important than the manner of how you have chosen to address it, which is a deliberate attempt at playing down the significance.' There were a few claps. 'I put forward that the person in question, whom I know to be a woman, show us the watch right *now*, right here *tonight*, so that we can see it with our own eyes and therefore allow the matter to be dropped and for our minds to be put at rest.'

There was a healthy applause to this suggestion.

The representative looked uncomfortable, she turned to look at her colleagues. Some nodded, some shook their heads, others looked bored, some shrugged and left it up to her.

'I'm concerned only with the welfare of the person in question, Mr O'Mara,' she addressed him. 'I hardly see it fair that she has arrived here only this week and is also faced with this. Her anonymity is vital. Surely you can appreciate that.'

This wasn't so strongly supported by people, but there was a light round of clapping from a few dozen and I silently thanked them and cursed Grace for confirming my sex.

An elderly woman standing beside the man speaking from the audience shot up out of her seat. 'Ms Burns, our wellbeing is more important, and the wellbeing of all the villagers. Isn't it more important that if once again we have heard rumours of somebody's belongings going missing we have a right to know if it's true?'

There were noises of support from among the crowd. Grace Burns held her hand up to her forehead to block the harsh stage lights in order to see the person belonging to the voice. 'But, Catherine, it *will* be revealed to you tomorrow after the person has come to me. Whatever the outcome it will be dealt with appropriately.'

'This doesn't just affect the Irish community,' a southern American male voice called out. Everybody looked around. The voice came from a man standing at the back. 'Remember what happened the last time there were rumours of things going missing?'

There were mumbles of agreement and nods.

'Everybody here remember a guy called James Ferrett?' he shouted now, addressing the hall.

There were loud murmurs of 'yes' and heads nodded.

'A few years ago he told of the very same thing happening to him. The representatives did the same thing then as they are doing now,' he addressed the crowd who were unfamiliar with the story. 'Mr Ferrett was encouraged to follow the same procedure as our anonymous woman tonight and instead he disappeared. Whether it was to join the rest of his belongings or whether it was the work of the reps we will never know.'

There was uproar at this but he shouted over the noise. 'At least let us deal with it now before the person in question has a chance to escape once again without us learning about what is happening. It's not as though any harm will come to her, and it's our duty to know!'

There was huge applause to this. The entire community erupted. They didn't want another opportunity of finding a way back to go by. The rep was quiet for a while as the hall chanted around her. She made a motion for silence and the crowd died down.

'Very well,' she said loudly into the microphone and those two words bounced around my heart until I thought I would faint or laugh, which one I wasn't sure.

I looked to Bobby. 'Please pinch me,' I smiled, 'because this is all so ridiculous I feel as though I'm in one of those awful nightmares you laugh about the next day.'

'It's not funny, Sandy,' he warned. 'Don't tell them anything.'

I tried to hide a smile yet my heart pounded.

'Sandy Shortt,' the representative announced, 'could you please stand up?'

44

After Jack had left Sandy Shortt's family home, he drove to the Leitrim Arms, the local bar in the small village. Despite the early hour the pub was dark, lit by too few dusty wall lights, natural light blocked out by dark burgundy stained-glass windows. The floor was uneven, flagged with stones, and the wooden benches were covered with paisley cushions with foam spilling from the sides. There were a total of three men in the bar: two at opposite ends of the counter, pints in hand, necks craning to see the horseracing on the small television suspended from a bracket from the ceiling. The barman held court behind the counter, arms resting on the taps, head up, eyes glued to the race. There was anxious expectation painted on each of the men's faces, a monetary interest in the outcome obvious. The commentator's thick Cork accent speedily documented a second-by-second account of the race, speaking so fast, everybody couldn't help but hold his breath, adding to the atmosphere of suspense.

Catching the barman's attention, Jack ordered a pint of Guinness and chose to sit in the quiet snug at the far end of the bar, away from everyone. He had something important to do.

The barman took his gaze away from the television, choosing profession over obsession, and gave his pouring of the perfect pint his complete attention. He held the glass at a forty-five-degree angle close to the spout, preventing large bubbles from forming in the head. He

311

pulled the tap fully open and filled the glass seventy-five per cent full. He placed the pint on the counter, allowing the stout to settle before filling the rest of the glass.

Jack took Donal's police file out of his bag and placed it on the table before him, spreading out the pages one last time. This was his goodbye. This was the end, the final glance at all he had studied every day for the past year. The end of the search, the beginning of the rest of his life. He wanted to raise a glass to his brother one final time, one last drink together. He ran his eyes over the police reports, the long hours of dedicated police time, each page reminding him of the ups and downs, the hopes and disappointments of the previous year. It had been long and hard. He laid out the witness statements in a row, the reports from all of Donal's friends who had been with him that night. The anguish and tears, lost sleep and despair that had gone into trying to remember every last blurred detail of the night.

Jack placed Donal's photograph on the tall stool opposite him. One final pint with his brother. He smiled across at him. *I've done my best, Donal; I promise you I've done my best.* For the first time he believed it. There was no more he could do. With that thought came great relief. He looked down again at the pages before him. Alan O'Connor's face stared back at him from the passport photo attached at the corner. Another broken man, another life almost destroyed. Alan was far from reaching the point Jack had arrived at that day. Jack had lost his brother, a brother he didn't know as well as he should have but Alan had lost his greatest friend. He glanced at the statement he'd read a thousand times, if not more. Alan's full, detailed account of the doomed night matched Andrew, Paul and Gavin's accounts and those of the three girls they had met at the fast-food restaurant, though they had trouble barely remembering the beginning of their night, never mind the early hours of the next morning. The language of the report was awkward, stilted and foreign. It lacked emotion, relayed only the facts of the matter, times and places, who was there and what was said. No feelings to convey the fact a group of friends had been torn apart by the incident of this one night. The one night that changed a lifetime of nights.

Andrew, Paul, Gavin, Shane, Donal and I left Clohessy's on Howley's Quay at approximately 12.30 on Friday night. We went to the nite club, 'The Sin Bin' in the same building . . . Jack skipped the details of what happened inside the club. *Andrew, Paul, Gavin, Donal and I left the club at approximately 2 a.m. and walked two blocks to SuperMacs on O'Connell Street. Shane had met a girl in the nite club that none of us knew and went home with her* . . . He skipped a few lines. *All of us sat down in a booth on the right-hand side of the chipper closest to the counter, to eat our burgers and chips. We got talking to three girls who were also in the chipper. We asked them to join us and we all sat in the booth. There were eight of us: me, Andrew, Paul, Gavin, Donal, Collette, Samantha and Fiona. Donal sat on the outside, on the edge of the seat beside Fiona, and opposite me. We made plans to go back to a party at Fiona's house* . . . Jack skipped to the most import-ant part. *I asked Donal if he was going to the party and he said yes and that was the last conversation we had that night. He didn't tell me he was leaving the chipper. I started talking to Collette and when I turned around Donal was gone. That was at 3 a.m. approximately.*

They had all relayed the same story. It was just a normal lads' Friday night out. Pub, night club, chipper, nothing out of the ordinary for them to remember; just the fact that their best friend went missing. Each of Donal's friends relayed different final conversations, nobody noticed him leave the chipper apart from the girl named Fiona, who was sitting beside him and only noticed that he was not beside her when she turned around and saw him walking out of the chipper. She said he had fallen against the doorframe as he left and a few girls by the door had seen him and laughed. Later, none of these girls could offer any more information than that. The chipper was full of people all thrown out of night clubs at the same time, and the CCTV in the chipper did not film the booth that Donal had been seated at. The queues forming at the counter and the pockets of people standing around unable to get a table blocked the booths. Still, there was nothing to see but Donal walking out of the chipper, bumping his shoulder on the doorframe as everyone had witnessed. CCTV filmed him at the nearby ATM where he withdrew €30, he was seen again stumbling down Arthur's Quay, and then his trace was lost.

Jack thought back to the last time he had spoken to Alan and felt guilty for putting him under such pressure to try to remember more. Alan had clearly already been squeezed for every last drop of detail of the night by the Gardaí. Jack had felt that in some way his brother going missing was his fault, that as an older brother there was something that he should have done, was supposed to do to make it right. His mother died feeling that same responsibility. Was there anyone that didn't blame themselves? He recalled his conversation with Alan, how only a few days ago he had admitted the same.

I hope you find him, Jack. I keep going back over that night again and again, wishing I'd left with him.

On the counter, the creamy head of the Guinness began to separate from the dark body. It was still foggy but was becoming clearer.

I keep going back over that night again and again, wishing I'd left with him.

Jack's heart caught in his throat. He fumbled through the pages to find Alan's statement again. *We all made plans to go back to a party at Fiona's house. I asked Donal if he was going to the party and he said yes and that was the last conversation we had that night. He didn't tell me he was leaving the chipper.*

The barman topped off the pint by pushing the tap

forward slightly, allowing the head to rise just proud of the rim.

Jack sat up straight, focused his mind, didn't lose his head. Thoughts began to rise to the top and he felt close to something. He kept reading and rereading the police report while simultaneously going over in his mind the conversation with Alan from only days ago.

The stout didn't overflow or run down the glass.

Jack controlled his breathing and kept his fear contained.

The barman delivered the pint to the snug and hesitated at the entrance, unsure of where to put the Guinness with the table a mess of papers.

'Just put it down anywhere,' Jack said. The barman made a circular motion with the pint in the air, trying to decide where to plant it and finally brought it down to the table, rushing back to where the men were shouting at the television, urging their horse on. Jack's eyes moved down the ruby-black belly of the body of the pint, right down to the base of the glass. The barman had placed it on Alan's statement, next to the sentence he had read over and over again. Everything was drawing him back to that sentence. *I asked Donal if he was going to the party and he said yes and that was the last conversation we had that night. He didn't tell me he was leaving the chipper.*

Jack was trembling but he didn't know why. He raised the shaking glass into the air and smiled wobbly at his brother's photo. He put the glass to his lips and took a big slug of the thick liquid. At the same time the warm stout slid down his throat, the memory of Alan's next sentence fired itself at him.

I really thought he'd be OK getting a taxi down that way, you know?

The Guinness caught in his throat and he began to cough, leaning away from the table to hack it up.

'You OK?' the barman shouted over.

'Yes! Go on, ya boya!' The two men in the bar

celebrated the victory of their horse, clapping their hands and cheering, giving Jack a fright.

Jack's mind ran through a million excuses, defences, mistakes and whether he'd misheard. He thought of Sandy's diary entry to visit written in red capital letters, he thought of the worried face of Mrs O'Connor – *You think he done something wrong?* She knew. She had known all along. Chills ran through him. Anger fired through his veins. He slammed the pint down on the table, the white ring left on the inside of the glass. His legs went weak as rage and fear took over his body.

He didn't remember leaving the pub, he didn't remember calling Alan and he didn't remember driving back to Limerick in record time to meet him. Looking back on those hours there was very little he knew about that night other than what people told him. The one thing he did recall was Alan's forlorn voice, now ringing constantly in his head: *I keep going back over that night again and again wishing I'd left with him. I really thought he'd be OK getting a taxi down that way, you know?* The contradicting voice from his statement shouted even louder: *I asked Donal if he was going to the party and he said yes and that was the last conversation we had that night.*

The last conversation we had.

He had lied. And why would he do that?

45

I stood up from my chair and the eyes of thousands of people turned to look at me, study me, form opinions, judge, hang me, and burn me at the stake. I spotted Helena in the front row, clearly distressed by how this was all playing out. Her hands were clasped tightly to her chest as though in prayer and her eyes glistened with welling tears. I smiled at her, feeling sorry for her. For *her*. She nodded at me encouragingly. Joseph, on the stage, did the same. I wasn't sure what to fear and I suppose that's why I didn't. I didn't understand what was going on, why it mattered so hugely that something of mine had gone missing, why something that seemed so positive could be turned into something so negative. The one thing I did understand was that those who had been here longer than me were fearful for me, and that was enough. Already over the last few days, life had been even more uncomfortable for me with people following me around, questioning me as to whether I knew their families. I wasn't keen on it getting any worse.

The representative fixed her eyes on me. 'Welcome, Sandy. I know it doesn't seem fair to do this so publicly but you have witnessed the reason for having to do it this way.'

I nodded.

'I must ask you, this rumour of your belongings going missing,' she paused, clearly not wanting to ask the question for fear of the answer, 'could you please confirm how this isn't true?'

317

'You're leading her!' one man shouted out, and others hushed him.

'This is not a courtroom,' the rep said angrily. 'Please allow Ms Shortt to speak.'

'The rumour,' I looked around to the thousands of faces, some of which were listening to the translation of my words in their headphones, 'is most definitely not true.' There was a babble of voices again so I raised my voice. 'Though I do understand where it has come from. I was waving to somebody and my watch flew from my wrist and landed in the nearby field. I enlisted some people to help me find it. It's really not a big deal.'

'And they found it?' Grace Burns said, unable to hide the relief from her voice.

'Yes,' I lied.

'Show it to us!' one man shouted out and a few hundred more agreed.

Grace sighed. 'Are you wearing this watch now?'

I froze and looked down at my bare wrist. 'Em . . . no, because the clasp broke as it fell to the ground and it hasn't been fixed yet.'

'Bring the watch!' a woman shouted.

'No!' I shouted back, and everyone quietened. I felt Bobby look at me in surprise. 'With respect to you all, I feel that this whole thing is no more than a ludicrous witch-hunt. I have given you my word that my watch has not gone missing and I refuse to continue with this charade by bringing it here to masquerade around the hall. I haven't been here long enough to understand why it is exactly you are all behaving this way but if you all wish to welcome me here as you should, then please, allow my word to be enough.'

That didn't go down well.

'Please, Ms Shortt,' Grace said worriedly. 'I suggest the best thing for you to do is to leave the hall and retrieve the watch. Jason will accompany you.' A man dressed in a black suit, lean and slenderly built, with a posture so perfect it could only have come from the army, arrived at the end of my row. He held his arm out towards the door.

'I don't know this man.' I grasped at straws. 'I'm not going with him.'

Grace looked confused first, and then wary. 'Well, you have to bring the watch to us whether you like it or not so who would the best person be to accompany you?'

I thought quickly. 'The man beside me.'

Bobby jumped to attention.

Grace strained her eyes to see, there was a flash of recognition, and she nodded. 'Very well, they will both go with you. We will move on with the session while you're gone.'

The Dutch Representative took to the stage to talk about the plans for more mills but nobody took any notice of him. All eyes were on us as we walked down the long aisle of the hall. People who stood at the back parted for us and we were swallowed up through the huge doors. Once outside, Bobby gave me big eyes, not wanting to speak in front of our companion.

'We have to collect my watch from Bobby's shop,' I explained calmly to Jason. 'He was supposed to fix the clasp for me.'

Bobby nodded, finally understanding.

We arrived outside the door of the Lost and Found shop, the brightly coloured odd socks decorating the front. It was dark outside now, the village like a ghost town with everybody in the Community Hall waiting for me, waiting for news of whether it was possible to leave Here or not.

'I'd like to wait here for Bobby.' I stopped walking and stayed on the veranda looking out to the black forest. Jason didn't say anything, but stood back with his hands joined before him and waited with me.

'What are you, secret service?' I teased, looking him up and down. He didn't smile, just looked away. 'Matrix bad guy? Man in black? Johnny Cash über fan?' He didn't answer. I sighed. 'Are you here to make sure I don't run away?' I asked him.

He didn't answer.

'Would you shoot at me if I did?' I said smartly. 'Asking you to accompany me,' I tutted. 'What do they think I am, a criminal?' I turned to him. 'Just for the record, I don't appreciate you being here.'

He stared straight ahead.

Bobby interrupted the uncomfortable silence, banging the door behind him. 'Right, got it.'

I took it from his hand and examined it.

'Is that yours?' Jason spoke for the first time, studying my face.

It was silver with a mother-of-pearl face but that's where the similarities ended. Instead of a linked bracelet it was chunky; instead of a rectangular face, this was round.

'Yep,' I said confidently. 'That's my watch all right.'

Jason took it in his hands and wrapped it around my wrist. It was hugely oversized even for my wrist. 'Bobby,' Jason rubbed his eyes wearily, 'get her another watch. One that fits, this time.'

We both looked at him in surprise.

'*That's* what I'm here for,' he said smartly, returning to his spot on the veranda.

Bobby quickly headed back to the shop and Jason called after him, 'Oh, and make sure the clasp is broken. You said you weren't wearing it because it was broken, right?'

I nodded, still silent.

'Well, that shut you up,' he said, looking back out to the forest.

Jason, Bobby and I walked back quickly to the Community Hall in silence, me holding the watch tightly in my hands. Just before Jason pulled open the door, I stopped him.

'What happens now?' I asked, anxiety building up inside me.

'Well, I assume you go in there and,' he thought about it and finally shrugged his shoulders, 'lie.' He pulled the door open and thousands of faces turned to look at us.

The Dutch Representative's speech immediately quietened and Grace Burns moved forward to the microphone. Anxiety was written all over her face. Bobby and Jason stayed at the door, Bobby nodded encouragingly and I began to walk forward up the long aisle to the stage at the top. If I hadn't been so uneasy I would have laughed at the irony of it. Gregory would have done anything to get me up the aisle, and his gift of the watch had finally succeeded.

I reached the top and handed the watch to Grace. She studied it, but I questioned how on earth she was to know whether it was my watch or not. It all seemed so ridiculous. It was all an act. To make those who were unsettled here feel more secure so they wouldn't rise up and demand to find a way out.

'How do we know it's her watch?' one person shouted out, and I rolled my eyes.

'Her name is engraved on the back!' someone shouted, and my blood turned cold. There were only a few people who knew that. I looked immediately to Joseph, but from the look on his face I knew it wasn't him. He was looking angrily at Helena, who was looking even more angrily to . . . Joan. Joan sat in the front row, with a red face, beside the man who had shouted out. She must have overheard. She looked apologetically to Helena and me. I looked away, not knowing how to feel, not truly knowing what any possible outcome could be.

'Is this true?' The representative looked at me.

'I assure you it's true,' the man shouted out again.

My face said it all, I'm sure.

She turned the watch over to look for my name at the back. She seemed pleased. 'Sandy Shortt is engraved on the back.'

There was a loud sigh and more talk within the audience.

'Sandy, thank you for co-operating. You may leave

now and enjoy your life here with us. I hope people will be more welcoming towards you from now on,' she smiled warmly.

Stunned, I took the watch, unable to believe that Bobby had managed to engrave my name in such a short space of time. I quickly walked back down the aisle while people clapped and smiled at me, some apologising, others still not convinced but probably never would be. I grabbed Bobby by the hand and led him out of the hall.

'Bobby!' I laughed once we were a safe distance away from the Community Hall. 'How the hell did you manage that?'

Bobby looked horrified. 'Manage what?'

'To engrave my name so quickly!'

'I didn't,' he said in shock.

'What?' I turned the watch over. A clear metallic back stared back at me.

'Come on, let's get inside,' Bobby said, unlocking the door to the shop while looking around him uncertainly.

In the shadows there was a noise and Jason stepped out.

I jumped.

'Sorry to startle you,' he said in his robot-like tone. 'Sandy,' emotion slipped into his voice and his body loosened as he stepped into the light of the porch, 'I just wondered if you knew my wife, Alison?' he asked awkwardly. 'Alison Rice? We're from Galway. Spiddal.' He swallowed hard, his aggressive appearance softened and vulnerable, concern written all over his face.

Still taken by surprise at his sudden appearance, I ran the name through my mind a few times. Not familiar with it, I shook my head slowly. 'Sorry.'

'OK.' He cleared his throat and straightened up, the hardness returning as though the question had never passed his lips. 'Grace Burns wanted me to tell you that she requests a meeting with you in her office first thing in the morning.' And he disappeared back into the darkness.

46

Jack felt the anger pumping through his veins. The muscles in his face twitched as they jumped around under his skin, psyching themselves up for the big fight as he tried to control his breathing, control his temper. His back teeth felt like they'd been ground to the bone on the drive there. His cheeks were hot, and throbbed along with the rest of his body. He clenched and unclenched his fists while walking through the crowded Limerick city pub.

He spotted Alan sitting alone at a small table with a pint before him, a stool sat in front of him, waiting for Jack. Alan looked up and waved, a smile stretched across his face and in that face Jack could see the ten-year-old that used to call round to their house every day. He prepared to fire himself at Alan but stopped. Instead he diverted to the toilet, where he stood at the sink, splashing water on his face, panting as though he'd run a marathon. It was all he could do to stop himself reaching out and wanting to kill Alan himself.

What had he done? What on earth had Alan done?

47

The week that Jenny-May Butler went missing, the Gardaí came to Leitrim National School. We were all especially excited because it was rare that our principal graced our humble selves with his presence, particularly in our classrooms. As soon as we caught sight of his stern, accusing face, butterflies fluttered in everyone's stomachs, each of us instantly hoping we weren't in trouble even though we knew we'd done nothing wrong. But such was his power. Our main reason for excitement was due to him disrupting our religion lesson to whisper loudly into Ms Sullivan's ear. Loud whispering in the classroom by teachers always meant something important was happening. We were allowed to abandon our studies that morning and told to queue in single file at the door with our fingers on our lips. For teachers, our placing our fingers on our lips didn't usually have the desired effect, the finger not being a suitable silencer as it was indeed a finger, not a zip, and it was, more importantly, our own finger, which we had the ability to remove at any stage. But that day when we entered the school hall, none of us said a word, because at the top of the very unusually silent room were two members of the Gardaí Síochána. One woman and one man, dressed head to toe in navy blue.

We sat on the floor in the middle of the hall with the other fourth-classers. Up the front were junior and senior infants, the older you were, the further back you were allowed to be. The sixth-classers always coolly took their places in the back row. Very quickly the hall was filled. The teachers lined up against the walls on the outside aisles like prison wardens, and every now and then clicked their fingers with an angry face at someone who was whispering or who was trying to make themselves more comfortable on the cold and slightly dirty gym floor, but who was seen to be fidgeting too much.

Our principal introduced the two guards to us, explaining that they were from the local garda station and were here to talk about a very important issue. He told us that we would be asked questions later in class about what they had said by our teachers. I looked over at our teachers when he announced this and noticed a few suddenly straightening themselves up to listen. Then the male garda began talking, he introduced himself as Garda Rogers and his colleague Garda Brannigan, and while he slowly walked the width of the top of the room with his hands behind his back he explained how we shouldn't trust strangers, how we shouldn't get into their cars, not even when they tell us that our parents have told them to collect us. That made me think of refusing to get into my uncle Fred's car on Wednesday afternoons when he collected me and I almost laughed out loud. He told us that we should always speak up if we notice someone getting friendlier than they should. If someone approaches us or we witness anybody else being approached we should tell our parents or teachers straight away. I was ten years old and I remember thinking about when I was seven and I saw Joey Harrison being collected by a weird man at school. I told my teacher at the time and she gave out to me because it was his dad and she thought I was being rude.

Also at ten years of age, almost eleven, this safety talk was old news. But I supposed that particular safety talk was especially for the five- and six-year-olds, who sat in the front rows of the hall, picking their noses, scratching their heads, looking at the ceiling. A front row of little grasshoppers. At that point I had no desire to join the Guards. It wasn't that day's free lesson in safety that set off my ambition; it was the odd socks. I also knew the talk was due to Jenny-May's disappearance that week. Everybody had been acting weirdly about it all week. Our teacher had even left the classroom in tears a few times whenever her eyes fell upon Jenny-May's empty seat. I was secretly delighted, which I knew was wrong but it was the first week of peace I'd gotten at school for years. For once I didn't feel Jenny-May's balls of paper hitting my head as she blew them through a straw, and whenever I answered a question in class I didn't hear sniggers behind me. I *knew* that a really terrible and sad thing had happened but I just couldn't *feel* sad.

We said a prayer in class every morning for the first few weeks after she went missing, praying for Jenny-May's safety, praying for her family and praying that she would be found. The prayer got shorter and shorter as the weeks went by and then suddenly one Monday, when we came back after the weekend, Ms Sullivan just left out that prayer without mentioning a thing. Everybody's desks were rearranged in a different shape in the room and, bam!, everything went back to normal. I found that even weirder than Jenny-May going missing in the first place. I spent the first few minutes of that day looking at everybody reciting their poem like they were crazy, but the teacher gave out to me for not learning the poem I had spent two hours learning the night before and she picked on me for the rest of the day.

After Garda Rogers had finished his safety talk, it was Garda Brannigan's turn to talk more specifically about Jenny-May. She spoke in softer tones about how, if anybody knew anything or had any information about something they saw over the last few weeks or months, they should go to room four beside the staffroom as she and Garda Rogers would be there for the day. My face burned because I felt like she was talking directly to me. I looked around, paranoia, feeling as though this entire event had been staged for me just to confess all that I knew. No one looked at me oddly apart from James Maybury, who picked a scab on his elbow and flicked it at me. Our teacher clicked her fingers at him, which had little effect as the damage had already been done and he wasn't afraid, nor did he care much about clicking fingers.

When the talk was over we were once again encouraged by our teachers to go to room four to talk to the Gardaí and then we were given our lunch break, which was a stupid idea because nobody was going to bother missing time playing in the yard by going to the guards. As soon as we got back into our classroom and Ms Sullivan told us to take our maths books out, hands suddenly shot into the air. People just suddenly seemed to remember vital evidence. But what else could Ms Sullivan do? And so the Gardaí found themselves with a very long queue of students of all ages outside their door, some of whom had never even met Jenny-May Butler.

Room four was nicknamed the interrogation room, and the story of what went on inside became more and more exaggerated with each pupil that left and rejoined their friends. There were so many pupils with alleged information that the guards had to come back the next day, but not without a stern announcement to each class that although everybody's help was very much appreciated, garda time was very precious and students should only go to room four if they had something very important to tell them. By the second day, I had already been refused access to room four by my teacher twice on account of the first request to go taking place during the history lesson and the second during Irish.

'But I like Irish, miss,' I protested.

'Good, then you'll be happy to stay,' she snapped, before ordering me to read an entire chapter aloud from the book.

I had no alternative but to raise my hand during art

class on Friday afternoon. *Everybody* loved art class. Ms Sullivan looked at me in surprise.

'Can I go now, miss?'

'To the toilet?'

'No, to room four.'

She looked surprised but finally took me seriously and I was given permission to leave art class to the sound of 'ooooooooh' from everybody else.

I knocked on the door to room four and Garda Rogers opened the door. He must have been six foot tall. At ten years old I was already very tall at five foot five and I was happy finally to see someone tower over me, even if he was intimidating, dressed in a garda uniform, and I was about to confess to him.

'Another maths class?' he smiled broadly.

'No,' I said so quietly I could barely hear myself. 'Art.'

'Oh.' He raised his thick caterpillar-eyebrows with surprise.

'I'm responsible,' I said quickly.

'Well, that's good, but I don't think missing one maths class makes you irresponsible, although don't tell your teacher I said that.' He touched his nose.

'No,' I said, taking a deep breath. 'I mean I'm responsible for Jenny-May going missing.'

This time he didn't smile. He opened the door wider. 'Come on in.'

I looked around the room. It was nothing like the rumours that had been going around the last two days. Jemima Hayes said that someone told her friend that someone told her that someone hadn't been allowed to leave the room to go to the toilet and had to wee in his pants. The room was non-threatening, with a couch up against one wall, small table in the centre and a plastic school chair opposite that. There was no sign of a wet chair.

'Sit down there.' He pointed to the couch. 'Make yourself comfortable. What's your name?'

'Sandy Shortt.'

'You're tall for your age, though, aren't you, Miss Shortt?' he laughed, and I smiled politely even though I'd heard it a million times. He stopped himself laughing. 'So, tell me, what makes you think you were responsible for Jenny-May's disappearance, as you called it?'

I frowned. 'What do you call it?'

'Well, we don't know for sure if . . . I mean there's nothing to suggest . . .' He sighed. 'Just tell me why you think you're responsible.' He motioned for more.

'Well, Jenny-May didn't like me,' I began slowly, suddenly becoming nervous.

'Oh, I'm sure that's not true,' he said kindly. 'What makes you think that?'

'She used to call me a lanky slut and throw stones at me.'

'Oh.' He fell silent.

I took a breath. 'Then last week she found out that I told my friend Emer that I didn't think she was as good at King/Queen as everybody thought she was and she got really angry and stormed over to me and Emer and challenged us to a game – well, not us actually, because she didn't say anything to Emer, just me. She doesn't like Emer either but she doesn't like me more, and I was the one that said it so we were supposed to play this game the next day, me and Jenny-May, and whoever won meant that they were the undisputed champions and nobody could say that they weren't good because the fact that they'd won would prove it. She also knew that I fancied Stephen Spencer and she always used to shout stuff at me just so he wouldn't like me, but I knew that she liked him too. Well, it was obvious because they French-kissed in the bushes at the end of the road a few times for dares but I don't think that he really liked her and maybe he's happy she's gone now too, so he'll be left alone, but I'm not saying I think he did anything to make her disappear. Anyway, the day we were supposed to play King/Queen I saw Jenny-May Butler cycling past my house down the road and she gave me a bad look and I knew she was going to beat me that day at King/Queen and that things would be even worse than they already were and—' I stopped talking and pursed my lips, not sure whether to say what I felt next.

'What happened, Sandy?'

I gulped hard.

'Did you do something?'

I nodded and he moved in, shuffling his backside closer to the edge of his chair.

'What did you do?'

'I . . . I . . .'

'It's OK. You can tell me.'

'I wished her away,' I said it quickly, like pulling a plaster from my skin, quick and easy.

'I'm sorry, you what?'

'I wished her away.'

'Whisht? Is that a weapon of some—'

'No, *wished*. I *wished* that she'd disappear.'

'Ah.' Realisation dawned and he sat back slowly in his chair. 'I understand now.'

'No, you're just saying that you do but you don't really. I really did wish for her to be gone, much more than I've ever wished for anything to be gone in my whole entire life, even more than when my uncle Fred stayed over in our house for a month after he split up from Aunt Isabel and he smoked and drank and stunk the place out and I really wanted him gone but not as much as I wanted Jenny-May gone, and a few hours after me wishing that, Mrs Butler came over to our house and told us she was missing.'

He leaned forward again. 'So you saw Jenny-May a few hours before Mrs Butler came over to your house?'

I nodded.

'What time was this at?'

I shrugged.

'Is there anything that could remind you of what time it was? Think back – what were you doing? Was there anybody else around?'

'I had just opened the door to my grandma and

granddad. They came over for lunch and I was giving Grandma a hug when I saw her cycling by. That's when I made the wish.' I winced.

'So this was lunchtime. Was she with anyone?' He was on the edge of his seat now, ignoring my concern over my wishing her away. He asked question after question about what Jenny-May was doing, who she was with, how did she look, what was she wearing, where did it look like she was going – lots of questions over and over again until my head hurt and I could barely think what the answers were any more. It turned out that I was such a good help to them because I was the last person to see her, that I was allowed to go home early that day. Another benefit to Jenny-May's disappearance.

A few nights before the Gardaí came to the school I had begun to feel guilty about Jenny-May disappearing. I watched a documentary with my dad about how one hundred and fifty thousand people in Washington DC all arranged to think positive thoughts at the same time and the crime rate went down, which proved that positive and negative thinking had a real effect. But then Garda Rogers told me that it wasn't my fault Jenny-May Butler was gone, that wishing for something to happen didn't actually make it happen, and so I became a lot more realistic after that.

And there I was, standing outside the office of Grace Burns twenty-four years later, about to knock on the door and feeling exactly the same as when I was ten. I had that same feeling of being responsible for something beyond my control but I also held the belief in some childish way that ever since I was ten years old, I had been secretly, silently and subconsciously wishing I'd discover a place like this.

48

'Jack, is everything OK?' Alan asked, as soon as Jack had taken his seat opposite him at the low bar table. Concern was written all over his face and doubt crept in on Jack again.

'I'm fine,' Jack replied, putting down his drink, settling on the stool, trying to keep the anger out of his voice, feeling confused.

'You look like shit.' His eyes dropped to Jack's leg, which was bouncing away steadily.

'Everything's OK.'

'You're sure?' Alan narrowed his eyes.

'Yeah.' He took a slug of Guinness, his mind going back to the memory that had hit him with his last taste. Alan's lie.

'So what's up?' Alan said. 'You sounded like there was a fire, on the phone. Something important to tell me?'

'No, no fire.' Jack looked around, avoiding eye contact, doing everything he could do to stop himself from throwing a punch. He needed to approach this properly, and tried to relax. His leg stopped bouncing, he leaned in to the table and stared into his pint. 'It's just this past week I've been looking for Donal, and it's brought everything back, y'know?'

Alan sighed and stared into his pint too. 'Yeah, I know. I think about it every day.'

'About what?'

Alan looked up quickly. 'What do you mean?'

'I mean what kind of things do you think about every day?' Jack tried to take the interrogative tone out of his voice.

'I don't know what you mean. I think about the whole thing,' Alan frowned.

'Well, *I* think about how I wish I'd been there that night, how I wish I'd known Donal better because if I had then maybe . . .' Jack held his hands up, 'maybe, maybe, maybe. Maybe I'd know where to look, maybe I'd know the places or people he went to for safety or for privacy. Anything like that, you know? Maybe there were some people he was running from, people he got involved with. We didn't talk much about private things and every day I think about the fact that if I'd been a better brother maybe I'd have found him. Maybe he'd be sitting right here beside us having a pint.'

They both naturally looked to the empty stool beside them.

'Don't think stuff like that, Jack. You were a good bro—'

'Don't,' Jack interrupted, raising his voice.

Alan stopped in surprise. 'Don't what?'

Jack looked him directly in the eyes. 'Don't lie.'

Fear, uncertainty entered Alan's face and Jack knew his intuition was correct. Alan looked around the room anxiously but Jack stopped him. 'You don't need to tell me I was a good brother because I know I wasn't. Don't lie to make me feel better.'

Alan seemed relieved by this answer. 'OK, you were a shit brother,' he smiled, and they both laughed.

'As much as I've been giving myself a hard time for not being there that night, deep down I know that even if I'd been there, the same thing probably would have happened. Because I know you had his back, you've always had his back.'

Alan smiled sadly into his pint.

'Last time we talked, you blamed yourself for not leaving with Donal that night.' Jack picked up a soggy beer mat and began peeling the outer label off slowly.

'I know what it's like to blame yourself: it's not good. I've been going to see some people, to help sort my head out.' He scratched his head awkwardly. 'They told me all this stuff about blaming yourself was normal. I thought it'd be important to tell you that. Over a pint.'

'Thanks,' Alan said quietly, 'I appreciate that.'

'Yeah, well . . . at least you got to have a conversation with him before he left, right?'

Alan's face said he wasn't sure where this was going, but Jack's voice was still non-threatening and he'd managed to calm himself completely now, to ignore what he guessed.

'You're lucky. The rest of the lads didn't notice him leave.'

'I didn't either.' Alan began fidgeting.

'No, you did,' Jack said. 'You said so last week.' He took another slug of Guinness and looked around, trying to keep the conversation casual. 'Busy here, isn't it? Didn't think it would be, so early in the evening.' He looked at his watch: six p.m. It felt like days since he had met Sandy's mother, not hours. 'Last week you said you wished you'd left with him and you thought he'd be safe getting a taxi down that way.'

Alan looked uncomfortable. 'I didn—'

'You did, man,' Jack interrupted and laughed. 'I may be losing my mind but I do remember that. I was happy to hear it, though.'

'Yeah?'

'Yeah,' Jack nodded happily, 'because it meant that he didn't just wander off, you know? He let someone know and it also makes sense what he was doing walking in that direction. That must make you feel better. The other lads, they're frustrated with themselves for not noticing. They blame themselves for not seeing him leave. At least you don't have that on your head.'

Alan was fidgeting. 'Yeah, I suppose so.' He took his bag of tobacco out of his shirt pocket. 'I'm going outside for a smoke. I'll be back in a minute.'

'Hang on a minute,' Jack said. 'I'll finish off this pint and go out with you.'

'You don't smoke.'

'I took it back up,' Jack lied. The last thing he wanted was for Alan to disappear. He would only get one chance to do this. 'Why is it so busy this evening?' he said, looking around.

Alan relaxed. 'I dunno.' He took out the skins and began to sprinkle the tobacco inside. 'It's a Saturday, I suppose.'

'Should we get a taxi down by Arthur's Quay tonight?' Jack asked casually. 'I left the car at home.'

'What do you mean?'

'That's where you told Donal to go for a cab, isn't it?'

Alan snorted and swallowed, cleaning his nostrils, making a sound but not answering the question. He slowly rolled the cigarette between his hands; Jack could see he was thinking. Trying to work it all out in his head.

'It's probably not such a good idea to recommend it to anyone now,' Jack said a little too angrily.

Alan stopped playing with his cigarette and looked at Jack. 'What's going on, Jack?'

'There are a few things running through my mind.' He scratched his forehead with his thumb and noticed his fingers tremble with anger. Alan looked up and saw them too. His eyes narrowed. 'I lost contact with the woman who was helping me look for Donal,' Jack explained, hearing his voice shaking but having no control over it. 'And that's driven me half insane. But mostly what's bothering me,' he spoke through gritted teeth, 'is the fact you told the guards and my family and everyone that would listen that you hadn't noticed Donal leave. Then last week you told me that you *had* noticed him leave. In fact you'd even spoken to him, in fact you'd even told him which way to go for a taxi.'

Alan's eyes got wider and wider as he spoke. His hands began to fidget more, he moved uncomfortably in his seat and a bead of sweat formed above his top lip.

'It doesn't make sense, Alan. And it might not even be a big deal but can you tell me why you lied for an entire year about the fact you told my brother, your best friend, to walk to an area for a taxi that would cause him to disappear?' The anger began to rise, and the volume of his voice with it.

Alan started to tremble. 'I had nothing to do with it.'

'With what?'

'With Donal going missing. I had nothing to do with it.' He went to stand up but Jack reached out and pushed him down by the shoulder. The bag of tobacco spilled to the carpet. Jack kept his hand there firmly, holding him down.

'Well then, who did?' he said angrily.

'I don't know.'

Jack dug his fingers into Alan's shoulder blade. He was just skin and bone.

'Jesus Christ, do we have to do this here?' Alan said in pain, trying to squirm out of Jack's grasp but failing.

Jack leaned in. 'Do what here? Is there some place else you'd like to go? The garda station maybe?'

'I didn't do anything,' Alan hissed. 'I swear.'

'Then why did you lie?'

'I didn't lie,' he said with big wide eyes, which looked like they'd never told the truth in his life. 'I don't exactly have a clean sheet as it is. I thought the guards would think I'd something to do with it.'

Their faces were only inches apart now. 'Tell me the truth.'

'I have.'

'He was your best friend, Alan, he was always there for you—'

'I know, I know,' he interrupted, holding his trembling nicotine-stained fingers to his head. Tears began to form in his eyes and he stared down at the table, his whole body shuddering.

'You can either tell me and make me understand, or I go to the guards,' Jack threatened.

It felt like hours before Alan built up the nerve to speak again. 'Donal got involved in something,' he said so quietly Jack had to move his head even closer. Their heads were practically touching now.

'You're a liar.'

'I'm not a liar.' Alan's head shot up, and Jack could see for once he was telling the truth. 'I was working for these lads—'

'What lads?'

'I can't say.'

Jack reached across and grabbed his collar. 'Who are they?'

'I'm helping you as much as I can, Jack,' Alan croaked, colour rising quickly in his face.

Jack loosened his grip slightly, enough for Alan to be able to breathe, and listened.

'They brought Donal in to program some stuff onto their computer. I suggested him as he'd got his degree and all, but he saw and heard a few things he shouldn't have and they got angry. I told them he wouldn't say a word but Donal was threatening to talk.'

'About what?' Anger was firing through Jack. He couldn't believe after one year of searching, the answer was right here at home, the truth lying with his brother's best friend.

'I can't tell you that,' Alan said through gritted teeth, spittle spilling from the sides of his mouth. 'I couldn't talk Donal out of snitching. He was trying to get me on the straight and narrow but he didn't understand how serious they were. He wouldn't listen.' His entire body trembled and Jack's eyes filled as he waited. Alan's voice broke and the shame was evident as he whispered, 'They were only supposed to knock him around a bit, warn him off, give him a scare.'

It was as though red powder fell before Jack's eyes. The anger pumped violently within him. 'And you walked him straight into it.' His voice was hoarse. Jack jumped out of his chair, pushed his hand up against Alan's throat and forced him off his chair. He fell back against the wall and the mirror behind Alan's head smashed with the force. The pub was silenced and people leaped out of the way of the two men. Jack threw Alan's head hard against the wall again. 'Where is he?' he hissed, his face up against Alan's.

Alan made choking sounds and Jack squeezed his grip tighter. Alan tried to speak and Jack remembered himself and loosened his grip. 'Where is his body?'

When he got his answer, he let go of Alan's throat and backed away, dropping him from his grip as if he was a dirty rag. He allowed Garda Graham Turner, who had been sitting nearby, to take over, and Jack left the pub to find his brother. This time he could say goodbye properly. This time the brothers would both finally be at rest.

49

'Hello, Sandy.' Grace Burns smiled at me from behind her desk. Her office was a boxroom at the back of a planning office. Inside were models of buildings and layouts of future plans for the surrounding lands.

I took a seat before her desk. 'Thank you for saving me from the angry mob last night,' I joked.

'No problem.' But her smile quickly faded. 'Tell me what's really happening, Sandy. Is your watch missing?'

After talking to Joseph, Helena and Bobby late into the night about what was the best thing do, they all agreed that I should lie. I didn't agree.

'Yes, it's missing,' I responded. Her eyes widened and she sat up straight in her chair. 'But the last thing I want to do is make a big deal of it,' I warned. 'I cannot explain how it disappeared, just as I can't explain how I arrived here. No amount of questions from your colleagues or scientists or people who consider themselves to be experts can help this situation. I don't want that GI Joe following me around any more either. I don't know anything. You must give me your word that you won't spread this news because I will not be co-operative.'

'I understand,' she said. 'In the time that I've been here there have been a few people I know of that have reported the same thing but we have been unable to learn anything, just as all of our studies have had little success in discovering how we arrived here. The people I knew of either moved town because word got out and life became too difficult under the gaze of everybody in the village, or else it was a false alarm and they found whatever it was they thought they'd lost. The two people that we did actually have the opportunity to work with closely just couldn't provide us with anything solid to work on. They knew nothing about why and how it was happening and most of us have realised that it's an impossible thing to understand.'

'Where are they now?'

'One passed away, another is living in another village. You're definitely sure your watch is gone?'

'It's gone,' I assured her.

'Is this the only thing that has disappeared?'

This is where I chose to lie. I nodded. 'And believe me, there's no better person at searching than me.' I looked around her room while she studied me.

'What is it that you do back home, Sandy?' She rested her chin on her hand and gazed intently at me, trying to solve the puzzle in her own mind.

'I run a missing persons agency.'

She laughed, but her smile faded when she realised she was laughing alone. 'You search for missing people?'

'And help people reunite, find long-lost relatives, adopted children's biological parents, that kind of thing,' I rattled off.

Her eyes widened with each example. 'So your case is certainly very different from the others I spoke about.'

'Or it's coincidental.'

She mulled that over but didn't comment. 'So that's how you know so much about the people here.'

'Only some people. Only the people in the play. By the way, the dress rehearsal is on tonight. Helena wanted me to invite you.' I remembered how Helena had hammered it into my head before I left the house that morning. 'It's *The Wizard of Oz* but it's not a musical, Helena is stressing to everybody. It's just her and Dennis O'Shea's interpretation,' I laughed. 'Orla Keane is playing the role of Dorothy. I'm actually quite looking forward to it,' I realised for the first time. 'The idea for the play was initially just my way of having a chance to talk to the potential cast without raising suspicions. We thought it would be far cleverer than knocking on doors and relaying stories of home, but perhaps we should have put a bit more thought into it. I didn't realise how quickly people talk here.'

'Word gets around fast,' Grace replied, still in a daze. She leaned in further. 'Were you looking for someone in particular when you arrived here?'

'Donal Ruttle,' I said, still hoping I'd find him.

'No.' She shook her head. 'The name isn't familiar.'

'He's now twenty-five years old, from Limerick, and would have arrived here last year.'

'He's definitely not in this village anyway.'

'I don't think he's here at all, I'm afraid,' I thought aloud, feeling instant sympathy for Jack Ruttle.

'I'm from Killybeggs in Donegal – I don't know if you know it . . .' Grace leaned forward again.

'Of course I do,' I smiled.

Her face softened. 'I'm married here but my maiden name is O'Donohue. My parents were Tony and Margaret O'Donohue. They have passed away now. I saw my dad's name in the obituaries in a newspaper I found six years ago. I've kept it.' She glanced over at her wall cabinet. 'Carol Dempsey,' she started up again, 'you know Carol? She's in the play too, I believe. Well, she's a Donegal woman too, as you'll know, and she informed me of my mother's death when she arrived a few years ago.'

'I'm sorry to hear that.'

'Yes, well . . .' she said gently. 'I'm an only child,' she explained, 'but I have an uncle Donie who moved to Dublin a few years before I arrived here.'

I nodded along with her, waiting for the story to begin but she fell silent and watched me. I shifted uneasily in my chair realising she was giving me information about her life to refresh my memory.

'I'm sorry, Grace,' I said softly. 'That might have been before I set up the agency. How long have you been here?'

'Fourteen years.' I must have looked at her with such pity because she quickly explained, 'I love it here, don't get me wrong. I have a wonderful husband and three gorgeous children and I wouldn't go back in a heartbeat, but I was just wondering . . .' she trailed off. 'I'm sorry.' She sat upright again and composed herself.

'It's OK, I'd want to know too,' I said gently, 'but I'm not familiar with the people you've mentioned. I'm sorry.'

There was a silence and I thought I'd upset her but when she spoke again she seemed fine.

'What made you want to find missing people? It's such an unusual career.'

I laughed. 'Now there's a question.' I thought back to when it all began. 'Two words,' I smiled. 'Jenny-May Butler. She lived across the road from me when I was a child in Leitrim, but she went missing when she was ten.'

'Yes,' Grace smiled, 'Jenny-May is as good a reason as any. What a character.'

It took me a moment to catch what she'd said. My heart leaped into my throat with the surprise. 'What? What did you say?'

50

'Come on, Bobby!' I yelled, poking my head in the door of Lost and Found.

'What?' he shouted from upstairs.

'Bring the camera, get your keys, lock up and let's go. We've got to go!' I allowed the door to swing shut and I paced up and down the veranda, Grace's words still ringing in my ears. She knew Jenny-May. She had given me directions. I had to go to her *now*. My excitement had gone way past boiling point and was overflowing, spilling from me as I waited impatiently outside for Bobby. I needed him to show me the way to Jenny-May's home in the forest, yet I didn't have the patience to explain what it was I wanted.

Bobby arrived at the door, looking bewildered. 'What the hell are you doing—' He stopped as soon as he saw the look on my face. 'What happened?'

'Get your things, Bobby, quick.' I pushed by him into the shop. 'I'll explain on the way. Bring the camera.' I hopped around him as he clumsily tried to gather his things, trying to keep up with the speed with which I was barking my orders. By the time he had finished locking up I was power-walking down the dusty street, aware that even more eyes were on me now, after the community gathering last night.

'Wait, Sandy!' I heard him panting behind me. 'What the hell happened to you? It's like you've a rocket shoved up your ass!'

'Maybe I have,' I smiled, racing on.

'Where are we going?' He jogged alongside me.

'Here.' I thrust the page of directions at him and kept walking.

'Hold on. Slow down,' he said, trying to read it and run alongside me at the same time. One of my strides equalled two of his but I kept walking none the less. 'Stop!' he shouted loudly in the market area, and others turned to stare. I finally stopped. 'If you want me to read this properly you have to tell me what the hell is happening.'

I spoke faster than I had ever spoken before in my life.

'OK, I think I got all that,' Bobby said, still slightly confused, 'but I've never been in this direction before.' He studied the map again. 'We'll have to ask Helena or Joseph.'

'No! We've no time! We have to go *now*,' I whined like an impatient child. 'Bobby, I've been waiting for this moment for the past twenty-four years of my life. Please do not delay me now when I'm so close.'

'Yes, Dorothy, but it will take a bit more than following the yellow brick road,' he said sarcastically.

Despite my frustration I laughed.

'I understand your haste but if I try to bring you to this place it will be another twenty-four years before we get there. I don't know this part of the woods, I have never heard of this Jenny-May person, and I don't have any friends who live that deep. If we get lost, we're in big trouble. Let's just go to Helena for help first.'

Although he was almost half my age, the boy made sense and so I grudgingly stomped my way to Helena and Joseph's house.

Helena and Joseph were sitting on the bench outside the front of their house, enjoying the relaxing atmosphere of Sunday lunchtime. Bobby, sensing my urgency, rushed straight to Helena and Joseph while Wanda jumped up from the ground where she was playing to run to me.

'Hi, Sandy,' she said, grabbing my hand and skipping alongside me as I walked towards the house.

'Hi, Wanda,' I said in a bored tone, but tried to hide my smile.

'What's that in your hand?'

'It's called Wanda's hand,' I said.

She rolled her eyes. 'No, the *other* hand.'

'It's a Polaroid camera.'

'Why?'

'Why is it a camera?'

'No. Why do you have it?'

'Because I want to take a photograph of somebody.'

'Who?'

'A girl I used to know.'

'Who?'

'A girl called Jenny-May Butler.'

'Was she your friend?'

'Not really.'

'Well then, why do you want to take a photograph of her?'

'I don't know.'

'Is it because you miss her?'

I was about to say no when I stopped myself. 'Actually I did miss her, very much.'

'And are you going to see her today?'

'Yes,' I smiled, grabbing Wanda under her armpits and swinging her around, much to her delight. 'I am going to see Jenny-May Butler *today*!'

Wanda began laughing uncontrollably and sang a song she pretended to know about a girl called Jenny-May, which she clearly was making up on the spot, much to my amusement.

'I'm going to come with you,' Helena said, breaking into Wanda's song, giving her a kiss on the top of her head. I took a photo of the two of them when they weren't looking.

'Stop wasting the cartridges,' Bobby barked at me, and I snapped his face too.

'No, Helena, I don't expect you to come.' I waved

the photos in the air to dry before placing them in my shirt pocket. 'You've got the dress rehearsal tonight. That's more important. Just explain to Bobby where it is.' I began to get jittery again.

She looked at her watch and I had a pang of longing for mine. 'It's just after one. The dress rehearsal isn't until seven; we'll be back in time. And besides, I want to go with you.' She touched my chin lightly and winked. 'This is far more important, plus I know exactly where we're going. This clearing is not much further on from where you and I met last week.'

Joseph made his way to me. He held out his hand. 'Safe trip, kipepeo girl.'

I took his hand with confusion. 'I'm coming back, Joseph.'

'I should hope so,' he smiled, and placed his other hand on my head. 'When you get back I shall tell you what a kipepeo girl is,' he smiled.

'Liar,' I said, narrowing my eyes.

'Right, let's go,' Helena said, throwing a lime-green pashmina over her shoulder.

We set off in the direction of the woods, Helena leading the way. At the edge of the woods a young woman appeared, looking dazed and confused as she gazed around the village.

'Welcome,' Helena said to her.

'Welcome,' Bobby said happily.

She looked with confusion from their faces to mine. 'Welcome,' I smiled, pointing her towards the registry office.

The routes Helena chose were cleared and well-travelled trails. The atmosphere reminded me of the first few days I had spent alone in these woods, wondering where I was. The scent of pine was rich, mixed with moss, bark and damp leaves. There was the foul smell of rotting leaves mixed with the sweet floral scents of the wild flowers. Mosquitoes hovered in small areas, darting in circular motions together. Red squirrels bounced from branch to branch, and occasionally

Bobby stopped to pick up an item of interest in our path. We couldn't walk fast enough as far as I was concerned. Yesterday I had thought the prospect of finding Jenny-May an impossibility; today I was going back the way I had come to actually see her.

Grace Burns had explained that Jenny-May had arrived in the village with an elderly Frenchman, who had been living deep in the woods for years. She had knocked on his door, seeking help when she had first arrived all those years ago. Seldom in the forty years he had lived Here had he ventured to the village, but twenty-four years ago he arrived at the registry office with the ten-year-old girl named Jenny-May Butler who insisted on him being her guardian, the only person she trusted. Despite his desire for solitude, he agreed to care for her, choosing to remain in his home in the woods but making sure Jenny-May went back and forth to school every day and formed and maintained friendships. She became fluent in French, choosing to speak it when in the village, meaning few of the Irish community were aware of her true roots. Jenny-May cared for her guardian until his dying day fifteen years ago, and she decided to remain in the home he made hers, outside of the village, rarely venturing to the village herself.

After twenty minutes we passed the clearing where I had met Helena and she insisted on stopping for a break. She drank from the canteen of water she had carried with her, and passed it to Bobby and me. I didn't feel the heat or the thirst on this hot day though. My mind was focused on Jenny-May. I wanted to keep moving, keep walking until we reached her. After that I had no idea what would happen.

'God, I've never seen you like this before,' Bobby said, staring at me oddly. 'It's as though you've ants in your pants.'

'She's always like that.' Helena closed her eyes and fanned her perspiring face.

I paced up and down beside Helena and Bobby, hopping around, kicking leaves and trying desperately to channel the adrenalin that was rushing through me. Feeling more anxious with every second they spent with me, they finally felt under pressure to move again, which I was glad of but felt guilty about.

The next part of the journey was further than Helena had thought. We walked for another thirty minutes before seeing a small wooden cabin in a clearing in the distance. Smoke was puffing from the chimney, following the direction of the tall pines until it overtook them, going where they couldn't go, up and out in the cloudless sky.

We stopped walking as soon as we saw the cabin in the distance. Helena was red in the face and tired, and I felt more guilty for bringing her on such a journey on this hot day. Bobby was looking at the cabin rather disappointedly, probably hoping for something far more luxurious than this. I, on the other hand, was more pumped up than ever. The sight of the humble home before me took my breath away. It was the home of a girl who had always boasted about wanting so much more, yet to me the sight of it was a dream, a perfect pretty little picture. Just like Jenny-May.

Tall pines stood protectively on two sides of the house. In front, there was a little garden amidst the large clearing, with small bushes, pretty flowers and what looked from afar to be a vegetable patch or herb garden. Mosquitoes and flies, when hit by the sun, looked like symbiotic creatures circling in the air, pockets of them scattered throughout the area. Streams of sunlight shone down through the trees, spotlighting centre stage.

'Oh, look,' Helena said, handing the water to Bobby as the front door of the cabin opened and out of it streamed a little girl with white-blonde hair. Her laughter echoed around the clearing and was carried over to us on the warm breeze. My hand went to my mouth. I must have made a sound, though I didn't hear it, because Bobby and Helena immediately looked to me. Tears welled in my eyes, as I watched the little girl, no older than five, exactly like the little girl I began my first day of school with. Then a female voice called from the house and my heart thudded.

'Daisy!'

Then a male voice: 'Daisy!'

Little Daisy ran around the front garden, giggling and twirling, her lemon dress floating around her on the wind. Then from the front door a man stepped out and began to chase her. Her giggling turned to screams of delight. He made terrifying noises behind her, teasing how he was going to catch her, which made her scream with laughter even more. Finally he caught her and spun her around in the air while she screamed for, 'More, more, more!' He stopped when both were out of breath and he carried her in his arms back towards the house. Just outside the door he stopped and turned around slowly to look straight at us.

He called into the house. We heard the female voice again but not her words. He stood there looking directly at us.

'Can I help you?' he called, holding his hand to his forehead to shield the sun from his eyes.

Helena and Bobby looked to me. I stared at the man and the child in his arms, speechless.

'Well, yes, thank you. We're looking for Jenny-May Butler,' Helena called politely. 'I'm not sure if we're at the right place.'

I had no doubt we were at the right place.

'Who is looking for her?' he asked politely. 'I'm sorry, I can't see you from here.' He began to take a few steps forward.

'Sandy Shortt is here for her,' Helena called.

Immediately a figure appeared at the door.

I heard my large intake of breath.

Long blonde hair, slim and pretty. The same but older. My age. The child in her was gone. She wore a loose-fitting white cotton dress and was barefoot. She held in her hand a tea cloth, which fell to the floor when she held her hand to her forehead to block out the sunlight and her eyes fell upon me.

'Sandy?' Her voice was older but the same. It quivered and was uncertain, displaying fear and joy all at the same time.

'Jenny-May,' I called back, hearing exactly the same tone in my voice.

Then I heard her cry as she slowly started to walk towards me and I heard myself cry as I took steps towards her. And I saw her arms reaching out and felt mine do the same. The distance between us grew smaller, the idea of her being before me becoming more real. Her tears were loud, mine too I was sure. We cried like children as we walked towards one another, studying faces, hair, bodies, and remembering: good things and bad. And then we were within each other's grasp and we fell into each other. Crying and hugging, moving to look at each other's face, wiping tears from one another's cheek and then holding on again. Never wanting to let go.

51

'Jack,' Garda Graham Turner said with surprise, 'what are you doing back here? We won't have results back from forensics for another few days and I promise you we'll contact you with the news.'

Time had got to Donal's body before them and had spared it no mercy. He had yet to be officially identified although Jack and his family knew in their hearts it was Donal. Fresh and decaying flowers were found on the site that Alan had visited each week of the year. He had confessed his true story to police the previous night but had refused to give the names of the gang involved. Over the next few months he would stand trial, and Jack was glad his mother wasn't around to see the man she helped raise take part of the blame for the murder of her baby.

After discussing the night's events with his family, it was the early hours of the morning before Jack returned to Foynes. The town was still celebrating the festival with all the energy of its opening hours. He ignored the sounds of music and singing, and went into the bedroom to find Gloria lying asleep in bed. He sat on the bed beside her and watched her, her long black lashes resting on the tops of her rosy cheeks. Her mouth was slightly open, soft sounds of her breath causing her white chest to heave gently up and down. It was that hypnotic sound and sight that compelled him to do what he hadn't done for a year. He reached out to her, placed his hand on her shoulder and gently woke her from her slumber, finally inviting her into his world. When they had talked all night about the past year and all he had learned in past week, he finally felt tired and joined her in her sleep at last.

'I'm not here about Donal,' Jack explained, sitting down in the station on Sunday evening. 'We need to find Sandy Shortt.'

'Jack,' Graham rubbed his eyes wearily. His desk and the surrounding desks were covered in paperwork and phones rang all around him. 'We've been through this.'

'Not in enough detail. Now listen to me. Maybe Sandy got in touch with Alan and he panicked. You never know. Maybe they arranged to meet and he got nervous she was getting close to the truth and maybe he did something. I don't know what. I'm not even talking about murder. I know Alan's not capable of that but,' he paused, 'actually,' his pupils dilated with anger, 'maybe he did, maybe he got desperate and—'

'He didn't,' Graham interrupted. 'I've been through it over and over again with him. He doesn't know anything about her, he had never even heard of her. He had no clue about what I was talking about. All he knew was what you told him: that some unknown woman was helping you find Donal. That's all.' He looked Jack in the eyes and softened his tone. 'Please, Jack, give up on this.'

'Give up? Like everyone told me to when I was looking for Donal?'

Graham shifted in his seat uncomfortably.

'Alan was Donal's *best friend* and he lied about what happened to him for *one year*. He's in enough trouble already – do you think he's going to bother telling us about what he could have done to some woman he cares nothing about? Was I not right about Alan the first time?' Jack raised his voice.

Graham was silent for a long time, biting down on his already non-existent nail as he quickly made a decision. 'OK, OK.' He closed his tired eyes and focused. 'We'll start searching the site where her car was left.'

52

I have thought about that moment with Jenny-May long and hard for many hours, days and nights but I have no words for the time that we spent together that day. It was far too big for words. It was more important than words; it had more meaning than just words.

We stole away from the cabin, leaving Bobby, Helena, Daisy and Jenny-May's husband, Luc, to chat among themselves. We had a lot to say to one another. To explain our conversations would not do the moment justice because we talked about nothing. To explain how I felt, watching an older version of the pretty photo embedded in my memory come alive, would fall short of the enormity of my delight. Delight – not good enough a word. Relief, joy, pure ecstasy – still not even close.

I filled her in on local people she once knew who were doing things of no interest to anybody but her. She told me about her family, her life, all that she had done since I had seen her. I told her of mine. Not once did we speak about her treatment of me. Does that seem odd? It didn't then. It wasn't important. Not once did we mention where we both were. Does that seem odd too? Perhaps, but that wasn't important either. It wasn't about then, or where, it was just about now. This moment, today. We didn't notice the hours go by, we barely saw the sunset and the moonrise. We didn't feel the heat leave our skin and the evening breeze cooling it. We felt nothing, heard nothing, saw nothing but the stories, sounds and visions of our own minds, which we filled one another with. It is nothing to others but so much to me.

But it is perhaps enough to say that a part of me was set free that night, as, I sensed, was the case for Jenny-May. We never said it to one another, of course. But we both knew.

53

Helena called to us that she had to get back to the village for the dress rehearsal and so while they said their goodbyes, Jenny-May and I put our heads together and looked up to the camera in my hand and smiled. I took the photo and slid it into my shirt pocket. Jenny-May turned down her invitation to see the play, preferring to stay home with her family. We said we would meet again but we made no arrangements. Not out of any badness between us, but because I felt it had all been said, or not said but understood, and she probably did too. To know she was there was enough, and for her to know I was around probably was too. Sometimes that's all people ever really need. Just to know.

We borrowed a flashlight from Jenny-May as the sun was hiding behind the trees, leaving us bathed in blue light. Helena led the way back to the village. Eventually I could see the lights in the distance. Feeling dizzy with happiness, I took the photos from my pocket to study them once more while walking. I retrieved two and felt around for the third. It was gone.

'Oh, no,' I moaned, and stopped walking, immediately looking to the ground.

'What's wrong?' Bobby stopped walking and called to Helena to stop.

'The photograph of me and Jenny-May is gone.' I started to walk back the way I had come.

'Hold on, Sandy.' Bobby followed me, looking at the

357

ground. 'We've been walking for almost an hour now. It could be anywhere. We really have to get back to the Community Hall for the play; we're late as it is. You can take another photo with her tomorrow when it's bright.'

'No I can't,' I whinged, straining my eyes to see the ground in the evening light.

Helena, who so far hadn't said a word, stepped forward. 'You dropped it?'

That made me stop and look up at her. Her face was serious, her tone grave.

'I assume so. I doubt it leaped out and ran away on its own.'

'You know what I'm talking about.'

'No, I definitely dropped it. My pocket is open, see?' I showed them the shallow breast pocket. 'Why don't you two just go on ahead and I'll look around here for a little while.'

They looked unsure.

'We're less than five minutes away. I can see the pathway back we're so close,' I smiled. 'Honestly, I'll be OK. I have to find this photo and then I'll go straight to the Community Hall to see the play. I promise.'

Helena was looking at me oddly, obviously torn between helping me and helping the cast prepare for their dress rehearsal.

'I'm not leaving you on your own,' Bobby said.

'Here, Sandy, you take this torch. Bobby and I will be able to see our way from here. I know it's important for you to find it.' She handed over the torch and I thought I saw tears in her eyes.

'Helena, stop worrying!' I laughed. 'I'll be OK.'

'I know you will, sweetheart.' She leaned over and, taking me by surprise, planted a quick kiss on my cheek and gave me a quick tight hug. 'Be careful.'

Bobby smiled at me over Helena's shoulder. 'She's not going to die, you know, Helena.'

Helena slapped him playfully over the head. 'Come on with me. I need you to bring all the costumes over from the shop a.s.a.p., Bobby! You promised I'd have them yesterday!'.

'Well, that was before David Copperfield here was called to the Community Hall!' he defended himself.

Helena glared at him.

'OK, OK!' He backed away from her. 'Hope you find it, Sandy.' He winked at me before following Helena back down the path. I heard them nagging and teasing one another for a while until the sounds of their voices disappeared and they entered the village.

I turned around and immediately started scanning the ground. I could pretty much remember the way we had come. It seemed to be one main pathway, very rarely did we come across a choice of others, and so with my eyes peeled to the floor, I made my way back deeper into the forest.

Helena and Bobby rushed around backstage, fixing costumes, last-minute broken zips and sewing tears, going over lines with nervous cast members and giving final pep talks to a panicked crew. Helena hurried out to her seat in the auditorium beside Joseph before the performance began and finally relaxed for the first time in the last hour.

'Is Sandy not with you?' Joseph asked, looking around.

'No,' Helena said, staring straight ahead, refusing to look at her husband. 'She stayed behind in the forest.'

Joseph took his wife's hand and whispered, 'Along the Kenyan coast where I come from, there is a forest called the Arabuko-Sokoke Forest.'

'Yes, you've talked about it,' Helena acknowledged.

'There, there are kipepeo girls, butterfly farmers who help keep the forest preserved.'

Helena looked up at him, finally learning the meaning of the nickname.

He smiled. 'They are known as guardians of the forest.'

'She stayed in the forest to find a photograph of her

and Jenny-May. She thinks she dropped it.' Helena's eyes began to fill and Joseph squeezed her hand.

The curtains on stage parted.

At times I thought I saw the white of the photograph glowing in the moonlight and I would wander off the track to search among the weeds and undergrowth, chasing small birds and creatures away with my flashlight. After half an hour I was sure I should have reached the first clearing by now. I shone the torch all around me, looking for something familiar but it was just trees, trees and more trees. But then again I had been walking far slower and so it would take me longer to get there. I decided to keep walking in the same direction. It was black now, and around me owls hooted and creatures moved in their natural habitat, startled to find me where I didn't belong. I didn't plan on being there much longer. I shivered, the cool evening now turning to cold. I shone the torch straight ahead, deciding that I'd dropped the photograph closer to Jenny-May's house than I thought.

'Where am I?' Orla Keane stepped onto the stage as Dorothy Gale, looking around the community hall that for the night was a grand theatre. Thousands of faces stared back at her. 'What is this strange land?'

Thirty minutes later, sweating, panting and dizzy from jogging around in different directions, I recognised the first clearing up ahead. I stopped running and leaned over to hold on to a tree, to steady myself and catch my breath. I breathed a sigh of relief and was taken aback by the realisation I'd been more anxious about being lost than I'd thought.

'I need a heart,' Derek sang. 'I need a brain,' Bernard announced theatrically. 'And I need courage,' Marcus said quietly in his bored tone. The audience laughed as they all hopped off with Dorothy stage right, arm in arm.

*   *   *

It was brighter in the clearing, the moon shining down without the trees acting as a shield. The floor of the clearing was blue and in the centre I could see a small white square sheet glistening. Despite my tiredness and the pain in my chest, I began to run towards the photograph. I knew I was out longer than I had intended to be and I had promised Helena I would be there for her. A mixture of emotions rushed through me as I felt such pressure to find the photograph and be there for Helena and my new friends. I wasn't concentrating as I stupidly ran at top speed in the dark, in Barbara Langley's heeled shoes. I landed unevenly on a rock and felt my ankle twist. The pain shot up my leg, forcing me off balance. The ground came up to meet me quickly before there was anything I could do to stop it.

'You mean I had the power inside myself to go home all the time?' Orla Keane said innocently. The audience laughed.

'Yes, Dorothy,' Carol Dempsey, dressed as the good witch Glinda, said in her usual gentle tones. 'Just click your heels together and say the words.'

Helena grabbed Joseph's hand tighter and he squeezed back.

Orla Keane closed her eyes and began to click her heels together. 'There's no place like home,' she said, pulling everyone into her mantra. 'There's no place like home.'

Joseph looked across at his wife and saw a tear roll down her face. He raised a thumb to stop it from dropping from her chin. 'Our kipepeo has flown.'

Helena nodded and another tear fell.

I felt everything go from under me, my head smashed violently against something hard. I felt the pain shoot down my spine and everything went black.

*   *   *

On stage Orla Keane tapped her ruby slippers together one last time before disappearing in a puff of smoke, compliments of Bobby's firecrackers. 'There's no place like home.'

54

'I don't think she's here.' Graham walked towards Jack in the wooded area of Glin. In the distance fireworks were going off over Foynes as the village celebrated the last few moments of the Irish Coffee Festival. They both stopped to look up.

'I have a feeling you might be right,' Jack finally admitted. They had spent the last few hours searching the scene where Sandy had deserted her car and, despite the fact it had fallen dark mid-search Jack had insisted they continue. They were not practical searching conditions and he could see the others checking their watches. 'Thanks for letting me try,' Jack said as they walked along the pathway back to the car.

Suddenly there was a loud crash; a sound as though a tree had come down. A thud and a female cry. The men both froze and each looked at the other.

'Which way did that come from?' Graham asked, spinning around, shining his flashlight in every direction. They heard groaning coming from further up on their left and all involved rushed to find her. Jack's flashlight fell upon Sandy, lying on her back, her leg looking dislocated, blood on her hand and staining her clothes.

'Oh my God.' Jack rushed forward and kneeled down by her side. 'She's here!' he called to the others, and they hurried over, crowding around her.

'OK, let's move back, give her space.' Graham radioed for an ambulance.

'I don't want to move her. Her head is bleeding heavily

and it looks like her leg's broken too. Oh God, Sandy, talk to me.'

Her eyes fluttered open. 'Who are you?'

'I'm Jack Ruttle,' he said, relieved she'd opened her eyes.

'Keep her talking, Jack,' Graham said.

'Jack?' Her eyes widened in surprise. 'Are you missing too?'

'What? No,' he frowned. 'No, I'm not missing.' He looked at Graham worriedly. Graham made motions to keep her talking.

'Where am I?' she asked in confusion, looking around. She tried to move her head and called out in pain.

'Don't move. An ambulance is on its way. You're in Glin, in Limerick.'

'Glin?' she repeated.

'Yes, we were supposed to meet here last week, remember?'

'Am I home?' Her eyes filled with tears, which quickly fell over her mud-streaked face. 'Donal,' she said suddenly, stopping her tears, 'Donal wasn't there.'

'Donal wasn't where?'

'I was in this place, Jack. Oh my God, this place where all the missing people were. Helena, Bobby, Joseph, Jenny-May, oh my God, Helena's play – I'm missing her play.' Tears fell quickly now. 'I need to get up,' she struggled to move. 'I have to go to the dress rehearsal.'

'You have to wait for the ambulance to come, Sandy. Don't move.' He looked back to Graham. 'She's delusional. Where the hell is the ambulance?'

Graham radioed again. 'On its way.'

'Who did this to you, Sandy? Tell me who did this and we'll get them, I promise.'

'Nobody did.' She looked confused. 'I fell. I told you I was in the place . . . where's my photograph, I've lost a photograph. Oh, Jack, I've something to tell you,' she said softly now. 'It's about Donal.'

'Go on,' he urged.

'He wasn't there. He wasn't in . . . the place with everyone else. He's not missing.'

'I know,' Jack said sadly. 'We found him this morning.'

'I'm so sorry.'

'How did you know?'

'He wasn't there, with all the missing people,' she mumbled, her eyes fluttering closed.

'Stay with me, Sandy,' Jack said with urgency in his voice.

My eyes opened to bright white, and my lids felt heavy. I looked around but to move my sockets was sore. My head pounded. I groaned.

'Sweetheart . . .' My mum's face appeared from above.

'Mum.' I instantly began crying and she reached out her arms to hold me.

'It's OK, sweetheart, it's OK now,' she said soothingly, while smoothing down my hair on my head.

'I've missed you so much,' I cried into her shoulder ignoring the pulsing pain around the rest of my body.

Her patting stopped when I said that, the shock of my words freezing her, and then it slowly began again. I felt Dad kiss the top of my head.

'I missed you, Dad,' I continued crying.

'We've missed you too, love.' His voice shook as he spoke.

'I found the place,' I said excitedly, the sounds and visions around me still blurred and faraway. My own voice was muffled. 'I found the place where all the missing things go.'

'Yes, sweetheart, Jack told us,' Mum said in a worried tone.

'No, I'm not mad, I didn't imagine it. I was really there.'

'Yes,' she hushed me, 'you need to rest, sweetheart.'

'The photographs are in my shirt pocket,' I explained,

trying to explain all the details clearly, but it felt muddled in my head. 'It's not my shirt pocket, it's Barbara Langley from Ohio's. I found it. I put them in my pocket.'

'The guards didn't find anything, honey,' Dad said quietly, not wanting anyone else to hear. 'There aren't any photographs.'

'They must have fallen out,' I mumbled, getting tired of trying to explain. 'Is Gregory here?' I asked.

'No, shall we call him?' my mother asked excitedly. 'I wanted to call him but Harold wouldn't let me.'

'Call him,' was the last thing I remember saying.

I awoke in my childhood bedroom and stared at the same floral wallpaper I was forced to look at all throughout my teens. I had hated it then, I couldn't wait to see the back of it, but now it gave me a strange sense of comfort. I smiled, feeling delighted to be home for the first time in my life. There was no bag by the door, no feeling of claustrophobia or fear of losing things. I had been at home now for three days, catching up on sleep and resting my injured and weary body. I had broken my leg, twisted my ankle and had stitches on the crown of my head but I was home and I was happy. I often thought of Helena, Bobby, Joseph and Wanda, and felt a longing to be with them but knew that they would understand what had happened, and wondered if they perhaps understood the entire time.

There was a knock on the door.

'Enter,' I called.

Gregory peeked his head around, then entered with a tray of food in his hands.

I groaned. 'Not more food. I think you're all trying to fatten me up.'

'We're trying to make you well again,' he said sombrely, placing the tray on the bed. 'Mrs Butler brought you the flowers.'

'That's so sweet of her,' I said gently. 'Do you still think I'm crazy?' I asked.

I had told him about where I had been as soon as I

had felt well enough to explain it properly. My parents had also obviously asked him to talk to me about it as it was issue number one on the agenda, although he was keen not to take the role of counsellor. Not any more. That was then, this is now.

He avoided the question. 'I spoke to Jack Ruttle today.'

'Good. I hope you apologised.'

'I definitely apologised.'

'Good,' I repeated, 'because if it wasn't for him I would literally be lying in a ditch somewhere. My own partner didn't care enough to join the search party,' I huffed.

'Honestly, Sandy, if I joined a search party every time you disappeared . . .' he trailed off. He had meant it as a joke but it changed the mood.

'Well, it won't be happening again.'

He looked unsure.

'I promise, Gregory. I've found what I was looking for.' I reached out to touch his cheek.

He smiled but I was sure it would take time before he'd truly believe me. The past few days I had questioned whether I believed myself.

'What did Jack say on the phone?'

'That he went back to the place where he'd found you to look for the photographs you've been talking about and he didn't find anything.'

'Does *he* think I'm crazy?'

'Probably, but he still loves you because he's convinced you and your mum helped him find his brother.'

'He's a sweet guy. If it wasn't for him . . .' I repeated, trailing off just to annoy Gregory.

'If you didn't already have a broken leg, I'd break it for you,' he threatened, but then became serious again. 'You know how your mum received a phone call from the Sheens? The people who bought your grandparents' house all those years ago?'

'Yes.' I tore the crust off a slice of toast and put it

in my mouth. 'I thought that was weird. I can't believe they were ringing to tell her they were moving.'

Gregory cleared his throat. 'Actually, well, that's not why they called; your dad concocted that story.'

'What? Why?' I put the toast down, no longer hungry.

'He didn't want to worry you.'

'Tell me, Gregory.'

'Well, your parents may not agree with me but I think it's important you know that they'd actually called to say that they'd found a teddy bear belonging to you. A Mr Pobbs, lying underneath a bed in the spare room with your name engraved on his striped pyjamas.'

I gasped. 'Everything's turning up again.'

'They found this particularly unusual because they had used that room as storage for a number of years and only turned it back into a bedroom last month. They had never noticed the teddy bear before.'

'Why didn't anyone tell me?'

'Your parents didn't want to upset you again, with you talking about this missing place and—'

'It's not a missing place, it's a place where missing people and things go,' I said angrily, realising once again how stupid it sounded.

'OK, OK, calm down.' He ran his fingers through his hair and leaned his elbows on his knees.

'What's wrong?'

'Nothing.'

'Gregory, I know when something's wrong with you. Tell me.'

'Well,' he wrung his hands together, 'after their phone call I gave further thought to your . . . theory.'

I rolled my eyes with frustration. 'What disorder do you think I have now?'

'Let me finish,' he raised his voice and an angry silence fell between us. After a while he spoke again. 'When I was emptying your hospital bag I found this in your shirt pocket.'

I held my breath as he removed something from his top pocket.

The photograph of me with Jenny-May.

I took it from his hands as though it were the most fragile thing in the world. Trees framed the photograph.

'Do you believe me now?' I whispered, running my finger over her face.

He shrugged. 'You know how my mind works, Sandy. For me this kind of thinking is nonsensical.' I looked to him angrily. '*But*,' he said firmly before I had a chance to snap, 'this is very difficult to explain.'

'That's good enough for now,' I accepted, holding the photograph close to me.

'I'm sure Mrs Butler would want to see that,' he said.

'Do you think?' I was unsure.

He thought about it. 'I think she's the only woman you could show it to. I think she's the only woman you *should* show it to.'

'But how could I explain it?'

He looked at me, spread his hands apart and shrugged. 'This time, you're the one with the answer.'

55

Sometimes, people can go missing right before our very eyes. Sometimes, people discover you, even though they've been looking at you the entire time. Sometimes, we lose sight of ourselves when we're not paying enough attention.

Days later, when I was feeling fit enough to venture outside on my crutches, under the gaze of Gregory and my parents, I hobbled my way across the road to Mrs Butler's house with the photograph of her daughter in my pocket. The lantern-shaped porch light provided a warm orange glow above the door and drew me in, like a moth to a flame. I took a deep breath and knocked on the door, once again feeling a responsibility and knowing that I'd wished for this moment my entire life.

We all get lost once in a while, sometimes by choice, sometimes due to forces beyond our control. When we learn what it is our soul needs to learn, the path presents itself. Sometimes we see the way out but wander further and deeper despite ourselves; the fear, the anger or the sadness preventing us returning. Sometimes we prefer to be lost and wandering, sometimes it's easier. Sometimes we find our own way out. But regardless, always, we are found.

Huge thank you (and farewell) Maxine Hitchcock for all you've done on my first four books – I'll miss you for the rest of the journey, but hope our paths will cross again sometime.

Thanks Lynne Drew, Amanda Ridout and the HarperCollins team for the fantastic support.

Thank you Marianne Gunn O'Connor for continuing to inspire and motivate me.

Also thanks to the incredibly supportive Pat Lynch and Vicki Satlow and thank you to Dermot Hobbs and John-Paul Moriarty.

Special thanks to David, Mimmie, Dad, Georgina, Nicky and all my family; Kellys, Aherns, Keoghans, and of course, the Witches of Eastwick – Paula Pea, Susana and SJ.

Thank you to all those who read my books – for the greatest motivation of all.

Thanks for the Memories

Prologue

Close your eyes and stare into the dark.

My father's advice when I couldn't sleep as a little girl. He wouldn't want me to do that now but I've set my mind to the task regardless. I'm staring into that immeasurable blackness that stretches far beyond my closed eyelids. Though I lie still on the ground, I feel perched at the highest point I could possibly be; clutching at a star in the night sky with my legs dangling above cold black nothingness. I take one last look at my fingers wrapped around the light and let go. Down I go, falling, then floating, and, falling again, I wait for the land of my life.

I know now, as I knew as that little girl fighting sleep, that behind the gauzed screen of shut-eye, lies colour. It taunts me, dares me to open my eyes and lose sleep. Flashes of red and amber, yellow and white speckle my darkness. I refuse to open them. I rebel and I squeeze my eyelids together tighter to block out the grains of light, mere distractions that keep us awake but a sign that there's life beyond.

But there's no life in me. None that I can feel, from where I lie at the bottom of the staircase. My heart beats quicker now, the lone fighter left standing in the ring, a red boxing glove pumping victoriously into the air, refusing to give up. It's the only part of me that cares, the only part that ever cared. It fights to pump the blood around to heal, to replace what I'm losing. But it's all leaving my body as quickly as it's sent; forming a deep black ocean of its own around me where I've fallen.

Rushing, rushing, rushing. We are always rushing. Never have enough time here, always trying to make our way there.

Need to have left here five minutes ago, need to be there now. The phone rings again and I acknowledge the irony. I could have taken my time and answered it now.

Now, not then.

I could have taken all the time in the world on each of those steps. But we're always rushing. All, but my heart. That slows now. I don't mind so much. I place my hand on my belly. If my child is gone, and I suspect this is so, I'll join it there. There . . . where? Wherever. It; a heartless word. He or she so young; who it was to become, still a question. But there, I will mother it.

There, not here.

I'll tell it: I'm sorry, sweetheart, I'm sorry I ruined your chances, my chance – our chance of a life together. But close your eyes and stare into the darkness now, like Mummy is doing, and we'll find our way together.

There's a noise in the room and I feel a presence.

'Oh God, Joyce, oh God. Can you hear me, love? Oh God. Oh God. Oh, please no, Good Lord, not my Joyce, don't take my Joyce. Hold on, love, I'm here. Dad is here.'

I don't want to hold on and I feel like telling him so. I hear myself groan, an animal-like whimper and it shocks me, scares me. I have a plan, I want to tell him. I want to go, only then can I be with my baby.

Then, not now.

He's stopped me from falling but I haven't landed yet. Instead he helps me balance on nothing, hover while I'm forced to make the decision. I want to keep falling but he's calling the ambulance and he's gripping my hand with such ferocity it's as though it is *he* who is hanging on to dear life. As though I'm all he has. He's brushing the hair from my forehead and weeping loudly. I've never heard him weep. Not even when Mum died. He clings to my hand with all of the strength I never knew his old body had and I remember that I am all he has and that he, once again just like before, is my whole world. The blood continues to rush through me. Rushing, rushing, rushing. We are always rushing. Maybe I'm rushing again. Maybe it's not my time to go.

I feel the rough skin of old hands squeezing mine, and their intensity and their familiarity force me to open my eyes. Light fills them and I glimpse his face, a look I never want to see again. He clings to his baby. I know I've lost mine; I can't let him lose his. In making my decision I already begin to grieve. I've landed now, the land of my life. And, still, my heart pumps on.

Even when broken it still works.

One Month Earlier

1

'Blood transfusion,' Dr Fields announces from the podium of a lecture hall in Trinity College's Arts building, 'is the process of transferring blood or blood-based products from one person into the circulatory system of another. Blood transfusions may treat medical conditions, such as massive blood loss due to trauma, surgery, shock and where the red-cell-producing mechanism fails.

'Here are the facts. Three thousand donations are needed in Ireland every week. Only three per cent of the Irish population are donors, providing blood for a population of almost four million. One in four people will need a transfusion at some point. Take a look around the room now.'

Five hundred heads turn left, right and around. Uncomfortable sniggers break the silence.

Dr Fields elevates her voice over the disruption. 'At least one hundred and fifty people in this room will need a blood transfusion at some stage in their lives.'

That silences them. A hand is raised.

'Yes?'

'How much blood does a patient need?'

'How long is a piece of string, dumb-ass,' a voice from the back mocks, and a scrunched ball of paper flies at the head of the young male enquirer.

'It's a very good question.' She frowns into the darkness, unable to see the students through the light of the projector. 'Who asked that?'

'Mr Dover,' someone calls from the other side of the room.

'I'm sure Mr Dover can answer for himself. What's your first name?'

'Ben,' he responds, sounding dejected.

Laughter erupts. Dr Fields sighs.

'Ben, thank you for your question – and to the rest of you, there is no such thing as a stupid question. This is what Blood For Life Week is all about. It's about asking all the questions you want, learning all you need to know about blood transfusions before you possibly donate today, tomorrow, the remaining days of this week on campus, or maybe regularly in your future.'

The main door opens and light streams into the dark lecture hall. Justin Hitchcock enters, the concentration on his face illuminated by the white light of the projector. Under one arm are multiple piles of folders, each one slipping by the second. A knee shoots up to hoist them back in place. His right hand carries both an overstuffed briefcase and a dangerously balanced Styrofoam cup of coffee. He slowly lowers his hovering foot down to the floor, as though performing a t'ai chi move, and a relieved smile creeps onto his face as calm is restored. Somebody sniggers and the balancing act is once again compromised.

Hold it, Justin. Move your eyes away from the cup and assess the situation. Woman on podium, five hundred kids. All staring at you. Say something. Something intelligent.

'I'm confused,' he announces to the darkness, behind which he senses some sort of life form. There are twitters in the room and he feels all eyes on him as he moves back towards the door to check the number.

Don't spill the coffee. Don't spill the damn coffee.

He opens the door, allowing shafts of light to sneak in again and the students in its line shade their eyes.

Twitter, twitter, nothing funnier than a lost man.

Laden down with items, he manages to hold the door open with his leg. He looks back to the number on the outside of the door and then back to his sheet, the sheet that, if he doesn't grab it that very second, will float to the ground. He makes a move to grab it. Wrong hand. Styrofoam cup of coffee falls to the ground. Closely followed by sheet of paper.

Damn it! There they go again, twitter, twitter. Nothing funnier than a lost man who's spilled his coffee and dropped his schedule.

'Can I help you?' The lecturer steps down from the podium.

Justin brings his entire body back into the classroom and darkness resumes.

'Well, it says here . . . well, it said there,' he nods his head towards the sodden sheet on the ground, 'that I have a class here now.'

'Enrolment for international students is in the exam hall.'

He frowns. 'No, I—'

'I'm sorry.' She comes closer. 'I thought I heard an American accent.' She picks up the Styrofoam cup and throws it into the bin, over which a sign reads 'No Drinks Allowed'.

'Ah . . . oh . . . sorry about that.'

'Mature students are next door.' She adds in a whisper, 'Trust me, you don't want to join this class.'

Justin clears his throat and corrects his posture, tucking the folders tighter under his arm. 'Actually I'm lecturing the History of Art and Architecture class.'

'You're lecturing?'

'Guest lecturing. Believe it or not.' He blows his hair up from his sticky forehead. *A haircut, remember to get a haircut. There they go again, twitter, twitter. A lost lecturer, who's spilled his coffee, dropped his schedule, is about to lose his folders and needs a haircut. Definitely nothing funnier.*

'Professor Hitchcock?'

'That's me.' He feels the folders slipping from under his arm.

'Oh, I'm so sorry,' she whispers. 'I didn't know . . .'

She catches a folder for him. 'I'm Dr Sarah Fields from the IBTS. The Faculty told me that I could have a half-hour with the students before your lecture, your permission pending, of course.'

'Oh, well, nobody informed me of that, but that's no problemo.' *Problemo?* He shakes his head at himself and makes for the door. *Starbucks, here I come.*

'Professor Hitchcock?'

He stops at the door. 'Yes.'

'Would you like to join us?'

I most certainly would not. There's a cappuccino and cinnamon muffin with my name on them. No. Just say no.

'Um . . . nn–es.' *Nes?* 'I mean yes.'

Twitter, twitter, twitter. Lecturer caught out. Forced into doing something he clearly didn't want to do by attractive young woman in white coat claiming to be a doctor of an unfamiliar initialised organisation.

'Great. Welcome.'

She places the folders back under his arm and returns to the podium to address the students.

'OK, attention, everybody. Back to the initial question of blood quantities. A car accident victim may require up to thirty units of blood. A bleeding ulcer could require anything between three and thirty units of blood. A coronary artery bypass may use between one and five units of blood. It varies, but with such quantities needed, now you see why we *always* want donors.'

Justin takes a seat in the front row and listens with horror to the discussion he's joined.

'Does anybody have any questions?'

Can you change the subject?

'Do you get paid for giving blood?'

More laughs.

'Not in this country, I'm afraid.'

'Does the person who is given blood know who their donor is?'

'Donations are usually anonymous to the recipient

but products in a blood bank are always individually traceable through the cycle of donation, testing, separation into components, storage and administration to the recipient.'

'Can anyone give blood?'

'Good question. I have a list here of contraindications to being a blood donor. Please all study it carefully and take notes if you wish.' Dr Fields places her sheet under the projector and her white coat lights up with a rather graphic picture of someone in dire need of a donation. She steps away and instead it fills the screen on the wall.

People groan and the word 'gross' travels around the tiered seating like a Mexican wave. Twice by Justin. Dizziness overtakes him and he averts his eyes from the image.

'Oops, wrong sheet,' Dr Fields says cheekily, slowly replacing it with the promised list.

Justin searches with great hope for needle or blood phobia in an effort to eliminate himself as a possible blood donor. No such luck – not that it mattered, as the chances of him donating a drop of blood to anyone are as rare as ideas in the morning.

'Too bad, Dover.' Another scrunched ball of paper goes flying from the back of the hall to hit Ben's head again. 'Gay people can't donate.'

Ben coolly raises two fingers in the air.

'That's discriminatory,' one girl calls out.

'It is also a discussion for another day,' Dr Fields responds, moving on. 'Remember, your body will replace the liquid part of the donation within twenty-four hours. With a unit of blood at almost a pint and everyone having eight to twelve pints of blood in their body, the average person can easily spare giving one.'

Pockets of juvenile laughter at the innuendo.

'Everybody, please.' Dr Fields claps her hands, trying desperately to get attention. 'Blood For Life Week is all about education as much as donation. It's all well and good that we can have a laugh and a joke but at this time I think it's important to note the fact that someone's *life*, be it woman, man or child, could be depending on you right now.'

How quickly silence falls upon the class. Even Justin stops talking to himself.

2

'Professor Hitchcock.' Dr Fields approaches Justin, who is arranging his notes at the podium while the students take a five-minute break.

'Please call me Justin, Doctor.'

'Please call me Sarah.' She holds out her hand.

Very 'Nice to meet you, Sarah.'

'I just want to make sure we'll see each other later?'

'Later?'

'Yes, later. As in . . . after your lecture,' she smiles.

Is she flirting? It's been so long, how am I supposed to tell? Speak, Justin, speak.

'Great. A date would be great.'

She purses her lips to hide a smile. 'OK, I'll meet you at the main entrance at six and I'll bring you across myself.'

'Bring me across where?'

'To where we've got the blood drive set up. It's beside the rugby pitch but I'd prefer to bring you over myself.'

'The blood drive . . .' He's immediately flooded with dread. 'Ah, I don't think that—'

'And then we'll go for a drink after?'

'You know what? I'm just getting over the flu so I don't think I'm eligible for donating.' He parts his hands and shrugs.

'Are you on antibiotics?'

'No, but that's a good idea, Sarah. Maybe I *should* be . . .' He rubs his throat.

'Oh, I think you'll be OK,' she grins.

'No, you see, I've been around some pretty infectious diseases lately. Malaria, smallpox, the whole lot. I was in a very tropical area.' He remembers the list of contraindications. 'And my brother, Al? Yeah, he's a leper.' *Lame, lame, lame.*

'Really.' She lifts an eyebrow and though he fights it with all his will, he cracks a smile. 'How long ago did you leave the States?'

Think hard, this could be a trick question. 'I moved to London three months ago,' he finally answers truthfully.

'Oh, lucky for you. If it was two months you wouldn't be eligible.'

'Now hold on, let me think . . .' He scratches his chin and thinks hard, randomly mumbling months of the year aloud. 'Maybe it *was* two months ago. If I work backwards from when I arrived . . .' He trails off, while counting his fingers and staring off into the distance with a concentrated frown.

'Are you afraid, Professor Hitchcock?' she smiles.

'Afraid? No!' He throws his head back and guffaws. 'But did I mention I have malaria?' He sighs at her failure to take him seriously. 'Well, I'm all out of ideas.'

'I'll see you at the entrance at six. Oh, and don't forget to eat beforehand.'

'Of course, because I'll be *ravenous* before my date with a giant homicidal needle,' he mumbles as he watches her leave.

The students begin filing back into the room and he tries to hide the smile of pleasure on his face, mixed as it is. Finally the class is his.

OK, my little twittering friends. It's pay-back time.

They're not yet all seated when he begins.

'Art,' he announces to the lecture hall, and he hears the sounds of pencils and notepads being extracted from bags, loud zips and buckles, tin pencil cases rattling; all new for the first day. Squeaky-clean and untarnished.

Shame the same can not be said for the students. 'The products of human creativity.' He doesn't stall to allow them time to catch up. In fact, it is time to have a little fun. His speech speeds up.

'The creation of beautiful or significant things.' He paces as he speaks, still hearing zipping sounds and rattling.

'Sir, could you say that again ple—'

'No,' he interrupts. 'Engineering,' he moves on, 'the practical application of science to commerce or industry.' Total silence now.

'Creativity and practicality. The fruit of their merger is architecture.'

Faster, Justin, faster!

'Architecture-is-the-transformation-of-ideas-into-a-physical-reality. The-complex-and-carefully-designed-structure-of-something-especially-with-regard-to-a-specific-period. To-understand-architecture-we-must-examine-the-relationship-between-technology-science-and-society.'

'Sir, can you—'

'No.' But he slows slightly. 'We examine how architecture through the centuries has been shaped by society, how it continues to be shaped, but also how it, in turn, shapes society.'

He pauses, looking around at the youthful faces staring up at him, their minds empty vessels waiting to be filled. So much to learn, so little time to do it in, such little passion within them to understand it truly. It is his job to give them passion. To share with them his experiences of travel, his knowledge of all the great masterpieces of centuries ago. He will transport them from the stuffy lecture theatre of the prestigious Dublin college to the rooms of the Louvre Museum, hear the echoes of their footsteps as he walks them through the Cathedral of St-Denis, to St-Germain-des-Prés and St-Pierre de Montmartre. They'll know not only dates and statistics but the smell of Picasso's paints, the feel of baroque marble, the sound of the bells of Notre-Dame

Cathedral. They'll experience it all, right here in this classroom. He will bring it all to them.

They're staring at you, Justin. Say something.

He clears his throat. 'This course will teach you how to analyse works of art and how to understand their historical significance. It will enable you to develop an awareness of the environment while also providing you with a deeper sensitivity to the culture and ideals of other nations. You will cover a broad range: history of painting, sculpture and architecture from Ancient Greece to modern times; early Irish art; the painters of the Italian Renaissance; the great Gothic cathedrals of Europe; the architectural splendours of the Georgian era and the artistic achievements of the twentieth century.'

He allows a silence to fall.

Are they filled with regret on hearing what lay ahead of them for the next four years of their lives? Or do their hearts beat wildly with excitement as his does, just thinking about all that is to come? Even after all these years, he still feels the same enthusiasm for the buildings, paintings and sculptures of the world. His exhilaration often leaves him breathless during lectures; he has to remember to slow down, not to tell them everything at once. Though he wants them to know everything, right now!

He looks again at their faces and has an epiphany.

You have them! They're hanging on your every word, just waiting to hear more. You've done it, they're in your grasp!

Someone farts and the room explodes with laughter.

He sighs, his bubble burst, and continues his talk in a bored tone. 'My name is Justin Hitchcock and in my special guest lectures scattered throughout the course, you will study the introduction to European painting such as the Italian Renaissance and French Impressionism. This includes the critical analysis of paintings, the importance of iconography and the various technical methods used by artists from the Book of Kells to modern day. There'll also be an introduction to European architecture. Greek temples to the present day, blah blah blah. Two volunteers to help me hand these out, please.'

And so it was another year. He wasn't at home in Chicago now; he had chased his ex-wife and daughter to live in London and was flying back and forth between there and Dublin for his guest lectures. A different country perhaps but another class of the same. First week and giddy. Another group displaying an immature lack of understanding of his passions; a deliberate turning of their backs on the possibility – no, not the possibility, the *surety* – of learning something wonderful and great.

It doesn't matter what you say now, pal, from here on in the only thing they'll go home remembering is the fart.

3

'What is it about fart jokes, Bea?'

'Oh, hi, Dad.'

'What kind of a greeting is that?'

'Oh, gee whizz, wow, Dad, so great to hear from you. It's been, what, ah shucks, three hours since you last phoned?'

'Fine, you don't have to go all porky pig on me. Is your darling mother home yet from a day out at her new life?'

'Yes, she's home.'

'And has she brought the delightful Laurence back with her?' He can't hold back his sarcasm, which he hates himself for but, unwilling to withdraw it and incapable of apologising, he does what he always does, which is to run with it, therefore making it worse. 'Laurence,' he drawls, 'Laurence of A— inguinal hernia.'

'Oh, you're such a geek. Would you ever give up talking about his trouser leg,' she sighs with boredom.

Justin kicks off the scratchy blanket of the cheap Dublin hotel he's staying in. 'Really, Bea, check it next time he's around. Those trousers are far too tight for what he's got going on down there. There should be a name for that. Something-itis.'

Balls-a-titis.

'There are only four TV channels in this dump, one in a language I don't even understand. It sounds like they're clearing their throats after one of your mother's terrible coq-au-vins. You know, in my wonderful home

back in Chicago, I had over two hundred channels.'
Dick-a-titis. Dickhead-a-titis. Ha!

'Of which none you watched.'

'But one had a choice not to watch those deplorable house-fixer-upper channels and music channels of naked women dancing around.'

'I appreciate *one* going through such an upheaval, Dad. It must be very traumatic for you, a sort-of grown man, while I, at sixteen years old, had to take this huge life adjustment of parents getting divorced and a move from Chicago to London all in my stride.'

'You got two houses and extra presents, what do you care?' he grumbles. 'And it was your idea.'

'It was my idea to go to *ballet school* in London, not for your marriage to end!'

'Oh, *ballet school*. I thought you said, "Break up, you *fool*." My mistake. Think we should move back to Chicago and get back together?'

'Nah.' He hears the smile in her voice and knows it's OK.

'Hey, you think I was going to stay in Chicago while you're all the way over this side of the world?'

'You're not even in the same country right now,' she laughs.

'Ireland is just a work trip. I'll be back in London in a few days. Honestly, Bea, there's nowhere else I'd rather be,' he assures her.

Though a Four Seasons would be nice.

'I'm thinking of moving in with Peter,' she says far too casually.

'So what is it about fart jokes?' he asks again, ignoring her. 'I mean what is it about the sound of expelling air that can stop people from being interested in some of the most incredible masterpieces ever created?'

'I take it you don't want to talk about me moving in with Peter?'

'You're a child. You and Peter can move into the wendy house, which I still have in storage. I'll set it up in the living room. It'll be real nice and cosy.'

'I'm eighteen. Not a child any more. I've lived alone away from home for two years now.'

'One year alone. Your mother left *me* alone the second year to join you, remember.'

'You and Mum met at my age.'

'And we did not live happily ever after. Stop imitating us and write your own fairy tale.'

'I would, if my overprotective father would stop butting in with his version of how the story should go.' Bea sighs and steers the conversation back to safer territory. 'Why are your students laughing at fart jokes, anyway? I thought your seminar was a one-off for post-grads who'd elected to choose your boring subject. Though why anybody would do that, is beyond me. You lecturing me on Peter is boring enough and I love him.'

Love! Ignore it and she'll forget what she said.

'It wouldn't be beyond you, if you'd listen to me when I talk. Along with my postgraduate classes, I was asked to speak to first-year students throughout the year too, an agreement I may live to regret, but no matter. On to my day job and far more pressing matters, I'm planning an exhibition at the Gallery on Dutch painting in the seventeenth century. You should come see it.'

'No, thanks.'

'Well, maybe my postgrads over the next few months will be more appreciative of my expertise.'

'You know, your students may have laughed at the fart joke but I bet at least a quarter of them donated blood.'

'They only did it because they heard they'd get a free KitKat afterward,' Justin huffs, rooting through the insufficiently filled mini-bar. 'You're angry at me for not giving blood?'

'I think you're an asshole for standing up that woman.'

'Don't use the word "asshole", Bea. Anyway, who told you that I stood her up?'

'Uncle Al.'

'Uncle Al is an asshole. And you know what else, honey? You know what the good doctor said today about donating blood?' He struggles with opening the film on the top of a Pringles box.

'What?' Bea yawns.

'That the donation is anonymous to the recipient. Hear that? *Anonymous*. So what's the point in saving someone's life if they don't even know you're the one who saved them?'

'Dad!'

'What? Come on, Bea. Lie to me and tell me you wouldn't want a bouquet of flowers for saving someone's life?'

Bea protests but he continues.

'Or a little basket of those, whaddaya call 'em muffins that you like, coconut—'

'Cinnamon,' she laughs, finally giving in.

'A little basket of cinnamon muffins outside your front door with a little note tucked into the basket saying, "Thanks, Bea, for saving my life. Anytime you want anything done, like your dry cleaning picked up, or your newspaper and a coffee delivered to your front door every morning, a chauffeur-driven car for your own personal use, front-row tickets to the opera . . ." Oh the list could go on and on.'

He gives up pulling at the film and instead picks up a corkscrew and stabs the top. 'It could be like one of those Chinese things; you know the way someone saves your life and then you're forever indebted to them. It could be nice having someone tailing you everyday; catching pianos flying out of windows and stopping them from landing on your head, that kind of thing.'

Bea calms herself. 'I hope you're joking.'

'Yeah, of course I'm joking.' Justin makes a face. 'The piano would surely kill them and that would be unfair.'

He finally pulls open the Pringles lid and throws the corkscrew across the room. It hits a glass on top of the minibar and it smashes.

'What was that?'

'House-cleaning,' he lies. 'You think I'm selfish, don't you?'

'Dad, you uprooted your life, left a great job, nice apartment and flew thousands of miles to another country just to be near me, of course I don't think you're selfish.'

Justin smiles and pops a Pringle into his mouth.

'But if you're not joking about the muffin basket, then you're definitely selfish. And if it was Blood For Life Week in my college, I would have taken part. But you have the opportunity to make it up to that woman.'

'I just feel like I'm being bullied into this entire thing. I was going to get my hair cut tomorrow, not have people stab at my veins.'

'Don't give blood if you don't want to, I don't care. But remember, if you do it, a tiny little needle isn't gonna kill you. In fact, the opposite may happen, it might save someone's life and you never know, that person could follow you around for the rest of your life leaving muffin baskets outside your door and catching pianos before they fall on your head. Now wouldn't that be nice?'

4

In a blood drive beside Trinity College's rugby pitch, Justin tries to hide his shaking hands from Sarah, while handing over his consent form and 'Health and Lifestyle' questionnaire, which frankly discloses far more about him than he'd reveal on a date. She smiles encouragingly and talks him through everything as though giving blood is the most normal thing in the world.

'Now I just need to ask you a few questions. Have you read, understood and completed the health and lifestyle questionnaire?'

Justin nods, words failing him in his clogged throat.

'And is all the information you've provided true and accurate to the best of your knowledge?'

'Why?' he croaks. 'Does it not look right to you? Because if it doesn't I can always leave and come back again another time.'

She smiles at him with the same look his mother wore before tucking him into bed and turning off the light.

'OK, we're all set. I'm just going to do a haemoglobin test,' she explains.

'Does that check for diseases?' He looks around nervously at the equipment in the van. *Please don't let me have any diseases. That would be too embarrassing. Not likely anyway. Can you even remember the last time you had sex?*

'No, this just measures the iron in your blood.' She takes a pinprick of blood from the pad of his finger. 'Blood is tested later for diseases and STDs.'

'Must be handy for checking up on boyfriends,' he jokes, feeling sweat tickle his upper lip. He studies his finger.

She quietens as she carries out the quick test.

Justin lies supine on a cushioned bench and extends his left arm. Sarah wraps a pressure cuff around his upper arm, making the veins more prominent, and she disinfects his inner elbow.

Don't look at the needle, don't look at the needle.

He looks at the needle and the ground swirls beneath him. His throat tightens.

'Is this going to hurt?' Justin swallows hard as his shirt clings to his saturated back.

'Just a little sting,' she smiles, approaching him with a cannula in her hand.

He smells her sweet perfume and it distracts him momentarily. As she leans over, he sees down her V-neck sweater. A black lace bra.

'I want you to take this in your hand and squeeze it repeatedly.'

'What?' he laughs nervously.

'The ball,' she smiles.

'Oh.' He takes a small soft ball into his hand. 'What does this do?' His voice shakes.

'It's to help speed up the process.'

He pumps at top speed.

Sarah laughs. 'Not yet. And not that fast, Justin.'

Sweat rolls down his back. His hair sticks to his sticky forehead. *You should have gone for the haircut, Justin. What kind of a stupid idea was this—* 'Ouch.'

'That wasn't so bad, was it?' she says softly, as though talking to a child.

Justin's heart beats loudly in his ears. He pumps the ball in his hand to the rhythm of his heartbeat. He imagines his heart pumping the blood, the blood flowing through his veins. He sees it reach the needle, go through the tube and he waits to feel faint. But the dizziness never comes and so he watches his blood run through the tube and down under the bed into the collection bag she has thoughtfully hidden below the bed on a scale.

'Do I get a KitKat after this?'

She laughs. 'Of course.'

'And then we get to go for drinks or are you just using me for my body?'

'Drinks are fine, but I must warn you against doing anything strenuous today. Your body needs to recover.'

He catches sight of her lace bra again. *Yeah, sure.*

Fifteen minutes later, Justin looks at his pint of blood with pride. He doesn't want it to go to some stranger, he almost wants to bring it to the hospital himself, survey the wards and present it to someone he really cares about, someone special, for it's the first thing to come straight from his heart in a very long time.

Present Day

5

I open my eyes slowly.

White light fills them. Slowly, objects come into focus and the white light fades. Orangey pink now. I move my eyes around. I'm in a hospital. A television high up on the wall. Green fills its screen. I focus more. Horses. Jumping and racing. Dad must be in the room. I lower my eyes and there he is with his back to me in an armchair. He thumps his fists lightly on the chair's arms, I see his tweed cap appearing and disappearing behind the back of the chair as he bounces up and down. The springs beneath him squeak.

The horse racing is silent. So is he. Like a silent movie being carried out before me, I watch him. I wonder if it's my ears that aren't allowing me to hear him. He springs out of his chair now faster than I've seen him move in a long time, and he raises his fist at the television, quietly urging his horse on.

The television goes black. His two fists open and he raises his hands up in the air, looks up to the ceiling and beseeches God. He puts his hands in his pockets, feels around and pulls the material out. They're empty and the pockets of his brown trousers hang inside out for all to see. He pats down his chest, feeling for money. Checks the small pocket of his brown cardigan. Grumbles. So it's not my ears.

He turns to feel around in his overcoat beside me and I shut my eyes quickly.

I'm not ready yet. Nothing has happened to me until

they tell me. Last night will remain a nightmare in my mind until they tell me it was true. The longer I close my eyes, the longer everything remains as it was. The bliss of ignorance.

I hear him rooting around in his overcoat, I hear change rattling and I hear the clunk as the coins fall into the television. I risk opening my eyes again and there he is back in his armchair, cap bouncing up and down, pounding his fists against the air.

My curtain is closed to my right but I can tell I share a room with others. I don't know how many. It's quiet. There's no air in the room; it's stuffy with stale sweat. The giant windows that take up the entire wall to my left are closed. The light is so bright I can't see out. I allow my eyes to adjust and finally I see. A bus stop across the road. A woman waits by the stop, shopping bags by her feet and on her hip sits a baby, bare chubby legs bouncing in the Indian summer sun. I look away immediately. Dad is watching me. He is leaning out over the side of the armchair, twisting his head around, like a child from his cot.

'Hi, love.'

'Hi.' I feel I haven't spoken for such a long time, and I expect to croak. But I don't. My voice is pure, pours out like honey. Like nothing's happened. But nothing has happened. Not yet. Not until they tell me.

With both hands on the arms of the chair he slowly pulls himself up. Like a seesaw, he makes his way over to the side of the bed. Up and down, down and up. He was born with a leg length discrepancy, his left leg longer than his right. Despite the special shoes he was given in later years, he still sways, the motion instilled in him since he learned to walk. He hates wearing those shoes and, despite our warnings and his back pains, he goes back to what he knows. I'm so used to the sight of his body going up and down, down and up. I recall as a child holding his hand and going for walks. How my arm would move in perfect rhythm with him. Being pulled up as he stepped down on his right leg, being pushed down as he stepped on his left.

He was always so strong. Always so capable. Always fixing things. Lifting things, mending things. Always with a screwdriver in his hand, taking things apart and putting them back together – remote controls, radios, alarm clocks, plugs. A handyman for the entire street. His legs were uneven, but his hands, always and for ever, steady as a rock.

He takes his cap off as he nears me, clutches it with both hands, moves it around in circles like a steering wheel as he watches me with concern. He steps onto his right leg and down he goes. Bends his left leg. His position of rest.

'Are you . . . em . . . they told me that . . . eh.' He clears his throat. 'They told me to . . .' He swallows hard and his thick messy eyebrows furrow and hide his glassy eyes. 'You lost . . . you lost, em . . .'

My lower lip trembles.

His voice breaks when he speaks again. 'You lost a lot of blood, Joyce. They . . .' He lets go of his cap with one hand and makes circular motions with his crooked finger, trying to remember. 'They did a transfusion of the blood thingy on you so you're em . . . you're OK with your bloods now.'

My lower lip still trembles and my hands automatically go to my belly, not long enough gone to even show swelling under the blankets. I look to him hopefully, only realising now how much I am still holding on, how much I have convinced myself the awful incident in the labour room was all a terrible nightmare. Perhaps I imagined my baby's silence that filled the room in that final moment. Perhaps there were cries that I just didn't hear. Of course it's possible – by that stage I had little energy and was fading away – maybe I just didn't hear the first little miraculous breath of life that everybody else witnessed.

Dad shakes his head sadly. No, it had been me that had made those screams instead.

My lip trembles more now, bounces up and down and I can't stop it. My body shakes terribly and I can't stop it either. The tears; they well, but I stop them from falling. If I start now I know I will never stop.

I'm making a noise. An unusual noise I've never heard before. Groaning. Grunting. A combination of both. Dad grabs my hand and holds it hard. The feel of his skin brings me back to last night, me lying at the end of the stairs. He doesn't say anything. But what can a person say? I don't even know.

I doze in and out. I wake and remember a conversation with a doctor and wonder if it was a dream. Lost your baby, Joyce, we did all we could . . . blood transfusion . . . Who needs to remember something like that? No one. Not me.

When I wake again the curtain beside me has been pulled open. There are three small children running around, chasing one another around the bed while their father, I assume, calls to them to stop in a language I don't recognise. Their mother, I assume, lies in bed. She looks tired. We catch eyes and smile at one another.

I know how you feel, her sad smile says, I know how you feel.

What are we going to do? my smile says back to her.

I don't know, her eyes say. I don't know.

Will we be OK?

She turns her head away from me, her smile gone.

Dad calls over to them. 'Where are you lot from then?'

'Excuse me?' her husband asks.

'I said where are you lot from then?' Dad repeats. 'Not from around here, I see.' Dad's voice is cheery and pleasant. No insults intended. No insults ever intended.

'We are from Nigeria,' the man responds.

'Nigeria,' Dad replies. 'Where would that be then?'

'In Africa.' The man's tone is pleasant too. Just an old man starved of conversation, trying to be friendly, he realises.

'Ah, Africa. Never been there myself. Is it hot there?

I'd say it is. Hotter than here. Get a good tan, I'd say, not that you need it,' he laughs. 'Do you get cold here?'

'Cold?' the African smiles.

'Yes, you know.' Dad wraps his arms around his body and pretends to shiver. 'Cold?'

'Yes,' the man laughs. 'Sometimes I do.'

'Thought so. I do too and I'm from here,' Dad explains. 'The chill gets right into my bones. But I'm not a great one for heat either. Skin goes red, just burns. My daughter, Joyce, goes brown. That's her over there.' He points at me and I close my eyes quickly.

'A lovely daughter,' the man says politely.

'Ah, she is.' Silence while I assume they watch me. 'She was on one of those Spanish islands a few months back and came back black, she did. Well, not as black as you, you know, but she got a fair ol' tan on her. Peeled, though. You probably don't peel.'

The man laughs politely. That's Dad. Never means any harm but has never left the country in his entire life. A fear of flying holds him back. Or so he says.

'Anyway, I hope your lovely lady feels better soon. It's an awful thing to be sick on your holliers.'

With that I open my eyes.

'Ah, welcome back, love. I was just talking to these nice neighbours of ours.' He seesaws up to me again, his cap in his hands. Rests on his right leg, goes down, bends his left leg. 'You know I think we're the only Irish people in this hospital. The nurse that was here a minute ago, she's from Sing-a-song or someplace like that.'

'Singapore, Dad,' I smile.

'That's it.' He raises his eyebrows. 'You met her already, did you? They all speak English, though, the foreigners do. Sure, isn't that better than being on your holidays and having to do all that signed-languagey stuff.' He puts his cap down on the bed and wiggles his fingers around.

'Dad,' I smile, 'you've never been out of the country in your life.'

'Haven't I heard the lads at the Monday Club talking about it? Frank was away in that place last week – oh, what's that place?' He shuts his eyes and thinks hard. 'The place where they make the chocolates?'

'Switzerland.'

'No.'

'Belgium.'

'No,' he says, frustrated now. 'The little round bally things all crunchy inside. You can get the white ones now but I prefer the original dark ones.'

'Maltesers?' I laugh, but feel pain and stop.

'That's it. He was in Maltesers.'

'Dad, it's Malta.'

'That's it. He was in Malta.' He is silent. 'Do they make Maltesers?'

'I don't know. Maybe. So what happened to Frank in Malta?'

He squeezes his eyes shut again and thinks. 'I can't remember what I was about to say now.'

Silence. He hates not being able to remember. He used to remember everything.

'Did you make any money on the horses?' I ask.

'A few bob. Enough for a few rounds at the Monday Club tonight.'

'But today is Tuesday.'

'It's on a Tuesday on account of the bank holiday,' he explains, seesawing around to the other side of the bed to sit down.

I can't laugh. I'm too sore and it seems some of my sense of humour was taken away with my child.

'You don't mind if I go, do you, Joyce? I'll stay if you want, I really don't mind, it's not important.'

'Of course it's important. You haven't missed a Monday night for twenty years.'

'Apart from bank holidays!' He lifts a crooked finger and his eyes dance.

'Apart from bank holidays,' I smile, and grab his finger.

'Well,' he takes my hand, 'you're more important than a few pints and a singsong.'

'What would I do without you?' My eyes fill again.

'You'd be just fine, love. Besides . . .' he looks at me warily, 'you have Conor.'

I let go of his hand and look away. What if I don't want Conor any more?

'I tried to call him last night on the hand phone but there was no answer. But maybe I tried the numbers wrong,' he adds quickly. 'There are so many more numbers on the hand phones.'

'Mobiles, Dad,' I say distractedly.

'Ah, yes. The mobiles. He keeps calling when you're asleep. He's going to come home as soon as he can get a flight. He's very worried.'

'That's nice of him. Then we can get down to the business of spending the next ten years of our married life trying to have babies.' Back to business. A nice little distraction to give our relationship some sort of meaning.

'Ah now, love . . .'

The first day of the rest of my life and I'm not sure I want to be here. I know I should be thanking somebody for this but I really don't feel like it. Instead I wish they hadn't bothered.

6

I watch the three children playing together on the floor of the hospital, little fingers and toes, chubby cheeks and plump lips – the faces of their parents clearly etched on theirs. My heart drops into my stomach and it twists. My eyes fill again and I have to look away.

'Mind if I have a grape?' Dad chirps. He's like a little canary swinging in a cage beside me.

'Of course you can. Dad, you should go home now, go get something to eat. You need your energy.'

He picks up a banana. 'Potassium,' he smiles, and moves his arms rigorously. 'I'll be jogging home tonight.'

'How did you get here?' It suddenly occurs to me that he hasn't been into the city for years. It all became too fast for him, buildings suddenly sprouting up where there weren't any, roads with traffic going in different directions from before. With great sadness he sold his car too, his failing eyesight too much of a danger for him and others on the roads. Seventy-five years old, his wife dead ten years. Now he has a routine of his own, content to stay around the local area, chatting to his neighbours, church every Sunday and Wednesday, Monday Club every Monday (apart from the bank holidays when it's on a Tuesday), butchers on a Tuesday, his crosswords, puzzles and TV shows during the days, his garden all the moments in between.

'Fran from next door drove me in.' He puts the banana down, still laughing to himself about his jogging joke, and pops another grape into his mouth. 'Almost had me killed two or three times. Enough to let me know there is a God if ever there was a time I doubted. I asked for seedless grapes; these aren't seedless,' he frowns. Liver-spotted hands put the bunch back on the side cabinet. He takes seeds out of his mouth and looks around for a bin.

'Do you still believe in your God now, Dad?' It comes out crueller than I mean to but the anger is almost unbearable.

'I do believe, Joyce.' As always, no offence taken. He puts the pips in his handkerchief and places it back in his pocket. 'The Lord acts in mysterious ways, in ways we often can neither explain nor understand, tolerate nor bear. I understand how you can question Him now – we all do at times. When your mother died I . . .' he trails off and abandons the sentence as always, the furthest he will go to being disloyal about his God, the furthest he will go to discussing the loss of his wife. 'But this time God answered all my prayers. He sat up and heard me calling last night. He said to me,' Dad puts on a broad Cavan accent, the accent he had as a child before moving to Dublin in his teens, '"No problem, Henry. I hear you loud and clear. It's all in hand so don't you be worrying. I'll do this for you, no bother at all." He saved you. He kept my girl alive and for that I'll be forever grateful to Him, sad as we may be about the passing of another.'

I have no response to that, but I soften.

He pulls his chair closer to my bedside and it screeches along the floor.

'And I believe in an afterlife,' he says a little quieter now. 'That I do. I believe in the paradise of heaven, up there in the clouds, and everyone that was once here is up there. Including the sinners, for God's a forgiver, that I believe.'

'Everyone?' I fight the tears. I fight them from falling. If I start I know I will never stop. 'What about my baby, Dad? Is my baby there?'

He looks pained. We hadn't spoken much about my

pregnancy. Early days and we were all worried, nobody more than he. Only days ago we'd had a minor falling-out over my asking him to store our spare bed in his garage. I had started to prepare the nursery, you see . . . Oh dear, the nursery. The spare bed and junk just cleared out. The cot already purchased. Pretty yellow on the walls. 'Buttercup Dream' with a little duckie border.

Five months to go. Some people, my father included, would think preparing the nursery at four months is premature but we'd been waiting six years for a baby, for this baby. Nothing premature about that.

'Ah, love, you know I don't know . . .'

'I was going to call him Sean if it was a boy,' I hear myself finally say aloud. I have been saying these things in my head all day, over and over, and here they are, spilling out of me instead of the tears.

'Ah, that's a nice name. Sean.'

'Grace, if it was a girl. After Mum. She would have liked that.'

His jaw sets at this and he looks away. Anyone who doesn't know him would think this has angered him. I know this is not the case. I know it's the emotion gathering in his jaw, like a giant reservoir, storing and locking it all away until absolutely necessary, waiting for those rare moments when the drought within him calls for those walls to break and for the emotions to gush.

'But for some reason I thought it was a boy. I don't know why but I just felt it somehow. I could have been wrong. I was going to call him Sean,' I repeat.

Dad nods. 'That's right. A fine name.'

'I used to talk to him. Sing to him. I wonder if he heard.' My voice is far away. I feel like I'm calling out from the hollow of a tree, where I hide.

Silence while I imagine a future that will never be with little imaginary Sean. Of singing to him every night, of marshmallow skin and splashes at bath time. Of kicking legs and bicycle rides. Of sandcastle architecture and foot-ball-related hot-headed tantrums. Anger at a missed life – no, worse – a lost life, overrides my thoughts.

'I wonder if he even knew.'

'Knew what, love?'

'What was happening. What he would be missing. Did he think I was sending him away? I hope he doesn't blame me. I was all he had and—' I stop. Torture over for now. I feel seconds away from screaming with such terror, I must stop. If I start my tears now I know I will never stop.

'Where is he now, Dad? How can you even die when you haven't even been born yet?'

'Ah, love.' He takes my hand and squeezes it again.

'Tell me.'

This time he thinks about it. Long and hard. He pats my hair, with steady fingers takes the strands from my face and tucks them behind my ears. He hasn't done that since I was a little girl.

'I think he's in heaven, love. Oh, there's no thinking involved – I know so. He's up there with your mother, yes he is. Sitting on her lap while she plays rummy with Pauline, robbing her blind and cackling away. She's up there all right.' He looks up and wags his forefinger at the ceiling. 'Now you take care of baby Sean for us, Gracie, you hear? She'll be tellin' him all about you, she will, about when you were a baby, about the day you took your first steps, about the day you got your first tooth. She'll tell him about your first day of school and your last day of school and every day in between, and he'll know all about you so that when you walk through those gates up there, as an old woman far older than me now, he'll look up from rummy and say, "Ah, there she is now. The woman herself. My mammy." Straight away he'll know.'

The lump in my throat, so huge I can barely swallow, prevents me from saying the thank you I want to express, but perhaps he sees it in my eyes as he nods in acknowledgement and then turns his attention back to the TV while I stare out the window at nothing.

'There's a nice chapel here, love. Maybe you should go visit, when you're good and ready. You don't even have to say anything, He won't mind. Just sit there and think. I find it helpful.'

I think it's the last place in the world I want to be.

'It's a nice place to be,' Dad says, reading my mind. He watches me and I can almost hear him praying for me to leap out of bed and grab the rosary beads he's placed by the bedside.

'It's a rococo building, you know,' I say suddenly, and have no idea what I'm talking about.

'What is?' Dad's eyebrows furrow and his eyes disappear underneath, like two snails disappearing into their shells. 'This hospital?'

I think hard. 'What were we talking about?'

Then he thinks hard. 'Maltesers. No!'

He's silent for a moment, then starts answering as though in a quick-fire round of a quiz.

'Bananas! No. Heaven! No. The chapel! We were talking about the chapel.' He flashes a million-dollar smile, jubilant he succeeded in remembering the conversation of less than one minute ago. He goes further now. 'And then you said it's a rickety building. But honestly it felt fine to me. A bit old but, sure, there's nothin' wrong with being old and rickety.' He winks at me.

'The chapel is a *rococo* building, not rickety,' I correct him, feeling like a teacher. 'It's famous for the elaborate stucco work which adorns the ceiling. It's the work of French stuccadore, Barthelemy Cramillion.'

'Is that so, love? When did he do that, then?' He moves his chair in closer to the bed. Loves nothing more than a *scéal*.

'In 1762.' So precise. So random. So natural. So inexplicable that I know it.

'That long? I didn't know the hospital was here since then.'

'It's been here since 1757,' I reply, and then frown. How on earth do I know that? But I can't stop myself, almost like my mouth is on autopilot, completely unattached to my brain. 'It was designed by the same man

417

who did Leinster House. Richard Cassells was his name. One of the most famous architects of the time.'

'I've heard of him, all right,' Dad lies. 'If you'd said Dick I'd have known straight away.' He chuckles.

'It was Bartholomew Mosse's brainchild,' I explain and I don't know where the words are coming from, don't know where the knowledge is coming from. From where else, I don't know. Like a feeling of *déjà vu* – these words, this feeling is familiar but I haven't heard them or spoken them in this hospital. I think maybe I'm making it up but I know somewhere deep inside that I'm correct. A warm feeling floods my body.

'In 1745 he purchased a small theatre called the New Booth and he converted it into Dublin's first lying-in hospital.'

'It stood here, did it? The theatre?'

'No, it was on George's Lane. This was all just fields. But eventually that became too small and he bought the fields that were here, consulted with Richard Cassells and in 1757 the new lying-in hospital, now known as the Rotunda, was opened by the Lord Lieutenant. On the eighth of December, if I recall correctly.'

Dad is confused. 'I didn't know you had an interest in that kind of thing, Joyce. How do you know all that?'

I frown. I didn't know I knew that either. Suddenly frustration overwhelms me and I shake my head aggressively.

'I want a haircut,' I add angrily, blowing my fringe off my forehead. 'I want to get out of here.'

'OK, love.' Dad's voice is quiet. 'A little longer, is all.'

7

Get a haircut! Justin blows his fringe out of his eyes and glares with dissatisfaction at his reflection in the mirror.

Until his image caught his eye, he was packing his bag to go back to London while whistling the happy tune of a recently divorced man who'd just been laid by the first woman since his wife. Well, the second time that year, but the first that he could recall with some small degree of pride. Now, standing before the full-length mirror, his whistling stalls, the image of his Fabio self failing miserably against the reality. He corrects his posture, sucks in his cheeks and flexes his muscles, vowing that now that the divorce cloud has lifted, he will get his body back in order. Forty-three years old, he is handsome and he knows it, but it's not a view that is held with arrogance. His opinions on his looks are merely understood with the same logic he applies to tasting a fine wine. The grape was merely grown in the right place, under the right conditions. Some degree of nurturing and love mixed with later moments of being completely trampled on and walked all over. He possesses the common sense enabling him to recognise he was born with good genes and features that were in proportion, in the right places. He should be neither praised nor blamed for this just as a less attractive person should not be viewed with flared nostrils and a media-obsessed induced smirk. It's just how it is.

At almost six feet, he is tall, his shoulders broad, his

hair still thick and chestnut brown, though greying at the sides. This he does not mind, he's had grey hairs since his twenties and has always felt they give him a distinguished look. Though there were some, afraid of the very nature of life, that viewed his salt-and-pepper sideburns as a thorn that would burst the bubble of their pretend life every time he was in their presence. They would come at him, bowing over and hunch-backed, and taking on the appearance of a sixteenth-century black-toothed tramp, thrusting hair dye at him as though it were a carafe of precious water from the fountain of eternal life.

For Justin, moving on and change are what he expects. He is not one for pausing, for becoming stuck in life, though he didn't expect his particular philos-ophy of ageing and greying to apply to his marriage. Jennifer left him two years ago to ponder this, though not just this, but for a great many other reasons too. So many, in fact, he wishes he had taken out a pen and notepad and listed them as she bellowed at him in her tirade of hate. In the initial dark lonely nights that followed, Justin held the bottle of dye in his hand and wondered if he gave in to his solid tight philosophy, would he make things all right? Would he wake up in the morning and Jennifer be in their bed; would the light scar on his chin have healed from where the wedding ring had landed; would the list of things about him she hated so much be the very things she loved? He sobered up then and emptied the dye down his rented accommodation kitchen sink, blackened stain-less steel that proved a reminder to him everyday of his decision to stay rooted in reality, until he moved to London to be closer to his daughter, much to his ex-wife's disgust.

Through strands of his long fringe hanging over his eyes, he has a vision of the man he expects to see. Leaner, younger, perhaps with fewer wrinkles around the eyes. Any faults, such as the expanding waistline, are partly due to age and partly of his own doing, because he took to beer and takeaways for comfort during his divorce process rather than walking or the occasional jog.

Repeated flashbacks of the previous night draw his eyes back to the bed, where he and Sarah finally got to know one another intimately. All day he definitely felt like the big man on campus and he was just seconds away from interrupting his talk on Dutch and Flemish painting to give details of his previous night's performance. First-year students in the midst of Rag Week, only three-quarters of the class had shown up after the previous night's foam party and those that were in attendance he was sure wouldn't notice if he launched into a detailed analysis of his lovemaking skills. He didn't test his assumptions, all the same.

Blood For Life Week is over, much to Justin's relief, and Sarah has moved on from the college, back to her base. On his return to Dublin this month he coincidentally bumped into her in a bar, that he just happened to know she frequented, and they went from there. He wasn't sure if he would see her again though his inside jacket pocket was safely padded with her number.

He has to admit that while the previous night was indeed delightful – a few too many bottles of Château Olivier, which, until last night he's always found disappointing despite its ideal location in Bordeaux, in a lively bar on the Green, followed by a trip to his hotel room – he feels much was missing from his conquest. He acquired some Dutch courage from his hotel minibar before calling round to see her, and by the time he arrived, he was already incapable of serious conversation or, more seriously, incapable of conversation – *Oh, for Christ's sake, Justin, what man do you know cares about the damn conversation?* But, despite ending up in his bed, he feels that Sarah did care about the conversation. He feels that perhaps there were things she wanted to say to him and perhaps did say while he saw those sad blue eyes boring into his and her rosebud lips opening and closing, but his Jameson whiskey wouldn't allow him to hear, instead singing over her words in his head like a petulant child.

With his second seminar in two months complete, Justin throws his clothes into his bag, happy to see the back of his miserable musty room. Friday afternoon, time to fly back to London. Back to his daughter, and his younger brother, Al, and sister-in-law, Doris, visiting from Chicago. He departs the hotel, steps out onto the cobbled side streets of Temple Bar and into his waiting taxi.

'The airport, please.'

'Here on holidays?' the driver asks immediately.

'No.' Justin looks out the window, hoping this will end the conversation.

'Working?' The driver starts the engine.

'Yes.'

'Where do you work?'

'A college.'

'Which one?'

Justin sighs. 'Trinity.'

'You the janitor?' Those green eyes twinkle playfully at him in the mirror.

'I'm a lecturer on Art and Architecture,' he says defensively, folding his arms and blowing his floppy fringe from his eyes.

'Architecture, huh? I used to be a builder.'

Justin doesn't respond and hopes the conversation will end there.

'So where are ye off to? Off on holiday?'

'Nope.'

'What is it then?

'I live in London.' *And my US social security number is . . .*

'And you work here?'

'Yep.'

'Would you not just live here?'

'Nope.'

'Why's that then?'

'Because I'm a guest lecturer here. A previous

colleague of mine invited me to give a seminar once a month.'

'Ah.' The driver smiles at him in the mirror as though he'd been trying to fool him. 'So what do you do in London?' His eyes interrogate him.

I'm a serial killer who preys on inquisitive cab drivers.

'Lots of different things.' Justin sighs and caves in as the driver waits for more. 'I'm the editor of the *Art and Architectural Review*, the only truly international art and architectural publication,' he says proudly. 'I started it ten years ago and still we're unrivalled. Highest selling magazine of its kind.' *Twenty thousand subscribers, you liar.*

There's no reaction.

'I'm also a curator.'

The driver winces. 'You've to touch dead bodies?'

Justin scrunches his face in confusion. 'What? No.' Then adds unnecessarily, 'I'm also a regular panelist on a BBC art and culture show.'

Twice in five years doesn't quite constitute regular, Justin. Oh, shut up.

The driver studies Justin now, in the rearview mirror. 'You're on TV?' He narrows his eyes. 'I don't recognise you.'

'Well, do you watch the show?'

'No.'

Well, then.

Justin rolls his eyes. He throws off his suit jacket, opens another of his shirt buttons and lowers the window. His hair sticks to his forehead. Still. A few weeks have gone by and he still hasn't been to the barber. He blows his fringe out of his eyes.

They stop at a red light and Justin looks to his left. A hair salon.

'Hey, would you mind pulling over on the left just for a few minutes?'

'Look, Conor, don't worry about it. Stop apologising,' I say into the phone tiredly. He exhausts me. Every little word with him drains me. 'Dad is here with me now and we're going to get a taxi to the house together, even though I'm perfectly capable of sitting in a car by myself.'

Outside the hospital, Dad holds the door open for me and I climb into the taxi. Finally I'm going home but I don't feel the relief I was hoping for. There's nothing but dread. I dread meeting people I know and having to explain what has happened, over and over again. I dread walking into my house and having to face the half-decorated nursery. I dread having to get rid of the nursery, having to replace it with a spare bed and filling the wardrobes with my own overflow of shoes and bags I'll never wear. As though a bedroom for them alone is as good a replacement as a child. I dread having to go to work instead of taking the leave I had planned. I dread seeing Conor. I dread going back to a loveless marriage with no baby to distract us. I dread living every day of the rest of my life while Conor drones on and on down the phone about wanting to be here for me, when it seems my telling him *not* to come home has been my mantra for the past few days. I know it would be common sense for me to want my husband to come rushing home to me – in fact, for my husband to want to come rushing home to me – but there are many buts in our marriage and this *incident* is not a regular normal occurrence. It deserves outlandish behaviour. To behave the right way, to do the adult thing feels wrong to me because I don't want anybody around me. I've been poked and prodded psychologically and physically. I want to be on my own to grieve. I want to feel sorry for myself without sympathetic words and clinical explanations. I want to be illogical, self-pitying, self-examining, bitter and lost for just a few more days, please, world, and I want to do it alone.

Though that is not unusual in our marriage.

Conor's an engineer. He travels abroad to work for months before coming home for one month and going off again. I used to get so used to my own company and routine that for the first week of him being home

I'd be irritable and wish he'd go back. That changed over time, of course. Now that irritability stretches to the entire month of him being home. And it's become glaringly obvious I'm not alone in that feeling.

When Conor took the job all those years ago, it was difficult being away from one another for so long. I used to visit him as much as I could but it was difficult to keep taking time off work. The visits got shorter, rarer, then stopped.

I always thought our marriage could survive anything as long as we both tried. But then I found myself having to try to try. I dug beneath the new layers of complexities we'd created over the years to get to the beginning of the relationship. What was it, I wondered, that we had then that we could revive? What was the thing that could make two people want to promise one another to spend every day of the rest of their lives together? Ah, I found it. It was a thing called love. A small simple word. If only it didn't mean so much, our marriage would be flawless.

My mind has wandered much while lying in that hospital bed. At times it has stalled in its wandering, like when entering a room and then forgetting what for. It stands alone dumbstruck. At those times it has been numb, and when staring at the pink walls I have thought of nothing but of the fact that I am staring at pink walls.

My mind has bounced from numbness to feeling too much, but on an occasion while wandering far, I dug deep to find a memory of when I was six years old and I had a favourite tea set given to me by my grandmother Betty. She kept it in her house for me to play with when I called over on Saturdays, and during the afternoons when my grandmother was 'taking tea' with her friends I would dress in one of my mother's pretty dresses from when she was a child and have afternoon tea with Aunt Jemima, the cat. The dresses never quite fit but I wore them all the same, and Aunt Jemima and I never did take to tea but we were both polite enough to keep up the pretence until my parents came to collect me at the end of the day. I told this story to Conor a few years ago and he laughed, missing the point.

It was an easy point to miss – I won't hold him accountable for that – but what my mind was shouting at him to understand was that I've increasingly found that people never truly tire of playing games and dressing up, no matter how many years pass. Our lies now are just more sophisticated; our words to deceive, more eloquent. From cowboys and Indians, doctors and nurses, to husband and wife, we've never stopped pretending. Sitting in the taxi beside Dad, while listening to Conor over the phone, I realise I've stopped pretending.

'Where is Conor?' Dad asks as soon as I've hung up.

He opens the top button of his shirt and loosens his tie. He dresses in a shirt and tie every time he leaves his house, never forgets his cap. He looks for the handle on the car door, to roll the window down.

'It's electronic, Dad. There's the button. He's still in Japan. He'll be home in a few days.'

'I thought he was coming back yesterday.' He puts the window all the way down and is almost blown away. His cap topples off his head and the few strands of hair left on his head stick up. He fixes the cap back on his head, has a mini battle with the button before finally figuring out how to leave a small gap at the top for air to enter the stuffy taxi.

'Ha! Gotcha,' he smiles victoriously, thumping his fist at the window.

I wait until he's finished fighting with the window to answer. 'I told him not to.'

'You told who what, love?'

'Conor. You were asking about Conor, Dad.'

'Ah, that's right, I was. Home soon, is he?'

I nod.

The day is hot and I blow my fringe up from my sticky forehead. I feel my hair sticking to the back of my clammy neck. Suddenly it feels heavy and greasy on my head. Brown and scraggy, it weighs me down and once again I have the overwhelming urge to shave it all off. I become agitated in my seat and Dad, sensing it again, knows not to say anything. I've been doing that all week: experiencing anger beyond comprehension, so that I want to drive my fists through the walls and punch the nurses. Then I become weepy and feel such loss inside me it's as if I'll never be filled again. I prefer the anger. Anger is better. Anger is hot and filling and gives me something to cling on to.

We stop at a set of traffic lights and I look to my left. A hair salon.

'Pull over here, please.'

'What are you doing, Joyce?'

'Wait in the car, Dad. I'll be ten minutes. I'm just going to get a quick haircut. I can't take it any more.'

Dad looks at the salon and then to the taxi driver and they both know not to say anything. The taxi directly in front of us indicates and moves over to the side of the road too. We pull up behind it.

A man ahead of us gets out of the car and I freeze with one foot out of the car, to watch him. He's familiar and I think I know him. He pauses and looks at me. We stare at one another for a while. Search each other's face. He scratches at his left arm; something that holds my attention for far too long. The moment is unusual and goose bumps rise on my skin. The last thing I want is to see somebody I know, and I look away quickly.

He looks away from me too and begins to walk.

'What are you doing?' Dad asks far too loudly, and I finally get out of the car.

I start walking towards the hair salon and it becomes clear that our destination is the same. My walk becomes mechanical, awkward, self-conscious. Something about him makes me disjointed. Unsettled. Perhaps it's the possibility of having to tell somebody there will be no baby. Yes, a month of non-stop baby talk and there will be no baby to show for it. Sorry, guys. I feel guilty for it, as though I've cheated my friends and family. The longest tease of all. A baby that will never be. My heart is twisted at the thought of it.

He holds open the door to the salon and smiles. Handsome. Fresh-faced. Tall. Broad. Athletic. Perfect. Is he glowing? I must know him.

'Thank you,' I say.

'You're welcome.'

We both pause, look at one another, back to the two identical taxis waiting for us by the pavement and back to one another. I think he's about to say something else but I quickly look away and step inside.

The salon is empty and two staff members are sitting down chatting. They are two men; one has a mullet, the other is bleached blond. They see us and spring to attention.

'Which one do you want?' the American says out of the side of his mouth.

'The blond,' I smile.

'The mullet it is then,' he says.

My mouth falls open but I laugh.

'Hello there, loves.' The mullet man approaches us. 'How can I help you?' He looks back and forth from the American to me. 'Who is getting their hair done today?'

'Well, both of us, I assume, right?' American man looks at me and I nod.

'Oh, pardon me, I thought you were together.'

I realise we are so close our hips are almost touching. We both look down at our adjoined hips, then up to join eyes and then we both take one step away in the opposite direction.

'You two should try synchronised swimming,' the hairdresser laughs, but the joke dies when we fail to react. 'Ashley, you take the lovely lady. Now come with me.' He leads his client to a chair. The American makes a face at me while being led away and I laugh again.

'Right, I just want two inches off, please,' the American says. 'The last time I got it done they took, like, twenty off. Please, just two inches,' he stresses.

'I've got a taxi waiting outside to take me to the airport, so as quick as possible too, please.'

His hairdresser laughs. 'Sure, no problem. Are you going back to America?'

The man rolls his eyes. 'No, I'm not going to America, I'm not going on holiday and I'm not going to meet anyone at arrivals. I'm just going to take a flight. Away. Out of here. You Irish ask a lot of questions.'

'Do we?'

'Y—' he stalls and narrows his eyes at the hairdresser.

'Gotcha,' the hairdresser smiles, pointing the scissors at him.

'Yes you did.' Gritted teeth. 'You got me good.'

I chuckle aloud and he immediately looks at me. He seems slightly confused. Maybe we do know each other. Maybe he works with Conor. Maybe I went to school with him. Or college. Perhaps he's in the property business and I've worked with him. I can't have; he's American. Maybe I showed him a property. Maybe he's famous and I shouldn't be staring. I become embarrassed and I turn away again quickly.

My hairdresser wraps a black cape around me and I steal another glance at the man beside me, in the mirror. He looks at me. I look away, then back at him. He looks away. And our tennis match of glances is played out for the duration of our visit.

'So what will it be for you, madam?'

'All off,' I say, trying to avoid my reflection but I feel cold hands on the sides of my hot cheeks, raising my head, and I am forced to stare at myself face to face. There is something unnerving about being forced to look at yourself when you are unwilling to come to terms with something. Something raw and real that you can't run away from. You can lie to yourself, to your mind and in your mind all of the time but when you look yourself in the face, well, you know that you're lying. I am not OK. That, I did not hide from myself, and the truth of it stared me in the face. My cheeks are sunken, small black rings below my eyes, red lines like eyeliner still sting from my night tears. But apart from that, I still look like me. Despite this huge change in my life, I look exactly the same. Tired, but me. I don't know what I'd expected. A totally changed woman, someone that people would look at and just know had been through a traumatic experience. Yet the mirror told me this: you can't know everything by looking at me. You can *never* know by looking at someone.

I'm five foot five, with medium-length hair that lands on my shoulders. My hair colour is midway between blonde and brown. I'm a medium kind of person. Not fat, not skinny; I exercise twice a week, jog a little, walk a little, swim a little. Nothing to excess, nothing not enough. Not obsessed, addicted to anything. I'm neither out-going nor shy, but a little of both, depending on my mood, depending on the occasion. I never overdo anything and enjoy most things I do. I'm seldom bored and rarely whine. When I drink I get tipsy but never fall over or get ill. I like my job, don't love it. I'm pretty, not stunning, not ugly; don't expect too much, am never too disappointed. I'm never overwhelmed or under it either; just nicely whelmed. I'm OK. Nothing spectacular but sometimes special. I look in the mirror and see this medium average person. A little tired, a little sad, but not falling apart. I look to the man beside me and I see the same.

'Excuse me?' the hairdresser breaks into my thoughts. 'You want it *all* off? Are you sure? You've such healthy hair.' He runs his fingers through it. 'Is this your natural colour?'

'Yes, I used to put a little colour in it but I stopped because of the—' I'm about to say 'baby'. My eyes fill and I look down but he thinks I'm nodding to my stomach, which is hidden under the gown.

'Stopped because of what?' he asks.

I continue to look at my feet, pretend to be doing something with my foot. An odd shuffle manoeuvre. I can't think of anything to say to him and so I pretend not to hear him. 'Huh?'

'You were saying you stopped because of something?'

'Oh, em . . .' Don't cry. Don't cry. If you start now you will never stop. 'Oh, I don't know,' I mumble, bending over to play with my handbag on the ground. It will pass, it will pass. Someday it will all pass, Joyce. 'Chemicals. I stopped because of chemicals.'

'Right, this is what it'll look like,' he takes my hair and ties it back. 'How about we do a Meg Ryan in *French Kiss*?' He pulls hairs out in all directions and I look like I've stuck my fingers in an electric socket. 'It's the sexy messy bed-head look. Or else we can do this.' He messes about with my hair some more.

'Can we hurry this along? I've got a taxi waiting outside too.' I look out the window. Dad is chatting to the taxi driver. They're both laughing and I relax a little.

'O . . . K. Something like this really shouldn't be rushed. You have a lot of hair.'

'It's fine. I'm giving you permission to hurry. Just cut it all off.' I look back to the car.

'Well, we must leave a few inches on it, darling.' He directs my face back towards the mirror. 'We don't want Sigourney Weaver in *Aliens*, do we? No GI Janes allowed in this salon. We'll give you a side-swept fringe, very sophisticated, very now. It'll suit you, I think, show off those high cheekbones. What do you think?'

I don't care about my cheekbones. I want it all off.

'Actually, how about we just do this?' I take the scissors from his hand, cut my ponytail, and then hand them both back to him.

He gasps. But it sounds more like a squeak. 'Or we could do that. A . . . bob.'

American man's mouth hangs open at the sight of my hairdresser with a large pair of scissors and ten inches of hair dangling from his hand. He turns to his and grabs the scissors before he makes another cut. 'Do not,' he points, 'do *that* to me!'

Mullet man sighs and rolls his eyes. 'No, of course not, sir.'

The American starts scratching his left arm again. 'I must have got a bite.' He tries to roll up his shirtsleeve and I squirm in my seat, trying to get a look at his arm.

'Could you please sit still?'

'Could you please sit still?'

The hairdressers speak in perfect unison. They look to one another and laugh.

'Something funny in the air today,' one of them comments and American man and I look at one another. Funny, indeed.

'Eyes back to the mirror, please, sir.' He looks away.

My hairdresser places a finger under my chin and tips my face back to the centre. He hands me my ponytail.

'Souvenir.'

'I don't want it.' I refuse to take my hair in my hands. Every inch of that hair was from a moment that has now gone. Thoughts, wishes, hopes, desires, dreams that are no longer. I want a new start. A new head of hair.

He begins to shape it into style now and as each strand falls I watch it drift to the ground. My head feels lighter.

The hair that grew the day we bought the cot. Snip.

The hair that grew the day we picked the nursery paint colours, bottles, bibs and baby grows. All bought too soon, but we were so excited . . . Snip.

The hair that grew the day we decided the names. Snip.

The hair that grew the day we announced it to friends and family. Snip.

The day of the first scan. The day I found out I was pregnant. The day my baby was conceived. Snip. Snip. Snip.

The more painful recent memories will remain at the root for another little while. I will have to wait for them to grow until I can be rid of them too and then all traces will be gone and I will move on.

I reach the till as the American pays for his cut.

'That suits you,' he comments, studying me.

I go to tuck some hair behind my ear self-consciously but there's nothing there. I feel lighter, light-headed, delighted with giddiness, giddy with delight.

'So does yours.'

'Thank you.'

He opens the door for me.

'Thank you.' I step outside.

'You're far too polite,' he tells me.

'Thank you,' I smile. 'So are you.'

'Thank you,' he nods.

We laugh. We both gaze at our taxis queuing up waiting, and look back at one another curiously. He gives me a smile.

'The first taxi or the second taxi?' he asks.

'For me?'

He nods. 'My driver won't stop talking.'

I study both taxis, see Dad in the second, leaning forward and talking to the driver.

'The first. My dad won't stop talking.'

He studies the second taxi where Dad has now pushed his face up against the glass and is staring at me as though I'm an apparition.

'The second taxi it is, then,' the American says, and walks to his taxi, glancing back twice.

'Hey,' I protest, and watch him, entranced.

I float to my taxi and we both pull our doors closed at the same time. The taxi driver and Dad look at me like they've seen a ghost.

'What?' My heart beats wildly. 'What happened? Tell me?'

'Your hair,' Dad simply says, his face aghast. 'You're like a boy.'

8

As the taxi gets closer to my home in Phisboro, my stomach knots tighter.

'That was funny how the man in front kept his taxi waiting too, Gracie, wasn't it?'

'Joyce. And yes,' I reply, my leg bouncing with nerves.

'Is that what people do now when they get their hairs cut?'

'Do what, Dad?'

'Leave taxis waiting outside for them.'

'I don't know.'

He shuffles his bum to the edge of the seat and pulls himself closer to the taxi driver. 'I say, Jack, is that what people do when they go to the barbers now?'

'What's that?'

'Do they leave their taxis outside waiting for them?'

'I've never been asked to do it before,' the driver explains politely.

Dad sits back satisfied. 'That's what I thought, Gracie.'

'It's Joyce,' I snap.

'Joyce. It's a coincidence. And you know what they say about coincidences?'

'Yep.' We turn the corner onto my street and my stomach flips.

'That there's no such thing as a coincidence,' Dad finishes, even though I've already said yes. 'Indeedy no,' he says to himself. 'No such thing. There's Patrick,' he waves. 'I hope he doesn't wave back.' He watches his friend from the Monday Club with two hands on his walking-frame. 'And David out with the dog.' He waves again although David is stopping to allow his dog to poop and is looking the other way. I get the feeling Dad feels rather grand in a taxi. It's rare he's in one, the expense being too much and everywhere he needs to go being within walking distance or a short bus hop away.

'Home sweet home,' he announces. 'How much do I owe you, Jack?' He leans forward again. He takes two five-euro notes out of his pocket.

'The bad news, I'm afraid . . . twenty euro, please.'

'What?' Dad looks up in shock.

'I'll pay, Dad, put your money away.' I give the driver twenty-five and tell him to keep the change. Dad looks at me like I've just taken a pint out of his hand and poured it down the drain.

Conor and I have lived in the red-brick terraced house in Phisboro since our marriage ten years ago. The houses have been here since the forties, and over the years we've pumped our money into modernising it. Finally it's how we want it, or it was until this week. A black railing encloses a small patch of a front garden where the rose bushes my mother planted preside. Dad lives in an identical house two streets away, the house I grew up in, though we're never done growing up, continually learning, and when I return to it I regress to my youth.

The front door to my house opens just as the taxi drives off. Dad's neighbour Fran smiles at me from my own front door. She looks at us awkwardly, failing to make eye contact with me each time she looks in my direction. I'll have to get used to this.

'Oh, your hair!' she says first, then gathers herself. 'I'm sorry, love, I meant to be out of here by the time you got home.' She opens the door fully and pulls a checked trolley-bag behind her. She is wearing a single Marigold glove on her right arm.

Dad looks nervous and avoids my eye.

'What were you doing, Fran? How on earth did you get into my house?' I try to be as polite as I can but the sight of someone in my house without my permission both surprises and infuriates me.

She pinks and looks to Dad. Dad looks at her hand and coughs. She looks down, laughs nervously and pulls off her single Marigold. 'Oh, your dad gave me a key. I thought that . . . well, I put down a nice rug in the hallway for you. I hope you like it.'

I stare at her with utter confusion.

'Never mind, I'll be off now.' She walks by me, grabs my arm and squeezes hard but still refuses to look at me. 'Take care of yourself, love.' She walks on down the road, dragging her trolley-bag behind her, her Nora Batty tights in rolls around her thick ankles.

'Dad,' I look at him angrily, 'what the hell is this?' I push into the house, looking at the disgusting dusty rug on my beige carpet. 'Why did you give a near-stranger my house keys so she could come in and leave a rug? I am not a charity!'

He takes off his cap and scrunches it in his hands. 'She's not a stranger, love. She's known you since the day you were brought home from the hospital—'

Wrong story to tell at this moment, and he knows it.

'I don't care!' I splutter. 'It's *my* house, not yours! You cannot just do that. I hate this ugly piece of shit rug!' I pick up one side of the clashing carpet, I drag it outside and then slam the door shut. I'm fuming and I look at Dad to shout at him again. He is pale and shaken. He is looking at the floor sadly. My eyes follow his.

Various shades of faded brown stains, like red wine, splatter the beige carpet. It has been cleaned in some places but the carpet hairs have been brushed in the opposite direction and give away that something once lay there. My blood.

I put my head in my hands.

Dad's voice is quiet, injured. 'I thought it would be best for you to come home with that gone.'

'Oh, Dad.'

'Fran has been here for a little while everyday now and has tried different things on it. It was me that suggested the rug,' he adds in a smaller voice. 'You can't blame her for that.'

I despise myself.

'I know you like all the nice new matching things in your house,' he looks around, 'but Fran or I wouldn't have the likes of that.'

'I'm sorry, Dad. I don't know what came over me. I'm sorry I shouted at you. You've been nothing but helpful this week. I'll . . . I'll call around to Fran at some stage and thank her properly.'

'Right,' he nods, 'I'll leave you at it, so. I'll bring the rug back to Fran. I don't want any of the neighbours seeing it outside on the path and telling her so.'

'No, I'll put it back where it was. It's too heavy for you to bring all the way around. I'll keep it for the time being and return it to her soon.' I open the front door and retrieve it from the outside path. I drag it back into the house with more respect, laying it down so that it hides the scene where I lost my baby.

'I'm so sorry, Dad.'

'Don't worry.' He seesaws up to me and pats my shoulder. 'You're having a hard time, that I know. I'm only round the corner if you need me for anything.'

With a flick of his wrist, his tweed cap is on his head and I watch him seesaw down the road. The movement is familiar and comforting, like the motion of the sea. He disappears round the corner and I close the door. Alone. Silence. Just me and the house. Life continues as though nothing has happened.

It seems as though the nursery upstairs vibrates through the walls and floor. Thump-thump. Thump-thump. As though like a heart, it's trying to push out the walls and send blood flowing down the stairs, through the hallways to reach every little nook and cranny. I walk away from the stairs, the scene of the crime, and wander around the rooms. It appears everything is exactly as it was, though on further inspection I see that Fran has tidied around. The cup of tea I was drinking is gone from the coffee table in the living room. The galley kitchen hums with the sound of the dishwasher Fran has set. The taps and draining boards glisten, the surfaces are gleaming. Straight through the kitchen the door leads to the back garden. My mum's rose bushes line the back wall. Dad's geraniums peep up from the soil.

Upstairs the nursery still throbs.

I notice the red light on the answering machine in the hall flashing. Four messages. I flick through the list of registered phone numbers and recognise friends' numbers. I leave the answering machine, not able to listen to their condolences quite yet. Then I freeze. I go back. I flick through the list again. There it is. Monday evening. 7.10 p.m. Again at 7.12 p.m. My second chance to take the call. The call I had foolishly rushed down the stairs for and sacrificed my child's life.

They have left a message. With shaking fingers, I press play.

'Hello, this is Xtra-vision, Phisboro calling about the DVD *The Muppet Christmas Carol*. It says on our system that it's one week late. We'd appreciate it if you could return it as soon as possible, please.'

I inhale sharply. Tears spring in my eyes. What did I expect? A phone call worthy of losing my baby? Something so urgent that I was right to rush for it? Would that somehow warrant my loss?

My entire body trembles with rage and shock. Breathing in shakily, I make my way into the living room. I look straight ahead to the DVD player. On top, is the DVD I rented while minding my goddaughter. I reach for the DVD, hold it tightly in my hands, squeeze it as though I can stop the life in it. Then I throw it hard across the room. It knocks our collection of photographs off the top of the piano, cracking the glass on our wedding photo, chipping the silver coating of another.

I open my mouth. And I scream. I scream at the top of my lungs, the loudest I can possibly go. It's deep and low and filled with anguish. I scream again and hold it for as long as I can. One scream after another from the pit of my stomach, from the depths of my heart. I let out deep howls that border on laughter, that are laced with frustration. I scream and I scream until I am out of breath and my throat burns.

Upstairs, the nursery continues to vibrate. Thump-thump, thump-thump. It beckons me, the heart of my home beating wildly. I go to the staircase, step over the rug and onto the stairs. I grab the banister, feeling too weak even to lift my legs. I pull myself upstairs. The thumping gets louder and louder with every step until I reach the top and face the nursery door. It stops throbbing. All is still now.

I trace a finger down the door, press my cheek to it, willing all that happened not to be so. I reach for the handle and open the door.

A half-painted wall of Buttercup Dream greets me. Soft pastels. Sweet smells. A cot with a mobile of little yellow ducks dangling above. A toy box decorated with giant letters of the alphabet. On a little rail hang two baby grows. Little booties on a dresser.

A bunny rabbit sits up enthusiastically inside the cot. He smiles stupidly at me. I take my shoes off and step barefoot onto the soft shagpile carpet, try to root myself in this world. I close the door behind me. There's not a sound. I pick up the rabbit and carry it around the room with me while I run my hands over the shiny new furniture, clothes and toys. I open a music box and watch as the little mouse inside begins to circle round and round after a piece of cheese to a mesmerising tinkling sound.

'I'm sorry, Sean,' I whisper, and my words catch in my throat. 'I'm so, so sorry.'

I lower myself to the soft floor, pull my legs close to me and hug the blissfully unaware bunny. I look again to the little mouse whose very being revolves around eternally chasing a piece of cheese he will never ever reach, let alone eat.

I slam the box shut and the music stops and I am left in silence.

9

'I can't find any food in the apartment; we're going to have to get take-out,' Justin's sister-in-law, Doris, calls into the living room as she roots through the kitchen cabinets.

'So maybe you know the woman,' Justin's younger brother, Al, sits on the plastic garden furniture chair in Justin's half-furnished living room.

'No, you see, that's what I'm trying to explain. It's *like* I know her but at the same time, I didn't know her at all.'

'You recognised her.'

'Yes. Well, no.' *Kind of.*

'And you don't know her name.'

'No. I definitely don't know her name.'

'Hey, is anyone listening to me in there or am I talking to myself?' Doris interrupts again. 'I said there's no food here so we're going to have to get take-out.'

'Yeah, sure, honey,' Al calls automatically. 'Maybe she's a student of yours or she went to one of your talks. You usually remember people you give talks to?'

'There's hundreds of people at a time,' Justin shrugs. 'And mostly they sit in darkness.'

'So that's a no then.' Al rubs his chin.

'Actually, forget the take-out,' Doris calls. 'You don't have any plates or cutlery – we're going to have to eat out.'

'And just let me get this clear, Al. When I say "recognise", I mean I didn't actually know her face.'

Al frowns.

'I just got a feeling. Like she was familiar.' *Yeah, that's it, she was familiar.*

'Maybe she just looked like someone you know.' *Maybe.*

'Hey, is anybody listening to me?' Doris interupts them, standing at the living-room door with her inchlong leopard-print nails on her skin-tight leather-trouserclad hips. Thirty-five-year-old Italian-American fast-talking Doris had been married to Al for the past ten years and is regarded by Justin as a lovable but annoying younger sister. Without an ounce of fat on her bones, everything she wears looks like it comes out of the closet of *Grease*'s Sandy post makeover.

'Yes, sure, honey,' Al says again, not taking his eyes off Justin. 'Maybe it was that *déjà vu* thingy.'

'Yes!' Justin clicks his fingers. 'Or perhaps *vécu*, or *senti*,' he rubs his chin, lost in thought. 'Or *visité*.'

'What the heck is that?' Al asks as Doris pulls over a cardboard box filled with books, to sit on, and joins them.

'*Déjà vu* is French for "already seen" and it describes the experience of feeling that one has witnessed or experienced a new situation previously. The term was coined by a French psychic researcher Emile Boirac, which expanded upon an essay that he wrote while at the University of Chicago.'

'Go the Maroons!' Al raises Justin's old trophy cup that he's drinking from, in the air, and then gulps down his beer.

Doris looks at him with disdain. 'Please continue, Justin.'

'Well, the experience of *déjà vu* is usually accompanied by a compelling sense of familiarity, and also a sense of eeriness or strangeness. The experience is most frequently attributed to a dream, although in some cases there is a firm sense that the experience genuinely happened in the past. *Déjà vu* has been described as remembering the future.'

444

'Wow,' Doris says breathily.

'So what's your point, bro?' Al belches.

'Well, I don't think this thing today with me and the woman was *déjà vu*,' Justin frowns and sighs.

'Why not?'

'Because *déjà vu* relates to just *sight* and I felt . . . oh, I don't know.' I *felt*. '*Déjà vécu* is translated as "already lived", which explains the experience that involves more than sight, but of having a weird knowledge of what is going to happen next. *Déjà senti* specifically means "already felt", which is exclusively a mental happening and *déjà visité* involves an uncanny knowledge of a new place, but that's less common. No,' he shakes his head, 'I definitely didn't feel like I had been at the salon before.'

They all go quiet.

Al breaks the silence. 'Well, it's definitely *déjà* something. Are you sure you didn't just sleep with her before?'

'Al.' Doris hits her husband across the arm. 'Why didn't you let me cut your hair, Justin, and who are we talking about anyway?'

'You own a doggie parlour.' Justin frowns.

'Dogs have hair,' she shrugs.

'Let me try to explain this,' Al interrupts. 'Justin saw a woman yesterday at a hair salon in Dublin and he says he recognised her but didn't know her face, and he felt that he knew her but didn't actually know her.' He rolls his eyes melodramatically, out of Justin's view.

'Oh my God,' Doris sings, 'I know what this is.'

'What?' Justin asks, taking a drink from a toothbrush holder.

'It's obvious.' She holds her hands up and looks from one brother to another for dramatic effect. 'It's past-life stuff.' Her face lights up. 'You knew the woman in a *paaast liiife*,' she pronounces the words slowly. 'I saw it on *Oprah*.' She nods her head, eyes wide.

'Not more of this crap, Doris. It's all she talks about now. She sees somethin' about it on TV and that's all I get, all the way from Chicago on the plane.'

'I don't think it's past-life stuff, Doris, but thanks.'

Doris tuts. 'You two need to have open minds about this kind of thing because you never know.'

'Exactly, you *never* know,' Al fires back.

'Oh, come on, guys. The woman was familiar, that's all. Maybe she just looked like someone I knew at home. No big deal.' *Forget about it and move on.*

'Well, you started it with your *déjà* stuff,' Doris huffs. 'How do you explain it?'

Justin shrugs. 'The optical pathway delay theory.'

They both stare at him, dumb-faced.

'One theory is that one eye may record what is seen fractionally faster than the other, creating that strong recollection sensation upon the same scene being viewed milliseconds later by the other eye. Basically it's the product of a delayed optical input from one eye, closely followed by the input from the other eye, which should be simultaneous. This misleads conscious awareness and suggests a sensation of familiarity when there shouldn't be one.'

Silence.

Justin clears his throat.

'Believe it or not, honey, I prefer your past-life thing,' Al snorts, and finishes his beer.

'Thanks, sweetie.' Doris places her hands on her heart, overwhelmed. 'Anyway as I was saying when I was *talking to myself* in the kitchen, there's no food, cutlery or crockery here so we'll have to eat out tonight. Look at how you're living, Justin. I'm worried about you,' Doris looks around the room with disgust and her back-combed hair-sprayed dyed red hair follows the movement. 'You've moved all the way over to this country on your own, you've got nothing but garden furniture and unpacked boxes in a basement that looks like it was built for students. Clearly Jennifer also got all the *taste* in the settlement too.'

'This is a Victorian masterpiece, Doris. It was a real find, and it's the only place I *could* find with a bit of history as well as having affordable rent. This is an expensive town.'

'I'm sure it was a gem hundreds of years ago but now it gives me the creeps and whoever built it is probably still hanging around these rooms. I can feel him watching me.' She shudders.

'Don't flatter yourself.' Al rolls his eyes.

'All the place needs is a bit of TLC and it'll be fine,' Justin says, trying to forget the apartment he loved and has recently sold in the affluent and historic neighbourhood of Old Town Chicago.

'Which is why I'm here.' Doris claps her hands with glee.

'Great.' Justin's smile is tight. 'Let's go get some dinner now. I'm in the mood for a steak.'

'But you're vegetarian, Joyce.' Conor looks at me as though I've lost my mind. I probably have. I can't remember the last time I've eaten red meat but I have a sudden craving for it now that we've sat down at the restaurant.

'I'm not vegetarian, Conor. I just don't like red meat.'

'But you've just ordered a medium-rare steak!'

'I know,' I shrug. 'I'm just one crazy cat.'

He smiles as if remembering there once was a wild streak in me. We are like two friends meeting up after years apart. So much to talk about but not having the slightest clue where to start.

'Have you chosen the wine yet?' the waiter asks Conor.

I quickly grab the menu. 'Actually I would like to order this one, please.' I point to the menu.

'Sancerre 1998. That's a very good choice, madam.'

'Thank you.' I have no idea whatsoever why I've chosen it.

Conor laughs. 'Did you just do eeny-meeny-miny-mo?'

I smile but get hot under the collar. I don't know why I've ordered that wine. It's too expensive and I usually drink white, but I act naturally because I don't want Conor to think I've lost my mind. He already thought I was crazy when he saw I'd chopped all my hair off. He needs to think I'm back to my normal self in order for me to say what I'm going to say tonight.

The waiter returns with the bottle of wine.

'You can do the tasting,' Al says to Justin, 'seeing as it was your choice.'

Justin picks up the glass of wine, dips his nose into the glass and inhales deeply.

I inhale deeply and then swivel the wine in the glass, watching for the alcohol to rise and sweep the sides. I take a sip and hold it on my tongue, suck it in and allow the alcohol to burn the inside of my mouth. Perfect.

'Lovely, thank you.' I place the glass on the table again.

Conor's glass is filled and mine is topped up.

'It's beautiful wine.' I begin to tell him the story.

'I found it when Jennifer and I went to France years ago,' Justin explains. 'She was there performing in the Festival des Cathédrales de Picardie with the orchestra, which was a memorable experience. In Versailles, we stayed in Hôtel du Berry, an elegant 1634 mansion full of period furniture. It's practically a museum of regional history – you probably remember my telling you about it. Anyway, on one of her nights off in Paris we found this beautiful little fish restaurant tucked away down one of the cobbled alleys of Montmartre. We ordered the special, seabass, but you know how much of a red wine fanatic I am – even with fish I prefer to drink red – so the waiter suggested we go for the Sancerre.

'You know I always thought of Sancerre as a white wine, as it's famous for using the Sauvignon grape, but as it turns out it also uses some Pinot Noir. *And* the great thing is that you can drink the red Sancerre cooled exactly like white, at twelve degrees. But when not chilled, it's also good with meat. Enjoy.' He toasts his brother and sister-in-law.

Conor is looking at me with a frozen face. 'Montmartre? Joyce, you've never been to Paris before. How do you know so much about wine? And who the hell is Jennifer?'

I pause, snap out of my trance and suddenly hear the words of the story I had just explained. I do the only thing I can do under the circumstances. I start laughing. 'Gotcha.'

'Gotcha?' he frowns.

'They're the lines to a movie I watched the other night.'

'Oh.' Relief floods his face and he relaxes. 'Joyce, you scared me there for a minute. I thought somebody had possessed your body.' He smiles. 'What film is it from?'

'Oh, I can't remember,' I wave my hand dismissively, wondering what on earth is going on with me and try to recall if I even watched a film any night during the past week.

'You don't like anchovies now?' he interrupts my thoughts, and looks down at the little collection of anchovies I've gathered in a pile at the side of my plate.

'Give them to me, bro,' Al says, lifting his plate closer to Justin's. 'I love 'em. How you can have a Caesar salad without anchovies is beyond me. Is it OK that I have anchovies, Doris?' he asks sarcastically. 'The doc didn't say anchovies are going to kill me, did he?'

'Not unless somebody stuffs them down your throat, which is quite possible,' Doris says through gritted teeth.

'Thirty-nine years old and I'm being treated like a kid.' Al looks wistfully at the pile of anchovies.

'Thirty-five years old and the only kid I have is my husband,' Doris snaps, picking an anchovy from the pile and tasting it. She ruffles her nose and looks around the restaurant. 'They call this an Italian restaurant? My mother and her family would roll in their graves if they knew this.' She blesses herself quickly. 'So, Justin, tell me about this lady you're seeing.'

Justin frowns. 'Doris, it's really no big deal, I told you I just thought I knew her.' *And she looked like she thought she knew you too.*

'No, not her,' Al says loudly with a mouthful of anchovies. 'She's talking about the woman you were banging the other night.'

'Al!' Food wedges in Justin's throat.

'Joyce,' Conor says with concern, 'are you OK?'

My eyes fill as I try to catch my breath from coughing.

'Here, have some water.' He pushes a glass in my face.

People around us are staring, concerned.

I'm coughing so much I can't even take a breath to drink. Conor gets up from his chair and comes around to me. He pats my back and I shrug him off, still coughing with tears running down my face. I stand up in panic, overturning my chair behind me in the process.

'Al, Al, do something. Oh, Madonn-ina Santa!' Doris panics. 'He's going purple.'

Al untucks his napkin from his collar and coolly places it on the table. He stands up and positions himself behind his brother. He wraps his arms around his waist, and pumps hard on his stomach.

On the second push, the food is dislodged from Justin's throat.

As a third person races to my aid, or rather to join the growing panicked discussion of how to perform the Heimlich manoeuvre, I suddenly stop coughing. Three faces stare at me in surprise while I rub my throat with confusion.

'Are you OK?' Conor asks, patting my back again.

'Yes,' I whisper, embarrassed by the attention we are

receiving. 'I'm fine, thank you. Everyone, thank you so much for your help.'

They are slow to back away.

'Please go back to your seats and enjoy your dinner. Honestly, I'm fine. Thank you.' I sit down quickly and rub my streaming mascara from my eyes, trying to ignore the stares. 'God, that was embarrassing.'

'That was odd; you hadn't even eaten anything. You were just talking and then, bam! You started coughing.'

I shrug and rub my throat. 'I don't know, something caught when I inhaled.'

The waiter comes over to take our plates away. 'Are you all right, madam?'

'Yes, thank you, I'm fine.'

I feel a nudge from behind me as our neighbour leans over to our table. 'Hey, for a minute there I thought you were going into labour, ha-ha! Didn't we, Margaret?' He looks at his wife and laughs.

'No,' Margaret says, her smile quickly fading and her face turning puce. 'No, Pat.'

'Huh?' He's confused. 'Well, *I* did anyway. Congrats, Conor.' He gives a suddenly pale Conor a wink. 'There goes sleep for the next twenty years, believe you me. Enjoy your dinner.' He turns back to face his table, and we hear murmured squabbling.

Conor's face falls and he reaches for my hand across the table. 'Are you OK?'

'That's happened a few times now,' I explain, and instinctively place my hand over my flat stomach. 'I've barely looked in the mirror since I've come home. I can't stand to look.'

Conor makes appropriate sounds of concern and I hear the words 'beautiful' and 'pretty' but I silence him. I need for him to listen and not to try to solve anything. I want him to know that I'm not trying to be pretty or beautiful but for once just to appear as I am. I want to tell him how I feel when I force myself to look in the mirror and study my body that now feels like a shell.

'Oh, Joyce.' His grip on my hand tightens as I speak, he squeezes my wedding ring into my skin and it hurts.

A wedding ring but no marriage.

I wriggle my hand a little to let him know to loosen his grip. Instead he lets go. A sign.

'Conor,' is all I say. I give him a look and I know he knows what I'm about to say. He's seen this look before.

'No, no, no, no, Joyce, not this conversation now.' He withdraws his hand from the table completely and holds his hands up in defence. 'You – *we* – have been through enough this week.'

'Conor, no more distractions.' I lean forward with urgency in my voice. 'We have to deal with us *now* or before we know it, ten years on we'll be wondering every single day of our miserable lives what *might* have been.'

We've had this conversation in some form or another on an annual basis over the last five years and I wait for the usual retort from Conor. That no one says marriage is easy, we can't expect it to be so, we promised one another, marriage is for life and he's determined to work at it. Salvage from the skip what's worth saving, my itinerant husband preaches. I focus on the centre flame's reflection in my dessert spoon while I wait for his usual comments. I realise minutes later they still haven't come. I look up and see he is battling tears and is nodding in what looks like agreement.

I take a breath. This is it.

Justin eyes the dessert menu.

'You can't have any, Al.' Doris plucks the menu out of her husband's hands and snaps it shut.

'Why not? Am I not allowed to even read it?'

'Your cholesterol goes up just reading it.'

Justin zones out as they squabble. He shouldn't be having any either. Since his divorce he's started to let himself go, eating as a comfort instead of his usual daily workout. He really shouldn't, but his eyes hover above one item on the menu like a vulture watching its prey.

'Any dessert for you, sir?' the waiter asks.

Go on.

'Yes. I'll have the . . .'

'Banoffee pie, please,' I blurt out to the waiter, to my own surprise.

Conor's mouth drops.

Oh dear. My marriage has just ended and I'm ordering dessert. I bite my lip and stop a nervous smile from breaking out.

To new beginnings. To the pursuit of . . . something-ness.

10

A grand chime welcomes me to my father's humble home. It's a sound far more than deserving of the two up-two down, but then, so is my father.

The sound teleports me back to my life within these walls and how I'd identified visitors by the sound of their call at the door. As a child, short piercing sounds told me that friends, too short to reach, were hopping up to punch the button. Fast and weak snippets of sound alerted me to boyfriends cowering outside, terrified of announcing their very existence, never mind their arrival, to my father. Late night unsteady, uncountable rings sang Dad's homecoming from the pub without his keys. Joyful, playful rhythms were family calls on occasions, and short, loud, continuous bursts like machine-gun fire warned us of door-to-door salespeople. I press the bell again, but not just because at ten a.m. the house is quiet and nothing stirs; I want to know what my call sounds like.

Apologetic, short and clipped. Almost doesn't want to be heard but needs to be. It says, sorry, Dad, sorry to disturb you. Sorry the thirty-three-year-old daughter you thought you were long ago rid of is back home after her marriage has fallen apart.

Finally I hear sounds inside and I see Dad's seesaw movement coming closer, shadowlike and eerie, in the distorted glass.

'Sorry, love,' he opens the door, 'I didn't hear you the first time.'

'If you didn't hear me then how did you know I rang?'

He looks at me blankly and then down at the suit-cases around my feet. 'What's this?'

'You . . . you told me I could stay for a while.'

'I thought you meant till the end of *Countdown*.'

'Oh . . . well, I was hoping to stay for a bit longer than that.'

'Long after I'm gone, by the looks of it.' He surveys his doorstep. 'Come in, come in. Where's Conor? Something happen to the house? You haven't mice again, have you? It's the time of the year for them all right, so you should have kept the windows and doors closed. Block up all the openings, that's what I do. I'll show you when we're inside and settled. Conor should know.'

'Dad, I've never called around to stay here because of mice.'

'There's a first time for everything. Your mother used to do that. Hated the things. Used to stay at your grand-mother's for the few days while I ran around here like that cartoon cat trying to catch them. Tom or Jerry, was it?' He squeezes his eyes closed tight to think, then opens them again, none the wiser. 'I never knew the difference but by God they knew it when I was after them.' He raises a fist, looks feisty for a moment while captured in the thought and then he stops suddenly and carries my suitcases into the hall.

'Dad?' I say, frustrated. 'I thought you understood me on the phone. Conor and I have separated.'

'Separated what?'

'Ourselves.'

'From what?'

'From each other!'

'What on earth are you talking about, Gracie?'

'Joyce. We're not together any more. We've split up.'

He puts the bags down by the hall's wall of photo-graphs, there to provide any visitor who crosses the threshold with a crash course of the Conway family history. Dad as a boy, Mum as a girl, Dad and Mum courting, married, my christening, communion, débutant ball and wedding. Capture it, frame it, display it; Mum and Dad's school of thought. It's funny how people mark their lives, the benchmarks they choose to decide when a moment is more of a moment than any other. For life is made of them. I like to think the best ones of all are in my mind, that they run through my blood in their own memory bank for no one else but me to see.

Dad doesn't pause for a moment at the revelations of my failed marriage and instead works his way into the kitchen. 'Cuppa?'

I stay in the hall looking around at the photos and breathe in that smell. The smell that's carried around everyday on every stitch of Dad's back, like a snail carries its home. I always thought it was the smell of Mum's cooking that drifted around the rooms and seeped into every fibre, including the wallpaper, but it's ten years since Mum has passed away. Perhaps the scent was her; perhaps it's still her.

'What are you doin' sniffin' the walls?'

I jump, startled and embarrassed at being caught, and make my way into the kitchen. It hasn't changed since I lived here and it's as spotless as the day Mum left it, nothing moved, not even for convenience's sake. I watch Dad move slowly about, resting on his left foot to access the cupboards below, and then using the extra inches of his right leg as his own personal footstool to reach above. The kettle boils too loudly for us to have a conversation and I'm glad of that because Dad grips the handle so tightly his knuckles are white. A teaspoon is cupped in his left hand, which rests on his hip, and it reminds me of how he used to stand with his cigarette, shielded in his cupped hand that'd be stained yellow from nicotine. He looks out to his immaculate garden and grinds his teeth. He's angry and I feel like a teenager once again, awaiting my talking-down.

'What are you thinking about, Dad?' I finally ask as soon as the kettle stops hopping about like a crammed

Hill 16 in Croke Park during an All-Ireland Final.

'The garden,' he replies, his jaw tightening once again.

'The garden?'

'That bloody cat from next door keeps pissing on your mother's roses.' He shakes his head angrily. 'Fluffy,' he throws his hands up, 'that's what she calls him. Well, Fluffy won't be so fluffy when I get my hands on him. I'll be wearin' one of them fine furry hats the Russians wear and I'll dance the *hopak* outside Mrs Henderson's front garden while she wraps a shiverin' *Baldy* up in a blanket inside.'

'Is that what you're really thinking about?' I ask incredulously.

'Well, not really, love,' he confesses, calming down. 'That and the daffodils. Not far off from planting season for spring. And some crocuses. I'll have to get some bulbs.'

Good to know my marriage breakdown isn't my dad's main priority. Nor his second. On the list after crocuses.

'Snowdrops too,' he adds.

It's rare I'm around the area so early on in the day. Usually I'd be at work showing property around the city. It's so quiet now with everyone at work, I wonder what on earth Dad does in this silence.

'What were you doing before I came?'

'Thirty-three years ago or today?'

'Today.' I try not to smile because I know he's serious.

'Quiz.' He nods at the kitchen table where he has a page full of puzzles and quizzes. Half of them are completed. 'I'm stuck on the number six. Have a look at that.' He brings the cups of tea to the table, managing not to spill a drop despite his swaying. Always steady.

'"Which of Mozart's operas was not well received by one especially influential critic who summed up the work as having 'Too many notes'?"' I read the clue aloud.

'Mozart,' Dad shrugs. 'Haven't a clue about that lad at all.'

'Emperor Joseph the Second,' I say.

'What's that now?' Dad's caterpillar eyebrows go up in surprise. 'How did you know that, then?'

I frown. 'I must have just heard it somwh— do I smell smoke?'

He sits up straight and sniffs the air like a bloodhound. 'Toast. I made it earlier. Had the setting on too high and burned it. They were the last two slices, as well.'

'Hate that.' I shake my head. 'Where's Mum's photograph from the hall?'

'Which one? There are thirty of her.'

'You've counted?' I laugh.

'Nailed them up there, didn't I? Forty-four photos in total, that's forty-four nails I needed. Went down to the hardware store and bought a pack of nails. Forty nails it contained. They made me buy a second packet just for four more nails.' He holds up four fingers and shakes his head. 'Still have thirty-six of them left over in the toolbox. What is the world comin' to at all, at all.'

Never mind terrorism or global warming. The proof of the world's downfall, in his eyes, comes down to thirty-six nails in a toolbox. He's probably right too.

'So where is it?'

'Right where it always is,' he says unconvincingly.

We both look at the closed kitchen door, in the direction of the hall table. I stand up to go out and check. These are the kinds of things you do when you have time on your hands.

'Ah ah,' he jerks a floppy hand at me, 'sit yourself down.' He rises. 'I'll go out and check.' He closes the kitchen door behind him, blocking me from seeing out. 'She's there all right,' he calls to me. 'Hello, Gracie, your daughter was worried about you. Thought she couldn't see you but sure, haven't you been there all along watchin' her sniffin' the walls, thinkin' the paper's on fire. But sure isn't it only madder she's gettin', leaving her husband and packing in her job.'

I haven't mentioned anything to him about taking leave from my job, which means Conor has spoken to him, which means Dad knew my exact intentions for being here from the very first moment he heard the doorbell ring. I have to give it to him, he plays stupid very well. He returns to the kitchen and I catch a glimpse of the photo on the hall table.

'Ah!' He looks at his watch in alarm. 'Ten twenty-five! Let's go inside quick!' He moves faster than I've seen him in a long time, grabbing his weekly television guide and his cup of tea and rushing into the television room.

'What are we watching?' I follow him into the living room, watching him with amusement.

'*Murder, She Wrote*, you know it?'

'Never seen it.'

'Oh, wait'll you see, Gracie. That Jessica Fletcher is a quare one for catching the murderers. Then over on the next channel we'll watch *Diagnosis Murder*, where the dancer solves the cases.' He takes a pen and circles it on the TV page.

I'm captivated by Dad's excitement. He sings along with the theme tune, making trumpet noises with his mouth.

'Come in here and lie on the couch and I'll put this over you.' He picks up a tartan blanket draped over the back of the green velvet couch and places it gently over me, tucking it in around my body so tightly I can't move my arms. It's the same blanket I rolled on as a baby, the same blanket they covered me with when I was home sick from school and was allowed to watch television on the couch. I watch Dad with fondness, remembering the tenderness he always showed me as a child, feeling right back there again.

Until he sits at the end of the couch and squashes my feet.

11

'What do you think, Gracie – will Betty be a millionaire by the end of the show?'

I have sat through an endless amount of half-hour morning shows over the last few days and now we are watching the *Antiques Roadshow*.

Betty is seventy years old, from Warwickshire, and is currently waiting with anticipation as the dealer tries to price the old teapot she has brought with her.

I watch the dealer handling the teapot delicately and a comfortable, familiar feeling overwhelms me. 'Sorry, Betty,' I say to the television, 'it's a replica. From the eighteenth century. The French used them but Betty's one was made in the early twentieth century. You can see from the way the handle is shaped. Clumsy craftsmanship.'

'Is that so?' Dad looks at me with interest.

We watch the screen intently and listen as the dealer repeats my remarks. Poor Betty is devastated but tries to pretend it was too precious a gift from her grandmother for her to have sold anyhow.

'Liar,' Dad shouts. 'Betty already had her cruise booked and her bikini bought. How do you know all that about the pots and the French, Gracie? Read it in one of your books maybe?'

'Maybe.' I have no idea. I get a headache thinking about this new-found knowledge.

Dad catches the look on my face. 'Why don't you call a friend or something? Have a chat.'

I don't want to but I know I should. 'I should probably give Kate a call.'

'The big-boned girl? The one who ploughed you with poteen when you were sixteen?'

'That's Kate,' I laugh. He has never forgiven her for that.

'What kind of a name is that, at all, at all. She was a messer, that girl. Has she come to anything?'

'No, not at all. She just sold her shop in the city for two million to become a stay-at-home mother.' I try not to laugh at the shock on his face.

His ears prick up. 'Ah, sure, give her a call. Have a chat. You women like to do that. Good for the soul, your mother always said. Your mother loved talking, was always blatherin' on to someone or other about somethin' or other.'

'Wonder where she got that from,' I say under my breath but just as if by a miracle, my father's rubbery-looking ears work.

'Her star sign is where she got it from. Taurus. Talked a lot of bull.'

'Dad!'

'What? Is it an admittance of hate? No. Nothing of the sort. I loved her with all my heart but the woman talked a lot of bull. Not enough to talk about a thing, I had to hear about how she felt about it too. Ten times over.'

'You don't believe in star signs,' I nudge him.

'I do too. I'm Libra. Weighing scales.' He rocks from side to side. 'Perfectly balanced.'

I laugh and escape to my bedroom to phone Kate. I enter the room, practically unchanged since the day I left it. Despite the rare occasion of guests staying over after I'd gone, my parents never removed my leftover belongings. The Cure stickers were still on the door and parts of the wallpaper were ripped from the tape that had secured my posters. As a punishment for ruining the walls, Dad forced me to cut the grass in the back garden, but while doing so I ran the lawnmower over a shrub in the bedding. He refused to speak to me for the rest of the day. Apparently it was the first year the shrub had blossomed since he'd planted it. I couldn't understand his frustration then, but after spending years of hard work cultivating a marriage, only for it to wither and die, I can now understand his plight. But I bet he didn't feel the relief I feel right now.

My box bedroom can only fit a bed and a wardrobe but it was my whole world. My only personal space to think and dream, to cry and laugh and wait until I became old enough to do all the things I wasn't allowed to do. My only space in the world then and, at thirty-three years old, my only space now. Who knew I'd find myself back again without any of the things I'd yearned for, and, even worse, still yearning for them? Not to be a member of The Cure or married to Robert Smith, but with no baby and no husband. The wallpaper is floral and wild; completely inappropriate for a space of rest. Millions of tiny brown flowers cluster together with tiny splashes of faded green stalks. No wonder I'd covered them with posters. The carpet is brown with lighter brown swirls, stained from spilled perfume and make-up. New additions to the room are old and faded brown leather suitcases lying on top of the wardrobe, gathering dust since Mum died. Dad never goes anywhere, a life without Mum, he decided long ago, enough of a journey for him.

The duvet cover is the newest introduction. New, as in, over ten years old; Mum purchased it when my room became the guest room. I moved out a year before she died, to live with Kate, and I wish everyday since that I hadn't, all those precious days of not waking up to hear her long yawns that turned into songs, talking to herself as she made her verbal diary with Gay Byrne's radio show on in the background. She loved Gay Byrne; her sole ambition in life being to meet him. The closest she got to that dream was when she and Dad got tickets to sit in the audience of *The Late Late Show* and she spoke about it for years. I think she had a thing for him. Dad hated him. I think he knew about her thing.

He likes to listen to him now, though, whenever he's on. I think he reminds him of a precious time spent with Mum, as though when we all hear Gay Byrne's voice, he hears Mum's instead. When she died, he surrounded himself with all the things she adored. He put Gay on the radio every morning, watched Mum's television shows, bought her favourite biscuits in his weekly shopping trip even though he never ate them. He liked to see them on the shelf when he opened the cupboard, liked to see her magazines beside his newspaper. He liked her slippers staying beside her armchair by the fire. He liked to remind himself that his entire world hadn't fallen apart. Sometimes we need all the glue we can get, just to hold ourselves together.

At sixty-five years old, he was too young to lose his wife. At twenty-three I was too young to lose my mother. At fifty-five she shouldn't have lost her life, but cancer, the thief of seconds, undetected until far too late, stole it from her and us all. Dad married late in life for that time, and didn't have me until he was forty-two years old. I think that there was somebody that broke his heart back then that he has never spoken of and that I've never asked about, but what he does say about that period is that he spent more days of his life waiting for Mum than actually being with her, but that every second spent looking for her and, eventually, remembering her, was worth it for all the moments in between.

Mum never met Conor but I don't know whether she would have liked him, though she was too polite ever to have shown it. Mum loved all kinds of people but particularly those with high spirit and energy, people that lived and exuded that life. Conor is pleasant. Always just pleasant. Never overexcited. Never, in fact, excited at all. Just pleasant, which is just another word for nice. Marrying a nice man gives you a nice marriage but never anything more. And nice is OK when it's among other things but never when it stands alone.

Dad would talk to anyone anywhere and not have

a feeling about them one way or another. The only negative thing he ever said about Conor was, 'Sure, what kind of man likes *tennis*?' A GAA and soccer man, Dad had spat the word out as though just saying it had dirtied his mouth.

Our failure to produce a child didn't do much to sway Dad's opinion. He blamed it on the tennis but particularly on the little white shorts Conor sometimes wore, whenever pregnancy test after pregnancy test failed to show blue. I know he said it all to put a smile on my face; sometimes it worked, other times it didn't, but it was a safe joke because we all knew it wasn't the tennis shorts or the man wearing them that was the problem.

I sit down on the duvet cover bought by Mum, not wanting to crease it. A two-pillow and duvet cover set from Dunnes with a matching candle for the windowsill, which has never been lit and has lost its scent. Dust gathers on the top, incriminating evidence that Dad is not keeping up with his duties, as if at seventy-five years old the removal of dust from anywhere but his memory shelf should be a priority. But the dust has settled and so let it stay.

I turn on my mobile, which has been switched off for days, and it begins to beep as a dozen messages filter through. I have already made my calls to those near, dear and nosy. Like pulling off a Band-Aid; don't think about it, move quickly and it's almost painless. Flip open the phonebook and bam, bam, bam: three minutes each. Quick snappy phone calls made by a strangely upbeat woman who'd momentarily inhabited my body. An incredible woman, in fact, positive and perky, yet emotional and wise at all the right times. Her timing impeccable, her sentiments so poignant I almost wanted to write them down. She even attempted a bit of humour, which some members of the near, dear and nosy coped well with while others seemed almost insulted – not that she cared, for it was her party and she was crying if she wanted to. I've met her before, of course; she whizzes around to me for the occasional trauma, steps into my shoes and takes over the hard parts. She'll be back again, no doubt.

No, it will be a long time before I can speak in my own voice to people other than the woman I am calling now.

Kate picks up on the fourth ring.

'Hello,' she shouts and I jump. There are manic noises in the background, as though a mini-war has broken out.

'Joyce!' she yells and I realise I'm on speakerphone. 'I've been *calling* you and *calling* you. Derek, SIT DOWN. MUMMY IS NOT HAPPY! Sorry, I'm just doing the school run. I've to bring six kids home, then a quick snack before I bring Eric to basketball and Jayda to swimming. Want to meet me there at seven? Jayda is getting her ten-metre badge today.'

Jayda howls in the background about hating ten-metre badges.

'How can you hate it when you've never had one?' Kate snaps. Jayda howls even louder and I have to move the phone from my ear. 'JAYDA! GIVE MUMMY A BREAK! DEREK, PUT YOUR SEATBELT ON! If I have to brake suddenly, you will go FLYING through the windscreen and SMASH YOUR FACE IN. Hold on, Joyce.'

There is silence while I wait.

'Gracie!' Dad yells. I run to the top of the stairs in panic, not used to hearing him shout like that since I was a child.

'Yes? Dad! Are you OK?'

'I got seven letters,' he shouts.

'You got *what*?'

'Seven letters!'

'What does that mean?'

'In *Countdown*!'

I stop panicking and sit on the top stair in frustration. Suddenly Kate's voice is back and it sounds as though calm has been restored.

'OK, you're off speakerphone. I'll probably be arrested for holding the phone, not to mention cast off the car-pool list, like I give a flying fuck about that.'

'I'm telling my mammy you said the f word,' I hear a little voice.

'Good. I've been wanting to tell her that for years,' Kate murmurs to me and I laugh.

'FUCK, FUCK, FUCK, FUCK,' I hear a crowd of kids chanting.

'Jesus, Joyce, I better go. See you at the leisure centre at seven? It's my only break. Or else I have tomorrow. Tennis at three or gymnastics at six? I can see if Frankie is free to meet up too.'

Frankie. Christened Francesca but refuses to answer to it. Dad was wrong about Kate. She may have sourced the poteen but technically it was Frankie that held my mouth open and poured it down my throat. As a result of this version of the story never being told, he thinks Frankie's a saint, very much to Kate's annoyance.

'I'll take gymnastics tomorrow,' I smile as the children's chanting gets louder. Kate's gone and there's silence.

'GRACIE!' Dad calls again.

'It's *Joyce*, Dad.'

'I got the conundrum!'

I make my way back to my bed and cover my head with a pillow.

A few minutes later Dad arrives at the door, scaring the life out of me.

'I was the only one that got the conundrum. The contestants hadn't a clue. Simon won anyway, goes through to tomorrow's show. He's been the winner for three days now and I'm half bored lookin' at him. He has a funny-looking face; you'd have a right laugh if you saw it. Don't think Carol likes him much either and she's after losin' loads of weight again. Do you want a HobNob? I'm going to make another cuppa.'

'No, thanks.' I put the pillow back over my head. He uses so many *words*.

'Well, I'm having one. I have to eat with my pills. Supposed to take it at lunch but I forgot.'

'You took a pill at lunch, remember?'

'That was for my heart. This is for my memory. Short-term memory pills.'

I take the pillow off my face to see if he's being serious. 'And you forgot to take it?'

He nods.

'Oh, Dad.' I start to laugh while he looks on as though I'm having an episode. 'You are medicine enough for me. Well, you need to get stronger pills. They're not working, are they?'

He turns his back and makes his way down the hall, grumbling, 'They'd bloody well work if I remembered to take them.'

'Dad,' I call to him and he stops at the top of the stairs. 'Thanks for not asking any questions about Conor.'

'Sure, I don't need to. I know you'll be back together in no time.'

'No we won't,' I say softly.

He walks a little closer to my room. 'Is he stepping out with someone else?'

'No he's not. And I'm not. We don't love each other. We haven't for a long time.'

'But you married him, Joyce. Didn't I bring you down the aisle myself?' He looks confused.

'What's that got to do with anything?'

'You both promised each other in the house of our Lord, I heard you myself with my own ears. What is it with you young people these days, breaking up and remarrying all the time? What happened to keeping promises?'

I sigh. How can I answer that? He begins to walk away again.

'Dad.'

He stops but doesn't turn round.

'I don't think you're thinking of the alternative. Would you rather I kept my promise to spend the rest of my life with Conor, but not love him and be unhappy?'

'If you think your mother and I had a perfect marriage then you're wrong because there's no such thing. No one's happy all the time, love.'

'I understand that, but what if you're *never* happy. Ever.'

He thinks about that for what looks like the first time and I hold my breath until he finally speaks. 'I'm going to have a HobNob.'

Halfway down the stairs he shouts back rebelliously, 'A *chocolate* one.'

12

'I'm on a vacation, bro, why are you dragging me to a gym?' Al half-walks half-skips alongside Justin in an effort to keep up with his lean brother's long strides.

'I have a date with Sarah next week,' Justin power-walks from the tube station, 'and I need to get back into shape.'

'I didn't realise you were *out* of shape,' Al pants, and wipes trickles of sweat from his brow.

'The divorce cloud was preventing me from working out.'

'The divorce cloud?'

'Never heard of it?'

Al, unable to speak, shakes his head and wobbles his chins like a turkey.

'The cloud moves to take the shape of your body, wraps itself nice and tight around you so that you can barely move. Or breathe. Or exercise. Or even *date*, let alone *sleep* with other women.'

'Your divorce cloud sounds like my marriage cloud.'

'Yeah, well, that cloud has moved on now.' Justin looks up at the grey London sky, closes his eyes for a brief moment and breathes in deeply. 'It's time for me to get back into action.' He opens his eyes and walks straight into a lamppost. 'Jesus, Al!' He doubles over, head in his hands. 'Thanks for the warning.'

Al's beetroot face wheezes back at him, words not coming easily. Or at all.

'Never mind *my* having to work out, look at yourself. Your doctor's already told you to drop a few hundred pounds.'

'Fifty pounds . . .' gasp, 'aren't exactly . . .' gasp, 'a few *hundred*, and don't start on me too.' Gasp. 'Doris is bad enough.' Wheeze. Cough. 'What she knows about dieting is beyond me. The woman doesn't eat. She's afraid to bite a nail in case they've too many calories.'

'Doris's nails are real?'

'Them and her hair is about all. I gotta hold on to something.' Al looks around, flustered.

'Too much information,' Justin says, misunderstanding. 'I can't believe Doris's *hair* is real too.'

'All but the colour. She's a brunette. Italian, of course. Dizzy.'

'Yeah, she is a bit dizzy. All that past-life talk about the woman at the hair salon,' Justin laughs. *So how do you explain it?*

'I meant *I'm* dizzy.' Al glares at him and reaches out to hold on to the nearby railing.

'Oh . . . I knew that, I was kidding. It looks like we're almost here. Think you can make it another hundred yards or so?'

'Depends on the "or so",' Al snaps.

'It's about the same as the week *or so* vacation that you and Doris were planning on taking. Looks like that's turning into a month.'

'Well, we wanted to surprise you, and Doug is well able to take care of the shop while I'm gone. The doc advised me to take it easy, Justin. With heart conditions being in the family history, I really need to rest up.'

'You told the doctor there's a history of heart conditions in the family?' Justin asks.

'Yeah, Dad died of a heart attack. Who else would I be talkin' about?'

Justin is silent.

'Besides, you won't be sorry, Doris will have your apartment done up so nice that you'll be glad we stayed. You know she did the doggie parlour all by herself?'

Justin's eyes widen.

'I know,' Al beams proudly. 'So, how many of these seminars will you be doing in Dublin? Me and Doris might accompany you on one of your trips over there, you know, see the place Dad was from.'

'Dad was from Cork.'

'Oh. Does he still have family there? We could go and trace our roots, what do you think?'

'That's not such a bad idea.' Justin thinks of his schedule. 'I have a few more seminars ahead. You probably won't be here that long, though.' He eyes Al sideways, testing him. 'And you can't come next week because I'm mixing that trip with a date with Sarah.'

'You're really hot on this girl?'

His almost forty-year-old brother's vocabulary never ceases to amaze Justin. 'Am I hot on this girl?' he repeats, amused and confused all at the same time. *Good question. Not really, but she's company. Is that an acceptable answer?*

'Did she have you at "I vant your blood"?' Al chuckles.

'Wow, that was uncanny,' Justin says. 'Sarah, too, is a vampire from Transylvania. Let's do an hour at the gym.' He changes the subject. 'I don't think "resting up" is going to make you any better. That's what got you into this state in the first place.'

'*One hour?*' Al almost explodes. 'What are you planning on doing on the date, rock-climbing?'

'It's just lunch.'

Al rolls his eyes. 'What, you have to chase and kill your food? Anyway, you wake up tomorrow morning after your first work-out for a whole year, you won't be able to *walk*, never mind screw.'

I wake up to the sound of banging pots and pans coming from downstairs. I expect to be in my own bedroom at home and it takes me a moment to remember. And then I remember everything, all over again. My daily morning pill as usual, hard to swallow. One of these days I'll wake up and I'll just know. I'm not sure which scenario I prefer; the moments of forget-fulness are such bliss.

I didn't sleep well last night between the thoughts in my head and the sound of the cistern flushing every hour after Dad's toilet breaks. When he was asleep, his snores rattled through the walls of the house.

Despite the interruptions, my dreams during my rare moments of sleep are still vivid in my mind. They almost feel real, like memories, though who's to know how real even they are, with all the altering our minds do? I remember being in a park, though I don't think I was me. I twirled a young girl with white-blonde hair around in my arms while a woman with red hair looked on smiling, with a camera in her hand. The park was colourful with lots of flowers and we had a picnic . . . I try to remember the song I'd been hearing all night but it fails me. Instead I hear Dad downstairs singing 'The Auld Triangle', an old Irish song he has sung at parties all of my life and probably most of his too. He'd stand there, eyes closed, pint in hand, a picture of bliss as he sang his story of how 'the auld triangle went jingle jangle'.

I swing my legs out of the bed and groan with pain, suddenly feeling an ache in both legs from my hips, right down my thighs, all the way down to my calf muscles. I try to move the rest of my body and feel paralysed with the pain too; my shoulders, biceps, triceps, back muscles and torso. I massage my muscles with complete confusion and make a note in my head to go to the doctor, just in case it's something to be worried about. I'm sure it's my heart, either looking for more attention, or so full of pain it has needed to ooze its ache around the rest of my body just to relieve itself. Each throbbing muscle is an extension of the pain I feel inside, though a doctor will tell me it's due to the thirty-year-old bed I slept on, manufactured before the time people claimed nightly back support as their God-given right. Potayto, potato.

I throw a dressing gown around me and slowly, as

stiff as a board, make my way downstairs, trying my best not to bend my legs.

The smell of smoke is in the air again and I notice as I'm passing the hall table that Mum's photograph once again isn't there. Something urges me to slide open the drawer beneath the table and there she is, lying face down in the drawer. Tears spring in my eyes, angry that something so precious has been hidden away. It has always meant more than a photograph to the both of us; it represents her presence in the house, pride of place to greet us whenever we come in the front door or down the stairs. I take deep breaths and decide to say nothing for now, assuming Dad has his reasons, though I can't think of any acceptable examples at this point. I slide the drawer closed and leave her where Dad has placed her, feeling like I'm burying her all over again.

When I limp into the kitchen, chaos greets me. There are pots and pans everywhere, tea towels, egg shells and what looks like the contents of the cupboards covering the counters. Dad is wearing an apron with an image of a woman in red lingerie and suspenders, over his usual sweater, shirt and trousers. On his feet are Manchester United slippers, shaped as large footballs.

'Morning, love.' He sees me and steps up onto his left leg to give me a kiss on the forehead.

I realise it's the first time in years somebody has made my breakfast for me, but it's also the first time for many years that Dad has had somebody to cook breakfast for. Suddenly the singing, the mess, the clattering pots and pans all make sense. He's excited.

'I'm making waffles!' he says with an American accent.

'Ooh, very nice.'

'That's what the donkey says, isn't it?'

'What donkey?'

'The one . . .' he stops stirring whatever is in the frying pan and closes his eyes to think, 'the story with the green man.'

'The Incredible Hulk?'

'No.'

'Well, I don't know any other green people.'

'You do, you know the one . . .'

'The Wicked Witch of the West?'

'No! There's no donkey in that! Think about stories with donkeys in them.'

'Is it a biblical tale?'

'Were there talking donkeys in the Bible, Gracie? Did Jesus eat waffles, do you think? Christ, we have it all wrong: it was waffles he was breaking at supper to share with the lads, and not bread after all!'

'My name is Joyce.'

'I don't remember Jesus eating waffles but, sure, won't I ask the crowd at the Monday Club? Maybe I've been reading the wrong Bible all my life.' He laughs at his own joke.

I look over his shoulder. 'Dad, you're not even making waffles!'

He sighs with exasperation. 'Am I a donkey? Do I look like a donkey to you? Donkeys make waffles, *I* make a good fry-up.'

I watch him poking the sausages around, trying to get all sides evenly cooked. 'I'll have sausages too.'

'But you're one of those vegetarianists.'

'Vegetarian. And I'm not any more.'

'Sure of course you're not. You've only been one since you were fifteen years old after seeing that show about the seals. Tomorrow I'll wake up and you'll be tellin' me you're a man. Saw it on the telly once. This woman, about the same age as you, brought her husband live on the telly in front of an audience to tell him that she decided that she wanted to turn her—'

Feeling frustrated with him, I blurt out, 'Mum's photo isn't on the hall table.'

Dad freezes, a reaction of guilt, and this makes me somewhat angry, as though before I had convinced myself that the mysterious midnight photograph-mover had broken in and done the dirty deed himself. I'd almost prefer that.

'Why?' is all I say.

He keeps himself busy, clattering with plates and cutlery now. 'Why what? Why are you walking like that is what I want to know?' Dad eyes my walk curiously.

'I don't know,' I snap, and limp across the room to take a seat at the table. 'Maybe it runs in the family.'

'Hoo hoo hoo,' Dad hoots and looks up at the ceiling, 'we've got a live one here, boss! Set the table like a good girl.'

He brings me right back and I can't help but smile. And so I set the table and Dad makes the breakfast and we both limp around the kitchen pretending everything is as it was and forever shall be. World without end.

13

'So, Dad, what are your plans for the day? Are you busy?'

A forkful of sausage, egg, bacon, pudding, mushroom and tomato stops on its way into my dad's open mouth. Amused eyes peer out at me from under his wildly wiry eyebrows.

'Plans, you say? Well, let's see, Gracie, while I go through the ol' schedule of events for the day. I was thinking of after I finish my fry in approximately fifteen minutes, I'd have another cuppa tea. Then while I'm drinking me tea I might sit down in this chair at this table, or maybe that chair where you are, the exact venue is TBD, as my schedule would say. Then I'll go through yesterday's answers of the crossword to see what we got correct and what was incorrect and then I'll find out the answer to the ones I couldn't figure out yesterday. Then I'll do the Dusoku, then the word game. I see we've to try and find *nautical* words today. *Seafaring*, *maritime*, *yachting*, yes, I'll be able to do that, sure I can see the word "boating" there on the first line already. Then I'm going to cut out my coupons and all that will fill my early morning right up, Gracie. Then I'd say I'll have another cuppa after all of that and then my programmes start. If you'd like to make an appointment, talk to Maggie.' He finally shovels the food into his mouth and egg drips down his chin. He doesn't notice and leaves it there.

I laugh. 'Who's Maggie?'

He swallows and smiles, amused at himself. 'I don't know why I said it.' He thinks hard and finally laughs. 'There was a fella I used to know in Cavan, this is goin' back sixty years now, Brendan Brady was his name. Whenever we'd be tryin' to make arrangements he'd say,' Dad deepens his voice, '"Talk to Maggie," like he was someone awful important.' She was either his wife or his secretary, I hadn't a clue. "Talk to Maggie,"' he repeats. 'Maggie was probably his mother,' he laughs, and continues eating.

'So basically, according to your schedule, you're doing exactly the same thing as yesterday.'

'Oh, no, it's not the same at all.' He thumbs through his TV guide and stabs a greasy finger on today's page. He looks at his watch and slides his finger down the page. He picks up his highlighter and marks another show. '*Animal Hospital* is on instead of the *Antiques Roadshow*. Not exactly the same day as yesterday at all, at all, how's about that. It'll be doggies and bunnies today instead of Betty's fake teapots. We might see her trying to sell the family dog for a few shillings. You might get that bikini on you after all, Betty.' He continues to draw a design around his shows on the TV page, his tongue licking the corners of his mouth in concentration as though he was decorating a manuscript.

'The Book of Kells,' I blurt out of nowhere, though that is nothing odd these days. My random ramblings are becoming something of the norm.

'What are you talking about now?' Dad stops his colouring and resumes eating.

'Let's go into town today. Do a tour of the city, go to Trinity College and look at the Book of Kells.'

Dad stares at me and munches. I'm not sure what he's thinking. He's probably thinking the same of me.

'You want to go to Trinity College. The girl who never wanted to set foot near the place for either studies or excursions with me and your mother, suddenly out of the blue wants to go. Sure, aren't "suddenly" and "out of the blue" one and the same? They shouldn't go together in a sentence, Henry,' he corrects himself.

'Yes, I want to go.' I suddenly, out of the blue, very much want to go to Trinity College.

'If you don't want to watch the *Animal Hospital* show just say so. You don't have to go darting into the city. There's such a thing as changing channels.'

'You're right, Dad, and I've been doing some of that recently.'

'Is that so? I hadn't noticed, what with your marriage breaking up, your not being a vegetarianist any more, your not mentioning a word about your job and your moving in with me, and all. There's been so much action around here, how's a man to tell if a channel's been changed or if a new show has just begun?'

'I need to do something new,' I explain. 'I have time for Frankie and Kate but everybody else . . . I'm just not ready right now. We need a change of schedule, Dad. I've got the big remote control of life in my hands and I'm ready to start pushing some buttons.'

He stares at me for a moment and puts a sausage in his mouth in response.

'We'll get a taxi into town and catch one of those tour buses, what do you think? MAGGIE!' I shout out at the top of my voice and it makes Dad jump. 'MAGGIE, DAD IS COMING INTO TOWN WITH ME TO HAVE A LOOK AROUND. IS THAT OK?'

I cock my ear and wait for a response. Happy I've received one, I nod and stand up. 'Right, Dad, it's been decided. Maggie says it's fine if you go into town. I'll have a shower and we'll leave in an hour. Ha! That rhymes.' I limp out of the kitchen, leaving my bewildered father behind with egg on his chin.

'I doubt Maggie said yes to me walkin' at this speed, Gracie,' Dad says, trying to keep up with me as we dodge pedestrians on Grafton Street.

'Sorry, Dad.' I slow down and link his arm. Despite his corrective footwear he still sways and I sway with him. Even if he was operated on to equal the length of his legs, I'd imagine he'd still sway, it's so much a part of who he is.

'Dad, are you ever going to call me Joyce?'

'What are you talkin' about? Sure, isn't that your name?'

I look at him with surprise. 'Do you not notice you always call me Gracie?'

He seems taken aback but makes no comment and keeps walking. Up and down, down and up.

'I'll give you a fiver, every time you call me Joyce today,' I smile.

'That's a deal, Joyce, Joyce, Joyce. Oh, how I love you, Joyce,' he chuckles. 'That's twenty quid already!' He nudges me and says seriously, 'I didn't notice I called you that, love. I'll do my best.'

'Thank you.'

'You remind me so much of her, you know.'

'Ah, Dad, really?' I'm touched; I feel my eyes prick with tears. He never says that. 'In what way?'

'You both have little piggy noses.'

I roll my eyes.

'I don't know why we're walking further away from Trinity College. Wasn't it there that you wanted to go to?'

'Yes, but the tour buses leave from Stephen's Green. We'll see it as we're passing. I don't really want to go in there now anyway.'

'Why not?'

'It's lunchtime.'

'And the Book of Kells goes off for an hour's break, does it?' Dad rolls his eyes. 'A ham sambo and a flask of tea and then it props itself back up on display, right as rain for the afternoon. Is that what you think happens? Because, not going just because it's lunchtime doesn't make any sense to me.'

'Well, it does to me.' And I don't know why it does but it just feels like the right direction to go in. Internal compass says so.

*　　*　　*

Justin darts through the front arch of Trinity College and bounds up the road to Grafton Street. Lunchtime with Sarah. He beats away the nagging voice within him telling him to cancel her. *Give her a chance. Give yourself a chance.* He needs to try, he needs to find his feet again, he needs to remember that not every meeting with a woman is going to be the same as the first time he laid eyes on Jennifer. The thump-thump, thump-thump feeling that made his entire body vibrate, the butterflies that did acrobatics in his stomach, the tingle when he brushed off her skin. He thought about how he'd felt on his date with Sarah. Nothing. Nothing but flattery that she was attracted to him and excitement that he was back out in the dating world again. Plenty of feelings about her and the situation but nothing *for* her. He had more of a reaction to the woman in the hair salon a few weeks ago and that was saying something. *Give her a chance. Give yourself a chance.*

Grafton Street is crowded at lunchtime, as though the gates to Dublin zoo have been opened and all the animals have flooded out, happy to escape confinement for an hour. He has finished work for the day, his seminar on his specialist subject, Copper as Canvas: 1575–1775, being a success with the third-year students who had elected to hear him speak.

Conscious that he'll be late for Sarah, he attempts to break into a run, but the aches and pains in his over-exercised body almost cripple him. Hating that Al's warnings were correct, instead he limps along, trailing behind what seem to be the two slowest people on Grafton Street. His plan to overtake them on either side is botched as people-traffic prevent him from leaving his lane. With impatience he slows, surrendering to the speed of the two before him, one of whom is singing happily to himself and swaying.

Drunk at this hour, honestly.

Dad takes his time, meandering up Grafton Street as though he has all the time in the world. I suppose he does, compared to everybody else, though a younger person would think differently. Sometimes he stops and points at things, joins circles of spectators to watch a street act and when we continue on, he steps out of line to really confuse the situation. Like a rock in a stream, he sends people flowing around him; he's a small diversion yet he's completely oblivious. He sings as we move up and down, down and up.

> 'Grafton Street's a wonderland,
> There's magic in the air,
> There's diamonds in the ladies' eyes and gold-
>   dust in their hair.
> And if you don't believe me,
> Come and see me there,
> In Dublin on a sunny summer morning.'

He looks at me and smiles and sings it all over again, forgetting some words and humming them instead.

During my busiest days at work, twenty-four hours just don't seem enough. I almost want to hold my hands out in the air and try to grasp the seconds and minutes as if I could stop them from moving on, like a little girl trying to catch bubbles. You can't hold on to time but somehow Dad appears to. I always wondered how on earth he filled his moments, as though my opening doors and talking about sunny angles, central heating and wardrobe space was worth so much more than his pottering. In truth, we're all just pottering, filling the time that we have here, only we like to make ourselves feel bigger by compiling lists of importance.

So this is what you do when it all slows down and the minutes that tick by feel a little longer than before. You take your time. You breathe slowly. You open your eyes a little wider and look at everything. Take it all in. Rehash stories of old, remember people, times and occasions gone by. Allow everything you see to remind you of something. Talk about those things. Stop and take your time to notice things and make those things you notice matter. Find out the answers you didn't know to yesterday's crosswords. *Slow down.* Stop trying to do everything now, now, now. Hold up the people behind you for all you care, feel them kicking at your heels but maintain your pace. Don't let anybody dictate your speed.

Though if the person behind me kicks my heels one more time . . .

The sun is so bright it's difficult to look straight ahead. It's as though it's sitting on the top of Grafton Street, another bowling ball ready to knock us all down. Finally we near the top of the street and escape of the human current is in sight. Dad suddenly stops walking, enthralled by the sight of a mime artist nearby. As I'm linking his arm, I'm forced to a sudden stop too, causing the person behind to run straight into me. One grand final kick of my heels. That is it.

'Hey!' I spin around. 'Watch it!'

He grunts at me in frustration and power-walks off. 'Hey yourself,' an American accent calls back.

I'm about to shout again but his voice silences me.

'Look at that,' Dad marvels, watching the mime trapped in an invisible box. 'Should I give him an invisible key to get out of that box?' He laughs again. 'Wouldn't that be funny, love?'

'No, Dad.' I examine the back of my road-rage nemesis, trying to recall the voice.

'You know de Valera escaped prison by using a key that was smuggled in to him in a birthday cake. Someone should tell this fella that story. Now where do we go from here?' He spins round beside me, looking about. He walks off in another direction, straight through a group of parading Hare Krishnas, without taking the slightest bit of notice.

The sandy duffel coat turns round again, throws me one last dirty look before he hurries on in a huff.

Still, I stare. If I was to reverse the frown. That smile. Familiar.

'Gracie, this is where you get the tickets. I've found it,' he shouts from afar.

'Hold on, Dad.' I watch after the duffel coat. Turn round one more time and show me your face, I plead.

'I'll just go get the tickets, so.'

'OK, Dad.' I continue to watch the duffel coat moving further away. I don't – correction, *can't* – move my eyes away from him. I mentally throw a cowboy's rope around his body and begin to pull him back towards me. His strides become smaller, his speed gradually slows.

He suddenly stops dead in his tracks. Yee-ha.

Please turn. I pull on the rope.

He spins round, searches the crowd. For me?

'Who are you?' I whisper.

'It's me!' Dad is beside me again. 'You're just standing in the middle of the street.'

'I know what I'm doing,' I snap. 'Here, go get the tickets.' I hold out some money.

I step away from the Hare Krishnas, keeping my eye on the duffel coat, hoping he'll see me. The crisp pale wool of his coat almost glows among the dark and gloomy colours of others around him. Around his sleeves, down his front like an autumn St Nicholas. I clear my throat and smooth down my shortened hair.

His eyes continue to search the street and then they ever so slowly fall upon mine. I remember him in the second it takes them to register me. 'Him' from the hair salon.

What now? Perhaps he won't recognise me at all. Perhaps he's just still angry that I shouted at him. I'm not sure what to do. Should I smile? Wave? Neither of us moves.

He holds up a hand. Waves. I look behind me first, to ensure it's me that his attention is on. Though I was so sure anyway, I would have bet my father on it. Suddenly Grafton Street is empty. And silent. Just me and him. Funny how that happened. How thoughtful of everyone. I wave back. He mouths something to me.

Hungry? Horny? No.

Sorry. He's sorry. I try to figure out what to mouth back but I'm smiling. Nothing can be mouthed when smiling, it's as impossible as whistling through a smile.

'I got the tickets!' Dad shouts. 'Twenty euro each – it's a crime, that is. Seeing is for free, I don't know how they can charge us to use our eyes. I'm planning to write a strongly worded letter to somebody about that. Next time you ask me why I stay in and watch my programmes I'll have it in mind to remind you that it's free. Two euro for my TV guide, one hundred and fifty for a *yearly* licence fee is better value than a *day* out with you,' he huffs. 'Expensive taxis into the town, lookin' at things in a city I've lived in and have looked at for free for sixty years.'

Suddenly I hear the traffic again, see the people crowding around, feel the sun and breeze on my face, feel my heart beating wildly in my chest as my blood rushes around in frenzied excitement. I feel Dad tugging on my arm.

'It's leaving now. Come on, Gracie, it's leaving. It's a bit of a walk up the road, we have to go. Near the Shelbourne Hotel. Are you OK? You look like you've seen a ghost and don't tell me you have because I've dealt with enough today already. Forty euro,' he mutters to himself.

A steady flow of pedestrians gather at the top of Grafton Street to cross the road, blocking my view of him. I feel Dad pulling me back and so I begin to move with him down Merrion Row, walking backwards, trying to keep him in sight.

'Damn it!'

'What's wrong, love? It's not far up the road at all. What on earth are you doing, walking backwards?'

'I can't see him.'

'Who, love?'

'A guy I think I know.' I stop walking backwards and stand in line with Dad, continuing to look down the street and scouring the crowds.

'Well, unless you know that you know him for sure, I wouldn't be stopping to chat in the city,' Dad says protectively. 'What kind of a bus is this at all, Gracie? It looks a bit odd, I'm not sure about this. I don't come to the city for a few years and look what the CIE do.'

I ignore him and let him lead the way onto the bus, while I'm busy looking the other way, searching furiously through the, curiously, plastic windows. The crowd finally move on from in front of where he stood to reveal nothing.

'He's gone.'

'Is that so? Can't have known him too well then, if he just ran off.'

I turn my attention to my father. 'Dad, that was the weirdest thing.'

'I don't care what you say, there's nothing weirder than this.' Dad looks around us in bewilderment.

Finally I too look around the bus and take in my surroundings. Everyone else is wearing a Viking helmet, with life jackets on their laps.

'OK, everybody,' the tour guide speaks into the microphone, 'we finally have everyone on board. Let's show our new arrivals what to do. When I say the word I want you all to rooooooar just like the Vikings did! Let me hear it!'

Dad and I jump in our seats, and I feel him cling to me, as the entire bus roars.

14

'Good afternoon, everybody, I'm Olaf the White, and welcome aboard the Viking Splash bus! Historically known as DUKWS, or Ducks, as they're more affectionately known. We are sitting in the amphibious version of the General Motors vehicle built during World War Two. Designed to withstand being driven onto beaches in fifteen-foot seas to deliver cargo or troops from ship to shore, they are now more commonly used as rescue and underwater recovery vehicles in the US, UK and other parts of the world.'

'Can we get off?' I whisper in Dad's ear.

He swats me away, enthralled.

'This particular vehicle weighs seven tonnes, is thirty-one feet long and eight feet wide. It has six wheels and can be driven in rear-wheel or all-wheel drive. As you can see, it has been mechanically rebuilt and outfitted with comfortable seats, a roof, roll down sides to protect you from the elements, because as you all know, after we see the sites around the city, we have a "splashdown" into the water with a fantastic trip around the Grand Canal Docklands!'

Everyone cheers and Dad looks at me, eyes wide like a little boy.

'Sure, no wonder it was twenty euro. A bus that goes into the water. A *bus*? That goes into the *water*? I've never seen the likes of it. Wait till I tell the lads at the Monday Club about this. Big mouth Donal won't be able to beat this story for once.' He turns his attention back to the tour operator, who, like everyone else on the bus, is wearing a Viking helmet with horns. Dad collects two, props one on his head and hands the other, which has blonde side plaits attached, to me.

'Olaf, meet Heidi.' I pop it on my head and turn to Dad.

He roars quietly in my face.

'Sights along the way include our famous city cathedrals, St Patrick's and Christchurch, Trinity College, Government buildings, Georgian Dublin . . .'

'Ooh, you'll like this one,' Dad elbows me.

'. . . and of course *Viking Dublin*!'

Everyone roars again, including Dad, and I can't help but laugh.

'I don't understand why we're celebrating a bunch of oafs who raped and pillaged their way around our country.'

'Oh, would you ever lighten up, at all, and have the craic?'

'And what do we do when we see a *rival* DUKW on the road?' the tour guide asks.

There's a mixture of boos and roars.

'OK, let's go!' Olaf says enthusiastically.

Justin frantically searches over the shaven heads of a group of Hare Krishnas who have begun to parade by him and obstruct his view of his woman in the red coat. A sea of orange togas, they smile at him merrily through their bell-ringing and drum-beating. He hops up and down on the spot, trying to get a view down Merrion Row.

Before him, a mime artist, dressed in a black leotard, with a painted white face, red lips and a striped hat, appears suddenly. They stand opposite one another, each waiting for the other to do something, Justin praying for the mime to grow bored and leave. He doesn't. Instead, the mime squares his shoulders, looks mean, parts his legs and lets his fingers quiver around his holster area.

Keeping his voice down, Justin speaks politely, 'Hey, I'm really not in the mood for this. Would you mind playing with someone else, please?'

Looking forlorn, the mime begins to play an invisible violin.

Justin hears laughter and realises he has an audience. *Great.*

'Yeah, that's funny. OK, enough now.'

Ignoring the antics, Justin distances himself from the growing crowd and continues to search down Merrion Row for the red coat.

The mime appears beside him again, holds his hand to his forehead and searches the distance as though at sea. His herd of spectators follow, bleating and snap-happy. An elderly Japanese couple take a photograph.

Justin grits his teeth and speaks quietly, hoping nobody but the mime can hear. 'Hey, asshole, do I look like I'm having fun?'

With lips of a ventriloquist, a gruff Dublin accent responds, 'Hey, asshole, do I look like I give a shit?'

'You wanna play like this? Fine. I'm not sure whether you're trying to be Marcel Marceau or Coco the clown but your little pantomime street performance is insulting to both of them. This crowd might find your stolen routines from Marceau's repertoire amusing but I don't. Unlike me, they're not aware that you've failed to notice the fact that Marceau used these routines to tell a story or sketch a theme or character. He did not just randomly stand on a street trying to get out of a box nobody could see. Your lack of creativity and technique gives a bad name to mimes all over the world.'

The mime blinks once and proceeds to walk against an invisible strong wind.

'Here I am!' a voice calls beyond the crowd.

There she is! She recognised me!

Justin shuffles from foot to foot, trying to catch sight of her red coat.

The crowd turns and parts, to reveal Sarah, looking excited by the scene.

The mime mimicks Justin's obvious disappointment, plastering a look of despair on his face and hunching his back so that his arms hang low and his hands almost scrape the ground.

'Oooooooo,' go the crowd, and Sarah's face falls.

Justin nervously replaces his look of disappointment with a smile. He makes his way through the crowd, greets Sarah quickly and leads her speedily away from the scene while the crowd clap and some drop coins into a container nearby.

'Don't you think that was a bit rude? Maybe you should have given him some change or something,' she says, looking over her shoulder apologetically at the mime, who is covering his face and moving his shoulders up and down violently in a false fit of tears.

'I think the gentleman in the leotard was a bit rude.' Distracted, Justin continues to look around for the red coat as they make their way to the restaurant for lunch, which Justin now definitely wants to cancel.

Tell her you feel sick. No. She's a doctor, she'll ask too many questions. Tell her you have unfortunately made a mistake and that you have a lecture, right now. Tell her, tell her!

But instead he finds himself continuing to walk with her, his mind as active as Mount St Helens, his eyes jumping around like an addict needing a fix. In the basement restaurant, they are led to a quiet table in the corner. Justin eyes the door.

Yell 'FIRE' and run!

Sarah shuffles her coat off her shoulders to reveal much flesh, and pulls her chair closer to his.

Such a coincidence he bumped, quite literally, into the woman from the salon again. Though maybe it wasn't such a big deal; Dublin's a small town. Since being here he's learned that everyone pretty much knows everyone, or somebody related to somebody, that someone once knew. But the woman, he would definitely have to stop calling her that. He should give her a name. *Angelina.*

'What are you thinking about?' Sarah leans across the table and gazes at him.

Or Lucille. 'Coffee. I'm thinking about coffee. I'll have a black coffee, please,' he says to the waitress clearing their table. He looks at her name badge. *Jessica*. No, his woman wasn't a Jessica.

'You're not eating?' Sarah asks, disappointed and confused.

'No, I can't stay as long as I'd hoped. I have to get back to the college earlier than planned.' His leg bounces beneath the table, hitting the surface and rattling the cutlery. The waitress and Sarah eye him peculiarly.

'Oh, OK, well,' she studies the menu, 'I'll have a chef's salad and a glass of the house white, please,' she says to the waitress and then to Justin, 'I have to eat or I'll collapse, I hope you don't mind.'

'No problem,' he smiles. *Even though you ordered the biggest fucking salad on the menu. How about the name, Susan? Does my woman look like a Susan? My woman? What the hell is wrong with me?*

'We are now turning into Dawson Street, so named after Joshua Dawson, who also designed Grafton, Anne and Henry Streets. On your right you will see the Mansion House, which houses the Lord Mayor of Dublin.'

All horned Viking helmets turn to the right. Video cameras, digital cameras and camera phones are suspended from the the open windows.

'You think this is what the Vikings did, way back when, Dad? Went clickety-click with their cameras at buildings that weren't even built yet?' I whisper.

'Oh, shut up,' he says loudly, and the tour operator stops speaking, shocked.

'Not you.' Dad waves a hand at him. 'Her.' He points, and the entire bus looks at me.

'To your right you will see St Anne's Church, which was designed by Isaac Wells in 1707. The interior dates back to the seventeenth century,' Olaf continues to the thirty-strong crew of Vikings aboard.

'Actually the Romanesque façade wasn't added until 1868, and that was designed by Thomas Newenham Deane,' I whisper to Dad.

'Oh,' Dad says slowly at this, eyes widening. 'I didn't know that.'

My eyes widen at my own piece of information. 'Me neither.'

Dad chuckles.

'We are now on Nassau Street, we will pass Grafton Street on the left in just a moment.'

Dad starts singing, 'Grafton Street's a wonderland.' Loudly.

The American woman in front of us turns around, her face beaming. 'Oh, do you know that song? My father used to sing that song. He was from Ireland. Oh, I would love to hear it again; can you sing it for us?'

A chorus of, 'Oh, yes, please do . . .' from around us.

No stranger to singing in public, the man who sings weekly at the Monday Club begins singing and the entire bus joins in, moving from side to side. Dad's voice reaches out beyond the plastic fold-up windows of the DUKW and into the ears of pedestrians and traffic going by.

I take another mental photograph of Dad sitting beside me, singing with his eyes closed, two horns propped on top of his head.

Justin watches with growing impatience as Sarah slowly picks at her salad. Her fork playfully pokes at a piece of chicken; the chicken hangs on, falls off, grabs on again and manages to hang on while she waves it around, using it as a sledgehammer to knock pieces of lettuce over to see what's beneath. Finally she stabs a piece of tomato and as she lifts the fork to her mouth, the same piece of chicken falls off again. That was the third time she'd done that.

'Are you sure you're not hungry, Justin? You seem to be really studying this plate,' she smiles, waving another forkful of food around, sending red onion and cheddar cheese tumbling back to the plate. It was like one step forward, two steps back every time.

'Yeah, sure, I wouldn't mind having some.' He'd already ordered and finished a bowl of soup in the time it had taken her to have five mouthfuls.

'You want me to feed it to you?' she flirts, moving it in circular motions towards his mouth.

'Well, I want more on it than that, for a start.'

She spears a few other pieces of food.

'More,' he says, keeping an eye on his watch. The more food he can squeeze in his mouth, the quicker this frustrating experience will be over. He knows that his woman, *Veronica*, is probably long gone by now, but sitting here, watching Sarah burn more calories playing with her food than ingesting them, isn't going to confirm that for him.

'OK, here comes the aeroplane,' she sings.

'More.' At least half of it has fallen again during its 'take-off'.

'More? How can you possibly fit more on the fork, never mind in your mouth?'

'Here, I'll show you.' Justin takes the fork from her and begins stabbing at as much as he can. Chicken, corn, lettuce, beetroot, onion, tomato, cheese; he manages it all. 'Now, if the lady pilot would like to bring her plane in to land . . .'

She giggles. 'This is *not* going to fit in your mouth.'

'I have a pretty big mouth.'

She shovels it in, laughing all the while, barely fitting it all into Justin's mouth. When he's finally swallowed it all, he looks at his watch and then again at her plate.

'OK, now you do it.' *You're such a shit, Justin.*

'No way,' she laughs.

'Come on.' He gathers as much food as possible, including the same piece of chicken she's deserted four times and 'flies' it into her open mouth.

She laughs while trying to fit it all in. Barely able to breathe, chew, swallow or smile, she still tries to look pretty. For almost a full minute she's unable to speak in her attempts to chew as ladylike as possible. Juices, dressing and food dribble down her chin and when she finally swallows, her lipstick-smudged mouth smiles at him to reveal a great big piece of lettuce stuck between her teeth.

'That was fun,' she smiles.

Helen. Like Helen of Troy, so beautiful she could start a war.

'Are you finished? Can I take the plate?' the waitress asks.

Sarah begins to answer, 'N—' but Justin jumps in.

'Yes, we are, thank you.' He avoids Sarah's stare.

'Actually I'm not quite finished, thank you,' Sarah says sternly. The plate is replaced.

Justin's leg bounces beneath the table, his impatience growing. *Salma. Sexy Salma.* An awkward silence falls between them.

'I'm sorry, Salma, I don't mean to be rude—'

'Sarah.'

'What?'

'My name is Sarah.'

'I know that. It's just that—'

'You called me Salma.'

'Oh. What? Who's Salma? God. Sorry. I don't even know a Salma, honestly.'

She speeds up her eating, obviously dying to get away from him now.

He says more softly, 'It's just that I have to get back to the college—'

'Earlier than planned. You said.' She smiles quickly and her face falls immediately as she looks back down at her plate. She pierces the food with purpose now. Playtime over. Time to eat. Food fills her mouth instead of words.

Justin cringes inside, knowing his behaviour is uncharacteristically rude. *Now say it like you mean it, you jerk.* He stares at her: beautiful face, great body, intelligent woman. Dressed smartly in a trouser suit, long legs, big lips. Long elegant fingers, neat French-manicured nails, a smart bag to match her shoes by her feet. Professional, confident, intelligent. There is absolutely nothing wrong with this woman at all. It is Justin's own distraction that is the problem, the feeling that a part of him is somewhere else. A part of him, in fact, that feels so nearby, he is almost compelled to run out and catch it. Right now running seems like a good idea but the problem is he doesn't know what he is trying to catch, or who. In a city of one million people, he can't expect to walk outside this door and find the same woman standing on the pavement. And is it worth leaving the beautiful woman sitting with him in this restaurant, in order just to chase a good idea?

He stops bouncing his leg up and down and settles back into his chair, no longer at the edge of his seat or ready to dive for the door the second she puts down her knife and fork.

'Sarah,' he sighs, and means it this time when he says, 'I'm very sorry.'

She stops forking food into her mouth and looks up at him, chews quickly, dabs at her lips with a napkin and swallows. Her face softens. 'OK.'

She wipes away the crumbs around her plate, shrugging. 'I'm not looking for a marriage here, Justin.'

'I know, I know.'

'Lunch is all this is.'

'I know that.'

'Or shall we say just coffee, in case mentioning the former sends you running out the fire exit yelling "Fire"?' She acknowledges his empty cup and flicks at imaginary crumbs now.

He reaches out to grab her hand and stop her fidgeting. 'I'm sorry.'

'OK,' she repeats.

The air clears, the tension evaporates, her plate is cleared away.

'I suppose we should get the check—'

'Have you always wanted to be a doctor?'

'Whoa.' She pauses midway opening her wallet. 'It's just intense either way with you, isn't it?' But she's smiling.

'I'm sorry.' Justin shakes his head. 'Let's have a coffee before we leave. Hopefully I'll have time to stop this from being the worst date you've ever been on.'

'It's not.' She shakes her head, smiling. 'But it's a close second. It was almost the worst but you pulled it right back there with the doctor question.'

Justin smiles. 'So. Have you?'

She nods. 'Ever since James Goldin operated on me when I was in Junior Infants. What do you call it, kindergarten? Anyway, I was five years old and he saved my life.'

'Wow. That's young for a serious operation. It must have had a huge effect.'

'Profound. I was in the yard at lunch break, I fell during a game of hopscotch and hurt my knee. The rest of my friends were discussing amputation but James Goldin came running over and straight away gave me mouth-to-mouth. Just like that, the pain went away. And that's when I knew.'

'That you wanted to be a doctor?'

'That I wanted to marry James Goldin.'

Justin smiles. 'And did you?'

'Nah. Became a doctor instead.'

'You're good at it.'

'Yes, because you can tell that from a needle insertion at a blood donation,' she smiles. 'Everything OK in that department?'

'My arm's a little itchy but it's fine.'

'Itchy? It shouldn't be itchy, let me see.'

He goes to roll up his sleeve and stops. 'Could I ask you something?' He squirms a little in his chair. 'Is there any way that I can find out where my blood went?'

'Where? As in, which hospital?'

'Well, yeah, or even better, do you know *who* it went to?'

She shakes her head. 'The beauty of this is that it's completely anonymous.'

'But someone, somewhere would know, wouldn't they? In hospital records or even *your* office records?'

'Of course. Products in a blood bank are always individually traceable. It's documented throughout the entire process of donation, testing, separation into components, storage and administration to the recipient but—'

'There's a word I hate.'

'Unfortunately for you, you can't know who received your donation.'

'But you just said that it's documented.'

'That information can't be released. But all our details are kept in a secure computerised database where all your donor details are kept. Under the Data Protection Act you have the right to access your donor records.'

'Will those records tell me who received my blood?'

'No.'

'Well, then, I don't want to see them.'

'Justin, the blood you donated was not transfused directly into somebody's body exactly as it came from your vein. It was broken up and separated into red blood cells, white blood cells, platelets—'

'I know, I know, I know all of that.'

'I'm sorry that there's nothing I can do. Why are you so keen to know?'

He thinks about it for a while, drops a brown sugar cube into his coffee and stirs it around. 'I'm just interested to know who I helped, if I helped them at all and if I did, how they are. I feel like . . . no, it sounds stupid, you'll think I'm insane. It doesn't matter.'

'Hey, don't be silly,' she says soothingly. 'I already think you're insane.'

'I hope that's not your medical opinion.'

'Tell me.' Her piercing blue eyes watch him over the brim of her coffee cup as she sips.

'This is the first time I've said this aloud, so forgive me for speaking while I think. At first, it was a ridiculous macho ego trip. I wanted to know whose life I saved. Which lucky person I'd sacrificed my precious blood for.'

Sarah smiles.

'But then over the last few days I haven't been able to stop thinking about it. I feel differently. Genuinely different. Like I've given something away. Something precious.'

'It is precious, Justin. We need more donors all the time.'

'I know, but not – not like that. I just feel like there's someone out there walking around with something inside them that I gave them and now I'm missing something—'

'The body replaces the liquid part of your donation within twenty-four hours.'

'No, I mean, I feel like I've given something away, a part of me, and that somebody else has been completed because of that part of me and . . . my God, this sounds crazy. I just want to know who that person is. I just feel like there's a part of me missing and I need to get out there and grab it.'

'You can't get your blood back, you know,' Sarah jokes weakly, and they both fall into deep thought; Sarah looking sadly into her coffee, Justin trying to make sense of his jumbled words.

'I should never try to discuss something so illogical with a doctor, I suppose,' he says.

'You sound like a lot of people I know, Justin. You're just the first person I've heard blame it on a blood donation.'

Silence.

'Well,' Sarah reaches behind her chair to get her coat, 'you're in a rush so we should really move now.'

They make their way down Grafton Street in a comfortable silence that's occasionally dotted with small talk. They automatically stop walking at the Molly Malone statue, across the road from Trinity College.

'You're late for your class.'

'No, I've got a little while before I—' He looks at his watch and then remembers his earlier excuse. He feels his face redden. 'Sorry.'

'It's OK,' she repeats.

'I feel like this whole lunch date has been me saying sorry and you saying that it's OK.'

'It really is OK,' she laughs.

'And I really am—'

'Stop!' She holds her hand to his mouth to hush him. 'Enough.'

'I really had a lovely time,' he says awkwardly. 'Should we . . . you know, I'm feeling really uncomfortable right now with her watching us.'

They look to their right and Molly stares down at them with her bronze eyes.

Sarah laughs. 'You know maybe we could make arrangements to—'

'Roooooaaaaaaaaarrrrrrrrr!!'

Justin almost leaps out of his skin with fright, startled by the intense screaming coming from the bus stopped at the traffic lights beside him. Sarah yelps with fright and her hand flies to her chest. Beside them more than a dozen men, women and children, all wearing Viking helmets, are waving their fists in the air and laughing and roaring at passers-by. Sarah and the dozens of others crowded around them on the pavement start laughing, some roar back, most ignore them.

Justin, whose breath has caught in his throat, is silent, for he can't take his eyes off the woman laughing uproariously with an old man; a helmet on her head, long blonde plaits flowing each side.

'We certainly got them, Joyce,' the old man laughs, roaring lightly in her face and waving his fist.

She looks surprised at first, then hands him a five-euro note, much to his delight, and they both continue laughing.

Look at me, Justin wills her. Her eyes stay on the old man's as he holds the note up to the light to check its authenticity. Justin looks to the traffic lights, which are still red. He has time yet for her to see him. *Turn around! Look at me just once!* The pedestrian lights flash to amber. He doesn't have much time.

Her head remains turned, completely lost in conversation.

The lights turn green and the bus slowly moves off up Nassau Street. He starts to walk alongside it, willing her with everything he has to look at him.

'Justin!' Sarah calls. 'What are you doing?'

He keeps on walking alongside the bus, quickening his pace and finally breaking out into a jog. He can hear Sarah calling after him but he can't stop.

'Hey!' he calls.

Not loud enough; she doesn't hear him. The bus picks up speed and Justin's jog breaks out into a run, the adrenalin surging through his body. The bus is beating him, speeding up. He's losing her.

'Joyce!' he blurts out. The surprising sound of his own yell is enough to stop him in his tracks. What on earth is he doing? He doubles over to rest his hands on his knees, tries to catch his breath, tries to centre himself in the whirlwind he feels caught up in. He looks back at the bus one last time. A Viking helmet appears from the window, blonde plaits moving from side to side like a pendulum. He can't make out the face but with just one head, just one person looking out from that bus and back at him, he knows it has to be her.

The whirlwind stops momentarily while he holds up a hand in salute.

A hand appears out the window and the bus rounds the corner onto Kildare Street, leaving Justin to, once again, watch her disappear from sight with his heart beating so wildly, he's sure the pavement is pounding beneath him. He may not have the slightest clue what is going on but there is one thing he knows now for sure.

Joyce. Her name is Joyce.

He looks down the empty street.

But who are you, Joyce?

'Why are you hanging your head out of the window?' Dad pulls me in, wild with worry. 'You might not have much to live for but, for Christsake, you owe it to yourself to live it.'

'Did you hear somebody calling my name?' I whisper to Dad, my mind a whirl.

'Oh, she's hearing voices now,' he grumbles. '*I* said your bloody name and you gave me a fiver for it, don't you remember?' He snaps it before her face and turns his attention back to Olaf.

'On your left is Leinster House, the building that now houses the National Parliament of Ireland.'

Snappedy-snap, clickety-click, flash-flash, record.

'Leinster House was originally known as Kildare House after the Earl of Kildare commissioned it to be built. On his becoming the Duke of Leinster, it was renamed. Parts of the building, which was formerly the Royal College of Surgeons—'

'Science,' I say loudly, still largely lost in thought.

'Pardon me?' He stops talking and heads turn once again.

'I was just saying that,' my face flushes, 'it was the Royal College of Science.'

'Yes, that's what I said.'

'No, you said "surgeons",' the American woman in front of me speaks out.

'Oh,' he gets flustered. 'Excuse me, I'm mistaken. Parts of the building, which was formerly the . . . the Royal College of,' he looks pointedly at me, '*Science*, have served as the seat of the Irish government since 1922 . . .'

I tune out.

'Remember I told you about the guy who designed the Rotunda hospital?' I whisper to Dad.

'I do. Dick somebody.'

'Richard Cassells. He designed this too. It's been

claimed that it formed a model for the design of the White House.'

'Is that so?' Dad says.

'Really?' The American woman twists around in her seat to face me. She speaks loudly. Very loudly. Too loudly. 'Honey, did you hear that? This lady says the guy who designed this, designed the White House.'

'No, I didn't actually—'

Suddenly I notice the tour operator has stopped talking and is currently glaring at me with as much love as a Viking Dragon for a Sea Cat. All eyes, ears and horns are on us.

'Well, I said it's been *claimed* that it formed a *model* for the design of the White House. There aren't any certainties as such,' I say quietly, not wanting to be dragged into this. 'It's just that James Hoban, who won the competition for the design of the White House in 1792, was an Irishman.'

They stare expectantly at me.

'Well, he studied architecture in Dublin and would have more than likely studied the design of Leinster House,' I finish off quickly.

The people around me ooh, aah and talk amongst one another about that titbit of information.

'We can't hear you!' someone at the top of the bus shouts out.

'Stand up, Gracie.' Dad pushes me up.

'Dad . . .' I slap him away.

'Hey, Olaf, give her the microphone!' the woman shouts to the tour operator. He grudgingly hands it over and folds his arms.

'Eh, hello.' I tap it with my finger and blow into the mike.

'You have to say, "Testing one, two, three," Gracie.'

'Eh, testing one, two—'

'We can hear you,' Olaf the White snaps.

'OK, well,' I repeat my comments, and the people up front nod with interest.

'And this is all part of your government's buildings

too?' the American woman points to the buildings either side.

I look uncertainly at Dad and he nods at me with encouragement. 'Well, actually no. The building to the left is the National Library and the National Museum is on the right.' I go to sit down again and Dad whooshes my backside back up. They are all still looking at me for more. The tour guide looks sheepish.

'Well, a bit of interesting information *may be* that the National Library and the National Museum were originally home of the Dublin Museum of Science and Art, which opened in 1890. Both were designed by Thomas Newenham Deane and his son Thomas Manly Deane after a competition held in 1885 and were constructed by the Dublin contractors J. and W. Beckett, who demonstrated the best of Irish craftsmanship in their construction. The Museum is one of the best surviving examples of Irish decorative stonework, wood-carving and ceramic tiling. The National Library's most impressive feature is the entrance rotunda. Internally this space leads up an impressive staircase to the magnif-icent reading room with its vast vaulted ceiling. As you can see for yourselves, the exterior of the building is characterised by its array of columns and pilasters in the Corinthian order and the rotunda with its open veranda and corner pavilions framing the composition. In the—'

Loud clapping interrupts my talk – single, loud clap-ping, coming only from one person: Dad. The rest of the bus is silent. A child, asking her mother if they can roar again, breaks it. An imaginary piece of tumble-weed blows down the aisle, landing at a grinning Olaf the White.

'I, em, I wasn't finished,' I say quietly.

Dad claps louder in response, and one man, who is sitting alone in the back row, joins in nervously.

'And . . . that's all I know,' I say quickly, sitting down.

'How do you know all that?' the woman in front asks.

'She's an estate agent,' Dad says proudly.

The woman's brow creases, she makes an 'oh' shape with her mouth and turns around again to face an extremely satisfied-looking Olaf. He grabs the microphone from me.

'Now everybody, let's roooooooaaaaaar!'

The silence is broken as everybody comes to life again, while each muscle and organ in my body cringes into a foetal position.

Dad leans into me and crushes me against the window. He moves his head close to whisper in my ear and our helmets knock against one another.

'How did you know all that, love?'

As though I'd used all of my words up in that tirade, my mouth opens and closes but nothing comes out. How on earth did I know all of that?

15

My ears immediately sizzle as soon I enter the school gymnasium that same evening, and spy Kate and Frankie huddled together on the bleachers, looking deep in conversation with concern etch-a-sketched across their faces. Kate looks as though Frankie's just told her that her father's passed away, a face I'm familiar with as I was the one to give her that look, with that very news, five years ago at Arrivals in Dublin airport when she'd cut short her holiday to rush to his side. Now Kate is talking and Frankie looks as though her dog's been hit by a car, a face I'm also familiar with, as I was once again the one to deliver the news, and the blow, that broke three of the sausage dog's legs. Now Kate looks as though she's been caught in the act as she glances in my direction. Frankie freezes too. Looks of surprise, then guilt and then a smile to make me think they've just been discussing the weather, rather than the events in my life, which are as changeable as.

I wait for the usual Lady of Trauma to fill my shoes. To give me a little break while she offers the usual insightful comments that keep inquisitors at bay; explaining one's recent loss as more of a continuous journey rather than a dead end, giving one the invaluable opportunity to gain strength and learn about oneself, and thereby turning this terribly tragic affair into something hugely positive. Usual Lady of Trauma does not arrive, knowing this is no easy gig for her. She is well aware the two people who currently hug me tight can see through her words and right to the heart of me.

My friends' hugs are longer and tighter; consist of extra squeezes and pats, which alternate between a circular rubbing motion and a light pitter-pattering on the back, both of which I find surprisingly comforting. The pity in their faces hammers home my great loss and my stomach feels queasy and my head fully loaded again. I realise that swaddling myself in a nest with Dad does not hold the super healing powers I'd hoped for, for every time I leave the house and meet somebody new, I have to go through it over again. Not just the entire rigmarole, but I have to feel it all, all over again, which is a far more tiring thing than words. Wrapped in Kate and Frankie's arms I could easily morph into the baby that they in their minds are coddling, but I don't, because if I start now, I know I'll never stop.

We sit on the bleachers away from the other parents where few sit together but most take time that is precious and rare to be alone to read or think or watch their children doing unimpressive sideways tumbles on the blue rubber mats. I spot Kate's children, six-year-old Eric and my five-year-old goddaughter, Jayda, the *Muppet Christmas Carol* fanatic I have sworn not to hold anything against. They are enthusiastically hopping about and chirping like crickets, pulling their underwear from in between the cheeks of their behinds and tripping over untied shoelaces. Eleven-month-old Sam sleeps beside us in a stroller, blowing bubbles from his chubby lips. I watch him fondly, then remember again and look away. Ah, remembering. That old chestnut.

'How's work, Frankie?' I ask, wanting everything to be as it was.

'Busy as usual,' she responds, and I detect guilt, perhaps even embarrassment.

I envy her normality, possibly even her boredom. I envy that her today was the same as her yesterday.

'Still buying low, selling high?' Kate pipes up.

Frankie rolls her eyes. 'Twelve years, Kate.'

'I know, I know,' Kate bites her lip and tries not to laugh.

'Twelve years, I've had this job and twelve years you've being saying that. It's not even funny any more. In fact I don't recall it *ever* being, and yet you persist.'

Kate laughs. 'It's just that, I have absolutely no idea what it is that you do. Something in the stock market?'

'Manager, deputy head corporate treasury and investor solutions desk,' Frankie tells her.

Kate stares back blankly, then sighs. 'So many words to say that you work at a desk.'

'Oh, I'm sorry, what do you do all day, again? Wipe shitty asses and make organic banana sandwiches?'

'There are other aspects to being a mother, Frankie,' Kate puffs. 'It is my responsibility to prepare three human beings so that if, God forbid, something happens to me, or when they are adults, they will be able to live and function and succeed responsibly in the world all by themselves.'

'And you mush organic bananas,' Frankie adds. 'No, no, hold on, is that before or after the preparation of three human beings? Before.' She nods to herself. 'Yes, definitely mush bananas and *then* prepare human beings. Got it.'

'All I'm saying is, you have, what, *seven* words to describe your paper-pushing job?'

'I believe it's eight.'

'I have one. *One*.'

'Well, I don't know. Is "car-pooler" one or two words? Joyce, what do you think?'

I stay out of it.

'The point I'm trying to make is that the word "mum",' she says, irritated, 'a teeny, tiny little word that *every* woman with a child is called, fails to describe the plethora of duties. If I was doing what I do everyday in your company, I'd be running the fucking place.'

Frankie shrugs nonchalantly. 'Sorry, but I don't think

I care. And I can't speak for my colleagues, but personally I like to make my own banana sandwiches and wipe my own behind.'

'Really?' Kate lifts an eyebrow. 'I'm surprised you don't have some poor man you picked up along the way, do that for you.'

'Nope, I'm still searching for that special one,' Frankie smiles back sweetly.

They do this all the time: talk at each other, never to each other, in an odd bonding ritual that seems to pull them closer when it would do the opposite to anybody else. In the silence that follows they both have time to figure out what exactly they were talking about in my company. Ten seconds later Kate kicks Frankie. Oh, yes. The mention of children.

When something tragic has happened, you'll find that you, the tragic*ee*, become the person that has to make everything comfortable for everyone else.

'How's Crapper?' I fill their uncomfortable silence and ask after Frankie's dog.

'He's doing well; his legs are healing nicely. Still howls when he sees your photograph, though. Sorry I had to move it from the fireplace.'

'Doesn't matter. In fact I was going to ask you to move it. Kate, you can get rid of my wedding photo too.'

Divorce talk. Finally.

'Ah, Joyce,' she shakes her head and looks at me sadly, 'that's my favourite photo of me. I looked so good at your wedding. Can I not just cut Conor out?'

'Or draw a little moustache on him,' Frankie adds. 'Or better yet, give him a personality. What colour should that be?'

I bite my lip guiltily to hide a smile that threatens to crawl from the corner of my lips. I'm not used to this kind of talk of my ex. It's disrespectful and I'm not sure I'm completely comfortable with it. But it is funny. Instead I look away to the children on the floor.

'OK, everybody.' The gymnastics instructor claps his

hands for attention and the crickets' hopping and chirping momentarily subsides. 'Spread out on the mat. We're going to do backwards rolls. Place your hands flat on the floor, fingers pointing towards your shoulders as you roll back to a stand. Like this.'

'Well, looky-look at our little flexible friend,' Frankie remarks.

One by one the children roll backwards to a perfect stand. Until it gets to Jayda, who rolls over one side of her head in the most awkward way, kicks another child in the shins and then gets onto her knees before finally jumping to a stand. She strikes a Spice Girl pose in all of her pink sparkling glory, with peace fingers and all, thinking nobody has noticed her error. The instructor ignores her.

'Preparing a human being for the world,' Frankie repeats smartly. 'Yip. You'd be running the fucking place all right.' Frankie turns to me and softens her voice. 'So, Joyce, how are you?'

I have debated whether to tell them, whether to tell anyone. Short of carting me off to the madhouse I have no idea how anybody will react to what's been happening to me, or even how they should react. But after today's experience, I side with the part of my brain that is anxious to reveal.

'This is going to sound really odd so bear with me on this.'

'It's OK.' Kate grabs my hand. 'You say whatever you want. Just release.'

Frankie rolls her eyes.

'Thanks.' I slowly slip my hand out of hers. 'I keep seeing this guy.'

Kate tries to register this. I can see her trying to link it with the loss of my baby or my looming divorce, but she can't.

'I think I know him but at the same time, I know I don't. I've seen him precisely three times now, the most recent being today, when he chased after my Viking bus. And I think he called out my name. Though I may have imagined that because how on earth could he know my name? Unless he knows me, but that brings me back to my being sure that he really doesn't. What do you think?'

'Hold on, I'm way back at the Viking bus part,' Frankie slows me down. 'You say you have a Viking bus.'

'I don't *have* one. I was on one. With Dad. It goes into the water too. You wear helmets with horns and go "aaaagh" at everyone.' I go close to their faces and wave my fists at them.

They stare back blankly.

I sigh and slide back on the bench. 'So anyway, I keep seeing him.'

'OK,' Kate says slowly, looking at Frankie.

There's an awkward silence as they worry about my sanity. I join with them on that.

Frankie clears her throat. 'So this man, Joyce, is he young, old, or indeed a Viking upon your magic bus that travels the high waters?'

'Late thirties, early forties. He's American. We got our hair cut together. That's where I saw him first.'

'Which is lovely, by the way.' Kate gently fingers a few front strands.

'Dad thinks I look like Peter Pan,' I smile.

'So maybe he remembers you from the hair salon,' Frankie reasons.

'It even felt weird at the salon. There was a . . . recognition or a *something*.'

Frankie smiles. 'Welcome to the world of singledom.' She turns to Kate, whose face is scrunched up in disagreement. 'When's the last time Joyce allowed herself a little flirt with someone? She's been married for so long.'

'Please,' Kate says patronisingly to Frankie. 'If you think that's what happens when you're married then you're sorely mistaken. No wonder you're afraid to get married.'

'I'm not afraid, I just don't agree with it. You know, just today I was watching a make-up show—'

'Oh, here we go.'

'Shut up and listen. And the make-up expert said that because the skin is so sensitive around the eye, you must apply cream with your *ring finger* because it is the finger with the *least power*.'

'Wow,' Kate says drily. 'You sure have revealed us married folk for the fools that we are.'

I rub my eyes wearily. 'I know I sound insane, I'm tired and probably imagining things where there is nothing to be imagined. The man I'm supposed to have on the brain is Conor and he's not. He's really not at all. I don't know if it's a delayed reaction and next month I'm going to fall apart, start drinking and wear black everyday—'

'Like Frankie,' Kate butts in.

'But right now, I feel nothing but relieved,' I continue. 'Isn't that terrible?'

'Is it OK for me to feel relieved too?' Kate asks.

'You hated him?' I ask sadly.

'No. He was fine. He was nice. I just hated you not being happy.'

'I hated him,' Frankie chirps up.

'We spoke briefly yesterday. It was odd. He wanted to know if he could take the espresso machine.'

'The bastard,' Frankie spits.

'I really don't care about the espresso machine. He can have it.'

'It's mind games, Joyce. Be careful. First it's the espresso machine and then it's the house and then it's your soul. And then it's that emerald ring that belonged to his grandmother that he claims you stole but that you recall more than clearly that when you first went to his house for lunch he said, "help yourself" and there it was.' She scowls.

I look to Kate for help.

'Her break-up with Lee.'

'Ah. Well, it's not going to get like your break-up with Lee.'

Frankie grumbles.

'Christian went for a pint with Conor last night,' Kate says. 'Hope you don't mind.'

'Of course I don't. They're friends. Is he OK?'

'Yeah, he seemed fine. He's upset about the, you know . . .'

'Baby. You can say the word. I'm not going to fall apart.'

'He's upset about the baby and disappointed the marriage didn't work but I think he thinks it's the right thing to do. He's going back to Japan in a few days. He also said you're both putting the house on the market.'

'I don't like being there any more and we bought it together, so it's the right thing to do.'

'But are you sure? Where will you live? Is your dad not driving you insane?'

As a tragicee and future divorcee, you'll also find that people will question you on the biggest decision you've ever made in your life as though you hadn't thought about it at all before, as though, through their twenty questions and many dubious faces, they're going to shine light on something that you missed the first time or hundredth time round during your darkest hours.

'Funnily enough, no,' I smile as I think about him. 'He's actually having the opposite effect. Though he's only managed to call me Joyce once in a week. I'm going to stay with him until the house is sold and I find somewhere else to live.'

'That story about the man . . . apart from him, how are you *really*? We haven't seen you since the hospital and we were so worried.'

'I know. I'm sorry about that.' I'd refused to see them when they came to visit, and I'd sent Dad out to the corridor to send them home, which of course he didn't, and so they'd sat by my side for a few minutes while I stared at the pink wall, thinking about the fact I was staring at a pink wall, and then they left. 'I really appreciated you coming, though.'

'No you didn't.'

'OK, I didn't then, but I do now.'

I think about that, about how I am now, *really*. Well, they asked.

'I eat meat now. And I drink red wine. I hate anchovies and I listen to classical music. I particularly love the *JK Ensemble* with John Kelly on Lyric FM, who doesn't play Kylie and I don't mind. Last night I listened to Handel's "*Mi restano le lagrime*" from Act Three Scene One of *Alcina* before going to sleep, and I actually knew the words but have no idea how. I know a lot about Irish architecture but not as much as I know about French and Italian. I've read *Ulysses* and can quote from it *ad nauseam* when I couldn't even finish the audio book before. Only today I wrote a letter to the council telling them how their cramming yet another new ugly modern block into an area in which its buildings are mostly older, less fashionable constructs means that not only is the nation's heritage seriously under threat but the sanity of its citizens too. I thought my father was the only person who wrote strongly worded letters. That's not such a big deal in itself, the big deal is that two weeks ago I'd have been *excited* about the prospect of showing these properties. Today I'm particularly vexed about talk of bulldozing a hundred-year-old building in Old Town, Chicago, and so I plan to write another letter. I bet you're wondering how I knew about that. Well, I read it in the recent edition of the *Art and Architectural Review*, the only truly international art and architectural publication. I'm a subscriber now.' I take a breath. 'Ask me anything, because I'll probably know the answer and I've no idea how.'

Stunned, Kate and Frankie look at one another.

'Maybe with the stress of constantly worrying about you and Conor over with, you're able to concentrate on things more,' Frankie suggests.

I consider that but not for long. 'I dream almost every night about a little girl with white-blonde hair who every night gets bigger. And I hear music – a song I don't know. When I'm not dreaming about her I have vivid dreams of places I've never been, eating foods I've never tasted and surrounded by strange people that I seem to know so well. A picnic in a park with a woman with red hair. A man with green feet. And sprinklers.' I think hard. 'Something about sprinklers.

'When I wake up I have to remember all over again that my dreams are not real and that my reality is not a dream. I find that next to impossible, but not completely, because Dad is there with a smile on his face and sausages on the frying pan, chasing a cat called Fluffy around the garden and for some unknown reason hiding Mum's photograph in the hall drawer. And after the first few moments of my waking day when everything is crap, all those other things become the only things on my mind. And a man I can't get out of my head, but not Conor, as you'd assume, the love of my life that I've just separated from. No, I keep thinking about an American man that I don't even know.'

The girls' eyes are filled, their faces a mixture of sympathy, worry and confusion.

I don't expect them to say anything – they probably think I'm crazy – and so I look out to the kids again on the gymnasium floor and watch as Eric takes to the balance beam, a four-inch-wide beam covered in thin leather. The instructor calls out to him to do aeroplane arms. Eric's face is a picture of nervous concentration. He stops walking as he slowly lifts his arms. The instructor offers words of encouragement and a small proud smile lifts onto Eric's face. He raises his eyes briefly to see if his mother is watching and in that one moment, loses balance and falls straight down, the beam quite unfortunately landing between his legs. His face is one of horror.

Frankie snorts again. Eric howls. Kate runs to her child. Sam continues to blow bubbles.

I leave.

16

Driving back to Dad's, I try not to glance at my house as I pass. My eyes lose the battle with my mind and I see Conor's car parked outside. Since our final meal together at the restaurant we have talked a few times, each conversation varying in degrees of affection for one another, the last, at the lower end of the scale. The first call came late at night the day after our final meal; Conor asking just one last time if we were doing the right thing. His slurred words and soft voice drifted in my ear as I lay on my bed in my childhood box bedroom and stared at the ceiling, just as I did during those all-night phone calls when we first met. Living with my father at thirty-three years of age after a failed marriage, and a vulnerable husband on the other end of the phone . . . it was so easy right then to remember the greatest times we'd ever spent together and go back on our decision. But more often than not, the easy decisions are the wrong decisions, and sometimes we feel like we're going backwards when we're actually moving forward.

The next phone call was a little more stern, an embarrassed apology and a mention of something legal related. The next, a frustrated enquiry into why my solicitor hadn't replied to his solicitor yet. The next, him telling me his newly pregnant sister was going to take the cot, something that made me fly into a jealous rage as soon as I rang off and throw the phone in the bin. The last was to tell me he'd boxed everything up, he was leaving

517

for Japan in a few days. And could he have the espresso machine?

But each time I hung up the phone, I felt that my weak goodbye wasn't a goodbye. It was more of a 'see you around'. I knew that there was always a chance to back out, that he'd be around for a little while longer, that our words weren't really final.

I pull the car over and stare up at the house we've lived in for almost ten years. Didn't it deserve more than a few weak goodbyes?

I ring the doorbell and there's no answer. Through the front window I can see everything in boxes, the walls naked, the surfaces bare, the stage set for the next family to move in and tread the boards. I turn my key in the door and step inside, making a noise so as not to surprise him. I'm about to call his name when I hear the soft tinkle of music drifting from upstairs. I make my way up to the half-decorated nursery and find Conor sitting on the soft carpet, tears streaming down his face as he watches the mouse chase the cheese. I cross the room and reach for him. On the floor, I hold him close and rock him gently. I close my eyes and drift away.

He stops crying and looks up at me slowly. 'What?'

'Hmm?' I snap out of my trance.

'You said something. In Latin.'

'No, I didn't.'

'Yes you did. Just there.' He dries his eyes. 'Since when do you speak Latin?'

'I don't.'

'Right,' he says sharply. 'Well, what does the one phrase that you do know mean?'

'I don't know.'

'You must know, you just said it.'

'Conor, I don't recall saying anything.' He glares at me, something pretty close to hate and I swallow hard.

A stranger stares back at me in a tense silence.

'OK.' He gets to his feet and moves towards the door. No more questions, no more trying to understand me. He no longer cares. 'Patrick will be acting as my solicitor now.'

Fantastic, his shit-head brother.

'OK,' I whisper.

He stops at the door and turns round, grinds his jaw as his eyes take in the room. A last look at everything, including me, and he's gone.

The final goodbye.

I have a restless night in bed at Dad's as more images flash through my mind like lightning, so fast and sharp they light up my head with an urgent bolt and then are gone again. Back to black.

A church. Bells ringing. Sprinklers. A tidal wave of red wine. Old buildings with shop fronts. Stained glass.

A view through banisters of a man with green feet, closing a door behind him. A baby in my arms. A girl with white-blonde hair. A familiar song.

A casket. Tears. Family dressed in black.

Park swings. Higher and higher. My hands pushing a child. Me swinging as a child. A seesaw. A chubby young boy raising me higher in the air, as he lowers himself to the ground. Sprinklers again. Laughter. Me and the same boy in swimming togs. Suburbs. Music. Bells. A woman in a white dress. Cobbled streets. Cathedrals. Confetti. Hands, fingers, rings. Shouting. Slamming.

The man with green feet closing the door.

Sprinklers again. A chubby young boy chasing me and laughing. A drink in my hand. My head down a toilet. Lecture halls. Sun and green grass. Music.

The man with green feet outside in the garden, holding a hose in his hand. Laughter. The girl with the white-blonde hair playing in the sand. The girl laughing on a swing. Bells again.

View from the banisters of the man with green feet closing a door. A bottle in his hand.

A pizza parlour. Ice-cream sundaes.

Pills in his hand too. The man's eyes seeing mine

before the door closes. My hand on a doorknob. The door opening. Empty bottle on the ground. Bare feet with green soles. A casket.

Sprinklers. Rocking back and forth. Humming that song. Long blonde hair covering my face and in my small hand. Whispers of a phrase . . .

I open my eyes with a gasp, heart drumming in my chest. The sheets are wet beneath me; my body is soaked in sweat. I fumble in the darkness for the bedside lamp. With tears in my eyes that I refuse to allow to fall, I reach for my mobile and dial with trembling fingers.

'Conor?' My voice is shaking.

He mumbles incoherently for a little while until he awakens. 'Joyce, it's three a.m.,' he croaks.

'I know, I'm sorry.'

'What's wrong? Are you OK?'

'Yes, yes, I'm fine, it's just that, well, I – I had a dream. Or a nightmare or maybe it was neither, there were flashes of, well . . . lots of places and people and things and,' I stop myself and try to focus. '*Perfer et obdura; dolor hic tibi proderit olim?*'

'What?' he says groggily.

'The Latin that I said earlier, is that what I said?'

'Yeah, it sounds like it. Jesus, Joyce—'

'Be patient and tough; someday this pain will be useful to you,' I blurt out. 'That's what it means.'

He is quiet and then he sighs. 'OK, thanks.'

'Somebody told me that, if not when I was a child, but tonight, they told me.'

'You don't have to explain.'

Silence.

'I'm going back to sleep now.'

'OK.'

'Are you OK, Joyce? Do you want me to call someone for you or . . . ?'

'No, I'm fine. Perfect.' My voice catches in my throat. 'Good night.'

He's gone.

A single tear rolls down my cheek and I wipe it away before it reaches my chin. Don't start, Joyce. Don't you dare start now.

17

As I make my way downstairs the following morning, I spy Dad placing Mum's photograph back on the hall table. He hears me approaching, whips out his handkerchief from his pocket and pretends he's dusting it.

'Ah, there she is. Muggins has risen from the dead.'

'Yes, well, the toilet flushing every fifteen minutes kept me awake for most of the night.' I kiss the top of his almost hairless head and go into the kitchen. I sniff the smoky atmosphere again.

'I'm very sorry that my prostate is bothering *your* sleep.' He studies my face. 'What's wrong with your eyes?'

'My marriage is over and so I decided to spend the night crying,' I explain matter-of-factly, hands on hips, sniffing the air.

He softens a bit but sticks the knife in regardless. 'I thought that's what you wanted.'

'Yes, Dad, you're absolutely right, the past few weeks have been every girl's dream.'

He moves up and down, down and up to the kitchen table, takes his usual seat in the path of the sun's beam, props his glasses on the base of his nose and continues his Sudoku. I watch him for a while, feeling mesmerised by his simplicity and then continue my sniffing mission.

'Did you burn toast again?' He doesn't hear me and keeps scribbling away. I check the toaster. 'It's on the right setting, I don't understand how it's still burning.' I look inside. No crumbs. I check the bin, no toast thrown out. I sniff the air again, grow suspicious and watch Dad from the corner of my eye. He fidgets.

'You're like that Fletcher woman or that Monk man, snooping around. You'll find no corpses here,' he says without looking up from his puzzle.

'Yes, but I'll find *something*, won't I?'

His head jerks up, quickly. Nervously. Aha. I narrow my eyes.

'What's up with you at all, at all?'

I ignore him, and race around the kitchen, opening presses, searching inside each of them.

He looks worried. 'Have you lost your mind? What are you doing?'

'Did you take your pills?' I ask, coming across the medicine cabinet.

'What pills?'

With a response like that, there's definitely something up.

'Your heart pills, memory pills, vitamin pills.'

'No, no and . . .' he thinks for a while, 'no.'

I bring them over to him, line them up on the table. He relaxes a little. Then I continue searching the cupboards and I feel him tense. I pull on the cereal cupboard knob—

'Water!' he shouts, and I jump and bang the door closed.

'Are you OK?'

'Yes,' he says calmly. 'I just need a glass of water for my pills. Glasses are in that cupboard over there.' He points to the other end of the kitchen.

Suspiciously, I fill a glass with water and deliver it to him. I return to the cereal cupboard.

'Tea!' he shouts. 'Sure, we'll have a cup of tea. Sit down there and I'll make it for you. You've been through such a tough time and you've been great about it all. So brave. Trophy brave, as a man says. Now sit down there and I'll fetch you a cuppa. A nice bit of cake as well. Battenburg – you liked that as a wee one. Always tried to take the marzipan off when no one was lookin', the greedy goat that you were.' He tries to steer me away.

'Dad,' I warn. He stops dithering and sighs in surrender.

I open the cupboard door and look inside. Nothing odd, or out of place, just the porridge I eat every morning and Sugar Puffs that I never touch. Dad looks satisfied, lets out a hearty harrumph-ing sound and makes his way back to the table. Hold on a minute. I open the press again and reach for the Sugar Puffs that I never eat and never see Dad eat. As soon as I lift it I know that it's empty of cereal. I look inside.

'Dad!'

'Ah what, love?'

'Dad, you promised me!' I hold the packet of cigarettes in front of his face.

'I only had one, love.'

'You have not had *only* one. That smell of smoke every morning is not burned toast. You lied to me!'

'One a day is hardly going to kill me.'

'That's exactly what it's going to do. You've had bypass surgery, you're not supposed to smoke at all! I turn a blind eye to your morning fry-ups but this, this is unacceptable,' I tell him.

Dad rolls his eyes and he holds his hand up like a puppet's mouth, mimicking me as he snaps it open and closed in my face.

'That's it, I'm calling your doctor.'

His mouth drops, he jumps out of his chair. 'No, love, don't do that.'

I march out to the hall and he chases after me. Up, down, down, up, up, down. Goes down on his right, bends his left.

'Ah, you wouldn't do that to me. If the cigarettes don't kill me, she will. She's a battleaxe, that woman.'

I pick up the phone that's beside Mum's photograph and dial the emergency number I've memorised. The first number that comes to my mind when I need to help the most important person in my life.

'If Mum knew what you were doing she would go berserk – oh.' I stall. 'That's why you hide the photograph?'

Dad looks down at his hands and nods sadly. 'She made me promise I'd stop. If not for me, for her. I didn't want her to see,' he adds in a whisper as though she can hear us.

'Hello?' There's a response on the other end of the phone. 'Hello? Is that you, Dad?' a young girl with an American accent says.

'Oh,' I snap out of it and Dad looks pleading at me. 'Pardon me,' I speak into the phone. 'Hello?'

'Oh, I'm sorry, I saw an Irish number and thought you were my dad,' the voice on the other end explains.

'That's OK,' I say, confused.

Dad is standing before me with his hands together in prayer.

'I was looking for . . .' Dad shakes his head wildly and I stall.

'Tickets to the show?' the girl asks.

I frown. 'To what show?'

'The Royal Opera House.'

'Sorry, who is this? I'm confused.'

Dad rolls his eyes and sits on the bottom stair.

'I'm Bea.'

'Bea.' I look at Dad questioningly and he shrugs. 'Bea who?'

'Well, who is this?' Her tone is harder.

'My name is Joyce. I'm sorry, Bea, I think I've dialled the wrong number. You said you saw an Irish number? Have I called America?'

'No, don't worry.' Happy there isn't a stalker at the other end, her tone is friendly again. 'You've called London,' she explains. 'I saw the Irish number and thought you were my dad. He's flying back tonight to make it to my show tomorrow and I was worried because I'm still a student and it's such a huge deal and I thought he was . . . sorry, I have absolutely no idea why I'm explaining this to you but I'm so nervous,' she laughs and takes a deep breath. 'Technically, this is his emergency number.'

'Funny, I dialled my emergency number too,' I say faintly.

We both laugh.

'Oh, weird,' she says.

'Your voice is familiar, Bea. Do I know you?'

'I don't think so. Don't know anyone in Ireland apart from my dad, who is a man and American, so unless you're my dad trying to be funny . . .'

'No, no, I'm not trying to be . . .' I feel weak at the knees. 'This may sound like a stupid question but, are you blonde?'

Dad holds his head in his hands and I hear him groan.

'Yeah! Why, do I sound blonde? Maybe that's not such a good thing,' she laughs.

I have a lump in my throat and must stop speaking. 'Just a silly guess,' I force out.

'Good guess,' she says curiously. 'Well, I hope everything's OK. You said you dialled your emergency number?'

'Yes, thanks, everything's fine.'

Dad looks relieved.

She laughs. 'Well, this is weird. I better go. Nice talking to you, Joyce.'

'Nice talking to you too, Bea. Best of luck with your ballet show.'

'Oh, sweet, thank you.'

We say our goodbyes and with a shaking hand I replace the handset.

'You silly dope, did you just dial the Americas?' Dad says, putting his glasses on and pressing a button on the phone. 'Joseph down the road showed me how to do this when I was getting the cranky calls. You can see who's called you and who you've called too. Turns out it was Fran bumping off her hand phone. The grandchildren got it for her last Christmas and she's done nothing with it but wake me up at all hours. Anyway, there it is. First few numbers are 0044. Where's that?'

'That's the UK.'

'Why on earth did you do that? Were you trying to trick me? Christ, that alone was enough to give me a heart attack.'

'Sorry, Dad.' I lower myself to the bottom stair, feeling shaky. 'I don't know where I got that number from.'

'Well, that sure taught me a lesson,' he says insincerely. 'I'll never smoke again. No siree, Bob. Give me those cigarettes and I'll throw them out.'

I hold my hand out, feeling dazed.

He snaps the packet up and shoves it deep into his trouser pocket. 'I hope you'll be paying for that phone call because my pension certainly won't be.' He narrows his eyes. 'What's up with you?'

'I'm going to London,' I blurt out.

'What?' His eyes almost pop out of his head. 'Christ Almighty, Gracie, it's just one thing after another with you.'

'I have to find some answers to . . . something. I have to go to London. Come with me,' I urge, standing up and stepping towards him.

He begins to walk backward with his hand held protectively over his pocket containing the cigarettes.

'I can't go,' he says nervously.

'Why not?'

'Sure, I've never been away from here in my life!'

'All the more reason to go away now,' I urge him intensely. 'If you're going to smoke, you might as well see outside of Ireland before you kill yourself.'

'There are numbers I can call about being spoken to like that. Don't you think that I haven't heard about all of that abuse carry-on that children do to their elderly parents?'

'Don't play the victim, you know I'm looking out for you. Come to London with me, Dad. Please.'

'But, but,' he keeps moving backward, his eyes wide, 'I can't miss the Monday Club.'

'We'll go tomorrow morning, be back before Monday, I promise.'

'But, I don't have a passport.'

'You just need photo ID.'

We're approaching the kitchen now.

'But we've nowhere to stay.' He passes through the door.

'We'll book a hotel.'

'It's too expensive.'

'We'll share a room.'

'But I won't know where anything is in London.'

'I know my way; I've been plenty of times.'

'But . . . but,' he bumps into the kitchen table and can move back no further. His face is a picture of terror. 'I've never been on a plane before.'

'There's nothing to it. You'll probably have a great time up there. And I'll be right beside you, talking to you the whole time.'

He looks unsure.

'What is it?' I ask gently.

'What will I pack? What will I need for over there? Your mother usually packed all my going-away bags.'

'I'll help you pack,' I smile, getting excited. 'This is going to be so much fun – you and me on our first overseas holiday!'

Dad looks excited for a moment, then the excitement fades. 'No, I'm not going. I can't swim. If the plane goes down, I can't swim. I don't want to go over the seas. I'll fly with you somewhere but not over the seas.'

'Dad, we live on an island; *everywhere* we go outside of this country, has to be over the sea. And there are life jackets on the plane.'

'Is that so?'

'Yeah, you'll be fine,' I assure him. 'They show you what to do in case of emergencies, but believe me there won't be one. I've flown dozens of times without so much as a hiccup. You'll have a great time. And imagine all the things you'll have to tell the gang at the Monday

Club? They'll hardly believe their ears, they'll want to hear your stories all day.'

A smile slowly creeps onto Dad's lips and he concedes, 'Big mouth Donal would have to listen to someone else tell a more interesting story, for a change. I think Maggie might be able to clear a spot for me in the schedule, all right.'

18

'Fran's outside, Dad. We have to go!'

'Hold on, love, I'm just making sure everything's OK.'

'Everything's fine,' I assure him. 'You've checked five times already.'

'You can never be too sure. You hear these stories of televisions malfunctioning and toasters exploding and people coming back from their holidays to a pile of smouldering ashes instead of their house.' He checks the socket switches in the kitchen for the umpteenth time.

Fran beeps the horn again.

'I swear one of these days I'm going to throttle that woman. Beep, beep, beep yourself,' he calls back, and I laugh.

'Dad,' I take his hand, 'we really have to go now. The house will be fine. All your friends that live around will keep an eye on it. Any little noise outside and their noses are pressed up against their windows. You know that.'

He nods and looks about, his eyes watering.

'We'll have great fun, really we will. What are you worried about?'

'I'm worried about that damn Fluffy cat, comin' into my garden and pissin' on my plants. I'm worried that the stranglers will suffocate my poor petunias and snapdragons, and that there'll be no one to keep an eye on my chrysanthemums. What if there's wind and rain when we're away? I haven't staked them yet and the flowers get heavy and might break. Do you know how long the magnolia took to settle? Planted it when you were a wee one, while your mother was lying out catchin' the sun on her legs and laughin' at Mr Henderson, God rest his soul, who was peekin' out the curtains at her from next door.'

Beep, beeeeeeep. Fran presses down on the horn.

'It's only a few days, Dad. The garden will be fine. You can get to work on it as soon as you get back.'

'OK, so.' He takes a last look around and makes his way to the door.

I watch his figure swaying. Dressed in his Sunday finest; a three-piece suit, shirt and tie, extra-shined shoes and his tweed cap, of course, which he'd never be seen without outside the house. He looks as though he's jumped straight from the photographs on the wall beside him. He stalls at the hall table and reaches for the photograph of Mum.

'You know your mother was always at me to go to London with her.' He pretends to wipe a smudge on the glass but really he runs his finger over Mum's face.

'Bring her with you, Dad.'

'Ah, no, that'd be silly,' he says confidently, but looks at me unsurely. 'Wouldn't it?'

'I think it'd be a great idea. The three of us will go and have a great time.'

His eyes tear up again and with a simple nod of the head, he slides the photo frame into his overcoat pocket and exits the house to more of Fran's beeping.

'Ah, there you are, Fran,' he calls to her as he sways down the garden path. 'You're late, we've been waiting for you for ages.'

'I was beeping, Henry – did you not hear me?'

'Were you now?' He gets into the car. 'You should press it a little harder the next time; we couldn't hear a thing in there.'

As I slide the key into the lock the phone sitting just inside the hall begins ringing. I look at my watch.

Seven a.m. Who on earth would be calling at seven a.m.?

Fran's car beeps again and I turn round angrily and see Dad leaning over Fran's shoulder, pushing his hand down on the steering wheel.

'There you go now, Fran. We'll hear you the next time. Come on, love, we've a plane to catch!' he laughs uproariously.

I ignore the ringing phone and hurry to the car with the bags.

'There's no answer.' Justin paces the living room in a panic. He tries the number again. 'Why didn't you tell me about this yesterday, Bea?'

Bea rolls her eyes. 'Because I didn't think it'd be such a big deal. People get wrong numbers all the time.'

'But it wasn't a wrong number.' He stops walking and taps his foot impatiently to the sound of the rings. 'That's exactly what it was.'

Answering machine. Damn it! Do I leave a message?

He hangs up and frantically dials again.

Bored with his antics, Bea sits on the garden furniture in the living room and looks around the dust-sheet-covered room and the walls filled with dozens of colour samples. 'When is Doris going to have this place finished?'

'After she starts,' Justin snaps, dialling again.

'My ears are burning,' Doris sings, appearing at the door in a pair of leopard-print overalls, her face heavily made up as usual. 'Found these yesterday, aren't they adorable?' she laughs. 'Buzzy-Bea, sweetie, so lovely to see you!' She rushes to her niece and they embrace. 'We are so excited about your performance tonight, you have no idea. Little Buzzy-Bea all grown up and performing in the *Royal Opera House*.' Her voice rises to a screech. 'Oh, we are so proud, aren't we, Al?'

Al enters the room with a chicken leg in his hand. 'Mmm hhm.'

Doris looks him up and down with disgust, and then back to her niece. 'A bed for the spare room arrived yesterday morning so you'll actually have something to sleep on when you stay, won't that be a treat?' She glares at Justin. 'Also, I got some paint and fabric samples so we can start planning your room design but I'm only designing according to feng shui rules. I won't hear of anything else.'

Bea freezes. 'Oh gee, great.'

'I know we'll have such fun!'

Justin glares at his daughter. 'That's what you get for withholding information.'

'What information? What's going on?' Doris ties her hair up in a cerise-pink scarf and makes a bow at the top of her head.

'Dad is having a conniption fit,' Bea explains.

'I told him to go to the dentist already. He has an abscess, I'm sure of it,' Doris says matter-of-factly.

'I told him too,' Bea agrees.

'No, not that. The woman,' Justin says intensely. 'Remember the woman I was telling you about?'

'Sarah?' Al asks.

'No!' Justin responds as though that was the most ridiculous answer ever given.

'Who can keep up with you?' Al shrugs him off. 'Certainly not Sarah, especially when you're running at top speed after buses, leaving her behind.'

Justin cringes. 'I apologised.'

'To her voice mail,' he chuckles. 'She is never going to answer your calls again.'

I wouldn't blame her.

'The *déjà vu* woman?' Doris gasps, realising.

'Yes.' Justin gets excited. 'Her name is Joyce and she called Bea yesterday.'

'She *may not* have.' Bea's protests falls on deaf ears. 'A woman named Joyce rang yesterday. But I do believe there's more than one Joyce in the world.'

Ignoring her, Doris gasps again. 'How can this be? How do you know her name?'

'I heard somebody call her that on a Viking bus. And *yesterday* Bea got a *phone call*, on her *emergency* number, that no one but me has, from a *woman in Ireland*.' Justin pauses for dramatic effect. 'Called Joyce.'

There's a silence. Justin nods his head knowingly. 'Yep, I know, Doris. Spooky, huh?'

Frozen in place, Doris widens her eyes. 'Spooky, all right. Besides from the Viking bus.' She turns to Bea. 'You're eighteen years old and you've given your father an *emergency* number?'

Justin groans with frustration and starts dialling again.

Bea's cheeks pink. 'Before he moved over, Mum wouldn't let him call at certain hours because of the time difference. So I got another number. It's not technically an emergency number but he's the only one that has it and every time he calls he seems to have done something wrong.'

'Not true,' Justin objects.

'Sure,' Bea responds breezily, flicking through a magazine. 'And I'm not moving in with Peter.'

'You're right, you're *not*. Peter,' he spits out the name, 'picks strawberries for a living.'

'I love strawberries,' Al offers his support. 'If it wasn't for Petey, I wouldn't eat 'em.'

'Peter is an *IT consultant*.' Bea holds her hands out in confusion.

Choosing this moment to butt in, Doris turns to Justin. 'Sweetie, you know I'm all for this stuff with the *déjà vu* lady—'

'Joyce, her name is Joyce.'

'Whatever, but you got nothing but a coincidence. And I'm all for coincidences but this is . . . well, a pretty dumb one.'

'I have not got nothing, Doris, and that sentence is atrociously wrong on so many grammatical levels, you wouldn't believe. I have got a *name* and now I have a *number*.' He kneels before Doris and squeezes her face in his hands, pushing her cheeks together so that her lips puff out. 'And that, Doris Hitchcock, means that I got something!'

'It also makes you a stalker,' Bea says under her breath.

You are now leaving Dublin. We hope you enjoyed your stay.

Dad's rubber ears go back on his head, his bushy eyebrows lift upward.

'You'll tell all the family that I'm asking for them, won't you, Fran?' Dad says a little nervously.

'Of course I will, Henry. You'll have a great time.' Fran's eyes smile at me knowingly in the rearview mirror.

'I'll see them all when I come back,' Dad adds, closely watching a plane as it disappears to the skies. 'It's off behind the clouds now,' he says, looking at me unsurely.

'The best part,' I smile.

He relaxes a little.

Fran pulls over at the drop-off section, busy with people conscious they can't stay for more than a minute and are quickly unloading bags, hugging, taxi drivers being paid, other drivers being moved on. Dad stands still, like the rock thrown into the stream again, and takes it all in, as I lift the bags from the boot. Eventually he snaps out of it and turns his attention to Fran, suddenly filled with warm affection for a woman he usually can't stop bickering about. Then he surprises us all by offering her a hug, awkward as it is.

Once inside, in the hustle and bustle of one of Europe's busiest airports, Dad holds on to my arm tightly with one hand and with the other, pulls along the weekend bag I've lent him. It had taken me the entire day and night to convince him it wasn't anything like the tartan trolley-bags Fran and all the other older ladies use for their shopping. He looks around now and I see him registering men with similar bags. He looks happy, if not a little confused. We go to the computers to check in.

'What are you doing? Getting the sterling pounds out?'

'It's not an ATM, this is check-in, Dad.'

'Do we not speak to a person?'

'No, this machine does it for us.'

'I wouldn't trust this yoke.' He looks over the shoulder of the man beside us. 'Excuse me, is your yokey-mabob working for you?'

'*Scusi?*'

Dad laughs. 'Scoozy-woozy to you too.' He looks back at me with a grin on his face. 'Scoozy. That's a good one.'

'*Mi dispiace tanto, signore, la prego di ignorarlo, è un vecchio sciocco e non sa cosa dice,*' I apologise to the Italian man, who seemed more than taken aback by Dad's comments. I have no idea what I've said but he returns my smile and continues checking in.

'You speak Italian?' Dad looks surprised but I haven't time to respond as he hushes me as an announcement is made. 'Whisht, Gracie, it might be for us. We better hurry.'

'We have two hours until our flight.'

'Why did we come so early?'

'We have to.' I'm already getting tired now and the tireder I get, the shorter the answers get.

'Who says?'

'Security.'

'Security who?'

'Airport security. Through there.' I nod in the direction of the metal detectors.

'Where do we go now?' he asks once I retrieve our boarding passes from the machine.

'To check our bags in.'

'Can we not carry them on?'

'No.'

'Hello,' the lady behind the counter smiles, and takes my passport and Dad's ID.

'Hello,' Dad says chirpily, a saccharine smile forcing itself through the wrinkles of his permanently grumpy face.

I roll my eyes. Always a sucker for the ladies.

'How many bags are you checking in?'

'Two.'

'Did you pack your own bags?'

'Yes.'

'No.' Dad nudges me and frowns. 'You packed my bag for me, Gracie.'

I sigh. 'Yes, but you were with me, Dad. We packed it together.'

'Not what she asked.' He turns back to the lady. 'Is that OK?'

'Yes.' She continues, 'Did anybody ask you to carry anything for them on the plane?'

'N—'

'Yes,' Dad interrupts me again. 'Gracie put a pair of her shoes in my bag because they wouldn't fit in hers. We're only going for a couple of days, you know, and she brought three pairs. *Three.*'

'Do you have anything sharp or dangerous in your hand luggage – scissors, tweezers, lighters or anything like that?'

'No,' I say.

Dad squirms and doesn't respond.

'Dad,' I elbow him, 'tell her no.'

'No,' he finally says.

'Well done,' I snap.

'Have a pleasant trip.' She hands us back our IDs.

'Thank you. You have very nice lipstick,' Dad adds before I pull him away.

I take deep breaths as we approach the security gates and I try to remind myself that this is Dad's first time in an airport and that if you've never heard the questions before, particularly if you're a seventy-five-year-old, I agree they would seem quite strange.

'Are you excited?' I ask, trying to make the moment enjoyable.

'Delirious, love.'

I give up and keep to myself.

I collect a clear plastic bag and fill it with my make-up and his pills, and we make our way through the maze that is the security queue.

'I feel like a little mouse,' Dad comments. 'Will there be cheese at the end of this?' He gives a wheezy laugh. Then we are through to the metal detectors.

'Just do what they say,' I tell him while taking off my belt and jacket. 'You won't cause any trouble, will you?'

'Trouble? Why would I cause trouble? What are you doing? Why are you taking your clothes off, Gracie?'

I groan quietly.

'Sir, could you please remove your shoes, belt, over-coat and cap?'

'What?' Dad laughs at him.

'Remove your shoes, belt, overcoat and cap.'

'I will do no such thing. You want me walking around in my socks?'

'Dad, just do it,' I tell him.

'If I take my belt off, my trousers will fall down,' he says angrily.

'You can hold them up with your hands,' I snap.

'Christ Almighty,' he says loudly.

The young man looks round to his colleagues.

'Dad, just do it,' I say more firmly now. An extremely long queue of irritated seasoned travellers who already have their shoes, belts and coats off, is forming behind us.

'Empty your pockets, please.' An older and angrier-looking security man steps in.

Dad looks uncertain.

'Oh my God, Dad, this is not a joke. Just do it.'

'Can I empty them away from her?'

'No, you'll do it right here.'

'I'm not looking.' I turn away, baffled.

I hear clinking noises as Dad empties his pockets.

'Sir, you were told you could not bring these things through with you.'

I spin round to see the security man holding a lighter and toe-nail clippers in his hands, the packet of ciga-rettes is in the tray with the photograph of Mum. And a banana.

'Dad!' I say.

'Stay out of this, please.'

'Don't speak to my daughter like that. I didn't know I couldn't bring them. She said scissors and tweezers and water and—'

'OK, we understand, sir, but we're going to have to take these from you.'

'But that's my good lighter, you can't take it from me! And what'll I do without my clippers?'

'We'll buy new ones,' I say through gritted teeth. 'Now just do what they say.'

'OK,' he waves his hands rudely at them, 'keep the damn things.'

'Sir, please remove your cap, jacket, shoes and belt.'

'He's an old man,' I say to the security guard in a low voice so that the gathering crowd behind us don't hear. 'He needs a chair to sit on to take off his shoes. And he shouldn't have to take them off as they're corrective footwear. Can you not just let him through?'

'The nature of his right shoe means that we must check it,' the man begins to explain but Dad overhears and explodes.

'Do you think I have a BOMB IN MY SHOE? Sure, what kind of eejit would do that? Do you think I have a BOMB sittin' on my head under my cap or in my belt? Is my banana really a GUN, do you think?' He waves the banana around at the staff, making shooting sounds. 'Are you all gone loony in here?'

Dad reaches for his cap. 'Or maybe I've a GRENADE under my—'

He doesn't have the opportunity to finish as everything goes crazy. He is whisked away before my eyes and I am taken to a small cell-like room and ordered to wait.

19

After fifteen minutes of sitting alone in the sparse interrogation room with nothing but a table and chair, I hear the door in the next room open, then close. I hear the squeak of chair legs and then Dad's voice, as always, louder than everyone else's. I move closer to the wall and press my ear up against it.

'Who are you travelling with?'

'Gracie.'

'Are you sure about that, Mr Conway?'

'Of course! She's my daughter, ask her yourself!'

'Her passport tells us her name is Joyce. Is she lying to us, Mr Conway? Or are you lying?'

'I'm not lying. Oh, I meant Joyce, I meant to say Joyce.'

'Are you changing your story now?'

'What story? I got the name wrong, is all. My wife is Gracie, I get confused.'

'Where is your wife?'

'She's not with us any more. She's in my pocket. I mean the photograph of her is in my pocket. At least, it *was* in my pocket until the lads out there took her and put her in the tray. Will I get my toe-nail clippers back, do you think? They cost me a bit.'

'Mr Conway, you were told sharp items and lighter fluid is not permitted on the flights.'

'I know that, but my daughter, Gracie, I mean, Joyce, went mad at me yesterday when she found my pack of smokes hidden in the Sugar Puffs and I didn't want to take the lighter out of my pocket or she'd lose the head again. I apologise for that, though. I wasn't intending to blow up the plane or anything.'

'Mr Conway, please refrain from using such language. Why did you refuse to take off your shoes?'

'I have holes in me socks!'

There is a silence.

'I'm seventy-five years old, young man. Why on earth do I have to take my shoes off? Did you think I was going to blow the plane up with a rubber shoe? Or maybe it's the insoles you're worried about. Maybe you're right, you can never tell the damage a man can do with a good insole—'

'Mr Conway, please don't use such language and refrain from smart-aleck behaviour or you will not be allowed on the plane. What was the reason for your refusal to remove your belt?'

'My trousers would have fallen down! I'm not like all these kids now, I don't wear a belt to look *groovy*, as they say. Where I come from you wear it because it keeps your pants up. And you'd be arrestin' me for a whole lot more than this, if it didn't, believe you me.'

'You haven't been arrested, Mr Conway. We just need to ask you some questions. Behaviour such as yours is prohibited at this airport, so we need to ascertain if you are a threat to the safety of our passengers.'

'What do you mean, a threat?'

The security officer clears his throat. 'Well, it means finding out if you are a member of any gangs or terrorist organisations before we reconsider allowing you through.'

I hear Dad roar with laughter.

'You must understand that planes are very confined spaces and we can't allow anybody on that we aren't sure of. We have the right to choose who we allow onboard our aircraft.'

'The only threat I'd be in a confined space is when I've had a good curry from my local. And terrorist organisations? I am, all right. The Monday Club is all

I'm a member of. Meet every Monday except on bank holidays when we meet on a Tuesday. A bunch of lads and lasses like me gettin' together for a few pints and a singsong is all it is. Though if you're lookin' for juice, Donal's family were pretty heavily involved in the IRA all right.'

I hear the man questioning him clear his throat again. 'Donal?'

'Donal McCarthy. Ah, leave him alone, he's ninety-seven, and I'm talkin' about way back when his dad fought. The only rebellious thing he's able to do now is whack the chessboard with his cane and that's only because he's frustrated he can't play. Arthritis in both his hands. Could do with gettin' it in his mouth, if you ask me. Talkin' is all he does. Annoys Peter no end but they've never gotten along since he courted his daughter and broke her heart. She's seventy-two. Have you ever heard anything more ridiculous? Had a wandering eye, she claimed, but sure, he's as cock-eyed as they come. His eye wanders without him even knowing it. I wouldn't blame the man for that, though he does like to domi-nate the conversations every week. I can't wait for him to listen to me for a change.' Dad laughs and sighs in the long pause that follows. 'Do you think I could get a cuppa?'

'We won't be much longer, Mr Conway. What is the nature of your visit to London?'

'I'm going because my daughter dragged me here, last minute. She gets off the phone yesterday morning and looks at me with a face as white as a sheet. I'm off to London, she says, like it's somethin' you just do last minute. Ah, maybe it is what you young people do, but not for me. Not what I'm used to at all, at all. Never been on a plane before, you see. So she says wouldn't it be fun if we both go away? And usually I'd say no, I've loads to be doin' in my garden. Have to put down the lilies, tulips, daffodils and hyacinths in time for the spring, you see, but she says live a little and I felt like peltin' her because it's more livin' I've been doing than her. But because of recent, well, troubles, shall we say, I decided to come with her. And that's no crime, is it?'

'What recent troubles, Mr Conway?'

'Ah, my Gracie—'

'Joyce.'

'Yes, thank you. My Joyce, she's been goin' through a rough patch. Lost her little baby a few weeks back, you see. Had been years trying to have one with a fella that plays tennis in little white shorts and things finally looked great but she had an accident, fell, you see and she lost the little one. Lost a little of herself too, if I'm to be honest with you. Lost the husband too just last week, but don't you be feelin' sorry for her about that. She lost somethin' all right but, mind you, she got a little somethin' she never had before. Can't put my finger on exactly what, but whatever it is, I don't think it's such a bad thing. Generally things aren't goin' right for her and sure, what kind of a father would I be to let her go off on her own in this state? She's got no job, no baby, no husband, no mother and soon no house, and if she wants to go to London for a break, even if it is last minute, then she sure as hell is entitled to go without any more people stopping her from what she wants.

'Here, take my bloody cap. My Joyce wants to go to London and you fellows should let her. She's a good girl, never did a thing wrong in her life. She has nothing right now but me and this trip, as far as I can see. So here, take it. If I have to go without my cap and my shoes and my belt and my coat, well then, that's fine by me, but my Joyce isn't going to London without me.'

Well, if that isn't enough to break a girl.

'Mr Conway, you do know that you get your clothing back once you go through the metal detector?'

'What?' he shouts. 'Why the hell didn't she tell me that? All this feckin' nonsense for nothing. Honestly, you'd think she almost *wants* the trouble sometimes. OK, lads, you can take my things. Will we still make the flight, do you think?'

Any tears that had welled very quickly dried.

Finally the door to my cell opens and, with a single nod, I'm a free woman.

'Doris, you cannot move the stove in the kitchen. Al, tell her.'

'Why not?'

'Honey, first of all it's heavy and second of all, it's gas. You are not qualified to move around kitchen appliances,' Al explains, and prepares to bite into a doughnut.

Doris whisks it away from him, leaving him to lick dribbles of jam from his fingers. 'You two don't seem to understand that it's bad feng shui to have a stove facing a door. The person at the stove may instinctively want to glance back at the door, which creates a feeling of unease, which can lead to accidents.'

'Perhaps removing the stove altogether will be a safer option for Dad.'

'You have to give me a break,' Justin sighs, sitting down at the new kitchen table and chairs. 'All the place needs is furniture and a lick of paint, not for you to restructure the entire place according to yoda.'

'It is not according to yoda,' Doris huffs. 'Donald Trump follows feng shui, you know.'

'Oh, *well then*,' Al and Justin say in unison.

'Yes, well then. Maybe if you did what he did, you'd be able to walk up the stairs without having to take a lunch-break halfway up,' she snaps at Al. 'Just because you sell tyres, sweetie, it doesn't mean you have to wear them too.'

Bea's mouth drops and Justin tries not to laugh. 'Come on, sweetheart, let's get out of here before it turns to violence.'

'Where are you two going? Can I come?' Al asks.

'I'm going to the dentist and Bea has rehearsals for tonight.'

'Good luck, Blondie.' Al ruffles her hair. 'We'll be cheering for you.'

'Thanks.' She grinds her teeth and fixes her hair. 'Oh,

that reminds me. One more thing about the woman on the phone, Joyce?'

What, what, what? 'What about her?'

'She knows that I'm blonde.'

'How did she know?' Doris asks, with surprise.

'She said she just guessed. But that's not it. Before she hung up she said, "Best of luck with your ballet show."'

'So she's a thoughtful lucky-guesser,' Al shrugs.

'Well, I was thinking about it afterward and I don't remember telling her anything about my show being specifically ballet.'

Justin immediately looks to Al, a little more concerned now that it involves his daughter, but adrenalin still surges. 'What do you think?'

'I think, watch your back, bro. She could be a fruit cake.' He stands up and heads to the kitchen, rubbing his stomach. 'Actually, that's not a bad idea. Fruit cake.'

Deflated, Justin looks hopefully at his daughter. 'Did she sound like a fruit cake?'

'I dunno,' Bea shrugs. 'What does a fruit cake sound like?'

Justin, Al and Bea all turn to stare at Doris.

'What?' she squeals.

'No,' Bea shakes her head wildly at her father. 'Nothing like that, at all.'

'What's this for, Gracie?'

'It's a sick bag.'

'What does this do?'

'It's for hanging your coat up.'

'Why is that there?'

'It's a table.'

'How do you get it down?'

'By unlatching it, at the top.'

'Sir, please leave your table-top up until after take-off.'

Silence.

'What are they doing outside?'

'Loading the bags.'

'What's that yoke?'

'An ejector seat for people who ask three million questions.'

'What's it, really?'

'For reclining your chair.'

'Sir, could you stay upright until after take-off, please?'

Silence.

'What does that do?'

'Air conditioning.'

'What about that?'

'A light.'

'And that one?'

'Yes, sir, can I help you?'

'Eh, no, thanks.'

'You pressed the button for assistance.'

'Oh, is that what that little woman on the button is for? I didn't know. Can I have a drink of water?'

'We can't serve drinks until after take-off, sir.'

'Oh, OK. That was a fine display you did earlier. You were the image of my friend Edna when you had that oxygen mask on. She used to smoke sixty a day, you see.'

The air stewardess makes an *oh* shape with her mouth.

'I feel very safe now, but what if we go down over land?' He raises his voice and the passengers around us look our way. 'Surely the life jackets are hopeless, unless we blow our whistles while we're flying through the air and hope someone below hears us and catches us. Do we not have parachutes?'

'There's no need to worry, sir, we won't go down over land.'

'OK. That's very reassuring, indeed. But if we do, tell the pilot to aim for a hay stack or something.'

I take deep breaths and pretend that I don't know him. I continue reading my book, *The Golden Age of Dutch Painting: Vermeer, Metsu and Terborch*, and convince myself this was not the bad idea it's turning out to be.

'Where are the toilets?'

'To the top and on the left but you can't go until after take-off.'

Dad's eyes widen. 'And when will that be?'

'In just a few minutes.'

'In just a few minutes, that,' he takes the sick bag out from the seat pocket, 'won't be used for what it's supposed to be used for.'

'We will be in the air in just a few minutes more, I assure you.' The stewardess quickly leaves before he asks another question.

I sigh.

'Don't you be sighing until after take-off,' Dad says, and the man next to me laughs and pretends to turn it into a cough.

Dad looks out the window and I revel in the moment of silence.

'Oh oh oh,' he sings, 'we're moving now, Gracie.'

As soon as we're off the ground, the wheels moan as they're brought back up and then we are light in the air. Dad is suddenly quiet. He is turned sideways in his chair, head filling the window, watching as we reach the beginning of the clouds, mere wisps at first. The plane bumps around as it pushes through the clouds. Dad is agog as we're surrounded by white on all sides of the plane, his head darts around looking at every window possible, and then suddenly it is blue and calm above the fluffy world of clouds. Dad blesses himself. He pushes his nose up against the window, his face lit by the nearby sun, and I take a mental photograph for my own hall of memories.

The seatbelt fasten sign goes off with a bing and cabin crew announce that we may now use electronic devices, the facilities, and that food and refreshments will be served shortly. Dad takes down the table-top, reaches into his pocket and takes out his photograph of Mum. He places her down on the table, facing out

the window. He reclines his chair and they both watch
the endless sea of white clouds disappear further below
us and don't say a word for the remainder of the
flight.

20

'Well, I must say, that was absolutely marvellous. Marvellous indeed.' Dad pumps the pilot's hand up and down enthusiastically.

We are standing by the just-opened door of the plane, with a queue of hundreds of irritated passengers huffing and puffing down our necks. They are like greyhounds whose trap has opened, the bunny has been fired off ahead of them and all that blocks their path is, well, Dad. The usual rock in the stream.

'And the *food*,' Dad continues to the cabin crew, 'it was excellent, just excellent.'

He's eaten a ham roll and a cup of tea.

'I can't believe I was eating in the sky,' he laughs. 'Well done again, just marvellous. Nothing short of miraculous, I'd say. My Lord.' He pumps the pilot's hand again, as though he's meeting JFK.

'OK, Dad, we should move on now. We're holding everybody up.'

'Oh, is that so? Thanks again, folks. 'Bye now. Might see you on the way back,' he shouts over his shoulder, as I pull him away.

We make our way through the tunnel adjoining the plane to the terminal and Dad says hello and tips his hat to everyone we pass.

'You really don't have to say hello to everybody, you know.'

'It's nice to be important, Gracie, but it's more impor-tant to be nice. Particularly when in another country,' says the man who hasn't left the province of Leinster for ten years.

'Will you stop shouting?'

'I can't help it. My ears feel funny.'

'Either yawn or hold your nose and blow. It will help your ears to pop.'

He stands by the conveyor belt, purple-faced, with his cheeks puffed out and his fingers over his nose. He takes a deep breath and pushes. He lets out a fart.

The conveyor belt jerks into motion and like flies around a carcass, people suddenly swoop in front of us to block our view, as though their life depends on grabbing their bags this very second.

'There's your bag.' I step forward.

'I'll get it, love.'

'No, I will. You'll hurt your back.'

'Step back, love, I can do it.' He passes over the yellow line and grabs his bag, only to realise that the strength he once had is gone and he finds himself walking alongside it, while tugging away. Ordinarily I would rush to help him but I'm doubled over laughing. All I can hear is Dad saying, 'Excuse me, excuse me,' to people who are standing over the yellow line, as he tries to keep up with his moving luggage. He does a full lap of the conveyor belt and by the time he gets back to where I stand (though I'm still doubled over) somebody has the common sense to help the out-of-breath grumbling old man.

He pulls his bag over to me, his face scarlet, his breathing heavy.

'I'll let you get your own bag,' he says, pulling his cap further down over his eyes with embarrassment.

I wait for our bags while Dad wanders around baggage claim 'acquainting himself with London'. After the incident at Dublin airport, the satellite navigational voice in my head has continuously nagged at me to make a U-turn *right now* but somewhere inside, another part of me is under strict orders to soldier on, feeling convinced this trip is the right thing to do. Now I'm wondering what exactly *this* is. As I collect my bag from the belt, I am aware that there is not a clear purpose for this trip at all. A wild-goose chase is all it is. Instinct alone, caused by a confusing conversation with a girl named Bea, has caused me to fly to another country with my seventy-five-year-old father, who has never left Ireland in his life. Suddenly what seemed like the 'only thing to do' at the time, has now occurred to me as being completely irrational behaviour.

What does it mean to dream about somebody you've never met, almost every night, and then have a chance encounter with them over the phone? I had called my dad's emergency number; she had answered her dad's emergency phone number. What message is in that? What am I supposed to learn? Is it a mere coincidence that an ordinary right-thinking person would ignore or am I right to think and feel that something more lies beneath this? My hope is that this trip will have some answers for me. Panic begins to build as I watch Dad reading a poster on the far side of the room. I have no idea what to do with him.

Suddenly Dad's hand flies to his head and then his chest and he darts towards me with a manic look in his eyes. I make a grab for his pills.

'Gracie,' he gasps.

'Here, quickly, take these.' My hand trembles as I hold out the pills and bottle of water.

'What on earth are you doing?'

'Well, you looked . . .'

'I looked what?'

'Like you were going to have a heart attack!'

'That's because I bloody well will, if we don't get out of here quick.' He grabs my arm and starts to pull me along.

'What's wrong? Where are we going?'

'We're going to Westminster.'

'What? Why? No! Dad, we have to go to the hotel to leave our bags.'

He stops walking and whips around, pushes his face

close to mine, almost aggressively. His voice shakes with the adrenalin. 'The *Antiques Roadshow* are having a valuation day today from nine thirty to four thirty in the afternoon in a place called Banqueting House. If we leave now we can start queuing. I'm not going to miss seeing it on the telly and then come all the way to London just to miss seeing it in the flesh. Sure we might even get to see Michael Aspel. *Michael Aspel*, Gracie. Christ Almighty, let's get out of here.'

His pupils are dilated, he's all fired up. He shoots off through the sliding doors, with nothing to declare but temporary insanity, and takes a confident left.

I stand in the arrivals hall, while men in suits approach me with placards from all sides. I sigh and wait. Dad appears from the direction he went in, seesawing and pulling his bag behind him at top speed.

'You could have told me that was the wrong way,' he says, passing me and heading in the opposite direction.

Dad rushes through Trafalgar Square, pulling his suitcase behind him and scattering a flock of pigeons into the sky. He's not interested in acquainting himself with London any more; he has only Michael Aspel and the treasures of the blue-rinse brigade in sight. Finally, after we've taken a few wrong turns since surfacing from the tube station, Banqueting House is eventually in view, a seventeenth-century former royal palace, and though I am sure I have never visited it before, it stands before me, a familiar sight.

Once deep in the queue, I study the single drawer that is in the hands of the old man in front of us. Behind us, a woman is rolling out a tea cup from a pile of newspapers to show somebody else in the queue. All around me there is excited and rather innocent and polite chatter, and the sun is shining as we wait outside to enter the reception area of Banqueting House. There are TV vans, camera and sound people going in and out of the building, and cameras filming the long queue while a woman with a microphone picks people out of the crowd to interview. Many people in the queue have brought deck chairs, picnic baskets of scones and finger sandwiches, and canteens of tea and coffee, and as Dad looks around with a grumbling stomach I feel like a guilty mother who hasn't properly equipped her child. I'm also concerned for Dad that we won't make it past the front door.

'Dad, I don't want to worry you but I really think that we're supposed to have something with us.'

'What do you mean?'

'Like an object. Everybody else has things with them to be valued.'

Dad looks around and notices for the first time. His face falls.

'Maybe they'll make an exception for us,' I add quickly but I doubt it.

'What about these cases?' He looks down at our bags.

I try not to laugh. 'I got them in TK Maxx; I don't think they'll be interested in valuing them.'

Dad laughs. 'Maybe I'll give them my undies, Gracie, what you think? There's a fine bit of history in them.'

I make a face and he waves his hand dismissively.

We shuffle along slowly in the queue and Dad has a great time chatting to everybody about his life and his exciting trip with his daughter. After queuing for an hour and a half, we have been invited to two houses for afternoon tea and Dad has taken note from the gentleman behind us on how to stop the mint in his garden from taking over his rosemary. Up ahead, just beyond the doors, I see an elderly couple being turned away due to having no items with them. Dad sees this too and looks at me, his eyes worried. It will be us next.

'Eh . . .' I look around quickly for something.

Both entrance doors have been held open for the flowing crowd. Just inside the main entrance, behind the opened door is a wooden waste basket posing as an umbrella stand, holding a few forgotten and broken umbrellas. While no one is looking I turn it upside down, emptying the few scrunched balls of paper and broken umbrellas out. I kick them behind the door just in time to hear, 'Next.'

I carry it up to the reception desk and Dad's eyes almost pop out of his head at the sight of me.

'Welcome to Banqueting House,' the young woman greets us.

'Thank you,' I smile innocently.

'How many objects have you brought today?' she asks.

'Oh, just the one.' I raise the bin onto the table.

'Oh, wow, fantastic.' She runs her fingers along it and Dad gives me a look, that if for any second I had forgotten which of us was the parent, I am quickly reminded. 'Have you been to a valuation day before?'

'No.' Dad shakes his head wildly. 'But I see it on the telly all the time. Big fan, I am. Even when Hugh Scully was host.'

'Wonderful,' she smiles. 'Once you enter the hall you'll see there are many queues. Please join the queue for the appropriate discipline.'

'What queue should we join for this thing?' Dad looks at the item as though there's a bad smell.

'Well, what is it?' she smiles.

Dad looks at me baffled.

'We were hoping you'd tell us that,' I say politely.

'I'd suggest miscellaneous, and though that is the busiest table, we try to move it along as quickly as possible for you by having four experts. Once you reach the expert's table, simply show your item and he or she will tell you all about it.'

'Which table do we go to for Michael Aspel?'

'Unfortunately Michael Aspel isn't actually an expert, he is the host, so he doesn't have a table of his own, but we do have twenty other experts that will be available to answer your questions.'

Dad looks devastated.

'There is the chance that your item may be chosen for television,' she adds quickly, sensing Dad's disappointment. 'The expert shows the object to the television team and a decision is made whether to record it, depending on rarity, quality, what the expert can say about the object and, of course, value. If your object is chosen, you'll be taken to our waiting room and made up before talking to the expert about your object in front of the camera for about five minutes. You would meet Michael Aspel under those circumstances. And the exciting news is that for the first time, we are broadcasting the show live, in, ooh let's see,' she examines her watch, 'in one hour.'

Dad's eyes widen. 'But five *minutes*? To talk about that thing?' Dad explodes and she laughs.

'Do bear in mind that we have to see two thousand people's items before the show,' she says to me with a knowing look.

'We understand. We're just here to enjoy the day, isn't that right, Dad?'

He doesn't hear; he's busy looking around for Michael Aspel.

'Do enjoy your day,' the woman says finally, calling the next person in line forward.

As soon as we enter the busy hall, I immediately look up at the ceiling of the double-cubed room, already knowing what to expect: nine huge canvases commissioned by Charles I, to fill the panelled ceiling.

'Here you go, Dad.' I hand him the waste basket. 'I'm going to take a look around this beautiful building while you look at the junk people are putting inside it.'

'It's not junk, Gracie. I once saw the show where a man's collection of walking sticks went for sixty thousand sterling pounds.'

'Wow, in that case you should show them your shoe.'

He tries not to laugh.

'Off you go to have a look around and I'll meet you back here.' He starts to wander away before he even finishes the sentence. Dying to get rid of me.

'Have fun,' I wink.

He smiles broadly and looks around the hall with such happiness, my mind takes another photograph.

As I wander the rooms of the only part of Whitehall Palace to survive a fire, the feeling that I've been here before comes over me in a giant wave and I find a quiet corner and secretly produce my mobile.

'Manager, deputy head corporate treasury and investor solutions desk, Frankie speaking.'

'My God, you weren't lying. That's a ridiculous amount of words.'

'Joyce! Hi!' Her voice is hushed and behind her, the stock-trading in the Irish Financial Services Centre offices, sounds manic.

'Can you talk?'

'For a little bit, yeah. How are you?'

'I'm fine. I'm in London. With Dad.'

'What? With your dad? Joyce, I've told you before it's not polite to bind and gag your father. What are you doing there?'

'I just decided to come over last minute.' For what, I have no idea. 'We're currently at the *Antiques Roadshow*. Don't ask.'

I leave the quiet rooms behind me and enter the gallery of the main hall. Below me I can see Dad wandering around the crowded hall with the bin in his hands. I smile as I watch him.

'Have we ever been to Banqueting House together?'

'Refresh my memory, where is it, what is it and what does it look like?'

'It's at the Trafalgar Square end of Whitehall. It's a seventeenth-century former royal palace designed by Inigo Jones in 1619. Charles I was executed on a scaffold in front of the building. I'm in a room now, with nine canvases covering the panelled ceiling.' What does it look like? I close my eyes. 'From memory, the roofline is balustrade. The street façade has two orders of engaged columns, Corinthian over Ionic, above a rusticated basement, which lock together in a harmonious whole.'

'Joyce?'

'Yes?' I snap out of it.

'Are you reading from a tourist guide?'

'No.'

'Our last trip to London consisted of Madame Tussaud's, a night in G-A-Y and a party back in a man named Gloria's flat. It's happening again, isn't it? That thing you were talking about?'

'Yes.' I slump into a chair in the corner, feel a rope beneath me and jump back up. I quickly move away from the antique chair, looking around for security cameras.

'Has your being in London got anything to do with the American man?'

'Yes,' I whisper.

'Oh, Joyce—'

'No, Frankie, listen. Listen and you'll understand. I hope. Yesterday I panicked about something and called Dad's doctor, a number that is practically engraved in my head, as it should be. I couldn't possibly get it wrong, right?'

'Right.'

'Wrong. I ended up dialling a UK number and a girl named Bea answered the phone. She'd seen an Irish number and thought it was her dad calling. So from our short conversation I figure out that her dad is American but was in Dublin and was travelling to London last night to see her in a show today. And she has blonde hair. I think Bea is the little girl I keep dreaming about seeing on the swings and playing in the sand, all at different ages.'

Frankie is quiet.

'I know I sound insane, Frankie, but this is what's happening. I have no explanation for it.'

'I know, I know,' she says quickly. 'I've known you practically all my life – this is *not* something you'd be inclined to make up – but even as I take you seriously please do keep in consideration the fact that you've had a traumatic time and what you're currently experiencing could be due to high levels of stress.'

'I've already considered that.' I groan and hold my head in my hands. 'I need help.'

'We'll only consider insanity as a last resort. Let me think for a second.' She sounds as though she's writing it down. 'So basically, you have seen this girl, Bea—'

'Maybe Bea.'

'OK, OK, let's just say it is Bea. You've seen her grow up?'

'Yes.'

'To what age?'

'From birth to I don't know . . .'

'Teenager, twenties, thirties?'

'Teenager.'

'OK, so who else is in the scenes with Bea?'

'Another woman. With a camera.'

'But never your American man?'

'No. So he probably has nothing to do with this at all.'

'Let's not rule anything out. So when you view Bea and the lady with the camera, are you part of the scene or viewing them as an outsider?'

I close my eyes and think hard, see my hands pushing the swing, holding hands, taking a photograph of the girl and her mother in the park, feeling the water from the sprinklers spray and tickle my skin . . . 'No, I'm part of it. They can see me.'

'OK.' She is silent.

'What, Frankie, what?'

'I'm figuring it out. Hold on. OK. So you see a child, a mother and they both see you?'

'Yes.'

'Would you say that in your dreams you're viewing this girl grow up through the eyes of a father?'

Goose bumps form on my skin.

'Oh my God,' I whisper. The American man?

'I take it that's a yes,' Frankie says. 'OK, we're on

to something here. I don't know what, but it's something very weird and I can't believe I'm even entertaining these thoughts. But what the hell, I only have a million other things to do. What else do you dream about?'

'It's all very fast, images just flashing by.'

'Try and remember.'

'Sprinklers in a garden. A chubby young boy. A woman with long red hair. I hear bells. See old buildings with shop fronts. A church. A beach. I'm at a funeral. Then at college. Then with the woman and young girl. Sometimes she's smiling and holding my hand, sometimes she's shouting and slamming doors.'

'Hmm . . . she must be your wife.'

I bury my head in my hands. 'Frankie, this sounds so ridiculous.'

'Who cares? When has life ever made sense? Let's keep going.'

'I don't know, the images are all so abstract. I can't make any sense of it.'

'What you should do is, every time you get a flash of something, or suddenly know something you never knew, then write it down and tell me. I'll help you figure this out.'

'Thank you.'

'So apart from the place you're in now, what kinds of things do you suddenly just know about?'

'Em . . . mostly buildings.' I look around and then up at the ceiling. 'And art. I spoke Italian to a man at the airport. And Latin, I spoke Latin to Conor the other day.'

'Oh God.'

'I know. I think he wants to have me sent away.'

'Well, we won't let him do that. Yet. OK so, buildings, art, languages. Wow, Joyce, it's like you've gotten a crash course in an entire college education you never had. Where is the culturally ignorant girl I once knew and loved?'

I smile. 'She's still here.'

'OK, one more thing. My boss has called me for a meeting this afternoon. What is it about?'

'Frankie, I don't have psychic powers!'

The door to the gallery opens and a flustered-looking young girl with a headset over her head rushes in. She approaches almost every woman on her way in, asking for me.

'Joyce Conway?' she asks me, out of breath.

'Yes.' My heat beats a mile a minute. Please let Dad be OK. Please, God.

'Is your father Henry?'

'Yes.'

'He wants you to join him in the green room.'

'He *what*? In the *what*?'

'He's in the green room. He's going live with Michael Aspel in just a few minutes with his item and he wants you to join him because he says you know more about it. We really have to move now, there's very little time and we need to get you made up.'

'Live with Michael Aspel . . .' I trail off. I realise I'm still holding the phone. 'Frankie,' I say, dazed, 'put on BBC, quick. You're about to witness me getting into very big trouble.'

<h1 style="text-align:center">21</h1>

I half-walk, half-run behind the girl with the headset, to get to the green room, and arrive panting and nervous to see Dad sitting on a make-up chair facing a mirror lit up by bulbs, tissue tucked into his collar, a cup and saucer in his hand, his bulbous nose being powdered for his close-up.

'Ah, there you are, love,' Dad says grandly. 'Everybody, this is my daughter and she'll be the one to tell us all about my lovely piece here that caught the eye of Michael Aspel.' This is followed by a chuckle and he sips on his tea. 'There's Jaffa Cakes over there if you want them.'

Evil little man.

I look around the room at all the interested, nodding heads, and force a smile onto my face.

Justin squirms uncomfortably in his chair in the dentist's waiting room, with his throbbing swollen cheek, sandwiched between two old dears carrying on a conversation about someone they know called Rebecca, who should leave a man called Timothy.

Shut up, shut up, shut up!

The 1970s television in the corner, which is covered by a lace cloth and fake flowers, announces that the *Antiques Roadshow* is about to begin.

Justin groans. 'Does anybody mind if I change the channel?'

'I'm watching it,' says a young boy no older than seven years old.

'Charming,' Justin smiles at him with loathing, then looks to his mother for backup.

Instead she shrugs. 'He's watching it.'

Justin grunts in frustration.

'Excuse me.' Justin finally interrupts the women to his right and left. 'Would one of you ladies like to swap places with me, so that you can continue this conversation more privately?'

'No, don't worry, love, there's nothing private about this conversation, believe you me. Eavesdrop all you like.'

The smell of her breath silently tiptoes under his nostrils again, tickles them with a feather duster and runs off with an evil giggle.

'I wasn't eavesdropping. Your *lips* were quite literally in my *ear*, and I'm not sure if Charlie or Graham or Rebecca would appreciate that.' He turns his nose away.

'Oh, Ethel,' one laughs, 'he thinks we're talking about *real* people.'

How foolish I am.

Justin turns his attention back to the television in the corner, which the other six people in the room are glued to.

'. . . And welcome to our first *live Antiques Roadshow* special . . .'

Justin sighs loudly again.

The little boy narrows his eyes at him and raises the volume with the remote control that is firmly within his grasp.

'. . . coming to you from Banqueting House, London.'

Oh, I've been there. A nice example of Corinthian and Ionic locked together in a harmonious whole.

'We have had over two thousand people spilling through our doors since nine thirty this morning, and only moments ago those doors have closed, leaving us to display the best pieces for you to view at home. Our first guests come from—'

Ethel leans across Justin and rests her elbow on his thigh. 'So anyway, Margaret—'

He zones in on the television so as not to grab both their heads and smash them together.

'So what do we have here?' Michael Aspel asks. 'Looks like a designer waste basket to me,' he says as the camera takes a close-up on the piece propped on the table.

Justin's heart begins to palpitate.

'Do you want me to change it now, mister?' The boy flicks through the channels at top speed.

'No!' he shouts, breaking through Margaret and Ethel's conversation and reaching out dramatically into thin air as though he can stop the waves from changing the channel. He falls to the carpet on his knees, before the television. Margaret and Ethel jump and go silent. 'Go back, go back, go back!' he shouts at the boy.

The boy's lower lip begins to tremble as he looks to his mother.

'There's no need to shout at him.' She holds his head to her chest, protectively.

He grabs the remote control from the boy and flicks through the channels at top speed. He stops when he comes upon the close-up of Joyce, whose eyes are looking uncertainly to the left and right, as though she has just landed in the cage of a Bengal tiger at feeding time.

In the Irish Financial Services Centre, Frankie is racing through the offices searching for a television. She finds one, surrounded by dozens of suits studying the figures that are racing by on the screen.

'Excuse me! Coming through!' she shouts, pushing her way through. She rushes to the TV and starts fiddling with the buttons to cries of abuse from the men and women around her.

'I'll just be one minute, the market won't crash in all of the *two minutes* this will take.' She flicks around and finds Joyce and Henry live on BBC.

She gasps and holds her hands up to her mouth. And then she laughs and throws her fist at the screen. 'You go, Joyce!'

The team around her quickly shuffles off to find another screen, apart from one man who seems pleased by the change in channel and decides to stay and watch.

'Oh, that's a nice piece,' he comments, leaning back against the desk and folding his arms.

'*Em* . . .' Joyce is saying, 'well, we found it . . . I mean we *put* it, put this beautiful . . . extraordinarily . . . eh, wooden . . . bucket, outside of our house. Well, not *outside*,' she quickly withdraws that statement on seeing the appraiser's reaction. '*Inside*. We put it inside our front porch so that it's protected from the weather, you see. For umbrellas.'

'Yes, and it may have been used for that too,' he says. 'Where did you get it from?'

Joyce's mouth opens and closes for a few seconds and Henry jumps in. He is standing upright with his hands clasped over his belly. His chin is raised, there is a glint in his eye and he ignores the expert and takes on a posh accent to direct his answer at Michael Aspel, whom he addresses as though he's the Pope.

'Well, Michael, I was given this by my great-great-grandfather Joseph Conway, who was a farmer in Tipperary. He gave it to my grandfather Shay, who was also a farmer. My grandfather gave it to my father, Paddy-Joe, who was also a farmer in Cavan and then when he died, I took it.'

'I see, and do you have any idea where your great-great- grandfather may have got this?'

'He probably stole it from the Brits,' Henry jokes, and is the only one to laugh. Joyce elbows her father, Frankie snorts, and on the floor before the television in a dentist's waiting room in London, Justin throws his head back and laughs loudly.

'Well, the reason I ask is because this is a fabulous item you have. It's a rare nineteenth-century English Victorian era upright jardinière planter—'

'I love gardening, Michael,' Henry interrupts the expert, 'do you?'

Michael smiles at him politely and the expert continues, 'It has wonderful hand-carved Black Forest-style plaques set in the Victorian ebonised wood framing on all four sides.'

'Country English or French décor, what do you think?' Frankie's work colleague asks her.

She ignores him, concentrating on Joyce.

'Inside it has what looks like an original tole-painted tin liner. Superb condition, ornate patterns carved into the solid wood panels. We can see here that two of the sides have a floral motif and the other two sides are figural, one with the centre lion's head and the other with griffin figures. Very striking indeed and an absolutely wonderful piece to have by your front door too.'

'Worth a few quid, is it?' Henry asks, dropping the posh accent.

'We'll get to that part,' the expert says. 'While it is in good condition, it appears there would have been feet, quite likely wooden. There are no splits or warping in the sides, there is an original tole-painted tin removable liner and the finger ring handles on the sides are intact. So bearing all that in mind, how much do you think it's worth?'

'Frankie!' Frankie hears her boss calling her from across the room. 'What's this I hear about you messing with the monitors?'

Frankie stands up, turns her back and while blocking the television with her body, attempts to turn the channel back.

'Ah,' her colleague tuts. 'They were just about to announce the value. That's the best bit.'

'Step aside,' her boss frowns.

Frankie moves to display the stock market figures racing across the screen. She smiles brightly, showing all her teeth, and then sprints back to her desk.

*   *   *

In the dental surgery's waiting room, Justin is glued to the television, glued to Joyce's face.

'Is she a friend, love?' Ethel asks.

Justin studies Joyce's face and smiles, 'Yes she is. Her name is Joyce.'

Margaret and Ethel ooh and aah.

On screen, Joyce's father or at least who Justin assumes him to be, turns to Joyce and shrugs.

'What would you say, love? How much lolly for Dolly?'

Joyce smiles tightly. 'I really wouldn't have the slightest idea how much it's worth.'

'How does between one thousand five hundred to one thousand seven hundred pounds sound to you?' the expert asks.

'Sterling pounds?' the old man asks, flabbergasted.

Justin laughs.

The camera zooms in on Joyce and her father's face. They are both astonished, so gobsmacked, in fact, that neither of them can say anything.

'Now there's an impressive reaction,' Michael laughs. 'Good news from this table, let's go over to our porcelain table to see if any of our other collectors here in London, have been as lucky.'

'Justin Hitchcock,' the receptionist announces.

The room is quiet. They all look around at one another.

'Justin,' she repeats, raising her voice.

'That must be him on the floor,' Ethel says. 'Yoohoo!' she sings and gives him a kick with her comfortable shoe. 'Are you Justin?'

'Somebody's in love, ooohey-ooohey,' Margaret sings while Ethel makes kissing noises.

'Louise,' Ethel says to the receptionist, 'why don't I go in now while this young man runs down to Banqueting House to see his lady? I'm tired of waiting.' She stretches her left leg out and makes pained expressions.

Justin stands and wipes the carpet hairs from his

trousers. 'I don't know why you're both waiting here anyway, at your age. You should just leave your teeth here and then come back later when the dentist's finished with them.'

He exits the room as a year-old copy of *Homes and Gardens* flies at his head.

22

'Actually, that's not a bad idea.' Justin stops following the receptionist down the hallway to the surgery, as adrenalin once again surges through his body. 'That's exactly what I'll do.'

'You're going to leave your teeth here?' she says drily, in a strong Liverpool accent.

'No, I'm going to Banqueting House,' he says, hopping about with excitement.

'Great, Dick. Can Anne come too? Let's be sure to ask Aunt Fanny first.' She glares at him, killing his excitement. 'I don't care what's going on with you, you're not escaping again. Come now. Dr Montgomery won't be happy if you don't show for your appointment again,' she urges him along.

'OK, OK, hold on. My tooth is fine now.' He holds out his hands and shrugs like it's all no big deal. 'All gone. No pain at all. In fact, chomp, chomp, chomp,' he says as he snaps his teeth together. 'Look, completely gone. What am I even doing here? Can't feel a thing.'

'Your eyes are watering.'

'I'm emotional.'

'You're delusional. Come on.' She continues to lead him down the corridor.

Dr Montgomery greets him with a drill in his hand, 'Hello, Clarisse,' he says, and breaks his heart laughing. 'Just joking. Trying to run off on me again, Justin?'

'No. Well, yes. Well, no, not run off exactly but I

realised that there's somewhere else I should be and . . .'

All throughout his explanation, the firm-handed Dr Montgomery and his equally strong assistant manage to usher him into the chair, and by the time he's finished his excuse he realises he's wearing a protective gown and reclining.

'Blah blah blah, was all I heard, I'm afraid, Justin,' Dr Montgomery says cheerily.

He sighs.

'You're not going to fight me today?' Dr Montgomery snaps two surgical gloves onto his hands.

'As long as you don't ask me to cough.'

Dr Montgomery laughs as Justin reluctantly opens his mouth.

The red light on the camera goes off and I grab Dad's arm.

'Dad, we have to go now,' I say with urgency.

'Not now,' Dad responds in a David Attenborough-style loud whisper. 'Michael Aspel is right over there. I can see him, standing behind the porcelain table, tall, charming, more handsome than I thought. He's looking around for someone to talk to.'

'Michael Aspel is very busy in his natural habitat, presenting a live television show.' I dig my fingernails into Dad's arm. 'I don't think talking to you is very high on his priority list right now.'

Dad looks slightly wounded, and not from my finger-nails. He lifts his chin high in the air, which I know from down the years has an invisible string attached to his pride. He prepares to approach Michael Aspel, who is standing alone by the porcelain table with his finger in his ear.

'Must get waxy build-up, like me,' Dad whispers. 'He should use that stuff you got for me. Pop! Comes right out.'

'It's an earpiece, Dad. He's listening to the people in the control room.'

'No, I think it's a hearing aid. Let's go over to him

and remember to speak up and mouth your words clearly. I have experience with this.'

I block his path and leer over him in the most intimidating way possible. Dad steps onto his left leg and immediately rises near enough to my eyelevel.

'Dad, if we do not leave this place right now, we will find ourselves locked in a cell. Again.'

Dad laughs, 'Ah, don't exaggerate, Gracie.'

'I'm *bloody* Joyce,' I hiss.

'All right, bloody Joyce, no need to get your bloody knickers in a twist.'

'I don't think you understand the seriousness of our situation. We have just stolen a seventeen-hundred-pound Victorian waste basket from a once-upon-a-time royal palace and talked about it live on air.'

Dad looks at me quickly, his bushy eyebrows raised halfway up his forehead. For the first time in a long time I can see his eyes. They look alarmed. And rather watery and yellow at the corners, and I make a note to ask him about that later, when we are not running from the law. Or the BBC.

The production girl I chased in order to find Dad gives me wide eyes from across the room. My heart beats in panic and I look around quickly. Heads are turning to stare at us. They know.

'OK, we have to go now. I think they know.'

'It's no big deal. We'll put it back.' He speaks as though it *is* a big deal. 'We haven't even taken it off the premises – that's no crime.'

'OK, it's now or never. Grab it quick, so we can put it back and get out of here.'

I scan the crowd to make sure nobody big and burly is coming towards us, cracking their knuckles and swinging a baseball bat. Just the young girl with the headset, and I'm sure I can take her on, and if not, Dad can hit her on the head with his clunky corrective shoe.

Dad grabs the waste basket from the table and tries to hide it in the inside of his coat. The coat barely makes it a third of the way around and I look at him bizarrely and he removes it. We make our way through the crowd, ignoring congrats and well-wishes from those who seem to think we've won the lottery. I see the young girl with the headset pushing her way through the crowd too.

'Quick, Dad, quick.'

'I'm going as fast as I can.'

We make it to the door of the hall, leaving the crowd behind, and start towards the main entrance. I look back before closing it behind me, and catch the girl with the headset, talking into her mike, urgently. She starts to run but gets caught behind two men in brown overalls carrying a wardrobe across the floor. I grab the wooden bin from Dad's hands and immediately we speed up. Down the stairs, we grab our bags from the cloakroom and then up and down, down and up, all the way along the marble-floored hallway.

Dad reaches for the gold oversized handle on the main door and we hear, 'Stop! Wait!'

We stop abruptly and slowly turn to look at one another, fearfully. I mouth 'Run' at Dad. He sighs dramatically, rolls his eyes and steps down on his right leg, bending his left as a way of reminding me of his struggles with walking, let alone running.

'Where are you two going in such a hurry?' the man asks, making his way towards us.

We slowly turn round, and I prepare to defend our honour.

'It was her,' Dad says straight away, thumb pointed at me.

My mouth falls open.

'It was both of you, I'm afraid,' he smiles. 'You left your microphone and packs on. Worth a bit, these are.' He fiddles around the back of Dad's trousers and unclips his battery pack. 'Could have gotten into a bit of trouble if you'd escaped with this,' he laughs.

Dad looks relieved until I ask nervously, 'Were these turned on, the entire time?'

'Eh,' he studies the pack and flicks the switch to the 'off' position. 'They were.'

'Who would have heard us?'

'Don't worry, they wouldn't have broadcasted your sound while they went to the next item.'

I breath a sigh of relief.

'But internally, whoever was wearing headphones on the floor would have heard,' he explains, removing Dad's mike. 'Oh, and the control room too,' he adds.

He turns to me next and I get into an embarrassing muddle as he pulls the pack from the waistband of my trousers and in doing so tugs the string of my thong, which it's mistakenly attached to.

'Ooowwwwww!' I yelp, and it echoes around the corridor.

'Sorry.' The sound man's face reddens while I fix myself. 'Pitfall of the job.'

'Perk, my friend, perk,' Dad smiles.

After he shuffles back to the fair, we place the umbrella stand back by the entrance door while no one is looking, fill it with the broken umbrellas and exit the scene of the crime.

'So, Justin, any news?' Dr Montgomery asks.

Justin, who is reclined in the chair, with two surgically gloved hands *and* apparatus shoved in his mouth, is unsure of how to answer, and decides to blink once having seen that on television. Then unsure of what exactly that signal means, he blinks twice to confuse matters.

Dr Montgomery misses his code and chuckles, 'Cat got your tongue?'

Justin rolls his eyes.

'I might start getting offended one of these days, if people continue to ignore me when I ask questions.' He chuckles again and leans in over Justin, giving him a good view up his nostrils.

'Arrrgggh,' he flinches as the cool prong hits his sore point.

'Hate to say I told you so,' Dr Montgomery continues, 'but that would be a lie. The cavity that you wouldn't let me look at during your last visit has become infected and now the tissue is inflamed.'

He taps around some more.

'Aaaahh.' Justin makes some gurgling sounds from the back of his throat.

'I should write a book on dentistry language. Everybody makes all sorts of sounds that only I can understand. What do you think, Rita?'

Rita with the glossy lips doesn't care much.

Justin gurgles some expletives.

'Now, now,' Dr Montgomery's smile fades for a moment. 'Don't be rude.'

Startled, Justin concentrates on the television suspended from the wall in the corner of the room. Sky News's red banner at the bottom of the screen screams it's breaking news again and though it's muted and too far away for him to read what exactly it is that they are breaking, it provides a welcome distraction from Dr Montgomery's dismal jokes and calms his urge to jump out of the chair and grab the first taxi he can find, straight to Banqueting House.

The broadcaster is currently standing outside Westminster, but as Justin can't hear a thing he has no idea what it's related to. He studies the man's face and tries to lip-read while Dr Montgomery comes at him with what looks like a needle. His eyes widen as he catches sight of something on the television. His pupils melt into his eyes, blackening them.

Dr Montgomery smiles as he holds it before Justin's face. 'Don't worry, Justin. I know how much you hate needles but it's necessary for a numbing effect. You need a filling in another tooth before that gets an abscess as well. It won't hurt, it will just feel slightly odd.'

Justin's eyes grow wider as he watches the television and he tries to sit up. For once, Justin doesn't care about the needle. He must try to communicate this as best as possible. Unable to move or close his mouth, he begins to make deep noises from the back of his throat.

'OK, don't panic. Just one more minute. I'm nearly there.'

He leans over Justin again, blocking his view of the television, and Justin squirms in his seat, trying to see the screen.

'My goodness, Justin, please stop it. The needle won't kill you, but I might if you don't stop wriggling.' Chuckle, chuckle.

'Ted, I think maybe we should stop,' his assistant says, and Justin looks at her with grateful eyes.

'Is he having a fit of some sort?' Dr Montgomery asks her and then raises his voice at Justin as though he has suddenly become hearing-impaired. 'I say, are you having a fit of some sort?'

Justin rolls his eyes and makes more noises from the back of his throat.

'TV? What do you mean?' Dr Montgomery looks up at Sky News and finally removes his fingers from Justin's mouth.

All three focus on the television screen, the other two concentrating on the news while Justin watches the background where Joyce and her father have wandered into the path of the camera's angle, them in the forefront, Big Ben in the background. Seemingly unaware, they carry out what looks like a seriously heated conversation, their hands gesturing wildly.

'Look at those two idiots at the back,' Dr Montgomery laughs.

Suddenly Joyce's father pushes his suitcase over to Joyce and then storms off in the other direction, leaving Joyce alone with two bags, and throwing her hands up with frustration.

'Yeah, thanks, that's very mature,' I shout after Dad who has just stormed off, leaving his suitcase behind with me. He is going in the wrong direction. Again. Has been since we left the Banqueting House but refuses to admit it and also refuses to get a taxi to the hotel as he is on a penny-saving mission.

He is still within my sights and so I sit on my case and wait for him to realise the error of his ways and come back. It's evening now and I just want to get to the hotel and have a bath. My phone rings.

'Hi, Kate.'

She is laughing hysterically.

'What's up with you?' I smile. 'Well, it's nice to hear *somebody* is in a good mood.'

'Oh, Joyce,' she catches her breath and I imagine she's wiping her teared-up eyes. 'You are the best dose of medicine, you really are.'

'What do you mean?' I can hear children's laughter in the background.

'Do me a favour and raise your right hand.'

'Why?'

'Just do it. It's a game the kids taught me,' she giggles.

'OK,' I sigh, and raise my right hand.

I hear the kids howl with laughter in the back.

'Tell her to wiggle her right foot,' Jayda shouts down the phone.

'OK,' I laugh. This is putting me in a much better mood. I wiggle my right foot and they laugh again. I can even hear Kate's husband howling in the back-ground, which suddenly makes me uncomfortable again. 'Kate, what exactly is this?'

Kate can't answer, she's laughing so much.

'Tell her to hop up and down!' Eric shouts.

'No.' I'm irritated now.

'She did it for Jayda,' he begins to whinge, and I sense tears.

I quickly hop up and down.

They howl again.

'By any chance,' Kate wheezes through her laugher, 'is there anyone around you who has the time?'

'What are you talking about?' I frown, looking around. I see Big Ben behind me, still not sure of the joke, and as I turn back round only then see the camera crew in the distance. I stop hopping.

'What on earth is that woman doing?' Dr Montgomery steps closer to the television. 'Is she dancing?'

'Oo han ee ha?' Justin says, feeling the effects of his numbed mouth.

'Of course I can see her,' he responds. 'I think she's doing the hokey cokey. See? You put your left leg in,' he begins to sing. 'Left leg out. In. Out. In. Out. Shake it all about.' He dances around. Rita rolls her eyes.

Justin, relieved that his sightings of Joyce aren't all in his mind, begins to bounce up and down in his seat, impatiently. *Hurry! I need to get to her.*

Dr Montgomery glances at him curiously, pushes Justin back in the chair and places the instruments in his mouth again. Justin gurgles and makes noises from the back of his throat.

'It's no good explaining it to me, Justin, you're not going anywhere until I have filled this cavity. You'll have to take antibiotics for the abscess, then when you come back I'll either extract it or use endodontic treatment. Whatever I'm in the mood for,' he laughs girlishly. 'And whoever this Joyce lady is, you can thank her for curing your fear of needles. You didn't even notice I'd injected you.'

'Aah haa ooo aaa aa ee a.'

'Oh, well, good for you, old boy. I donated blood before too, you know. Satisfying isn't it?'

'Aa. Ooo aaa iii uuuu.'

Dr Montgomery throws his head back and laughs. 'Oh, don't be silly, they'll never tell you who the blood has gone to. Besides it's been separated into different parts, platelets, red blood cells and what have you.'

Justin gurgles again.

The dentist laughs again. 'What kind of muffins do you want?'

'Aa.'

'Banana,' he considers this. 'Prefer chocolate, myself. Air, Rita, please.'

A bewildered Rita puts the tube into Justin's mouth.

23

I succeed in hailing a black cab and I send the driver in the direction of the dapper old man who is easily spotted on the pavement swaying in horizontal motions like a drunken sailor, amidst the crowd's vertical stream. Like a salmon, he swims upstream, pushing against the throngs of people going in the opposite direction. Not doing it just for the sake of it, not to be deliberately different, or even noticing he's the odd one out.

Seeing him now reminds me of a tale he told me when I was so small he seemed to me to be as gigantic as our neighbour's oak tree that loomed over our garden wall, raining acorns onto our grass. This, during the months when outside playtime was interrupted by afternoons spent staring out the window at the grey world, and, outside, wearing mitts that hung from strings through my coat sleeves. The howling wind would blow the giant oak tree's branches from side to side, leaves going swish swash, left to right, just like my dad, a skittle wavering at the end of a bowling alley. But neither of them fell under the wind's force. Not like the acorns, that leapt from their branches like panicked parachutist pushed out unawares or excited wind worshippers falling to their knees.

When my dad was as sturdy as an oak tree and when I was bullied at school for sucking my thumb, he recalled the Irish myth of how an ordinary salmon had eaten hazelnuts that had fallen into the Fountain of Wisdom. In doing so, the salmon gained all the knowledge in the world, and the first to eat the salmon's flesh would, in turn, gain this knowledge. The poet Finneces spent seven long years fishing for this salmon and when he'd finally caught it, he instructed his young apprentice, Fionn, to prepare it for him. When spattered with hot fat from the cooking salmon, Fionn immediately sucked on his burned thumb to ease his pain. In doing so, he gained incredible knowledge and wisdom. For the rest of his life, when he didn't know what to do, all he had to do was suck on his thumb and the knowledge would come.

He told me that story way back when I sucked my thumb and when he was as big as an oak tree. When Mum's yawns sounded like songs. When we were all together. When I had no idea there would ever come a time when we wouldn't be. When we used to have chats in the garden, under the weeping willow. Where I always used to hide and where he always found me. When nothing was impossible and when the three of us, together forever, was a given.

I smile now as I watch my great big salmon of knowledge moving upstream, weaving in and out of the pedestrians pounding the pavements towards him.

Dad looks up, sees me, gives me two fingers and keeps walking.

Ah.

'Dad,' I call out the open window, 'come on, get in the car.'

He ignores me and holds a cigarette to his mouth, inhaling long and hard, so much so that his cheeks concave.

'Dad, don't be like this. Just get in the car and we'll go to the hotel.'

He continues walking, looks straight ahead, as stubborn as anything. I've seen this face so many times before, arguing with Mum over spending too late and too often at the pub, arguments with the Monday Club gang about the political state of their country, at a restaurant when his beef is handed to him not resembling a piece of charcoal as he so wishes. The 'I'm right, you're wrong' look that has set his chin in that defiant stance, jutting outward like Cork and Kerry's rugged coastline to the rest of the land. A defiant chin, a troubled head.

'Look, we don't even have to talk. You can ignore me in the car too. And in the hotel. Don't talk to me all night, if it'll make you feel better.'

'You'd like that, wouldn't you?' he huffs.

'Honestly?'

He looks at me.

'Yes.'

He tries not to smile. Scratches the corner of his mouth with his yellow-stained cigarette fingers to hide how he softens. The smoke rises into his eyes and I think of his yellow eyes, think of how piercingly blue they used to be when, as a little girl, legs swinging, chin on my hands, I'd watch him sitting at the kitchen table, while he dismantled a radio or a clock or a plug. Piercing blue eyes, alert, busy, like a CAT scan sourcing a tumour. His cigarette squashed between his lips, to the side of his mouth like Popeye, the smoke drifting into his squinted eyes, perhaps staining them the yellow that he sees through now. The colour of age, like old newspapers dipped in time.

I'd watch him, transfixed, afraid to speak, afraid to breathe, afraid to break the spell he'd cast on the contraption he was fixing. Like the surgeon who'd operated on his heart during his bypass surgery ten years ago, there he was, youth on his side, connecting wires, clearing blockages, his shirtsleeves rolled to just below his elbows, the muscles in his arms tanned from the gardening, flexing and unflexing as his fingers tackled the problem. His fingernails, always with a trace of dirt under the surface. His right forefinger and middle finger, yellow from the nicotine. Yellow, but steady. Uneven, but steady.

Finally he stops walking. He throws his cigarette on the ground and stomps it out with his chunky shoe. The cab stops. I throw the life-saving ring around his body and we pull him out of his stream of defiance and into the boat. Always a chancer, always lucky, he'd fall into a river and come out dry, with fish in his pockets. He sits in the car without a word to me, his clothes, breath and fingers smelling of smoke. I bite my lip to stop from saying anything and prepare to have my thumb burned.

He is silent for a record amount of time. Ten, maybe fifteen, minutes. Finally words start spilling out of his mouth, as though they'd been queuing up impatiently behind his closed lips during the rare silence. As though they'd been fired from his heart and, as usual, not from his head, catapulted to his mouth, only this time to find themselves bounce against the walls of closed lips. Instead of being allowed out into the world, they build up like paranoid fat cells, afraid of the food never coming. But now the lips open and the words fly out in all directions like projectile vomit.

'You may have got a sherbet but I hope you know that I haven't a sausage.' He raises his chin, which pulls on the invisible string attached to his pride. He appears pleased with the collection of words that have strung themselves together for him on this particular occasion.

'What?'

'You heard me.'

'Yes, but . . .'

'Sherbet dab, *cab*. Sausage and mash, *cash*,' he explains. 'It's the ol' Chitty Chitty.'

I try to work that out in my head.

'Bang Bang, *rhyming slang*,' he finishes. 'He knows exactly what I'm talking about,' he nods at the driver.

'He can't hear you.'

'Why? Is he Mutt and Jeff?'

'What?'

'Deaf.'

'No,' I nod my head, feeling dazed and tired. 'When the red light is off, they can't hear you.'

'Like Joe's hearing aid,' Dad responds. He leans

forward and flicks the switch in the back of the cab. 'Can you hear me?' he shouts.

'Yeah, mate.' The driver looks at him in the mirror. 'Loud and clear.'

Dad smiles and flicks the switch again. 'Can you hear me now?'

There is no response, the driver quickly glances at him in the rearview mirror, concern wrinkling his forehead, while trying also to keep an eye on the road.

Dad chuckles.

I bury my face in my hands.

'This is what we do to Joe,' he says mischievously. 'Sometimes he can go a whole day without realising we turned his hearing aid off. He just thinks that no one's saying anything. Every half-hour he shouts, "JAYSUS, IT'S VERY QUIET IN HERE!"' Dad laughs and flicks the switch again, ''Allo, guv,' Dad says pleasantly.

'All right, Paddy,' the driver responds.

I wait for Dad's gnarled fist to go through the slit in the window. It doesn't. Instead his laughter filters through.

'I feel like being on my tod tonight. I say, could you tell me where there's a good jack near my hotel, so I can go for a pig without my teapot.'

The young driver studies Dad's innocent face in the mirror, always meaning well, never intending insults. But he doesn't respond and continues driving.

I look away so Dad isn't embarrassed, but I feel rather superior and hate myself for it. Moments later, at a set of traffic lights, the hatch opens and the driver passes a piece of paper through.

'There's a list of a few there, mate. I'd suggest the first one, that's my favourite. Does good loop and tucker right about now, if you know what I mean,' he smiles and winks.

'Thank you.' Dad's face lights up. He studies the paper closely as though it's the most precious thing he's ever been given, then folds it carefully and slides it into his top pocket, proudly. 'It's just that this one here, is being a merry ol' soul, if you know what *I* mean. Make sure she gives you a good bit of rifle.'

The driver laughs and pulls over at our hotel. I examine it from the cab and am pleasantly surprised. The three-star hotel is right in the heart of the city, only ten minutes' walk from main theatres, Oxford Street, Piccadilly and Soho. Enough to keep us either out of trouble. Or rightin it.

Dad gets out of the car and pulls his case along to the revolving doors at the hotel entrance. I watch him while waiting for my change. The doors are going around so fast, I can see him trying to time his entrance. Like a dog afraid to jump into the cold sea, he inches forward, then stops, jerks forward again and stops. Finally he makes a run for it and his suitcase gets stuck outside, jamming the revolving doors and trapping him inside.

I take my time getting out of the cab. I lean in the passenger's side window to the sound of Dad rapping on the glass behind me.

'Help! Someone!' I hear Dad call.

'By the way, what did he call me?' I ask the driver, calmly ignoring the calls behind me.

'A merry old soul?' he asks with a grin. 'You don't want to know.'

'Tell me,' I smile.

'It means arsehole,' he laughs, and then he pulls away, leaving me at the side of the street with my mouth gaping.

I notice the knocking has quietened and turn to see that Dad has been freed at last. I hurry inside.

'I can't give you a credit card, but I can give you my word,' Dad is saying slowly and loudly to the woman behind the reception desk. 'And my word is as good as my honour.'

'It's OK, here you go.' I slide my credit card across the counter to the young lady.

'Why can't people just pay with paper money these days?' Dad says, leaning further over the counter. 'It's more trouble that the youth of today are getting themselves into, debt after debt because they want this, they want that, but they don't want to work for it so they use those plastic thingies. Well, that's not free money, I can tell you that.' He nods his head with finality. 'You'll only ever lose with one of those.'

No one responds.

The receptionist smiles at him politely and taps away on the computer. 'You're sharing a room?' she asks.

'Yes,' I respond with dread.

'Two Uncle Teds, I hope?'

She frowns.

'Beds,' I say quietly. 'He means beds.'

'Yes, they're twin beds.'

'Is it an en-suite?' He leans in, trying to see her name badge. 'Breda, is it?' he asks.

'Aakaanksha. And, yes, sir, all our rooms are en-suite,' she says politely.

'Oh,' he looks impressed. 'Well, I hope your lifts are working because I can't take the apples, my Cadbury's playin' up.'

I squeeze my eyes together tightly.

'Apples and pears, *stairs*. Cadbury snack, *back*,' he says with the same voice he used to say nursery rhymes to me as a little girl.

'I see. Very good, Mr Conway.'

I take the key and head towards the elevator, hearing his little voice repeating a question over and over again as he follows me through the foyer. I hit the button for the third floor and the doors close.

The room is standard and it's clean, and that's good enough for me. Our beds are far enough apart for my liking, there's a television and a mini-bar, which hold Dad's attention while I run a bath.

'I wouldn't mind a drop of fine,' he says, his head disappearing into the mini-bar.

'You mean wine.'

'Fine and dandy, *brandy*.'

I finally slide down into the hot soothing bathwater,

the suds rise like the foam atop an ice-cream float. They tickle my nose and cover my body, overflow and float to the ground, where they slowly fade with a crackling sound. I lie back and close my eyes, feeling tiny bubbles all over my body pop as soon as they touch my skin . . . There's a knock on the door.

I ignore it.

Then it goes again, a little more loudly this time.

Still I don't answer.

BANG! BANG!

'What?' I shout.

'Oh, sorry, thought you'd fallen asleep or something, love.'

'I'm in the bath.'

'I know that. You have to be careful in those things. Could nod off and slip under the water and drown. Happened to one of Amelia's cousins. You know Amelia. Visits Joseph sometimes, down the road. But she doesn't drop by as much as before on account of the bath accident.'

'Dad, I appreciate your concern but I'm fine.'

'OK.'

Silence.

'Actually, it's not that, Gracie. I'm just wonderin' how long you'll be in there for?'

I grab the yellow rubber duck sitting at the side of the bath and I strangle it.

'Love?' he asks in a little voice.

I hold the duck under the water, trying to drown it. Then I let go, it bobs to the top again, the same silly eyes staring back at me. I take a deep breath, breathe out slowly.

'About twenty minutes, Dad, is that OK?'

Silence.

I close my eyes again.

'Eh, love. It's just that you've been in there twenty minutes already and you know how my prostate is—'

I don't hear any more, because I'm climbing out of the bath with all the gracefulness of a piranha at feeding time. My feet squeak on the bathroom floor, water splashes in all directions.

'Everything OK in there, Shamu?' Dad laughs uproariously at his own joke.

I throw a towel around me and open the door.

'Ah, Willy's been freed,' he smiles.

I bow and hold my arm out to the toilet. 'Your chariot awaits you, sir.'

Embarrassed, he shuffles inside and closes the door behind him. It locks.

Wet and shivering, I browse through the half-bottles of red wine in the mini-bar. I pick one up and study the label. Immediately an image flashes through my mind, so vivid, I feel like my body has been transported.

A picnic basket with this bottle inside, an identical label, red and white chequered cloth laid out on the grass, a little girl with blonde hair twirling, twirling in a pink tutu. The wine swirling, swirling in a glass. The sound of her laughter. Birds twittering. Children's laughter far off, a dog barking. I am lying on the chequered cloth, barefoot, trousers rolled above my ankles. *Hairy* ankles. I feel a hot sun beating down on my skin, the little girl dances and twirls before the sun, sometimes blocking the harshness of light, other times spinning in the other direction to send the glare into my eyes. A hand appears before me, a glass of red wine in it. I look to her face. Red hair, lightly freckled, smiling adoringly. At me.

'Justin,' she's singing. 'Earth to Justin!'

The little girl is laughing and twirling, the wine is swirling, the long red hair is blowing in the light breeze . . .

Then it's gone. I'm back in the hotel room, standing before the mini-bar, my hair dripping bath water onto the carpet. Dad is studying me, watching me curiously, hand suspended in the air as though he's not sure whether to touch me or not.

'Earth to Joyce,' he's singing.

I clear my throat. 'You're done?'

Dad nods and his eyes follow me to the bathroom. On the way there, I stop and turn. 'By the way, I've booked a ballet show for tonight if you'd like to come. We need to leave in an hour.'

'OK, love,' he nods softly, and watches after me with a familiar look of worry in his eyes. I've seen that look as a child, I've seen it as an adult and a million times in between. It's as though I've taken the stabilisers off my bicycle for the very first time and he's running along beside me, holding on tight, afraid to let me go.

24

Dad breathes heavily beside me and links my arm tightly as we slowly make our way to Covent Garden. Using my other hand I pat down my pockets, feeling for his heart pills.

'Dad, we're definitely getting a taxi back to the hotel and I'm not taking no for an answer.'

Dad stops and stares ahead, he takes deep breaths.

'Are you OK? Is it your heart? Should we sit down? Stop and take a rest? Go back to the hotel?'

'Shut up and turn round, Gracie. It's not just my heart that takes my breath away, you know.'

I spin round and there it is, the Royal Opera House, its columns illuminated for the evening performance, a red carpet lining the pavement outside and crowds filing through the doors.

'You have to take your moments, love,' Dad says, taking in the sight before him. 'Don't just go head first into everything, like a bull seeing red.'

Having booked our tickets so late we are seated in the lower slips almost at the top of the tremendous theatre. The position is unlucky, yet we are fortunate to have got tickets at all. The view of the stage is restricted, yet the view of the boxes opposite is perfect. Squinting through the binoculars situated beside the seat, I spy on the people filling the boxes. No sign of my American man. *Earth to Justin?* I hear the woman's voice in my head and wonder if Frankie's theory about seeing the world from his eyes was correct.

Dad is enthralled by our view. 'We've got the best seats in the house, love, look.' He leans over the balcony and his tweed cap almost falls off his head. I grab his arm and pull him back. He takes the photograph of Mum from his pocket and places her on the velvet balcony ledge. 'Best seat in the house, indeed,' he says, his eyes filling.

The voice over the intercom system counts latecomers down and finally the cacophony of the orchestra dies down, the lights dim and there is silence before the magic begins. The conductor taps and the orchestra play the opening bars of Tchaikovsky's ballet. Apart from Dad snorting when the male principal dancer appears on stage wearing tights, it runs smoothly and we are both entranced by the story of *Swan Lake*. I look away from the prince's coming-of-age party and study those sitting in the boxes. Their faces are lit, their eyes dancing along with the dancers they follow. It's as though a music box has been opened, spilling music and light from it and all those watching have been enchanted, captured by its magic. I continue to spy at them through my opera glasses, moving from left to right, a row of unfamiliar faces until . . . My eyes widen as I reach the familiar face, the man from the hair salon I now know from Bea's biography in the programme, to be Mr Hitchcock. *Justin Hitchcock?* He watches the stage, entranced, leaning so far over the balcony it looks as though he'll topple over the ledge.

Dad elbows me. 'Would you stop looking around you, and keep your eye on the stage. He's about to kill her.'

I turn to face the stage and try to hold my eyes on the prince leaping about with his crossbow, but I can't. A magnetic pull turns my face back down to the box, anxious to see who Mr Hitchcock is sitting with. My heart is drumming so loudly I only realise now it's not part of Tchaikovsky's score. Beside him is the woman with long red hair and lightly freckled face, who holds the camera in my dreams. Beside her is a sweet-looking gentleman and behind them, squashed together are a young man pulling uncomfortably at his tie, a woman with big curly red hair and a large round man. I flick through my memory files like I'm going through Polaroids. The chubby boy from the sprinkler scene and seesaw? Perhaps. But the other two, I don't know. I move my eyes back to Justin Hitchcock and smile, finding his face more entertaining than the action on stage.

Suddenly the music changes, the light reflecting on his face flickers and his expression changes. I know instantly that Bea is on stage, and I turn to watch. There she is among the flock of swans, moving about so gracefully in perfect unison, dressed in a white fitted corset dress with raggedy long white tutu, similar to feathers. Her long blonde hair is tied up in a bun, covered by a neat headdress. I recall the image of her in the park as a little girl, twirling and twirling in her tutu and I'm filled with pride. How far she has come. How grown up she is now. My eyes fill.

'Oh, look, Justin,' Jennifer says breathily beside him.

He is looking. He can't take his eyes off his daughter, a vision in white, dancing in perfect unison with the flock of swans, not a movement out of place. She looks so grown up, so . . . how did that happen? It seems like only yesterday she was twirling for him and Jennifer in the park across from their house, a little girl with a tutu and dreams and now . . . His eyes fill and he looks beside him to Jennifer, to share a look, share the moment but at the same time, she reaches for Laurence's hand. He looks away quickly, back to his daughter. A tear falls and he reaches into his front pocket for his handkerchief.

A handkerchief is raised to my face, catches my tear before it drips from my chin.

'What are you crying for?' Dad says loudly, dabbing at my chin roughly, as the curtain lowers for the interval.

'I'm just so proud of Bea.'

'Who?'

'Oh, nothing . . . I just think it's a beautiful story. What do you think?'

'I think those lads have definitely got socks down their tights.'

I laugh and wipe my eyes. 'Do you think Mum's enjoying it?'

He smiles and stares at the photo. 'She must be, she hasn't turned round once since it started. Unlike you, who's got ants in her pants. If I'd known you were so keen on binoculars I'd have taken you out bird-watching long ago.' He sighs and looks around. 'The lads at the Monday Club won't believe this at all. Donal McCarthy, you better watch out,' he chuckles.

'Do you miss her?'

'It's been ten years, love.'

It stings that he can be so dismissive. I fold my arms and look away, silently fuming.

Dad leans closer and nudges me. 'And everyday, I miss her more than I did the day before.'

Oh. I immediately feel guilty for wishing that on him.

'It's like my garden, love. Everything grows. Including love. And with that growing everyday how can you expect missing her to ever fade away? Everything builds, including our ability to cope with it. That's how we keep going.'

I shake my head, in awe of some of the things he comes out with. Philosophical and otherwise. And this from a man who's been calling me his teapot (lid, *kid*) since we landed.

'And I just thought you liked pottering,' I smile.

'Ah, there's a lot to be said for pottering. You know Thomas Berry said that gardening is an active participation in the deepest mysteries of the universe? There are lessons in pottering.'

'Like what?' I try not to smile.

'Well, even a garden grows stranglers, love. It grows

them naturally, all by itself. They creep up and choke the plants that are growing from the very same soil as they are. We each have our demons, our self-destruct button. Even in gardens. Pretty as they may be. If you don't potter, you don't notice them.'

He eyes me and I look away, choosing to clear my already-clear throat.

Sometimes I wish he'd just stick to laughing at men in tights.

'Justin, we're going to the bar, are you coming?' Doris asks.

'No,' he says, in a huff like a child, folding his arms.

'Why not?' Al squeezes further into the box to sit beside him.

'I just don't want to.' He picks up the opera glasses and starts fiddling with them.

'But you'll be here on your own.'

'So?'

'Mr Hitchcock, would you like me to get you a drink?' Bea's boyfriend, Peter, asks.

'Mr Hitchcock was my father, you can call me Al. Like the song.' He punches him playfully on the shoulder but it knocks him back a few steps.

'OK, Al, but I actually meant Justin.'

'*You* can call me Mr Hitchcock.' Justin looks at him like there's a bad smell in the room.

'We don't have to sit with Laurence and Jennifer, you know.'

Laurence. Laurence of Ahernia who has elephantitis of the—

'Yes we do, Al, don't be ridiculous,' Doris interrupts.

Al sighs. 'Well, give Petey an answer, do you want us to bring you back a drink?'

Yes. But Justin can't bring himself to say it and instead shakes his head sulkily.

'OK, we'll be back in fifteen.'

Al gives him a comforting brotherly pat on his shoulder before they all leave him alone in the box to stew over Laurence and Jennifer and Bea and Chicago and London and Dublin and now Peter, and how exactly his life has ended up.

Two minutes later and already tired of feeling sorry for himself, he looks through the opera glasses and begins spying on the trickles of people seated below him who'd stayed in their seats for the interval. He spots a couple fighting, snapping at one another. Another couple kissing, reaching for their coats and then disappearing quickly to the exits. He spies a mother giving out to her son. A group of women laughing together. A couple saying nothing to one another or who have nothing to say to one another. He'd prefer the former. Nothing exciting. He moves to the boxes opposite. They are empty, everyone choosing to have their pre-ordered drinks in the nearby bar. He cranes his neck up higher. *How on earth can anyone see anything from there?* Here, there are a small number of people, like everyone else, just chatting. He moves along from right to left. Then stops. Rubs his eyes. Sure he is imagining it. He squints back through the opera glasses again and sure enough, there she is. With the old man. Every scene in his life was beginning to be like a page from *Where's Wally?*

She is looking through her opera glasses too, scanning the crowd below them both. Then she raises her opera glasses, moves slowly to the right and . . . they both freeze, staring at one another through the lenses. He slowly lifts his arm. Waves.

She slowly does the same. The old man beside her puts his glasses on and squints in his direction, mouth opening and closing the entire time.

Justin holds his hand up, intends to make a 'wait' sign. *Hold on, I'm coming up to you.* He holds his forefinger up, as though he's just thought of an idea. *One minute. Hold on, I'll be one minute,* he tries to signal.

She gives him the thumbs-up and he breaks into a smile.

He drops the opera glasses and stands up immediately,

taking note of where exactly she is sitting. The door to the box opens and in walks Laurence.

'Justin, I thought maybe we could have a word,' he says politely, drumming his fingers on the back of the chair that separates them.

'No, Laurence, not now, sorry.' He tries to move past him.

'I promise not to take up too much of your time. Just a few minutes while we're alone. To clear the air, you know?' He opens the button of his blazer, smooths down his tie and closes his button again.

'Yeah, I appreciate that, buddy, I really do, but I'm in a really big hurry right now.' He tries to inch by him but Laurence moves to block him.

'A hurry?' he says, raising his eyebrows. 'But the interval is just about over and . . . ah,' he stops, realising. 'I see. Well, I just thought I'd give it a try. If you're not ready to have the discussion yet, that's understandable.'

'No, it's not that.' Justin looks through his opera glasses and up at Joyce, feeling panicked. She's still there. 'It's just that I really am in a hurry to get to somebody. I have to go, Laurence.'

Jennifer walks in just as he says that. Her face is stony.

'Honestly, Justin. Laurence just wanted to be a gentleman and talk to you like an *adult*. Something, it seems, you have forgotten how to be. Though I don't know why I'm surprised about that.'

'No, no, look, Jennifer.' *I used to call you Jen. So formal now, a lifetime away from that memorable day in the park when they were all so happy, so in love.* 'I *really* don't have time for this right now. You don't understand, I have to go.'

'You can't go. The ballet is about to begin in a few minutes and your daughter will be onstage. Don't tell me you're walking out on her too, because of some ridiculous male pride.'

Doris and Al enter the box, Al's size alone completely

crowding the small space and blocking his path to the door. Al holds a pint of cola in his hand and an oversized bag of crisps.

'Tell him, Justin.' Doris folds her arms and taps her long fake pink nails against her thin arms.

Justin groans. 'Tell him what?'

'*Remind* him of the heart disease in your family so that he may think twice before eating and drinking that crap.'

'What heart disease?' Justin holds his hands to his head while on the other side of him, Jennifer drones on and on in what sounds like Charlie Brown's teacher's voice. 'Wah, wah, wah' is all he hears.

'Your *father*, dying of a *heart attack*,' she says impatiently.

Justin freezes.

'The doc didn't say that it would necessarily happen to me,' Al moans to his wife.

'He said there was a good chance. If there's a history in the family.'

Justin's voice sounds to him as though it's coming from somewhere else. 'No, no, I really don't think you have to worry about that, Al.'

'See?' He looks at Doris.

'That's not what the doctor said, sweetheart. We have to be more careful if it runs in the family.'

'No, it doesn't run in the—' Justin stalls. 'Look, I really have to go now.' He tries to move in the crowded box.

'No, you will not,' Jennifer blocks him. 'You are not going anywhere until you *apologise* to Laurence.'

'It's really all right, Jen,' Laurence says awkwardly.

I call her Jen, not you!

'No, it's not, sweetheart.'

I'm her sweetheart, not you!

Voices come at him from all sides, wah wah wah, he is unable to make out the words. He feels hot and sweaty, dizziness grips him.

Suddenly the lights dim and the music begins and he

has no choice but to take his seat again, beside a fuming Jennifer, an insulted Laurence, a silent Peter, a worried Doris and a hungry Al, who decides to munch loudly in his left ear, on the packet of potato chips.

He sighs and looks up at Joyce.

Help.

It seems the squabble in Mr Hitchcock's box has ended, but as the lights are going down, they are all still standing. When the lights lift again, they are all seated with stony faces, apart from the large man at the back, who is eating a large bag of crisps. I have ignored Dad all throughout the last few moments, choosing instead to invest my time in a crashcourse in lip-reading. If I have been successful, their conversation involved Carrot Top and barbecued bananas.

Deep inside, my heart drums like a *djembe*, its deep bass and slap reaching down into my chest. I feel it in the base of my throat, throbbing, and all because he saw me, he wanted to come to me. I feel relieved that following my instincts, however flighty, paid off. It takes me a few minutes to be able to focus on anything other than Justin, but when I calm my nerves slightly I turn my attention back to the stage where Bea takes my breath away and causes me to sniffle through her performance like a proud aunt. It occurs to me so strongly right now that the only people privy to those wonderful happy memories in the park are Bea, her mother, father . . . and me.

'Dad, can I ask you something?' I lean close to him and whisper.

'He's just after telling that girl that he loves her but she's the wrong girl,' he rolls his eyes. 'Eejit. The swan girl was in white and that one is in black. They don't look alike at all.'

'She could have changed for the ball. No one wears the same thing everyday.'

He looks me up and down. 'You only took your bathrobe off *one day* last week. Anyway, what's up with you?'

'Well, it's that, I, em, something has happened and, well . . .'

'Spit it out for Christsake, before I miss anything else.'

I give up whispering in his ear and turn to face him. 'I've been given something, or more, something very special has been *shared* with me. It's completely inexplicable and it doesn't make any sense at all, in an Our Lady of Knock kind of way, you know?' I laugh nervously and quickly stop, on seeing his face.

No, he doesn't know. Dad looks angry I've used Mary's apparition in County Mayo during the 1870s as an example of nonsense.

'OK, perhaps that was a bad example. What I mean is, it breaks every rule I've ever known. I just don't understand *why*.'

'Gracie,' Dad lifts his chin, 'Knock, like the rest of Ireland, suffered great distress over the centuries from invasion, evictions and famines, and Our Lord sent His Mother, the Blessed Virgin, to visit with His oppressed children.'

'No,' I hold my hands over my face, 'I don't mean why did Mary appear, I mean why has this . . . this *thing* happened to me? This thing I've been given.'

'Oh. Well, is it hurting anyone? Because if it's not and if you've been given it, I'd as soon stop callin' it a "thing" and start referring to it as a "gift". Look at them dancing. He thinks she's the swan girl. Surely he can see her face. Or is it like Superman when he takes the glasses off and suddenly he's completely different, even though it's as clear as day that it's the same person?'

A gift. I'd never thought of it like that. I look over at Bea's parents, beaming with pride, and I think of Bea before the interval, floating around with her flock of swans. I shake my head. No. No one is being hurt.

'Well, then,' Dad shrugs.

'But I don't understand *why* and *how* and—'

'What is it with people these days?' he hisses, and

the man beside me turns round. I whisper my apologies.

'In my day, something *just was*. None of this analysis a hundred times over. None of these college courses with people graduating with degrees in Whys and Hows and Becauses. Sometimes, love, you just need to forget all of those words and enrol in a little lesson called "Thank You". Look at this story here,' he points at the stage. 'Do you hear anybody here giving out about the fact *she*, a *woman*, has been turned into a *swan*? Have you heard anything more ludicrous in your life?'

I shake my head, smiling.

'Have you met anyone lately who happens to have been turned into a swan?'

I laugh and whisper, 'No.'

'Yet look at it. This bloody thing has been famous the world over for centuries. We have non-believers, atheists, intellects, cynicists, *him*.' He nods his head at the man who shushed us. 'All kinds of what-have-yous in here tonight, but all of them want to see that fella in the tights end up with that swan girl, so she'll be able to get out of that lake. Only with the love of one who has never loved before, can the spell be broken. Why? Who the hell cares why? Do you think your woman with the feathers is going to ask *why*? No. She's going to say *thank you* because then she can move on and wear nice dresses and go for walks, instead of having to peck at soggy bread in a stinky lake every day for the rest of her life.'

I have been stunned to silence.

'Now, *whisht*, we're missing the performance. She wants to kill herself now, look? Talk about being dramatic.' He places his elbows on the balcony and leans in closer to the stage, his left ear tilted towards the stage more than his eyes, quite literally eavesdropping.

25

During the standing ovation, Justin spies Joyce's father helping her into a red coat, the same one from their Grafton Street collision. She begins to move to her nearby exit with her father in tow.

'Justin,' Jennifer scowls at her ex-husband, who is more busy spying through his opera glasses up at the ceiling than at his daughter bowing on stage.

He puts the glasses down and claps loudly, cheering.

'Hey, guys, I'm going to go to the bar and keep some good seats for us.' He starts moving towards the door.

'It's already reserved,' Jennifer shouts after him, over the applause.

He holds his hand up to his ear and shakes his head. 'Can't hear you.'

He escapes and runs down the corridors, trying to find his way upstairs to the lower slips. The curtains must have fallen for the final time as people begin to exit their boxes, crowding the corridors and making it impossible for Justin to push past.

He has a change of plan: he'll rush to the exit and wait for her there. That way he can't miss her.

'Let's get a drink, love,' Dad says as we slowly amble behind the crowd exiting the theatre. 'I saw a bar on this floor.'

We stop to read some directions.

'There's the Amphitheatre bar, this way,' I say, looking out constantly for Justin Hitchcock.

A woman usher announces that the bar is open only for cast, crew and family members.

'That's great, we'll have some peace and quiet so,' Dad says to her, tipping his cap as he walks by. 'Oh, you should have seen my granddaughter up there. Proudest day of my life,' he says, putting his hand on his heart.

The woman smiles and allows us entry.

'Come on, Dad.' After we've bought our drinks, I drag him deep into the room to sit at a table in the far corner, away from the growing crowd.

'If they try to throw us out, Gracie, I'm not leaving my pint. I just sat down.'

I wring my hands nervously and perch on the edge of my seat, looking around for him. *Justin*. His name rolls around in my head, plays around my tongue like a contented pig in muck.

People filter out of the bar until all that is left are family, crew and cast members. Nobody approaches us again to usher us out, perhaps one of the perks of being with an old man. Bea's mother enters with the two unknown people from the box, and the chubby man I recognise. But no Mr Hitchcock. My eyes dart around the room.

'There she is,' I whisper.

'Who?'

'One of the dancers. She was one of the swans.'

'How do you know? They all looked the same. Even the nancy boy thought they were the same. Sure, didn't he profess his love to the wrong woman? The bloody eejit.'

There's no sign of Justin and I begin to worry that this is another wasted opportunity. Perhaps he has left early and isn't coming to the bar at all.

'Dad,' I say urgently, 'I'm just going to take a look around for somebody. Please do *not* move from this chair. I'll be back soon.'

'The only moving I'll be doing is this.' He picks up his pint and moves it to his lips. He takes a gulp of

Guinness, closes his eyes and savours the taste, leaving a white moustache around his lips.

I hurry out of the bar and wander around the huge theatre, not sure where to start looking. I stand outside the nearby gents' toilets for a few moments but he doesn't appear. I look over at the box he was seated in but it's empty.

Justin gives up standing by the exit door as the last few people trickle by him. He must have missed her and he was stupid to think there was only one exit. He sighs with frustration. He wishes he could transport himself back in time to the day in the salon and relive the moment properly this time. His pocket vibrates, snapping him out of his daydream.

'Bro, where the heck are you?'

'Hi, Al. I saw the woman again.'

'The Sky News woman?'

'Yeah!'

'The Viking woman?'

'Yeah, yeah, her.'

'The *Antiques Roadshow* wo—'

'YES! For Christsake, do we have to go through this again?'

'Hey, did you ever think that maybe she's a stalker?'

'If she's a stalker, then why am I always chasing her?'

'Oh, yeah. Well, maybe you're the stalker and you don't know it.'

'Al . . .' Justin grits his teeth.

'Whatever, hurry back up here before Jennifer has a conniption fit. Another one.'

Justin sighs. 'I'm coming.'

He snaps his phone shut and takes one last look down the street. Among the crowd something catches his eye, a red coat. Adrenalin surges. He races outside, pushes past the slowly filtering crowd, his heart pounding, his eyes not budging from the coat.

'Joyce!' he calls. 'Joyce, wait!' he shouts louder.

She keeps walking, unable to hear him.

He bumps and pushes, getting cursed at and prodded by people he pushes by until finally she's just inches from him.

'Joyce,' he says breathlessly, reaching out and grabbing her arm. She spins around, a face twisted in surprise and fright. A face of a stranger.

She hits him over the head with her leather bag.

'Ow! Hey! Jesus!'

Apologising, he slowly makes his way back to the theatre, trying to catch his breath, rubbing his sore head, cursing and grumbling to himself with frustration. He reaches for the main door. It doesn't open. He tries it again gently, then rattles it slightly a few times. Within seconds, he pulls and pushes the door with full force, kicking at the door with frustration.

'Hey, hey, hey! We're closed! Theatre's closed!' a member of staff informs him from behind the glass.

When I return to the bar, I thankfully find Dad sitting in the corner where I'd left him. Only this time he's not alone. Perched on the chair beside him, her head close to his as though in deep conversation, is Bea. I panic and rush over to them.

'Hi.' I approach them, terrified by what verbal diarrhoea may have slipped out of his mouth already.

'Ah, there you are, love. Thought you'd abandoned me. This nice girl came to see if I was OK, seeing as someone tried to throw me out again.'

'I'm Bea,' she smiles, and I can't help but notice how grown-up she has become. How self-assured and confident she is. I almost feel like telling her that the last time I'd seen her she was 'yay high', but I stop myself from gushing at her extraordinary transformation into adulthood.

'Hello, Bea.'

'Do I know you?' Frown lines appear on her porcelain forehead.

'Em . . .'

'This is my daughter, Gracie,' Dad butts in, and for once I don't correct him.

'Oh, Gracie,' Bea shakes her head. 'No. I was thinking of someone else. Nice to meet you.'

We shake hands and I hold on for a little too long perhaps, entranced by the feel of her real skin, not just a memory. I quickly let go.

'You were wonderful tonight. I was so proud,' I say breathily.

'Proud? Oh, yes, your father told me you designed the costumes,' she smiles. 'They were beautiful. I'm surprised I hadn't met you until now, we had been dealing with Linda for all the fittings.'

My mouth drops, Dad shrugs nervously and sips on what looks to be a new pint. A fresh lie for a fresh pint. The price of his soul.

'Oh, I didn't design them . . . I just . . .' You just what, Joyce? 'I just supervised,' I say dumbly. 'What else has he been telling you?' I nervously sit down and look around for her father, hoping this isn't the moment he chooses to enter and greet me in the midst of this ridiculous lie.

'Well, just as you arrived he was telling me about how he'd saved a swan's life,' she smiles.

'Single-handedly,' they both add in unison and laugh.

'Ha ha,' I force out and it sounds fake. 'Is that true?' I ask him doubtfully.

'Oh, ye of little faith.' Dad takes another gulp of Guinness. Seventy-five years old and he's already had a brandy and a pint: he'll be on his ear in no time. God knows what he'd be saying then. We'll have to leave soon.

'Well, you know what, girls, it's great to save a life, it really, really is,' Dad says from his high horse. 'Unless you've done it, you have no idea.'

'My father, the hero,' I smile.

Bea laughs at Dad. 'You sound exactly like my father.'

My ears perk up. 'Is he here?'

She looks around. 'No, not yet. I don't know *where*

he is. Probably hiding from my mom and her new boyfriend, not to mention my boyfriend,' she laughs. 'But that's another story. Anyway he considers himself Superman—'

'Why?' I interrupt and try to rein myself in.

'About a month ago, he donated blood,' she smiles and holds her hands up. 'Ta-da! That's it!' She laughs. 'But he thinks he's some kind of hero that's saved somebody's life. I mean, I don't know, maybe he has. It's *all* he talks about. He donated it at a mobile unit at the college where he was giving a seminar – you guys probably know it, it's in Dublin. Trinity College? Anyway, I wouldn't mind, but he only did it because the doctor was cute and for that Chinese thing, what do you call it? The thing where you save someone's life and they're forever indebted to you or something like that?'

Dad shrugs. 'I don't speak Chinese. Or know any. She eats the food all the time, though.' He nods his head at me. 'Rice with eggs, or something.' He ruffles his nose.

Bea laughs. 'Anyway, he figured if he was going to save someone's life he deserved to be thanked every day for the rest of his life by the person he *saved*.'

'How would they do that, then?' Dad leans in.

'By delivering a muffin basket, do his dry cleaning, a newspaper and coffee delivered to his door every morning, a chauffeur-driven car, front-row tickets to the opera . . .' She rolls her eyes and then frowns. 'I can't remember what else but they were ridiculous things. Anyway, I told him he may as well have a slave if he wants that kind of treatment, not save someone's life.' She laughs and Dad does too.

I make an *oh* shape with my mouth but nothing comes out.

'Don't get me wrong, he's a really thoughtful guy,' she adds quickly, misunderstanding my silence. 'And I was proud of him for donating blood as he's absolutely terrified by needles. He has a *huge* phobia,' she explains to Dad, who nods along in agreement. 'That's him there.'

She opens her locket around her neck and if I have regained my power of speech, it is quickly lost again.

On one side of the locket is a photograph of Bea and her mother, and on the other side is the photograph of her and her father when she was a little girl, in the park on that summer day that is clearly imbedded in my memory. I remember how she jumped up and down with excitement and how it had taken us so long to get her to sit still. I remember the smell of her hair as she sat on my lap and pushed her head up against mine and shouted 'Cheeeeese!' so loudly she'd almost deafened me. She hadn't done that to me at all, of course, but I remember it with equal fondness as a day spent fishing with my father when I was a child, feel all the sensations of the day as clearly as the drink I now taste in my mouth and feel flowing down my throat. The cold of the ice, the sweetness of the mineral. It's all as real to me as the moments spent with Bea in the park.

'I'll have to put my glasses on to see this,' Dad says, moving closer and taking the gold locket in his old fingers. 'Where was this?'

'The park near where we used to live. In Chicago. I'm five years old there, with my dad, but I love this photograph. It was such a special day.' She looks at it fondly. 'One of the best.'

I smile too, remembering it.

'Photograph!' somebody in the bar calls out.

'Dad, let's get out of here,' I whisper while Bea is distracted by the commotion.

'OK, love, just after this pint—'

'No! Now!' I hiss.

'Group photo! Come on!' Bea says, grabbing Dad's arm.

'Oh!' Dad looks pleased.

'No, no no no no no.' I try to smile to hide my panic. 'We really must go now.'

'Just one photo, Gracie,' she smiles. 'We have to get the lady who's responsible for all these beautiful costumes.'

'No, I'm not—'

'Costume *supervisor*,' Bea corrects herself apologetically.

A woman on the other side of the group throws me a look of horror, on hearing this. Dad laughs. I'm stiff beside Bea, who throws one arm around me and the other arm around her mother.

'Everyone say Tchaikovsky!' Dad shouts.

'Tchaikovsky!' They all cheer and laugh.

I roll my eyes.

The camera flashes.

Justin enters the room.

The crowd breaks up.

I grab Dad, and run.

26

Back in our hotel room it's lights out for Dad, who climbs into bed in his brown paisley pyjamas, and for me, who is wearing more clothes in bed than I've worn for a long time.

The room is black, thick with shadows and still, apart from the flashing red digits in the time display panel at the bottom of the television. Lying flat and still on my back, I attempt to process the day's events. My body once again becomes the subject of much Zulu drumming as my heartbeat intensifies. I feel its pounding rebound against the springs in the mattress beneath me. Then the pulse in my neck vibrates so wildly it causes my ear drums to join in. Beneath my ribcage, it feels like two fists hammering to get out, and I watch the bedroom door and anticipate the arrival of an African tribe, ready to participate in the synchronised stamping of feet, at the end of my bed.

The reason for these internal war drums? Over and over again, my mind runs through the clanger Bea dropped only hours ago. The words fell from her mouth just like a cymbal falling from its drum set. Since then it has rolled around the floor and only now lands face down on the ground with a crash, ending my African orchestra. The revelation that Bea's dad, Justin, donated blood a month ago in Dublin, the same month I fell down the stairs and changed my life for ever, plays over and over in my mind. Coincidence? A resounding yes. Something more? A shaky possibility. A *hopeful* possibility.

When is a coincidence just a coincidence, though? And when, if at all, should it be seen as something more? At a time like this? When I am lost and desperate, grieving for a child that was never born, and tending to my wounds after a defeated marriage? This, I have found, is the time when what was once clear has instead become cloudy, and what was once considered bizarre has now become a possibility.

It is during troubled times like these that people see straight, though others watch with concern and try to convince them that they can't. Weighted minds are just so because of all of their new thoughts. When those who have passed through their troubles and come out the other side suddenly embrace their new beliefs whole-heartedly, it is viewed with cynicism by others. Why? Because when you're in trouble you look harder for answers than those who aren't, and it's those answers that help you through.

This blood transfusion – is it *the* answer or merely an answer I'm looking for? I find that, usually, answers present themselves. They are not hidden under rocks or camouflaged among trees. Answers are right there, in front of our eyes. But if you haven't cause to look, then of course you will probably never find them.

So, the explanation for the sudden arrival of alien memories, the reason for such a deep connection to Justin – I feel it running through my very veins. Is this the answer that my heart is currently raging within me to realise? It hops up and down now, like Skippy, trying to get my attention, trying to alert me to a problem. I breathe in slowly through my nose and exhale, I close my eyes gently and place my hands over my chest, feeling the thump-thump, thump-thump that is raging within me. Time to slow everything down now, time to get answers.

Taking the bizarre as a given for just one moment,

as people in trouble do: if I did indeed receive Justin's blood during my transfusion, then my heart is now sending his blood around my body. Some of the blood that once flowed through his veins, keeping him alive, now rushes through mine, helping to keep me alive. Something that came from his heart, that beat within him, that made him who he is, is now a part of me.

At first I shiver at the thought, goose bumps rising on my skin, but on further thought, I snuggle down into the bed and hug my body. I suddenly don't feel so lonely, feel glad of the company within me. Is this the reason for the connection I feel with him? That in flowing from his channels to mine, it enabled me to tune into his frequency and experience his personal memories and passions?

I sigh wearily, knowing nothing in my life makes sense any more, and not just since the day I fell down the stairs. I had been falling for quite some time before that. That day . . . that was the day I'd landed. The first day of the rest of my life, and quite possibly, thanks to Justin Hitchcock.

It has been a long day. The business at the airport, the *Antiques Roadshow*, then finally the clanger at the Royal Opera House. A tsunami of emotions has come crashing down upon me all in twenty-four hours, pulled me under and overwhelmed me. I smile now, remembering the events, the precious moments with Dad, from tea at his kitchen table to a mini-adventure in London. I offer a wide toothy grin to the ceiling above me and a thanks to beyond the ceiling.

From the darkness I hear a wheezing, short rasps drifting into the atmosphere.

'Dad?' I whisper. 'Are you OK?'

The wheezing gets louder and my body freezes.

'Dad?'

Then it's followed by a snort. And a loud guffaw.

'Michael Aspel,' he splutters through his laughter. 'Christ Almighty, Gracie.'

I smile with relief as his laughter intensifies, becomes

so much bigger than him that he almost can't bear it. I giggle at the sound of his laughter. He laughs harder on hearing me, and I at him. Our sounds fuel each other. The springs of the mattress beneath me squeak as my body shakes, causing us to roar even more. Thoughts of the umbrella stand, going live with Michael Aspel, the group cheering 'Tchaikovsky!' at the camera, the hilarity grows with each flickering scene.

'Oh, my stomach,' he howls.

I roll onto my side, hands on my belly.

Dad continues to wheeze and bangs his hand repeatedly on the side cabinet that separates us. I try to stop, the panic of a stiffening stomach sore but hilarious at the same time. I can't stop and Dad's high-pitched wheezing sets me off even more. I don't think I've ever heard him laugh so much and so heartily. From the pale light seeping through the window beside Dad, I see his legs rise in the air and kick around with glee.

'Oh. My. I. Can't. Stop.'

We wheeze and roar and laugh, sit up, lie down, roll around and try to catch our breaths. We stop momentarily and try to compose ourselves but it takes over our bodies again, laughing, laughing, laughing in the darkness, at nothing and everything.

Then we calm down and there is silence. Dad farts and we are off again.

Hot tears roll from the sides of my eyes and down my plumped cheeks, which ache from smiling and I squeeze them with my hands to stop. It occurs to me how close happiness and sadness are. So closely knitted together. Such a thin line, a thread-like divide that in the midst of emotions, it trembles, blurring the territory of exact opposites. The movement is minute, like the thin thread of a spider's web that quivers under a raindrop. Here in my moment of unstoppable cheek- and stomach-aching laughter, as my body rolls around, my stomach clenched, all the muscles taut, my body jumps about, is racked by emotion and therefore steps ever so slightly over the mark, and into sadness. Tears of sadness gush down my cheeks as my stomach continues to shake and ache with happiness.

I think of Conor and me; how quickly a moment of love was snapped away to a moment of hate. One comment to steal it all away. Of how love and war stand upon the very same foundations. How, in my darkest moments, my most fearful times, when faced, became my bravest. When feeling at your weakest you end up showing more strength, when at your lowest are suddenly lifted above higher than you've ever been. They all border one another, those opposites, and how quickly we can be altered. Despair can be altered by one simple smile offered by a stranger; confidence can become fear by the arrival of one uneasy presence. Just as Kate's son had wavered on the balance beam and in an instant his excitement had turned to pain. Everything is on the verge, always brimming the surface, a slight shake, a tremble sends things toppling. How similar emotions are.

Dad stops his laughter so abruptly it concerns me and I reach for the light.

Pitch-black so quickly becomes light.

He looks at me as though he's done something wrong, but is afraid to admit it. He throws the covers off his body and shuffles into the bathroom, grabbing his travel bag and hitting off everything in his path, refusing to meet my eyes. I look away. How quickly such comfort with someone can shift to awkwardness. How in the very second you reach a dead end, moments when you are convinced you know exactly where you're going are altered. A realisation in less than a second. A flicker.

Dad makes his way back to bed wearing a different pair of pyjama bottoms and with a towel tucked under his arm. I turn off the light, both of us quiet now. Light so quickly becomes darkness again. I continue to stare at the ceiling, feeling lost again when only moments ago I'd been found. My answers of only minutes ago are again transformed into questions.

'I can't sleep, Dad.' My voice sounds childlike.

'Close your eyes and stare into the dark, love,' Dad responds sleepily, sounding thirty years younger too.

Moments later his light snores are audible. Awake . . . and then gone.

A veil hangs between the two opposites, a mere slip of a thing that is transparent to warn us or comfort us. You hate now but look through this veil and see the possibility of love; you're sad now but look through to the other side and see happiness. Absolute composure to a complete mess – it happens so quickly, all in the blink of an eye.

'OK, I've gathered us all here today because—'

'Somebody died.'

'No, Kate,' I sigh.

'Well, it sounds like— Ow,' she yelps as Frankie, I assume, physically harms her for her tactlessness.

'So are you all red-bused out of it?' Frankie asks.

I'm seated at the desk in my hotel room, on the phone to the girls who are huddled around the phone in Kate's house with me on loudspeaker. I'd spent the morning looking around London with Dad, taking photographs of him standing awkwardly in front of anything resembling anything English: red buses, post boxes, police horses, pubs, Buckingham Palace, and a completely unaware transvestite, as he was so excited to see 'a real one', who was nothing like the local priest who'd lost his mind and wandered the streets wearing a dress, in his home town of Cavan when he was young.

While I sit at the desk, he is lying on his bed watching a rerun of *Strictly Come Dancing*, drinking a brandy and licking the sour cream and onion off Pringles before depositing the soggy crisps in the bin.

'NICE!' he shouts at the television, responding to Bruce Forsyth's catchphrase.

I've called a conference call to share the latest news, or more for help and a plea for sanity strengthening. I may have gone one wish too far, but a girl can always dream. Kate and Frankie are huddled around Kate's home phone.

'One of your kids just puked on me,' Frankie says. 'Your *kid* just puked on me.'

'Oh, that is not puke, that's just a little dribble.'

'No, *this* is dribble . . .'

There's silence.

'Frankie, you are disgusting.'

'OK, girls, girls, please can you two stop, just this once?'

'Sorry, Joyce, but I can't continue this conversation until it is out of here. It's crawling around biting things, climbing on things, drooling on things. It's very distracting. Can't Christian mind it?'

I try not to laugh.

'Do not call my child "it". And no, Christian is busy.'

'He's watching football.'

'He doesn't like to be disturbed, particularly by you. Ever.'

'Well, you're busy too. How do I get it to come with me?'

There's a silence.

'Come here, little boy,' Frankie says uneasily.

'His name is Sam. You're his godmother, in case you've forgotten that too.'

'No, I haven't forgotten *that*. Just his name.' Her voice strains, as though she's lifting weights. 'Wow, what do you feed it?'

Sam squeals like a pig.

Frankie snorts back.

'Frankie, give him to me. I'll bring him in to Christian.'

'OK, Joyce,' Frankie begins in Kate's absence, 'I've done some research on the information you gave me yesterday and I've brought some paperwork with me, hold on.' I hear papers being ruffled.

'What's this about?' Kate asks, returning.

'This is about Joyce jumping into the mind of the American man, thereby possessing his memories, skills and intelligence,' Frankie responds.

'What?' Kate shrieks.

'I found out that his name is Justin Hitchcock,' I say excitedly.

'How?' Kate asks.

'His surname was in his daughter's biography in last night's ballet programme, and his first name, well, I heard that in a dream.'

There's silence. I roll my eyes as I imagine them giving each other *that* look.

'What the hell is going on here?' Kate asks, confused.

'Google him, Kate,' Frankie orders. 'Let's see if he exists.'

'He exists, believe me,' I confirm.

'No, sweetie, you see, the way these stories work is, we're supposed to think you're crazy for a while before eventually believing you. So let us check up on him and then we'll go from there.'

I lean my chin on my hand and wait.

'While Kate's doing that, I looked into the idea of sharing memories—'

'What?' Kate shrieks again. 'Sharing memories? Are you both out of your mind?'

'No, just me,' I say tiredly, resting my head on the desk.

'Actually, surprisingly enough, it turns out that you're not clinically insane. On that count, anyway. I went online and did some research. It turns out you're not alone in feeling that.'

I sit up, suddenly alert.

'I came across websites with interviews with others who have admitted to experiencing somebody else's memories and who have also acquired their skills or tastes.'

'Oh, you two are having me on. I knew this was a set-up. I knew it was out of character for you to drop by, Frankie.'

'This isn't a set-up,' I assure Kate.

'So you're trying to tell me honestly that you've magically acquired somebody *else*'s skills.'

'She speaks Latin, French and Italian,' Frankie

explains. 'But we didn't say it was magically. *That* is ridiculous.'

'And what about tastes?' Kate is not convinced.

'She eats meat now,' Frankie says matter-of-factly.

'But why do you think these are somebody else's skills? Why can't she just have learned Latin, French and Italian by herself and decided that she likes meat all by herself, like a normal person? I suddenly like olives and have an aversion to cheese, does that mean my body has been possessed by an olive tree?'

'I don't think you're quite getting this. What makes you think olive trees don't like cheese?'

Silence.

'Look, Kate, I agree with you about the change of diet being a natural thing, but in all fairness, Joyce did learn three languages overnight without *actually* learning them.'

'Oh.'

'And I have dreams of Justin Hitchcock's private childhood moments.'

'Where the hell was I when all of this was happening?'

'Making me do the hokey cokey live on Sky News,' I huff.

I place the phone on loudspeaker and for the few minutes that follow, pace the room patiently and watch the time on the bottom of the television as both Frankie and Kate laugh heartily, on the other end.

Dad's tongue freezes mid-Pringle lick as his eyes follow me.

'What's that noise?' he finally asks.

'Kate and Frankie laughing,' I respond.

He rolls his eyes and continues licking his Pringles, attention back on a middle-aged male newsreader doing the rumba.

After three minutes, the laughter stops and I take them off loudspeaker.

'So as I was saying,' Frankie says, catching her breath, as though nothing had happened, 'what you're experiencing is quite normal – well, not normal, but there are other, eh . . .'

'Freaks?' Kate suggests.

'. . . *cases* where people have spoken of similar things. The only thing is, these are all people who have had heart transplants, which is nothing to do with what you've been through, so that blows that theory.'

Thump-thump, thump-thump. In my throat again.

'Hold on,' Kate butts in, 'one person says here that it's because she was abducted by aliens.'

'Stop reading my notes, Kate,' Frankie hisses. 'I wasn't going to mention her.'

'Listen,' I interrupt their squabbling, 'he donated blood. The same month that I went into hospital.'

'So?' Kate says.

'She received a blood transfusion,' Frankie explains. 'Not all that different to the heart transplant theory I just mentioned.'

We all go quiet.

Kate breaks the silence. 'OK, so, I still don't get it. Somebody explain.'

'Well, it's practically the same thing, isn't it?' I say. 'Blood comes from the heart.'

Kate gasps. 'It came straight from his heart,' she says dreamily.

'Oh, so now blood transfusions are romantic to you,' Frankie comments. 'Let me tell you about what I got from the Net. Due to reports from several heart transplant recipients claiming experiences of unexpected side effects, Channel Four made a documentary about whether it's possible that in receiving a transplanted organ, a patient could inherit some of their donor's memories, tastes, desires and habits as well. The documentary follows these people making contact with the donor families in the recipients' efforts to understand the new life within them. It questions science's understanding of how the memory works, featuring scientists who are pioneering research into the intelligence of the heart and the biochemical basis for memory in our cells.'

'So if they think that the heart holds more intelligence than we think, then the blood which is pumped from someone's heart could carry that intelligence. So in transfusing his blood, he transfused his memories too?' Kate asks. 'And his love of meat and languages,' she adds a little tartly.

Nobody wants to say yes to that question. Everybody wants to say no. Apart from me, who's had a night to warm to the idea already.

'Did *Star Trek* have an episode of this one time?' Frankie asks. 'Because if they didn't, they should have.'

'This can easily be solved,' Kate says excitedly. 'You can just find out who your blood donor was.'

'She can't.' Frankie, as usual, dampens her spirits. 'That kind of information is confidential. Besides, it's not as though she received all of his blood. He could only have donated less than a pint in one go. Then it's separated into white blood cells, red blood cells, plasma and platelets. What Joyce would have got, if Joyce received it at all, is only a part of his blood. It could even have been mixed with somebody else's.'

'His blood is still running through my body,' I add. 'It doesn't matter how much of it there is. And I remember feeling distinctly odd as soon as I opened my eyes in the hospital.'

A silence answers my ridiculous statement, as we all consider the fact that my feeling 'distinctly odd' had nothing to do with my transfusion and all to do with the unspeakable tragedy of losing my baby.

'We've got a Google hit for Mr Justin Hitchcock,' Kate fills the silence.

My heart beats rapidly. Please tell me I'm not making it all up, that he exists, that he's not a figment of my delusional mind. That the plans I've put in place already are not going to scare away some random person.

'OK, Justin Hitchcock was a hatmaker in Massachusetts. Hmm. Well, at least he's American. You have any knowledge of hats, Joyce?'

I think hard. 'Berets, bucket hats, fedoras, fishermen hats, ball caps, pork-pie hats, tweed caps.'

Dad stops licking his Pringle again and looks at me. 'Panama hat.'

'Panama hat,' I repeat to the girls.

'Newsboy caps, skull caps,' Kate adds.

'Top hat,' Dad says, and I pass this down the phone once again.

'Cowboy hat,' Frankie says, sounding deep in thought. She snaps out of it. 'Wait a minute, what are we doing? Anybody can name hats.'

'You're right, it doesn't feel right. Keep reading,' I urge.

'Justin Hitchcock moved to Deerfield in 1774 where he served as a soldier and fifer in the Revolution . . . I should probably stop reading this. Over two hundred years old is probably too much of a sugar daddy for you.'

'Hold on,' Frankie takes over, not wanting me to lose hope. 'There's another Justin Hitchcock below that. New York sanitation department—'

'No,' I say with frustration. 'I already know he exists. This is ridiculous. Add Trinity College to the search; he did a seminar there.'

Tap-tap-tap.

'No. Nothing for Trinity College.'

'Are you sure you spoke to his daughter?' Kate asks.

'Yes,' I say through gritted teeth.

'And did anybody see you talking to this girl?' she says sweetly.

I ignore her.

'I'm adding the words, art, architecture, French, Latin, Italian to the search,' Frankie says over the tap-tap-tap sound.

'Aha! Gotcha, Justin Hitchcock! *Guest* lecturer at Trinity College, Dublin. The Faculty of Arts and Humanities. Department of Art and Architecture. Bachelor's degree, Chicago, Master's degree, Chicago, Ph.D. Sorbonne University. Special interests are History of Italian Renaissance and Baroque Sculpture, Painting in Europe in 1600–1900. External responsibilities include founder and editor of the *Art and Architectural Review*. He is the co-author of *The Golden Age of Dutch Painting: Vermeer, Metsu and Terborch*, author of *Copper as Canvas: Paintings on Copper 1575–1775*. He has written over fifty articles in books, journals, dictionaries and conference proceedings.'

'So he exists,' Kate says, as though she's just found the Holy Grail.

Feeling more confident now I say, 'Try his name with the London National Gallery.'

'Why?'

'I have a hunch.'

'You and your hunches.' Kate continues reading, 'He is a curator of European Art at the National Gallery, London. Oh my God, Joyce, he works in London. You should go see him.'

'Hold your horses, Kate. She might freak him out and end up in a padded cell. He might not even be the donor,' Frankie objects. 'And even if he is, it doesn't explain anything.'

'It's him,' I say confidently. 'And if he was my donor, then it means something to me.'

'We'll have to figure out a way to find out,' Kate offers.

'It's him,' I repeat.

'So what are you going to do about it?' Kate asks.

I smile lightly and glance at the clock again. 'What makes you think I haven't done something already?'

Justin holds the phone to his ear and paces the small office in the National Gallery as much as he can, stretching the phone cord as far as it will go on each pace, which is not far. Three and a half steps up, five steps down.

'No, no, Simon, I said *Dutch* Portraits, though you're correct as there certainly will be *much* Dutch portraits,' he laughs. 'The Age of Rembrandt and Frans Hals,' he continues. 'I've written a book about that subject so it's something I'm more than familiar with.' *A half-written book you stopped working on two years ago, liar.*

'The exhibition will include sixty works, all painted between 1600 and 1680.'

There is a knock on the door.

'Just a minute,' he calls out.

The door opens anyway and his colleague, Roberta, enters. Though young, in her thirties, her back is hunched, her chin pressed to her chest as though she is decades older. Her eyes, mostly cast downward, occasionally flicker upwards to meet his before falling again. She is apologetic for everything, as always, constantly saying sorry to the world, as though her very presence offends. She tries to manoeuvre her way through the obstacle course that is his cluttered office to reach his desk. This she does the same way as she does through her life, as quietly and as invisibly as possible, which Justin would find admirable if it weren't quite so sad.

'Sorry, Justin,' she whispers, carrying a small basket in her hand. 'I didn't know you were on the phone, sorry. This was at reception for you. I'll just put it here. Sorry.' She backs away, barely making a sound as she tiptoes out of the room and closes the door silently behind her. A silent whirlwind that spins so gracefully and slowly it hardly appears to move at all, failing to uproot anything that lies around it.

He simply nods at her and then tries to concentrate on the conversation, picking up where he left off.

'It will range from small individual portraits meant for the private home to the large-scale group portraits of members of charitable institutions and civic guards.'

He stops pacing and eyes the hamper suspiciously, feeling as though something is about to jump out at him.

'Yes, Simon, in the Sainsbury Wing. If there's anything else you need to know please do contact me here at the office.'

He hurries his colleague off the phone and hangs up.

His hand pauses on the receiver, not sure whether to call for security. The small hamper seems alien and sweet, in his musty office, like a new-born baby in a cradle left on the dirty steps of an orphanage. Underneath the wicker handle, the contents are covered by a chequered cloth. He stands back and lifts it slowly, preparing to jump away at any moment.

A dozen or so muffins stare back at him.

His heart thumps and he quickly looks around his box-sized office, knowing nobody is with him, but his discomfort at receiving this surprise gift adds an eerie presence. He searches the basket for a card. Taped to the other side is a small white envelope. With what he realises now are shaking hands, he rips it rather clumsily from the basket. It hasn't been sealed and so he slides the card out. In the centre of the card in neat handwritten script it simply says:

Thank you . . .

28

Justin power-walks through the halls of the National Gallery, part of him obeying and the other part disobeying the 'no running in the halls' rule as he jogs three steps then walks three steps, jogs three steps and slows to a walk again. Goody Two-Shoes and the daredevil within him battling it out.

He spots Roberta tiptoeing through the hallway, making her way like a shadow to the private library where she has worked for the past five years.

'Roberta!' His daredevil is unleashed; disobeys the 'no shouting in the halls' rule, and his voice echoes and rebounds off the walls and high ceilings, deafening the ears of all in the portraits, loud enough to wilt van Gogh's sunflowers and to crack the mirror in the Arnolfini portrait.

It's also enough for Roberta to freeze and turn slowly, her eyes wide and terrified like a deer caught in the headlights. She blushes as the half-dozen members of the public turn to stare at her. Her gulp is visible from where he stands and Justin's immediately sorry for breaking her code, for pointing her out when she wanted to be invisible. He stops his power-walking and tries to walk quietly along the floors, glide as she does, in an attempt to retract the noise he had made. She stands, stiff as a board and as close to the wall as possible like an elegant climber, clinging to the walls and fences, preferring shelter and not noticing its own beauty. Justin wonders if her behaviour is as a consequence of her

627

career, or if being a librarian in the National Gallery had seemed attractive to her because of her way. He thinks the latter.

'Yes,' she whispers, wide-eyed and frightened.

'Sorry for shouting your name,' he says as quietly as he can.

Her face softens and her shoulders relax a little.

'Where did you get this hamper?' He holds it out to her.

'At reception. I was returning from my break when Charlie asked me to give it to you. Is there something wrong?'

'Charlie.' He thinks hard. 'He's at the Sir Paul Getty Entrance?'

She nods.

'OK, thank you, Roberta, I apologise for shouting.' He dashes off to the East Wing, his daredevil and good side clashing again in a remarkably confused half-run, half-walk combination, while the basket swings from his hand.

'Finished for the day, Little Red Riding Hood?' He hears a croaky chuckle.

Justin, noticing he was skipping along with the basket, stops abruptly and spins around to face Charlie, a security guard, over six foot tall.

'My, Grandmother, what an ugly head you have.'

'What do you want?'

'I was wondering who gave you this basket?'

'A delivery guy from . . .' Charlie moves over to behind his small desk and riffles through some papers. He retrieves a clipboard. 'Harrods. Zhang Wei,' he reads. 'Why? Something wrong with the muffins?' He runs his tongue over his teeth and clears his throat.

Justin's eyes narrow. 'How did you know they were muffins?'

Charlie refuses to meet his stare. 'Had to check, didn't I? This is the National Gallery. You can't expect me to accept a package without knowing what's in it.'

Justin studies Charlie, whose face has pinked. He

spies crumbs stuck to the crevices at the corners of his mouth and slight traces down his uniform. He removes the chequered cloth from his hamper and counts. Eleven muffins.

'Don't you think it's odd to send a person eleven muffins?'

'Odd?' Eyes wander, shoulders fidget. 'Dunno, mate. Never sent muffins to anyone in my life.'

'Wouldn't it seem more obvious to send a *dozen* muffins?'

Shoulders shrug. Fingers fidget. His eyes study everybody that enters the gallery, far more intently than usual. His body language tells Justin that he's finished with the conversation.

Justin whips out his cellphone as he exits to Trafalgar Square.

'Hello?'

'Bea, it's Dad.'

'I'm not talking to you.'

'Why not?'

'Peter told me what you said to him at the ballet last night,' she snaps.

'What did I do?'

'You interrogated him on his *intentions* all night.'

'I'm your father, that's my job.'

'No, what you did is the job of the Gestapo,' she fumes. 'I swear, I'm not speaking to you until you *apologise* to him.'

'Apologise?' he laughs. 'What for? I merely made a few enquiries into his past, in order to ascertain his agenda.'

'Agenda? He doesn't *have* an agenda!'

'So I asked him a few questions, so what? Bea, he's not good enough for you.'

'No, he's not good enough for *you*. Well, I don't care what you think of him, it's me that's supposed to be happy.'

'He picks *strawberries* for a living.'

'He is an *IT consultant*!'

'Then, who picks strawberries?' *Somebody picks strawberries.* 'Well, honey, you know how I feel about consultants. If they are *so amazing* at something why don't they do it themselves, instead of just making money telling people?'

'You're a lecturer, curator, reviewer, *whatever*. If you know so much why don't you just build a building or paint a damn picture yourself?' she shouts. 'Instead of just bragging to everybody about how much you know about them!'

Hmm.

'Sweetheart, let's not get out of control now.'

'No, you are the one out of control. You will apologise to Peter and if you do not, I will not answer your phone calls and you can deal with your little dramas all by yourself.'

'Wait, wait, wait. Just one question.'

'Dad, I—'

'Did-you-send-me-a-hamper-of-a-dozen-cinnamon-muffins?' he rushes out with.

'What? No!'

'No?'

'No muffins! No conversations, no *nothing*—'

'Now, now, sweetheart, there's no need for double negatives.'

'I'll have no more contact with you until you apologise,' she finishes.

'OK,' he sighs. 'Sorry.'

'Not to *me*. To *Peter*.'

'OK, but does that mean you won't be collecting my dry cleaning on your way over tomorrow? You know where it is, it's the one beside the tube station—'

The phone clicks. He stares at it in confusion. *My own daughter hung up on me? I knew this Peter was trouble.*

He thinks again about the muffins and dials again. He clears his throat.

'Hello.'

'Jennifer, it's Justin.'

'Hello, Justin.' Her voice is cold.

Used to be warm. Like honey. No, like hot caramel. It used to bounce from octave to octave when she heard his name, just like the piano music he'd wake on Sunday mornings to hear her play from the conservatory. But now?

He listens to the silence on the other end.

Ice.

'I'm just calling to see whether you'd sent me a hamper of muffins.' As soon as he's said it, he realises how ridiculous this call is. Of course she didn't send him anything. Why would she?

'I beg your pardon?'

'I received a basket of muffins to my office today along with a thank you note, but the note failed to reveal the sender's identity. I was wondering if it was you.'

Her voice is amused now. No, not amused, mocking. 'What would I have to thank you for, Justin?'

It's a simple question, but knowing her as he knows her, it has implications far beyond the words, and so Justin jumps up and snaps at the bait. The hook cuts through his lip and bitter Justin is back, the voice he grew so accustomed to during the demise of their . . . well, during *their* demise. She has reeled him right in.

'Oh, I don't know, twenty years of marriage, perhaps. A daughter. A good living. A roof over your head.' He knows it's a stupid statement. That before him, after him and even without him, she had and always would have a roof, of all things, over her head, but it's spurting out of him now and he can't stop and won't stop, for he is right and she is wrong and anger is spurring on every word, like a jockey whipping his horse as they near the finish line. 'Travel all over the world.' *Whip-crack-away!* 'Clothes, clothes and more clothes.' *Whip-crack-away!* 'A new kitchen when we didn't need one, a *conservatory*, for Christsake . . .' And he goes on, like a man from the nineteenth century who'd been keeping his wife accustomed to a good life she would otherwise have been without, ignoring the fact that she had made a good living herself, playing in an orchestra that travelled the world, making several trips that he had accompanied her on.

At the beginning of their married life they had no choice but to live with Justin's mother. They were young and had a baby to rear, the reason for their hasty marriage, and as Justin was still attending college by day, bar tending at night and working at an art museum at the weekend, Jennifer had made money playing the piano at an upmarket restaurant in Chicago. At the weekends, she would return home in the early hours of the morning, her back sore and tendonitis in her middle finger, but that all went out of his mind when she'd dangled the line with that seemingly innocent question. She had known that this tirade would come and he gobbles, gobbles, gobbles, munches on the bait that fills his mouth. Finally running out of things they have spent the last twenty years doing together, and out of steam, he stops.

Jennifer is silent.

'Jennifer?'

'Yes, Justin.' Icy.

Justin sighs with exhaustion. 'So, was it you?'

'It must have been one of your other women, because it most certainly wasn't me.'

Click and she's gone.

Rage bubbles inside him. Other women. *Other women! One* affair when he was twenty years old, a fumble in the dark with Mary-Beth Dursoa at college, *before* he and Jennifer were even married, and she carries on as though he was Don Juan. In their bedroom, he'd even put a print of *A Satyr Mourning over a Nymph* by Piero di Cosimo, which Jennifer had always loathed but he had always hoped would send her subliminal messages. In the painting there is a young girl semi-clothed who on first glance seems asleep but on further viewing has blood seeping from her throat. A satyr is mourning her. Justin's interpretation of the painting is that the woman, mistrusting her husband's fidelity, followed him into the woods. He was hunting, not going astray as she thought, and shot her by accident, thinking her rustling in the trees was an animal. Sometimes during his and Jennifer's darkest moments, when their hate raged during their toughest arguments, when their throats were red raw, their eyes stinging with tears, their hearts breaking from the pain, their heads pounding from the analysis, Justin would study the painting and envy the satyr.

Fuming, he charges down the North Terrace steps, sits down by one of the fountains, places the basket by his feet and bites into a muffin, scoffing it down so quickly he barely has time to taste it. Crumbs fall at his feet, attracting a flock of pigeons with intent in their beady black eyes. He goes to reach for another muffin but he is swarmed by overenthusiastic pigeons pecking at the contents of his basket, greedily. Peck, peck, peck – he watches dozens more flock towards him, coming in to land like fighter jets. Afraid of falling missiles from those that circle his head, he picks up his basket and shoos them away with all the butchness of an eleven-year-old.

He breezes in the front door of his home, leaving it open behind him, and is immediately greeted by Doris, with a paint palette in her hand.

'OK, so I've narrowed it down,' she begins, thrusting dozens of colours in his face.

Her long leopard-print nails are each decorated with a diamanté jewel. She wears an all-in-one snakeskin jumpsuit, and her feet wobble dangerously in patent lace-up ankle stilettos. Her hair is still its usual shock of red, her eyes catlike with inky eyeliner sweeping up from her corners of her eyes, her painted lips to match her hair remind him of Ronald McDonald. He watches them with severe irritation as they open and close.

The random words he hears are, 'Gooseberry Fool, Celtic Forest, English Mist and Woodland Pearl, all *calm* tones, would look so good in this room *or* Wild

Mushroom, Nomadic Glow and Sultana Spice. The Cappuccino Candy is one of my faves but I don't think it'll work next to that curtain, what do you think?'

She waves a fabric in front of his face and it tickles his nose, which tingles with such intensity it senses the fight that is about to brew. He doesn't respond but takes deep breaths and counts to ten in his mind. And when that doesn't work and she keeps listing paint colours, he keeps on going to twenty.

'Hello? Justin?' She snaps her fingers in his face. 'Hel-lo?'

'Maybe you should give Justin a break, Doris. He looks tired.' Al looks nervously at his brother.

'But—'

'Get your sultana spice behind over here,' he teases and she whoops.

'OK, but just one more thing. Bea will love her room done in Ivory Lace. And Petey too. Imagine how romantic this will be for—'

'ENOUGH!' Justin screams at the top of his lungs, not wanting his daughter's name and the word romantic to share the same sentence.

Doris jumps and stops talking immediately. Her hand flies to her chest. Al stops drinking, his bottle freezes just below his lips, his heavy breathing above the rim making ivory pipe music. Other than that, there's absolute silence.

'Doris,' Justin takes a deep breath and tries to speak as calmly as possible, 'enough of this please. Enough of this Cappuccino Nights—'

'Candy,' she interrupts, and quickly silences again.

'Whatever. This is a Victorian house, from the nineteenth century, not some painted lady from an episode of *Changing Rooms*.' He tries to restrain his emotions, his feelings insulted on behalf of the building. 'If you had mentioned Cappuccino Chocolate—'

'Candy,' she whispers.

'Whatever! To anyone during that time, you would have been instantly burned at the stake!'

She squeaks, insulted.

'It needs *sophistication*, it needs to be *researched*, it needs furniture *of* the period, colours *of* the period, not a room that sounds like Al's dinner menu.'

'Hey!' Al speaks up.

'I think it needs,' Justin takes a deep breath and says gently, 'somebody else for the job. Maybe it's just bigger than you thought it was going to be but I appreciate your help, really I do. Please tell me you understand.'

She nods slowly and he breathes a sigh of relief.

Suddenly the paint palettes go flying across the room as Doris lets rip, 'You pretentious little bastaaaaard!'

'Doris!' Al leaps up out of his armchair, or at least, makes a great attempt to.

Justin immediately takes steps back as she walks aggressively towards him, pointing her sparkly animal-print nail at him, like a weapon.

'Listen here, you silly little man. I have spent the last two weeks researching this dump of a basement in the kinds of libraries and places you wouldn't even think *exist*. I've been to dark, dingy dungeons where people smell of old . . . things.' Her nostrils flare and her voice deepens, threateningly. 'I purchased every historic period paint brochure that I could get my hands on and applied the colours in accordance with the colour rules at the end of the nineteenth century. I've shaken hands with people you don't even wanna know about, I've seen parts of London *I* didn't even wanna know about. I've looked through books so old, the dust mites were big enough to hand them to me from the shelves. I have matched the Dulux colours as closely as I possibly could to your historic period paint and I've been to second-hand, third-hand, even *antique* stores and seen furniture in such disgusting derelict conditions, I almost set up the ISPCF. I've seen things crawling around dining-room tables and sat in such rickety chairs I could smell the black death that killed the last person who died sitting right in it. I have sanded down so much pine, I have splinters in places you don't wanna see. So.' She prods him in the chest with her dagger nail as she emphasises each word that finally backs him up against the wall. 'Don't. Tell. Me. That *this* is too big for me.'

She clears her throat and stands up straight. The anger in her voice is replaced with a vulnerable 'poor me' tremble. 'But despite what you said, I will finish this project. I will go on undeterred. I will do it in spite of you and I will do it for your brother, who might be dead next month and you don't even care.'

'Dead?' Justin's eyes widen.

With that, she turns on her heel and storms off into her bedroom.

She sticks her head out of the doorway. 'By the way, just so you know, I would have banged the door behind me VERY LOUDLY to show just how angry I am but it's currently out in the backyard ready for sanding and priming, before I paint it . . .' and this she spits out rebelliously, 'Ivory Lace.'

Then she disappears again, without a bang.

I shift from foot to foot nervously outside the open door of Justin's home. Should I press the bell now? Simply call his name into the room? Would he call the police and have me arrested for trespassing? Oh, this was such a bad decision. Frankie and Kate had persuaded me to come here, to present myself to him. They had pumped me up to such a point I had hopped in the first taxi that came my way to Trafalgar Square, to catch him at the National Gallery before he left. I'd been so close to him as he'd been on the phone, heard his calls to people as he asked them about the basket. I'd felt oddly comfortable just watching him, without his knowing, unable to take my eyes off him, revelling in the secret thrill of being able to see him for who he is instead of viewing his life from his own memories.

His anger at whoever was on the phone – most likely his ex-wife, the woman with the red hair and freckles – convinced me it was the wrong time to approach him and so I'd followed him. *Followed*, not stalked. I'd taken my time while trying to build up the courage to talk to him. Would I mention the transfusion or not? Would he think I was crazy or be open to listening or, even better, open to believing?

But once on the tube, the timing again wasn't right. It was overcrowded, people were pushing and shoving, avoiding eye contact, never mind first-time introductions or conversations about studies into the possible intelligence of blood. And so after pacing up and down his road, feeling like both a schoolgirl with a crush and a stalker at the same time, I now find myself standing outside the door, with a plan. But my plan is once again being compromised as Justin and his brother Al begin to talk about something I know I shouldn't be hearing, about a family secret I am more than familiar with already.

I move my finger away from the doorbell, keep hidden from all the windows and I bide my time.

29

Justin looks to his brother in panic and searches quickly for something to sit on. He pulls over a giant paint tub and sits down, not noticing the wet white ring of paint around the top.

'Al, what was she talking about? About you being dead next month.'

'No, no, no,' Al laughs. 'She said, *might* be dead. That's distinctly different. Hey, you got away lightly there, bro. Good for you. I think that valium is really helping her. Cheers.' He holds up his bottle and downs the last of it.

'Hold on, hold on. Al, what are you talking about? There's something you haven't told me? What did the doctor say?'

'The doctor told me exactly what I've been telling you for the last two weeks. If any members of a person's immediate family developed coronary heart disease at a young age, i.e., a male under fifty-five years old, well then, we have an increased risk of coronary heart disease.'

'Have you high blood pressure?'

'A little.'

'Have you high cholesterol?'

'A lot.'

'So, all you do is make lifestyle changes, Al. It doesn't mean you're going to be struck down like . . . like . . .'

'Dad?'

'No.' He frowns and shakes his head.

'Coronary heart disease is the number-one killer of American males *and* females. Every thirty-three seconds an American will suffer some type of coronary event and almost every minute someone will die from it.' He looks at their mother's grandfather clock half-covered in a dust sheet. The minute hand moves. Al grabs his heart and starts groaning. His noises soon turn to laughter.

Justin rolls his eyes. 'Who told you that nonsense?'

'The pamphlets at the doc's office said so.'

'Al, you're not going to have a heart attack.'

'It's my fortieth birthday next week.'

'Yeah, I know.' Justin hits him playfully on the knee. 'That's the spirit, we'll have a big party.'

'That's what age Dad was when he died.' He lowers his eyes and peels the label from his beer.

'That's what this is about?' Justin's voice softens. 'Damnit, Al, that's what this is all about? Why didn't you say something earlier?'

'I just thought that I'd spend some time with you before, you know, just in case . . .' His eyes tear up and he looks away.

Tell him the truth.

'Al, listen, there's something you should know.' His voice trembles and he clears his throat, trying to control it. *You've never told anyone.* 'Dad was under a huge amount of pressure at work. He had a lot of difficulties, financial and otherwise, that he didn't tell anyone. Not even Mom.'

'I know, Justin. I know.'

'You know?'

'Yeah, I get it. He didn't just drop dead for no reason. He was stressed out of his mind. And I'm not, I know that. But ever since I was a kid, I've had this feeling hanging over me that it's gonna happen to me too. It's been playing on my mind for as long as I can remember and now that my birthday's next week and I'm not in the greatest of shape . . . Things have been real busy at the business and I haven't been looking after myself. Never could do it like you could, you know?'

'Hey, you don't have to explain it to me.'

'Remember that day we spent with him on the front lawn? With the sprinklers? Just hours before Mom found him . . . Well, remember the whole family playing around?'

'They were good times,' Justin smiles, fighting back the tears.

'You remember?' Al laughs.

'Like it was yesterday,' Justin says.

'Dad was holding the hose and spraying us both. He seemed in such good humour.' Al frowns with confusion and thinks for a while, then the smile returns. 'He'd brought Mom home a big bunch of flowers – remember she put that big flower in her hair?'

'The sunflower.' Justin nods along.

'And it was real hot. Do you remember it being real hot?'

'Yeah.'

'And Dad had his pants rolled up to his knees and his shoes and socks off. And the grass was getting all wet and his feet were all covered in grass and he just kept chasing us around and around . . .' He smiles into the distance. 'That was the last time I saw him.'

It wasn't for me.

Justin's memory flashes through the image of his father closing the living-room door. Justin had run into the house from the front yard to go to the bathroom; all that playing around with water was almost making him burst. As far as he knew, all the members of his family were still outside playing. He could hear his mom chasing and taunting Al, and Al, who was only five years old, screeching with laughter. But when he was coming downstairs, he spotted his dad coming out of the kitchen, walking down the hall. Justin, wanting to jump out and surprise him, crouched down and watched him from behind the banister.

But then he saw what was in his hand. He saw the bottle of liquid that was always locked away in the cabinet in the kitchen and only taken out on special occasions when his dad's family came over from Ireland to visit. When they all drank from that bottle they would change, they would sing songs that Justin had never heard before but that his dad knew every word of, and they would laugh and tell stories and sometimes cry. He wasn't sure why that bottle was in his dad's hands now. Did he want to sing and laugh and tell stories today? Did he want to cry?

Then Justin saw the bottle of pills in his hand too. He knew they were pills, because they were in the same container as the medicine Mom and Dad took when they were sick. He hoped his dad wasn't feeling sick now and he hoped he didn't want to cry. He watched as he closed the door behind him with the pills and bottle of alcohol in his hands. He should have known then what his dad was about to do but he didn't. Thinks of that moment over and over and tries to force himself to call out and stop him. But the nine-year-old Justin never hears him. He stays crouched on the stair, waiting for his dad to come out so he can jump out and surprise him. As time went by he began to feel that something wasn't right, but he didn't quite know why he felt that way and he didn't want to ruin the big surprise by checking on his dad.

After minutes that felt like hours, of nothing but silence from behind the door, Justin gulped and stood up. He could hear Al screaming with laughter outside. He could still hear Al laughing when he went inside and saw the green feet on the floor. He remembers the sight of those feet so vividly, Dad lying on the floor like a big green giant. He remembers following those feet and finding his dad on the floor, staring lifeless at the ceiling.

He didn't say anything. Didn't scream, didn't touch him, didn't kiss him, didn't try to help him because though he didn't understand much at that time, he knew that it was too late for help. He just slowly backed out of the room, closed the door behind him and ran out to the front lawn to his mom and younger brother.

Five minutes they had. Five more minutes of everything being exactly the same. He was nine years old on a sunny day with a mom and a dad and a brother, and he was happy and Mom was happy and the neighbours smiled at him normally like they did all the other kids, all the food they ate for dinner was made by his mom and when he was bad at school the teachers shouted at him, like they should. Five more minutes of everything being the same, until his mom went into the house and then it was all completely different, then everything changed. Five minutes later, he wasn't nine years old with a mom, a dad and a brother. He wasn't happy, neither was Mom, and the neighbours smiled at him with such a sadness he wished they didn't bother smiling at all. Everything they ate came from containers carried over by women that lived on the same street, who always looked sad too, and when he acted up at school the teachers just looked at him with that same face. Everyone had the same face. The five extra minutes wasn't long enough.

Mom told them Dad had suffered a heart attack. She told the entire family and anybody that came by with a home-cooked meal or pie.

Justin could never bring himself to tell anyone he knew the truth, half because he wanted to believe the lie and half because he thought his mother had started to believe it too. So he kept it to himself. He hadn't even told Jennifer, because saying it out loud made it true and he did not want to validate his father dying that way. And now, their mother gone, he was the only person who knew the truth about his dad. The story of their father's death that had been fabricated to help them had ended up hanging like a black cloud over Al and a burden for Justin.

He wanted to tell Al the truth right now, he really did. But how could it help him? Surely knowing the truth would be far worse, and he'd have to explain how and why he'd kept it from him all these years . . . But then he would no longer have to shoulder all the burden.

Perhaps there would be finally some release for him. It could help Al's fear of heart failure and they could deal with it together.

'Al, there's something I have to tell you,' Justin begins.

The doorbell rings suddenly. A sharp sting of a ring that startles them both from their thoughts, smashing the silence like a sledgehammer through glass. All their thoughts shatter and fall to pieces on the ground.

'Is someone gonna get that?' Doris yells, breaking the silence.

Justin walks to the door with a white ring of paint around his behind. The door is already ajar and he pulls it open further. Before him, on the railings, hangs his dry cleaning. His suits, shirts and sweaters all covered in plastic. Nobody is there. He steps outside and runs up the basement steps to see who has left them there, but apart from the skip, the front lawn is empty.

'Who is it?' Doris calls.

'Nobody,' Justin responds, confused. He unhooks his dry cleaning from the railing and carries it inside.

'You're telling me that cheap suit just pressed the doorbell itself?' she asks, still angry at him from before.

'I don't know. It's peculiar. Bea was going to collect this tomorrow. I hadn't arranged a delivery with the dry cleaners.'

'Maybe it's a special delivery, for being such a good customer because by the looks of it, they dry cleaned your entire wardrobe.' She eyes his choice of clothes with distaste.

'Yeah, and I'll bet the special delivery comes with a big bill,' he grumbles. 'I had a little falling-out with Bea earlier; maybe she organised this as an apology.'

'Oh, you are a stubborn man.' Doris rolls her eyes. 'Do you ever think for a second that it's *you* who should be making the apologies?'

Justin narrows his eyes at her. 'Did you talk to Bea?'

'Hey, look, there's an envelope on this side,' Al points out, interrupting the beginnings of another fight.

'There's your bill,' Doris laughs.

Justin's heart immediately leaps to his mouth as he catches sight of the familiar envelope. He throws the pile of clothes down on the dust sheet and rips off the envelope.

'Be careful! These have just been pressed.' Doris takes them and hangs them from the door frame.

He opens the envelope and gulps hard, reading the note.

'What does it say?' Al asks.

'It must be a death threat, look at his face,' Doris says excitedly. 'Or a begging letter. Some of those are so much fun. What's wrong with them and how much do they want?' she giggles.

Justin takes out the card he received on the muffin basket earlier, and he holds the two cards together so that they make a complete sentence. Reading the words causes a chill to run through his body.

Thank you . . . For Saving My Life.

30

I lie in the skip, breathless, heart beating at the speed of a humming bird's wings. I'm like a child playing hide and seek, with intense nervous excitement rolling around my tummy; like a dog on its back trying to rid itself of fleas. Please don't find me, Justin, don't find me like this, lying at the bottom of the skip in your garden, covered in plaster and dust. I hear his footsteps move further away, back down the steps to his basement flat and the door closes.

What on earth have I become? A coward. I chickened out and rang the doorbell to stop Justin telling the story about his father to Al and then, afraid of playing God to two strangers, I ran, leaped and landed in the bottom of a skip. How metaphorical. I'm not sure I'll ever be able to speak to him. I don't know how I'll ever find the words to explain how I'm feeling. The world is not a patient place: stories such as this are mostly for the pages of the *Enquirer* or double-page spreads in certain women's magazines. Beside my story would be a photograph of me, in my dad's kitchen, looking forlornly at the camera. With no make-up. No, Justin would never believe me if I told him – but actions speak louder than words.

Lying on my back, I stare up at the sky. Lying face down, the clouds stare right back down at me. They pass over the woman in the skip with curiosity, calling the stragglers behind them to come see. More clouds gather, eager to see what the others are grumbling about.

Then they too pass over, leaving me staring at blue and the occasional white wisp. I almost hear my mother laughing aloud, imagine her nudging her friends to come have a look at her daughter. I imagine her peeping over a cloud, hanging over too far like Dad in the balcony at the Royal Opera House. I smile, enjoying this now.

Now, as I brush dust, paint and wood from my clothes and clamber out of the skip, I try to remember what other things Bea mentioned her father wanted to have done, by the person he saved.

'Justin, calm down, for creep's sake. You're making me nervous.' Doris sits on a stepladder and watches Justin pace up and down the room.

'I can't calm down. Do you not understand what this means?' He hands her the two cards.

Her eyes widen. 'You saved someone's life?'

'Yeah.' He shrugs and stops pacing. 'It's really no big deal. Sometimes you just gotta do what you gotta do.'

'He donated blood,' Al interrupts his brother's failed attempt at modesty.

'*You* donated blood?'

'It's how he met Vampira, remember?' Al refreshes his wife's memory. 'In Ireland when they say, "Fancy a pint?" *beware*.'

'Her name is *Sarah* not Vampira.'

'So you donated blood to get a date.' Doris folds her arms. 'Is there nothing you do for the greater good of humanity or is it *all* just for yourself?'

'Hey, I have a heart.'

'Though a pint lighter than it was,' Al adds.

'I have donated plenty of my time to helping organisations – colleges, universities and galleries – which are in need of my expertise. Something I don't *have* to do, but which I have agreed to do *for them*.'

'Yeah and I bet you charge them per word. That's why he says "oops-a-daisies" instead of "shit" when he stubs his toe.'

Al and Doris dissolve into laughter, thumping and hitting each other in their fit.

Justin takes a deep breath. 'Let's get back to the matter at hand. *Who* is sending me these notes and running these errands?'

He begins pacing again and biting his nails. 'Maybe this is Bea's idea of a joke. She's the only person I had the conversation with about deserving thanks in return for saving a life.'

Please, don't be Bea.

'Man, you are selfish,' Al laughs.

'No.' Doris shakes her head, her long earrings whip against her cheeks with each movement, her back-brushed hairsprayed hair as still as a microphone head. 'Bea wants nothing to do with you until you apologise. No words can describe how much she hates you right now.'

'Well, thank God for that.' Justin continues pacing. 'But she must have told somebody or this wouldn't be happening. Doris, find out from Bea who she spoke to about this.'

'Huh.' Doris lifts her chin and looks away. 'You said some pretty nasty things to me before. I don't know if I can help you.'

Justin falls to his knees and shuffles over to her.

'Please, Doris, I'm begging you. I am so, so sorry for what I said. I had no idea how much time and effort you were putting into this place. I underestimated you. Without you, I'd still be drinking from a toothbrush holder and eating from a cat bowl.'

'Yeah, I meant to ask you about that,' Al interrupts his grovelling. 'You don't even have a cat.'

'So I'm a good interior designer?' Doris lifts her chin.

'A *great* designer.'

'How great?'

'Greater than . . .' he stalls. 'Andrea Palladio.'

Her eyes look to the left, look to the right. 'Is he better than Ty Pennington?'

'He was an Italian architect in the sixteenth century,

widely considered the most influential person in the history of Western architecture.'

'Oh. OK. You're forgiven.' She holds out her hand. 'Give me your phone and I'll call Bea.'

Moments later they are all seated around the new kitchen table listening to Doris's half of the phone conversation.

'OK, Bea told Petey, and the costume supervisor for *Swan Lake*. And her father.'

'The costume supervisor? Do you guys still have the programme?'

Doris disappears to her bedroom and returns with the ballet programme. She flicks through the pages.

'No,' Justin shakes his head on reading her biography, 'I met this woman that night and it's not her. But her father was there? I didn't see her father.'

Al shrugs.

'Well, these people aren't involved in this, I certainly didn't save her life or her father's. The person must be Irish or have received medical attention in an Irish hospital.'

'Maybe her dad's Irish, or was in Ireland.'

'Give me that programme, I'm calling the theatre.'

'Justin, you can't just call her up.' Doris dives for the programme in his hand, but he dodges her. 'What are you going to say?'

'All I need to know is if her father is Irish or was in Ireland during the past month. I'll make the rest up as I go along.'

Al and Doris look at each other worriedly while he leaves the kitchen to make the call.

'Did you do this?' Doris asks Al quietly.

'No way.' Al shakes his head, his chins wobbling.

Five minutes later Justin returns.

'She remembered me from last night and, no, it's not her or her father. So either Bea told somebody else or . . . it must be Peter fooling around. I'm gonna get that little kid and—'

'Grow up, Justin. It's not him,' Doris says sternly.

'Start looking elsewhere. Call the dry cleaners, call the guy who delivered the muffins.'

'I have already. They were charged to a credit card and they can't release the owner's details.'

'Your life is just one big mystery. Between the Joyce woman and these mysterious deliveries, you should hire a private investigator,' Doris responds. 'Oh! I just remembered.' She reaches into her pocket and hands him a piece of paper. 'Speaking of private investigators. I got this for you. I've had it for a few days but didn't say anything because I didn't want you going on a wild-goose chase and making a fool of yourself. But seeing as you're choosing to do that anyway, here.'

She hands him the piece of paper with Joyce's details.

'I called International Directory Enquiries and gave them the number of the Joyce person that showed up on Bea's phone last week. They gave me the address that goes with it. I think it'd be a better idea to find this woman, Justin. Forget this other person. It seems very odd behaviour to me. Who knows who's sending you these notes? Concentrate on the woman; a nice healthy relationship is what you need.'

He barely reads the page before putting it in his jacket pocket, totally uninterested, his mind elsewhere.

'You just jump from one woman to another, don't you?' Doris studies him.

'Hey, it could be the Joyce woman that's sending the messages,' Al pipes up.

Doris and Justin both look at him and roll their eyes.

'Don't be ridiculous, Al,' Justin dismisses him. 'I met her in a hair salon. Anyway, who says it's a woman that's doing this?'

'Well, it's obvious,' Al replies. 'Because you were given a *muffin basket*.' He scrunches up his nose. 'Only a woman would think of sending a muffin basket. Or a gay guy. And whoever it is, he or she – or maybe it's a he*she* – they know how to do calligraphy, which further backs up my theory. Woman, gay guy or tranny,' he sums up.

'*I* was the one who thought of the muffin basket!' Justin puffs. '*And* I do calligraphy.'

'Yeah, like I said. Woman, gay guy or tranny,' he grins.

Justin throws his hands up in exasperation and falls back in his chair. 'You two are no help.'

'Hey, I know who could help you.' Al sits up.

'Who?' Justin rests his chin on his fist, bored.

'Vampira,' he says spookily.

'I've already asked her for help. All I could see were my blood details in the database. Nothing about who received my donation. She won't tell me where my blood went and she won't ever speak to me again either.'

'On account of you running away from her after a Viking bus?'

'That had something to do with it.'

'Gee, Justin, you really have a beautiful way with women.'

'Well, at least *somebody* thinks I'm doing something right.' He stares at the two cards he's placed in the centre of the table.

Who are you?

'You don't have to ask Sarah straight out. Maybe you could snoop around a bit in her office,' Al gets excited.

'No, that would be wrong,' Justin says unconvincingly. 'I could get into trouble. I could get *her* into trouble and, besides, I've treated her so badly.'

'So a really lovely thing to do,' Doris says slyly, 'would be to drop by her office, and tell her you're sorry. As a friend.'

A smile slowly creeps onto each of their faces.

'But can you take a day off work next week, to go to Dublin?' Doris asks, breaking their evil moment.

'I've already accepted an invitation from the National Gallery in Dublin to give a talk on Terborch's *Woman Writing a Letter*,' Justin says excitedly.

'What's the painting of?' Al asks.

'A woman writing a letter, Sherlock,' Doris snorts.

'What a boring story.' Al scrunches up his nose. Then he and Doris settle down and watch as Justin reads the notes over and over, hoping to decipher a hidden code.

'*Man Reading a Note*,' Al says rather grandly, 'Discuss.'

He and Doris crack up again as Justin exits the room.

'Hey, where are you going?'

'Man booking a flight,' he winks.

31

At seven fifteen the next morning, just before Justin leaves his flat for work, he stands poised at the front door, hand on the door handle.

'Justin, where's Al? He wasn't in bed when I woke up.' Doris shuffles out of her bedroom in her slippers and robe. 'What on earth are you doing now, you funny little man?'

Justin holds a finger to his lips, hushing her, and jerks his head in the direction of the door.

'Is the blood person out there?' she whispers excitedly, kicking off her slippers and tiptoeing like a cartoon character, to join him at the door.

He nods excitedly.

They press their ears up against the door and Doris's eyes widen. *I can hear!* she mouths.

'OK, on three,' he whispers and they mouth together, *One, two—* He pulls the door open with full force. 'HA! Gotcha!' he shouts, striking an attacker's pose and pointing his finger with more aggression than intended.

'Aaaah!' the postman screams with fright, dropping envelopes by Justin's feet. He fires a package at Justin and holds another parcel by his head in defence.

'Aaaah!' Doris shouts.

Justin doubles over as the package hits between his legs. He falls to his knees, his face turning red as he gasps for air.

They all hold their chests, panting.

The postman remains cowered, his knees bent, his head covered by a package.

'Justin,' Doris picks up an envelope and hits Justin across the arm, 'you idiot! It's the postman.'

'Yes,' he rasps, and makes choking sounds. 'I can see that now.' He takes a moment to compose himself. 'It's OK, sir, you can lower your package now. I'm sorry to have frightened you.'

The postman slowly lowers the parcel, fear and confusion in his eyes. 'What was that about?'

'I thought you were someone else. I'm sorry, I was expecting . . . something else.' He looks to the envelopes on the floor. Bills. 'Is there nothing else for me?'

His left arm starts to niggle at him again. Tingling as though a mosquito has bitten him. He starts to scratch. Lightly at first and then he pats his inner elbow, smacking the itch away. The tingling becomes more intense and he digs his nail into his skin, scratching over and over. Beads of sweat break out on his forehead.

The postman shakes his head and starts to back away.

'Did nobody give you anything to deliver to me?' He climbs back to his feet and moves closer, unintentionally appearing threatening.

'No, I said no.' The postman rushes up the steps.

Justin looks after him, confused.

'Leave the man alone. You almost gave him a heart attack.' Doris continues picking up the envelopes. 'If you have that reaction to the real person, then you'll scare them off too. If you ever do meet this person, I advise you rethink the "Ha! Gotcha!" routine.'

Justin pulls up the sleeve of his shirt and examines his arm, expecting to find red lumps or a rash, but there are no marks on his skin apart from the scratch marks he has made himself.

'Are you on something?' Doris narrows her eyes.

'No!'

She shuffles back into the kitchen with a harrumphing sound. 'Al?' her voice echoes around the kitchen. 'Where are you?'

'Help! Help me! Someone!'

In the distance they hear Al's voice, muffled as though his mouth is stuffed with socks.

Doris gasps, 'Baby?' Justin hears the fridge door opening. 'Al?' She sticks her head in the fridge. She returns to the living room, shaking her head, alterting Justin to the fact that her husband was not in the fridge after all.

Justin rolls his eyes. 'He's outside, Doris.'

'Then for goodness' sake stop just standing there looking at me and help him!'

He opens the door and Al sits slumped on the ground at the base of the steps. Wrapped around his sweaty head, Rambo style, is one of Doris's tangerine head-bands, his T-shirt is soaked with sweat, beads of perspiration run down his face, his legs are spandex-clad and crumpled underneath him, still in the same position as when he'd fallen.

Doris pushes by Justin aggressively, and charges towards Al. She falls to her knees. 'Baby? Are you OK? Did you fall down the stairs?'

'No,' he says weakly, his chins resting on his chest.

'No, you're not OK or no, you didn't fall down the stairs?' she asks.

'The first one,' he says with exhaustion. 'No, the second. Hold on, what was the first?'

She shouts at him now as though he is deaf. 'The first was, are you OK? And the second was, did you fall down the stairs?'

'No,' he responds, rolling his head back to rest it against the wall.

'To which one? Will I call an ambulance? Do you need a doctor?'

'No.'

'No what, baby? Come on, don't go to sleep on me, don't you dare go anywhere.' She slaps his face. 'You have to stay conscious.'

Justin leans against the door frame and folds his arms, watching the two. He knows his brother is fine, lack of fitness being his only problem. He goes to the kitchen for some water for Al.

'My heart . . .' Al is panicking when Justin returns. His hands are scraping at his chest and he's gasping for air, stretching his head upwards and taking in gulps, like a goldfish reaching to the surface of the fish bowl for food.

'Are you having a heart attack?' Doris shrieks.

Justin sighs, 'He's not having a—'

'Stop it, Al!' Justin is interrupted by a screeching Doris. 'Don't you dare have a heart attack, do you hear me?' She picks up a newspaper from the ground, starts hitting Al across the arm with each word. 'Don't. You. Dare. Even. *Think*. Of. Dying. Before. Me. Al. Hitchcock.'

'Ow,' he rubs his arm, 'that hurts.'

'Hey, hey, hey!' Justin breaks it up. 'Give me that paper, Doris.'

'No!'

'Where did you get it?' He tries to grab it out of her hands but she dodges him each time.

'It was just there, beside Al,' she shrugs. 'Paperboy delivered it.'

'They don't have paperboys around here,' he explains.

'Then I guess it's Al's.'

'There's a coffee to-go too,' Al, finally getting his breath back, manages to say.

'A coffee-to-WHAT?' Doris screeches so loudly, a window from the neighbour's flat upstairs is banged closed loudly. This does not deter Doris. 'You bought a coffee?' She begins spanking him again with the newspaper. 'No wonder you're dying!'

'Hey,' he crosses his arms over his body protectively, 'it's not mine. It was outside the door with the newspaper when I got here.'

'It's mine.' Justin snatches the paper from Doris's hands and the coffee to-go that is on the ground beside Al.

'There's no note attached.' She narrows her eyes and

looks from one brother to the other and back. 'Trying to defend your brother is only going to kill him in the long run, you know.'

'I might do it more often, then,' he grumbles, shaking the newspaper and hoping for a note to fall out. He checks the coffee cup for a message. Nothing. Yet he's sure it's for him and whoever left it there can't be long gone. He focuses then on the front page. Above the headline, in the corner of the page he notices the instruction, 'P. 42.'

He can't open it quick enough and battles with the oversized pages to get to the correct point. Finally he opens it up on the classified pages. He scans the advertisements and birthday greetings and is about to close the paper altogether and join Doris in blaming Al for feeding his caffeine habit, when he spots it.

> 'Eternally grateful recipient wishes to thank Justin Hitchcock, donor and hero, for saving life. Thank you.'

He holds his head back and howls with laughter. Doris and Al look at him with surprise.

'Al,' Justin lowers himself to his knees before his brother, 'I need you to help me now.' His voice is urgent, the pitch going up and down with excitement. 'Did you see anybody when you were jogging back to the house?'

'No.' Al's head rolls tiredly from one side to the other. 'I can't think.'

'Think.' Doris slaps his face lightly.

'That's not entirely necessary, Doris.'

'They do it in the movies when they're looking for information. Go on, tell him, baby.' She nudges him a little more lightly.

'I don't know,' Al whinges.

'You make me sick,' she growls in his ear.

'Honestly, Doris, that's really not helping.'

'Fine,' she folds her arms, 'but it works for Horatio.'

'By the time I got to the house, I couldn't breathe, let alone see. I don't remember anyone. Sorry, bro. Man,

I was so scared. All of these black dots were in front of my eyes and I just couldn't see any more, I was getting so dizzy and—'

'OK,' Justin leaps to his feet and runs up the stairs to the front yard. He runs to the drive entrance and looks up and down the street. It's busier now; at seven thirty there is more life as people leave their homes to head for work and the traffic noise level has picked up.

'THANK YOU!' Justin shouts at the top of his lungs, his voice breaking through the quiet. A few people turn around to look at him but most keep their heads down as a light drizzle of October London rain begins to fall while another man loses his mind on a Monday morning in the city.

'I CAN'T WAIT TO READ THIS!' He waves the newspaper around in the air, shouting up the road and down so that he can be heard from all angles.

What do you say to someone whose life you saved? Say something deep. Say something funny. Say something philosophical.

'I'M GLAD YOU'RE ALIVE!' he shouts.

'Eh, thanks.' A woman scurries past him with her head down.

'EM, I WON'T BE HERE TOMORROW!' Pause. 'IN CASE YOU'RE PLANNING ON DOING THIS AGAIN.' He lifts the coffee into the air and waves it around, sending droplets to jump from the small drinking hole and burn his hand. Still hot. Whoever it was, they weren't here that long ago.

'EM. GETTING THE FIRST FLIGHT TO DUBLIN TOMORROW MORNING. ARE YOU FROM THERE?' he shouts to the wind. The breeze sends more crispy autumn leaves parachuting from their branches to the ground, where they land running, make a tapping sound, and scrape along the ground until it's safe to stop.

'ANYWAY, THANKS AGAIN.' He waves the paper in the air and turns to face the house.

Doris and Al are standing at the top of the stairs,

their arms folded, their faces a picture of concern. Al has caught his breath and composed himself but is leaning against the iron railings for support.

Justin tucks the newspaper under his arm, straightens himself up and tries to appear as respectable as possible. He puts his hand in his pocket and strolls back towards the house. Feeling a piece of paper in his hand, he retrieves it and reads it quickly before crumpling it in his hand and tossing it into the skip. He has saved a person's life just as he thought; he must focus on the most important matter at hand. He makes his way to the flat, trying to appear as dignified as possible.

From the bottom of the skip, beneath rolls of old tired smelly carpets, crushed tiles, paint tubs and plaster board, I lie in the discarded bath tub and listen as the voices recede and the door to the flat finally closes.

A crumpled ball of paper has landed nearby and as I reach for it, my shoulder knocks over a two-legged stool, which toppled onto me in my rush to leap into the skip. I locate the paper and open it up, smoothing out the edges. My heart starts its rumba beat again as I see my first name, Dad's address and his phone number scrawled upon it.

32

'Where on earth have you been? What happened to you, Gracie?'

'Joyce,' is my response as I burst into the hotel room, breathless and covered in paint and dust. 'Don't have time to explain.' I rush around the room, throwing my clothes into my bag, taking a change of clothes and hurrying by Dad, who's sitting on the bed, in order to get to the bathroom.

'I tried calling you on your hand phone,' Dad calls to me.

'Yeah? I didn't hear it ring.' I struggle to squeeze into my jeans, hopping around on one foot while I pull them up and brush my teeth at the same time.

I hear his voice saying something. Mumbles but no words.

'Can't hear you, brushing my teeth!'

Silence while I finish and then back to the room and he continues as though we didn't have five minutes of silence.

'That's because when I called it, I heard it ringing here in the bedroom. It was on top of your pillow. Just like one of those chocolates the nice ladies here leave behind.'

'Oh. OK.' I jump over his legs to get to the dressing table and reapply my make-up.

'I was worried about you,' he says quietly.

'You needn't have been.' I hop around with one shoe on, while searching everywhere for the other.

'So I called downstairs to reception to see if they knew where you were.'

'Yeah?' I give up looking for my shoe and concentrate on inserting my earrings. My fingers are trembling with the adrenalin of the Justin situation and my fingers become too big for the task at hand. The back of one earring falls to the floor. I get down on my hands and knees to find it.

'So then I walked up and down the road, checking all of the shops that I know you like, asking all the people in them if they'd seen you.'

'You did?' I say, distracted, feeling carpet burns through my jeans as I shuffle around the floor on my knees.

'Yes,' he says quietly again.

'Aha! Got it!' I find it beside the bin below the dresser. 'Where the hell is my shoe?'

'And along the way,' Dad continues, and I hold back my aggravation, 'I met a policeman and I told him I was very worried, and he walked me back to the hotel and told me to wait here for you but to call this number if you didn't come back after twenty-four hours.'

'Oh, that was nice of him.' I open the wardrobe, still searching for my shoe, and find it still full of Dad's clothes. 'Dad!' I exclaim. 'You forgot your other suit. And your good jumper!'

I look at him, I realise for the first time since I entered the room, and only now notice how pale he looks. How old he looks in this new soulless hotel room. Perched at the edge of his single bed, he's dressed in his three-piece suit, cap beside him on the bed, his case packed or half-packed and sitting upright right beside him. In one hand is the photograph of Mum, in the other is the card the policeman gave him. The fingers that hold them tremble; his eyes are red and sore-looking.

'Dad,' I say as panic builds inside me, 'are you OK?'

'I was worried,' he repeats again in the tiny voice

I'd as good as ignored since I'd entered the room. He swallows hard. 'I didn't know where you were.'

'I was visiting a friend,' I say softly, joining him on the bed.

'Oh. Well, this friend here was worried.' He gives a small smile. A weak smile and I'm jolted by how fragile he appears. He looks like an old man. His usual attitude, his jovial nature is gone. His smile disappears quickly and his trembling hands, usually steady as a rock, force the photoframe of Mum and the card from the policeman back into his coat pocket.

I look at his bag. 'Did you pack that yourself?'

'Tried to. Thought I got everything.' He looks away from the open wardrobe, embarrassed.

'OK, well, let's take a look in it and see what we have.' I hear my voice and it startles me to hear myself speaking to him as though addressing a child.

'Aren't we running out of time?' he asks. His voice is so quiet, I feel I should lower mine so as not to break him.

'No,' my eyes fill with tears and I speak more forcefully than I intend, 'we have all the time in the world, Dad.'

I look away and distract those tears from falling by lifting his case onto the bed and trying to compose myself. Day-to-day things, the ordinary, the mundane is what keeps the motor running. How extraordinary the ordinary really is, a tool we all use to keep going, a template for sanity.

When I open the case I feel my composure slip again but I keep talking, sounding like a delusional 1960s suburban TV mother, repeating the hypnotic mantra that everything's just dandy and swell. I 'oh, gosh' and 'shucks' my way through his suitcase, which is a mess, though I shouldn't be surprised as Dad has never had to pack a suitcase in his life. I think what upsets me is the possibility that at seventy-five years old, after ten years without his wife, he simply doesn't know how to, or else my being missing for a few hours has prevented him from accomplishing it. A simple thing like that, my big-as-an-oak-tree, steady-as-a-rock father cannot do. Instead he sits on the edge of the bed twisting his cap around in his gnarled fingers, liver spots like the skin of a giraffe, his fingers trembling in air as though wobbling on an invisible fingerboard and controlling the vibrato in my head.

Things have attempted to be folded but have failed, are crumpled in small balls with no order at all as though they have been packed by a child. I find my shoe inside some bathroom towels. I take my shoe out and put it on my foot without saying anything, as though it's the most normal thing in the world. The towels go back to where they belong. I start folding and packing all over again. His dirty under-wear, socks, pyjamas, vests, his washbag. I turn my back to take his clothes from the wardrobe and I take a deep breath.

'We have all the time in the world, Dad,' I repeat. Though this time, it's for my own benefit.

On the tube, on the way to the airport, Dad keeps checking his watch and fidgeting in his seat. Every time the tube stops at a station, he pushes the seat in front of him impatiently as if to move it along himself.

'Have you to be somewhere?' I smile.

'The Monday Club. He looks at me with worried eyes. He's never missed a week, not even when I was in hospital.

'But today is Monday.'

He fidgets. 'I just don't want to miss this flight. We might get stuck over here.'

'Oh, I think we'll make it.' I do my best to hide my smile. 'And there's more than one flight a day, you know.'

'Good.' He looks relieved and even impressed. 'I might even make evening Mass. Oh, they won't believe everything I tell them tonight,' he says with excitement. 'Donal will drop dead when everybody listens to me and not to him for a change.' He settles back into his seat and watches out the window as the blackness of the underground speeds by. He stares into the black, not seeing his own reflection but seeing somewhere else and someone else a long way off, a long time ago. While he's in another world, or the same world but a different time, I take out my mobile and start planning my next move.

'Frankie, it's me. Justin Hitchcock is getting the first plane to Dublin tomorrow morning and I need to know what he's doing stat.'

'How am I supposed to do that, Dr Conway?'

'I thought you had ways.'

'You're right, I do. But I thought you were the psychic one.'

'I'm certainly not pyschic and I'm not getting anything about where he could be going.'

'Are your powers fading?'

'I don't have powers.'

'Whatever. Give me an hour, I'll get back to you.'

Two hours later, just as Dad and I are about to board, I receive a phone call from Frankie.

'He's going to be in the National Gallery tomorrow morning at ten thirty. He's giving a talk on a painting called *Woman Writing a Letter*. It sounds fascinating.'

'Oh, it is, it's one of Terborch's finest. In my opinion.'

Silence.

'You were being sarcastic, weren't you?' I realise. 'OK, well, does your Uncle Tom still run that company?' I smile mischievously and Dad looks at me curiously.

'What are you planning?' Dad asks suspiciously once I've hung up the phone.

'I'm having a little bit of fun.'

'Shouldn't you get back to work? It's been weeks now. Conor called your hand phone while you were gone this morning, it slipped my mind to tell you. He's in Japan but I could hear him very clearly,' he says, impressed with either Conor or the phone company, I'm not sure which. 'He wanted to know why the house hadn't got a For Sale sign in the garden yet. He said that you were supposed to do that.' He looks worried, as though I've broken a world-old rule and now the house will explode if it doesn't have a For Sale sign dug into the ground.

'Oh, I haven't forgotten.' I'm agitated by Conor's call. 'I'm selling it myself. I have my first viewing tomorrow.'

He looks unsure and he's right to because I'm lying through my teeth, but all I have to do is go through my books and call around my list of clients who I know to be looking for a similar property. I can think of a few straight away.

'Your company knows this?' His eyes narrow.

'Yes,' I smile tightly. 'They can take the photos and put the sign up in a matter of hours. I know a few people in the estate agent world.'

He rolls his eyes.

We both look away, in a huff, and just so I don't feel that I'm lying, while we shuffle along the queue to board the plane, I text a few clients I showed properties to before I took my leave to see if they're interested in a viewing. Then I ask my trusty photographer to take the shots of the house. Just as we take our seats on the plane, I have already arranged the photographs and For Sale sign for later today and a viewing appointment for tomorrow. Both teachers at the local school, she and her husband will view the house during their lunch break. At the bottom of the text is the mandatory 'Was so sorry to hear about what happened. Have been thinking of you. See you tomorrow, Linda xx.'

I delete it straight away.

Dad looks at my thumb working over the buttons on my phone with speed. 'You writing a book?'

I ignore him.

'You'll get arthritis in your thumb and it's not much fun, I can tell you that.'

I press send and switch the phone off.

'You really weren't lying about the house?' he asks.

'No,' I say, confidently now.

'Well, I didn't know that, did I? I didn't know what to tell him.'

Score one to me.

'That's OK, Dad, you don't have to feel in the middle of all this.'

'Well, I am.'

Score one to him.

'Well, you wouldn't have been if you hadn't answered *my* phone.'

Two one.

'You were missing all morning – what was I supposed to do, ignore it?'

Two all.

'He was concerned about you, you know. He thought you should see someone. A professional person.'

Off the charts.

'Did he now?' I fold my arms, wanting to call him straight away and rant about all the things I hate about him and that have always annoyed me. The cutting of his toenails in bed, his nose-blowing every morning that almost rattled the house, his inability to let people finish their sentences, his stupid party coin trick that I fake laughed to every time he did it, including the first, his inability to sit down and have an adult conversation about our problems, his constant walking away during our fights . . . Dad interrupts from my silent torture of Conor.

'He said you called him in the middle of the night, spurting Latin.'

'Really?' I feel anger surge. 'What did you say?'

He looks out the window as we pick up speed down the runway.

'I told him you made a fine fluent Italian-speaking Viking too.' I see his cheeks lift and I throw my head back and laugh.

All even.

He suddenly grabs my hand. 'Thanks for all this,

love. I had a great time.' He gives my hand a squeeze and goes back to looking out the window as the green of the fields surrounding the runway goes racing by.

He doesn't let go of my hand, so I rest my head on his shoulder and close my eyes.

33

Justin walks through arrivals at Dublin airport on Tuesday morning, with his cellphone glued to his ear, listening once again to the sound of Bea's voice mail. He sighs and rolls his eyes before the beep, beyond bored now with her childish behaviour.

'Hi, honey, it's me. Dad. Again. Listen, I know you're angry with me, and at your age everything is oh-so-very-dramatic, but if you'd just listen to what I have to say, the odds are you'll agree with me and thank me for it when you're old and grey. I only want the best for you and I will not hang up this phone until I have convinced you . . .' He immediately hangs up.

Behind the barricade at arrivals is a man in a dark suit holding a large white placard with Justin's surname written in large capitals. Underneath are those two magical words, 'THANK YOU'.

Those words had captured his attention on billboards, newspapers, radio adverts and television adverts all day and every day, since the first note arrived. Whenever the words drifted from the lips of a passer-by, he did a double take, following them as though hypnotised, as though in them was contained a special encrypted code just for him. Those words floated in the air like the scent of freshly cut grass on a summer's day; more than a smell, they carried with them a feeling, a place, a time of year, a happiness, a celebration of change, of moving on. They transport him just as the hearing of a special song familiar from youth does, when nostalgia, like the tide, sweeps in and catches you on the sand, pulling you in and under when you least expect it, often when you least want it.

Those words were constantly in his head, *thank you, thank you, thank you*. The more he heard them and reread the short notes, the more alien they became, as though he was seeing the sequence of those particular letters for the first time in his life – like music notes, so familiar, so simple, but arranged in a different way, become pure masterpieces.

This transformation of everyday common things to something magical, this growing understanding that what he perceived to be was not at all, reminded him of when he was a child and spent long silent moments staring at his face in the mirror. Standing on a foot-stool so that he could reach, the more intensely he stared, the more his face began to morph into one he was wholly unfamiliar with. It wasn't the face his mind had so stubbornly convinced him he had, but instead he saw the real him: eyes further apart than he'd thought, one eyelid lower than the other, one nostril also ever so slightly lower, the corner of one side of his mouth turning downward, as though there was a line going through the centre of his face and with the drawing of that line everything was dragged south, like a knife through sticky chocolate cake. The surface, once smooth, drooped and hung. A quick glimpse and it was unno-ticeable. Careful analysis, before brushing his teeth at night, revealed he wore the face of a stranger.

Now he takes a step back from those two words, circles them a few times and views them from all angles. Just as with paintings in a gallery, the words themselves dictate the height at which they should be displayed, the angle from which they should be approached and the position from which they should best be contem-plated. He has found the correct angle now. He can now see the weight they hold, like pigeons, *and* the messages they carry, oysters with their pearls, bees on dutious guard of their queen and honey, with their barbed stings attached. They have a sense of purpose, the strength of beauty and ammunition. Rather than a polite utterance heard a thousand times a day, 'Thank you' now has meaning.

Without another thought about Bea, he flips his phone closed and approaches the man holding the sign. 'Hello.'

'Mr Hitchcock?' The six-foot man's eyebrows are so dark and thick Justin can barely see his eyes.

'Yes,' he says suspiciously. 'Is this car for a *Justin* Hitchcock?'

The man consults a piece of paper in his pocket. 'Yes, it is, sir. Is that still you or does it change things?'

'Ye-es,' he says slowly, contemplatively. 'That's me.'

'You don't seem so sure,' the driver says, lowering the sign. 'Where are you going this morning?'

'Shouldn't you know that?'

'I do. But the last time I let somebody in my car as unsure as you, I delivered an animal rights activist directly into an IMFHA meeting.'

Unfamiliar with the initials, Justin asks, 'Is that bad?'

'The President of the Irish Masters of Fox Hounds Association thought so. He was stuck at the airport with no car, while the lunatic I collected was splashing red paint around the conference room. Let's just say, in terms of a tip for me, it was what the hounds would call a "blank day".'

'Well, I don't think the *hounds* would call it anything, necessarily,' Justin jokes, 'unless they go "Ooo-ooo".' He lifts his chin and howls into the air, playfully.

The driver stares at him blankly.

Justin's face flushes. 'Well, I'm going to the National Gallery.' Pause. 'I'm *pro* the National Gallery. I'm going to talk about painting, not turn people into canvases as a method of venting my frustration. Though if my ex-wife was in the audience I'd run at her with a paint brush,' he laughs, and the driver responds with another glare.

'I wasn't expecting anybody to greet me,' Justin yaps

at the chauffeur's heels, out of the airport into the grey October day. 'Nobody at the Gallery informed me you'd be here,' he tests him as they hurry across the pedestrian walkway through the parachuting raindrops, which pull on their emergency cords as they plummet towards Justin's head and shoulders.

'I didn't know about the job until late last night when I got a call. I was supposed to be going to my wife's aunt's funeral today.' He roots around his pockets for the car parking ticket and slides it into the machine to validate it.

'Oh, I'm sorry to hear that.' Justin stops wiping away the raindrop parachuting casualties that have landed with a shplat on the shoulders of his brown corduroy jacket, and looks at the driver grimly, out of respect.

'So was I. I hate funerals.'

Curious response. 'Well, you wouldn't be alone in thinking that.'

He stops walking and turns to face Justin with a look of intense seriousness on his face. 'They always give me the giggles,' he says. 'Does that ever happen to you?'

Justin is unsure whether to take him seriously or not but the driver doesn't crack even the slightest smile. Justin pictures his father's funeral, goes back to when he was nine years old. The two families huddled together at the graveyard, all dressed head to toe in black like dung beetles around the dirty open hole in the ground where the casket was placed. His dad's family had flown over from Ireland, bringing with them the rain, which was unconventional for Chicago's hot summer. They stood beneath umbrellas, he close to his Aunt Emelda, who held the umbrella in one hand and another tightly on his shoulder, Al and his mother beside him under another umbrella. Al had brought along a fire engine, which he played with while the priest talked about their father's life. This annoyed Justin. In fact, everything and everybody annoyed Justin that day.

He hated Aunt Emelda's hand being there on his

shoulder, though he knew she was trying to be helpful. It felt heavy and tight, as though she was holding him back, afraid he'd escape from her, afraid he'd scuttle into the big hole in the ground where his father was going.

He'd greeted her that morning, dressed in his best suit, as his mother had requested in her new quiet voice, which Justin had to put his ear to her lips to hear. Aunt Emelda had pretended to be psychic just as she always did when they met one another after their long stints apart.

'I know just what you want, little soldier,' she'd said in her strong Cork accent, which Justin could barely understand and was never sure whether she'd just broken into a song or was speaking to him. She'd rummaged in her oversized handbag and dug out a soldier with a plastic smile and a plastic salute, quickly peeling off the price, and with it ripping off the soldier's name before handing it to him. Justin stared down at Colonel Blank, who saluted him with one hand and held a plastic gun in the other, and immediately mistrusted him. The blank-shooting plastic gun got lost in the heavy pile of black coats by the front door as soon as he'd pulled open the packet. As usual, Aunt Emelda's psychic powers had been tuned into the desires of the wrong nine-year-old boy, for Justin had not wanted this plastic soldier on this day of all days, and he couldn't help but imagine a young boy across town waiting for a plastic soldier for his birthday and instead being handed Justin's father by the tuft of his jet-black hair. However, he accepted her thoughtful gift with a smile as big and sincere as Colonel Blank's. Later that day, as he stood beside the hole in the ground, maybe for once Aunt Emelda could read his mind as her hand gripped him tighter and her nails dug into his bony shoulders as though holding him back. For Justin had thought about jumping into that damp dark hole.

He thought about what it would be like in the world down there. If he could escape the strong hand of his

Corkonian aunt and leap into the hole before anybody could catch him, maybe when the ground was closed over on top of them, like a grass carpet being rolled over, they would both be together. He wondered if they would have their own cosy world under the ground. He could have him all to himself, without having to share him with Mom or Al, and there they could play and laugh together, where it was darker. Maybe Dad just didn't like the light; maybe all he wanted was for the light to go away so that it wouldn't make his eyes squint and his fair skin burn and freckle and itch, as it always did when the sun came out. When that hot sun was in the sky it annoyed his dad, and he would have to sit in the shade while he and his mom and Al would play outside, Mom getting browner and browner by the day, his dad getting paler and more irritated by the heat. Maybe a break from the summer was all he wanted; for the itch and the frustration of light to go away.

As his casket was lowered into the hole, his mother let out howls that made Al cry too. Justin knew that Al wasn't crying because he missed his dad, he was crying because he was scared of Mom's reaction. She started crying when his grandma, his father's mother's sniffles became loud wails, and when Al started crying it broke the hearts of the entire congregation to see the young child left behind in tears. Even Dad's brother, Seamus, who always looked like he wanted to laugh, had a trembling lip and a vein that jutted out of his neck like a body-builder, which made Justin think there was another person inside Uncle Seamus, just bursting to get out if Uncle Seamus would let him.

People should never start crying. Because if they start . . . Justin felt like shouting out for them all to stop being so stupid; that Al wasn't crying because of his dad. He wanted to tell them that Al had little idea of what was really going on. He'd been concentrating on his fire engine all day and occasionally looking to Justin with a face so full of questions that he had to keep turning away.

There were men in suits that carried his dad's casket to this place. Men that weren't his uncles or his dad's friends. They weren't crying like everyone else, but they weren't smiling either. They didn't look bored but they didn't look interested. They looked as though they had been to Dad's funeral a hundred times already and they didn't care so much that he had died again but also didn't mind having to make another hole, carry him again and bury him again. He watched as the men with no smiles threw handfuls of soil onto the coffin, making drumming sounds against the wood. He wondered if that would wake his dad up from his summer slumber. He didn't cry like everyone else because he felt assured that Dad had finally escaped the light. His dad would no longer have to sit alone in the shade.

Justin realises the driver is staring at him intently. His head moves in close as though he's awaiting the answer to a very personal question concerning a rash and whether Justin has ever had one too.

'No,' Justin says quietly, clearing his throat and adjusting his eyes to the world of thirty-five years later. Time travel of the mind; a powerful thing.

'That's us over there.' The driver presses the button on his keys and the lights of an S-class Mercedes light up.

Justin's mouth drops. 'Do you know who organised this?'

'No idea.' The driver holds the door open for him. 'I just take the orders from my boss. Thought it was unusual having to write "Thank You" on the sign. Does that make sense to you?'

'Yes, it does but . . . it's complicated. Could you find out from your boss who's paying for this?' Justin sits into the back seat of the car, places his briefcase on the floor beside him.

'I could try.'

'That would be great.' *I'll have gotcha then!* Justin relaxes into the leather chair, stretches his legs out fully and closes his eyes, barely able to hold back his smile.

'I'm Thomas, by the way,' the driver introduces himself. 'I'm here for you all day so wherever you want to go after this, just let me know.'

'For the entire day?' Justin almost chokes on his free bottle of chilled water, which was waiting for him in the hand rest. He saved a rich person's life. Yes! He should have mentioned more to Bea than muffins and daily newspapers. A villa in the South of France. What an idiot he was not to have thought more quickly.

'Would your company not have organised this for you?' Thomas asks.

'No.' Justin shakes his head. 'Definitely not.'

'Maybe you've a fairy godmother you don't know about,' Thomas says, deadpan.

'Well, let's see what this pumpkin's made of,' Justin laughs.

'Won't get to test it in this traffic,' Thomas says, braking as they enter Dublin traffic, worsened by the grey rainy morning.

Justin presses the button on the door for heated seats and reclines as he feels his back and behind warming. He kicks off his shoes, reclines his chair and relaxes in comfort as he watches the miserable faces of those in buses glaring sleepily out of the fogged-up windows.

'After the Gallery, do you mind bringing me to D'Olier Street? I need to visit somebody in the blood donor clinic.'

'No problem, boss.'

The October gust huffs and puffs and attempts to blow the last of the leaves off the nearby trees. They hang on tight, like the nannies in *Mary Poppins*, who cling to the lampposts of Cherry Tree Lane in a desperate attempt to prevent their airborne competition from blowing them away from the big Banks job interview. The leaves, like many people this autumn, are not yet ready to let go. They cling on tight to yesterday, unable to have controlled their change in colour but, by God, putting up a fight before giving up the place that has been their home for two seasons. I watch as one leaf lets go, dances around in the air before falling to the ground. I pick it up and slowly twirl it around by its stalk in my hand. I'm not fond of autumn. Not fond of watching things so sturdy wither as they lose against nature, the higher power they can't control.

'Here comes the car,' I comment to Kate.

We're standing across the main road from the National Gallery, behind the parked cars, shaded by the trees rising above and over the gates of Merrion Square.

'You paid for *that*?' Kate says. 'You really are nuts.'

'Tell me something I don't know. Actually, I paid half. That's Frankie's uncle driving – he runs the company. Pretend you don't know him if he looks over.'

'I don't know him.'

'Good, that's convincing.'

'Joyce, I have never seen that man in my life.'

'Wow, that's *really* good.'

'How long are you going to keep this up, Joyce? The London thing sounded fun but really, all we know is that he donated blood.'

'To me.'

'We don't know that.'

'I know that.'

'You can't know that.'

'I can. That's the funny thing.'

She looks doubtful and stares at me with such a look of pity, it makes my blood boil.

'Kate, yesterday I had carpaccio and fennel for my dinner, and I spent the evening singing along to practically all the words of Pavarotti's *Ultimate Collection*.'

'I still don't understand how you think that it's this Justin Hitchcock man that's responsible for it. Remember that film *Phenomenon*? John Travolta just suddenly became a genius overnight.'

'He had a brain tumour that somehow increased his ability to learn,' I snap.

The Mercedes pulls up by the gates of the Gallery. The driver gets out of the car to open the door for Justin and he emerges, briefcase in hand, a beam from ear to ear, and I'm happy to see that next month's mortgage payment has gone to good use. I shall worry about that, and everything else in my life, when the time comes.

He still has the aura I felt from the day I first laid my eyes on him in the hair salon – a presence that makes my stomach walk a few flights of stairs and then climb the final ladder to the ten-metre diving platform at the Olympics final. He looks up at the Gallery, around at the park, and with that strong jawline he smiles, a smile that causes my stomach to do one bounce, two bounce, three bounce, before attempting the toughest dive of all, a reverse one-point-five somersault and then one, two, three and a half twists before entering the water, with a belly flop. My unsophisticated entry into the water shows I am not a seasoned nervous wreck. The dive, while terrifying, was quite pleasant and I'm open to taking those steps again.

The leaves around me rustle as another soft breeze blows and I'm not sure if I imagine that it carries to me the smell of his aftershave, the same scent as from the hair salon. I have a brief flash of him picking up a parcel wrapped in emerald-green paper, which sparkles under Christmas tree lights and surrounding candles. It's tied with a large red bow and my hands are momentarily his as he unties it slowly, carefully peels back the tape from the paper, taking care not to rip it. I am struck by his tenderness for the package, which has been lovingly wrapped, until his thoughts are momentarily mine and I am in on his plans to pocket the paper and use it on the unwrapped presents he has sitting out in the car. Inside is a bottle of aftershave and a shaving set. A Christmas gift from Bea.

'He's handsome,' Kate whispers. 'I support your stalking campaign one hundred per cent, Joyce.'

'It's not a stalking campaign,' I hiss, 'and I'd have done this if he was ugly.'

'Can I go in and listen to his talk?' Kate asks.

'No!'

'Why not? He's never seen me; he won't recognise me. Please, Joyce, my best friend believes she is connected to a complete stranger. At least I can go and listen to him to see what he's like.'

'What about Sam?'

'Do you want to mind him for a little while?'

I freeze.

'Oh, forget that,' she says quickly. 'I'll bring him in with me. I'll stay down the back and leave if he disturbs anyone.'

'No, no, it's OK. I can mind him.' I swallow and paste a smile on my face.

'Are you sure?' She looks unconvinced. 'I won't stay for the entire thing. I just want to see what he's like.'

'I'll be fine. Go.' I push her away gently. 'Go in and enjoy yourself. We'll be fine here, won't we?'

Sam puts his socked toe in his mouth in response.

'I promise I won't be long.' Kate leans into the stroller, gives her son a kiss and dashes across the road and into the Gallery.

'So . . .' I look around nervously. 'It's just you and me, Sean.'

He looks at me with his big blue eyes and mine instantly fill.

I look around to make sure nobody has heard me. I mean Sam.

Justin takes his place at the podium in the lecture hall in the basement of the National Gallery. A packed room of faces stares back at him and he is in his element. A late arrival, a young woman, enters the room, apologises and quickly takes a place among the crowd.

'Good morning, ladies and gentlemen, and thank you so much for making it here on this rainy morning. I am here to talk about this painting. *Woman Writing a Letter*, by Terborch, a Dutch Baroque artist from the seventeenth century who was largely responsible for the popularisation of the letter theme. This painting – well, not this painting alone – this genre of letter-writing is a personal favourite of mine, particularly when in this current age it seems a personal letter has almost become extinct.' He stops.

Almost but not quite, for there's somebody sending me notes.

He steps away from the podium, takes one step towards the audience and looks at the crowd, suspicion written upon his face. His eyes narrow as he studies his audience. He scans the rows, knowing that somebody here could be the mystery note-writer.

Somebody coughs, snapping him out of his trance, and he is back with them again. He is mildly flustered but continues where he left off.

'In an age when a personal letter has almost become extinct, this is a reminder of how the great masters of the Golden Age depicted the subtle range of human emotions affected by such a seemingly simple aspect of daily life. Terborch was not the only artist responsible for these images. I cannot go further on this subject without paying lip-service to Vermeer, Metsu and de Hooch, who all produced paintings of people reading, writing, receiving and dispatching letters, which I have written about in my book *The Golden Age of Dutch Painting: Vermeer, Metsu and Terborch*. Terborch's paintings use letter-writing as a pivot on which to turn complex psychological dramas and his are among the first works to link lovers through the theme of a letter.'

He studies the woman who arrived a little late as he says half of this and another young woman behind her for the second half, wondering if they are reading deeper into his words. He almost laughs aloud at himself at his assumption that, first, the person whose life he saved would be in this room; secondly, that it would be a young woman; and thirdly, attractive. Which makes him ask himself what exactly was he hoping to come out of this current drama?

I push Sam's stroller into Merrion Square, and we're instantly transported from the Georgian centre of the city to another world, shaded by mature trees and surrounded by colour. Burned oranges, reds and yellows of the autumn foliage litter the ground and, with each gentle breeze, hop alongside us like inquisitive robin redbreasts. I choose a bench along the quiet walk and turn Sam's stroller around so that he faces me. In the trees bordering the walk I hear twigs snapping as homes are being constructed and lunch prepared.

I watch Sam for a while, as he strains his neck to see the remaining leaves that refuse to surrender their branch, far above him. He points a tiny finger up at the sky and makes sounds.

'Tree,' I tell him, which makes him smile, and his mother is instantly recognisable.

The vision has the same effect as a boot hitting my stomach. I take a moment to catch my breath.

'Sam, while we're here we should really discuss something,' I say.

His smile widens.

'I have to apologise for something,' I clear my throat. 'I haven't been paying much attention to you lately, have I? The thing is . . .' I trail off and wait until a man has passed us by to continue. 'The thing is,' I lower my voice, 'I couldn't bear to look at you . . .' I trail off as his grin widens.

'Oh, here.' I lean over, remove his blanket and press the button to release his safety straps. 'Come up here to me.' I lift him out of the buggy and sit him on my lap. His body is warm and I hug him close. I breathe in the top of his head, candy, his wispy hairs so silky like velvet, his body so chubby and soft in my arms, I want to squeeze him tighter. 'The thing is,' I say quietly to the top of his head, 'it broke my heart to look at you, to cuddle you like I used to, because each time I saw you, I remembered what I'd lost.' He looks up at me and babbles in response. 'Though how could I ever be afraid to look at you?' I kiss his nose. 'I shouldn't have taken it out on you but you're not mine, and that's so hard.' My eyes fill and I let the tears fall. 'I wanted to have a little boy or girl so that just like when you smile, people could say, oh look, you're the picture of your mummy, or maybe that the baby would have my nose or my eyes because that's what people say to me. They say I look like my mum. And I love hearing that, Sam, I really do, because I miss her and I want to be reminded of her every single day. But looking at you was different. I didn't want to be reminded I'd lost my baby every single day.'

'Ba-ba,' he says.

I sniffle. 'Ba-ba gone, Sam. Sean for a boy, Grace for a girl.' I wipe my nose.

Sam, uninterested in my tears, looks away and studies a bird. He points a chubby finger again.

'Bird,' I say through my tears.

'Ba-ba,' he responds.

I smile and wipe my eyes as yet more stream down.

'But there's no Sean or Grace now.' I hug him tighter and let my tears fall, knowing that Sam won't be able to report my weeping to anybody.

The bird hops a few inches and then takes off, disappearing into the sky.

'Ba-ba gone,' Sam says, holding his hands out, palms up.

I watch it fly into the distance, still visible like a speck of dust against the pale blue sky. My tears stop. 'Ba-ba gone,' I repeat.

'What do we see in this painting?' Justin asks.

Silence as everyone views the projected image.

'Well, let us state the obvious first. A young woman sits at a table in a quiet interior. She is writing a letter. We see a quill moving across a sheet of paper. We do not know what she is writing but her soft smile suggests she is writing to a loved one or perhaps a lover. Her head tilts forward, exposing the elegant curve of her neck . . .'

While Sam is back in his buggy, drawing circles on paper with his blue crayon, or more likely, banging out dots on the paper, sending wax shrapnel all over his buggy, I produce my own pen and paper from my bag. I take my calligraphy pen in my hand and imagine I'm hearing Justin's words from across the road. I don't need to see the work of the *Woman Writing a Letter* on the canvas for it has been painted in my mind after Justin's years of intensive study during college and again during research for his book. I begin to write.

As part of a mother/daughter bonding activity when I was seventeen years old, during my goth phase, when I had dyed black hair, a white face and red lips that were victim to a lip-piercing, Mum enrolled us both in a calligraphy class at the local primary school. Every Wednesday at seven p.m.

Mum read in a rather new-age book that Dad didn't agree with that through partaking in activities with your children they would more easily, and of their own accord, open up and share things about their lives, rather than being forced to in a face-to-face, formal and almost interrogative-style sit-down, which Dad was more accustomed to.

The classes worked and, though I moaned and groaned when learning this uncool task, I opened up and told her all. Well, almost all. The rest she had the intuition to guess. I came away with a deeper love, respect and understanding of my mother as a person, a woman and not just as a mum. I also came away with a skill in calligraphy.

I find that when I put pen to paper and get into the rhythm of quick upward flicks, just as we were taught, it takes me back to those classes, transports me to those classrooms where I sat with my mother.

I hear her voice, I smell her scent and I replay our conversations, sometimes awkward as, because I'm seventeen, we dance around the personal, but we talk about it in our own way, finding a way of getting to the point in spite of that. It was a perfect activity for her to choose for me at seventeen, better than she ever knew. Calligraphy had rhythm, roots in Gothic style, it

was written in the vigour of the moment and it had
attitude. A uniform style of writing, but one that was
unique. A lesson to teach me that conformity may not
quite mean what I once thought that it had meant, for
there are many ways to express oneself in a world with
boundaries, without overstepping them.

Suddenly I look up from my page. 'Trompe l'oeil,' I
say aloud with a smile.

Sam looks up from his crayon banging and regards
me with interest.

'What does that mean?' Kate asks.

'Trompe l'oeil is an art technique involving extremely
realistic imagery in order to create the optical illusion
that the depicted objects really exist, instead of being
two-dimensional painting. It's derived from French,
trompe meaning "trick" and *l'oeil* meaning "eye",'
Justin tells the room. 'Trick the eye,' he repeats, looking
around at all the faces in the crowd.

Where are you?

34

'So how did that go?' Thomas the driver asks as Justin gets back into the car after his talk.

'I saw you standing at the back of the room. You tell me.'

'Well, I don't know much about art but you certainly knew how to talk a lot about one girl writing a letter.'

Justin smiles and reaches for another free bottle of water. He's not thirsty but it's there, and it's free.

'Were you looking for somebody?' Thomas asks.

'What do you mean?'

'In the crowd. I noticed you looking around a few times. A woman, is it?' he grins.

Justin smiles, and shakes his head. 'I have no idea. You'd think I was crazy if I told you.'

'So, what do you think?' I ask Kate as we walk around Merrion Square and she fills me in on Justin's lecture.

'What do I think?' she repeats, strolling slowly behind Sam's buggy. 'I think that it doesn't matter if he ate carpaccio and fennel yesterday because he seems like a lovely man anyway. I think that no matter what your reasons are for feeling connected to him or attracted to him, they're not important. You should stop all this running around and just introduce yourself.'

I shake my head. 'No can do.'

'Why not? He seemed to be interested when he was chasing your bus down the road, and when he saw you at the ballet. What's changed now?'

'He doesn't want anything to do with me.'

'How do you know that?'

'I know.'

'*How?* And don't tell me it's because of some mumbo-jumbo thing you saw in your tea leaves.'

'I drink coffee now.'

'You hate coffee.'

'*He* obviously doesn't.'

She does her best not to be negative but looks away.

'He's too busy looking for the woman whose life he saved; he's no longer interested in me. He had my contact details, Kate, and he never called. Not once. In fact, he went so far as to throw them in a skip, and don't ask me how I know that.'

'Knowing you, you were probably lying in the bottom of it.'

I keep tight-lipped.

Kate sighs. 'How long are you going to keep this up?'

I shrug. 'Not much longer.'

'What about work? What about Conor?'

'Conor and I are done. There's nothing more to say. Four years of separation and then we'll be divorced. As for work, I've already told them I'm going back next week – my diary is already full with appointments – and as for the house – shit!' I pull up my sleeve to find my watch. 'I have to get back. I'm showing the house in an hour.'

A quick kiss and I run for the nearest bus home.

'OK, this is it.' Justin stares out of the car window and up to the second floor, which houses the blood donor clinic.

'You're donating blood?' Thomas asks.

'No way. I'm just paying somebody a visit. I shouldn't be too long. If you see any police cars coming, start the engine.' He smiles, but it is unconvincing.

He nervously asks for Sarah at reception and is told to wait in the waiting room. Around him men and women on their lunch breaks from work sit in their suits and read the newspapers, waiting to be called for their blood donations.

He inches closer to the woman beside him, who's flicking through a magazine. He leans over her shoulder and as he whispers, she jumps.

'Are you sure you want to do this?'

Everyone in the room lowers their papers and magazines to stare at him. He coughs and looks away, pretending somebody else said it. On the walls around him are posters encouraging those in the room to donate, and there are also thank you posters of young children, survivors of leukaemia and other illnesses. He has already waited half an hour and checks his watch every minute, conscious he has a plane to catch. When the last person leaves him alone in the room, Sarah appears at the door.

'Justin.' She isn't icy, she isn't tough or angry. Quiet. Hurt. That's worse. He'd rather she was angry.

'Sarah.' He stands to greet her, is locked in an awkward half-embrace and a kiss on one cheek, which turns into two, a questionable third but is aborted and almost becomes a kiss on the lips. She pulls away, ending the farcical greeting.

'I can't stay long, I have to get to the airport for a flight, but I wanted to call by and see you face to face. Can we talk for a few minutes?'

'Yes, sure.' She enters the reception and sits down, arms still folded.

'Oh.' He looks around. 'Don't you have an office, or something?'

'This is nice and quiet.'

'Where is your office?'

Her eyes narrow with suspicion and he gives up that particular line of questioning and quickly takes a seat beside her.

'I'm here, really, to apologise for my behaviour the last time we met. Well, every time we met and every moment after that. I really am sorry.'

She nods, waiting for more.

Damn it, that's all I had! Think, think. You're sorry and . . .

'I didn't mean to hurt you. I got very distracted that day with those crazy Vikings. In fact, you could say I've been distracted by crazy Vikings almost every day for the last month or two and, uh . . .' *Think!* 'Could I go to the men's room? If you wouldn't mind. Please.'

She looks a little taken aback but directs him. 'Sure, it's straight down the hall at the end.'

Standing outside, which has a newly hammered 'For Sale' sign attached to the front wall, Linda and her husband, Joe, are pressing their faces up against the window and gawking into the living room. A protective feeling comes over me. Then as soon as it comes, it vanishes. Home is not a place – not this place, anyway.

'Joyce? Is that you?' Linda slowly lowers her sunglasses.

I give them a big wobbly smile, reaching into my pocket for the bunch of keys, which is already minus my car keys and furry ladybird that used to be on Mum's set. Even the set of keys have lost their heart, their playfulness; all they have now is their function.

'Your hair, you look so different.'

'Hi, Linda. Hi, Joe.' I hold out my hand to greet them.

Linda has other plans and reaches out to offer me a huge, tight hug.

'Oh, I'm so sorry for you.' She squeezes me. 'Poor you.'

A nice gesture, if perhaps I'd known her a bit longer than to show her three houses over a month ago, and even then she'd done the same with her hands on my practically flat stomach on learning I was pregnant. My body suddenly becoming everybody else's property, I'd found entirely annoying during my only month of being able to talk about it.

She lowers her voice to a whisper. 'Did they do that at the hospital?' She eyes my hair.

'Eh, no.' I laugh. 'They did that at the hair salon,' I chirp, my usual Lady of Trauma coming back to save the day. I turn the key in the door and allow them to enter first.

'Oh,' she breathes excitedly, and her husband smiles and takes her hand. I have a flashback of Conor and me ten years ago, coming to view the house, which had just been deserted by an old lady who had lived alone for the previous twenty years. I follow my younger self and him into the house and suddenly they are real and I am the ghost, remembering what we saw and listening to our conversation, replaying the moment again.

It had reeked inside, had old carpets, creaking floors, rotting windows and wallpaper that was so old it had just gone out of fashion for the third time round. It was disgusting and a money pit, and we loved it as soon as we stood where Linda and her husband stand right now.

We had it all ahead of us back then, when Conor was the Conor I loved and I was the old me; a perfect match. Then Conor became who he is now and I became the Joyce he no longer loved. As the house became more beautiful, our relationship became uglier. We could have lain on a cat-hair-infested rug on our first night in our home back then and would have been happy, but then every minute detail of what was wrong in our marriage we attempted to fix by getting a new couch, repairing the doors, replacing the draughty windows. If only we'd put that much time and concentration into ourselves; self-improvement rather than home improvement. Neither of us thought to fix the draught in our marriage. It whistled through the growing cracks while neither of us was paying attention until we both woke up one morning with cold feet.

'I'll show you around downstairs, but, em,' I look up at the nursery door, no longer vibrating as it had when I first returned home. It is just a door, quiet and still. Doing what a door does. Nothing. 'I'll let you wander around upstairs by yourselves.'

'Are the owners still living here?' Linda asks.

I look around. 'No. No, they're long gone.'

As Justin makes his way down the hall to the toilet, he examines each of the names on the doors, looking for Sarah's office. He has no idea where to start but maybe if he can find the folder that deals with blood taken from Trinity College in early autumn, then he'll be closer to finding out.

He sees her name on the door, raps on it gently. When he hears no response he enters and closes it quietly behind him. He looks around quickly, piles of folders on the shelves. He runs immediately to the filing cabinets and starts rifling through them. Moments later the door knob turns. He drops the file back into the cabinet, turns towards the door and freezes. Sarah looks at him, shocked.

'Justin?'

'Sarah?'

'What are you doing in my office?'

You're an educated man, think of something smart.

'I took a wrong turn.'

She folds her arms. 'Why don't you tell me the truth now?'

'I was on my way back and I saw your name on the door and I thought I'd come in and have a look around, see what your office is like. I have this thing, you see, where I believe that an office really represents what a person is like and I thought that if we're to have a future tog—'

'We're not going to have a future.'

'Oh. I see. But if we *were* to—'

'No.'

He scans her desk and his eyes fall upon a photograph of Sarah with her arms around a young blonde girl and a man. They pose happily together on a beach.

Sarah follows his gaze.

'That's my daughter, Molly.' She tightens her lips then, angry at herself for saying anything.

'You have a daughter?' He reaches for the frame, pauses before touching it and looks to her for permission first.

She nods, lips loosening, and he takes it in his hands. 'She's beautiful.'

'She is.'

'How old is she?'

'Six.'

'I didn't know you had a daughter.'

'You don't know a lot of things about me. You never stuck around long enough on our dates to talk about anything that wasn't about you.'

Justin cringes, his heart falls. 'Sarah, I'm so sorry.'

'So you said, so sincerely, right before you came into my office and started rooting around.'

'I wasn't rooting—'

Her look is enough to stop himself from telling another lie. She takes the photo frame from his hands, gently. Nothing about her is rough or aggressive. She is filled with disappointment; not for the first time an idiot like Justin has let her down.

'The man in the photo?'

She looks sad as she studies it and then places it back on the table.

'I would have been happy to tell you about him before,' she says softly. 'In fact, I remember trying to on at least two occasions.'

'I'm sorry,' he repeats, feeling so small he almost can't see over her desk. 'I'm listening now.'

'And I'm sure I remember you telling me you had a flight to catch,' she says.

'Right,' he nods, and makes his way to the door. 'I am so truly, very, very sorry. I am hugely embarrassed and disappointed in myself.' And he realises he actually means it from the bottom of his heart. 'I am going through some strange things at the moment.'

'Find me someone who isn't. We all have crap to deal with, Justin. Just please do not drag me into yours.'

'Right.' He nods again and offers another apologetic, embarrassed smile before exiting her office, rushing down the stairs and into the car, feeling two foot tall.

35

'What's that?'

'I don't know.'

'Just give it a wipe.'

'No, you do.'

'Have you seen something like that before?'

'Yeah, maybe.'

'What do you mean, maybe? You either have or you haven't.'

'Don't get smart with me.'

'I'm not, I'm just trying to figure it out. Do you think it will come off?'

'I've no idea. Let's ask Joyce.'

I hear Linda and Joe mumbling together in the hallway. I've left them to their own devices and have been standing in the galley kitchen, drinking a black coffee and staring out at my mother's rose bush at the back of the garden and seeing the ghosts of Joyce and Conor sunbathing on the grass during a hot summer with the radio blaring.

'Joyce, could we show you something for a moment?'

'Sure.'

I put the coffee cup down, pass the ghost of Conor making his lasagne specialty in the kitchen, pass the ghost of Joyce sitting in her favourite armchair in her pyjamas, eating a Mars bar, and make my way to the hall. They are on their hands and knees examining the stain by the stairs. My stain.

'I think it might be wine,' Joe says, looking up at

me. 'Did the owners say anything about the stain?'

'Eh . . .' My legs wobble slightly and for a moment I think my knees are going to go. I lean out to hold on to the banister and pretend to lean down and look at it more closely. I close my eyes. 'It's been cleaned a few times already, as far as I know. Would you be interested in keeping the carpet?'

Linda makes a face while she thinks, looks up and down the stairs, through the house, examining my choice of décor with a ruffled nose. 'No, I suppose not. I think wooden floors would be lovely. Don't you?' she asks Joe.

'Yeah,' he nods. 'A nice pale oak.'

'Yeah,' she agrees. 'No, I don't think we'd keep this carpet.' She turns her nose up again.

I haven't intended to keep the owners' details from them deliberately – there's no point as they'll see it on the contract anyway. I had assumed they knew that the property was mine, but it was their misunderstanding, and as they poked holes in the decorations, the choice of room layout, and funny noises and smells they weren't used to but that I had stopped noticing by now, I didn't think it would be necessary to make them uncomfortable by pointing it out now.

'You seem keen,' I smile, watching their faces aglow with warmth and excitement at finally finding a property they felt at home in.

'We are,' she grins. 'We have been so fussy up till now, as you well know. But now the situation has changed and we need to get out of that flat and find somewhere bigger as soon as we can, seeing as we're expanding, or I'm expanding,' she jokes nervously, and it's only then that I notice her small bump beneath her shirt, her belly button hard and protruding against the fabric.

'Oh, wow . . .' Lump to throat, wobble of knees again, eyes fill, please let this moment be over quickly, please make them look away from me. They have tact and so they do. 'That's fantastic, congratulations,' my voice says cheerily, and even I can hear how hollow it is, so devoid of sincerity, the empty words almost echo within themselves.

'So that room upstairs would be perfect.' Joe nods to the nursery.

'Oh, of course, that's just wonderful.' The 1960s surbuban housewife is back as I gosh, gee-whizz and shucks my way through the rest of the conversation.

'I can't believe they don't want any of the furniture,' Linda says, looking around.

'Well, they're both moving to smaller property and their belongings just won't fit there any more.'

'But they're not taking *anything*?'

'No,' I smile, looking around. 'Nothing but the rose bush in the back garden.'

And a suitcase of memories.

Justin falls into the car with a giant sigh.

'What happened to you?'

'Nothing. Could you just drive directly to the airport now, please? I'm a little behind time.' Justin places his elbow on the windowledge and covers his face with his hand, hating himself, hating the selfish miserable man he has become. He and Sarah weren't right for one another but what right had he to use her like that, to bring her down with him into his pit of desperation and selfishness?

'I've got something that will cheer you up,' Thomas says, reaching for the glove compartment.

'No, I'm really not in the—' Justin stops, seeing Thomas retrieve a familiar envelope from the compartment. He hands it over to him.

'Where did you get this?'

'My boss called me, told me to give it to you before you got to the airport.'

'Your boss.' Justin narrows his eyes. 'What's his name?'

Thomas is silent for a while. 'John,' he finally replies.

'John Smith?' Justin says, his voice thick with sarcasm.

'The very man.'

Knowing he'll squeeze no information from Thomas, he turns his attention back to the envelope. He circles it slowly in his hand, trying to decide whether to open it or not. He could leave it unopened and end all of this now, get his life back in order, stop trying to use people, take advantage. Meet a nice woman, treat her well.

'Well? Aren't you going to open it?' Thomas asks.

Justin continues to circle it in his hand.

'Maybe.'

Dad opens the door to me, his iPod in his ears, the control pad in his hand. He looks my outfit up and down.

'OOH, YOU LOOK VERY NICE TODAY, GRACIE,' he shouts at the top of his voice, and a man walking his dog across the road turns to stare. 'WERE YOU OUT SOMEWHERE SPECIAL?'

I smile. Light relief at last. I put my finger on my lips and take the earphones out of his ears.

'I was showing the house to some clients of mine.'

'Did they like it?'

'They're going to come back in a few days to measure. So that's a good sign. But being back over there, I realised there are so many things that I have to go through.'

'Haven't you been through enough? You don't need to sob for weeks just to make yourself feel OK about it.'

I smile. 'I mean that I have to go through *possessions*. Things I've left behind. I don't think they want a lot of the furniture. Would it be OK if I stored it in your garage?'

'My woodwork studio?'

'That you haven't been in for ten years.'

'I've been in there,' he says defensively. 'Oh, all right then, you can put your things in there. Will I ever get rid of you at all, at all?' he says with a slight smile on his face.

I sit at the kitchen table and Dad immediately busies himself, filling the kettle as he does for everyone who enters the kitchen.

'So how did the Monday Club go last night? I bet Donal McCarthy couldn't believe your story. What was his face like?' I lean in, excited to hear.

'He wasn't there,' Dad says, turning his back to me as he takes a cup and saucer out for himself and a mug for me.

'What? Why not? And you with your big story to tell him! The cheek of him. Well, you'll have next week, won't you?'

He turns around slowly. 'He died at the weekend. His funeral's tomorrow. Instead we spent the night talking about him and all his old stories that he told a hundred times.'

'Oh, Dad, I'm so sorry.'

'Ah, well. If he hadn't have gone over the weekend, he would have dropped dead when he'd heard I met Michael Aspel. Maybe it was just as well,' he smiles sadly. 'Ah, he wasn't such a bad man. We had a good laugh even if we did enjoy getting a rise out of one another.'

I feel for Dad. It is such a trivial thing compared with the loss of a friend, but he had been so excited to share his stories with his great rival.

We both sit in silence.

'You'll keep the rose bush, won't you?' Dad asks finally.

I know immediately what he's talking about. 'Of course I will. I thought that it'd look good in your garden.'

He looks out the window and studies his garden, probably deciding where he'll plant it.

'You have to be careful with moving, Gracie. Too much shock causes a serious, possibly a grave decline.'

I smile sadly. 'That's a bit dramatic, but I'll be fine, Dad. Thanks for caring.'

He keeps his back turned. 'I was talking about the roses.'

My phone rings, vibrates along the table and almost
hops off the edge.

'Hello?'

'Joyce, it's Thomas. I just left your young man off
at the airport.'

'Oh, thank you so much. Did he get the envelope?'

'Eh, yeah. About that: I gave it to him all right but
I've just looked in the back seat of the car and it's still
there.'

'What?' I jump up from the kitchen chair. 'Go back,
go back! Turn the car around! You have to give it to
him. He's forgotten it!'

'You see, the thing is, he wasn't too sure on whether
he wanted to open it or not.'

'What? Why?'

'I don't know, love! I gave it to him when he got
back into the car before we got to the airport, just like
you asked. He seemed very down and so I thought it'd
cheer him up a bit.'

'Down? Why? What was wrong with him?'

'Joyce, love, I don't know. All I know is he got into
the car a bit upset so I gave him the envelope and he
sat there looking at it and I asked him if he was going
to open it and he said maybe.'

'Maybe,' I repeat. Had I done something to upset
him? Had Kate said something to him? 'He was upset
when he came out of the Gallery?'

'No, not the Gallery. We stopped off at the blood
donor clinic on D'Olier Street before the airport.'

'He was donating blood?'

'No, he said he had to meet somebody.'

Oh my God, maybe he'd discovered it was me who'd
received his blood and he wasn't interested.

'Thomas, do you know if he opened it?'

'Did you seal it?'

'No.'

'Then there's no way of my knowing. I didn't see
him open it. I'm sorry. Do you want me to drop it at
your house on the way back from the airport?'

'Please.'

An hour later I meet Thomas at the door and he gives me the envelope. I can feel the tickets still inside and my heart falls. Why didn't Justin open it and take it with him?

'Here, Dad.' I slide the envelope across the kitchen table. 'A present for you.'

'What's in it?'

'Front-row seats to the opera for next weekend,' I say sadly, leaning my chin on my hand. 'It was a gift for somebody else, but he clearly doesn't want to go.'

'The opera.' Dad makes a funny face and I laugh. 'It's far from operas I was raised,' though he opens the envelope anyway as I get up to make some more coffee.

'Oh, I think I'll pass on this opera thing, love, but thanks anyway.'

I spin round. 'Oh, Dad, why? You liked the ballet and you didn't think that you would.'

'Yes, but I went to that with you. I wouldn't go to this on my own.'

'You don't have to. There are two tickets.'

'No, there aren't.'

'There definitely are. Look again.'

He turns the envelope upside down and shakes it. A loose piece of paper falls out and flutters to the table.

My heart skips a beat.

Dad props his glasses on the tip of his nose and peers down at the note. '"Accompany me",' he says slowly. 'Ah, love, that's awful nice of you—'

'Show me that.' I grab it from his hands, disbelievingly, and read it for myself. Then I read it again. And again and again.

'Accompany me? Justin.'

36

'He wants to meet me,' I tell Kate nervously, as I twirl a string from the end of my unravelling top around my finger.

'You're going to cut off your circulation, be careful,' Kate responds, motherly.

'Kate! Did you not hear me? I said he wants to meet me!'

'And so he should. Did you not think that this would eventually happen? Really, Joyce, you've been taunting the man for weeks. And if he did save your life, as you're insisting he did, wouldn't he want to meet the person whose life he saved? Boost his male ego? Come on, it's the equivalent to a white horse and a shiny suit of armour.'

'No it's not.'

'It is in his male eyes. His male *wandering* eyes,' she spits out aggressively.

My eyes narrow as I study her closely. 'Is everything OK? You're beginning to sound like Frankie.'

'Stop biting your lip, it's starting to bleed. Yes, everything's great. Just hunky-dory.'

'OK, here I am,' Frankie makes her announcement as she breezes through the door and joins us on the bleachers.

We are seated on a split-level viewing balcony at Kate's local swimming pool. Below us Eric and Jayda splash noisily in their swimming class. Beside us Sam is sitting in his stroller, looking around.

'Does he ever do anything?' Frankie watches him suspiciously.

Kate ignores her.

'Issue number one for discussion today is why do we have to constantly meet in these places with all these *things* crawling around?' She looks at all the toddlers. 'What happened to cool bars, new restaurants, shop openings? Remember we used to go out and have *fun*?'

'I have plenty of fucking fun,' Kate says a little too defensively and loudly. 'I am just one great big ball of fucking fun,' she repeats, and looks away.

Frankie doesn't hear the unusual tone in Kate's voice, or does hear it and decides to push anyway. 'Yes, at dinner parties for other couples who haven't been out for a month either. For me, that's not so fun.'

'You'll understand when you have kids.'

'I don't plan to have any. Is everything OK?'

'Yes, she's "hunky-dory",' I say to Frankie, using my fingers as inverted commas.

'Oh, I see,' Frankie says slowly and mouths 'Christian' at me.

I shrug.

'Is there anything you want to get off your chest?' Frankie asks.

'Actually, yes.' Kate turns to her with fire in her eyes. 'I'm tired of your little comments about my life. If you're not happy here or in my company, then piss off somewhere else, but just know that it'll be without me.' She turns away, her cheeks flushed with anger.

Frankie is silent for a moment as she observes her friend. 'OK,' she says perkily and turns to me. 'My car is parked outside; we can go to the new bar down the road.'

'We're not going anywhere,' I protest.

'Ever since you left your husband and your life has fallen apart, you've been no fun,' she says to me sulkily. 'And as for you, Kate, ever since you got that new Swedish nanny and your husband's been eyeing her up, *you've* been absolutely miserable. As for me, I'm tired of hopping from one night of meaningless sex with handsome strangers to another, and having to eat microwave dinners alone every evening. There, I've said it.'

My mouth falls open. So does Kate's. I can tell we are both trying our best to be angry with her but her comments are so spot on, it's actually quite humorous. She nudges me with her elbow and chuckles mischievously in my ear. The corners of Kate's lips begin to twitch too.

'I should have got a manny,' Kate finally says.

'Nah, I still wouldn't trust Christian,' Frankie responds. 'You're being paranoid, Kate,' she assures her seriously. 'I've been around there, I've seen him. He adores you and she is not attractive at all.'

'You think?'

'Uh-huh,' she nods, but when Kate looks away, mouths 'gorgeous' to me.

'Did you mean all that you said?' Kate says, brightening up.

'No.' Frankie throws her head back and laughs. 'I *love* meaningless sex. I need to do something about the microwave dinners, though. My doctor says I need more iron. OK,' she claps her hands, causing Sam to jump with fright, 'what's this session's meeting been called for?'

'Justin wants to meet Joyce,' Kate explains, and snaps at me, 'Stop biting your lip.'

I stop.

'Ooh, great,' Frankie says excitedly. 'So what's the problem?' She sees my look of terror.

'He's going to realise that I'm me.'

'As opposed to you being . . . ?'

'Someone else.' I bite my lip again.

'This is really reminding me of the old days. You are thirty-three years old, Joyce, why are you acting like a teenager?'

'Because she's in love,' Kate says, bored, turning to face the swimming pool and clapping her coughing daughter, Jayda, whose face is half under the water.

'She can't be in love.' Frankie rolls her nose up in disgust.

'Is that normal, do you think?' Kate, beginning to get worried about Jayda, tries to get our attention.

'Of course it's not normal,' Frankie responds. 'She hardly knows the guy.'

'Girls, eh, stop for a minute,' Kate tries to butt in.

'I know more about him than any other person will ever know,' I defend myself. 'Apart from himself.'

'Eh, lifeguard.' Kate gives up on us and calls gently to the woman sitting below us. 'Is she OK, do you think?'

'Are you in love?' Frankie looks at me as though I've just said I want to have a sex change.

I smile just as the lifeguard crashes into the water to save Jayda and a few kids scream.

'You'll have to take us over to Ireland with you,' Doris says with excitement, placing a vase on the kitchen windowsill. The flat is almost finished and she's arranging the finishing touches. 'They could be a nutcase and you'd never know. We need to be nearby just in case something happens. They could be a murderer, a serial stalker who dates people and then kills them. I saw something like that on *Oprah*.'

Al begins hammering nails into the wall and Justin joins in with the rhythm, gently and repeatedly bashing his head against the kitchen table in response.

'I am not taking you both to the opera with me,' Justin says.

'You took me along on a date with you when you and Delilah Jackson went out.' Al stops hammering and turns to him. 'Why should this be any different?'

'Al, I was twelve years old.'

'Still,' he shrugs, returning to his hammering.

'What if she's a celebrity?' Doris says excitedly. 'Oh my God, she could be! I think she is! Jennifer Aniston could be sitting in the front row of the opera and there could be a place free beside her. Oh my God, what if it is?' She turns to Al with wide eyes. 'Justin, you *have* to tell her I'm her biggest fan.'

'Whoa, whoa, whoa, hold on a minute, you're starting to hyperventilate. *How on earth* have you come to that conclusion? We don't even know if it's a woman. You are obsessed with celebrities,' Justin sighs.

'Yeah, Doris,' Al joins in. 'It's probably just a normal person.'

Justin rolls his eyes. 'Yeah,' he imitates his tone, 'because celebrities aren't normal people, they're really underworld beasts that grow horns and have three legs.'

With that both Al and Doris pause from their hammering and hanging duties to stare at him.

'We're going to Dublin tomorrow,' Doris says with an air of finality. 'It's your brother's birthday and a weekend in Dublin, in a very nice hotel like the Shelbourne Hotel – I've, I mean *Al* has always wanted to stay there – would be a perfect birthday present for him, from you.'

'I can't afford the Shelbourne Hotel, Doris.'

'Well, we'll need somewhere close to a hospital in case he has a heart attack. In any case, we're all going!' She claps her hands excitedly.

37

I'm on my way into the city to meet Kate and Frankie for help on what to wear to tonight's opera, when my phone rings.

'Hello?'

'Joyce, it's Steven.'

My boss.

'I just received another phone call.'

'That's really great but you don't have to call me when that happens.'

'It's another complaint, Joyce.'

'From who and about what?'

'That couple you showed the new cottage to yesterday?'

'Yes?'

'They've pulled out.'

'Oh, that's a shame,' I say, lacking all sincerity. 'Did they say why?'

'Yes, in fact they did. It seems a certain person in our company advised them that to recreate the look of the period cottage properly, they should demand that the builders carry out excess work. Guess what? The builders weren't entirely interested in their list that included,' I hear paper rustling and he reads aloud, '"Exposed beams, exposed brickwork, log-burning stove, open fires . . ." The list goes on. So now they've backed out.'

'It sounds reasonable enough to me. The builders were recreating period cottages without any period features. Does that make sense to you?'

'Who cares? Joyce, you were only supposed to let them in to measure for their couch. Douglas had sold this place to them already when you were . . . out.'

'Evidently, he didn't.'

'Joyce, I need you to stop turning our clients away. Do you need to be reminded that your job is to *sell*, and if you're not doing that then . . .'

'Then what?' I say haughtily, my head getting hot.

'Then nothing,' he softens. 'I know you've had a difficult time,' he begins awkwardly.

'That time is over and has nothing to do with my ability to sell a house,' I snap.

'Then sell one,' he finishes.

'Fine.' I snap my phone shut and glare out the bus window at the city. A week back at work and already I need a break.

'Doris, is this really necessary?' Justin moans from the bathroom.

'Yes!' she calls. 'This is what we're here for. We have to make sure you're going to look right tonight. Hurry up, you take longer than a woman to get changed.'

Doris and Al are sitting on the end of their bed in a Dublin hotel, not the Shelbourne, much to Doris's dismay. It is more of a Holiday Inn, but it's central to the city and shopping streets and that's good enough for her. As soon as they'd landed earlier that morning, Justin had been all set to show them around the sites, the museums, churches and castles, but Doris and Al had other things on their minds. Shopping. The Viking tour was as cultured as they got and Doris had howled when water had sprayed her in the face on entry into the River Liffey. They'd ended up rushing to the nearest rest room so that Al could wash the mascara out of her eye.

There were only hours to go until the opera, until he would finally discover the identity of this mystery person. He was filled with anxiety, excitement and nerves at the thought of it. It would be an evening of sheer torture or pleasantries depending on his luck. He had to figure out an escape plan if his worst-case scenario was to play out.

'Oh, hurry up, Justin,' Doris howls again and he fixes his tie and exits the bathroom.

'Work it, work it, work it!' Doris whoops as he strolls up and down the bedroom in his best suit. He pauses in front of them and fidgets awkwardly, feeling like a little boy in his communion suit.

He is greeted by silence. Al, who has been shovelling popcorn in his mouth at a serious speed, also stops.

'What?' he says nervously. 'Something wrong? Something on my face? Is there a stain?' He looks down, studying himself.

Doris rolls her eyes and shakes her head. 'Ha-ha very funny. Now seriously, stop wasting time and show us the real suit.'

'Doris!' Justin exclaims. 'This is the real suit!'

'That's your best suit?' she drawls, looking him up and down.

'I think I recognise that from our wedding.' Al's eyes narrow.

Doris stands up and picks up her handbag. 'Take it off,' she says calmly.

'What? Why?'

She takes a deep breath. 'Just take it off. Now.'

'These are too formal, Kate.' I turn my nose up at the dresses she has chosen. 'It's not a ball, I just need something . . .'

'Sexy,' Frankie says, waving a little dress in front of me.

'It's an opera, not a nightclub.' Kate whips it away from her. 'OK, look at this. Not formal, not slutty.'

'Yes, you could be a nun,' Frankie says sarcastically. They both turn away and continue to root through the rails.

'Aha! I got it,' Frankie announces.

'No, I've found the perfect one.'

They both spin round with the same dresses in their hand, Kate holding one in red, Frankie holding the black. I chew on my lip.

'Stop it!' they say in unison.

'Oh my God,' Justin whispers.

'What? You've never seen a pink pinstripe before? It's divine. Worn with this pink shirt and this pink tie, oh, it would be perfect. Oh, Al, I wish you'd wear suits like this.'

'I prefer the blue,' Al disagrees. 'The pink is a bit gay. Or maybe that's a good idea in case she turns out to be a disaster. You can tell her your boyfriend's waiting for you. I can back you up on that,' he offers.

Doris stares at him with loathing. 'See, isn't this so much better than that other thing you were wearing? Justin? Earth to Justin? What on earth are you looking at? Oh, she's pretty.'

'That's Joyce,' he whispers. He had once read that a blue-throated hummingbird had a heart rate of one thousand two hundred and sixty beats per minute, and he'd wondered how on earth anything could survive that. He understood now. With each beat, his heart pushed out blood and sent it flowing around his body. He felt his entire body throb, pulsate in his neck, his wrists, his heart, his stomach.

'That's Joyce?' Doris asks, shocked. 'The phone woman? Well, she looks . . . *normal*, Justin. What do you think, Al?'

Al looks her up and down and nudges his brother. 'Yeah, she looks real *normal*. You should ask her out once and for all.'

'Why are you both so surprised she looks normal?' Thump-thump. Thump-thump.

'Well, sweetie, the very fact that she exists is a surprise,' Doris snorts. 'The fact that she's *pretty* is damn near a miracle. Go on, ask her out for dinner tonight.'

'I can't tonight.'

'Why not?'
'I've got the opera!'
'Opera shopera. Who cares about that?'
'You have been talking about it non-stop for over a week. And now it's opera shopera?' Thump-thump. Thump-thump.

'Well, I didn't want to alarm you before but I was thinking about it on the plane on the way over and . . .' she takes a deep breath and touches his arm gently, 'it can't be Jennifer Aniston. There's just going to be some old lady sitting in the front row waiting for you with a bouquet of flowers that you don't even want, or some overweight guy with bad breath. Sorry, Al, I don't mean you.' She touches his arm apologetically.

Al misses the insult he's so upset about the bomb-shell she's dropped. 'What? But I brought my autograph book!'

Justin's heart beats the speed of a hummingbird's heart, his mind now at the speed of its wings. He can barely think, everything is happening too fast. Joyce, far more beautiful up close than he remembers, her newly short hair soft around her face. She is beginning to move away now. He has to do something quick. *Think, think, think!*

'Ask her out tomorrow night,' Al suggests.
'I can't! My exhibition is tomorrow.'
'Skip it. Call in sick.'
'I can't, Al! I've been working on this for months, I'm the damn curator, I *have* to be there.' Thump-thump, thump-thump.

'If you don't ask her out, I will.' Doris pushes him.
'She's busy with her friends.'
Joyce starts to move away.
Do something!
'Joyce!' Doris calls out.
'Jesus Christ.' Justin tries to turn round and scarper in the other direction but both Al and Doris block him.

'Justin Hitchcock,' a voice says loudly and he stops trying to break through their barrier and slowly turns round. The lady standing beside Joyce is familiar. She has a baby in a stroller beside her.

'Justin Hitchcock.' The girl reaches her hand out. 'Kate McDonald.' She shakes his hand firmly. 'I was at your talk last week in the National Gallery. It was incredibly interesting,' she smiles. 'I didn't know you knew Joyce,' she smiles brightly and elbows Joyce. 'Joyce, you never said! I was at Justin Hitchcock's talk just last week! Remember I told you? The painting about the woman and the letter? And the fact that she was writing it?'

Joyce's eyes are wide and startled. She looks from her friend to Justin and back again.

'She doesn't know me, exactly,' Justin finally speaks up and feels a slight tremble in his voice. The adrenalin is surging through him so much he feels as if he's about to take off like a rocket through the department store's roof. 'We've passed one another on many occasions but never had the opportunity to meet properly.' He holds out his hand. 'Joyce, I'm Justin.'

She reaches out to take his hand and static electricity rushes through as they get a quick shock from one another.

They both let go quickly. 'Whoa!' She pulls back and cradles her hand in the other, as though burned.

'Oooh,' Doris sings.

'It's static electricity, Doris. Caused when the air and materials are dry. They should use a humidifier in here,' Justin says like a robot, not moving his eyes from Joyce's face.

Frankie cocks her head and tries not to laugh. 'Charming.'

'I tell him that all the time,' Doris says angrily.

After a moment, Joyce extends her hand again to finish the handshake properly. 'Sorry, I just got a—'

'That's OK, I got it too,' he smiles.

'Nice to meet you, finally,' she says.

They remain holding hands, just staring at one another. A line of Doris, Justin and Al standing opposite Joyce's party of three.

Doris clears her throat noisily. 'I'm Doris, his sister-in-law.'

She reaches diagonally over Justin and Joyce's hand-shake to greet Frankie.

'I'm Frankie.'

They shake hands. While doing so, Al reaches over diagonally to shake hands with Kate. It becomes a hand-shaking marathon as they all greet at once, Justin and Joyce finally releasing hold of one another.

'Would you like to go for dinner tonight with Justin?' Doris blurts out.

'Tonight?' Joyce's mouth drops.

'She would *love* to,' Frankie answers for her.

'*Tonight*, though?' Justin turns to face Doris with wide eyes.

'Oh, it's no problem, Al and I want to eat alone anyway,' she nudges him. 'No point being the goose-berry,' she smiles.

'Are you sure you wouldn't rather stick to your *other* plans tonight?' Joyce says, slightly confused.

'Oh, no,' Justin shakes his head, 'I'd love to have dinner with you. Unless of course *you* have plans?'

Joyce turns to Frankie. 'Tonight? I have that *thing*, Frankie . . .'

'Oh, no, don't be silly. It doesn't really make a differ-ence now, does it?' She widens her eyes. 'We can have drinks any other time.' Frankie waves her hand dismis-sively. 'Where are you taking her?' She smiles sweetly at Justin.

'The Shelbourne Hotel?' Doris says. 'At eight?'

'Oh I've always wanted to eat there,' Kate sighs. 'Eight suits her fine,' she responds.

Justin smiles and looks at Joyce. 'Does it?'

Joyce seems to consider this, her mind ticking at the same rate as his heart.

'You're *absolutely* sure you're happy to cancel your other plans for tonight?' Frown lines appear on her forehead.

Her eyes bore into his and guilt overcomes him as

he thinks of whoever he is currently making arrangements to stand up.

He gives a single nod and is unsure of how convincing it seems.

Sensing this, Doris begins to pull him away. 'Well, it was wonderful to meet you all but we really better get back to shopping. Nice to meet you, Kate, Frankie, Joyce sweetie.' She gives her a quick hug. 'Enjoy dinner. At eight. Shelbourne Hotel. Don't forget now.'

'Red or black?' Joyce holds up the two dresses to Justin, before he's pulled away.

He considers this carefully. 'Red.'

'Black it is, then,' she smiles, mirroring their first and only conversation from the hair salon, the first day they met.

He laughs and allows Doris to drag him away.

38

'What the hell did you do that for, Doris?' Justin asks as they walk back towards their hotel.

'You've gone on and on about this woman for weeks and now you've finally got a date with her. What's so wrong with that?'

'I have *plans* tonight! I can't just stand the person up.'

'You don't even know who they are!'

'It doesn't matter, it's still rude.'

'Justin, seriously, listen to me. This whole Thank You message thing could honestly be somebody playing a cruel joke.'

He narrows his eyes with suspicion. 'Is it?'

'I honestly don't know.'

'I have no idea,' Al shrugs, beginning to pant.

Doris and Justin slow down immediately, taking baby steps.

Justin sighs.

'Would you rather risk going to something where you have no idea what or who to expect? Or go to dinner with a pretty lady, who you are absolutely crazy about and have been thinking about for weeks?'

'Come on,' Al joins in, 'when's the last time you felt like this about anyone? I don't even think you were like this with Jennifer.'

Justin smiles.

'So, bro, what's it gonna be?'

'You should really take something for that heartburn, Mr Conway,' I can hear Frankie telling Dad in the kitchen.

'Like what?' Dad asks, enjoying the company of two young ladies.

'Christian gets that all the time,' Kate says, and I hear Sam's babbling echo around the kitchen.

Dad babbles back at him, imitating his non-words.

'Oh, it's called, em . . .' Kate thinks, 'I can't remember what it's called.'

'You're the same as me,' Dad says to her. 'You've got CRAFT too.'

'What's that?'

'Can't. Remember. A. Fuc—'

'OK, I'm coming!' I call down the stairs to Kate, Frankie and Dad.

'Yahooo!' Frankie hollers.

'OK, I've got the camera ready!' Kate calls.

Dad starts making trumpet noises as I walk down the stairs and I start to laugh. I keep an eye on Mum's photo on the hall table as I walk down the steps, maintaining eye contact with her all the way as she looks up at me. I wink at her as I pass.

As soon as I step into the hall and turn to them in the kitchen, they all go quiet.

My smile fades. 'What's wrong?'

'Oh, Joyce,' Frankie whispers as though it's a bad thing, 'you look beautiful.'

I sigh with relief and join them in the kitchen.

'Do a twirl.' Kate films with the video camera.

I spin in my new red dress while Sam claps his podgy hands.

'Mr Conway, you haven't said anything!' Frankie nudges him. 'Isn't she beautiful?'

We all turn to face Dad, who has gone silent, eyes filled with tears. He nods up and down quickly, but no words come.

'Oh, Dad,' I reach out and wrap my arms around him, 'it's only a dress.'

'You look beautiful, love,' he manages to say. 'Go get him, kiddo.' He gives me a kiss on the cheek and hurries into the living room, embarrassed by his emotion.

'So,' Frankie says smiling, 'have you decided whether it's going to be dinner or the opera tonight?'

'I still don't know.'

'He asked you out to dinner,' Kate says. 'Why do you think he'd rather go to the opera.'

'Because firstly, *he* didn't ask me out for dinner. His sister-in-law did. And I didn't say yes. *You* did.' I glare at Kate. 'I think it's killing him not knowing whose life he saved. He didn't seem so convinced at the end, before he left the shop, did he?'

'Stop reading so much into it,' Frankie says. 'He asked you out so go out.'

'But he looked guilty to be standing the opera date up.'

'I don't know,' Kate disagrees. 'He seemed to really want you at that dinner.'

'It's a tough decision,' Frankie summarises. 'I would *not* like to be in your shoes.'

'Hey, they're my shoes,' Kate says, insulted. 'Why can't you just come clean and tell him that it's you?'

'My way of coming clean was supposed to be him seeing me at the opera. This was going to be it, the night he found out.'

'So go to dinner and tell him that it was you all along.'

'But what if he goes to the opera?'

We talk in circles for a while longer, and when they leave, I discuss the pros and cons of both situations with myself until my head is spinning so much I can't think any more. When the taxi arrives, Dad walks me to the door.

'I don't know what you girls were in such deep conversation about but I know you've to make a decision about something. Have you made it?' Dad asks softly.

'I don't know, Dad.' I swallow hard. 'I don't know what the right decision is.'

'Of course you do. You always take your own route, love. You always have.'

'What do you mean?'

He looks out to the garden. 'See that trail there?'

'The garden path?'

He shakes his head and points to a track in the lawn where the grass has been trampled on and the soil is slightly visible beneath. 'You made that path.'

'What?' I'm confused now.

'As a little girl,' he smiles. 'We call them "desire lines" in the gardening world. They're the tracks and trails that people make for themselves. You've always avoided the paths laid down by other people, love. You've always gone your own way, found your own way, even if you do eventually get to the same point as everybody else. You've never taken the official route,' he chuckles to himself. 'No, indeed you haven't. You're certainly your mother's daughter, cutting the corners, creating spontaneous paths, while I'd stick to the routes and make my way the long way round.' He smiles as he reminisces.

We both study the small well-worn ribbon of trampled grass across the garden leading to the path.

'Desire lines,' I repeat, seeing myself as a little girl, as a teenager, a grown woman, cutting across that patch, each time. 'I suppose desire isn't linear. There is no straightforward way of going where you want.'

'Do you know what you're going to do now?' he asks as the taxi arrives.

I smile and kiss him on his forehead. 'I do.'

39

I step out of the taxi at Stephen's Green and immediately see the crowds flowing towards the Gaiety Theatre, all dressed in their finest for the National Irish Opera's production. I have never been to an opera before, have only ever seen one on television, and my heart, tired of a body that can't keep up with it, is pounding to get out of my body and run into the building itself. I'm filled with nerves, with anticipation, and with the greatest hope I have ever felt in my life, that the final part of my plan will come together. I'm terrified that Justin will be angry that it's me, though why he would be, I've run through a hundred thousand times in my head and can't seem to come to any rational conclusion.

I stand halfway between the Shelbourne Hotel and the Gaiety Theatre, no less than three hundred yards between them. I look from one to the other, close my eyes and don't care how stupid I look in the middle of the road as people pass by me on this Saturday night. I wait to feel the pull. Which way to go. Right to the Shelbourne. Left to the Gaiety. My heart drums in my chest.

I turn to the left and stride confidently toward the theatre. Inside the bustling entrance foyer, I purchase a programme and make my way to my seat. No time for pre-performance drinks; if he shows up early and sees I'm not here I would never forgive myself. Front-row tickets – I could not believe my luck but I had called the very moment the tickets had gone on sale to secure these precious seats.

I take my seat in the red velvet chairs, my red dress falling down either side of me, my purse on my lap, Kate's shoes glistening on the floor before me. The orchestra are directly in front of me, tuning and rehearsing, dressed in black in their underworld of fabulous sounds.

The atmosphere is magical, the balconies drip from the side. Thousands of people buzzing with excitement, orchestra fine-tuning and striving for perfection, lots of bodies moving around, balconies like honeycombs, the air rich with perfumes and aftershaves, pure honey.

I look to my right at the empty chair and shiver with excitement.

An announcement explains that the performance will begin in five minutes, that those who are late will be forbidden entry until a break, but are able to stay outside and watch the performance on the screens until the ushers tell them it is an appropriate time to enter.

Hurry, Justin, hurry, I plead, my legs bouncing beneath me with nerves.

Justin speed-walks from his hotel and up Kildare Street. He is just out of the shower but already his skin feels moist, his shirt sticks to his back, his forehead glistens with sweat. He stops walking at the top of the road. The Shelbourne Hotel is directly beside him, the Gaiety Theatre two hundred yards to his right.

He closes his eyes and takes deep breaths. Breathes in the fresh October air of Dublin city.

Which way to go. Which way to go.

The performance has begun and I cannot take my eyes off the door to my right-hand side. Beside me is an empty seat whose very presence sends a lump to my throat. While onstage a woman sings with such emotion, much to my neighbours' annoyance beside and behind me, I can't help but turn my head to face the door.

Despite the announcement, a few people have been permitted entry and have moved quickly to their seats. If Justin does not come now, he may not be able to be seated until after the interval. I empathise with the woman singing before me, for the mere fact that, after all this time, a door and an usher being the only things separating us, is an opera in itself.

I turn round once more and my heart skips a beat as the door beside me opens.

Justin pulls on the door and as soon as he enters the room, all heads turn to stare at him. He looks around quickly for Joyce, his heart in his mouth, his fingers clammy and trembling.

The maître d' approaches. 'Welcome, sir. How can I help you?'

'Good evening. I've booked a table for two, under Hitchcock.' He looks around nervously, takes a handkerchief out of his pocket and dabs at his forehead nervously. 'Is she here yet?'

'No, sir, you are the first to arrive. Would you like me to show you to your table or would you rather have a drink before?'

'The table please.' If she arrives and sees he isn't at the table, he will never forgive himself.

He is led to a table for two in the centre of the dining room.

He sits in the chair that has been held out for him and immediately servers flow to his table, pouring water, laying his serviette on his lap, bringing bread rolls.

'Sir, would you like to see the menu or would you like to wait for the other party to arrive?'

'I'll wait, thank you.' He watches the door and takes this moment of being alone to calm himself.

It has been over an hour. There have been a few moments when people have entered and been shown their seats but none of those people have been Justin. The chair beside me remains empty and cold. The woman next to it, glances occasionally at it and at me who is twisted round, eye obsessively and possessively on the door, and she smiles politely, sympathetically. It brings tears to my eyes, a feeling of utter loneliness, in a room full of people, full of sound, full of song, I feel utterly alone. The interval begins, the curtain lowers, the house lights are raised and everybody stands up and exits to the bar, outside for cigarettes or to stretch their legs.

I sit and I wait.

The more lonely I feel, the more hope that springs in my heart. He may still come. He may still feel this is as important to him as it is to me. Dinner with a woman he's met once or an evening with a person whose life he helped save, a person who has done exactly what he wished and thanked him in all the ways he asked.

Perhaps it wasn't enough.

'Would you like to see the menu now, sir?'

'Em,' he looks at the clock. She's a half-hour late and his heart sinks but he remains hopeful. 'She's just running a little late, you see,' he explains.

'Of course, sir.'

'I'll have a look at the wine menu, please.'

'Of course, sir.'

The woman's lover is ripped from her arms and she pleads for him to be let go. She wails and howls and hollers in song, and beside me the woman sniffles. My eyes fill too, remembering Dad's face of pride when he saw me in my dress.

'Go get him,' he said.

Well, I didn't. I've lost another one. I've been stood up by a man who'd rather have dinner with me. As nonsensical as it should be, it is crystal clear to me. I wanted him to be here. I wanted the connection I felt, that he caused, to be the thing that brought us together, not a chance meeting in a department store, a few hours before. It seems so fickle for him to choose me over something far more important.

Perhaps I am viewing this the wrong way, though. Perhaps I should be happy he chose dinner with me. I look at my watch. Perhaps he is there right now, waiting for me. But what if I leave here and he arrives, missing me? No. I am best to stay put and not confuse matters.

My mind battles on, as events do on stage.

But if he is at the restaurant now, and I am here, then he is alone, has been alone for over an hour. Why then, wouldn't he give up on a date with me and run a few hundred yards to seek out the mystery date? Unless he has come. Unless he took one look through the door, saw that it was me and refused to come in. I am so overwhelmed by the thoughts in my head I tune out of the act, too muddled, completely ambushed by the questions in my head.

Before I know it, the opera is over. The seats are empty, the curtains are down on the stage, the lights are up. I walk out to the cold night air. The city is busy, filled with people enjoying their Saturday night out. My tears feel cold against my skin as the breeze hits them.

Justin empties the last of his second bottle of wine into his glass and slams it back onto the table unintentionally. He has lost all co-ordination by now, he can barely read the time on his watch but he knows it's gone past a reasonable hour for Joyce to show.

He has been stood up.

By the one woman he's had any sort of interest in since his divorce. Not counting poor Sarah. He had never counted poor Sarah.

I am a horrible person.

'I'm sorry to disturb you, sir,' the maître d' says politely, 'but we have received a phone call from your brother, Al?'

Justin nods.

'He wanted to pass on the message that he is still alive and that he hopes you are, em, well, that you're enjoying your night.'

'Alive?'

'Yes, sir, he said you would understand, as it's twelve o'clock. His birthday?'

'Twelve?'

'Yes, sir. I'm also sorry to tell you that we are closing for the evening. Would you like to settle your bill?'

Justin looks up at him, bleary-eyed, and tries to nod again but feels his head loll to one side.

'I've been stood up.'

'I'm sorry, sir.'

'Oh, don't be. I deserve it. I stood up a person I don't even know.'

'Oh. I see.'

'But they have been so kind to me. So, so kind. They gave me muffins and coffee, a car and a driver, and I've been so horrible to him or her.' He stops suddenly.

It might be still open!

'Here.' He thrusts his credit card at him. 'I might still have time.'

I stroll around the quiet streets of the neighbourhood, wrapping my cardigan tighter around me. I told the taxi driver to let me out round the corner so that I could get some air and clear my head before I return home. I also want to be rid of my tears by the time Dad sees me, who I'm sure is currently sitting up in his armchair as he used to do when I was younger, alert and eager to find out what had happened, though he would pretend to be asleep as soon as he heard the key in the door.

I walk by my old house, which I successfully managed to sell only days ago, not to the eager Linda and Joe, who found out it was my home and were afraid my bad luck was an omen for them and their unborn child, or more, that the stairs that caused my fall, would perhaps be too dangerous for Linda during her pregnancy. Nobody takes responsibility for their actions, I notice. It wasn't the stairs, it was me. I was rushing. It was my fault. Simple as that. Something I'm going to have to dig deep to forgive, as it shall never be forgotten.

Perhaps I've been rushing through my whole entire life, jumping into things head first without thinking them through. Running through the days without noticing the minutes. Not that the times when I slowed down and planned ever gave any more positive results. Mum and Dad had planned everything for their entire lives: summer holidays, a child, their savings, nights out. Everything was done by the book. Her premature departure from life was the one thing they had never bargained on. A blip that knocked everything off course.

Conor and I had teed-off straight for the trees and had bogeyed, big time.

The money for the house is to be halved and shared between Conor and me. I will have to start hunting for something smaller, something cheaper. I have no idea what he will do – an odd realisation.

I stop outside our old home and stare up at the red bricks, at the door we argued about what colour to paint, about the flowers we'd thought deeply about before planting. Not mine any more, but the memories are; the memories can't be sold. The building that housed my once-upon-a-time dreams stands for someone else now, as it did for the people before us, and I feel happy to let it go. Happy that was another time and that I can begin again, anew, though bearing the scars of before. They represent wounds that have healed.

It's midnight when I return to Dad's house and behind the windows is blackness. There isn't a single light on, which is unusual, as he usually leaves the porch light on, particularly if I'm out.

I open my bag to get my keys and bump against my mobile phone. It lights up to show I have missed ten calls, eight of which are from the house. I had it on silent at the opera and, knowing that Justin didn't have my number, I didn't think to look at it. I scramble for my keys, my hands trembling as I try to fit the key into the lock. They fall to the ground, the noise echoing in the silent dark street. I lower myself to my knees, not caring about my new dress, and shuffle around the concrete, feeling for the metal in the darkness. Finally, my fingers touch upon them and I'm through the door like a rocket, turning on all the lights.

'Dad?' I call in the hallway. Mum's photograph is on the floor, underneath the table. I pick it up and place it back where it belongs, trying to stay calm, but my heart is having its own idea.

No answer.

I walk to the kitchen and flick the switch. A full cup of tea sits on the kitchen table. A slice of toast with jam, with one bite taken from it.

'Dad?' I say more loudly now, walking into the living room and turning on the light.

His pills have all been spilled on the floor, all the containers opened and emptied, all the colours mixed.

I panic now, running back through the kitchen, through the hall, and run upstairs, turning on all the lights as I yell at the top of my lungs.

'DAD! DAD! WHERE ARE YOU? DAD, IT'S ME, JOYCE! DAD!' Tears are flowing now; I can barely speak. He is not in his bedroom, or the bathroom, not in my room or anywhere else. I pause on the landing, trying to listen in the silence to hear if he's calling. All I can hear is the drumbeat of my heart in my ears, in my throat.

'DAD!' I yell, my chest heaving, the lump in my throat threatening to seize my breath. I've nowhere else to look. I start pulling open wardrobes, searching under his bed. I grab a pillow from his bed and breathe in, holding it close to me and instantly soaking it with tears. I look out the back window and into the garden: no sign of him.

My knees too weak to stand, my head too clouded to think, I sink onto the top stair on the landing and try to figure out where he could be.

Then I think of the spilled pills on the floor and I yell the loudest I have *ever* shouted in my life. 'DAAAAAAD!'

Silence greets me and I have never felt so alone. More

alone than at the opera, more alone than in an unhappy marriage, more alone than when Mum died. Completely and utterly alone, the last person I have in my life, taken away from me.

Then.

'Joyce?' A voice calls from the front door, which I've left open. 'Joyce, it's me, Fran.' She stands there in her dressing gown and slippers, her eldest son standing behind her with a flashlight in his hand.

'Dad is gone.' My voice trembles.

'He's in the hospital, I was trying to call y—'

'What? Why?' I stand up and rush down the stairs.

'He thought he was having another heart—'

'I have to go. I have to go to him.' I rush around searching for my car keys. 'Which one is he in?'

'Joyce, relax, love, relax.' Fran's arms are around me. 'I'll drive you.'

<h1 align="center">40</h1>

I run down the corridors, examining each door, trying to find the correct room. I panic, my tears blinding my vision. A nurse stops me and helps me, tries to calm me. Knows instantly who I'm talking about. I shouldn't be allowed in at this time but she can tell I'm distraught, wants to calm me by showing me he's all right. She allows me a few minutes.

I follow her down a series of corridors and finally she leads me into his room. I see Dad lying in bed, tubes attached to his wrists and nose, his skin deathly pale, his body so small under the blankets in the bed.

'Was that you making all that fuss out there?' he asks, his voice sounding weak.

'Dad.' I try to remain calm but my voice comes out muffled.

'It's OK, love. I just got a shock, is all. Thought my heart was acting up again, went to take my pills but then I got dizzy and they all fell. Something to do with sugar, they tell me.'

'Diabetes, Henry,' the nurse smiles. 'The doctor will be around to explain it all to you in the morning.'

I sniffle, trying to remain calm.

'Ah, come here, you silly sod.' He lifts his arms towards me.

I rush to him and hug him tight, his body feeling frail but protective.

'I'm not going anywhere on you now. Hush, now.' He runs his hands through my hair and pats my back comfortingly. 'I hope I didn't ruin your night, now. I told Fran not to bother you.'

'Of course you should have called me,' I say into his shoulder. 'I got such a fright when you weren't home.'

'Well, I'm fine. You'll have to help me, though, with all this stuff,' he whispers. 'I told the doctor I understand but I don't really,' he says, a little worried. 'He's a real snooty type.' He ruffles up his nose.

'Of course I will.' I wipe my eyes and try to compose myself.

'So, how did it go?' he asks, perking up. 'Tell me all the good news.'

'He, em,' I purse my lips, 'he didn't show up.' My tears start again.

Dad is quiet; sad then angry, then sad again. He hugs me again, tighter this time.

'Ah, love,' he says gently. 'He's a bloody fool.'

41

Justin finishes explaining the story of his disastrous weekend to Bea, who is sitting on the couch, her mouth open in shock.

'I can't believe I missed all this. I'm so bummed!'

'Well, you wouldn't have missed it if you'd been talking to me,' Justin teases.

'Thank you for apologising to Peter. I appreciate it. He appreciates it.'

'I was acting like an idiot; just didn't want to admit my little girl was all grown up.'

'You better believe it,' she smiles. 'God,' she thinks back to his story, 'I still can't imagine somebody sending you all that stuff. Who could it be? The poor person must have waited and waited for you at the opera.'

Justin covers his face and winces. 'Please stop, it's killing me.'

'But you chose Joyce, anyway.'

He nods and smiles sadly.

'You must have really liked her.'

'She must have really not liked me because she didn't show up. No, Bea, I'm over it now. It's time to move on. I hurt too many people in the process of trying to find out. If you can't remember anyone else you told, then we'll never know.'

Bea thinks hard. 'I only told Peter, the costume supervisor and her father. But what makes you think it wasn't either of them?'

'I met the costume supervisor that night. She didn't

act like she knew me, and she's English – why would she have gone to Ireland for a blood transfusion? I called her and asked her about her father. Don't ask.' He sees off her glare. 'Anyway, turns out her father's Polish.'

'Hold on, where are you getting that from? She wasn't English, she was Irish,' Bea frowns. 'They both were.'

Thump-thump. Thump-thump.

'Justin,' Laurence enters the room with cups of coffee for him and Bea, 'I was wondering when you have a minute, if we could have a word.'

'Not now, Laurence,' Justin says, moving to the edge of his seat. 'Bea, where's your ballet programme? Her photograph's in it.'

'Honestly, Justin.' Jennifer arrives at the door with her arms folded. 'Could you please just be respectful for one moment. Laurence has something he wants to say and you owe it to him to listen.'

Bea runs to her room, pushing through the battling adults, and returns waving the programme in her hand, ignoring them. As does Justin.

He grabs it from her and flicks through it quickly. 'There!' he stabs his finger on the page.

'Guys,' Jennifer steps in between them, 'we really have to settle this now.'

'Not now, Mum. Please!' Bea yells. 'This is important!'

'And this is not?'

'That's not her.' Bea shakes her head furiously. 'That's not the woman I spoke to.'

'Well, what did she look like?' Justin is up on his feet now. Thump-thump. Thump-thump.

'Let me think, let me think.' Bea panics. 'I know! Mum!'

'What?' Jennifer looks from Justin to Bea with confusion.

'Where are the photographs we took of the first night I stood in for Charlotte in the ballet?'

'Oh, em—'

'Quick.'

'They're in the corner kitchen cupboard,' Laurence says, frowning.

'Yes, Laurence!' Justin punches the air. 'They're in the corner kitchen cupboard! Go get them, quick!'

Alarmed, Laurence runs into the kitchen, while Jennifer watches him with an open mouth. There is much shuffling of papers while Justin paces the floor at top speed and Jennifer and Bea watch him.

'Here they are.' He offers them forward and Bea snaps them out of his hand.

Jennifer tries to interject but Bea and Justin's speech and movements are on fast forward.

Bea shuffles through the photos at top speed. 'You weren't in the room at the time, Dad. You had disappeared somewhere but we all got a group photo and, here it is!' She rushes to her dad. 'That's them. The woman and her father, at the end.' She points.

Silence.

'Dad?'

Silence.

'Dad, are you OK?'

'Justin?' Jennifer moves in closer. 'He's gone very pale, get him a glass of water, Laurence, quick.'

Laurence rushes back to the kitchen.

'Dad.' Bea clicks her fingers in front of his eyes. 'Dad, are you with us?'

'It's her,' he whispers.

'Her who?' Jennifer asks.

'The woman whose life he saved.' Bea jumps up and down excitedly.

'*You* saved a woman's life?' Jennifer asks, shocked. '*You?*'

'It's Joyce,' he whispers.

Bea gasps. 'The woman who phoned me?'

He nods.

Bea gasps again. 'The woman you stood up?'

Justin closes his eyes, and silently curses himself.

'You saved a woman's life and then *stood her up*?' Jennifer laughs.

'Bea, where's your phone?'

'Why?'

'She called you, remember? Her number was in your phone.'

'Oh, Dad, that was ages ago. My phone log only holds ten recent numbers. That was weeks ago!'

'Damnit!'

'I gave it to Doris, remember? She wrote it down. You called the number from your flat!'

You threw it in the skip, you jerk! The skip! It's still there!

'Here.' Laurence runs in with the glass of water, panting.

'Laurence.' Justin reaches out, takes him by the cheeks and kisses his forehead. 'I give you my blessing. Jennifer,' he does the same and kisses her directly on the lips, 'good luck.'

He runs out of the apartment as Bea cheers him on, Jennifer wipes her lips with disgust and Laurence wipes the spilled water from his clothes.

As Justin sprints from the tube station to his house, rain pours from the clouds like a cloth being squeezed. He doesn't care, he just looks up to the sky and laughs, loving how it feels on his face, unable to believe that Joyce was the woman all along. He should have known. It all makes sense now, her asking him if he was sure he wanted to make new dinner plans, her friend being at his talk, all of it!

He turns the corner into his drive and sees the skip now filled to the brim with items. He jumps in and begins sorting through it.

From the window, Doris and Al stop packing their suitcases and watch him with concern.

'Damnit, I really thought he was getting back to normal,' Al says. 'Should we stay?'

'I don't know,' she replies worriedly. 'What on earth is he doing? It's ten o'clock at night – surely the neighbours will call the cops.'

His grey T-shirt is soaked through, his hair slicked back, water drips from his nose, his trousers are stuck to his skin. They watch him whooping and hollering as he throws the contents of the skip onto the ground beside it.

42

I lie in bed, staring at the ceiling, trying to process my life. Dad is still in hospital undergoing tests and will be home tomorrow. With nobody around, it has forced me to think about my life and I have worked my way through despair, guilt, sadness, anger, loneliness, depression, cynicism and have finally found my way to hope. Like an addict going cold turkey, I have paced the floors of these rooms with every emotion bursting from my skin. I have spoken aloud to myself, screamed, shouted, wept and mourned.

It's eleven p.m., dark, windy and cold outside as the winter months are fighting their way through, when the phone rings. Thinking it's Dad I hurry downstairs, grab the phone and sit on the bottom stair.

'Hello?'

'It was you all along.'

I freeze. My heart thuds. I move the phone from my ear and take a deep breath.

'Justin?'

'It was you all along, wasn't it?'

I'm silent.

'I saw the photograph of you and your father with Bea. That's the night she told you about my donation. About wanting thank yous.' He sneezes.

'Bless you.'

'Why didn't you say anything to me? All those times I saw you? Did you follow me or . . . or, what's going on, Joyce?'

'Are you angry with me?'

'No! I mean, I don't know. I don't understand. I'm so confused.'

'Let me explain.' I take a deep breath and try to steady my voice, try to speak through the heartbeat that is currently at the base of my throat. 'I didn't follow you to any of the places we met so please don't be concerned. I'm not a stalker. Something happened, Justin. Something happened when I received my transfusion and *whatever* that was, when your blood was transfused into mine, I suddenly felt connected to you. I kept turning up at places you were at, like the hair salon, the ballet. It was all a coincidence.' I'm speaking too fast now but I can't slow down. 'And then Bea told me you'd donated blood around the same time that I'd received it and . . .'

'What?'

I'm not sure what he means.

'You mean, you don't know for sure if it is my blood that you received? Because I couldn't find out, nobody would tell me. Did somebody tell you?'

'No. Nobody told me. They didn't need to. I—'

'Joyce.' He stops me and I'm immediately worried by his tone.

'I'm not some *weird* person, Justin. Trust me. I have never experienced what I have over the past few weeks.' I tell him the story. Of experiencing his skills, his knowledge, of sharing his tastes.

He is quiet.

'Say something, Justin.'

'I don't know what to say. It sounds . . . odd.'

'It is odd, but it's the truth. This will sound even worse but I feel like I've gained some of your memories too.'

'Really?' His voice is cold, far away. I'm losing him.

'Memories of the park in Chicago, Bea dancing in her tutu on the red chequered cloth, the picnic basket, the bottle of red wine. The cathedral bells, the ice-cream parlour, the seesaw with Al, the sprinklers, the—'

'Whoa, whoa, whoa. Stop now. Who are you?'

'Justin, it's me!'

'Who's told you these things?'

'Nobody, I just know them!' I rub my eyes tiredly. 'I know it sounds bizarre, Justin, I really do. I am a normal decent human being who is as cynical as they come but this is my life and these are the things that are happening to me. If you don't believe me then I'm sorry and I'll hang up and go back to my life, but please know that this is not a joke or a hoax or any kind of set-up.'

He is quiet for a while. And then, 'I want to believe you.'

'You feel something between us?'

'I feel that.' He speaks very slowly as though pondering every letter of every word. 'The memories, tastes and hobbies and whatever else of mine that you mentioned, are things that you could have seen me do or heard me say. I'm not saying you're doing this on purpose, maybe you don't even know it, but you've read my books; I mention many personal things in my books. You saw the photo in Bea's locket, you've been to my talks, you've read my articles. I may have revealed things about myself in them, in fact I know I have. How can I know that you knowing these things is through a transfusion? How do I know that – no offence – but that you're not some lunatic young woman who's convinced herself of some crazy story she read in a book or saw in a movie? How am I supposed to know?'

I sigh. I have no way of convincing him. 'Justin, I don't believe in anything right now, but I believe in this.'

'I'm sorry, Joyce,' he begins to end the conversation.

'No, wait,' I stop him. 'Is this it?'

Silence.

'Aren't you going to even try to believe me?'

He sighs deeply. 'I thought you were somebody else, Joyce. I don't know why because I'd never even met you, but I thought you were a different kind of person. This . . . this I don't understand. This, I find . . . it's not right, Joyce.'

Each sentence is a stab through my heart and a punch in my stomach. I could stand hearing this from anyone else in the world but not him. Anyone but him.

'You've been through a lot, by the sound of it, perhaps you should . . . talk to someone.'

'Why don't you believe me? Please, Justin. There must be something I can say to convince you. Something I know that you haven't written in an article or a book or told anyone in a lecture . . .' I trail off, thinking of something. No, I can't use that.

'Goodbye, Joyce. I hope everything works out for you, really I do.'

'Hold on! Wait! There is one thing. One thing that only you could know.'

He pauses. 'What?'

I squeeze my eyes shut and take a deep breath. Do it or don't do it. Do it or don't. I open my eyes and blurt it out, 'Your father.'

There's silence.

'Justin?'

'What about him?' His voice is ice cold.

'I know what you saw,' I say softly. 'How you could never tell anyone.'

'What the hell are you talking about?'

'I know about you being on the stairs, seeing him through the banisters. I see him too. I see him with the bottle and the pills closing the door. Then I see the green feet on the floor—'

'STOP IT!' he yells, and I'm shocked to silence.

But I must keep trying or I'll never have the opportunity to say these words again.

'I know how hard it must have been for you as a child. How hard it was to keep it to yourself—'

'You know nothing,' he says coldly. 'Absolutely nothing. Please stay away from me. I don't ever wish to hear from you again.'

'OK.' My voice is a whisper but it is to myself as he has already hung up.

I sit on the steps of the dark empty house and listen as the cold October wind rattles the building.

So that's that.

One Month Later

43

'Next time we should take the car, Gracie,' Dad says as we make our way down the road back from our walk in the Botanics. I link his arm and I'm lifted up and down with him as he sways. Up and down, down and up. The motion is soothing.

'No, you need the exercise, Dad.'

'Speak for yourself,' he mutters. 'Howya, Sean? Miserable day isn't it?' he calls across the street to the old man on his Zimmer frame.

'Terrible,' Sean shouts back.

'So what did you think of the apartment?' I broach the subject for the third time in the last few minutes. 'You can't dodge it this time.'

'I'm dodging nothing, love. Howya, Patsy? Howya, Suki?' He stops and bends down to pat the sausage dog. 'Aren't you a cute little thing,' he says, and we continue on. 'I hate that little runt. Barks all bloody night when she's away,' he mutters, pushing his cap down further over his eyes as a great big gust blows. 'Christ Almighty, are we gettin' anywhere at all, I feel like we're on one of those milltreads with this wind.'

'Treadmills,' I laugh. 'So come on, do you like the apartment or not?'

'I'm not sure. It seemed awful small and there was a funny man that went into the flat next door. Don't think I liked the look of him.'

'He seemed very friendly to me.'

'Ah, he would to you, and all.' He rolls his eyes and

747

shakes his head. 'Any man would do for you now, I'd say.'

'Dad!' I laugh.

'Good afternoon, Graham. Miserable day, isn't it?' he says to the neighbour passing.

'Awful day, Henry,' Graham responds, shoving his hands in his pockets.

'Anyway, I don't think you should take that apartment, Gracie. Hang on here a little longer until something more appropriate pops up. There's no point in taking the first thing you see.'

'Dad, we've seen ten apartments and you don't like any of them.'

'Is it for me to live in or for you?' he asks. Up and down. Down and up.

'For me.'

'Well, then, what do you care?'

'I value your opinion.'

'You do in your— Hello there, Kathleen!'

'You can't keep me at home for ever, you know.'

'For ever's been and gone, my love. There's no budging you. You're the Stonehenge of grown-up children living at home.'

'Can I go to the Monday Club tonight?'

'Again?'

'I've to finish off the game of chess I started with Larry.'

'Larry just keeps positioning his pawns so that you'll lean over and he can see down your top. That game will never end.' Dad rolls his eyes.

'Dad!'

'What? Well, you need to get more of a social life than hanging around with the likes of Larry and me.'

'I like hanging around with you.'

He smiles to himself, pleased to hear that.

We turn into Dad's house and sway up the small garden path to the front door.

The sight of what's on the doorstop stops me in my tracks.

A small hamper of muffins, covered in plastic wrapper and tied with a pink bow. I look at Dad, who steps right over them and unlocks the front door. His movement makes me question my eyesight. Have I imagined them?

'Dad! What are you doing?' Shocked, I look around behind me but nobody's there.

Dad winks at me, looks sad for a moment and then gives me a great big smile before closing the door in my face.

I reach for the envelope that is taped to the plastic and with trembling fingers slide the card out.

Thank you . . .

'I'm sorry, Joyce.' I hear a voice behind me that almost stops my heart and I twirl round.

There he is, standing at the garden gate, a bouquet of flowers in his gloved hands, the sorriest look on his face. He is wrapped up in a scarf and winter coat, the tip of his nose and cheeks red from the cold, his green eyes twinkling in the grey day. He is a vision; he takes my breath away with one look, his proximity to me almost too much to bear.

'Justin . . .' Then I'm utterly speechless.

'Do you think,' he takes a step forward, 'you could find it in your heart to forgive a fool like me?' He stands at the end of the garden, beside the gate.

I'm unsure what to say. It's been a month. Why now?

'On the phone, you hit a sore point,' he says, clearing his throat. 'Nobody knows that about my dad. Or knew that. I don't know how you did.'

'I told you how.'

'I don't understand it.'

'Neither do I.'

'But then I don't understand most ordinary things that happen everyday. I don't understand what my daughter sees in her boyfriend. I don't understand how my brother has defied the laws of science by not turning into an actual potato chip. I don't know how Doris can open the milk carton with such long nails. I don't understand why I didn't beat down your door a month ago and tell you how I felt . . . I don't understand so many simple things, I don't know why this should be any different.'

I take in the sight of his face, his curly hair covered by a woolly hat, his small nervous smile. He studies me back and I shiver, but not from the cold. I don't feel it now. The world has been heated up entirely for me. How kind. I thank beyond the clouds.

Frown lines appear on his forehead as he looks at me.

'What?'

'Nothing. You just remind me so much of somebody right now. It's not important.' He clears his throat, smiles, trying to pick up where he left off.

'Eloise Parker,' I guess, and his grin fades.

'How the hell do you know that?'

'She was your next-door neighbour who you had a crush on for years. When you were five years old you decided to do something about it and so you picked flowers from your front yard and brought them to her house. She opened the door before you got up the path and stepped outside wearing a blue coat and a black scarf,' I say, pulling my blue coat around me tighter.

'Then what?' he asks, shocked.

'Then nothing.' I shrug. 'You dropped them on the ground and chickened out.'

He shakes his head softly and smiles. 'How on earth . . . ?'

I shrug.

'What else do you know about Eloise Parker?' He narrows his eyes.

I smile and look away. 'You lost your virginity to her when you were sixteen, in her bedroom when her mom and dad were away on a cruise.'

He rolls his eyes and lowers the bouquet so that it

faces the ground. 'Now you see, *that* is not fair. You are not allowed to know stuff like that about me.'

I laugh.

'You were christened Joyce Bridget Conway but you tell everyone your middle name is Angeline,' he retaliates.

My mouth falls open.

'You had a dog called Bunny when you were a kid.' He lifts an eyebrow, cockily.

I narrow my eyes.

'You got drunk on poteen when you were,' he closes his eyes and thinks hard, 'fifteen. With your friends Kate and Frankie.'

He takes a step closer to me with each piece of knowledge and that smell, the smell of him I've dreamed to be near gets closer and closer.

'Your first French kiss was with Jason Hardy when you were ten, who everyone used to call Jason Hard-On.'

I laugh.

'You're not the only one who's allowed to know stuff.' He takes a step closer and can't move any nearer now. His shoes, the fabric of his thick coat, every part of him touches me.

My heart takes out a trampoline and enrols in a marathon session of leaping. I hope Justin doesn't hear it whooping with joy.

'Who told you all of that?' My words touch his face in a breath of cold smoke.

'Getting me here was a big operation,' he smiles. '*Big*. Your friends had me run through a series of tests to prove I was sorry enough to be deemed worthy of coming here.'

I laugh, shocked Frankie and Kate could finally agree on something, never mind keeping anything of this magnitude a secret.

Silence. We are so close, if I look up at him my nose will touch his chin. I keep looking down.

'You're still afraid to sleep in the dark,' he whispers,

taking my chin in his hand and lifting it so that I can look nowhere else but at him. 'Unless somebody's with you,' he adds with a small smile.

'You cheated on your first college paper,' I whisper.

'You used to hate art.' He kisses my forehead.

'You lie when you say you're a fan of the *Mona Lisa*.' I close my eyes.

'You had an invisible friend named Horatio until you were five.' He kisses my nose and I'm about to retaliate but his lips touch mine so softly, the words give up, fainting before they reach my voice box and sliding back to the memory bank where they came from.

I am faintly aware of Fran exiting her house and saying something to me, of a car driving by with a beep, but everything is blurred in the distance as I get lost in the moment with Justin, as I create a new memory for him, for me.

'Forgive me?' he says as he pulls away.

'I have no choice but to. It's in my blood,' I smile, and he laughs. I look down at the flowers in his hands, which have been crushed between us. 'Are you going to drop these on the ground too and chicken out?'

'Actually, they're not for you.' His cheeks redden even more. 'They're for somebody at the blood clinic who I really need to apologise to. I was hoping you would come with me, help explain the reason for my crazy behaviour, and maybe she could explain a few things to us in turn.'

I look back to the house and see Dad spying at us from behind the curtain. I look to him questioningly. He gives me the thumbs-up and my eyes fill.

'He was in on this too?'

'He called me a worthless silly sod and an up-to-no-good fool.' He makes a face and I laugh.

I blow Dad a kiss as I begin slowly to walk away. I feel him watching me, and feel Mum's eyes on me too, as I walk down the garden path, cut across the grass and follow the desire line I had created as a little girl, out onto the pavement leading away from the house I grew up in.

Though this time, I'm not alone.

Q&A with Cecelia

We gave you the chance to ask Cecelia questions about her books and the inspirations behind her writing. There was a great response and so we couldn't fit them all in here. But why not visit the website to read some more.

Where did you get your inspiration from? I absolutely love your work and have all of your books.   *Yvonne Blasius*

It is very difficult for me to say what exactly inspires me and where exactly I get my ideas from. The obvious answer is: life. I absorb everything around me. All the people I've met and all the places I've been, all the stories I've heard, music, books, absolutely anything and everything inspires me. I find that I'm constantly day dreaming, constantly imagining and creating scenarios in my head. I'm a creative person and so I allow my mind to wander, to go off on tangents, to take pathways off the beaten track and get lost. I ask questions and look for answers and then I try to think of more answers. I'm always open to new possibilities, to hearing the other side of the story, and then I like creating the third side of the story that nobody has thought of, or that perhaps people have thought of but have never thought through fully. I watch people, I listen to people, I try to see the world from their eyes. I like to view things from a different angle. I like climbing inside peoples heads and trying to imagine everything from their point of view. I can sit still for hours on end, staring at a wall, my body totally still but my mind going on the greatest adventures. I think that's just the way I am. Being a writer is a natural thing because it's something that's not forced. I don't try to think of ideas, ideas come to me. I don't try to create characters, they introduce themselves to me. I'm emotional and through the very action of feeling, I'm immediately inspired because it brings me to another place and connects me to writing.

I started to read *Thanks for the Memories* after having a miscarriage and it touched my heart so much that it made me cry but seemed to help. Had you been through it? Because you wrote everything that I felt. Thank you. *Rebecca Martins*

Thank you. I think it's important when I'm writing to really feel my way through the story. If I write something because I think it's sad or moving then it's really not good enough. I have to feel sad, I have to feel moved. I have to dig deep and use my own experiences of having felt loss, loneliness and deep sadness in order to be able to tell the story accurately. If I have a deep understanding of my character, then I have a deep understanding of their journey. Joyce's journey was one of loss and of grief and what grief is made up are a whole series of emotions – loneliness, deep sadness, anger, despair, feeling a lack of direction, confusion, feeling left behind – that as humans we all experience on a daily basis. And while all our journeys are different and we all deal with circumstances in different ways, what ties us together is our ability to feel the same emotions. My stories are very much emotion driven. It's so important to me that I do these feelings justice, knowing that people reading my books have possibly experienced what I'm writing about – particularly the issue of miscarriage where so many women suffer, and most of them secretly – means that I work so hard to make sure I'm writing about the subject accurately. My books of course are a means of entertainment and escapism, but if they can be of any comfort or help to somebody who is suffering then that is an amazing gift for me as a writer.

I was wondering how old were you when you knew you wanted to be an author? I am deciding between interior design, being an author (I love your books – I hope if I choose to be an author my books are half as good as yours!) or a photographer. Thanks for

answering and please keep writing - I absolutely LOVE your books!!
Kendall Tate

Funnily enough, I never knew that I wanted to be an author. Ever since I was seven or eight, I've been writing diaries every day, writing songs, poems, short stories. When I was fourteen I attempted my first novel, *Beans on Toast and a Bottle of Beer*, which I never managed to finish as school exams called. I knew from a young age that I wanted to do a Communications course at college that I'd heard about. It was very broad and practical and it involved documentary making, creative writing, journalism, radio production etc. Since an early age, if I was angry I felt compelled to write, when I was happy I felt compelled to write. Despite studying Journalism and Media Communications which involved a certain amount of writing, I still wasn't focused on getting into writing for a career. I wanted to do film production. But when I had finished college and I'd started writing *PS, I Love You*, it took over my life. I wrote all night and slept all day. I didn't leave the house for three months until the book was finished and I knew within the first week that it was something special. With my mother's encouragement I sent a few chapters away hoping for some advice. What I ended up getting months later was a book deal! Incredible! So what I'm saying is, writing is a passion, not just a profession. I would write if I wasn't published. I would write on my own time, all of the time and so if you wake up in the morning and feel compelled to do something, then that's what you should do.

How do you find all your ideas? How do you manage to create all these universes? How do you write? *Laëtitia Montassier*

Unlike some writers I don't have a daily routine for writing. Some people like to write nine-to-five, or have a specific word count that they like to achieve per day. I just like to write when I feel the moment's

right, when I feel like I've something to say, when the characters are ready to move ahead with the story. Thankfully, when I'm in the zone and I get swept away by the story, my hours could be all day, all night, and this could go on for weeks, consuming all of my time. Then I could take a few days off and do nothing but recharge my batteries. I think I'm an all-or-nothing writer. I have to immerse myself in the world that I'm creating. I find it difficult to have created this new world, with new characters, spend such intense moments with them, and then have to put the pen down in order to take a lunch break. That system doesn't work for me. I like to write long hand. I love physically writing, I love the feel of pen on paper, I love the flow of ideas from my mind, from my heart, onto the paper. It feels like a very natural way to tell a story, whereas writing purely on a computer feels very mechanical, as though there's a block between me and the story. After I write a chapter, I type a chapter and edit it as I go along, shaping the story and further developing the characters. When I write I have to see the picture in front of me, I always believe that if I can see it – and most importantly feel it – then I can write it. I smell the scents I'm writing about, I feel the emotions my characters are feeling, I see the rooms they're in. I totally immerse myself in the stories I tell and live the journey along with my characters.

I just want to ask a very simple question – do you believe in happily ever afters? *Caren Ong Yu Sze*

My books have often been compared to modern fairy tales and when I heard this at first, I didn't know whether I was comfortable with that description. What I feel about fairy tales is that, though uplifting, they are often unrealistic and the female characters are eventually rescued and whisked off into the sunset so that finding a man is their happily ever after. This isn't how I like stories to be, this isn't how I see real life. In my books my characters are on journeys of self-discovery. I introduce them to the reader just as they've hit their lowest point. I like to catch them

before they fall and help carry them along through their journey. In *PS, I Love You* we met Holly after she'd just lost Gerry; in *If You Could See Me Now* it was when Elizabeth had been left with a child to care for and she was at breaking point; for Sandy in *A Place Called Here* it was when she literally lost herself and her way in life; and in *Thanks for the Memories* it was when Joyce lost her child.

For me, a happy ending is when the person feels as though they're able to face the day, when they feel that they can get through the moments and they're happy to be alive. It's not about finding the man of your dreams, it's about finding the happiness within ourselves. Instead of being rescued by other people, my characters – through the help of friends and family – rescue themselves. They create their own futures. That, for me, is a happy ending, and I suppose that's what makes my stories 'modern fairy tales' and I'm comfortable with that now.

Dear Cecelia Ahern, when is your next book coming out and what is the title of that book? I love your books and I am waiting for your next book to be published. *Karlya Kang*

My next and sixth novel is called *The Gift* and it will be published October in Ireland and the UK. It's a story based around Christmas time that deals with the theme of time – how it's the most precious thing that we have and how often we take time, and whom we spend it with, for granted. The world is speeding up, people are increasingly busy, there's a pressure to balance work life with family life. So many people have said to me, "Oh if I could just be in two places at once," or "If I could just clone myself, I'd be able to get things done." Well my mind wandered, as it always does and I wondered, if we could be in two places at once, where would we choose to be? This story is about how a man called Lou Suffern has three opportunities to be in two places at the same time, and how he learns a harsh lesson about what's important. Because my books always carry a

message, I thought they'd lend themselves well to this fable style story. I adore Christmas stories, the magical feel of the period of time, where we at times revert to feeling like children again. It's also one of the busiest times of the year for people, pressures mount and for some, not so enjoyable as families are thrown together and old wounds are reopened. It felt like the perfect period to base the story around and a time when messages are learned and people take stock of their lives as they gather with family and friends as the year comes to an end.

What do you find most rewarding about writing novels? *Kayla Kirby*

Apart from the personal enjoyment that I get from writing novels, I love meeting and talking to my readers and hearing their feedback and listening to their personal. This gives me such encouragement to see that people connect with my work, that people enjoy and appreciate what I do and it also makes me eager to please my readers each time I write a new book. I always say that I write for myself because I'm so passionate about it and it gives me such joy but the most amazing thing is to know that one little idea that I've had while lying in bed, or making a coffee, or doing the washing or just going about the ordinary things in my life, can affect the lives of others all around the world, whether it's just for a moment of entertainment or a moment of comfort. Despite where we're from or what we've been through, despite never meeting in the past or never possibly meeting in the future, that we can all be connected by a story, that we're never alone, is such a rewarding thought.

Keep up to date with Cecelia!

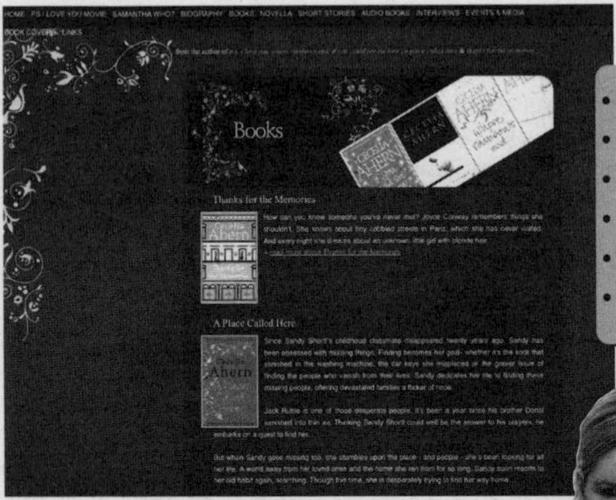

- **BOOKS**
- **NEWS**
- **INTERVIEWS**
- **EVENTS**
- **PHOTOS**
- **And much more!**

Log on to **WWW.cecelia-ahern.com**
for the latest Cecelia news,
photographs and interviews.

You'll also find details on all Cecelia's
books and short stories, as well as the
film adaptation of *PS I Love You*, and
information on *Samantha Who?*, a hit
US comedy co-created by Cecelia.

There are details of forthcoming events,
plus links to other Cecelia websites.

And why not sign up for the exclusive
HarperCollins Cecelia Ahern
newsletter while you're there?